The Collected Supernatural and Weird Fiction of Mary E. Wilkins Freeman

The Collected Supernatural and Weird Fiction of Mary E. Wilkins Freeman

Five Novelettes 'Evelina's Garden,' 'Silence', 'The Love of Parson Lord', 'The Buckley Lady,' and 'Giles Corey, Yeoman' and Nineteen Short Stories of the Strange and Unusual Including 'The Hall Bedroom', 'The Jade Bracelet', 'The Little Maid at the Door', 'The Gentle Ghost' and Others

Mary E. Wilkins Freeman

LEONAUR

The Collected
Supernatural and Weird
Fiction of
Mary E. Wilkins Freeman
Five Novelettes 'Evelina's Garden,' 'Silence',
'The Love of Parson Lord', 'The Buckley Lady,' and 'Giles Corey, Yeoman'
and Nineteen Short Stories of the Strange and Unusual Including
'The Hall Bedroom', 'The Jade Bracelet',
'The Little Maid at the Door', 'The Gentle Ghost' and Others
by Mary E. Wilkins Freeman

FIRST EDITION

Leonaur is an imprint of Oakpast Ltd

Copyright in this form © 2014 Oakpast Ltd

ISBN: 978-1-78282-315-5 (hardcover)
ISBN: 978-1-78282-316-2 (softcover)

http://www.leonaur.com

Publisher's Notes

The views expressed in this book are not necessarily
those of the publisher.

Contents

A Gentle Ghost

Out in front of the cemetery stood a white horse and a covered wagon. The horse was not tied, but she stood quite still, her four feet widely and ponderously planted, her meek white head hanging. Shadows of leaves danced on her back. There were many trees about the cemetery, and the foliage was unusually luxuriant for May. The four women who had come in the covered wagon remarked it. "I never saw the trees so forward as they are this year, seems to me," said one, gazing up at some magnificent gold-green branches over her head.

"I was sayin' so to Mary this mornin'," rejoined another. "They're uncommon forward, I think."

They loitered along the narrow lanes between the lots: four homely, middle-aged women, with decorous and subdued enjoyment in their worn faces. They read with peaceful curiosity and interest the inscriptions on the stones; they turned aside to look at the tender, newly blossomed spring bushes—the flowering almonds and the bridal wreaths. Once in a while they came to a new stone, which they immediately surrounded with eager criticism. There was a solemn hush when they reached a lot where some relatives of one of the party were buried. She put a bunch of flowers on a grave, then she stood looking at it with red eyes. The others grouped themselves deferentially aloof.

They did not meet any one in the cemetery until just before they left. When they had reached the rear and oldest portion of the yard, and were thinking of retracing their steps, they became suddenly aware of a child sitting in a lot at their right. The lot held seven old, leaning stones, dark and mossy, their inscriptions dimly traceable. The child sat close to one, and she looked up at the staring knot of women with a kind of innocent keenness, like a baby. Her face was small and fair and pinched. The women stood eying her.

"What's your name, little girl?" asked one. She had a bright flower in her bonnet and a smart lift to her chin, and seemed the natural spokeswoman of the party. Her name was Holmes. The child turned her head sideways and murmured something.

"What? We can't hear. Speak up; don't be afraid! What's your name?" The woman nodded the bright flower over her, and spoke with sharp pleasantness.

"Nancy Wren," said the child, with a timid catch of her breath.

"Wren?"

The child nodded. She kept her little pink, curving mouth parted.

"It's nobody I know," remarked the questioner, reflectively. "I guess she comes from—over there. She made a significant motion of her head towards the right. "Where do you live, Nancy?" she asked.

The child also motioned towards the right.

"I thought so," said the woman. "How old are you?"

"Ten."

The women exchanged glances. "Are you sure you're tellin' the truth?"

The child nodded.

"I never saw a girl so small for her age if she is," said one woman to another.

"Yes," said Mrs. Holmes, looking at her critically; "she is dreadful small. She's considerable smaller than my Mary was. Is there any of your folks buried in this lot?" said she, fairly hovering with affability and determined graciousness.

The child's upturned face suddenly kindled. She began speaking with a soft volubility that was an odd contrast to her previ-

8

ous hesitation.

"That's mother," said she, pointing to one of the stones, "an' that's father, an' there's John, an' Marg'ret, an' Mary, an' Susan, an' the baby, and here's—Jane."

The women stared at her in amazement. "Was it your—" began Mrs. Holmes; but another woman stepped forward, stoutly impetuous.

"Land! it's the Blake lot!" said she. "This child can't be any relation to 'em. You hadn't ought to talk so, Nancy."

"It's so," said the child, shyly persistent. She evidently hardly grasped the force of the woman's remark.

They eyed her with increased bewilderment. "It can't be," said the woman to the others. "Every one of them Blakes died years ago."

"I've seen Jane," volunteered the child, with a candid smile in their faces.

Then the stout woman sank down on her knees beside Jane's stone, and peered hard at it.

"She died forty year ago this May," said she, with a gasp. "I used to know her when I was a child. She was ten years old when she died. You ain't ever seen her. You hadn't ought to tell such stories."

"I ain't seen her for a long time," said the little girl.

"What made you say you'd seen her at all?" said Mrs. Holmes, sharply, thinking this was capitulation.

"I did use to see her a long time ago, an' she used to wear a white dress, an' a wreath on her head. She used to come here an' play with me."

The women looked at each other with pale, shocked faces; one nervous; one shivered. "She ain't quite right," she whispered. "Let's go." The women began filing away. Mrs. Holmes, who came last, stood about for a parting word to the child.

"You can't have seen her," said she, severely, "an' you are a wicked girl to tell such stories. You mustn't do it again, remember."

Nancy stood with her hand on Jane's stone, looking at her.

"She did," she repeated, with mild obstinacy.

"There's somethin' wrong about her, I guess," whispered Mrs. Holmes, rustling on after the others.

"I see she looked kind of queer the minute I set eyes on her," said the nervous woman.

When the four reached the front of the cemetery they sat down to rest for a few minutes. It was warm, and they had still quite a walk, nearly the whole width of the yard, to the other front corner where the horse and wagon were.

They sat down in a row on a bank; the stout woman wiped her face; Mrs. Holmes straightened her bonnet.

Directly opposite across the street stood two houses, so close to each other that their walls almost touched. One was a large square building, glossily white, with green blinds; the other was low, with a facing of whitewashed stone-work reaching to its lower windows, which somehow gave it a disgraced and menial air; there were, moreover, no blinds.

At the side of the low building stretched a wide ploughed field, where several halting old figures were moving about plant-ing. There was none of the brave hope of the sower about them. Even across the road one could see the feeble stiffness of their attitudes, the half-palsied fling of their arms.

"I declare I shouldn't think them old men over there would ever get that field planted," said Mrs. Holmes, energetically watchful. In the front door of the square white house sat a girl with bright hair. The yard was full of green light from two tall maple-trees, and the girl's hair made a brilliant spot of colour in the midst of it.

"That's Flora Dunn over there on the door-step, ain't it?" said the stout woman.

"Yes. I should think you could tell her by her red hair."

"I knew it. I should have thought Mr. Dunn would have hated to have had their house so near the poor-house. I declare I should!"

"Oh, he wouldn't mind," said Mrs. Holmes; "he's as easy as old Tilly. It wouldn't have troubled him any if they'd set it right

10

in his front yard. But I guess *she* minded some. I heard she did. John said there wa'n't any need of it. The town wouldn't have set it so near, if Mr. Dunn had set his foot down he wouldn't have it there. I s'pose they wanted to keep that big field on the side clear; but they would have moved it along a little if he'd made a fuss. I tell you what 'tis, I've 'bout made up my mind—I dun know as it's Scripture, but I can't help it—if folks don't make a fuss they won't get their rights in this world. If you jest lay still an' don't rise up, you're goin' to get stepped on. If people like to be, they can; I don't."

"I should have thought he'd have hated to have the poorhouse quite so close," murmured the stout woman.

Suddenly Mrs. Holmes leaned forward and poked her head among the other three. She sat on the end of the row. "Say," said she, in a mysterious whisper, "I want to know if you've heard the stories 'bout the Dunn house?"

"No; what?" chorused the other women, eagerly. They bent over towards her till the four faces were in a knot.

"Well," said Mrs. Holmes, cautiously, with a glance at the bright-headed girl across the way—"I heard it pretty straight— they say the house is haunted."

The stout woman sniffed and straightened herself. "Haunted!" repeated she.

"They say that ever since Jenny died there's been queer noises 'round the house that they can't account for. You see that front chamber over there, the one next to the poorhouse; well, that's the room, they say."

The women all turned and looked at the chamber windows, where some ruffled white curtains were fluttering.

"That's the chamber where Jenny used to sleep, you know," Mrs. Holmes went on; "an' she died there. Well, they said that before Jenny died, Flora had always slept there with her, but she felt kind of bad about goin' back there, so she thought she'd take another room. Well, there was the awfulest moanin' an' takin' on up in Jenny's room, when she did, that Flora went back there to sleep."

11

"I shouldn't thought she could," whispered the nervous woman, who was quite pale.

"The moanin' stopped jest as soon as she got in there with a light. You see Jenny was always terrible timid an' afraid to sleep alone, an' had a lamp burnin' all night, an' it seemed to them jest as if it really was her, I s'pose."

"I don't believe one word of it," said the stout woman, getting up. "It makes me all out of patience to hear people talk such stuff, jest because the Dunns happen to live opposite a graveyard."

"I told it jest as I heard it," said Mrs. Holmes, stiffly.

"Oh, I ain't blamin' you; it's the folks that start such stories that I ain't got any patience with. Think of that dear, pretty little sixteen-year-old girl hauntin' a house!"

"Well, I've told it jest as I heard it," repeated Mrs. Holmes, still in a tone of slight umbrage. "I don't ever take much stock in such things myself."

The four women strolled along to the covered wagon and climbed in. "I declare," said the stout woman, conciliatingly, "I dun know when I've bad such an outin'. I feel as if it had done me good. I've been wantin' to come down to the cemetery for a long time, but it's most more'n I want to walk. I feel real obliged to you, Mis' Holmes."

The others climbed in. Mrs. Holmes disclaimed all obligations gracefully, established herself on the front seat, and shook the reins over the white horse. Then the party jogged along the road to the village, past outlying farmhouses and rich green meadows, all freckled gold with dandelions. Dandelions were in their height; the buttercups had not yet come.

Flora Dunn, the girl on the doorstep, glanced up when they started down the street; then she turned her eyes on her work; she was sewing with nervous haste.

"Who were those folks, did you see, Flora?" called her mother, out of the sitting-room.

"I didn't notice," replied Flora, absently.

Just then the girl whom the women had met came lingeringly out of the cemetery and crossed the street.

"There's that poor little Wren girl," remarked the voice in the sitting-room.

"Yes," assented Flora. After a while she got up and entered the house. Her mother looked anxiously at her when she came into the room.

"I'm all out of patience with you, Flora," said she. "You're jest as white as a sheet. You'll make yourself sick. You're actin' dreadful foolish."

Flora sank into a chair and sat staring straight ahead with a strained, pitiful gaze. "I can't help it; I can't do any different," said she. "I shouldn't think you'd scold me, mother."

"Scold you; I ain't scoldin' you, child; but there ain't any sense in your doin' so. You'll make yourself sick, an' you're all I've got left. I can't have anything happen to you, Flora." Suddenly Mrs. Dunn burst out in a low wail, hiding her face in her hands.

"I don't see as you're much better yourself, mother," said Flora, heavily.

"I don't know as I am," sobbed her mother; "but I've got you to worry about besides—everything else. Oh, dear! oh, dear, dear!"

"I don't see any need of your worrying about me." Flora did not cry, but her face seemed to darken visibly with a gathering melancholy like a cloud. Her hair was beautiful, and she had a charming delicacy of complexion; but she was not handsome, her features were too sharp, her expression too intense and nervous. Her mother looked like her as to the expression; the features were widely different. It was as if both had passed through one corroding element which had given them the similarity of scars. Certainly a stranger would at once have noticed the strong resemblance between Mrs. Dunn's large, heavy-featured face and her daughter's thin, delicately outlined one—a resemblance which three months ago had not been perceptible.

"I see, if you don't," returned the mother. "I ain't blind."

"I don't see what you are blaming me for."

"I ain't blamin' you, but it seems to me that you might jest as

13

well let me go up there an' sleep as you."

Suddenly the girl also broke out into a wild cry. "I ain't going to leave her. Poor little Jenny! poor little Jenny! You needn't try to make me, mother; I won't!"

"Flora, don't!"

"I won't! I won't! I won't! Poor little Jenny! Oh, dear! oh, dear!"

"What if it is so? What if it is—*her*? Ain't she got me as well as you? Can't her mother go to her?"

"I won't leave her. I won't! I won't !"

Suddenly Mrs. Dunn's calmness seemed to come uppermost, raised in the scale by the weighty impetus of the other's distress. "Flora," said she, with mournful solemnity, "you mustn't do so; it's wrong. You mustn't wear yourself all out over something that maybe you'll find out wasn't so some time or other."

"Mother, don't you think it is—don't you?"

"I don't know what to think, Flora." Just then a door shut somewhere in the back part of the house. "There's father," said Mrs. Dunn, getting up; "an' the fire ain't made."

Flora rose also, and went about helping her mother to get supper. Both suddenly settled into a rigidity of composure; their eyes were red, but their lips were steady. There was a resolute vein in their characters; they managed themselves with wrenches, and could be hard even with their grief. They got tea ready for Mr. Dunn and his two hired men; then cleared it away, and sat down in the front room with their needlework. Mr. Dunn, a kindly, dull old man, was in there too, over his newspaper. Mrs. Dunn and Flora sewed intently, never taking their eyes from their work.

Out in the next room stood a tall clock, which ticked loudly; just before it struck the hours it made always a curious grating noise. When it announced in this way the striking of nine, Mrs. Dunn and Flora exchanged glances; the girl was pale, and her eyes looked larger. She began folding up her work. Suddenly a low moaning cry sounded through the house, seemingly from the room overhead. "There it is!" shrieked Flora. She caught up a lamp and ran. Mrs. Dunn was following, when her husband, sitting near the door, caught bold of her dress with a bewildered air; he had been dozing. "What's the matter?" said he, vaguely.

"Don't you hear it? Didn't you hear it, father?"

The old man let go of her dress suddenly. "I didn't hear nothin'," said he.

"Hark!"

But the cry, in fact, had ceased. Flora could be heard moving about in the room overhead, and that was all. In a moment Mrs. Dunn ran upstairs after her. The old man sat staring. "It's all dum foolishness," he muttered, under his breath. Presently he fell to dozing again, and his vacantly smiling face lopped forward. Mr. Dunn, slow-rained, patient, and unimaginative, had had his evening naps interrupted after this manner for the last three months, and there was as yet no cessation of his bewilderment. He dealt with the simple, broad lights of life; the shadows were beyond his speculation. For his consciousness his daughter Jenny had died and gone to heaven; he was not capable of listening for her ghostly moans in her little chamber overhead, much less of hearing them with any credulity.

When his wife came downstairs finally she looked at him, sleeping there, with a bitter feeling. She felt as if set about by an icy wind of loneliness. Her daughter, who was after her own kind, was all the one to whom she could look for sympathy and understanding in this subtle perplexity which had come upon her. And she would rather have dispensed with that sympathy, and heard alone those piteous, uncanny cries, for she was wild with anxiety about Flora. The girl had never been very strong. She looked at her distressfully when she came down the next morning.

"Did you sleep any last night?" said she.

"Some," answered Flora.

Soon after breakfast they noticed the little Wren girl stealing across the road to the cemetery again. "She goes over there all the time," remarked Mrs. Dunn. " I b'lieve she runs away. See her look behind her."

"Yes," said Flora, apathetically.

It was nearly noon when they heard a voice from the next house calling, "Nancy! Nancy! Nancy Wren!" The voice was loud and imperious, but slow and evenly modulated. It indicated well its owner. A woman who could regulate her own angry voice could regulate other people. Mrs. Dunn and Flora heard it understandingly.

"That poor little thing will catch it when she gets home," said Mrs. Dunn.

"Nancy! Nancy! Nancy Wren!" called the voice again.

"I pity the child if Mrs. Gregg has to go after her. Mebbe she's fell asleep over there. Flora, why don't you run over there an' get her?"

The voice rang out again. Flora got her hat and stole across the street a little below the house, so the calling woman should not see her. When she got into the cemetery she called in her turn, letting out her thin sweet voice cautiously. Finally she came directly upon the child. She was in the Blake lot, her little slender body, in its dingy cotton dress, curled up on the ground close to one of the graves. No one but Nature tended those old graves now, and she seemed to be lapsing them gently back to her own lines, at her own will. Of the garden shrubs which had been planted about them not one was left but an old low-spraying white rose-bush, which had just gotten its new leaves. The Blake lot was at the very rear of the yard, where it verged upon a light wood, which was silently stealing its way over its own proper boundaries. At the back of the lot stood a thicket of little thin trees, with silvery twinkling leaves. The ground was quite blue with houstonias.

The child raised her little fair head and stared at Flora, as if just awakened from sleep. She held her little pink mouth open, her innocent blue eyes had a surprised look, as if she were suddenly gazing upon a new scene.

"Where's she gone?" asked she, in her sweet, feeble pipe.

"Where's who gone?"

"Jane."

"I don't know what you mean. Come, Nancy, you must go home now."

"Didn't you see her?"

"I didn't see anybody," answered Flora, impatiently. "Come!"

"She was right here."

"What do you mean?"

"Jane was standin' right here. An' she had her white dress on, an' her wreath."

Flora shivered, and looked around her fearfully. The fancy of the child was overlapping her own nature. There wasn't a soul here. "You've been dreaming, child. Come!"

"No, I wasn't. I've seen them blue flowers an' the leaves winkin' all the time. Jane stood right there." The child pointed with her tiny finger to a spot at her side. "She hadn't come for a long time before," she added. " She's stayed down there." She pointed at the grave nearest her.

"You mustn't talk so," said Flora, with tremulous severity. "You must get right up and come home. Mrs. Gregg has been calling you and calling you. She won't like it."

Nancy turned quite pale around her little mouth, and sprang to her feet. "Is Mis' Gregg comin'?"

"She will come if you don't hurry."

The child said not another word. She flew along ahead through the narrow paths, and was in the almshouse door before Flora crossed the street.

"She's terrible afraid of Mrs. Gregg," she told her mother when she got home. Nancy had disturbed her own brooding a little, and she spoke more like herself.

"Poor little thing! I pity her," said Mrs. Dunn. Mrs. Dunn did not like Mrs. Gregg.

Flora rarely told a story until she had ruminated awhile over it herself. It was afternoon, and the two were in the front room at their sewing, before she told her mother about "Jane."

"Of course she must have been dreaming," Flora said.

"She must have been," rejoined her mother.

But the two looked at each other, and their eyes said more

17

than their tongues. Here was a new marvel, new evidence of a kind which they had heretofore scented at, these two rigidly walking New England souls; yet walking, after all, upon narrow paths through dark meadows of mysticism. If they never lost their footing, the steaming damp of the meadows might come in their faces.

This fancy, delusion, superstition, whichever one might name it, of theirs had lasted now three months—ever since young Jenny Dunn had died. There was apparently no reason why it should not last much longer, if delusion it were; the temperaments of these two women, naturally nervous and imaginative, overwrought now by long care and sorrow, would perpetuate it.

If it were not delusion, pray what exorcism, what spell of book and bell, could lay the ghost of a little timid child who was afraid alone in the dark?

The days went on, and Flora still hurried up to her chamber at the stroke of nine. If she were a moment late, sometimes if she were not, that pitiful low wail sounded through the house.

The strange story spread gradually through the village. Mrs. Dunn and Flora were silent about it, but Gossip is herself of a ghostly nature, and minds not keys nor bars.

There was quite an excitement over it. People affected with morbid curiosity and sympathy came to the house. One afternoon the minister came and offered a prayer. Mrs. Dunn and Flora received them all with a certain reticence; they did not concur in their wishes to remain and hear the mysterious noises for themselves. People called them "dreadful close." They got more satisfaction out of Mr. Dunn, who was perfectly ready to impart all the information in his power and his own theories in the matter.

"I never heard a thing but once," said he, "an' then it sounded more like a cat to me than anything. I guess mother and Flora air kinder nervous."

The spring was waxing late when Flora went upstairs one night with the oil low in her lamp. She had neglected filling it that day. She did not notice it until she was undressed; then she thought to herself that she must blow it out. She always kept a lamp burning all night, as she had in timid little Jenny's day. Flora herself was timid now.

So she blew the light out. She had barely laid her head upon the pillow when the low moaning wail sounded through the room. Flora sat up in bed and listened, her hands clinched. The moan gathered strength and volume; little broken words and sentences, the piteous ejaculations of terror and distress, began to shape themselves out of it.

Flora sprang out of bed, and stumbled towards her west window—the one on the almshouse side. She leaned her head out, listening a moment. Then she called her mother with wild vehemence. But her mother was already at the door with a lamp. When she entered, the moans ceased.

"Mother," shrieked Flora, "it ain't Jenny. It's somebody over there—at the poor-house. Put the lamp out in the entry, and come back here and listen."

Mrs. Dunn set out the lamp and came back, closing the door. It was a few minutes first, but presently the cries recommenced.

"I'm goin' right over there," said Mrs. Dunn. "I'm goin' to dress myself an' go over there. I'm goin' to have this affair sifted now."

"I'm going too," said Flora.

It was only half-past nine when the two stole into the almshouse yard. The light was not out in the room on the ground-floor, which the overseer's family used for a sitting-room. When they entered, the overseer was there asleep in his chair, his wife sewing at the table., and an old woman in a pink cotton dress, apparently doing nothing. They all started, and stared at the intruders.

"Good-evenin'," said Mrs. Dunn, trying to speak composedly. "We thought we'd come in; we got kind of started. Oh, there 'tis now! What is it, Mis' Gregg?"

In fact, at that moment, the wail, louder and more distinct, was heard.

"Why, it's Nancy," replied Mrs. Gregg, with dignified surprise. She was a large woman, with a masterly placidity about her. "I heard her a few minutes ago," she went on; "an' I was goin' up there to see to her if she hadn't stopped."

Mr. Gregg, a heavy, saturnine old man, with a broad bristling face, sat staring stupidly. The old woman in pink calico surveyed them all with an impersonal grin.

"Nancy!" repeated Mrs. Dunn, looking at Mrs. Gregg. She had not fancied this woman very much, and the two had not fraternized, although they were such near neighbours. Indeed, Mrs. Gregg was not of a sociable nature, and associated very little with anything but her own duties.

"Yes; Nancy Wren," she said, with gathering amazement. "She cries out this way 'most every night. She's ten years old, but she's as afraid of the dark as a baby. She's a queerchild. I guess mebbe she's nervous. I don't know but she's got notions into her head, stayin' over in the graveyard so much. She runs away over there every chance she can get, an' she goes over a queer rigmarole about playin' with Jane, and her bein' dressed in white an' a wreath. I found out she meant Jane Blake, that's buried in the Blake lot. I knew there wa'n't any children round here, an' I thought I'd look into it. You know it says 'Our Father,' an' 'Our Mother,' on the old folks' stones. An' there she was, callin' them father an' mother. You'd thought they was right there. I've got 'most out o' patience with the child. I don't know nothin' about such kind of folks." The wail continued. "I'll go right up there," said Mrs. Gregg, determinately, taking a lamp.

Mrs. Dunn and Flora followed. When they entered the chamber to which she led them they saw little Nancy sitting up in bed, her face pale and convulsed, her blue eyes streaming with tears, her little pink mouth quivering.

"Nancy—" began Mrs. Gregg, in a weighty tone. But Mrs. Dunn sprang forward and threw her arms around the child.

"You got frightened, didn't you?" whispered she; and Nancy clung to her as if for life.

A great wave of joyful tenderness rolled up in the heart of the bereaved woman. It was not, after all, the lonely and fearfully wandering little spirit of her dear Jenny; she was peaceful and blessed, beyond all her girlish tumults and terrors; but it was this little living girl. She saw it all plainly now. Afterwards it seemed to her that anyone but a woman with her nerves strained, and her imagination unhealthily keen through watching and sorrow, would have seen it before.

She held Nancy tight, and soothed her. She felt almost as if she held her own Jenny. "I guess I'll take her home with me, if you don't care," she said to Mrs. Gregg.

"Why, I don't know as I've got any objections, if you want to," answered Mrs. Gregg, with cold stateliness. "Nancy Wren has had everything done for her that I was able to do," she added, when Mrs. Dunn had wrapped up the child, and they were all on the stairs. "I ain't coaxed an' cuddled her, because it ain't my way. I never did with my own children."

"Oh, I know you've done all you could," said Mrs. Dunn, with abstracted apology. " I jest thought I'd like to take her home tonight. Don't you think I'm blamin' you, Mis' Gregg." She bent down and kissed the little tearful face on her shoulder: she was carrying Nancy like a baby. Flora had hold of one of her little dangling hands.

"You shall go right upstairs an' sleep with Flora," Mrs. Dunn whispered in the child's ear, when they were going across the yard; "an' you shall have the lamp burnin' all night, an' I'll give you a piece of cake before you go."

It was the custom of the Dunns to visit the cemetery and carry flowers to Jenny's grave every Sunday afternoon. Next Sunday little Nancy went with them. She followed happily along, and did not seem to think of the Blake lot. That pitiful fancy, if fancy it were, which had peopled her empty childish world with ghostly kindred, which had led into it an angel playmate in white robe and crown, might lie at rest now. There was no more need for it. She had found her place in a nest of living hearts, and she was getting her natural food of human love.

21

They had dressed Nancy in one of the little white frocks which Jenny had worn in her childhood, and her hat was trimmed with some ribbon and rose-buds which had adorned one of the dead young girl's years before.

It was a beautiful Sunday. After they left the cemetery they strolled a little way down the road. The road lay between deep green meadows and cottage yards. It was not quite time for the roses, and the lilacs were turning gray. The buttercups in the meadows had blossomed out, but the dandelions had lost their yellow crowns, and their filmy skulls appeared. They stood like ghosts among crowds of golden buttercups; but none of the family thought of that; their ghosts were laid in peace.

A Symphony in Lavender

It was quite late in the evening, dark and rainy, when I arrived, and I suppose the first object in Ware, outside of my immediate personal surroundings, which arrested my attention was the Munson house. When I looked out of my window the next morning it loomed up directly opposite, across the road, dark and moist from the rain of the night before. There were so many elm-trees in front of it and in front of the house I was in, that the little pools of rain-water, still standing in the road here and there, did not glisten and shine at all, although the sun was bright and quite high. The house itself stood back far enough to allow of a good square yard in front, and was raised from the street-level the height of a face-wall. Three or four steps led up to the front walk.

On each side of the steps, growing near the edge of the wall, was an enormous lilac-tree in full blossom. I could see them tossing their purple clusters between the elm branches: there was quite a wind blowing that morning. A hedge of lilacs, kept low by constant cropping, began at the blooming lilac-trees, and reached around the rest of the yard at the top of the face wall. The yard was gay with flowers, laid out in fantastic little beds, all bordered trimly with box. The house was one of those square, solid, white-painted, green-blinded edifices which marked the wealth and importance of the dweller therein a half-century or so ago, and still cast a dim halo of respect over his memory. It had no beauty in itself, being boldly plain and glaring, like all of its kind but the green waving boughs of the elms and lilacs and the undulating shadows they cast toned it down, and gave it an air of coolness and quiet and lovely reserve. I began to feel a sort of pleasant, idle curiosity concerning it as I stood there at my chamber window, and after breakfast, when I had gone into the sitting-room, whose front windows also faced that way, I took occasion to ask my hostess, who had come in with me, who lived there.

"Of course it is nobody I have ever seen or heard of," said I; "but I was looking at the house this morning, and have taken a fancy to know."

Mrs. Leonard gazed reflectively across at the house, and then at me. It was an odd way she always had before speaking.

"There's a maiden lady lives there," she answered, at length, turning her gaze from me to the house again, "all alone; that is, all alone except old Margaret. She's always been in the family— ever since Caroline was a baby, I guess: a faithful old creature as ever lived, but she's pretty feeble now. I reckon Caroline has to do pretty much all the work, and I don't suppose she's much company, or much of anything but a care. There she comes now."

"Who?" said I, feeling a little bewildered.

"Why, Caroline—Caroline Munson."

A slim, straight little woman, with a white pitcher in her hand, was descending the stone steps between the blooming lilac-trees opposite. She had on a lilac-coloured calico dress and a white apron. She wore no hat or bonnet, and her gray hair seemed to be arranged in a cluster of soft little curls at the top of her head. Her face, across the street, looked like that of a woman of forty, fair and pleasing.

"She's going down to Mrs. Barnes's after milk," Mrs. Leonard explained. "She always goes herself, every morning just about this time. She never sends old Margaret ; I reckon she ain't fit to go. I guess she can do some things about the house, but when it comes to travelling outside Caroline has to do it herself."

Then Mrs. Leonard was called into the kitchen, and I thought over the information, at once vague and definite, I had received, and watched Miss Caroline Munson walk down the shady street.

24

She had a pretty, gentle gait.

About a week later I received an invitation to take tea with her. I was probably never more surprised in my life, as I had not the slightest acquaintance with her. I had sometimes happened to watch her morning pilgrimages down the street after milk, and occasionally had observed her working over her flower-beds in her front yard. That was all, so far as I was concerned; and I did not suppose she knew there was such a person as myself in existence. But Mrs. Leonard, who was also bidden, explained it.

"It's Caroline's way," said she. "She's always had a sort of mania for asking folks to tea. Why, I reckon there's hardly a fortnight, on an average, the year round, but what she invites somebody or other to tea. I suppose she gets kind of dull, and there's a little excitement about it, getting ready for company. Anyhow, she must like it, or she wouldn't ask people. She probably has heard you were going to board here this summer—Ware's a little place you know, and folks hear everything about each other—and thought she would invite you over with me. You had better go; you'll enjoy it. It's a nice place to go to, and she's a beautiful cook, or Margaret is; I don't know which does the cooking, but I guess they both have a hand in it. Anyhow, you'll have a pleasant time. We'll take our sewing, and go early—by three o'clock. That's the way people go out to take tea in Ware."

So the next afternoon, at three o'clock, Mrs. Leonard and I sallied across the street to Miss Caroline Munson's. She met us at the door, in response to a tap of the old-fashioned knocker. Her manner of greeting us was charming from its very quaintness. She hardly said three words, but showed at the same time a simple courtesy and a pleased shyness, like a child overcome with the delight of a tea-party in her honour. She ushered us into a beautiful old parlour on the right of the hall, and we seated ourselves with our sewing. The conversation was not very brisk nor very general so far as I was concerned. There was scarcely any topic of common interest to the three of us, probably. Mrs. Leonard was one of those women who converse only of matters pertaining to themselves or their own circle of acquaintances, and seldom digress. Miss Munson I could not judge of as to conversational habits, of course; she seemed now to be merely listening with a sort of gentle interest, scarcely saying a word herself, to Mrs. Leonard's remarks. I was a total stranger to Ware and Ware people, and consequently could neither talk nor listen to much purpose.

But I was interested in observing Miss Munson. She was a nice person to observe, for if she was conscious of being an object of scrutiny, she did not show it. Her eyes never flashed up and met mine fixed upon her, with a suddenness startling and embarrassing to both of us. I could stare at her as guilelessly and properly as I could at a flower.

Indeed, Miss Munson did make me think of a flower, and of one prevalent in her front yard, too—a lilac: there was that same dull bloom about her, and a shy, antiquated grace. A lilac always does seem a little older than some other flowers. Miss Munson, I could now see, was probably nearer fifty than forty. There were little lines and shadows in her face that one could not discern across the street. It seemed to me that she must have been very lovely in her youth, with that sort of loveliness which does not demand attention, but holds it with no effort. An exquisite, delicate young creature, she ought to have been, and had been, unless her present appearance told lies.

Lilac seemed to be her favourite colour for gowns, for she wore that afternoon a delicious old-fashioned lilac muslin that looked as if it had been laid away in lavender every winter for the last thirty years. The waist was cut surplice fashion, and she wore a dainty lace handkerchief tucked into it. Take it altogether, I suppose I never spent a pleasanter afternoon in my life, although it was pleasant in a quiet, uneventful sort of a way. There was an atmosphere of gentle grace and comfort about everything about Miss Munson, about the room, and about the lookout from the high, deep-seated windows. There was not one vivid tint in that parlour; everything had the dimness of age over it. All the brightness was gone out of the carpet. Large, shadowy figures sprawled over the floor, their indistinctness giving them the suggestion of grace, and the polish on the mahogany furniture was too dull to reflect the light. The gilded scrolls on the wall-paper no longer shone, and over some of the old engravings on the walls a half-transparent film that looked like mist had spread. Outside, a cool green shadow lay over the garden, and soft, lazy puffs of lilac-scented air came in at the windows. Oh, it was all lovely, and it was so little trouble to enjoy it.

I liked, too, the tea which came later. The dining-room was as charming in its way as the parlour, large and dark and solid, with some beautiful quaint pieces of furniture in it. The china was pink and gold; and I fancied to myself that Miss Munson's grandmother had spun the table linen, and put it away in a big chest, with rose leaves between the folds. I do believe the sur-roundings and the circumstances imparted a subtle flavour to everything I tasted, which gave rise to something higher than mere gustatory delight, or maybe it was my mood; but it cer-tainly seemed to me that I had never before enjoyed a tea so much.

After that day, Miss Munson and I became very well ac-quainted. I got into the habit of running over there very often; she seldom came to see me. It was tacitly understood between us that it was pleasanter for me to do the visiting.

I do not know how she felt towards me—I think she liked me—but I began to feel an exceeding, even a loving, interest in her. All that I could think of sometimes, when with her, was a person walking in a garden and getting continually delicious lit-tle sniffs of violets, so that he certainly knew they were near him, although they were hidden somewhere under the leaves, and he could not see them. There would not be a day that Miss Mun-son would not say things that were so many little hints of a rare sweetness and beauty of nature, which her shyness and quietness did not let appear all at once.

She was rather chary always of giving very broad glimpses of herself. I was always more or less puzzled and evaded by her, though she was evidently a sincere, childlike woman, with a liking for simple pleasures. She took genuine delight in picking a little bunch of flowers in her garden for a neighbour, and in giving those little tea-parties. She was religious in an innocent, unquestioning way, too. I oftener than not found an open Bible near her when I came in, and she talked about praying as simply as one would about breathing.

But the day before I left Ware she told me a very peculiar story, by which she displayed herself to me all at once in a fuller light, although she revealed such a character that I was, in one way, none the less puzzled. She and I were sitting in her parlour. She was feeling sad about my going, and perhaps that led her to confide in me. Anyway, she looked up, suddenly, after a little silence.

"Do you," she said, "believe in dreams?"

"That is a question I can't answer truthfully," I replied, laughing. I don't really know whether I believe in dreams or not."

"I don't know either," she said, slowly, and she shuddered a little. "I have a mind to tell you," she went on, "about a dream I had once, and about something that happened to me afterwards. I never did tell anyone, and I believe I would like to. That is, if you would like to have me," she asked, as timidly as a child afraid of giving trouble.

I assured her that I would, and, after a little pause, she told me this:

"I was about twenty-two," she said, " and father and mother had been dead, one four, the other six years. I was living alone here with Margaret, as I have ever since. I have thought sometimes that it was my living alone so much, and not going about with other girls more, that made me dream as much as I did, but I don't know. I always used to have a great many dreams, and some of them seemed as if they must mean something; but this particular one, in itself and in its effect on my after-life, was very singular."

"It was in spring, and the lilacs were just in bloom, when I dreamed it. I thought I was walking down the road there under the elm-trees. I had on a lilac muslin gown, and I carried a basket of flowers on my arm. They were mostly white, or else the very faintest pink-lilies and roses. I had gone down the street a little way, when I saw a young man coming towards me. He had on a broad-brimmed soft hat and a velvet coat, and carried something that looked odd under his arm. When he came nearer I could see that he had a handsome dark face, and that he was carrying an artist's easel. When he reached me he stopped and looked down into my face and then at my basket of flowers. I stopped too—I could not seem to help it in my dream—and gazed down at the ground. I was afraid to look at him, and I trembled so that the lilies and roses in my basket quivered.

Finally he spoke. "Won't you give me one of your flowers," he said—'just one?'

I gathered courage to glance up at him then, and when his eyes met mine it did seem to me that I wanted to give him one of those flowers more than anything else in the world. I looked into my basket, and had my fingers on the stem of the finest lily there, when something came whirring and fanning by my face and settled on my shoulder, and when I turned my head, with my heart beating loud, there was a white dove.

"But, somehow, I seemed in my dream to forget all about the dove in a minute, and I looked away in the young man's face again, and lifted the lily from the basket as I did so.

"But his face did not look to me as it did before, though I still wanted to give him the lily just as much. I stood still, gazing at him, for a moment; there was, in my dream, a sort of fascination over me which would not let me take my eyes from him. As I gazed, his face changed more and more to me, till finally—I cannot explain it—it looked at once beautiful and repulsive. I wanted at once to give him the lily and would have died rather than give it to him, and I turned and fled, with my basket of flowers and my dove on my shoulder, and a great horror of something, I did not know what, in my heart. Then I woke up all of a tremble."

Miss Munson stopped. "What do you think of the dream?" she said, in a few minutes. "Do you think it possible that it could have had any especial significance, or should you think it merely a sleeping vagary of a romantic, imaginative girl?"

"I think that would depend entirely upon after-events," I answered; "they might or might not prove its significance."

"Do you think so?" she said, eagerly. "Well, it seemed to me that they did, but the worst of it has been I have never been quite sure—never quite sure. But I will tell you, and you shall judge. A year from the time I dreamed that dream, I actually met that same young man one morning in the street. I had on my lilac gown, and I held a sprig of lilac in my hand; I had broken it off the bush as I came along. He almost stopped for a second when he came up to me, and looked down into my face. I was terribly startled, for I recognised at once the man of my dream, and I can't tell you how horrible and uncanny it all seemed for a minute. There was the same handsome dark face; there were the broad hat, and the velvet coat, and the easel under the arm. Well, he passed on, and I did; but I was in a flutter all day, and his eyes seemed to be looking into mine continually.

"A few days afterwards he called upon me with Mrs. Graves, a lady who used to live in Ware and take boarders: she moved away some years ago. I learned that he was an artist. His name was—no, I will not tell you his name: he is from your city, and well known. He had engaged board with Mrs. Graves for the summer. After that there was scarcely a day but I saw him. We were both entirely free to seek each other's society, and we were together a great deal. He used to take me sketching with him, and he would come here at all hours of the day as unconcernedly as a brother might. He would sit beside me in the parlour and watch me sew, and in the kitchen and watch me cook. He was very boyish and unconventional in his ways, and I used to think it charming.

"We soon grew to care a great deal about each other, of course, although he said nothing about it to me for a long time. I knew from the first that I loved him dearly, but from the first there was, as there was in my dream, a kind of horror of him along with the love: it kept me from being entirely happy. The night before he went away he spoke. We had been to walk, and were standing here at my door. He asked me to marry him. I looked up in his face, and felt just as I did in my dream about giving him the flower, when all of a sudden his face looked different to me, just as it did in the dream. I cannot explain it. It was as if I saw no more of the kindness and the love in it, only something else—evil—and the same horror came over me.

"I don't know how I looked to him as I stood gazing up at him, but he turned very pale, and started back. 'My God! Caroline,' he said, 'what is it?'

"I don't know what I said, but it must have expressed my sudden repulsion very strongly; for, after a few bitter words, he left me, and I went into the house. I never saw him again. I have seen his name in the papers, and that is all.

"Now I want to know," Miss Munson went on, "if you think that my dream was really sent to me as a warning, or that I fancied it all, and wrecked—no, I won't say wrecked—dulled the happiness of my whole life for a nervous whim?"

She looked questioningly at me, an expression at once serious and pitiful on her delicate face. I hardly knew what to say. It was obvious that I could form no correct opinion unless I knew the man. I wondered if I did. There was an artist of about the right age whom I thought of. If he were the one—well, I think Miss Munson was right.

She saw that I hesitated. "Never mind," she said, rising with her usual quiet, gentle smile on her lips, "you don't know any more than I do, and I never shall know in this world. All I hope is that it was what God meant, and not what I imagined. We won't talk any more about it. I liked to tell you, for some reason or other, that is all. Now I am going to take you into the garden and pick your last poesy for you."

After I had gone down the stone steps with my hands full of verbenas and pansies, I turned and looked up at her standing so mild and sweet between the lilac-trees, and said goodbye again. That was the last time I saw her.

The next summer when I came to Ware the blinds on the front of the Munson house were all closed, and the little flower-beds in the front yard were untended; only the lilacs were in blossom, for they had the immortal spring for their gardener.

"Miss Munson died last winter," said Mrs. Leonard looking reflectively across the street. "She was laid out in a lilac-coloured cashmere gown; it was her request. She always wore lilac, you know. Well" (with a sigh), "I do believe that Caroline Munson, if she is an angel—and I suppose she is—doesn't look much more different from what she did before than those lilacs over there do from last year's ones."

A Far-Away Melody

The clothes-line was wound securely around the trunks of four gnarled, crooked old apple-trees, which stood promiscuously about the yard back of the cottage. It was tree-blossoming time, but these were too aged and sapless to blossom freely, and there was only a white bough here and there shaking itself triumphantly from among the rest, which had only their new green leaves. There was a branch occasionally which had not even these, but pierced the tender green and the flossy white in hard, gray nakedness. All over the yard, the grass was young and green and short, and had not yet gotten any feathery heads. Once in a while there was a dandelion set closely down among it.

The cottage was low, of a dark-red colour, with white facings around the windows, which had no blinds, only green paper curtains.

The back door was in the centre of the house, and opened directly into the green yard, with hardly a pretence of a step, only a flat, oval stone before it.

Through this door, stepping cautiously on the stone, came presently two tall, lank women in chocolate-coloured calico gowns, with a basket of clothes between them. They set the basket underneath the line on the grass, with a little clothespin bag beside it, and then proceeded methodically to hang out the clothes. Everything of a kind went together, and the best things on the outside line, which could be seen from the street in front of the cottage.

The two women were curiously alike. They were about the same height, and moved in the same way. Even their faces were so similar in feature and expression that it might have been a difficult matter to distinguish between them. All the difference, and that would have been scarcely apparent to an ordinary observer, was a difference of degree, if it might be so expressed. In one face the features were both bolder and sharper in outline, the eyes were a trifle larger and brighter, and the whole expression more animated and decided than in the other.

One woman's scanty drab hair was a shade darker than the other's, and the negative fairness of complexion, which generally accompanies drab hair, was in one relieved by a slight tinge of warm red on the cheeks.

This slightly intensified woman had been commonly considered the more attractive of the two, although in reality there was very little to choose between the personal appearance of these twin sisters, Priscilla and Mary Brown. They moved about the clothesline, pinning the sweet white linen on securely, their thick, white-stockinged ankles showing beneath their limp calicoes as they stepped, and their large feet in cloth slippers flattening down the short, green grass. Their sleeves were rolled up, displaying their long, thin, muscular arms, which were sharply pointed at the elbows.

They were homely women; they were fifty and over now, but they never could have been pretty in their teens, their features were too irredeemably irregular for that. No youthful freshness of complexion or expression could have possibly done away with the impression that they gave. Their plainness had probably only been enhanced by the contrast, and these women, to people generally, seemed better-looking than when they were young. There was an honesty and patience in both faces that showed all the plainer for their homeliness.

One, the sister with the darker hair, moved a little quicker than the other, and lifted the wet clothes from the basket to the line more frequently. She was the first to speak, too, after they had been hanging out the clothes for some little time in silence.

She stopped as she did so, with a wet pillow-case in her hand, and looked up reflectively at the flowering apple-boughs overhead, and the blue sky showing, between, while the sweet spring wind ruffled her scanty hair a little.

"I wonder, Mary," said she, " if it would seem so very queer to die a mornin' like this, say. Don't you believe there's apple branches a-hangin' over them walls made out of precious stones, like these, only there ain't any dead limbs among 'em, an' they're all covered thick with flowers? An' I wonder if it would seem such an awful change to go from this air into the air of the New Jerusalem." Just then a robin hidden somewhere in the trees began to sing. "I s'pose," she went on, "that there's angels instead of robins, though, and they don't roost up in trees to sing, but stand on the ground, with lilies growin' round their feet, maybe, up to their knees, or on the gold stones in the street, an' play on their harps to go with the singin'."

The other sister gave a scared, awed look at her. "Lor, don't talk that way, sister," said she. "What has got into you lately? You make me crawl all over, talkin' so much about dyin'. You feel well, don't you?"

"Lor, yes," replied the other, laughing, and picking up a clothespin for her pillowcase; "I feel well enough, an' I don't know what has got me to talkin' so much about dyin' lately, or thinkin' about it. I guess it's the spring weather. P'r'aps flowers growin' make anybody think of wings sproutin' kinder naterally. I won't talk so much about it if it bothers you, an' I don't know but it's sorter nateral it should. Did you get the potatoes before we came out, sister?"—with an awkward and kindly effort to change the subject.

"No," replied the other, stooping over the clothes-basket. There was such a film of tears in her dull blue eyes that she could not distinguish one article from another.

Well, I guess you had better go in an' get 'em, then they ain't worth anything, this time of year, unless they soak a while, an I'll finish hangin' out the clothes while you do it."

"Well, p'r'aps I'd better," the other woman replied, straightening herself up from the clothes-basket. Then she went into the house without another word; but down in the damp cellar, a minute later, she sobbed over the potato barrel as if her heart would break. Her sister's remarks had filled her with a vague apprehension and grief which she could not throw off. And there was something little singular about it. Both these women had always been of a deeply religious cast of mind. They had studied the Bible faithfully, if not understandingly, and their religion had strongly tinctured their daily life. They knew almost as much about the Old Testament prophets as they did about their neighbours; and that was saying a good deal of two single women in a New England country town. Still this religious element in their natures could hardly have been termed spirituality. It deviated from that as much as anything of religion—which is in one way spirituality itself—could.

Both sisters were eminently practical in all affairs of life, down to their very dreams, and Priscilla especially so. She had dealt in religion with the bare facts of sin and repentance, future punishment and reward. She had dwelt very little, probably, upon the poetic splendours of the Eternal City, and talked about them still less. Indeed, she had always been reticent about her religious convictions, and had said very little about them even to her sister.

The two women, with God in their thoughts every moment, seldom had spoken his name to each other. For Priscilla to talk in the strain that she had today, and for a week or two previous, off and on, was, from its extreme deviation from her usual custom, certainly startling.

Poor Mary, sobbing over the potato barrel, thought it was a sign of approaching death. She had a few superstitious-like grafts upon her practical, commonplace character.

She wiped her eyes finally, and went upstairs with her tin basin of potatoes, which were carefully washed and put to soak by the time her sister came in with the empty basket.

At twelve exactly the two sat down to dinner in the clean kitchen, which was one of the two rooms the cottage boasted.

The narrow entry ran from the front door to the back. On one side was the kitchen and living-room; on the other, the room where the sisters slept. There were two small unfinished lofts overhead, reached by a step-ladder through a little scuttle in the entry ceiling: and that was all. The sisters had earned the cottage and paid for it years before, by working as tailoresses. They had, besides, quite a snug little sum in the bank, which they had saved out of their hard earnings. There was no need for Priscilla and Mary to work so hard, people said; but work hard they did, and work hard they would as long as they lived. The mere habit of work had become as necessary to them as breathing

Just as soon as they had finished their meal and cleared away the dishes, they put on some clean starched purple prints, which were their afternoon dresses, and seated themselves with their work at the two front windows; the house faced southwest, so the sunlight streamed through both. It was a very warm day for the season, and the windows were open. Close to them in the yard outside stood great clumps of lilac bushes. They grew on the other side of the front door too; a little later the low cottage would look half-buried in them. The shadows of their leaves made a dancing net-work over the freshly washed yellow floor.

The two sisters sat there and sewed on some coarse vests all the afternoon. Neither made a remark often. The room, with its glossy little cooking-stove, its eight-day clock on the mantel, its chintz-cushioned rocking-chairs, and the dancing shadows of the lilac leaves on its yellow floor, looked pleasant and peaceful.

Just before six o'clock a neighbour dropped in with her cream pitcher to borrow some milk for tea, and she sat down for a minute's chat after she had got it filled. They had been talking a few moments on neighbourhood topics, when all of a sudden Priscilla let her work fall and raised her hand. "Hush!" whispered she.

The other two stopped talking, and listened, staring at her wonderingly, but they could hear nothing.

"What is it, Miss Priscilla?" asked the neighbour, with round blue eyes. She was a pretty young thing, who had not been married long.

"Hush! Don't speak. Don't you hear that beautiful music?" Her ear was inclined towards the open window, her hand still raised warningly, and her eyes fixed on the opposite wall beyond them.

Mary turned visibly paler than her usual dull paleness, and shuddered. "I don't hear any music," she said. "Do you, Miss Moore?"

"No-o," replied the caller, her simple little face beginning to put on a scared look, from a vague sense of a mystery she could not fathom.

Mary Brown rose and went to the door, and looked eagerly up and down the street. "There ain't no organ-man in sight any-where," said she, returning, "an' I can't hear any music, an' Miss Moore can't, an' we're both sharp enough o' hearing'. You're jest imaginin' it, sister."

"I never imagined anything in my life," returned the other, "an' it ain't likely I'm goin' to begin now. It's the beautifulest music. It comes from over the orchard there. Can't you hear it? But it seems to me it's growin' a little fainter like now. I guess it's movin' off, perhaps."

Mary Brown set her lips hard. The grief and anxiety she had felt lately turned suddenly to unreasoning anger against the cause of it; through her very love she fired with quick wrath at the beloved object. Still she did not say much, only, "I guess it must be movin' off," with a laugh, which had an unpleasant ring in it.

After the neighbour had gone, however, she said more, standing before her sister with her arms folded squarely across her bosom. "Now, Priscilla Brown," she exclaimed, "I think it's about time to put a stop to this. I've heard about enough of it. What do you s'pose Miss Moore thought of you? Next thing it'll be all over town that you're gettin' spiritual notions. Today it's mu-sic that nobody else can hear, an' yesterday you smelled roses, and there ain't one in blossom this time o' year, and all the time you're talkin' about dyin'. For my part, I don't see why you ain't as likely to live as I am. You're uncommon hearty on vittles. You ate a pretty good dinner today for a dyin' person."

"I didn't say I was goin' to die," replied Priscilla, meekly: the two sisters seemed suddenly to have changed natures. "An' I'll try not to talk so, if it plagues you. I told you I wouldn't this mornin', but the music kinder took me by surprise like, an' I thought maybe you an' Miss Moore could hear it. I can jest hear it a little bit now, like the dyin' away of a bell."

"There you go agin!" cried the other, sharply. "Do, for mercy's sake, stop, Priscilla. There ain't no music."

"Well, I won't talk any more about it," she answered, patiently; and she rose and began setting the table for tea, while Mary sat down and resumed her sewing, drawing the thread through the cloth with quick, uneven jerks.

That night the pretty girl neighbour was aroused from her first sleep by a distressed voice at her bedroom window, crying, "Miss Moore! Miss Moore!"

She spoke to her husband, who opened the window. "What's wanted?" he asked, peering out into the darkness.

"Priscilla's sick," moaned the distressed voice; "awful sick. She's fainted, an' I can't bring her to. Go for the doctor—quick! quick! *quick!* The voice ended in a shriek on the last word, and the speaker turned and ran back to the cottage, where, on the bed, lay a pale, gaunt woman, who had not stirred since she left it. Immovable through all her sister's agony, she lay there, her features shaping themselves out more and more from the shadows, the bedclothes that covered her limbs taking on an awful rigidity.

"She must have died in her sleep," the doctor said, when he came, "without a struggle."

When Mary Brown really understood that her sister was dead, she left her to the kindly ministrations of the good women who are always ready at such times in a country place, and went and sat by the kitchen window in the chair which her sister had occupied that afternoon.

There the women found her when the last offices had been

done for the dead.

"Come home with me tonight," one said; "Miss Green will stay with *her*," with a turn of her head towards the opposite room, and an emphasis on the pronoun which distinguished it at once from one applied to a living person.

"No," said Mary Brown; "I'm a goin' to set here an' listen." She had the window wide open, leaning her head out into the chilly night air.

The women looked at each other; one tapped her head, another nodded hers. "Poor thing!" said a third.

"You see," went on Mary Brown, still speaking with her head leaned out of the window, "I was cross with her this afternoon because she talked about hearin' music. I was cross, an' spoke up sharp to her, because I loved her, but I don't think she knew. I didn't want to think she was goin' to die, but she was. An' she heard the music. It was true. An' now I'm a-goin' to set here an' listen till I hear it too, an' then I'll know she 'ain't laid up what I said agin me, an' that I'm a-goin' to die too."

They found it impossible to reason with her; there she sat till morning, with a pitying woman beside her, listening all in vain for unearthly melody.

Next day they sent for a widowed niece of the sisters, who came at once, bringing her little boy with her. She was a kindly young woman, and took up her abode in the little cottage, and did the best she could for her poor aunt, who, it soon became evident, would never be quite herself again. There she would sit at the kitchen window and listen day after day. She took a great fancy to her niece's little boy, and used often to hold him in her lap as she sat there. Once in a while she would ask him if he heard any music. "An innocent little thing like him might hear quicker than a hard, unbelievin' old woman like me," she told his mother once.

She lived so for nearly a year after her sister died. It was evident that she failed gradually and surely, though there was no apparent disease. It seemed to trouble her exceedingly that she never heard the music she listened for. She had an idea that she could not die unless she did, and her whole soul seemed filled with longing to join her beloved twin sister, and be assured of her forgiveness. This sister-love was all she had ever felt, besides her love of God, in any strong degree; all the passion of devotion of which this homely, commonplace woman was capable was centred in that, and the unsatisfied strength of it was killing her. The weaker she grew, the more earnestly she listened. She was too feeble to sit up, but she would not consent to lie in bed, and made them bolster her up with pillows in a rocking-chair by the window. At last she died, in the spring, a week or two before her sister had the preceding year. The season was a little more advanced this year, and the apple-trees were blossomed out further than they were then. She died about ten o'clock in the morning. The day before, her niece had been called into the room by a shrill cry of rapture from her: "I've heard it! I've heard it!" she cried. "A faint sound o' music, like the dyin' away of a bell."

The Shadows on the Wall

"Henry had words with Edward in the study the night before Edward died," said Caroline Glynn.

She was elderly, tall, and harshly thin, with a hard colourlessness of face. She spoke not with acrimony, but with grave severity. Rebecca Ann Glynn, younger, stouter and rosy of face between her crinkling puffs of gray hair, gasped, by way of assent. She sat in a wide flounce of black silk in the corner of the sofa, and rolled terrified eyes from her sister Caroline to her sister Mrs. Stephen Brigham, who had been Emma Glynn, the one beauty of the family. She was beautiful still, with a large, splendid, full-blown beauty; she filled a great rocking-chair with her superb bulk of femininity, and swayed gently back and forth, her black silks whispering and her black frills fluttering. Even the shock of death (for her brother Edward lay dead in the house,) could not disturb her outward serenity of demeanour. She was grieved over the loss of her brother: he had been the youngest, and she had been fond of him, but never had Emma Brigham lost sight of her own importance amidst the waters of tribulation. She was always awake to the consciousness of her own stability in the midst of vicissitudes and the splendour of her permanent bearing.

But even her expression of masterly placidity changed before her sister Caroline's announcement and her sister Rebecca Ann's gasp of terror and distress in response.

"I think Henry might have controlled his temper, when poor

Edward was so near his end," said she with an asperity which disturbed slightly the roseate curves of her beautiful mouth.

"Of course he did not *know*," murmured Rebecca Ann in a faint tone strangely out of keeping with her appearance.

One involuntarily looked again to be sure that such a feeble pipe came from that full-swelling chest.

"Of course he did not know it," said Caroline quickly. She turned on her sister with a strange sharp look of suspicion. "How could he have known it?" said she. Then she shrank as if from the other's possible answer. "Of course you and I both know he could not," said she conclusively, but her pale face was paler than it had been before.

Rebecca gasped again. The married sister, Mrs. Emma Brigham, was now sitting up straight in her chair; she had ceased rocking, and was eyeing them both intently with a sudden accentuation of family likeness in her face. Given one common intensity of emotion and similar lines showed forth, and the three sisters of one race were evident.

"What do you mean?" said she impartially to them both. Then she, too, seemed to shrink before a possible answer. She even laughed an evasive sort of laugh. "I guess you don't mean anything," said she, but her face wore still the expression of shrinking horror.

"Nobody means anything," said Caroline firmly. She rose and crossed the room toward the door with grim decisiveness.

"Where are you going?" asked Mrs. Brigham.

"I have something to see to," replied Caroline, and the others at once knew by her tone that she had some solemn and sad duty to perform in the chamber of death.

"Oh," said Mrs. Brigham.

After the door had closed behind Caroline, she turned to Rebecca.

"Did Henry have many words with him?" she asked.

"They were talking very loud," replied Rebecca evasively, yet with an answering gleam of ready response to the other's curiosity in the quick lift of her soft blue eyes.

Mrs. Brigham looked at her. She had not resumed rocking. She still sat up straight with a slight knitting of intensity on her fair forehead, between the pretty rippling curves of her auburn hair.

"Did you—hear anything?" she asked in a low voice with a glance toward the door.

"I was just across the hall in the south parlour, and that door was open and this door ajar," replied Rebecca with a slight flush.

"Then you must have—"

"I couldn't help it."

"Everything?"

"Most of it."

"What was it?"

"The old story."

"I suppose Henry was mad, as he always was, because Edward was living on here for nothing, when he had wasted all the money father left him."

Rebecca nodded with a fearful glance at the door.

When Emma spoke again her voice was still more hushed. "I know how he felt," said she. "He had always been so prudent himself, and worked hard at his profession, and there Edward had never done anything but spend, and it must have looked to him as if Edward was living at his expense, but he wasn't."

"No, he wasn't."

"It was the way father left the property—that all the children should have a home here—and he left money enough to buy the food and all if we had all come home."

"Yes."

"And Edward had a right here according to the terms of father's will, and Henry ought to have remembered it."

"Yes, he ought."

"Did he say hard things?"

"Pretty hard from what I heard."

"What?"

"I heard him tell Edward that he had no business here at all, and he thought he had better go away."

"What did Edward say?"

"That he would stay here as long as he lived and afterward, too, if he was a mind to, and he would like to see Henry get him out; and then—"

"What?"

"Then he laughed."

"What did Henry say."

"I didn't hear him say anything, but—"

"But what?"

"I saw him when he came out of this room."

"He looked mad?"

"You've seen him when he looked so."

Emma nodded; the expression of horror on her face had deepened.

"Do you remember that time he killed the cat because she had scratched him?"

"Yes. Don't!"

Then Caroline re-entered the room. She went up to the stove in which a wood fire was burning—it was a cold, gloomy day of fall—and she warmed her hands, which were reddened from recent washing in cold water.

Mrs. Brigham looked at her and hesitated. She glanced at the door, which was still ajar, as it did not easily shut, being still swollen with the damp weather of the summer. She rose and pushed it together with a sharp thud which jarred the house. Rebecca started painfully with a half exclamation. Caroline looked at her disapprovingly.

"It is time you controlled your nerves, Rebecca," said she.

"I can't help it," replied Rebecca with almost a wail. "I am nervous. There's enough to make me so, the Lord knows."

"What do you mean by that?" asked Caroline with her old air of sharp suspicion, and something between challenge and dread of its being met.

Rebecca shrank.

"Nothing," said she.

"Then I wouldn't keep speaking in such a fashion."

Emma, returning from the closed door, said imperiously that it ought to be fixed, it shut so hard.

"It will shrink enough after we have had the fire a few days," replied Caroline. "If anything is done to it it will be too small; there will be a crack at the sill."

"I think Henry ought to be ashamed of himself for talking as he did to Edward," said Mrs. Brigham abruptly, but in an almost inaudible voice.

"Hush!" said Caroline, with a glance of actual fear at the closed door.

"Nobody can hear with the door shut."

"He must have heard it shut, and—"

"Well, I can say what I want to before he comes down, and I am not afraid of him."

"I don't know who is afraid of him! What reason is there for anybody to be afraid of Henry?" demanded Caroline.

Mrs. Brigham trembled before her sister's look. Rebecca gasped again. "There isn't any reason, of course. Why should there be?"

"I wouldn't speak so, then. Somebody might overhear you and think it was queer. Miranda Joy is in the south parlour sewing, you know."

"I thought she went upstairs to stitch on the machine."

"She did, but she has come down again."

"Well, she can't hear."

"I say again I think Henry ought to be ashamed of himself. I shouldn't think he'd ever get over it, having words with poor Edward the very night before he died. Edward was enough sight better disposition than Henry, with all his faults. I always thought a great deal of poor Edward, myself."

Mrs. Brigham passed a large fluff of handkerchief across her eyes; Rebecca sobbed outright.

"Rebecca," said Caroline admonishingly, keeping her mouth stiff and swallowing determinately.

"I never heard him speak a cross word, unless he spoke cross to Henry that last night. I don't know, but he did from what Rebecca overheard," said Emma.

"Not so much cross as sort of soft, and sweet, and aggravating," sniffled Rebecca.

"He never raised his voice," said Caroline; "but he had his way."

"He had a right to in this case."

"Yes, he did."

"He had as much of a right here as Henry," sobbed Rebecca, "and now he's gone, and he will never be in this home that poor father left him and the rest of us again."

"What do you really think ailed Edward?" asked Emma in hardly more than a whisper. She did not look at her sister.

Caroline sat down in a nearby armchair, and clutched the arms convulsively until her thin knuckles whitened.

"I told you," said she.

Rebecca held her handkerchief over her mouth, and looked at them above it with terrified, streaming eyes.

"I know you said that he had terrible pains in his stomach, and had spasms, but what do you think made him have them?"

"Henry called it gastric trouble. You know Edward has always had dyspepsia."

Mrs. Brigham hesitated a moment. "Was there any talk of an—examination?" said she.

Then Caroline turned on her fiercely.

"No," said she in a terrible voice. "No."

The three sisters' souls seemed to meet on one common ground of terrified understanding though their eyes. The old-fashioned latch of the door was heard to rattle, and a push from without made the door shake ineffectually. "It's Henry," Rebecca sighed rather than whispered. Mrs. Brigham settled herself after a noiseless rush across the floor into her rocking-chair again, and was swaying back and forth with her head comfortably leaning back, when the door at last yielded and Henry Glynn entered. He cast a covertly sharp, comprehensive glance at Mrs. Brigham with her elaborate calm; at Rebecca quietly huddled in the corner of the sofa with her handkerchief to her face and only one small reddened ear as attentive as a dog's uncovered and revealing her alertness for his presence; at Caroline sitting with a strained composure in her armchair by the stove. She met his eyes quite firmly with a look of inscrutable fear, and defiance of the fear and of him.

Henry Glynn looked more like this sister than the others. Both had the same hard delicacy of form and feature, both were tall and almost emaciated, both had a sparse growth of gray blond hair far back from high intellectual foreheads, both had an almost noble aquilinity of feature. They confronted each other with the pitiless immovability of two statues in whose marble lineaments emotions were fixed for all eternity.

Then Henry Glynn smiled and the smile transformed his face. He looked suddenly years younger, and an almost boyish recklessness and irresolution appeared in his face. He flung himself into a chair with a gesture which was bewildering from its incongruity with his general appearance. He leaned his head back, flung one leg over the other, and looked laughingly at Mrs. Brigham.

"I declare, Emma, you grow younger every year," he said.

She flushed a little, and her placid mouth widened at the corners. She was susceptible to praise.

"Our thoughts today ought to belong to the one of us who will *never* grow older," said Caroline in a hard voice.

Henry looked at her, still smiling. "Of course, we none of us forget that," said he, in a deep, gentle voice, "but we have to speak to the living, Caroline, and I have not seen Emma for a long time, and the living are as dear as the dead."

"Not to me," said Caroline.

She rose, and went abruptly out of the room again. Rebecca also rose and hurried after her, sobbing loudly.

Henry looked slowly after them.

"Caroline is completely unstrung," said he. Mrs. Brigham rocked. A confidence in him inspired by his manner was stealing over her. Out of that confidence she spoke quite easily and naturally.

"His death was very sudden," said she.

Henry's eyelids quivered slightly but his gaze was unswerving.

"Yes," said he; "it was very sudden. He was sick only a few hours."

"What did you call it?"

"Gastric."

"You did not think of an examination?"

"There was no need. I am perfectly certain as to the cause of his death."

Suddenly Mrs. Brigham felt a creep as of some live horror over her very soul. Her flesh prickled with cold, before an inflection of his voice. She rose, tottering on weak knees.

"Where are you going?" asked Henry in a strange, breathless voice.

Mrs. Brigham said something incoherent about some sewing which she had to do, some black for the funeral, and was out of the room. She went up to the front chamber which she occupied. Caroline was there. She went close to her and took her hands, and the two sisters looked at each other.

"Don't speak, don't, I won't have it!" said Caroline finally in an awful whisper.

"I won't," replied Emma.

That afternoon the three sisters were in the study, the large front room on the ground floor across the hall from the south parlour, when the dusk deepened.

Mrs. Brigham was hemming some black material. She sat close to the west window for the waning light. At last she laid her work on her lap.

"It's no use, I cannot see to sew another stitch until we have a light," said she.

Caroline, who was writing some letters at the table, turned to Rebecca, in her usual place on the sofa.

"Rebecca, you had better get a lamp," she said.

Rebecca started up; even in the dusk her face showed her

agitation.

"It doesn't seem to me that we need a lamp quite yet," she said in a piteous, pleading voice like a child's.

"Yes, we do," returned Mrs. Brigham peremptorily. "We must have a light. I must finish this tonight or I can't go to the funeral, and I can't see to sew another stitch."

"Caroline can see to write letters, and she is farther from the window than you are," said Rebecca.

"Are you trying to save kerosene or are you lazy, Rebecca Glynn?" cried Mrs. Brigham. "I can go and get the light myself, but I have this work all in my lap."

Caroline's pen stopped scratching.

"Rebecca, we must have the light," said she.

"Had we better have it in here?" asked Rebecca weakly.

"Of course! Why not?" cried Caroline sternly.

"I am sure I don't want to take my sewing into the other room, when it is all cleaned up for tomorrow," said Mrs. Brigham.

"Why, I never heard such a to-do about lighting a lamp."

Rebecca rose and left the room. Presently she entered with a lamp—a large one with a white porcelain shade. She set it on a table, an old-fashioned card-table which was placed against the opposite wall from the window. That wall was clear of bookcases and books, which were only on three sides of the room. That opposite wall was taken up with three doors, the one small space being occupied by the table. Above the table on the old-fash-ioned paper, of a white satin gloss, traversed by an indeterminate green scroll, hung quite high a small gilt and black-framed ivory miniature taken in her girlhood of the mother of the family. When the lamp was set on the table beneath it, the tiny pretty face painted on the ivory seemed to gleam out with a look of intelligence.

"What have you put that lamp over there for?" asked Mrs. Brigham, with more of impatience than her voice usually re-vealed. "Why didn't you set it in the hall and have done with it. Neither Caroline nor I can see if it is on that table."

"I thought perhaps you would move," replied Rebecca

hoarsely.

"If I do move, we can't both sit at that table. Caroline has her paper all spread around. Why don't you set the lamp on the study table in the middle of the room, then we can both see?"

Rebecca hesitated. Her face was very pale. She looked with an appeal that was fairly agonizing at her sister Caroline.

"Why don't you put the lamp on this table, as she says?" asked Caroline, almost fiercely. "Why do you act so, Rebecca?"

"I should think you *would* ask her that," said Mrs. Brigham. "She doesn't act like herself at all."

Rebecca took the lamp and set it on the table in the middle of the room without another word. Then she turned her back upon it quickly and seated herself on the sofa, and placed a hand over her eyes as if to shade them, and remained so.

"Does the light hurt your eyes, and is that the reason why you didn't want the lamp?" asked Mrs. Brigham kindly.

"I always like to sit in the dark," replied Rebecca chokingly. Then she snatched her handkerchief hastily from her pocket and began to weep. Caroline continued to write, Mrs. Brigham to sew.

Suddenly Mrs. Brigham as she sewed glanced at the opposite wall. The glance became a steady stare. She looked intently, her work suspended in her hands. Then she looked away again and took a few more stitches, then she looked again, and again turned to her task. At last she laid her work in her lap and stared concentratedly. She looked from the wall around the room, taking note of the various objects; she looked at the wall long and intently. Then she turned to her sisters.

"What *is* that?" said she.

"What?" asked Caroline harshly; her pen scratched loudly across the paper.

Rebecca gave one of her convulsive gasps.

"That strange shadow on the wall," replied Mrs. Brigham.

Rebecca sat with her face hidden: Caroline dipped her pen in the inkstand.

"Why don't you turn around and look?" asked Mrs. Brigham

in a wondering and somewhat aggrieved way.

"I am in a hurry to finish this letter, if Mrs. Wilson Ebbit is going to get word in time to come to the funeral," replied Caroline shortly.

Mrs. Brigham rose, her work slipping to the floor, and she began walking around the room, moving various articles of furniture, with her eyes on the shadow.

Then suddenly she shrieked out:

"Look at this awful shadow! What is it? Caroline, look, look! Rebecca, look! *What is it?*"

All Mrs. Brigham's triumphant placidity was gone. Her handsome face was livid with horror. She stood stiffly pointing at the shadow.

"Look!" said she, pointing her finger at it. "Look! What is it?"

Then Rebecca burst out in a wild wail after a shuddering glance at the wall:

"Oh, Caroline, there it is again! There it is again!"

"Caroline Glynn, you look!" said Mrs. Brigham. "Look! What is that dreadful shadow?"

Caroline rose, turned, and stood confronting the wall.

"How should I know?" she said.

"It has been there every night since he died," cried Rebecca.

"Every night?"

"Yes. He died Thursday and this is Saturday; that makes three nights," said Caroline rigidly. She stood as if holding herself calm with a vise of concentrated will.

"It—it looks like—like—" stammered Mrs. Brigham in a tone of intense horror.

"I know what it looks like well enough," said Caroline. "I've got eyes in my head."

"It looks like Edward," burst out Rebecca in a sort of frenzy of fear. "Only—"

"Yes, it does," assented Mrs. Brigham, whose horror-stricken tone matched her sister's, "only— Oh, it is awful! What is it,

Caroline?"

"I ask you again, how should I know?" replied Caroline. "I see it there like you. How should I know any more than you?"

"It *must* be something in the room," said Mrs. Brigham, staring wildly around.

"We moved everything in the room the first night it came," said Rebecca; "it is not anything in the room."

Caroline turned upon her with a sort of fury. "Of course it is something in the room," said she. "How you act! What do you mean by talking so? Of course it is something in the room."

"Of course, it is," agreed Mrs. Brigham, looking at Caroline suspiciously. "Of course it must be. It is only a coincidence. It just happens so. Perhaps it is that fold of the window curtain that makes it. It must be something in the room."

"It is not anything in the room," repeated Rebecca with obstinate horror.

The door opened suddenly and Henry Glynn entered. He began to speak, then his eyes followed the direction of the others'. He stood stock still staring at the shadow on the wall. It was life size and stretched across the white parallelogram of a door, half across the wall space on which the picture hung.

"What is that?" he demanded in a strange voice.

"It must be due to something in the room," Mrs. Brigham said faintly.

"It is not due to anything in the room," said Rebecca again with the shrill insistency of terror.

"How you act, Rebecca Glynn," said Caroline.

Henry Glynn stood and stared a moment longer. His face showed a gamut of emotions—horror, conviction, then furious incredulity. Suddenly he began hastening hither and thither about the room. He moved the furniture with fierce jerks, turning ever to see the effect upon the shadow on the wall. Not a line of its terrible outlines wavered.

"It must be something in the room!" he declared in a voice which seemed to snap like a lash.

His face changed. The inmost secrecy of his nature seemed

evident until one almost lost sight of his lineaments. Rebecca stood close to her sofa, regarding him with woeful, fascinated eyes. Mrs. Brigham clutched Caroline's hand. They both stood in a corner out of his way. For a few moments he raged about the room like a caged wild animal. He moved every piece of furniture; when the moving of a piece did not affect the shadow, he flung it to the floor, the sisters watching.

Then suddenly he desisted. He laughed and began straightening the furniture which he had flung down.

"What an absurdity," he said easily. "Such a to-do about a shadow."

"That's so," assented Mrs. Brigham, in a scared voice which she tried to make natural. As she spoke she lifted a chair near her.

"I think you have broken the chair that Edward was so fond of," said Caroline.

Terror and wrath were struggling for expression on her face. Her mouth was set, her eyes shrinking. Henry lifted the chair with a show of anxiety.

"Just as good as ever," he said pleasantly. He laughed again, looking at his sisters. "Did I scare you?" he said. "I should think you might be used to me by this time. You know my way of wanting to leap to the bottom of a mystery, and that shadow does look—queer, like—and I thought if there was any way of accounting for it I would like to without any delay."

"You don't seem to have succeeded," remarked Caroline dryly, with a slight glance at the wall.

Henry's eyes followed hers and he quivered perceptibly.

"Oh, there is no accounting for shadows," he said, and he laughed again. "A man is a fool to try to account for shadows."

Then the supper bell rang, and they all left the room, but Henry kept his back to the wall, as did, indeed, the others.

Mrs. Brigham pressed close to Caroline as she crossed the hall. "He looked like a demon!" she breathed in her ear.

Henry led the way with an alert motion like a boy; Rebecca brought up the rear; she could scarcely walk, her knees trembled so.

"I can't sit in that room again this evening," she whispered to Caroline after supper.

"Very well, we will sit in the south room," replied Caroline. "I think we will sit in the south parlour," she said aloud; "it isn't as damp as the study, and I have a cold."

So they all sat in the south room with their sewing. Henry read the newspaper, his chair drawn close to the lamp on the table. About nine o'clock he rose abruptly and crossed the hall to the study. The three sisters looked at one another. Mrs. Brigham rose, folded her rustling skirts compactly around her, and began tiptoeing toward the door.

"What are you going to do?" inquired Rebecca agitatedly.

"I am going to see what he is about," replied Mrs. Brigham cautiously.

She pointed as she spoke to the study door across the hall; it was ajar. Henry had striven to pull it together behind him, but it had somehow swollen beyond the limit with curious speed. It was still ajar and a streak of light showed from top to bottom. The hall lamp was not lit.

"You had better stay where you are," said Caroline with guarded sharpness.

"I am going to see," repeated Mrs. Brigham firmly.

Then she folded her skirts so tightly that her bulk with its swelling curves was revealed in a black silk sheath, and she went with a slow toddle across the hall to the study door. She stood there, her eye at the crack.

In the south room Rebecca stopped sewing and sat watching with dilated eyes. Caroline sewed steadily. What Mrs. Brigham, standing at the crack in the study door, saw was this:

Henry Glynn, evidently reasoning that the source of the strange shadow must be between the table on which the lamp stood and the wall, was making systematic passes and thrusts all over and through the intervening space with an old sword which had belonged to his father. Not an inch was left unpierced. He seemed to have divided the space into mathematical sections. He brandished the sword with a sort of cold fury and calculation; the blade gave out flashes of light, the shadow remained unmoved. Mrs. Brigham, watching, felt herself cold with horror.

Finally Henry ceased and stood with the sword in hand and raised as if to strike, surveying the shadow on the wall threateningly. Mrs. Brigham toddled back across the hall and shut the south room door behind her before she related what she had seen.

"He looked like a demon!" she said again. "Have you got any of that old wine in the house, Caroline? I don't feel as if I could stand much more."

Indeed, she looked overcome. Her handsome placid face was worn and strained and pale.

"Yes, there's plenty," said Caroline; "you can have some when you go to bed."

"I think we had all better take some," said Mrs. Brigham. "Oh, my God, Caroline, what—"

"Don't ask and don't speak," said Caroline.

"No, I am not going to," replied Mrs. Brigham; "but—"

Rebecca moaned aloud.

"What are you doing that for?" asked Caroline harshly.

"Poor Edward," returned Rebecca.

"That is all you have to groan for," said Caroline. "There is nothing else."

"I am going to bed," said Mrs. Brigham. "I sha'n't be able to be at the funeral if I don't."

Soon the three sisters went to their chambers and the south parlour was deserted. Caroline called to Henry in the study to put out the light before he came upstairs. They had been gone about an hour when he came into the room bringing the lamp which had stood in the study. He set it on the table and waited a few minutes, pacing up and down. His face was terrible, his fair complexion showed livid; his blue eyes seemed dark blanks of awful reflections.

Then he took the lamp up and returned to the library. He

set the lamp on the centre table, and the shadow sprang out on the wall. Again he studied the furniture and moved it about, but deliberately, with none of his former frenzy. Nothing affected the shadow. Then he returned to the south room with the lamp and again waited. Again he returned to the study and placed the lamp on the table, and the shadow sprang out upon the wall. It was midnight before he went upstairs. Mrs. Brigham and the other sisters, who could not sleep, heard him.

The next day was the funeral. That evening the family sat in the south room. Some relatives were with them. Nobody entered the study until Henry carried a lamp in there after the others had retired for the night. He saw again the shadow on the wall leap to an awful life before the light.

The next morning at breakfast Henry Glynn announced that he had to go to the city for three days. The sisters looked at him with surprise. He very seldom left home, and just now his practice had been neglected on account of Edward's death. He was a physician.

"How can you leave your patients now?" asked Mrs. Brigham wonderingly.

"I don't know how to, but there is no other way," replied Henry easily. "I have had a telegram from Doctor Mitford."

"Consultation?" inquired Mrs. Brigham.

"I have business," replied Henry.

Doctor Mitford was an old classmate of his who lived in a neighbouring city and who occasionally called upon him in the case of a consultation.

After he had gone Mrs. Brigham said to Caroline that after all Henry had not said that he was going to consult with Doctor Mitford, and she thought it very strange.

"Everything is very strange," said Rebecca with a shudder.

"What do you mean?" inquired Caroline sharply.

"Nothing," replied Rebecca.

Nobody entered the library that day, nor the next, nor the next. The third day Henry was expected home, but he did not arrive and the last train from the city had come.

"I call it pretty queer work," said Mrs. Brigham. "The idea of a doctor leaving his patients for three days anyhow, at such a time as this, and I know he has some very sick ones; he said so. And the idea of a consultation lasting three days! There is no sense in it, and *now* he has not come. I don't understand it, for my part."

"I don't either," said Rebecca.

They were all in the south parlour. There was no light in the study opposite, and the door was ajar.

Presently Mrs. Brigham rose—she could not have told why; something seemed to impel her, some will outside her own. She went out of the room, again wrapping her rustling skirts around that she might pass noiselessly, and began pushing at the swollen door of the study.

"She has not got any lamp," said Rebecca in a shaking voice.

Caroline, who was writing letters, rose again, took a lamp (there were two in the room) and followed her sister. Rebecca had risen, but she stood trembling, not venturing to follow.

The doorbell rang, but the others did not hear it; it was on the south door on the other side of the house from the study. Rebecca, after hesitating until the bell rang the second time, went to the door; she remembered that the servant was out.

Caroline and her sister Emma entered the study. Caroline set the lamp on the table. They looked at the wall. "Oh, my God," gasped Mrs. Brigham, "there are—there are *two*—shadows." The sisters stood clutching each other, staring at the awful things on the wall. Then Rebecca came in, staggering, with a telegram in her hand. "Here is—a telegram," she gasped. "Henry is—dead."

Luella Miller

Close to the village street stood the one-storey house in
which Luella Miller, who had an evil name in the village, had
dwelt. She had been dead for years, yet there were those in
the village who, in spite of the clearer light which comes on a
vantage-point from a long-past danger, half believed in the tale
which they had heard from their childhood. In their hearts, although they scarcely would have owned it, was a survival of the
wild horror and frenzied fear of their ancestors who had dwelt
in the same age with Luella Miller. Young people even would
stare with a shudder at the old house as they passed, and children
never played around it as was their wont around an untenanted
building. Not a window in the old Miller house was broken: the
panes reflected the morning sunlight in patches of emerald and
blue, and the latch of the sagging front door was never lifted,
although no bolt secured it.

Since Luella Miller had been carried out of it, the house
had had no tenant except one friendless old soul who had no
choice between that and the far-off shelter of the open sky. This
old woman, who had survived her kindred and friends, lived in
the house one week, then one morning no smoke came out of
the chimney, and a body of neighbours, a score strong, entered
and found her dead in her bed. There were dark whispers as to
the cause of her death, and there were those who testified to
an expression of fear so exalted that it showed forth the state
of the departing soul upon the dead face. The old woman had
been hale and hearty when she entered the house, and in seven

days she was dead; it seemed that she had fallen a victim to some uncanny power. The minister talked in the pulpit with covert severity against the sin of superstition; still the belief prevailed. Not a soul in the village but would have chosen the almshouse rather than that dwelling. No vagrant, if he heard the tale, would seek shelter beneath that old roof, unhallowed by nearly half a century of superstitious fear.

There was only one person in the village who had actually known Luella Miller. That person was a woman well over eighty, but a marvel of vitality and unextinct youth. Straight as an arrow, with the spring of one recently let loose from the bow of life, she moved about the streets, and she always went to church, rain or shine. She had never married, and had lived alone for years in a house across the road from Luella Miller's.

This woman had none of the garrulousness of age, but never in all her life had she ever held her tongue for any will save her own, and she never spared the truth when she essayed to present it. She it was who bore testimony to the life, evil, though possibly wittingly or designedly so, of Luella Miller, and to her personal appearance. When this old woman spoke—and she had the gift of description, although her thoughts were clothed in the rude vernacular of her native village—one could seem to see Luella Miller as she had really looked. According to this woman, Lydia Anderson by name, Luella Miller had been a beauty of a type rather unusual in New England. She had been a slight, pliant sort of creature, as ready with a strong yielding to fate and as unbreakable as a willow. She had glimmering lengths of straight, fair hair, which she wore softly looped round a long, lovely face. She had blue eyes full of soft pleading, little slender, clinging hands, and a wonderful grace of motion and attitude.

"Luella Miller used to sit in a way nobody else could if they sat up and studied a week of Sundays," said Lydia Anderson, "and it was a sight to see her walk. If one of them willows over there on the edge of the brook could start up and get its roots free of the ground, and move off, it would go just the way Luella Miller used to. She had a green shot silk she used to wear, too, and a hat with green ribbon streamers, and a lace veil blowing across her face and out sideways, and a green ribbon flyin' from her waist. That was what she came out bride in when she married Erastus Miller. Her name before she was married was Hill. There was always a sight of "l's" in her name, married or single. Erastus Miller was good lookin', too, better lookin' than Luella. Sometimes I used to think that Luella wa'n't so handsome after all. Erastus just about worshiped her. I used to know him pretty well. He lived next door to me, and we went to school together. Folks used to say he was waitin' on me, but he wa'n't. I never thought he was except once or twice when he said things that some girls might have suspected meant somethin'. That was before Luella came here to teach the district school. It was funny how she came to get it, for folks said she hadn't any education, and that one of the big girls, Lottie Henderson, used to do all the teachin' for her, while she sat back and did embroidery work on a cambric pocket-handkerchief.

"Lottie Henderson was a real smart girl, a splendid scholar, and she just set her eyes by Luella, as all the girls did. Lottie would have made a real smart woman, but she died when Luella had been here about a year—just faded away and died: nobody knew what ailed her. She dragged herself to that schoolhouse and helped Luella teach till the very last minute. The committee all knew how Luella didn't do much of the work herself, but they winked at it. It wa'n't long after Lottie died that Erastus married her. I always thought he hurried it up because she wa'n't fit to teach. One of the big boys used to help her after Lottie died, but he hadn't much government, and the school didn't do very well, and Luella might have had to give it up, for the committee couldn't have shut their eyes to things much longer.

"The boy that helped her was a real honest, innocent sort of fellow, and he was a good scholar, too. Folks said he overstudied, and that was the reason he was took crazy the year after Luella married, but I don't know. And I don't know what made Erastus Miller go into consumption of the blood the year after he was married: consumption wa'n't in his family. He just grew weaker and weaker, and went almost bent double when he tried to wait on Luella, and he spoke feeble, like an old man. He worked terrible hard till the last trying to save up a little to leave Luella. I've seen him out in the worst storms on a wood-sled—he used to cut and sell wood—and he was hunched up on top lookin' more dead than alive. Once I couldn't stand it: I went over and helped him pitch some wood on the cart—I was always strong in my arms. I wouldn't stop for all he told me to, and I guess he was glad enough for the help. That was only a week before he died. He fell on the kitchen floor while he was gettin' breakfast. He always got the breakfast and let Luella lay abed. He did all the sweepin' and the washin' and the ironin' and most of the cookin'.

"He couldn't bear to have Luella lift her finger, and she let him do for her. She lived like a queen for all the work she did. She didn't even do her sewin'. She said it made her shoulder ache to sew, and poor Erastus's sister Lily used to do all her sewin'. She wa'n't able to, either; she was never strong in her back, but she did it beautifully. She had to, to suit Luella, she was so dreadful particular. I never saw anythin' like the fagottin' and hemstitchin' that Lily Miller did for Luella. She made all Luella's weddin' outfit, and that green silk dress, after Maria Babbit cut it. Maria she cut it for nothin', and she did a lot more cuttin' and fittin' for nothin' for Luella, too. Lily Miller went to live with Luella after Erastus died. She gave up her home, though she was real attached to it and wa'n't a mite afraid to stay alone. She rented it and she went to live with Luella right away after the funeral."

Then this old woman, Lydia Anderson, who remembered Luella Miller, would go on to relate the story of Lily Miller. It seemed that on the removal of Lily Miller to the house of her dead brother, to live with his widow, the village people first began to talk. This Lily Miller had been hardly past her first youth, and a most robust and blooming woman, rosy-cheeked, with curls of strong, black hair overshadowing round, candid temples and bright dark eyes. It was not six months after she had taken up her residence with her sister-in-law that her rosy colour faded and her pretty curves became wan hollows. White shadows began to show in the black rings of her hair, and the light died out of her eyes, her features sharpened, and there were pathetic lines at her mouth, which yet wore always an expression of utter sweetness and even happiness. She was devoted to her sister; there was no doubt that she loved her with her whole heart, and was perfectly content in her service. It was her sole anxiety lest she should die and leave her alone.

"The way Lily Miller used to talk about Luella was enough to make you mad and enough to make you cry," said Lydia Anderson. "I've been in there sometimes toward the last when she was too feeble to cook and carried her some blancmange or custard—somethin' I thought she might relish, and she'd thank me, and when I asked her how she was, say she felt better than she did yesterday, and asked me if I didn't think she looked better, dreadful pitiful, and say poor Luella had an awful time takin' care of her and doin' the work—she wa'n't strong enough to do anythin'—when all the time Luella wa'n't liftin' her finger and poor Lily didn't get any care except what the neighbours gave her, and Luella eat up everythin' that was carried in for Lily. I had it real straight that she did. Luella used to just sit and cry and do nothin'.

"She did act real fond of Lily, and she pined away considerable, too. There was those that thought she'd go into a decline herself. But after Lily died, her Aunt Abby Mixter came, and then Luella picked up and grew as fat and rosy as ever. But poor Aunt Abby begun to droop just the way Lily had, and I guess somebody wrote to her married daughter, Mrs. Sam Abbot, who lived in Barre, for she wrote her mother that she must leave right away and come and make her a visit, but Aunt Abby wouldn't go. I can see her now. She was a real good-lookin' woman, tall and large, with a big, square face and a high forehead that looked of itself kind of benevolent and good.

"She just tended out on Luella as if she had been a baby, and when her married daughter sent for her she wouldn't stir one inch. She'd always thought a lot of her daughter, too, but she said Luella needed her and her married daughter didn't. Her daughter kept writin' and writin', but it didn't do any good. Finally she came, and when she saw how bad her mother looked, she broke down and cried and all but went on her knees to have her come away. She spoke her mind out to Luella, too. She told her that she'd killed her husband and everybody that had anythin' to do with her, and she'd thank her to leave her mother alone.

"Luella went into hysterics, and Aunt Abby was so frightened that she called me after her daughter went. Mrs. Sam Abbot she went away fairly cryin' out loud in the buggy, the neighbours heard her, and well she might, for she never saw her mother again alive. I went in that night when Aunt Abby called for me, standin' in the door with her little green-checked shawl over her head. I can see her now. 'Do come over here, Miss Anderson,' she sung out, kind of gasping for breath. I didn't stop for anythin'. I put over as fast as I could, and when I got there, there was Luella laughin' and cryin' all together, and Aunt Abby trying to hush her, and all the time she herself was white as a sheet and shakin' so she could hardly stand. 'For the land sakes, Mrs. Mixter,' says I, 'you look worse than she does. You ain't fit to be up out of your bed.'

"'Oh, there ain't anythin' the matter with me,' says she. Then she went on talkin' to Luella. 'There, there, don't, don't, poor little lamb,' says she. 'Aunt Abby is here. She ain't goin' away and leave you. Don't, poor little lamb.'

"'Do leave her with me, Mrs. Mixter, and you get back to bed,' says I, for Aunt Abby had been layin' down considerable lately, though somehow she contrived to do the work.

"'I'm well enough,' says she. 'Don't you think she had better have the doctor, Miss Anderson?'

"'The doctor,' says I, 'I think *you* had better have the doctor. I think you need him much worse than some folks I could mention.' And I looked right straight at Luella Miller laughin' and cryin' and goin' on as if she was the centre of all creation. All the time she was actin' so—seemed as if she was too sick to sense anythin'—she was keepin' a sharp lookout as to how we took it out of the corner of one eye. I see her. You could never cheat me about Luella Miller. Finally I got real mad and I run home and I got a bottle of valerian I had, and I poured some boilin' hot water on a handful of catnip, and I mixed up that catnip tea with most half a wineglass of valerian, and I went with it over to Luella's. I marched right up to Luella, a-holdin' out of that cup, all smokin'. 'Now,' says I, 'Luella Miller, *You swaller this!*'

"'What is—what is it, oh, what is it?' she sort of screeches out. Then she goes off a-laughin' enough to kill.

"'Poor lamb, poor little lamb,' says Aunt Abby, standin' over her, all kind of tottery, and tryin' to bathe her head with camphor.

"'*You swaller this right down,*' says I. And I didn't waste any ceremony. I just took hold of Luella Miller's chin and I tipped her head back, and I caught her mouth open with laughin', and I clapped that cup to her lips, and I fairly hollered at her: 'Swaller, swaller, swaller!' and she gulped it right down. She had to, and I guess it did her good. Anyhow, she stopped cryin' and laughin' and let me put her to bed, and she went to sleep like a baby inside of half an hour. That was more than poor Aunt Abby did. She lay awake all that night and I stayed with her, though she tried not to have me; said she wa'n't sick enough for watchers. But I stayed, and I made some good cornmeal gruel and I fed her a teaspoon every little while all night long. It seemed to me as if she was jest dyin' from bein' all wore out.

"In the mornin' as soon as it was light I run over to the Bisbees and sent Johnny Bisbee for the doctor. I told him to tell the doctor to hurry, and he come pretty quick. Poor Aunt Abby didn't seem to know much of anythin' when he got there. You couldn't hardly tell she breathed, she was so used up. When the doctor had gone, Luella came into the room lookin' like a baby in her ruffled nightgown. I can see her now. Her eyes were as blue and her face all pink and white like a blossom, and she looked at Aunt Abby in the bed sort of innocent and surprised. 'Why,' says she, 'Aunt Abby ain't got up yet?'

"'No, she ain't,' says I, pretty short.

"'I thought I didn't smell the coffee,' says Luella.

"'Coffee,' says I. 'I guess if you have coffee this mornin' you'll make it yourself.'

"'I never made the coffee in all my life,' says she, dreadful astonished. 'Erastus always made the coffee as long as he lived, and then Lily she made it, and then Aunt Abby made it. I don't believe I *can* make the coffee, Miss Anderson.'

"'You can make it or go without, jest as you please,' says I.

"'Ain't Aunt Abby goin' to get up?' says she.

"'I guess she won't get up,' says I, 'sick as she is.' I was gettin' madder and madder. There was somethin' about that little pink-and-white thing standin' there and talkin' about coffee, when she had killed so many better folks than she was, and had jest killed another, that made me feel 'most as if I wished somebody would up and kill her before she had a chance to do any more harm.

"'Is Aunt Abby sick?' says Luella, as if she was sort of ag-grieved and injured.

"'Yes,' says I, 'she's sick, and she's goin' to die, and then you'll be left alone, and you'll have to do for yourself and wait on yourself, or do without things.' I don't know but I was sort of hard, but it was the truth, and if I was any harder than Luella Miller had been I'll give up. I ain't never been sorry that I said it. Well, Luella, she up and had hysterics again at that, and I jest let her have 'em. All I did was to bundle her into the room on the other side of the entry where Aunt Abby couldn't hear her, if she wa'n't past it—I don't know but she was—and set her down hard in a chair and told her not to come back into the other room, and she minded. She had her hysterics in there till she got tired. When she found out that nobody was comin' to coddle her and do for her she stopped.

"At least I suppose she did. I had all I could do with poor Aunt Abby tryin' to keep the breath of life in her. The doctor had told me that she was dreadful low, and give me some very strong medicine to give to her in drops real often, and told me real particular about the nourishment. Well, I did as he told me real faithful till she wa'n't able to swaller any longer. Then I had her daughter sent for. I had begun to realize that she wouldn't last any time at all. I hadn't realized it before, though I spoke to Luella the way I did. The doctor he came, and Mrs. Sam Abbot, but when she got there it was too late; her mother was dead. Aunt Abby's daughter just give one look at her mother layin' there, then she turned sort of sharp and sudden and looked at me.

"'Where is she?' says she, and I knew she meant Luella.

"'She's out in the kitchen,' says I. 'She's too nervous to see folks die. She's afraid it will make her sick.'

"The doctor he speaks up then. He was a young man. Old Doctor Park had died the year before, and this was a young fellow just out of college. 'Mrs. Miller is not strong,' says he, kind of severe, 'and she is quite right in not agitating herself.'

"'You are another, young man; she's got her pretty claw on you,' thinks I, but I didn't say anythin' to him. I just said over to Mrs. Sam Abbot that Luella was in the kitchen, and Mrs. Sam Abbot she went out there, and I went, too, and I never heard anythin' like the way she talked to Luella Miller. I felt pretty hard to Luella myself, but this was more than I ever would have dared to say. Luella she was too scared to go into hysterics. She jest flopped. She seemed to jest shrink away to nothin' in that kitchen chair, with Mrs. Sam Abbot standin' over her and talkin' and tellin' her the truth. I guess the truth was most too much for her and no mistake, because Luella presently actually did faint away, and there wa'n't any sham about it, the way I always suspected there was about them hysterics. She fainted dead away and we had to lay her flat on the floor, and the doctor he came runnin' out and he said somethin' about a weak heart dreadful fierce to Mrs. Sam Abbot, but she wa'n't a mite scared. She faced him jest as white as even Luella was layin' there lookin' like death and the doctor feelin' of her pulse.

"'Weak heart,' says she, 'weak heart; weak fiddlesticks! There ain't nothin' weak about that woman. She's got strength enough to hang onto other folks till she kills 'em. Weak? It was my poor mother that was weak: this woman killed her as sure as if she had taken a knife to her.'

"But the doctor he didn't pay much attention. He was bendin' over Luella layin' there with her yellow hair all streamin' and her pretty pink-and-white face all pale, and her blue eyes like stars gone out, and he was holdin' onto her hand and smoothin' her forehead, and tellin' me to get the brandy in Aunt Abby's room, and I was sure as I wanted to be that Luella had got somebody else to hang onto, now Aunt Abby was gone, and I thought of poor Erastus Miller, and I sort of pitied the poor young doctor, led away by a pretty face, and I made up my mind I'd see what I could do.

"I waited till Aunt Abby had been dead and buried about a month, and the doctor was goin' to see Luella steady and folks were beginnin' to talk; then one evenin', when I knew the doctor had been called out of town and wouldn't be round, I went over to Luella's. I found her all dressed up in a blue muslin with white polka dots on it, and her hair curled jest as pretty, and there wa'n't a young girl in the place could compare with her. There was somethin' about Luella Miller seemed to draw the heart right out of you, but she didn't draw it out of ME. She was settin' rocking in the chair by her sittin'-room window, and Maria Brown had gone home. Maria Brown had been in to help her, or rather to do the work, for Luella wa'n't helped when she didn't do anythin'.

"Maria Brown was real capable and she didn't have any ties; she wa'n't married, and lived alone, so she'd offered. I couldn't see why she should do the work any more than Luella; she wa'n't any too strong; but she seemed to think she could and Luella seemed to think so, too, so she went over and did all the work—washed, and ironed, and baked, while Luella sat and rocked. Maria didn't live long afterward. She began to fade away just the same fashion the others had. Well, she was warned, but she acted real mad when folks said anythin': said Luella was a poor, abused woman, too delicate to help herself, and they'd

68

ought to be ashamed, and if she died helpin' them that couldn't help themselves she would—and she did.

"'I s'pose Maria has gone home,' says I to Luella, when I had gone in and sat down opposite her.

"'Yes, Maria went half an hour ago, after she had got supper and washed the dishes,' says Luella, in her pretty way.

"'I suppose she has got a lot of work to do in her own house tonight,' says I, kind of bitter, but that was all thrown away on Luella Miller. It seemed to her right that other folks that wa'n't any better able than she was herself should wait on her, and she couldn't get it through her head that anybody should think it *wa'n't* right.

"'Yes,' says Luella, real sweet and pretty, 'yes, she said she had to do her washin' tonight. She has let it go for a fortnight along of comin' over here.'

"'Why don't she stay home and do her washin' instead of comin' over here and doin' *your* work, when you are just as well able, and enough sight more so, than she is to do it?' says I.

"Then Luella she looked at me like a baby who has a rattle shook at it. She sort of laughed as innocent as you please. 'Oh, I can't do the work myself, Miss Anderson,' says she. 'I never did. Maria *has* to do it.'

"Then I spoke out: 'Has to do it I' says I. 'Has to do it!' She don't have to do it, either. Maria Brown has her own home and enough to live on. She ain't beholden to you to come over here and slave for you and kill herself.'

"Luella she jest set and stared at me for all the world like a doll-baby that was so abused that it was comin' to life.

"'Yes,' says I, 'she's killin' herself. She's goin' to die just the way Erastus did, and Lily, and your Aunt Abby. You're killin' her jest as you did them. I don't know what there is about you, but you seem to bring a curse,' says I. 'You kill everybody that is fool enough to care anythin' about you and do for you.'

"She stared at me and she was pretty pale.

"'And Maria ain't the only one you're goin' to kill,' says I. 'You're goin' to kill Doctor Malcom before you're done with him.'

"Then a red colour came flamin' all over her face. 'I ain't goin' to kill him, either,' says she, and she begun to cry.

"'Yes, you *be!*' says I. Then I spoke as I had never spoke before. You see, I felt it on account of Erastus. I told her that she hadn't any business to think of another man after she'd been married to one that had died for her: that she was a dreadful woman; and she was, that's true enough, but sometimes I have wondered lately if she knew it—if she wa'n't like a baby with scissors in its hand cuttin' everybody without knowin' what it was doin'.

"Luella she kept gettin' paler and paler, and she never took her eyes off my face. There was somethin' awful about the way she looked at me and never spoke one word. After awhile I quit talkin' and I went home. I watched that night, but her lamp went out before nine o'clock, and when Doctor Malcom came drivin' past and sort of slowed up he see there wa'n't any light and he drove along. I saw her sort of shy out of meetin' the next Sunday, too, so he shouldn't go home with her, and I begun to think mebbe she did have some conscience after all. It was only a week after that that Maria Brown died—sort of sudden at the last, though everybody had seen it was comin'. Well, then there was a good deal of feelin' and pretty dark whispers. Folks said the days of witchcraft had come again, and they were pretty shy of Luella.

"She acted sort of offish to the doctor and he didn't go there, and there wa'n't anybody to do anythin' for her. I don't know how she *did* get along. I wouldn't go in there and offer to help her—not because I was afraid of dyin' like the rest, but I thought she was just as well able to do her own work as I was to do it for her, and I thought it was about time that she did it and stopped killin' other folks. But it wa'n't very long before folks began to say that Luella herself was goin' into a decline jest the way her husband, and Lily, and Aunt Abby and the others had, and I saw myself that she looked pretty bad. I used to see her goin' past from the store with a bundle as if she could hardly crawl, but I remembered how Erastus used to wait and 'tend when he couldn't hardly put one foot before the other, and I didn't go out to help her.

"But at last one afternoon I saw the doctor come drivin' up like mad with his medicine chest, and Mrs. Babbit came in after supper and said that Luella was real sick.

"'I'd offer to go in and nurse her,' says she, 'but I've got my children to consider, and mebbe it ain't true what they say, but it's queer how many folks that have done for her have died.'

"I didn't say anythin', but I considered how she had been Erastus's wife and how he had set his eyes by her, and I made up my mind to go in the next mornin', unless she was better, and see what I could do; but the next mornin' I see her at the window, and pretty soon she came steppin' out as spry as you please, and a little while afterward Mrs. Babbit came in and told me that the doctor had got a girl from out of town, a Sarah Jones, to come there, and she said she was pretty sure that the doctor was goin' to marry Luella.

"I saw him kiss her in the door that night myself, and I knew it was true. The woman came that afternoon, and the way she flew around was a caution. I don't believe Luella had swept since Maria died. She swept and dusted, and washed and ironed; wet clothes and dusters and carpets were flyin' over there all day, and every time Luella set her foot out when the doctor wa'n't there there was that Sarah Jones helpin' of her up and down the steps, as if she hadn't learned to walk.

"Well, everybody knew that Luella and the doctor were goin' to be married, but it wa'n't long before they began to talk about his lookin' so poorly, jest as they had about the others; and they talked about Sarah Jones, too.

"Well, the doctor did die, and he wanted to be married first, so as to leave what little he had to Luella, but he died before the minister could get there, and Sarah Jones died a week afterward.

"Well, that wound up everything for Luella Miller. Not another soul in the whole town would lift a finger for her. There got to be a sort of panic. Then she began to droop in good earnest. She used to have to go to the store herself, for Mrs. Babbit was afraid to let Tommy go for her, and I've seen her goin' past and stoppin' every two or three steps to rest. Well, I stood it as long as I could, but one day I see her comin' with her arms full and stoppin' to lean against the Babbit fence, and I run out and took her bundles and carried them to her house. Then I went home and never spoke one word to her though she called after me dreadful kind of pitiful. Well, that night I was taken sick with a chill, and I was sick as I wanted to be for two weeks. Mrs. Babbit had seen me run out to help Luella and she came in and told me I was goin' to die on account of it. I didn't know whether I was or not, but I considered I had done right by Erastus's wife.

"That last two weeks Luella she had a dreadful hard time, I guess. She was pretty sick, and as near as I could make out nobody dared go near her. I don't know as she was really needin' anythin' very much, for there was enough to eat in her house and it was warm weather, and she made out to cook a little flour gruel every day, I know, but I guess she had a hard time, she that had been so petted and done for all her life.

"When I got so I could go out, I went over there one morning. Mrs. Babbit had just come in to say she hadn't seen any smoke and she didn't know but it was somebody's duty to go in, but she couldn't help thinkin' of her children, and I got right up, though I hadn't been out of the house for two weeks, and I went in there, and Luella she was layin' on the bed, and she was dyin'.

"She lasted all that day and into the night. But I sat there after the new doctor had gone away. Nobody else dared to go there. It was about midnight that I left her for a minute to run home and get some medicine I had been takin', for I begun to feel rather bad.

"It was a full moon that night, and just as I started out of my door to cross the street back to Luella's, I stopped short, for I saw something."

Lydia Anderson at this juncture always said with a certain defiance that she did not expect to be believed, and then proceeded in a hushed voice:

"I saw what I saw, and I know I saw it, and I will swear on my death bed that I saw it. I saw Luella Miller and Erastus Miller, and Lily, and Aunt Abby, and Maria, and the doctor, and Sarah, all goin' out of her door, and all but Luella shone white in the moonlight, and they were all helpin' her along till she seemed to fairly fly in the midst of them. Then it all disappeared. I stood a minute with my heart poundin', then I went over there. I thought of goin' for Mrs. Babbit, but I thought she'd be afraid. So I went alone, though I knew what had happened. Luella was layin' real peaceful, dead on her bed."

This was the story that the old woman, Lydia Anderson, told, but the sequel was told by the people who survived her, and this is the tale which has become folklore in the village.

Lydia Anderson died when she was eighty-seven. She had continued wonderfully hale and hearty for one of her years until about two weeks before her death.

One bright moonlight evening she was sitting beside a window in her parlour when she made a sudden exclamation, and was out of the house and across the street before the neighbour who was taking care of her could stop her. She followed as fast as possible and found Lydia Anderson stretched on the ground before the door of Luella Miller's deserted house, and she was quite dead.

The next night there was a red gleam of fire athwart the moonlight and the old house of Luella Miller was burned to the ground. Nothing is now left of it except a few old cellar stones and a lilac bush, and in summer a helpless trail of morning glories among the weeds, which might be considered emblematic of Luella herself.

Old Woman Magoun

The hamlet of Barry's Ford is situated in a sort of high valley among the mountains. Below it the hills lie in moveless curves like a petrified ocean; above it they rise in green-cresting waves which never break. It is *Barry's* Ford because at one time the Barry family was the most important in the place; and *Ford* because just at the beginning of the hamlet the little turbulent Barry River is fordable. There is, however, now a rude bridge across the river.

Old Woman Magoun was largely instrumental in bringing the bridge to pass. She haunted the miserable little grocery, wherein whiskey and hands of tobacco were the most salient features of the stock in trade, and she talked much. She would elbow herself into the midst of a knot of idlers and talk.

"That bridge ought to be built this very summer," said Old Woman Magoun. She spread her strong arms like wings, and sent the loafers, half laughing, half angry, flying in every direction. "If I were a *man*," said she, "I'd go out this very minute and lay the fust log. If I were a passel of lazy men layin' round, I'd start up for once in my life, I would." The men cowered visibly—all except Nelson Barry; he swore under his breath and strode over to the counter.

Old Woman Magoun looked after him majestically. "You can cuss all you want to, Nelson Barry," said she; "I ain't afraid of you. I don't expect you to lay any log of the bridge, but I'm goin' to have it built this very summer." She did. The weakness of the masculine element in Barry's Ford was laid low before such

74

strenuous feminine assertion.

Old Woman Magoun and some other women planned a treat—two sucking pigs, and pies, and sweet cake—for a reward after the bridge should be finished. They even viewed leniently the increased consumption of ardent spirits.

"It seems queer to me," Old Woman Magoun said to Sally Jinks, "that men can't do nothin' without havin' to drink and chew to keep their sperits up. Lord! I've worked all my life and never done nuther."

"Men is different," said Sally Jinks.

"Yes, they be," assented Old Woman Magoun, with open contempt.

The two women sat on a bench in front of Old Woman Magoun's house, and little Lily Barry, her granddaughter, sat holding her doll on a small mossy stone near by. From where they sat they could see the men at work on the new bridge. It was the last day of the work.

Lily clasped her doll—a poor old rag thing—close to her childish bosom, like a little mother, and her face, round which curled her long yellow hair, was fixed upon the men at work. Little Lily had never been allowed to run with the other children of Barry's Ford. Her grandmother had taught her everything she knew—which was not much, but tending at least to a certain measure of spiritual growth—for she, as it were, poured the goodness of her own soul into this little receptive vase of another. Lily was firmly grounded in her knowledge that it was wrong to lie or steal or disobey her grandmother. She had also learned that one should be very industrious. It was seldom that Lily sat idly holding her doll-baby, but this was a holiday because of the bridge.

She looked only a child, although she was nearly fourteen; her mother had been married at sixteen. That is, Old Woman Magoun said that her daughter, Lily's mother, had married at sixteen; there had been rumours, but no one had dared openly gainsay the old woman. She said that her daughter had married Nelson Barry, and he had deserted her. She had lived in her mother's house, and Lily had been born there, and she had died when the baby was only a week old. Lily's father, Nelson Barry, was the fairly dangerous degenerate of a good old family. Nelson's father before him had been bad. He was now the last of the family, with the exception of a sister of feeble intellect, with whom he lived in the old Barry house. He was a middle-aged man, still handsome.

The shiftless population of Barry's Ford looked up to him as to an evil deity. They wondered how Old Woman Magoun dared brave him as she did. But Old Woman Magoun had within her a mighty sense of reliance upon herself as being on the right track in the midst of a maze of evil, which gave her courage. Nelson Barry had manifested no interest whatever in his daughter. Lily seldom saw her father. She did not often go to the store which was his favourite haunt. Her grandmother took care that she should not do so.

However, that afternoon she departed from her usual custom and sent Lily to the store.

She came in from the kitchen, whither she had been to baste the roasting pig. "There's no use talkin'," said she, "I've got to have some more salt. I've jest used the very last I had to dredge over that pig. I've got to go to the store."

Sally Jinks looked at Lily. "Why don't you send her?" she asked.

Old Woman Magoun gazed irresolutely at the girl. She was herself very tired. It did not seem to her that she could drag herself up the dusty hill to the store. She glanced with covert resentment at Sally Jinks. She thought that she might offer to go. But Sally Jinks said again, "Why don't you let her go?" and looked with a languid eye at Lily holding her doll on the stone.

Lily was watching the men at work on the bridge, with her childish delight in a spectacle of any kind, when her grandmother addressed her.

"Guess I'll let you go down to the store an' git some salt, Lily," said she.

The girl turned uncomprehending eyes upon her grandmother at the sound of her voice. She had been filled with one of the innocent reveries of childhood. Lily had in her the making of an artist or a poet. Her prolonged childhood went to prove it, and also her retrospective eyes, as clear and blue as blue light itself, which seemed to see past all that she looked upon. She had not come of the old Barry family for nothing. The best of the strain was in her, along with the splendid staunchness in humble lines which she had acquired from her grandmother.

"Put on your hat," said Old Woman Magoun; "the sun is hot, and you might git a headache." She called the girl to her, and put back the shower of fair curls under the rubber band which confined the hat. She gave Lily some money, and watched her knot it into a corner of her little cotton handkerchief. "Be careful you don't lose it," said she, "and don't stop to talk to anybody, for I am in a hurry for that salt. Of course, if anybody speaks to you, answer them polite, and then come right along."

Lily started, her pocket-handkerchief weighted with the small silver dangling from one hand, and her rag doll carried over her shoulder like a baby. The absurd travesty of a face peeped forth from Lily's yellow curls. Sally Jinks looked after her with a sniff.

"She ain't goin' to carry that rag doll to the store?" said she.

"She likes to," replied Old Woman Magoun, in a half-shamed yet defiantly extenuating voice.

"Some girls at her age is thinkin' about *beaux* instead of rag dolls" said Sally Jinks.

The grandmother bristled. "Lily ain't big nor old for her age," said she. "I ain't in any hurry to have her git married. She ain't none too strong."

"She's got a good colour," said Sally Jinks. She was crocheting white cotton lace, making her thick fingers fly. She really knew how to do scarcely anything except to crochet that coarse lace; somehow her heavy brain or her fingers had mastered that.

"I know she's got a beautiful colour," replied Old Woman Magoun, with an odd mixture of pride and anxiety, "but it comes an' goes."

"I've heard that was a bad sign," remarked Sally Jinks, loosening some thread from her spool.

"Yes, it is," said the grandmother. "She's nothin' but a baby, though she's quicker than most to learn."

Lily Barry went on her way to the store. She was clad in a scanty short frock of blue cotton; her hat was tipped back, forming an oval frame for her innocent face. She was very small, and walked like a child, with the clap-clap of little feet of babyhood. She might have been considered, from her looks, under ten.

Presently she heard footsteps behind her; she turned around a little timidly to see who was coming. When she saw a handsome, well-dressed man, she felt reassured. The man came alongside and glanced down carelessly at first, then his look deepened. He smiled, and Lily saw he was very handsome indeed, and that his smile was not only reassuring but wonderfully sweet and compelling.

"Well, little one," said the man, "where are you bound, you and your dolly?"

"I am going to the store to buy some salt for grandma," replied Lily, in her sweet treble. She looked up in the man's face, and he fairly started at the revelation of its innocent beauty. He regulated his pace by hers, and the two went on together. The man did not speak again at once. Lily kept glancing timidly up at him, and every time that she did so the man smiled and her confidence increased. Presently when the man's hand grasped her little childish one hanging by her side, she felt a complete trust in him. Then she smiled up at him. She felt glad that this nice man had come along, for just here the road was lonely.

After a while the man spoke. "What is your name, little one?" he asked, caressingly.

"Lily Barry."

The man started. "What is your father's name?"

"Nelson Barry," replied Lily.

The man whistled. "Is your mother dead?"

"Yes, sir."

"How old are you, my dear?"

"Fourteen," replied Lily.

The man looked at her with surprise. "As old as that?"

Lily suddenly shrank from the man. She could not have told why. She pulled her little hand from his, and he let it go with no remonstrance. She clasped both her arms around her rag doll, in order that her hand should not be free for him to grasp again.

She walked a little farther away from the man, and he looked amused.

"You still play with your doll?" he said, in a soft voice.

"Yes, sir," replied Lily. She quickened her pace and reached the store.

When Lily entered the store, Hiram Gates, the owner, was behind the counter. The only man besides in the store was Nelson Barry. He sat tipping his chair back against the wall; he was half asleep, and his handsome face was bristling with a beard of several days' growth, and darkly flushed. He opened his eyes when Lily entered, the strange man following. He brought his chair down on all fours, and he looked at the man—not noticing Lily at all—with a look compounded of defiance and uneasiness.

"Hullo, Jim!" he said.

"Hullo, old man!" returned the stranger.

Lily went over to the counter and asked for the salt, in her pretty little voice. When she had paid for it and was crossing the store, Nelson Barry was on his feet.

"Well, how are you, Lily? It is Lily, isn't it?" he said.

"Yes, sir," replied Lily, faintly.

Her father bent down and, for the first time in her life, kissed her, and the whiskey odour of his breath came into her face.

Lily involuntarily started, and shrank away from him. Then she rubbed her mouth violently with her little cotton handkerchief, which she held gathered up with the rag doll.

"Damn it all! I believe she is afraid of me," said Nelson Barry, in a thick voice.

"Looks a little like it," said the other man, laughing.

"It's that damned old woman," said Nelson Barry. Then he smiled again at Lily. "I didn't know what a pretty little daughter I was blessed with," said he, and he softly stroked Lily's pink cheek under her hat.

Now Lily did not shrink from him. Hereditary instincts and nature itself were asserting themselves in the child's innocent, receptive breast.

Nelson Barry looked curiously at Lily. "How old are you, anyway, child?" he asked.

"I'll be fourteen in September," replied Lily.

"But you still play with your doll?" said Barry, laughing kindly down at her.

Lily hugged her doll more tightly, in spite of her father's kind voice. "Yes, sir," she replied.

Nelson glanced across at some glass jars filled with sticks of candy. "See here, little Lily, do you like candy?" said he.

"Yes, sir."

"Wait a minute."

Lily waited while her father went over to the counter. Soon he returned with a package of the candy.

"I don't see how you are going to carry so much," he said, smiling. "Suppose you throw away your doll?"

Lily gazed at her father and hugged the doll tightly, and there was all at once in the child's expression something mature. It became the reproach of a woman. Nelson's face sobered.

"Oh, it's all right, Lily," he said; "keep your doll. Here, I guess you can carry this candy under your arm."

Lily could not resist the candy. She obeyed Nelson's instructions for carrying it, and left the store laden. The two men also left, and walked in the opposite direction, talking busily.

When Lily reached home, her grandmother, who was watching for her, spied at once the package of candy.

"What's that?" she asked, sharply.

"My father gave it to me," answered Lily, in a faltering voice. Sally regarded her with something like alertness.

"Your father?"

"Yes, ma'am."

"Where did you see him?"

"In the store."

"He gave you this candy?"

"Yes, ma'am."

"What did he say?"

"He asked me how old I was, and—"

"And what?"

"I don't know," replied Lily; and it really seemed to her that she did not know, she was so frightened and bewildered by it all, and, more than anything else, by her grandmother's face as she questioned her.

Old Woman Magoun's face was that of one upon whom a long-anticipated blow had fallen. Sally Jinks gazed at her with a sort of stupid alarm.

Old Woman Magoun continued to gaze at her grandchild with that look of terrible solicitude, as if she saw the girl in the clutch of a tiger. "You can't remember what else he said?" she asked, fiercely, and the child began to whimper softly.

"No, ma'am," she sobbed. "I—don't know, and—"

"And what? Answer me."

"There was another man there. A real handsome man."

"Did he speak to you?" asked Old Woman Magoun.

"Yes, ma'am; he walked along with me a piece," confessed Lily, with a sob of terror and bewilderment.

"What did _he_ say to you?" asked Old Woman Magoun, with a sort of despair.

Lily told, in her little, faltering, frightened voice, all of the conversation which she could recall. It sounded harmless enough, but the look of the realization of a long-expected blow never left her grandmother's face.

The sun was getting low, and the bridge was nearing completion. Soon the workmen would be crowding into the cabin for their promised supper. There became visible in the distance, far up the road, the heavily plodding figure of another woman who had agreed to come and help. Old Woman Magoun turned again to Lily.

"You go right upstairs to your own chamber now," said she.

"Good lord! ain't you goin' to let that poor child stay up and see the fun?" said Sally Jinks.

"You jest mind your own business," said Old Woman Magoun, forcibly, and Sally Jinks shrank. "You go right up there now, Lily," said the grandmother, in a softer tone, "and grandma will bring you up a nice plate of supper."

"When be you goin' to let that girl grow up?" asked Sally Jinks, when Lily had disappeared.

"She'll grow up in the Lord's good time," replied Old Woman Magoun, and there was in her voice something both sad and threatening. Sally Jinks again shrank a little.

Soon the workmen came flocking noisily into the house. Old Woman Magoun and her two helpers served the bountiful supper. Most of the men had drunk as much as, and more than, was good for them, and Old Woman Magoun had stipulated that there was to be no drinking of anything except coffee during supper.

"I'll git you as good a meal as I know now," she said, "but if I see any one of you drinkin' a drop, I'll run you all out. If you want anything to drink, you can go up to the store afterward. That's the place for you to go to, if you've got to make hogs of yourselves. I ain't goin' to have no hogs in my house."

Old Woman Magoun was implicitly obeyed. She had a curious authority over most people when she chose to exercise it. When the supper was in full swing, she quietly stole upstairs and carried some food to Lily. She found the girl, with the rag doll in her arms, crouching by the window in her little rocking-chair—a relic of her infancy, which she still used.

"What a noise they are makin', grandma!" she said, in a terrified whisper, as her grandmother placed the plate before her on a chair.

"They've 'most all of 'em been drinkin'. They air a passel of hogs," replied the old woman.

"Is the man that was with—with my father down there?" asked Lily, in a timid fashion. Then she fairly cowered before the look in her grandmother's eyes.

"No, he ain't; and what's more, he never will be down there if I can help it," said Old Woman Magoun, in a fierce whisper. "I know who he is. They can't cheat me. He's one of them Willises—that family the Barrys married into. They're worse than the Barrys, ef they *have* got money. Eat your supper, and put him out of your mind, child."

It was after Lily was asleep, when Old Woman Magoun was alone, clearing away her supper dishes, that Lily's father came. The door was closed, and he knocked, and the old woman knew at once who was there. The sound of that knock meant as much to her as the whir of a bomb to the defender of a fortress. She opened the door and Nelson Barry stood there.

"Good-evening, Mrs. Magoun," he said.

Old Woman Magoun stood before him, filling up the doorway with her firm bulk.

"Good-evening, Mrs. Magoun," said Nelson Barry again.

"I ain't got no time to waste," replied the old woman, harshly. "I've got my supper dishes to clean up after them men."

She stood there and looked at him as she might have looked at a rebellious animal which she was trying to tame. The man laughed.

"It's no use," said he. "You know me of old. No human being can turn me from my way when I am once started in it. You may as well let me come in."

Old Woman Magoun entered the house, and Barry followed her.

Barry began without any preface. "Where is the child?" asked he.

"Upstairs. She has gone to bed."

"She goes to bed early."

"Children ought to," returned the old woman, polishing a plate.

Barry laughed. "You are keeping her a child a long while," he remarked, in a soft voice which had a sting in it.

"She *is* a child," returned the old woman, defiantly.

"Her mother was only three years older when Lily was

born."

The old woman made a sudden motion toward the man which seemed fairly menacing. Then she turned again to her dishwashing.

"I want her," said Barry.

"You can't have her," replied the old woman, in a still stern voice.

"I don't see how you can help yourself. You have always acknowledged that she was my child."

The old woman continued her task, but her strong back heaved. Barry regarded her with an entirely pitiless expression.

"I am going to have the girl, that is the long and short of it," he said, "and it is for her best good, too. You are a fool, or you would see it."

"Her best good?" muttered the old woman.

"Yes, her best good. What are you going to do with her, anyway? The girl is a beauty, and almost a woman grown, although you try to make out that she is a baby. You can't live forever."

"The Lord will take care of her," replied the old woman, and again she turned and faced him, and her expression was that of a prophetess.

"Very well, let Him," said Barry, easily. "All the same I'm going to have her, and I tell you it is for her best good. Jim Willis saw her this afternoon, and—"

Old Woman Magoun looked at him. "Jim Willis!" she fairly shrieked.

"Well, what of it?"

"One of them Willises!" repeated the old woman, and this time her voice was thick. It seemed almost as if she were stricken with paralysis. She did not enunciate clearly.

The man shrank a little. "Now what is the need of your making such a fuss?" he said. "I will take her and Isabel will look out for her."

"Your half-witted sister?" said Old Woman Magoun.

"Yes, my half-witted sister. She knows more than you think."

"More wickedness."

"Perhaps. Well, a knowledge of evil is a useful thing. How are you going to avoid evil if you don't know what it is like? My sister and I will take care of my daughter."

The old woman continued to look at the man, but his eyes never fell. Suddenly her gaze grew inconceivably keen. It was as if she saw through all externals.

"I know what it is!" she cried. "You have been playing cards and you lost, and this is the way you will pay him."

Then the man's face reddened, and he swore under his breath.

"Oh, my God!" said the old woman; and she really spoke with her eyes aloft as if addressing something outside of them both. Then she turned again to her dish-washing.

The man cast a dogged look at her back. "Well, there is no use talking. I have made up my mind," said he, "and you know me and what that means. I am going to have the girl."

"When?" said the old woman, without turning around.

"Well, I am willing to give you a week. Put her clothes in good order before she comes."

The old woman made no reply. She continued washing dishes. She even handled them so carefully that they did not rattle.

"You understand," said Barry. "Have her ready a week from today."

"Yes," said Old Woman Magoun, "I understand."

Nelson Barry, going up the mountain road, reflected that Old Woman Magoun had a strong character, that she understood much better than her sex in general the futility of withstanding the inevitable.

"Well," he said to Jim Willis when he reached home, "the old woman did not make such a fuss as I expected."

"Are you going to have the girl?"

"Yes; a week from today. Look here, Jim; you've got to stick to your promise."

"All right," said Willis. "Go you one better."

The two were playing at cards in the old parlour, once magnificent, now squalid, of the Barry house. Isabel, the half-witted sister, entered, bringing some glasses on a tray. She had learned with her feeble intellect some tricks, like a dog. One of them was the mixing of sundry drinks. She set the tray on a little stand near the two men, and watched them with her silly simper.

"Clear out now and go to bed," her brother said to her, and she obeyed.

Early the next morning Old Woman Magoun went up to Lily's little sleeping-chamber, and watched her a second as she lay asleep, with her yellow locks spread over the pillow. Then she spoke. "Lily," said she—"Lily, wake up. I am going to Greenham across the new bridge, and you can go with me."

Lily immediately sat up in bed and smiled at her grandmother. Her eyes were still misty, but the light of awakening was in them.

"Get right up," said the old woman. "You can wear your new dress if you want to."

Lily gurgled with pleasure like a baby. "And my new hat?" asked she.

"I don't care."

Old Woman Magoun and Lily started for Greenham before Barry's Ford, which kept late hours, was fairly awake. It was three miles to Greenham. The old woman said that, since the horse was a little lame, they would walk. It was a beautiful morning, with a diamond radiance of dew over everything. Her grandmother had curled Lily's hair more punctiliously than usual. The little face peeped like a rose out of two rows of golden spirals. Lily wore her new muslin dress with a pink sash, and her best hat of a fine white straw trimmed with a wreath of rosebuds; also the neatest black open-work stockings and pretty shoes. She even had white cotton gloves. When they set out, the old, heavily stepping woman, in her black gown and cape and bonnet, looked down at the little pink fluttering figure. Her face was full of the tenderest love and admiration, and yet there was something terrible about it. They crossed the new bridge—a primitive structure built of logs in a slovenly fashion. Old Woman

Magoun pointed to a gap.

"Jest see that," said she. "That's the way men work."

"Men ain't very nice, be they?" said Lily, in her sweet little voice.

"No, they ain't, take them all together," replied her grandmother.

"That man that walked to the store with me was nicer than some, I guess," Lily said, in a wishful fashion. Her grandmother reached down and took the child's hand in its small cotton glove. "You hurt me, holding my hand so tight," Lily said presently, in a deprecatory little voice.

The old woman loosened her grasp. "Grandma didn't know how tight she was holding your hand," said she. "She wouldn't hurt you for nothin', except it was to save your life, or somethin' like that." She spoke with an undertone of tremendous meaning which the girl was too childish to grasp. They walked along the country road. Just before they reached Greenham they passed a stone wall overgrown with blackberry-vines, and, an unusual thing in that vicinity, a lusty spread of deadly nightshade full of berries.

"Those berries look good to eat, grandma," Lily said.

At that instant the old woman's face became something terrible to see. "You can't have any now," she said, and hurried Lily along.

"They look real nice," said Lily.

When they reached Greenham, Old Woman Magoun took her way straight to the most pretentious house there, the residence of the lawyer, whose name was Mason. Old Woman Magoun bade Lily wait in the yard for a few moments, and Lily ventured to seat herself on a bench beneath an oak-tree; then she watched with some wonder her grandmother enter the lawyer's office door at the right of the house. Presently the lawyer's wife came out and spoke to Lily under the tree. She had in her hand a little tray containing a plate of cake, a glass of milk, and an early apple. She spoke very kindly to Lily; she even kissed her, and offered her the tray of refreshments, which Lily accepted gratefully. She sat eating, with Mrs. Mason watching her, when Old Woman Magoun came out of the lawyer's office with a ghastly face.

"What are you eatin'?" she asked Lily, sharply. "Is that a sour apple?"

"I thought she might be hungry," said the lawyer's wife, with loving, melancholy eyes upon the girl.

Lily had almost finished the apple. "It's real sour, but I like it; it's real nice, grandma," she said.

"You ain't been drinkin' milk with a sour apple?"

"It was real nice milk, grandma."

"You ought never to have drunk milk and eat a sour apple," said her grandmother. "Your stomach was all out of order this mornin', an' sour apples and milk is always apt to hurt anybody."

"I don't know but they are," Mrs. Mason said, apologetically, as she stood on the green lawn with her lavender muslin sweeping around her. "I am real sorry, Mrs. Magoun. I ought to have thought. Let me get some soda for her."

"Soda never agrees with her," replied the old woman, in a harsh voice. "Come," she said to Lily, "it's time we were goin' home."

After Lily and her grandmother had disappeared down the road, Lawyer Mason came out of his office and joined his wife, who had seated herself on the bench beneath the tree. She was idle, and her face wore the expression of those who review joys forever past. She had lost a little girl, her only child, years ago, and her husband always knew when she was thinking about her. Lawyer Mason looked older than his wife; he had a dry, shrewd, slightly one-sided face.

"What do you think, Maria?" he said. "That old woman came to me with the most pressing entreaty to adopt that little girl."

"She is a beautiful little girl," said Mrs. Mason, in a slightly husky voice.

"Yes, she is a pretty child," assented the lawyer, looking pityingly at his wife; "but it is out of the question, my dear. Adopting a child is a serious measure, and in this case a child who comes from Barry's Ford."

"But the grandmother seems a very good woman," said Mrs. Mason.

"I rather think she is. I never heard a word against her. But the father! No, Maria, we cannot take a child with Barry blood in her veins. The stock has run out; it is vitiated physically and morally. It won't do, my dear."

"Her grandmother had her dressed up as pretty as a little girl could be," said Mrs. Mason, and this time the tears welled into her faithful, wistful eyes.

"Well, we can't help that," said the lawyer, as he went back to his office.

Old Woman Magoun and Lily returned, going slowly along the road to Barry's Ford. When they came to the stone wall where the blackberry-vines and the deadly nightshade grew, Lily said she was tired, and asked if she could not sit down for a few minutes. The strange look on her grandmother's face had deepened. Now and then Lily glanced at her and had a feeling as if she were looking at a stranger.

"Yes, you can set down if you want to," said Old Woman Magoun, deeply and harshly.

Lily started and looked at her, as if to make sure that it was her grandmother who spoke. Then she sat down on a stone which was comparatively free of the vines.

"Ain't you goin' to set down, grandma?" Lily asked, timidly.

"No; I don't want to get into that mess," replied her grandmother. "I ain't tired, I'll stand here."

Lily sat still; her delicate little face was flushed with heat. She extended her tiny feet in her best shoes and gazed at them. "My shoes are all over dust," said she.

"It will brush off," said her grandmother, still in that strange voice.

Lily looked around. An elm-tree in the field behind her cast a spray of branches over her head; a little cool puff of wind came on her face. She gazed at the low mountains on the horizon, in the midst of which she lived, and she sighed, for no reason that she knew. She began idly picking at the blackberry-vines; there were no berries on them; then she put her little fingers on the berries of the deadly nightshade. "These look like nice berries," she said.

Old Woman Magoun, standing stiff and straight in the road, said nothing.

"They look good to eat," said Lily.

Old Woman Magoun still said nothing, but she looked up into the ineffable blue of the sky, over which spread at intervals great white clouds shaped like wings.

Lily picked some of the deadly nightshade berries and ate them. "Why, they are real sweet," said she. "They are nice." She picked some more and ate them.

Presently her grandmother spoke. "Come," she said, "it is time we were going. I guess you have set long enough."

Lily was still eating the berries when she slipped down from the wall and followed her grandmother obediently up the road.

Before they reached home, Lily complained of being very thirsty. She stopped and made a little cup of a leaf and drank long at a mountain brook. "I am dreadful dry, but it hurts me to swallow," she said to her grandmother when she stopped drinking and joined the old woman waiting for her in the road. Her grandmother's face seemed strangely dim to her. She took hold of Lily's hand as they went on. "My stomach burns," said Lily, presently. "I want some more water."

"There is another brook a little farther on," said Old Woman Magoun, in a dull voice.

When they reached that brook, Lily stopped and drank again, but she whimpered a little over her difficulty in swallowing. "My stomach burns, too," she said, walking on, "and my throat is so dry, grandma." Old Woman Magoun held Lily's hand more tightly. "You hurt me holding my hand so tight, grandma," said Lily, looking up at her grandmother, whose face she seemed to see through a mist, and the old woman loosened her grasp.

When at last they reached home, Lily was very ill. Old Woman Magoun put her on her own bed in the little bedroom out of the kitchen. Lily lay there and moaned, and Sally Jinks came in.

"Why, what ails her?" she asked. "She looks feverish."

Lily unexpectedly answered for herself. "I ate some sour apples and drank some milk," she moaned.

"Sour apples and milk are dreadful apt to hurt anybody," said Sally Jinks. She told several people on her way home that Old Woman Magoun was dreadful careless to let Lily eat such things.

Meanwhile Lily grew worse. She suffered cruelly from the burning in her stomach, the vertigo, and the deadly nausea. "I am so sick, I am so sick, grandma," she kept moaning. She could no longer see her grandmother as she bent over her, but she could hear her talk.

Old Woman Magoun talked as Lily had never heard her talk before, as nobody had ever heard her talk before. She spoke from the depths of her soul; her voice was as tender as the coo of a dove, and it was grand and exalted. "You'll feel better very soon, little Lily," said she.

"I am so sick, grandma."

"You will feel better very soon, and then —"

"I am sick."

"You shall go to a beautiful place."

Lily moaned.

"You shall go to a beautiful place," the old woman went on.

"Where?" asked Lily, groping feebly with her cold little hands. Then she moaned again.

"A beautiful place, where the flowers grow tall."

"What colour? Oh, grandma, I am so sick."

"A blue colour," replied the old woman. Blue was Lily's favourite colour. "A beautiful blue colour, and as tall as your knees, and the flowers always stay there, and they never fade."

"Not if you pick them, grandma? Oh!"

"No, not if you pick them; they never fade, and they are so sweet you can smell them a mile off; and there are birds that sing, and all the roads have gold stones in them, and the stone walls

91

are made of gold."

"Like the ring grandpa gave you? I am so sick, grandma."

"Yes, gold like that. And all the houses are built of silver and gold, and the people all have wings, so when they get tired walking they can fly, and —"

"I am so sick, grandma."

"And all the dolls are alive," said Old Woman Magoun. "Dolls like yours can run, and talk, and love you back again."

Lily had her poor old rag doll in bed with her, clasped close to her agonized little heart. She tried very hard with her eyes, whose pupils were so dilated that they looked black, to see her grandmother's face when she said that, but she could not. "It is dark," she moaned feebly.

"There where you are going it is always light," said the grandmother, "and the commonest things shine like that breast-pin Mrs. Lawyer Mason had on today."

Lily moaned pitifully, and said something incoherent. Delirium was commencing. Presently she sat straight up in bed and raved; but even then her grandmother's wonderful compelling voice had an influence over her.

"You will come to a gate with all the colours of the rainbow," said her grandmother; "and it will open, and you will go right in and walk up the gold street, and cross the field where the blue flowers come up to your knees, until you find your mother and she will take you home where you are going to live. She has a little white room all ready for you, white curtains at the windows, and a little white looking-glass, and when you look in it you will see —"

"What will I see? I am so sick, grandma."

"You will see a face like yours, only it's an angel's; and there will be a little white bed, and you can lay down an' rest."

"Won't I be sick, grandma?" asked Lily. Then she moaned and babbled wildly, although she seemed to understand through it all what her grandmother said.

"No, you will never be sick any more. Talkin' about sickness won't mean anything to you."

It continued. Lily talked on wildly, and her grandmother's great voice of soothing never ceased, until the child fell into a deep sleep, or what resembled sleep; but she lay stiffly in that sleep, and a candle flashed before her eyes made no impression on them.

Then it was that Nelson Barry came. Jim Willis waited outside the door. When Nelson entered he found Old Woman Magoun on her knees beside the bed, weeping with dry eyes and a might of agony which fairly shook Nelson Barry, the degenerate of a fine old race.

"Is she sick?" he asked, in a hushed voice.

Old Woman Magoun gave another terrible sob, which sounded like the gasp of one dying.

"Sally Jinks said that Lily was sick from eating milk and sour apples," said Barry, in a tremulous voice. "I remember that her mother was very sick once from eating them."

Lily lay still, and her grandmother on her knees shook with her terrible sobs.

Suddenly Nelson Barry started. "I guess I had better go to Greenham for a doctor if she's as bad as that," he said. He went close to the bed and looked at the sick child. He gave a great start. Then he felt of her hands and reached down under the bedclothes for her little feet. "Her hands and feet are like ice," he cried out. "Good God! why didn't you send for someone—for me—before? Why, she's dying; she's almost gone!"

Barry rushed out and spoke to Jim Willis, who turned pale and came in and stood by the bedside.

"She's almost gone," he said, in a hushed whisper.

"There's no use going for the doctor; she'd be dead before he got here," said Nelson, and he stood regarding the passing child with a strange sad face—unutterably sad, because of his incapability of the truest sadness.

"Poor little thing, she's past suffering, anyhow," said the other man, and his own face also was sad with a puzzled, mystified sadness.

Lily died that night. There was quite a commotion in Barry's

Ford until after the funeral, it was all so sudden, and then everything went on as usual. Old Woman Magoun continued to live as she had done before. She supported herself by the produce of her tiny farm; she was very industrious, but people said that she was a trifle touched, since every time she went over the log bridge with her eggs or her garden vegetables to sell in Greenham, she carried with her, as one might have carried an infant, Lily's old rag doll.

The Witch's Daughter

It was well for old Elma Franklin that Cotton Mather had passed to either the heaven or hell in which he believed; it was well that the Salem witchcraft days were over, although not so long ago, or it would have fared ill with her. As it was, she was shunned, and at the same time cringed to. People feared to fear her. Witches were no longer accused in court, and put to torture and death, but human superstitions die hard. The heads thereof may be cut off, but their noxious bodies of fear and suspicions writhe long. People in that little New England village, which was as stiff and unyielding as its own poplar-trees which sentinelled so many of its houses, knew nothing of that making of horns which averts the evil eye. They shuddered upon their orthodox heights at the idea of the sign of the cross, but many would have fain taken refuge therein for the easing of their unquiet imaginations when they dwelt upon old Elma Franklin.

Many a woman whispered to another under promise of strict secrecy that she was sure that Elma bore upon her lean, withered body the witch-sign; many a man, when he told his neighbor of the death of his cow or horse, nodded furtively toward old Elma's dwelling. In truth, old Elma's appearance alone, had it been only a few years ago, would have condemned her. Lean was she, and withered in a hard brown fashion like old leather. Her eyes were of a blue so bright that people said they felt like swooning before their glance; and what right had a woman, so old and wrinkled, with a head of golden hair like a young girl's? Her own hair, too, and she would wear no wig like other decent women of less than her age. And what right had she with that flower-like daughter Daphne?

Young creatures like Daphne are not born of women like Elma Franklin, who must have been old sixteen years agone. Daphne was sixteen. Daphne had a Greek name and Greek beauty. She was very small, but very perfect, and finished like an ivory statue whose sculptor had toiled for his own immortality. Daphne had golden hair like her mother's, but it waved in a fashion past finding out over her little ears, whose tips showed below like the pointed petals of pink roses, and her chin and cheeks curved as clearly as a rose, and her nose made a rapture of her profile, and her neck was long and slowly turning, and her eyes were not blue like her mother's, but sweet and dark, and gently regardant, and her hands were as white and smooth as lilies, whereas hands had never been seen so knotted and wickedly veined as if with unholy clawing as her mother's.

Daphne led however, as lonely a life as her mother. People were afraid. Dark stories, vile stories, were whispered among that pitiless, bigoted people. Old Elma and Daphne lived alone in their poor little cottage, although in the midst of fertile fields, and they fed on the milk of their two cows, and the eggs of their chickens, and the vegetables of their garden, and the honey of their bees. Old Elma hived them when they swarmed with never any protection for that strange face and those hands of hers, and people said the bees were of an evil breed, and familiars of old Elma's, and durst not sting her. Young men sometimes cast eyes askance at Daphne, but turned away, and old Elma knew the reason why, and she hated them; for hatred prospered in her heart, coming as she did of a strong and fierce race.

Elma combed her daughter's wonderful golden locks, and dressed her in fine stuff made of a store which she had in a great carved chest in the garret, and would have had the girl go to meeting where she could be seen and admired; but Daphne went once, and was ever after afraid to venture, because of the black looks cast upon her, which seemed to sear her gentle heart, for the girl was so gentle that she seemed to have no voice of insistence for her own rights. When her mother chid her, saying, with the disappointment of a great love, that she had with her own hands fashioned her wonderful gown of red shot with golden threads and embroidered with silver flowers, and had wrought with fine needlework her lace kerchief and her mitts and her scarf, and that it was a shame that she must needs, with all this goodly apparel, slink beside her own hearth and be seen of no one, the girl only kissed her mother on her leathery brown cheek, and smiled like an angel.

Daphne was a maiden of few words, and that would have enticed lovers had it not been for her mother. However, at last came Harry Edgelake, and he was bolder than the rest, and the moment he set eyes upon the girl clad in green with a rose in her hair and a rose at her breast, spinning in a cool shadow at her mother's door, his heart melted, and he swore that he would wed her, came she of a whole witch-tribe. But Harry had more than he recked at first to deal with in the way of opposition. He came of a long line of eminent ministers of the Word, and his grandfather and father still survived, and were of the Cotton Mather strain. Although they talked none, they would, if the good old days had endured, have had old Elma up before the judges; for all the cattle in the precinct, and all the poor crops, and every thunder tempest and lightning stroke, and all strange noises they laid at her door, nodding at each other and whispering.

Therefore when it came to their ears that Harry, who had just come home from Harvard, and was to be, had he a call, a minister of the Word, like themselves, had been seen standing and chatting by the hour beside the witch's daughter as she spun in the shade with her golden head shining out in it like a star, he was sternly reasoned with. And when he heeded not the counsel of his elders, but was seen strolling down lovers' lane with the maid, great stress was laid to bear upon him, and he was sent away to Boston town, and Daphne watched and he came not, and old Elma watched the girl watch in vain, and her evil passions grew; for evil surely dwelt in her heart, as in most human hearts, and she had been sorely dealt with and badgered, and the girl was her one delight of life, and the girls' sorrow was her own magnified into the most cruel torture that a heart can bear and live.

And whether she were a witch or not, much brooding upon the suspicion with which people regarded her had made her uncertain of herself, and she owned a strange book of magic, over which she loved to pore when the cry of the hounds of her kind was in her ears, and she resolved one night, when a month had passed and she knew her daughter to be pining for her lover, that if she were indeed witch as they said, she would use witchcraft.

The moon was at the full, and the wide field behind her cottage, which had been shorn for hay for the cows, glittered like a silver shield, and upon the silver shield were little wheels also like silver woven by spiders for their prey, and strange lights of dew blazed out here and there like stars. And old Elma led her daughter out into the field, and Elma wore a sad-cooluured gown which made her passing like the passing of a shadow, and Daphne was all in white, which made her passing like that of a moonbeam; and the mother took her daughter by the arm, and she so loved her that she hurt her.

"Mother, you hurt me, you hurt me!" moaned Daphne, and directly the mother's grasp of the little fair arm was as if she touched a newborn babe.

"What aileth thee, sweetheart?" she whispered, but the girl only sobbed gently.

"It is for thy lover, and not a maid in the precinct so fair and good," said the mother, in her fierce old voice.

And Daphne sobbed again, and the mother gathered her in her arms.

"Sweetheart, thy mother will compel love for thee," she whispered, and the girl shrank away in fear, for there was something strange in her mother's voice.

"I want no witchery," she whispered.

"Nay, but this is good witchery, to call true love to true love."

"If love cannot be called else, I want not love at all."

"But, sweetheart, this is not black but white witchery."

"I want none, and besides—"

"Besides?"

The girl said no more, but the mother knew that it was because of her that the lover had fled, and not because of lack of love.

"See, sweetheart," said old Elma, "I know a charm."

"I will have no charm, mother; I tell thee I will have no charm."

"Sweetheart, watch thy mother cross the field from east to west and from north to south, and criss-cross like the spiders' webs, and see if thou thinkest it harmful witchcraft."

"I will not, mother," said the girl, but she watched.

And old Elma crossed the field from east to west and from north to south, and crisscrossed like the spiders' webs, and ever after her trailed lines of brighter silver than the dew which lay up the field, until the whole was like a wonderful web, and in the midst shone a great silver light as if the moon had fallen there, although still in the sky.

Then came old Elma to her daughter, and her face in the strange light was fair and young. "Daughter, daughter," said the mother, "but follow the lines of light thy mother's feet have made and come to the central light, and thy lover shall be there."

But the daughter stood in her place, like a white lily whose roots none could stir save to her death. "I follow not, mother," she said. "It would be to his soul's undoing, and better I love his soul and its fair salvation than his body and his heart in this world."

And the mother was silent, for she truly knew not as to the spell whether it concerned the soul's salvation.

But she had still another spell, which she had learned from her strange book. "Then stay, daughter," said old Elma, and straightway she crossed the paths of light which she made, and they vanished, and the meadow became as before, but in the midst old Elma stood, and said strange words under her breath, and waved her arms, while her daughter watched her fearfully. And as she watched, Daphne saw spring up, in the meadow in the space over which her mother's long arms waved, a patch of white lilies, which gave out lights like no lilies of earth, and their wonderful scent came in her face. And her mother hurried back, and in her hurrying was like a black shadow passing over the meadow.

"And go to the patch of lilies, sweetheart," she said, "and in the time which it takes thee to reach them thy lover will have gone over the forests and the waters, and he will meet thee in the lilies."

But Daphne stood firm in her place. "I go not, mother," she said. "It would be to his dear soul's undoing, and better I love his soul and his soul's heaven than I love him and myself."

Then down lay old Elma upon the silver shield of the meadow like a black shadow at her daughter's feet.

"Then is there but one way left, sweetheart," came her voice from among the meadow grasses like the love-song of a stricken mother-bird. "There is but one way, sweet daughter of mine. Step thou over thy mother's body, darling, and cross to the patch of lilies, and I swear to thee, by the Christ and the Cross and all that the meeting-folk hold sacred, that thou shalt have thy lover, and his soul shall not miss heaven, neither his soul nor thine."

"And thine?"

"I am thy mother."

And Daphne stood firm. "Better I love thee, mother," she said, "than heaven on earth with my lover; better I love thee than his weal or mine in this world, better than all save his dear soul."

"I tell thee, sweet, cross my body, and his soul and thy soul shall be safe."

"But thy life on earth, and thy soul?"

"I am thy mother."

"I will not go."

Then came a wail of despair from old Elma at her daughter's feet upon the silver shield of the meadow, and then she was raised up by young Harry Edgelake, and she stood with her leathern old face like an angel's for pure joy and forgetfulness of self. For her daughter stood in her lover's arms and his voice sounded like a song.

"Nothing on earth and nothing in heaven shall part me from thee, who hold my soul dearer than myself, and thy mother dearer than thyself, for, witch or no witch, thy mother has shown me thy angel in the meadow tonight," he said.

Old Elma stood watching them with her face of pure joy, and all the fierceness and the bitter grief of injury received from those whom she had not injured faded from her heart. She forgot the strange book which she had studied, she forgot her power of strange deeds, she forgot herself, and remembered nothing, nothing save her daughter and her love, and such bliss possessed her that she could stand no longer upon the silver shield of the meadow. She sank down slowly as a flower sinks when its time has come before the sun and the wind which have given it life, and she lay still at the feet of her daughter and the youth, and they stooped over her and they knew that she had been no witch, but a great lover.

Evelina's Garden

On the south a high *arbor-vitæ* hedge separated Evelina's garden from the road. The hedge was so high that when the school-children lagged by, and the secrets behind it fired them with more curiosity than those between their battered book covers, the tallest of them by stretching up on tiptoe could not peer over. And so they were driven to childish engineering feats, and would set to work and pick away sprigs of the *arbor-vitæ* with their little fingers, and make peep-holes—but small ones, that Evelina might not discern them. Then they would thrust their pink faces into the hedge, and the enduring fragrance of it would come to their nostrils like a gust of aromatic breath from the mouth of the northern woods, and peer into Evelina's garden as through the green tubes of vernal telescopes.

Then suddenly hollyhocks, blooming in rank and file, seemed to be marching upon them like platoons of soldiers, with detonations of colour that dazzled their peeping eyes; and, indeed, the whole garden seemed charging with its mass of riotous bloom upon the hedge. They could scarcely take in details of marigold and phlox and pinks and London-pride and cock's-combs, and prince's-feather's waving overhead like standards.

Sometimes also there was the purple flutter of Evelina's gown; and Evelina's face, delicately faded, hung about with softly drooping gray curls, appeared suddenly among the flowers, like another flower uncannily instinct with nervous melancholy.

Then the children would fall back from their peep-holes, and huddle off together with scared giggles. They were afraid of

Evelina. There was a shade of mystery about her which stimulated their childish fancies when they heard her discussed by their elders. They might easily have conceived her to be some baleful fairy entrenched in her green stronghold, withheld from leaving it by the fear of some dire penalty for magical sins. Summer and winter, spring and fall, Evelina Adams never was seen outside her own domain of old mansion-house and garden, and she had not set her slim lady feet in the public highway for nearly forty years, if the stories were true.

People differed as to the reason why. Some said she had had an unfortunate love-affair, that her heart had been broken, and she had taken upon herself a vow of seclusion from the world, but nobody could point to the unworthy lover who had done her this harm. When Evelina was a girl, not one of the young men of the village had dared address her. She had been set apart by birth and training, and also by a certain exclusiveness of manner, if not of nature. Her father, old Squire Adams, had been the one man of wealth and college learning in the village. He had owned the one fine old mansion-house, with its white front propped on great Corinthian pillars, overlooking the village like a broad brow of superiority.

He had owned the only coach and four. His wife during her short life had gone dressed in rich brocades and satins that rustled loud in the ears of the village women, and her nodding plumes had dazzled the eyes under their modest hoods. Hardly a woman in the village but could tell—for it had been handed down like a folk-lore song from mother to daughter—just what Squire Adams's wife wore when she walked out first as bride to meeting. She had been clad all in blue.

"Squire Adams's wife, when she walked out bride, she wore a blue satin brocade gown, all wrought with blue flowers of a darker blue, cut low neck and short sleeves. She wore long blue silk mitts wrought with blue, blue satin shoes, and blue silk clocked stockings. And she wore a blue crape mantle that was brought from over seas, and a blue velvet hat, with a long blue ostrich feather curled over it—it was so long it reached her shoulder, and waved when she walked; and she carried a little blue crape fan with ivory sticks." So the women and girls told each other when the squire's bride had been dead nearly seventy years.

The blue bride attire was said to be still in existence, packed away in a cedar chest, as the squire had ordered after his wife's death. "He stood over the woman that took care of his wife whilst she packed the things away, and he never shed a tear, but she used to hear him a-goin' up to the north chamber nights, when he couldn't sleep, to look at 'em," the women told.

People had thought the squire would marry again. They said Evelina, who was only four years old, needed a mother, and they selected one and another of the good village girls. But the squire never married. He had a single woman, who dressed in black silk, and wore always a black wrought veil over the side of her bonnet, come to live with them, to take charge of Evelina. She was said to be a distant relative of the squire's wife, and was much looked up to by the village people, although she never did more than interlace, as it were, the fringes of her garments with theirs. "She's stuck up," they said, and felt, curiously enough, a certain pride in the fact when they met her in the street and she ducked her long chin stiffly into the folds of her black shawl by way of salutation.

When Evelina was fifteen years old this single woman died, and the village women went to her funeral, and bent over her lying in a last helpless dignity in her coffin, and stared with awed freedom at her cold face. After that Evelina was sent away to school, and did not return, except for a yearly vacation, for six years to come. Then she returned, and settled down in her old home to live out her life, and end her days in a perfect semblance of peace, if it were not peace.

Evelina never had any young school friend to visit her; she had never, so far as any one knew, a friend of her own age. She lived alone with her father and three old servants. She went to meeting, and drove with the squire in his chaise. The coach was never used after his wife's death, except to carry Evelina to and from school. She and the sSquire also took long walks, but they never exchanged aught but the merest civilities of good-days and nods with the neighbours whom they met, unless indeed the Squire had some matter of business to discuss. Then Evelina stood aside and waited, her fair face drooping gravely aloof. She was very pretty, with a gentle high-bred prettiness that impressed the village folk, although they looked at it somewhat askance.

Evelina's figure was tall, and had a fine slenderness; her silken skirts hung straight from the narrow silk ribbon that girt her slim waist; there was a languidly graceful bend in her long white throat; her long delicate hands hung inertly at her sides among her skirt folds, and were never seen to clasp anything; her softly clustering fair curls hung over her thin blooming cheeks, and her face could scarce be seen, unless, as she seldom did, she turned and looked full upon one. Then her dark blue eyes, with a little nervous frown between them, shone out radiantly; her thin lips showed a warm red, and her beauty startled one.

Everybody wondered why she did not have a lover, why some fine young man had not been smitten by her while she had been away at school. They did not know that the school had been situated in another little village, the counterpart of the one in which she had been born, wherein a fitting mate for a bird of her feather could hardly be found. The simple young men of the countryside were at once attracted and intimidated by her. They cast fond sly glances across the meeting-house at her lovely face, but they were confused before her when they jostled her in the doorway and the rose and lavender scent of her lady garments came in their faces. Not one of them dared accost her, much less march boldly upon the great Corinthian-pillared house, raise the brass knocker, and declare himself a suitor for the squire's daughter.

One young man there was, indeed, who treasured in his heart an experience so subtle and so slight that he could scarcely believe in it himself. He never recounted it to mortal soul, but kept it as a secret sacred between himself and his own nature, but something to be scoffed at and set aside by others.

It had happened one Sabbath day in summer, when Evelina had not been many years home from school, as she sat in the meeting-house in her Sabbath array of rose-colored satin gown, and white bonnet trimmed with a long white feather and a little wreath of feathery green, that of a sudden she raised her head and turned her face, and her blue eyes met this young man's full upon hers, with all his heart in them, and it was for a second as if her own heart leaped to the surface, and he saw it, although afterward he scarce believed it to be true.

Then a pallor crept over Evelina's delicately brilliant face. She turned it away, and her curls falling softly from under the green wreath on her bonnet brim hid it. The young man's cheeks were a hot red, and his heart beat loudly in his ears when he met her in the doorway after the sermon was done. His eager, timorous eyes sought her face, but she never looked his way. She laid her slim hand in its cream-colored silk mitt on the squire's arm; her satin gown rustled softly as she passed before him, shrinking against the wall to give her room, and a faint fragrance which seemed like the very breath of the unknown delicacy and exclusiveness of life came to his bewildered senses.

Many a time he cast furtive glances across the meeting-house at Evelina, but she never looked his way again. If his timid boy-eyes could have seen her cheek behind its veil of curls, he might have discovered that the colour came and went before his glances, although it was strange how she could have been conscious of them; but he never knew.

And he also never knew how, when he walked past the squire's house of a Sunday evening, dressed in his best, with his shoulders thrust consciously back, and the windows in the westering sun looked full of blank gold to his furtive eyes, Evelina was always peeping at him from behind a shutter, and he never dared go in. His intuitions were not like hers, and so nothing happened that might have, and he never fairly knew what he knew. But that he never told, even to his wife when he married; for his hot young blood grew weary and impatient with this vain courtship, and he turned to one of his village-mates, who met him fairly halfway, and married her within a year.

On the Sunday when he and his bride first appeared in the meeting-house Evelina went up the aisle behind her father in an array of flowered brocade, stiff with threads of silver, so wonderful that people all turned their heads to stare at her. She wore also a new bonnet of rose-colored satin, and her curls were caught back a little, and her face showed as clear and beautiful as an angel's.

The young bridegroom glanced at her once across the meeting-house, then he looked at his bride in her gay wedding finery with a faithful look.

When Evelina met them in the doorway, after meeting was done, she bowed with a sweet cold grace to the bride, who courtesied blushingly in return, with an awkward sweep of her foot in the bridal satin shoe. The bridegroom did not look at Evelina at all. He held his chin well down in his stock with solemn embarrassment, and passed out stiffly, his bride on his arm.

Evelina, shining in the sun like a silver lily, went up the street, her father stalking beside her with stately swings of his cane, and that was the last time she was ever seen out at meeting. Nobody knew why.

When Evelina was a little over thirty her father died. There was not much active grief for him in the village; he had really figured therein more as a stately monument of his own grandeur than anything else. He had been a man of little force of character, and that little had seemed to degenerate since his wife died. An inborn dignity of manner might have served to disguise his weakness with any others than these shrewd New-Englanders, but they read him rightly. "The squire wa'n't ever one to set the river a-fire," they said. Then, moreover, he left none of his property to the village to build a new meeting-house or a townhouse. It all went to Evelina.

People expected that Evelina would surely show herself in her mourning at meeting the Sunday after the squire died, but she did not. Moreover, it began gradually to be discovered that she never went out in the village street nor crossed the boundaries of her own domains after her father's death. She lived in the great house with her three servants—a man and his wife, and the woman who had been with her mother when she died. Then it was that Evelina's garden began. There had always been a garden at the back of the squire's house, but not like this, and only a low fence had separated it from the road. Now one morning in the autumn the people saw Evelina's manservant, John Darby, setting out the *arbor-vitæ* hedge, and in the spring after that there were ploughing and seed-sowing extending over a full half-acre, which later blossomed out in glory.

Before the hedge grew so high Evelina could be seen at work in her garden. She was often seen stooping over the flower-beds in the early morning when the village was first astir, and she moved among them with her watering-pot in the twilight—a shadowy figure that might, from her grace and her constancy to the flowers, have been Flora herself.

As the years went on, the *arbor-vitæ* hedge got each season a new growth and waxed taller, until Evelina could no longer be seen above it. That was an annoyance to people, because the quiet mystery of her life kept their curiosity alive, until it was in a constant struggle, as it were, with the green luxuriance of the hedge.

"John Darby had ought to trim that hedge," they said. They accosted him in the street: "John, if ye don't cut that hedge down a little it 'll all die out." But he only made a surly grunting response, intelligible to himself alone, and passed on. He was an Englishman, and had lived in the squire's family since he was a boy.

He had a nature capable of only one simple line of force, with no radiations or parallels, and that had early resolved itself into the service of the squire and his house. After the squire's death he married a woman who lived in the family. She was much older than himself, and had a high temper, but was a good servant, and he married her to keep her to her allegiance to Evelina. Then he bent her, without her knowledge, to take his own attitude toward his mistress. No more could be gotten out of John

Darby's wife than out of John Darby concerning the doings at the squire's house. She met curiosity with a flash of hot temper, and he with surly taciturnity, and both intimidated.

The third of Evelina's servants was the woman who had nursed her mother, and she was naturally subdued and undemonstrative, and rendered still more so by a ceaseless monotony of life. She never went to meeting, and was seldom seen outside the house. A passing vision of a long white-capped face at a window was about all the neighbours ever saw of this woman.

So Evelina's gentle privacy was well guarded by her own household, as by a faithful system of domestic police. She grew old peacefully behind her green hedge, shielded effectually from all rough bristles of curiosity. Every new spring her own bloom showed paler beside the new bloom of her flowers, but people could not see it.

Some thirty years after the squire's death the man John Darby died; his wife, a year later. That left Evelina alone with the old woman who had nursed her mother. She was very old, but not feeble, and quite able to perform the simple household tasks for herself and Evelina. An old man, who saved himself from the almshouse in such ways, came daily to do the rougher part of the garden-work in John Darby's stead. He was aged and decrepit; his muscles seemed able to perform their appointed tasks only through the accumulated inertia of a patiently toilsome life in the same tracks. Apparently they would have collapsed had he tried to force them to aught else than the holding of the ploughshare, the pulling of weeds, the digging around the roots of flowers, and the planting of seeds.

Every autumn he seemed about to totter to his fall among the fading flowers; every spring it was like Death himself urging on the resurrection; but he lived on year after year, and tended well Evelina's garden, and the gardens of other maiden-women and widows in the village. He was taciturn, grubbing among his green beds as silently as a worm, but now and then he warmed a little under a fire of questions concerning Evelina's garden. "Never see none sech flowers in nobody's garden in this town, not sence I knowed 'nough to tell a pink from a piny," he would mumble. His speech was thick; his words were all uncouthly slurred; the expression of his whole life had come more through his old knotted hands of labour than through his tongue. But he would wipe his forehead with his shirt sleeve and lean a second on his spade, and his face would change at the mention of the garden. Its wealth of bloom illumined his old mind, and the roses and honeysuckles and pinks seemed for a second to be reflected in his bleared old eyes.

There had never been in the village such a garden as this of Evelina Adams's. All the old blooms which had come over the seas with the early colonists, and started as it were their own colony of flora in the new country, flourished there. The naturalized pinks and phlox and hollyhocks and the rest, changed a little in colour and fragrance by the conditions of a new climate and soil, were all in Evelina's garden, and no one dreamed what they meant to Evelina; and she did not dream herself, for her heart was always veiled to her own eyes, like the face of a nun. The roses and pinks, the poppies and heart's-ease, were to this maiden-woman, who had innocently and helplessly outgrown her maiden heart, in the place of all the loves of life which she had missed. Her affections had forced an outlet in roses; they exhaled sweetness in pinks, and twined and clung in honeysuckle-vines. The daffodils, when they came up in the spring, comforted her like the smiles of children; when she saw the first rose, her heart leaped as at the face of a lover.

She had lost the one way of human affection, but her feet had found a little single side-track of love, which gave her still a zest in the journey of life. Even in the winter Evelina had her flowers, for she kept those that would bear transplanting in pots, and all the sunny windows in her house were gay with them. She would also not let a rose leaf fall and waste in the garden soil, or a sprig of lavender or thyme. She gathered them all, and stored them away in chests and drawers and old china bowls— the whole house seemed laid away in rose leaves and lavender. Evelina's clothes gave out at every motion that fragrance of dead flowers which is like the fragrance of the past, and has a sweetness like that of sweet memories. Even the cedar chest where Evelina's mother's blue bridal array was stored had its till heaped with rose leaves and lavender.

When Evelina was nearly seventy years old the old nurse who had lived with her her whole life died. People wondered then what she would do. "She can't live all alone in that great house," they said. But she did live there alone six months, until spring, and people used to watch her evening lamp when it was put out, and the morning smoke from her kitchen chimney. "It ain't safe for her to be there alone in that great house," they said.

But early in April a young girl appeared one Sunday in the old squire's pew. Nobody had seen her come to town, and nobody knew who she was or where she came from, but the old people said she looked just as Evelina Adams used to when she was young, and she must be some relation. The old man who had used to look across the meeting-house at Evelina, over forty years ago, looked across now at this young girl, and gave a great start, and his face paled under his gray beard stubble. His old wife gave an anxious, wondering glance at him, and crammed a peppermint into his hand. "Anything the matter, father?" she whispered; but he only gave his head a half-surly shake, and then fastened his eyes straight ahead upon the pulpit. He had reason to that day, for his only son, Thomas, was going to preach his first sermon therein as a candidate. His wife ascribed his nervousness to that. She put a peppermint in her own mouth, and sucked it comfortably.

"That's all 'tis," she thought to herself. "Father always was easy worked up," and she looked proudly up at her son sitting on the hair-cloth sofa in the pulpit, leaning his handsome young head on his hand, as he had seen old divines do. She never dreamed that her old husband sitting beside her was possessed of an inner life so strange to her that she would not have known him had she met him in the spirit. And, indeed, it had been so always, and she had never dreamed of it. Although he had been faithful to his wife, the image of Evelina Adams in her youth, and that one love-look which she had given him, had never left his soul, but had given it a guise and complexion of which his nearest and dearest knew nothing.

It was strange, but now, as he looked up at his own son as he arose in the pulpit, he could seem to see a look of that fair young Evelina, who had never had a son to inherit her beauty. He had certainly a delicate brilliancy of complexion, which he could have gotten directly from neither father nor mother; and whence came that little nervous frown between his dark blue eyes? His mother had blue eyes, but not like his; they flashed over the great pulpit Bible with a sweet fire that matched the old memory in his father's heart.

But the old man put the fancy away from him in a minute; it was an old one, which his stern common-sense always overcame. It was impossible that Thomas Merriam should resemble Evelina Adams; indeed, people always called him the very image of his father.

The father tried to fix his mind upon his son's sermon, but presently he glanced involuntarily across the meeting-house at the young girl, and again his heart leaped and his face paled; but he turned his eyes gravely back to the pulpit, and his wife did not notice. Now and then she thrust a sharp elbow in his side to call his attention to a grand point in their son's discourse. The odour of peppermint was strong in his nostrils, but through it all he seemed to perceive the rose and lavender scent of Evelina Adams's youthful garments. Whether it was with him simply the memory of an odour, which affected him like the odour itself, or not, those in the vicinity of the squire's pew were plainly aware of it.

The gown which the strange young girl wore was, as many an old woman discovered to her neighbour with loud whispers, one of Evelina's, which had lain away in a sweet-smelling chest since her old girlhood. It had been somewhat altered to suit the fashion of a later day, but the eyes which had fastened keenly upon it when Evelina first wore it up the meeting-house aisle could not mistake it. "It's Evelina Adams's lavender satin made over," one whispered, with a sharp hiss of breath, in the other's ear.

The lavender satin, deepening into purple in the folds, swept in a rich circle over the knees of the young girl in the squire's pew. She folded her little hands, which were encased in Evelina's cream-colored silk mitts, over it, and looked up at the young minister, and listened to his sermon with a grave and innocent dignity, as Evelina had done before her. Perhaps the resemblance between this young girl and the young girl of the past was more one of mien than aught else, although the type of face was the same. This girl had the same fine sharpness of feature and delicately bright color, and she also wore her hair in curls, although they were tied back from her face with a black velvet ribbon, and did not veil it when she drooped her head, as Evelina's used to do.

The people divided their attention between her and the new minister. Their curiosity goaded them in equal measure with their spiritual zeal. "I can't wait to find out who that girl is," one woman whispered to another.

The girl herself had no thought of the commotion which she awakened. When the service was over, and she walked with a gentle maiden stateliness, which seemed a very copy of Evelina's own, out of the meeting-house, down the street to the squire's house, and entered it, passing under the stately Corinthian pillars, with a last purple gleam of her satin skirts, she never dreamed of the eager attention that followed her.

It was several days before the village people discovered who she was. The information had to be obtained, by a process like mental thumb-screwing, from the old man who tended Evelina's garden, but at last they knew. She was the daughter of a cousin of Evelina's on the father's side. Her name was Evelina Leonard; she had been named for her father's cousin. She had been finely brought up, and had attended a Boston school for young ladies. Her mother had been dead many years, and her father had died some two years ago, leaving her with only a very little money, which had now all gone, and Evelina Adams had invited her to live with her. Evelina Adams had herself told the old gardener, seeing his scant curiosity was somewhat awakened by the sight of the strange young lady in the garden, but he seemed to have almost forgotten it when the people questioned him.

"She'll leave her all her money, most likely," they said, and they looked at this new Evelina in the old Evelina's perfumed gowns with awe.

However, in the space of a few months the opinion upon this matter was divided. Another cousin of Evelina Adams's came to town, and this time an own cousin: a widow in fine black bombazine, portly and florid, walking with a majestic swell, and, moreover, having with her two daughters, girls of her own type, not so far advanced. This woman hired one of the village cottages, and it was rumoured that Evelina Adams paid the rent. Still, it was considered that she was not very intimate with these last relatives. The neighbours watched, and saw, many a time, Mrs. Martha Loomis and her girls try the doors of the Adams house, scudding around angrily from front to side and back, and knock and knock again, but with no admittance.

"Evelina she won't let none of 'em in more'n once a week," the neighbours said. It was odd that, although they had deeply resented Evelina's seclusion on their own accounts, they were rather on her side in this matter, and felt a certain delight when they witnessed a crestfallen retreat of the widow and her daughters. "I don't s'pose she wants them Loomises marchin' in on her every minute," they said.

The new Evelina was not seen much with the other cousins, and she made no acquaintances in the village. Whether she was to inherit all the Adams property or not, she seemed, at any rate, heiress to all the elder Evelina's habits of life. She worked with her in the garden, and wore her old girlish gowns, and kept almost as closely at home as she. She often, however, walked abroad in the early dusk, stepping along in a grave and stately fashion, as the elder Evelina had used to do, holding her skirts away from the dewy road-side weeds, her face showing out in the twilight like a white flower, as if it had a pale light of its own.

Nobody spoke to her; people turned furtively after she had passed and stared after her, but they never spoke. This young Evelina did not seem to expect it. She passed along with the lids cast down over her blue eyes, and the rose and lavender scent of her garments came back in their faces.

But one night when she was walking slowly along, a full half-mile from home, she heard rapid footsteps behind, and shrank a little closer to the wall, that whoever it was might have room to pass, and the young minister, Thomas Merriam, came up beside her and spoke.

"Good-evening," said he, and his voice was a little hoarse through nervousness.

Evelina started, and turned her fair face up toward his. "Good-evening," she responded, and curtsied as she had been taught at school, and stood closer to the wall, that he might pass; but Thomas Merriam paused also.

"I—" he began, but his voice broke. He cleared his throat angrily, and went on. "I have seen you in meeting," he said, with a kind of defiance, more of himself than of her. After all, was he not the minister, and had he not the right to speak to everybody in the congregation? Why should he embarrass himself?

"Yes, sir," replied Evelina. She stood drooping her head before him, and yet there was a certain delicate hauteur about her. Thomas was afraid to speak again. They both stood silent for a moment, and then Evelina stirred softly, as if to pass on, and Thomas spoke out bravely. "Is your cousin, Miss Adams, well?" said he.

"She is pretty well, I thank you, sir."

"I've been wanting to—call," he began; then he hesitated again. His handsome young face was blushing crimson.

Evelina's own colour deepened. She turned her face away. "Cousin Evelina never sees callers," she said, with grave courtesy; "perhaps you did not know. She has not for a great many years."

"Yes, I did know it," returned Thomas Merriam; "that's the reason I haven't called."

"Cousin Evelina is not strong," remarked the young girl, and there was a savour of apology in her tone.

"But—" stammered Thomas; then he stopped again. "May I—has she any objections to—anybody's coming to see you?"

Evelina started. "I am afraid Cousin Evelina would not approve," she answered, primly. Then she looked up in his face, and a girlish piteousness came into her own. "I am very sorry," she said, and there was a catch in her voice.

Thomas bent over her impetuously. All his ministerial state fell from him like an outer garment of the soul. He was young, and he had seen this girl Sunday after Sunday. He had written all his sermons with her image before his eyes, he had preached to her, and her only, and she had come between his heart and all the nations of the earth in his prayers. "Oh," he stammered out, "I am afraid you can't be very happy living there the way you do. Tell me —"

Evelina turned her face away with sudden haughtiness. "My cousin Evelina is very kind to me, sir," said she.

"But—you must be lonesome with nobody—of your own age—to speak to," persisted Thomas, confusedly.

"I never cared much for youthful company. It is getting dark; I must be going," said Evelina. "I wish you good-evening, sir."

"Sha'n't I—walk home with you?" asked Thomas, falteringly.

"It isn't necessary, thank you, and I don't think Cousin Evelina would approve," she replied, primly; and her light dress fluttered away into the dusk and out of sight like the pale wing of a moth.

Poor Thomas Merriam walked on with his head in a turmoil. His heart beat loud in his ears. "I've made her mad with me," he said to himself, using the old rustic schoolboy vernacular, from which he did not always depart in his thoughts, although his ministerial dignity guarded his conversations. Thomas Merriam came of a simple homely stock, whose speech came from the emotions of the heart, all unregulated by the usages of the schools. He was the first for generations who had aspired to col-

116

lege learning and a profession, and had trained his tongue by the models of the educated and polite. He could not help, at times, the relapse of his thoughts, and their speaking to himself in the dialect of his family and his ancestors. "She's 'way above me, and I ought to ha' known it," he further said, with the meekness of an humble but fiercely independent race, which is meek to itself alone. He would have maintained his equality with his last breath to an opponent; in his heart of hearts he felt himself below the scion of the one old gentle family of his native village.

This young Evelina, by the fine dignity which had been born with her and not acquired by precept and example, by the sweetly formal diction which seemed her native tongue, had filled him with awe. Now, when he thought she was angered with him, he felt beneath her lady-feet, his nostrils choked with a spiritual dust of humiliation.

He went forward blindly. The dusk had deepened; from either side of the road, from the mysterious gloom of the bushes, came the twangs of the katydids, like some coarse rustic quarrellers, each striving for the last word in a dispute not even dignified by excess of passion.

Suddenly somebody jostled him to his own side of the path. "That you, Thomas? Where you been?" said a voice in his ear.

"That you, father? Down to the post-office."

"Who was that you was talkin' with back there?"

"Miss Evelina Leonard."

"That girl that's stayin' there—to the old squire's?"

"Yes." The son tried to move on, but his father stood before him dumbly for a minute. "I must be going, father. I've got to work on my sermon," Thomas said, impatiently.

"Wait a minute," said his father. "I've got something to say to ye, Thomas, an' this is as good a time to say it as any. There ain't anybody 'round. I don't know as ye'll thank me for it—but mother said the other day that she thought you'd kind of an idea—she said you asked her if she thought it would be anything out of the way for you to go up to the squire's to make a call. Mother she thinks you can step in anywheres, but I don't know.

I know your book-learnin' and your bein' a minister has set you up a good deal higher than your mother and me and any of our folks, and I feel as if you were good enough for anybody, as far as that goes; but that ain't all. Some folks have different startin'-points in this world, and they see things different; and when they do, it ain't much use tryin' to make them walk alongside and see things alike.

"Their eyes have got different cants, and they ain't able to help it. Now this girl she's related to the old squire, and she's been brought up different, and she started ahead, even if her father did lose all his property. She 'ain't never eat in the kitchen, nor been scart to set down in the parlor, and satin and velvet, and silver spoons, and cream-pots 'ain't never looked anything out of the common to her, and they always will to you. No matter how many such things you may live to have, they'll always get a little the better of ye. She'll be 'way above 'em; and you won't, no matter how hard you try. Some ideas can't never mix; and when ideas can't mix, folks can't."

"I never said they could," returned Thomas, shortly. "I can't stop to talk any longer, father. I must go home."

"No, you wait a minute, Thomas. I'm goin' to say out what I started to, and then I sha'n't ever bring it up again. What I was comin' at was this: I wanted to warn ye a little. You mustn't set too much store by little things that you think mean consider'ble when they don't. Looks don't count for much, and I want you to remember it, and not be upset by 'em."

Thomas gave a great start, and coloured high. "I'd like to know what you mean, father," he cried, sharply.

"Nothin'. I don't mean nothin', only I'm older'n you, and it's come in my way to know some things, and it's fittin' you should profit by it. A young woman's looks at you don't count for much. I don't s'pose she knows why she gives 'em herself half the time; they ain't like us. It's best you should make up your mind to it; if you don't, you may find it out by the hardest. That's all. I ain't never goin' to bring this up again."

"I'd like to know what you mean, father." Thomas's voice

shook with embarrassment and anger.

"I ain't goin' to say anything more about it," replied the old man. "Mary Ann Pease and Arabella Mann are both in the settin'-room with your mother. I thought I'd tell ye, in case ye didn't want to see 'em, and wanted to go to work on your sermon."

Thomas made an impatient ejaculation as he strode off. When he reached the large white house where he lived he skirted it carefully. The chirping treble of girlish voices came from the open sitting-room window, and he caught a glimpse of a smooth brown head and a high shell comb in front of the candle-light. The young minister tiptoed in the back door and across the kitchen to the back stairs. The sitting-room door was open, and the candle-light streamed out, and the treble voices rose high. Thomas, advancing through the dusky kitchen with cautious steps, encountered suddenly a chair in the dark corner by the stairs, and just saved himself from falling. There was a startled outcry from the sitting-room, and his mother came running into the kitchen with a candle.

"Who is it?" she demanded, valiantly. Then she started and gasped as her son confronted her. He shook a furious warning fist at the sitting-room door and his mother, and edged toward the stairs. She followed him close. "Hadn't you better jest step in a minute?" she whispered. "Them girls have been here an hour, and I know they're waitin' to see you." Thomas shook his head fiercely, and swung himself around the corner into the dark crook of the back stairs. His mother thrust the candle into his hand. "Take this, or you'll break your neck on them stairs," she whispered.

Thomas, stealing up the stairs like a cat, heard one of the girls call to his mother—"Is it robbers, Mis' Merriam? Want us to come an' help tackle 'em?"—and he fairly shuddered; for Evelina's gentle-lady speech was still in his ears, and this rude girlish call seemed to jar upon his sensibilities.

"The idea of any girl screeching out like that!" he muttered. And if he had carried speech as far as his thought, he would have added, "when Evelina is a girl!"

He was so angry that he did not laugh when he heard his mother answer back, in those conclusive tones of hers that were wont to silence all argument: "It ain't anything. Don't be scared. I'm coming right back." Mrs. Merriam scorned subterfuges. She took always a silent stand in a difficulty, and let people infer what they would. When Mary Ann Pease inquired if it was the cat that had made the noise, she asked if her mother had finished her blue and white counterpane.

The two girls waited a half-hour longer, then they went home. "What do you s'pose made that noise out in the kitchen?" asked Arabella Mann of Mary Ann Pease, the minute they were out-of-doors.

"I don't know," replied Mary Ann Pease. She was a broad-backed young girl, and looked like a matron as she hurried along in the dusk.

"Well, I know what I think it was," said Arabella Mann, moving ahead with sharp jerks of her little dark body.

"What?"

"It was him."

"You don't mean—"

"I think it was Thomas Merriam, and he was tryin' to get up the backstairs unbeknownst to anybody, and he run into something."

"What for?"

"Because he didn't want to see *us*."

"Now, Arabella Mann, I don't believe it! He's always real pleasant to me."

"Well, I do believe it, and I guess he'll know it when I set foot in that house again. I guess he'll find out I didn't go there to see him! He needn't feel so fine, if he is the minister; his folks ain't any better than mine, an we've got 'nough sight handsomer furniture in our parlour."

"Did you see how the tallow had all run down over the candles?"

"Yes, I did. She gave that candle she carried out in the kitchen to him, too. Mother says she wasn't never any kind of a house-keeper."

"Hush! Arabella: here he is coming now."

But it was not Thomas; it was his father, advancing through the evening with his son's gait and carriage. When the two girls discovered that, one tittered out quite audibly, and they scuttled past. They were not rivals; they simply walked faithfully side by side in pursuit of the young minister, giving him as it were an impartial choice. There were even no heart-burnings between them; one always confided in the other when she supposed herself to have found some slight favour in Thomas's sight; and, indeed, the young minister could scarcely bow to one upon the street unless she flew to the other with the news.

Thomas Merriam himself was aware of all this devotion on the part of the young women of his flock, and it filled him with a sort of angry shame. He could not have told why, but he despised himself for being the object of their attention more than he despised them. His heart sank at the idea of Evelina's discovering it. What would she think of him if she knew all those young women haunted his house and lagged after meeting on the chance of getting a word from him? Suppose she should see their eyes upon his face in meeting-time, and decipher their half-unconscious boldness, as he had done against his will.

Once Evelina had looked at him, even as the older Evelina had looked at his father, and all other looks of maidens seemed to him like profanations of that, even although he doubted afterward that he had rightly interpreted it. Full it had seemed to him of that tender maiden surprise and wonder, of that love that knows not itself, and sees its own splendour for the first time in another's face, and flees at the sight. It had happened once when he was coming down the aisle after the sermon and Evelina had met him at the door of her pew. But she had turned her head quickly, and her soft curls flowed over her red cheek, and he doubted ever after if he had read the look aright. When he had gotten the courage to speak to her, and she had met him with the gentle coldness which she had learned of her lady aunt and her teacher in Boston, his doubt was strong upon him.

The next Sunday he looked not her way at all. He even tried faithfully from day to day to drive her image from his mind with prayer and religious thoughts, but in spite of himself he would lapse into dreams about her, as if borne by a current of nature too strong to be resisted. And sometimes, upon being awakened from them, as he sat over his sermon with the ink drying on his quill, by the sudden outburst of treble voices in his mother's sitting-room below, the fancy would seize him that possibly these other young damsels took fond liberties with him in their dreams, as he with Evelina, and he resented it with a fierce maidenliness of spirit, although he was a man. The thought that possibly they, over their spinning or their quilting, had in their hearts the image of himself with fond words upon his lips and fond looks in his eyes, filled him with shame and rage, although he took the same liberty with the delicately haughty maiden Evelina.

But Thomas Merriam was not given to undue appreciation of his own fascination, as was proved by his ready discouragement in the case of Evelina. He had the knowledge of his conquests forced upon his understanding until he could no longer evade it. Every day were offerings laid upon his shrine, of pound-cakes and flaky pies, and loaves of white bread, and cups of jelly, whereby the culinary skill of his devotees might be proved. Silken purses and beautiful socks knitted with fancy stitches, and holy book-marks for his Bible, and even a wonderful bed-quilt, and a fine linen shirt with hem-stitched bands, poured in upon him. He burned with angry blushes when his mother, smiling meaningly, passed them over to him. "Put them away, mother; I don't want them," he would growl out, in a distress that was half comic and half pathetic.

He would never taste of the unctuous viands which were brought to him. "How you act, Thomas!" his mother would say. She was secretly elated by these feminine libations upon the altar of her son. They did not grate upon her sensibilities, which were not delicate. She even tried to assist two or three of the young women in their designs; she would often praise them and their handiwork to her son—and in this she was aided by an old woman aunt of hers who lived with the family. "Nancy Winslow is as handsome a girl as ever I set eyes on, an' I never see any nicer sewin'," Mrs. Merriam said, after the advent of the linen shirt, and she held it up to the light admiringly. "Jest look at that hem-stitchin'!" she said.

"I guess whoever made that shirt calkilated 'twould do for a weddin' one," said old Aunt Betty Green, and Thomas made an exclamation and went out of the room, tingling all over with shame and disgust.

"Thomas don't act nateral," said the old woman, glancing after him through her iron-bound spectacles.

"I dun'no' what's got into him," returned his mother.

"Mebbe they foller him up a leetle too close," said Aunt Betty. "I dun'no' as I should have ventured on a shirt when I was a gal. I made a satin vest once for Joshua, but that don't seem quite as p'inted as a shirt. It didn't scare Joshua, nohow. He asked me to have him the next week."

"Well, I dun'no'," said Mrs. Merriam again. "I kind of wish Thomas would settle on somebody, for I'm pestered most to death with 'em, an' I feel as if 'twas kind of mean takin' all these things into the house."

"They've 'bout kept ye in sweet cake, 'ain't they, lately?"

"Yes; but I don't feel as if it was jest right for us to eat it up, when 'twas brought for Thomas. But he won't touch it. I can't see as he has the least idee of any one of them. I don't believe Thomas has ever seen anybody he wanted for a wife."

"Well, he's got the pick of 'em, a-settin' their caps right in his face," said Aunt Betty.

Neither of them dreamed how the young man, sleeping and eating and living under the same roof, beloved of them since he entered the world, holding himself coldly aloof from this crowd of half innocently, half boldly ardent young women, had set up for himself his own divinity of love, before whom he consumed himself in vain worship. His father suspected, and that was all, and he never mentioned the matter again to his son.

After Thomas had spoken to Evelina the weeks went on, and they never exchanged another word, and their eyes never met. But they dwelt constantly within one another's thoughts, and were ever present to each other's spiritual vision. Always as the young minister bent over his sermon-paper, laboriously tracing out with sputtering quill his application of the articles of the orthodox faith, Evelina's blue eyes seemed to look out at him between the fierce doctrines like the eyes of an angel. And he could not turn the pages of the Holy Writ unless he found some passage therein which to his mind treated directly of her, setting forth her graces like a prophecy.

"*The fairest among women*," read Thomas Merriam, and nodded his head, while his heart leaped with the satisfied delight of all its fancies at the image of his love's fair and gentle face. "*Her price is far above rubies*," read Thomas Merriam, and he nodded his head again, and saw Evelina shining as with gold and pearls, more precious than all the jewels of the earth. In spite of all his efforts in those days, when Thomas Merriam studied the Scriptures he was more nearly touched by those old human hearts which throbbed down to his through the ages, welding the memories of their old loves to his living one until they seemed to prove its eternity, than by the Messianic prophecies. Often he spent hours upon his knees, but arose with Evelina's face before his very soul in spite of all.

And as for Evelina, she tended the flowers in the elder Evelina's garden with her poor cousin, whose own love-dreams had been illustrated as it were by the pinks and lilies blooming around them when they had all gone out of her heart, and Thomas Merriam's half-bold, half-imploring eyes looked up at her out of every flower and stung her heart like bees. Poor young Evelina feared much lest she had offended Thomas, and yet her own maiden decorum had been offended by him, and she had offended it herself, and she was faint with shame and distress when she thought of it. How had she been so bold and shameless as to give him that look in the meeting-house? and how had he been so cruel as to accost her afterward? "She had done right for the maintenance of her own maiden dignity," she told herself, and yet she feared lest she had angered him and hurt him.

"Suppose he had been fretted by her coolness?" she thought, and then a great wave of tender pity went over her heart, and she would almost have spoken to him of her own accord. But then she would reflect how he continued to write such beautiful sermons, and prove so clearly and logically the tenets of the faith; and how could he do that with a mind in distress? Scarcely could she herself tend the flower-beds as she should, nor set her embroidery stitches finely and evenly, she was so ill at ease. It must be that Thomas had not given the matter an hour's worry, since he continued to do his work so faithfully and well. And then her own heart would be sorer than ever with the belief that his was happy and at rest, although she would chide herself for it.

And yet this young Evelina was a philosopher and an analyst of human nature in a small way, and some slight comfort she got out of a shrewd suspicion that the heart of a man might love and suffer on a somewhat different principle from the heart of a woman. "It may be," thought Evelina, sitting idle over her embroidery with far-away blue eyes, "that a man's heart can always turn a while from love to other things as weighty and serious, although he be just as fond, while a woman's heart is always fixed one way by loving, and cannot be turned unless it breaks. And it may be wise," thought young Evelina, "else how could the state be maintained and governed, battles for independence be fought, and even souls be saved, and the gospel carried to the heathen, if men could not turn from the concerns of their own hearts more easily than women? Women should be patient," thought Evelina, "and consider that if they suffer 'tis due to the lot which a wise Providence has given them."

And yet tears welled up in her earnest blue eyes and fell over her fair cheeks and wet the embroidery—when the elder Evelina was not looking, as she seldom was. The elder Evelina was kind to her young cousin, but there were days when she seemed to dwell alone in her own thoughts, apart from the whole world, and she seldom spoke either to Evelina or her old servant-man.

Young Evelina, trying to atone for her former indiscretion and establish herself again on her height of maiden reserve in Thomas Merriam's eyes, sat resolutely in the meeting-house of a Sabbath day, with her eyes cast down, and after service she glided swiftly down the aisle and was out of the door before the young minister could much more than descend the pulpit stairs, unless he ran an indecorous race.

And young Evelina never at twilight strolled up the road in the direction of Thomas Merriam's home, where she might quite reasonably hope to meet him, since he was wont to go to the store when the evening stage-coach came in with the mail from Boston.

Instead she paced the garden paths, or, when there was not too heavy a dew, rambled across the fields; and there was also a lane where she loved to walk. Whether or not Thomas Merriam suspected this, or had ever seen, as he passed the mouth of the lane, the flutter of maidenly draperies in the distance, it so happened that one evening he also went a-walking there, and met Evelina. He had entered the lane from the highway, and she from the fields at the head. So he saw her first afar off, and could not tell fairly whether her light muslin skirt might not be only a white flowering bush.

For, since his outlook upon life had been so full of Evelina, he had found that often the most common and familiar things would wear for a second a look of her to startle him. And many a time his heart had leaped at the sight of a white bush ahead stirring softly in the evening wind, and he had thought it might be she. Now he said to himself impatiently that this was only another fancy; but soon he saw that it was indeed Evelina, in a light muslin gown, with a little lace kerchief on her head. His handsome young face was white; his lips twitched nervously; but he reached out and pulled a spray of white flowers from a bush, and swung it airily to hide his agitation as he advanced.

As for Evelina, when she first espied Thomas she started and half turned, as if to go back; then she held up her white ker-chiefed head with gentle pride and kept on. When she came up to Thomas she walked so far to one side that her muslin skirt was in danger of catching and tearing on the bushes, and she never raised her eyes, and not a flicker of recognition stirred her sweet pale face as she passed him.

But Thomas started as if she had struck him, and dropped his spray of white flowers, and could not help a smothered cry that was half a sob, as he went on, knocking blindly against the bushes. He went a little way, then he stopped and looked back with his piteous hurt eyes. And Evelina had stopped also, and she had the spray of white flowers which he had dropped, in her hand, and her eyes met his. Then she let the flowers fall again, and clapped both her little hands to her face to cover it, and turned to run; but Thomas was at her side, and he put out his hand and held her softly by her white arm.

"Oh," he panted, "I—did not mean to be—too presuming, and offend you. I—crave your pardon —"

Evelina had recovered herself. She stood with her little hands clasped, and her eyes cast down before him, but not a quiver stirred her pale face, which seemed turned to marble by this last effort of her maiden pride. "I have nothing to pardon," said she. "It was I, whose bold behaviour, unbecoming a modest and well-trained young woman, gave rise to what seemed like pre-sumption on your part." The sense of justice was strong within her, but she made her speech haughtily and primly, as if she had learned it by rote from some maiden school-mistress, and pulled her arm away and turned to go; but Thomas's words stopped her.

"Not—unbecoming if it came—from the heart," said he, bro-kenly, scarcely daring to speak, and yet not daring to be silent.

Then Evelina turned on him, with a sudden strange pride that lay beneath all other pride, and was of a nobler and truer sort. "Do you think I would have given you the look that I did if it had not come from my heart?" she demanded. "What did you take me to be—false and a jilt? I may be a forward young woman, who has overstepped the bounds of maidenly decorum, and I shall never get over the shame of it, but I am truthful, and I am no jilt."The brilliant colour flamed out on Evelina's cheeks. Her blue eyes met Thomas's with that courage of innocence and nature which dares all shame. But it was only for a second; the tears sprung into them. "I beg you to let me go home," she said, pitifully; but Thomas caught her in his arms, and pressed her troubled maiden face against his breast.

"Oh, I love you so!" he whispered—"I love you so, Evelina, and I was afraid you were angry with me for it."

"And I was afraid," she faltered, half weeping and half shrinking from him, "lest you were angry with me for betraying the state of my feelings, when you could not return them."And even then she used that gentle formality of expression with which she had been taught by her maiden preceptors to veil decorously her most ardent emotions. And, in truth, her training stood her in good stead in other ways; for she presently commanded, with that mild dignity of hers which allowed of no remonstrance, that Thomas should take away his arm from her waist, and give her no more kisses for that time.

"It is not becoming for any one," said she, "and much less for a minister of the gospel. And as for myself, I know not what Mistress Perkins would say to me. She has a mind much above me, I fear."

"Mistress Perkins is enjoying her mind in Boston," said Thomas Merriam, with the laugh of a triumphant young lover.

But Evelina did not laugh. "It might be well for both you and me if she were here," said she, seriously. However, she tempered a little her decorous following of Mistress Perkins's precepts, and she and Thomas went hand in hand up the lane and across the fields.

There was no dew that night, and the moon was full. It was after nine o'clock when Thomas left her at the gate in the fence which separated Evelina Adams's garden from the field, and watched her disappear between the flowers. The moon shone full on the garden. Evelina walked as it were over a silver dap-

128

ple, which her light gown seemed to brush away and dispel for a moment. The bushes stood in sweet mysterious clumps of shadow.

Evelina had almost reached the house, and was close to the great althea bush, which cast a wide circle of shadow, when it seemed suddenly to separate and move into life.

The elder Evelina stepped out from the shadow of the bush. "Is that you, Evelina?" she said, in her soft melancholy voice, which had in it a nervous vibration.

"Yes, Cousin Evelina."

The elder Evelina's pale face, drooped about with gray curls, had an unfamiliar, almost uncanny, look in the moonlight, and might have been the sorrowful visage of some marble nymph, lovelorn, with unceasing grace. "Who—was with you?" she asked.

"The minister," replied young Evelina.

"Did he meet you?"

"He met me in the lane, Cousin Evelina."

"And he walked home with you across the field?"

"Yes, Cousin Evelina."

Then the two entered the house, and nothing more was said about the matter. Young Evelina and Thomas Merriam had agreed that their affection was to be kept a secret for a while. "For," said young Evelina, "I cannot leave Cousin Evelina yet a while, and I cannot have her pestered with thinking about it, at least before another spring, when she has the garden fairly growing again."

"That is nearly a whole year; it is August now," said Thomas, half reproachfully, and he tightened his clasp of Evelina's slender fingers.

"I cannot help that," replied Evelina. "It is for you to show Christian patience more than I, Thomas. If you could have seen poor Cousin Evelina, as I have seen her, through the long winter days, when her garden is dead, and she has only the few plants in her window left! When she is not watering and tending them she sits all day in the window and looks out over the garden and the naked bushes and the withered flower-stalks. She used not to be so, but would read her Bible and good books, and busy herself somewhat over fine needle-work, and at one time she was compiling a little floral book, giving a list of the flowers, and poetical selections and sentiments appropriate to each. That was her pastime for three winters, and it is now nearly done; but she has given that up, and all the rest, and sits there in the window and grows older and feebler until spring. It is only I who can divert her mind, by reading aloud to her and singing; and sometimes I paint the flowers she loves the best on card-board with water-colours. I have a poor skill in it, but Cousin Evelina can tell which flower I have tried to represent, and it pleases her greatly. I have even seen her smile. No, I cannot leave her, nor even pester her with telling her before another spring, and you must wait, Thomas," said young Evelina.

And Thomas agreed, as he was likely to do to all which she proposed which touched not his own sense of right and honour. Young Evelina gave Thomas one more kiss for his earnest pleading, and that night wrote out the tale in her journal. "It may be that I overstepped the bounds of maidenly decorum," wrote Evelina, "but my heart did so entreat me," and no blame whatever did she lay upon Thomas.

Young Evelina opened her heart only to her journal, and her cousin was told nothing, and had little cause for suspicion. Thomas Merriam never came to the house to see his sweetheart; he never walked home with her from meeting. Both were anxious to avoid village gossip, until the elder Evelina could be told.

Often in the summer evenings the lovers met, and strolled hand in hand across the fields, and parted at the garden gate with the one kiss which Evelina allowed, and that was all.

Sometimes when young Evelina came in with her lover's kiss still warm upon her lips the elder Evelina looked at her wistfully, with a strange retrospective expression in her blue eyes, as if she were striving to remember something that the girl's face called to mind. And yet she could have had nothing to remember except dreams.

And once, when young Evelina sat sewing through a long summer afternoon and thinking about her lover, the elder Evelina, who was storing rose leaves mixed with sweet spices in a jar, said, suddenly, "He looks as his father used to."

Young Evelina started. "Whom do you mean, Cousin Evelina?" she asked, wonderingly; for the elder Evelina had not even glanced at her, nor even seemed to address her at all.

"Nothing," said the elder Evelina, and a soft flush stole over her withered face and neck, and she sprinkled more cassia on the rose leaves in the jar.

Young Evelina said no more; but she wondered, partly because Thomas was always in her mind, and it seemed to her naturally that nearly everything must have a savour of meaning of him, if her cousin Evelina could possibly have referred to him and his likeness to his father. For it was commonly said that Thomas looked very like his father, although his figure was different. The young man was taller and more firmly built, and he had not the meek forward curve of shoulder which had grown upon his father of late years.

When the frosty nights came Thomas and Evelina could not meet and walk hand in hand over the fields behind the squire's house, and they very seldom could speak to one another. It was nothing except a "good-day" on the street, and a stolen glance, which set them both a-trembling lest all the congregation had noticed, in the meeting-house. When the winter set fairly in they met no more, for the elder Evelina was taken ill, and her young cousin did not leave her even to go to meeting. People said they guessed it was Evelina Adams's last sickness, and they furthermore guessed that she would divide her property between her cousin Martha Loomis and her two girls and Evelina Leonard, and that Evelina would have the house as her share.

Thomas Merriam heard this last with a satisfaction which he did not try to disguise from himself, because he never dreamed of there being any selfish element in it. It was all for Evelina. Many a time he had looked about the humble house where he had been born, and where he would have to take Evelina after he had married her, and striven to see its poor features with her eyes—not with his, for which familiarity had tempered them. Often, as he sat with his parents in the old sitting-room, in which he had kept so far an unquestioning belief, as in a friend of his childhood, the scales of his own personality would fall suddenly from his eyes. Then he would see, as Evelina, the poor, worn, humble face of his home, and his heart would sink. "I don't see how I ever can bring her here," he thought. He began to save, a few cents at a time out of his pitiful salary, to at least beautify his own chamber a little when Evelina should come. He made up his mind that she should have a little dressing-table, with an oval mirror, and a white muslin frill around it, like one he had seen in Boston.

"She shall have that to sit before while she combs her hair," he thought, with defiant tenderness, when he stowed away another shilling in a little box in his trunk. It was money which he ordinarily bestowed upon foreign missions; but his Evelina had come between him and the heathen. To procure some dainty furnishings for her bridal-chamber he took away a good half of his tithes for the spread of the gospel in the dark lands. Now and then his conscience smote him, he felt shamefaced before his deacons, but Evelina kept her first claims. He resolved that another year he would hire a piece of land, and combine farming with his ministerial work, and so try to eke out his salary, and get a little more money to beautify his poor home for his bride.

Now if Evelina Adams had come to the appointed time for the closing of her solitary life, and if her young cousin should inherit a share of her goodly property and the fine old mansion-house, all necessity for anxiety of this kind was over. Young Evelina would not need to be taken away, for the sake of her love, from all these comforts and luxuries. Thomas Merriam rejoiced innocently, without a thought for himself.

In the course of the winter he confided in his father; he couldn't keep it to himself any longer. Then there was another reason. Seeing Evelina so little made him at times almost doubt the reality of it all. There were days when he was depressed, and inclined to ask himself if he had not dreamed it. Telling somebody gave it substance.

His father listened soberly when he told him; he had grown old of late.

"Well," said he, "she 'ain't been used to living the way you have, though you have had advantages that none of your folks ever had; but if she likes you, that's all there is to it, I s'pose."

The old man sighed wearily. He sat in his armchair at the kitchen fireplace; his wife had gone in to one of the neighbours, and the two were alone.

"Of course," said Thomas, simply, "if Evelina Adams shouldn't live, the chances are that I shouldn't have to bring her here. She wouldn't have to give up anything on my account—you know that, father."

Then the young man started, for his father turned suddenly on him with a pale, wrathful face. "You ain't countin' on that!" he shouted. "You ain't countin' on that—a son of mine countin' on anything like that!"

Thomas coloured. "Why, father," he stammered, "you don't think—you know, it's all for *her*—and they say she can't live anyway. I had never thought of such a thing before. I was wondering how I could make it comfortable for Evelina here."

But his father did not seem to listen. "Countin' on that!" he repeated. "Countin' on a poor old soul, that 'ain't ever had anything to set her heart on but a few posies, dyin' to make room for other folks to have what she's been cheated out on. Countin' on that!" The old man's voice broke into a hoarse sob; he got up, and went hurriedly out of the room.

"Why, father!" his son called after him, in alarm. He got up to follow him, but his father waved him back and shut the door hard.

"Father must be getting childish," Thomas thought, wonderingly. He did not bring up the subject to him again.

Evelina Adams died in March. One morning the bell tolled seventy long melancholy tones before people had eaten their breakfasts. They ran to their doors and counted. "It's her," they

133

said, nodding, when they had waited a little after the seventieth stroke. Directly Mrs. Martha Loomis and her two girls were seen hustling importantly down the road, with their shawls over their heads, to the squire's house. "Mis' Loomis can lay her out," they said. "It ain't likely that young Evelina knows anything about such things. Guess she'll be thankful she's got somebody to call on now, if she 'ain't mixed much with the Loomises." Then they wondered when the funeral would be, and the women furbished up their black gowns and bonnets, and even in a few cases drove to the next town and borrowed from relatives; but there was a great disappointment in store for them.

Evelina Adams died on a Saturday. The next day it was announced from the pulpit that the funeral would be private, by the particular request of the deceased. Evelina Adams had carried her delicate seclusion beyond death, to the very borders of the grave. Nobody, outside the family, was bidden to the funeral, except the doctor, the minister, and the two deacons of the church. They were to be the bearers. The burial also was to be private, in the squire's family burial-lot, at the north of the house. The bearers would carry the coffin across the yard, and there would not only be no funeral, but no funeral procession, and no hearse. "It don't seem scarcely decent," the women whispered to each other; "and more than all that, she ain't goin' to be *seen*." The deacons' wives were especially disturbed by this last, as they might otherwise have gained many interesting particulars by proxy.

Monday was the day set for the burial. Early in the morning old Thomas Merriam walked feebly up the road to the squire's house. People noticed him as he passed. "How terrible fast he's grown old lately!" they said. He opened the gate which led into the squire's front yard with fumbling fingers, and went up the walk to the front door, under the Corinthian pillars, and raised the brass knocker.

Evelina opened the door, and started and blushed when she saw him. She had been crying; there were red rings around her blue eyes, and her pretty lips were swollen. She tried to smile at

Thomas's father, and she held out her hand with shy welcome.

"I want to see her," the old man said, abruptly.

Evelina started, and looked at him wonderingly. "I—don't believe—I know who you mean," said she. "Do you want to see Mrs. Loomis?"

"No; I want to see her."

"*Her?*"

"Yes, *her.*"

Evelina turned pale as she stared at him. There was something strange about his face. "But—Cousin Evelina," she faltered—"she—didn't want—Perhaps you don't know: she left special directions that nobody was to look at her."

"I *want to see her*," said the old man, and Evelina gave way. She stood aside for him to enter, and led him into the great north parlor, where Evelina Adams lay in her mournful state. The shutters were closed, and one on entering could distinguish nothing but that long black shadow in the middle of the room. Young Evelina opened a shutter a little way, and a slanting shaft of spring sunlight came in and shot athwart the coffin. The old man tiptoed up and leaned over and looked at the dead woman. Evelina Adams had left further instructions about her funeral, which no one understood, but which were faithfully carried out. She wished, she had said, to be attired for her long sleep in a certain rose-coloured gown, laid away in rose leaves and lavender in a certain chest in a certain chamber. There were also silken hose and satin shoes with it, and these were to be put on, and a wrought lace tucker fastened with a pearl brooch.

It was the costume she had worn one Sabbath day back in her youth, when she had looked across the meeting-house and her eyes had met the then young Thomas Merriam's; but nobody knew nor remembered; even young Evelina thought it was simply a vagary of her dead cousin's.

"It don't seem to me decent to lay away anybody dressed so," said Mrs. Martha Loomis; "but of course last wishes must be respected."

The two Loomis girls said they were thankful nobody was to

see the departed in her rose-colored shroud.

Even old Thomas Merriam, leaning over poor Evelina, cold and dead in the garb of her youth, did not remember it, and saw no meaning in it. He looked at her long. The beautiful colour was all faded out of the yellow-white face; the sweet full lips were set and thin; the closed blue eyes sunken in dark hollows; the yellow hair showed a line of gray at the edge of her old woman's cap, and thin gray curls lay against the hollow cheeks. But old Thomas Merriam drew a long breath when he looked at her. It was like a gasp of admiration and wonder; a strange rapture came into his dim eyes; his lips moved as if he whispered to her, but young Evelina could not hear a sound. She watched him, half frightened, but finally he turned to her. "I 'ain't seen her—fairly," said he, hoarsely—"I 'ain't seen her, savin' a glimpse of her at the window, for over forty year, and she 'ain't changed not a look. I'd have known her anywheres. She's the same as she was when she was a girl. It's wonderful—wonderful!"

Young Evelina shrank a little. "We think she looks natural," she said, hesitatingly.

"She looks jest as she did when she was a girl and used to come into the meetin'-house. She *is* jest the same," the old man repeated, in his eager, hoarse voice. Then he bent over the coffin, and his lips moved again. Young Evelina would have called Mrs. Loomis, for she was frightened, had he not been Thomas's father, and had it not been for her vague feeling that there might be some old story to explain this which she had never heard. "Maybe he was in love with poor Cousin Evelina, as Thomas is with me," thought young Evelina, using her own leaping-pole of love to land straight at the truth. But she never told her surmise to anyone except Thomas, and that was long afterward, when the old man was dead. Now she watched him with her blue dilated eyes. But soon he turned away from the coffin and made his way straight out of the room, without a word. Evelina followed him through the entry and opened the outer door. He turned on the threshold and looked back at her, his face working.

"Don't ye go to lottin' too much on what ye're goin' to get

through folks that have died an' not had anything," he said; and he shook his head almost fiercely at her.

"No, I won't. I don't think I understand what you mean, sir," stammered Evelina.

The old man stood looking at her a moment. Suddenly she saw the tears rolling over his old cheeks. "I'm much obliged to ye for lettin' of me see her," he said, hoarsely, and crept feebly down the steps.

Evelina went back trembling to the room where her dead cousin lay, and covered her face, and closed the shutter again. Then she went about her household duties, wondering. She could not understand what it all meant; but one thing she understood—that in some way this old dead woman, Evelina Adams, had gotten immortal youth and beauty in one human heart. "She looked to him just as she did when she was a girl," Evelina kept thinking to herself with awe. She said nothing about it to Mrs. Martha Loomis or her daughters. They had been in the back part of the house, and had not heard old Thomas Merriam come in, and they never knew about it.

Mrs. Loomis and the two girls staid in the house day and night until after the funeral. They confidently expected to live there in the future. "It isn't likely that Evelina Adams thought a young woman no older than Evelina Leonard could live here alone in this great house with nobody but that old Sarah Judd. It would not be proper nor becoming," said Martha Loomis to her two daughters; and they agreed, and brought over many of their possessions under cover of night to the squire's house during the interval before the funeral.

But after the funeral and the reading of the will the Loomises made sundry trips after dusk back to their old home, with their best petticoats and cloaks over their arms, and their bonnets dangling by their strings at their sides. For Evelina Adams's last will and testament had been read, and therein provision was made for the continuance of the annuity heretofore paid them for their support, with the condition affixed that not one night should they spend after the reading of the will in the house known as the Squire Adams house. The annuity was an ample one, and would provide the widow Martha Loomis and her daughters, as it had done before, with all the needfuls of life; but upon hearing the will they stiffened their double chins into their kerchiefs with indignation, for they had looked for more.

Evelina Adams's will was a will of conditions, for unto it she had affixed two more, and those affected her beloved cousin Evelina Leonard. It was notable that "beloved" had not preceded her cousin Martha Loomis's name in the will. No pretence of love, when she felt none, had she ever made in her life. The entire property of Evelina Adams, spinster, deceased, with the exception of Widow Martha Loomis's provision, fell to this beloved young Evelina Leonard, subject to two conditions—firstly, she was never to enter into matrimony, with any person whomsoever, at any time whatsoever; secondly, she was never to let the said spinster Evelina Adams's garden, situated at the rear and southward of the house known as the Squire Adams house, die through any neglect of hers.

Due allowance was to be made for the dispensations of Providence: for hail and withering frost and long-continued drouth, and for times wherein the said Evelina Adams might, by reason of being confined to the house by sickness, be prevented from attending to the needs of the growing plants, and the verdict in such a case was to rest with the minister and the deacons of the church. But should this beloved Evelina love and wed, or should she let, through any wilful neglect, that garden perish in the season of flowers, all that goodly property would she forfeit to a person unknown, whose name, enclosed in a sealed envelope, was to be held meantime in the hands of the executor, who had also drawn up the will, Lawyer Joshua Lang.

There was great excitement in the village over this strange and unwonted will. Some were there who held that Evelina Adams had not been of sound mind, and it should be contested. It was even rumoured that Widow Martha Loomis had visited Lawyer Joshua Lang and broached the subject, but he had dismissed the matter peremptorily by telling her that Evelina Adams, spinster, deceased, had been as much in her right mind at the time of drawing the will as anybody of his acquaintance.

"Not setting store by relations, and not wanting to have them under your roof, don't go far in law nor common-sense to send folks to the mad-house," old Lawyer Lang, who was famed for his sharp tongue, was reported to have said. However, Mrs. Martha Loomis was somewhat comforted by her firm belief that either her own name or that of one of her daughters was in that sealed envelope kept by Lawyer Joshua Lang in his strong-box, and by her firm purpose to watch carefully lest Evelina prove derelict in fulfilling the two conditions whereby she held the property.

Larger peep-holes were soon cut away mysteriously in the high *arbor-vitæ* hedge, and therein were often set for a few moments, when they passed that way, the eager eyes of Mrs. Martha or her daughter Flora or Fidelia Loomis. Frequent calls they also made upon Evelina, living alone with the old woman Sarah Judd, who had been called in during her cousin's illness, and they strolled into the garden, spying anxiously for withered leaves or dry stalks. They had at every opportunity interviewed the old man who assisted Evelina in her care of the garden concerning its welfare. But small progress they made with him, standing digging at the earth with his spade while they talked, as if in truth his wits had gone therein before his body and he would uncover them.

Moreover, Mrs. Martha Loomis talked much slyly to mothers of young men, and sometimes with bold insinuations to the young men themselves, of the sad lot of poor young Evelina, condemned to a solitary and loveless life, and of her sweetness and beauty and desirability in herself, although she could not bring the old squire's money to her husband. And once, but no more than that, she touched lightly upon the subject to the young minister, Thomas Merriam, when he was making a pastoral call.

"My heart bleeds for the poor child living all alone in that great house," said she. And she looked down mournfully, and did not see how white the young minister's face turned. "It seems almost a pity," said she, furthermore—"Evelina is a good house-keeper, and has rare qualities in herself, and so many get poor wives nowadays—that some godly young man should not court her in spite of the will. I doubt, too, if she would not have a happier lot than growing old over that garden, as poor Cousin Evelina did before her, even if she has a fine house to live in and a goodly sum in the bank. She looks pindling enough lately. I'll warrant she has lost a good ten pound since poor Evelina was laid away, and —"

But Thomas Merriam cut her short. "I see no profit in dis-cussing matters which do not concern us," said he, and only his ministerial estate saved him from the charge of impertinence.

As it was, Martha Loomis coloured high. "I'll warrant he'll look out which side his bread is buttered on; ministers always do," she said to her daughters after he had gone. She never dreamed how her talk had cut him to the heart.

Had he not seen more plainly than anyone else, Sunday after Sunday, when he glanced down at her once or twice cautiously from his pulpit, how weary-looking and thin she was grow-ing? And her bright colour was well-nigh gone, and there were pitiful downward lines at the corners of her sweet mouth. Poor young Evelina was fading like one of her own flowers, as if some celestial gardener had failed in his care of her. And Thomas saw it, and in his heart of hearts he knew the reason, and yet he would not yield.

Not once had he entered the old squire's house since he at-tended the dead Evelina's funeral, and stood praying and eulo-gizing, with her coffin between him and the living Evelina, with her pale face shrouded in black bombazine. He had never spo-ken to her since, nor entered the house; but he had written her a letter, in which all the fierce passion and anguish of his heart was cramped and held down by formal words and phrases, and poor young Evelina did not see beneath them. When her lover wrote her that he felt it inconsistent with his Christian duty and the higher aims of his existence to take any further steps toward a matrimonial alliance, she felt merely that Thomas either cared no more for her, or had come to consider, upon due reflection, that she was not fit to undertake the responsible position of a minister's wife. "It may be that in some way I failed in my attendance upon Cousin Evelina," thought poor young Evelina, "or it may be that he thinks I have not enough dignity of character to inspire respect among the older women in the church." And sometimes, with a sharp thrust of misery that shook her out of her enforced patience and meekness, she wondered if indeed her own loving freedom with him had turned him against her, and led him in his later and sober judgment to consider her too light-minded for a minister's wife.

"It may be that I was guilty of great indecorum, and almost indeed forfeited my claim to respect for maidenly modesty, inasmuch as I suffered him to give me kisses, and did almost bring myself to return them in kind. But my heart did so entreat me, and in truth it seemed almost like a lack of sincerity for me to wholly withstand it," wrote poor young Evelina in her journal at that time; and she further wrote: "It is indeed hard for one who has so little knowledge to be fully certain of what is or is not becoming and a Christian duty in matters of this kind; but if I have in any manner, through my ignorance or unwarrantable affection, failed, and so lost the love and respect of a good man, and the opportunity to become his helpmeet during life, I pray that I may be forgiven—for I sinned not wilfully—that the lesson may be sanctified unto me, and that I may live as the Lord order, in Christian patience and meekness, and not repining."

It never occurred to young Evelina that possibly Thomas Merriam's sense of duty might be strengthened by the loss of all her cousin's property should she marry him, and neither did she dream that he might hesitate to take her from affluence into poverty for her own sake. For herself the property, as put in the balance beside her love, was lighter than air itself. It was so light that it had no place in her consciousness. She simply had thought, upon hearing the will, of Martha Loomis and her daughters in possession of the property, and herself with Thomas, with perfect acquiescence and rapture.

Evelina Adams's disapprobation of her marriage, which was supposedly expressed in the will, had indeed, without reference to the property, somewhat troubled her tender heart, but she told herself that Cousin Evelina had not known she had promised to marry Thomas; that she would not wish her to break her solemn promise. And furthermore, it seemed to her quite reasonable that the condition had been inserted in the will mainly through concern for the beloved garden.

"Cousin Evelina might have thought perhaps I would let the flowers die when I had a husband and children to take care of," said Evelina. And so she had disposed of all the considerations which had disturbed her, and had thought of no others.

She did not answer Thomas's letter. It was so worded that it seemed to require no reply, and she felt that he must be sure of her acquiescence in whatever he thought best. She laid the letter away in a little rosewood box, in which she had always kept her dearest treasures since her school days. Sometimes she took it out and read it, and it seemed to her that the pain in her heart would put an end to her in spite of all her prayers for Christian fortitude; and yet she could not help reading it again.

It was seldom that she stole a look at her old lover as he stood in the pulpit in the meeting-house, but when she did she thought with an anxious pang that he looked worn and ill, and that night she prayed that the Lord would restore his health to him for the sake of his people.

It was four months after Evelina Adams's death, and her garden was in the full glory of midsummer, when one evening, toward dusk, young Evelina went slowly down the street. She seldom walked abroad now, but kept herself almost as secluded as her cousin had done before her. But that night a great restlessness was upon her, and she put a little black silk shawl over her shoulders and went out. It was quite cool, although it was midsummer. The dusk was deepening fast; the katydids called back and forth from the way-side bushes. Evelina met nobody for some distance. Then she saw a man coming toward her, and her heart stood still, and she was about to turn back, for she thought for a minute it was the young minister. Then she saw it was his father, and she went on slowly, with her eyes downcast. When she met him she looked up and said good-evening, gravely, and would have passed on, but he stood in her way.

"I've got a word to say to ye, if ye'll listen," he said.

Evelina looked at him tremblingly. There was something strained and solemn in his manner. "I'll hear whatever you have to say, sir," she said.

The old man leaned his pale face over her and raised a shaking forefinger. "I've made up my mind to say something," said he. "I don't know as I've got any right to, and maybe my son will blame me, but I'm goin' to see that ye have a chance. It's been borne in upon me that women folks don't always have a fair chance. It's jest this I'm goin' to say: I don't know whether you know how my son feels about it or not. I don't know how open he's been with ye. Do you know jest why he quit ye?"

Evelina shook her head. "No," she panted—"I don't—I never knew. He said it was his duty."

"Duty can get to be an idol of wood and stone, an' I don't know but Thomas's is," said the old man. "Well, I'll tell ye. He don't think it's right for him to marry ye, and make you leave that big house, and lose all that money. He don't care anything about it for himself, but it's for you. Did you know that?"

Then Evelina grasped the old man's arm hard with her little fingers.

"You don't mean that—was why he did it!" she gasped.

"Yes, that was why."

Evelina drew away from him. She was ashamed to have Thomas's father see the joy in her face. "Thank you, sir," she said. "I did not understand. I—will write to him."

"Maybe my son will think I have done wrong coming betwixt him and his idees of duty," said old Thomas Merriam, "but sometimes there's a good deal lost for lack of a word, and I wanted ye to have a fair chance an' a fair say. It's been borne in upon me that women folks don't always have it. Now ye can do jest as ye think best, but you must remember one thing—riches ain't all. A little likin' for ye that's goin' to last, and keep honest and faithful to ye as long as ye live, is worth more; an' it's worth more to women folks than 'tis to men, an' it's worth enough to them. My son's poorly. His mother and I are worried about him. He don't eat nor sleep—walks his chamber nights. His mother don't know what the matter is, but he let on to me some time since."

"I'll write a letter to him," gasped Evelina again. "Good-night, sir." She pulled her little black silk shawl over her head and hastened home, and all night long her candle burned, while her weary little fingers toiled over pages of foolscap-paper to convince Thomas Merriam fully, and yet in terms not exceeding maidenly reserve, that the love of his heart and the companion-ship of his life were worth more to her than all the silver and gold in the world. Then the next morning she despatched it, all neatly folded and sealed, and waited.

It was strange that a letter like that could not have moved Thomas Merriam, when his heart too pleaded with him so hard to be moved. But that might have been the very reason why he could withstand her, and why the consciousness of his own weakness gave him strength. Thomas Merriam was one, when he had once fairly laid hold of duty, to grasp it hard, although it might be to his own pain and death, and maybe to that of oth-ers. He wrote to poor young Evelina another letter, in which he emphasized and repeated his strict adherence to what he believed the line of duty in their separation, and ended it with a prayer for her welfare and happiness, in which, indeed, for a second, the passionate heart of the man showed forth. Then he locked himself in his chamber, and nobody ever knew what he suffered there. But one pang he did not suffer which Evelina would have suffered in his place. He mourned not over nor real-ized the grief of her tender heart when she should read his letter, otherwise he could not have sent it. He writhed under his own pain alone, and his duty hugged him hard, like the iron maiden of the old tortures, but he would not yield.

As for Evelina, when she got his letter, and had read it through, she sat still and white for a long time, and did not seem to hear when old Sarah Judd spoke to her. But at last she rose up and went to her chamber, and knelt down, and prayed for a long time; and then she went out in the garden and cut all the most beautiful flowers, and tied them in wreaths and bouquets, and carried them out to the north side of the house, where her cousin Evelina was buried, and covered her grave with them. And then she knelt down there and hid her face among them, and said, in a low voice, as if in a listening ear, "I pray you, Cousin Evelina, forgive me for what I am about to do."

And then she returned to the house, and sat at her needle-work as usual; but the old woman kept looking at her, and asking if she were sick, for there was a strange look in her face.

She and old Sarah Judd had always their tea at five o'clock, and put the candles out at nine, and this night they did as they were wont. But at one o'clock in the morning young Evelina stole softly down the stairs with her lighted candle, and passed through into the kitchen; and a half-hour after she came forth into the garden, which lay in full moonlight, and she had in her hand a steaming teakettle, and she passed around among the shrubs and watered them, and a white cloud of steam rose around them. Back and forth she went to the kitchen; for she had heated the great copper wash-kettle full of water; and she watered all the shrubs in the garden, moving amid curling white wreaths of steam, until the water was gone. And then she set to work and tore up by the roots with her little hands and trampled with her little feet all the beautiful tender flower-beds; all the time weeping, and moaning softly: "Poor Cousin Evelina! poor Cousin Evelina! Oh, forgive me, poor Cousin Evelina!"

And at dawn the garden lay in ruin, for all the tender plants she had torn up by the roots and trampled down, and all the stronger-rooted shrubs she had striven to kill with boiling water and salt.

Then Evelina went into the house, and made herself tidy as well as she could when she trembled so, and put her little shawl

145

over her head, and went down the road to the Merriams' house. It was so early the village was scarcely astir, but there was smoke coming out of the kitchen chimney at the Merriams'; and when she knocked, Mrs. Merriam opened the door at once, and stared at her.

"Is Sarah Judd dead?" she cried; for her first thought was that something must have happened when she saw the girl standing there with her wild pale face.

"I want to see the minister," said Evelina, faintly, and she looked at Thomas's mother with piteous eyes.

"Be you sick?" asked Mrs. Merriam. She laid a hard hand on the girl's arm, and led her into the sitting-room, and put her into the rocking-chair with the feather cushion. "You look real poorly," said she. "Sha'n't I get you a little of my elderberry wine?"

"I want to see him," said Evelina, and she almost sobbed.

"I'll go right and speak to him," said Mrs. Merriam. "He's up, I guess. He gets up early to write. But hadn't I better get you something to take first? You do look sick."

But Evelina only shook her head. She had her face covered with her hands, and was weeping softly. Mrs. Merriam left the room, with a long backward glance at her. Presently the door opened and Thomas came in. Evelina stood up before him. Her pale face was all wet with tears, but there was an air of strange triumph about her.

"The garden is dead," said she.

"What do you mean?" he cried out, staring at her, for indeed he thought for a minute that her wits had left her.

"The garden is dead," said she. "Last night I watered the roses with boiling water and salt, and I pulled the other flowers up by their roots. The garden is dead, and I have lost all Cousin Evelina's money, and it need not come between us any longer." She said that, and looked up in his face with her blue eyes, through which the love of the whole race of loving women from which she had sprung, as well as her own, seemed to look, and held out her little hands; but even then Thomas Merriam could not

146

understand, and stood looking at her.

"Why—did you do it?" he stammered.

"Because you would have me no other way, and—I couldn't bear that anything like that should come between us," she said, and her voice shook like a harp-string, and her pale face went red, then pale again.

But Thomas still stood staring at her. Then her heart failed her. She thought that he did not care, and she had been mistaken. She felt as if it were the hour of her death, and turned to go. And then he caught her in his arms.

"Oh," he cried, outbreaking with a great sob, "the Lord make me worthy of thee, Evelina!"

There had never been so much excitement in the village as when the fact of the ruined garden came to light. Flora Loomis, peeping through the hedge on her way to the store, had spied it first. Then she had run home for her mother, who had in turn sought Lawyer Lang, panting bonnetless down the road. But before the lawyer had started for the scene of disaster, the minister, Thomas Merriam, had appeared, and asked for a word in private with him. Nobody ever knew just what that word was, but the lawyer was singularly uncommunicative and reticent as to the ruined garden.

"Do you think the young woman is out of her mind?" one of the deacons asked him, in a whisper.

"I wish all the young women were as much in their minds; we'd have a better world," said the lawyer, gruffly.

"When do you think we can begin to move in here?" asked Mrs. Martha Loomis, her wide skirts sweeping a bed of uprooted verbenas.

"When your claim is established," returned the lawyer, shortly, and turned on his heel and went away, his dry old face scanning the ground like a dog on a scent. That afternoon he opened the sealed document in the presence of witnesses, and the name of the heir to whom the property fell was disclosed. It was "Thomas Merriam, the beloved and esteemed minister of this parish," and young Evelina would gain her wealth instead of losing it by her marriage. And furthermore, after the declaration of the name of the heir was this added: "This do I in the hope and belief that neither the greed of riches nor the fear of them shall prevent that which is good and wise in the sight of the Lord, and with the surety that a love which shall triumph over so much in its way shall endure, and shall be a blessing and not a curse to my beloved cousin Evelina Leonard."

Thomas Merriam and Evelina were married before the leaves fell in that same year, by the minister of the next village, who rode over in his chaise, and brought his wife, who was also a bride, and wore her wedding-dress of a pink and pearl shot silk. But young Evelina wore the blue bridal array which had been worn by old Squire Adams's bride, all remodelled daintily to suit the fashion of the times; and as she moved, the folds shook out the fragrance of roses and lavender of the old summers during which it had been laid away, like sweet memories.

A New England Prophet

At half past six o'clock a little company of people passed down the village street in the direction of the Lennox farmhouse.

They advanced in silence, stepping along the frozen ridges of the road. It was cold, but there was no snow. There was a young moon shining through thin white clouds like *nebulæ*.

Now and then, as the company went on, new recruits were gathered from the scattered houses. A man would emerge darkly from a creaking gate, with maybe a second and third dark figure following, with a flirt of feminine draperies. "There's Deacon Scranton," or "There's Thomas Jennings and his wife and Ellen," the people would murmur to each other.

Once a gleam of candle-light from an open door lay across the road in advance, and wavered into darkness with a slam of the door when the company drew near. Then a solitary woman came ponderously down the front walk, seeming to jar the frozen earth with the jolt of her great feminine bulk. "There's Abby Mosely," somebody muttered. Sometimes two young girls fluttered out of a door-yard, clinging together with nervous giggles and outcries, which were soon hushed. They moved along with the others, their little cold fingers clinging together with a rigid clutch. It was as if a strange, solemn atmosphere surrounded this group moving along the country road in the starlit night. Whoever came into their midst felt it, and his emotions changed involuntarily as respiration changes on a mountain-top.

When the party reached a windy hill-top in sight of the

lighted windows of the Lennox house in the valley below, it numbered nearly twenty. Halfway down the hill somebody else joined them. He had been standing ahead of them, waiting in the long shadow of a poplar, and they had not discerned him until they were close to him. Then he stepped forward and the shadow of the tree was left motionless. The young girls half screamed, he appeared so suddenly, and their nerves were strained. The elders made a solemn hushed murmur of greeting. They knew as soon as he moved that he was Isaac Penfield. He had a martial carriage of his shoulders, he was a captain in the militia, and he wore an ash-coloured cloak, which distinguished him.

The young girls cast glances, bolder from the darkness, toward his stately ash-coloured shoulders and the proudly set pale gleam of his face. Not one of them who had not her own lover but had her innocent secret dreams about this Isaac Penfield. Now, had a light shone out suddenly in the darkness, their dreams would have shown in their faces.

One slender girl slunk softly around in the rear darkness and crept so close to Isaac Penfield that his ash-coloured cloak, swinging out in the wind, brushed her cheek. He did not notice her; indeed, after his first murmur of salutation, he did not speak to anyone.

They all went in silence down the hill, and flocked into the great yard of the Lennox house. There was a red flicker of light in the kitchen windows from the great hearth fire, but a circle of dark heads and shoulders hid the fire itself from the newcomers. There was evidently a number of people inside.

Deacon Scranton raised the knocker, and the door was opened immediately. Melissa Lennox stood there holding a candle in a brass candlestick, with the soft light streaming up in her fair face. She looked through it with innocent, anxious blue eyes at the company. "Won't you walk in?" she said, tremulously, and the people passed into the south entry, and through the door on the left into the great Lennox kitchen. Some dozen persons who had come from the other end of the village were already there.

Isaac Penfield entered last. Melissa did not see him until he stepped suddenly within her radius of candle-light. Then she started, and bent her head before him, blushing. The candle shook in her outstretched hand.

Isaac Penfield took the candle without a word and set it on the stairs. Then he took Melissa's slim right hand in his, and stood a moment looking down at her bent head, with its parted gloss of hair. His forehead was frowning, and yet he half smiled with tender triumph.

"Come out in the front yard with me a moment," he whispered. He pulled her with gentle force toward the door, and the girl yielded, after a faint murmur of expostulation.

Out in the front yard Isaac Penfield folded a corner of his ash-coloured cloak around Melissa's slender shoulders.

"Now I want you to tell me, Melissa," he whispered. "You are not still carried away by all this?" He jerked his head toward the kitchen windows.

Melissa trembled against the young man's side under the folds of his cloak.

"You are not, after all I said to you, Melissa?"

She nodded against his breast, with a faint sob.

"I hoped you would do as I asked you, and cut loose from this folly," Isaac Penfield said, sternly.

"Father—says—it's true. Oh, I am afraid—I am afraid! My sins are so great, and I cannot hide from the eyes of the Lord. I am afraid!"

Isaac Penfield tightened his clasp of the girl's trembling figure, and bent his head low down over hers. "Melissa, dear, can't you listen to me?" he whispered.

Suddenly the kitchen door opened, and a new light streamed across the entry.

"Melissa, where be you?" called a woman's voice, high-pitched and melancholy.

"There's mother calling," Melissa said, in a frightened whisper, and she broke away and ran into the house.

Her mother stood in the kitchen door. "Where have you been?" she began. Then she stopped, and looked at Isaac Penfield

151

with a half-shrinking, half-antagonistic air. This stalwart young man, radiant with the knowledge of his own strength, represented to this delicate woman, who was held to the earth more by the tension of nerves than the weight of matter, the very pride of life, the material power which she was to fear and fight for herself and for her daughter.

"I thought I would step into your meeting tonight, if I were permitted," Isaac Penfield said.

Mrs. Lennox looked at him with deep blue eyes under high, thin temples. "All are permitted who listen to the truth with the right spirit," said she, and turned shortly and glided into the kitchen. Melissa and Isaac followed.

The company sat in wide semicircles, three deep, before the fire. In the open space between the first semicircle and the fire, his wide arm-chair on the bricks of the broad hearth, half facing the company, sat Solomon Lennox. Near him sat his deaf-and-dumb son Alonzo. He held up a great slate so the firelight fell upon it, and marked upon it with a grating pencil. He screwed his face with every stroke, so it seemed that one watching attentively might discern the picture itself from his changing features.

Alonzo Lennox was fourteen years old, but he looked no more than ten, and he had been deaf and dumb from his birth. The firelight gave a reddish tinge to his silvery blond hair, spreading out stiffly from the top of his head over his ears like the thatch of a hut. His delicate irregular profile bent over the slate; now and then a spasm of silent merriment shook his narrow chest, and the surrounding people looked at him with awe. They regarded it as the mystic ecstasy of a seer.

Melissa and her mother had slid softly through the semi-circles to the chairs they had left. Isaac Penfield stood on the outskirts, towering over all the people, refusing a seat which somebody offered him. He threw off his ash-coloured cloak and held it on his arm. His costume of fine broadcloth and flowered satin and glittering buttons surpassed any there, as did his face and his height and his carriage; and, more than all, he stood among the others raised upon a spiritual eminence, unseen, but none the less real, which his ancestors had reared for him before his birth. The Penfield name had been a great one in that vicinity for three generations. Once Penfields had owned the greater part of the township. Isaac's father, and his grandfather before him, had been esquires, and held as nearly the position of lords of this little village as was possible in New England. Now this young man was the last of his race, living, with his housekeeper and an old servant, in the Penfield homestead; and the village adulation which had been accorded to his ancestors was his also in a large measure.

Tonight, as he entered, people glanced at him, away from Alonzo and his slate, but only for a moment. The matter under discussion that night was too solemn and terrible to be lost sight of long.

In about ten minutes after Isaac Penfield entered, the boy gave a shout, grating and hideous, with a discord of human thoughts and senses in it. A shudder passed over the company like a wind.

Alonzo Lennox sprang up and waved the slate, and his father reached out for it. "Give it to me," he demanded, sternly, as if the boy could hear. But Alonzo gave another shout, and leaped aside, and waved the slate out of his father's reach. Then he danced lightly up and down on the tips of his toes, shaking his head and flinging out fantastic heels. His shock of hair flew out wildly, and looked like a luminous crown; the firelight struck his dilated eyes, and they gleamed red.

The people watched him with sobbing breaths and pale faces, all except Isaac Penfield and one other. Isaac stood looking at him, with his mouth curling in a scornful smile. Solomon Lennox stood aside with a startled air, then he caught the boy firmly by the arm and grasped the slate.

Alonzo grinned impishly in his father's face, then he let go the slate, and sank down on his stool in the chimney-corner. There he sat submissive and inactive, except for the cunning, sharp flash of his blue eyes under his thatch of hair.

Solomon Lennox held the slate to the light and looked at it, while the people waited breathless, their pale intent faces bent forward. Then he handed the slate, without a word, to the man at the end of the first semicircle, and it was circulated through the entire company. As one passed the slate to another a shuddering thrill like an electric shock seemed to be passed with it, and there was a faint murmur of horror.

Isaac Penfield held the slate longest, and examined it closely. Drawn with a free hand, which certainly gave evidence of some inborn artistic skill aside from aught else, were great sweeping curves of wings upbearing an angel with a trumpet at his mouth. Under his feet were lashing tongues as of flames, with upturned faces of agony in the midst of them. And everywhere, between the wings and the angel and the flames and the faces, were, in groups of five, those grotesque little symbols of the sun, a disk with human features therein, which one sees in the almanacs.

After Isaac Penfield had finished looking at the mystic slate he passed it to Solomon Lennox's elder brother, Simeon, who sat at his right. The old man's hard shaven jaws widened in a sardonic grin; his small black eyes twinkled derisively over the drawings. "Pretty pictures," he said, half aloud. Then he passed the slate along with a contemptuous chuckle, which was heard in the solemn stillness all over the room.

Solomon Lennox gave a furious glance in his brother's direction. "This is no time nor season for scoffers!" cried he. And his voice seemed to shock the air like a musket-shot.

Simeon Lennox chuckled again. Solomon's right hand clinched. He arose; then sat down again, with his mouth compressed. He sat still until the slate had gone its rounds and returned to the boy, who sat contemplating it with uncouth delight; then he stood up, and the words flowed from his mouth in torrents. Never at a loss for subject-matter of speech was Solomon Lennox. By the fluency of his discourse he might well have been thought inspired. He spoke of visions of wings and holy candlesticks and beasts and cups of abomination as if he had with his own eyes seen them like the prophet of old. He expounded strange and subtle mathematical calculations and erratic interpretations of history as applied to revelation with a fervour which brought conviction to his audience. He caught the slate from his deaf-and-dumb son, and explained the weird characters thereon. The five suns were five days. Five times the sun should arise in the east, as it had done from the creation; then should the angel, upborne on those great white wings, sound his trumpet, and the flames burst forth from the lower pit, and those upturned faces in the midst of them gnash with despair.

"Repent, for the day of the Lord is at hand!" shouted Solomon Lennox at the close of his arguments, and his voice itself rang like a trumpet full of all intonations and reverberations, of awe and dread. "Repent, for the great and dreadful day of the Lord is at hand! Repent while there is yet time, while there is yet a foothold on the shore of the lake of fire! Repent, repent! Prepare your ascension robes! Renounce the world, and all the lust and the vanity thereof! Repent, for the day of judgment is here! Soon shall ye choke with the smoke of the everlasting burning, soon shall your eyes be scorched with the fiery scroll of the heavens, your ears be deafened with the blast of the trumpet of wrath, and the cry against you of your own sins! Repent, repent, repent!"

Solomon Lennox's slight figure writhed with his own emotion as with internal fire; the veins swelled out on his high bald forehead; his eyes blazed with fanatical fire. Aside from the startling nature of his discourse, he himself was a marvel, and a terror to his neighbours. His complete deviation from a former line of life produced among them the horror of the supernatural. He affected them like his own ghost. He had always been a man of few and quiet words, who had never expressed his own emotions in public beyond an inaudible, muttered prayer at a conference meeting, and now this flood of fiery eloquence from him seemed like a very convulsion of human nature.

When a great physical malady is epidemic there are often isolated cases in remote localities whose connection with the main disturbance cannot be established. So in this little New England village, far from a railroad, scarcely reached by the news of the day, Solomon Lennox had developed within himself, with seeming spontaneity, some of the startling tenets of Joseph Miller, and had established his own small circle of devoted disciples and followers. It was as if some germs of a great spiritual disturbance had sought, through some unknown medium, this man's mind as their best ripening place.

After Solomon had arisen one night in conference meeting and poured forth his soul to his startled neighbours in a strain of fiery prophecy, Millerite publications had been sent for, and he had strengthened his own theories with those of the original leader, although in many respects his maintained a distinct variance.

The effect of Solomon's prophecies had been greatly enhanced by the drawings of his deaf-and-dumb son. Alonzo Lennox's slate, covered with rude representations of beasts and trumpets and winged creatures—the weird symbolic figures of the prophet Daniel—had aroused a great tumult of awe and terror in the village. And the more so because the boy had never learned the language of the deaf and dumb, and had no ordinary and comprehensible means of acquiring information upon such topics.

Tonight, as his father spoke, he kept his blue eyes upon his face with such a keen look that it seemed almost impossible that he did not hear and comprehend every word. Unbelievers in this new movement were divided between the opinion that Lonny Lennox had heard more than folks had given him credit for right along, and the one that he understood by some strange power which the loss of his other faculties had sharpened.

"The boy has developed the sixth sense," Isaac Penfield thought as he watched his intent face upturned toward his father's; and he also thought impatiently that he should be cuffed and sent to bed for his uncanny sharpness. He grew more and more indignant as the time went on and the excitement deepened. He watched Melissa grow paler and paler, and finally press her slender hands over her face, and shake with sobs, and made a sudden motion as if he would go to her. Then he restrained himself, and muttered something between his teeth.

Old Simeon Lennox watched him curiously, then he hit him in the side with a sharp elbow. "Made up your mind to go up in our family chariot on the last day?" he whispered, with a hoarse whistle of breath in Isaac's ear. Then he leaned back, with a long cackle of laughter in his throat, which was unheard in the din of his brother's raging voice and the responsive groans and sobs.

Isaac Penfield coloured, and kept his eyes straight forward and his head up with a haughty air. Presently the old man nudged him again, with the sharpness of malice protected by helplessness. "Guess," he whispered, craning up to the young man's handsome, impatient face—"guess you 'ain't much opinion of all this darned tomfoolery neither."

Isaac shook his head fiercely.

"Well," said the old man, "let 'em go it," and he cackled with laughter again.

After Solomon Lennox had finished his fervid appeal, two or three offered prayers, and many testified and confessed sins, and professed repentance, and terror of the wrath to come, in hoarse, strained voices, half drowned by sobs and cries.

It was nearly midnight before Solomon Lennox declared the meeting at a close, and recommended the brethren and sisters to repair to their homes, not to sleep, but to pray, and appointed another session for the next forenoon, for these meetings of terror-stricken and contrite souls were held three times a day—morning, afternoon, and evening. In those days the housewives' kitchen tables were piled high with unwashed dishes, the hearths were unswept and the fires low, the pantry shelves were bare, and often the children went to bed with only the terrors of the judgment for sustenance.

In those days the cattle grew lean, and stood lowing piteously long after nightfall at the pasture bars. Even the horses turned in their stalls at every footfall and whinnied for food. Men lost all thought for their earthly goods in their fierce concern for their own souls.

The people flocked out of Solomon Lennox's kitchen, some with rapt eyes, some white-faced and trembling, huddling together as if with a forlorn hope that human companionship might avail somewhat even against divine judgment. The deaf-and-dumb boy went sleepily out of the room and upstairs with his candle, leaving his slate on the hearthstone. Isaac Penfield stood a few minutes looking irresolutely at Melissa, who sat still with her hands pressed tightly over her face, as if she were weeping. Her mother stood near her, talking to Abby Mosely, who was Simeon Lennox's housekeeper. The woman was fairly gasping with emotion; her broad shawled bosom heaved.

"Repent!" cried Mrs. Lennox, loud, in her ears, like an echo of her husband. "Repent; there is yet time! There are five days before the heavens open! Repent!" Her nervous hands served to intensify her weak, straining voice. They pointed and threatened in the woman's piteous, scared face. Isaac started to approach Melissa; then her mother half turned and seemed to shriek out her warning cry toward him, and he tossed his gray cloak over his shoulders, strode out of the room, and out of the house.

Old Simeon Lennox lingered behind the others.

"I'm a-comin' right along, Abby," he called to his housekeeper when she started to leave the room. "If ye go to bed afore I come, mind ye put the cat out, so she won't get afoul of that pig meat in the pantry." Simeon spoke with cool disregard of the distressed sobs and moans with which the woman was making her exit.

"D'ye hear what I say, Abby?" he called, sharply, when she did not reply.

The housekeeper groaned a faint assent over her shoulder as she crossed the threshold.

"Well, mind ye don't forgit it," said Simeon, "for I tell ye what 'tis, if that cat does git afoul of that pig meat, there'll be a jedgment afore Thursday."

The old man clamped leisurely across the room, drew an armchair close to the fire, and settled into it with a grunting yawn.

"Fire feels good," he remarked. His voice was thick, for he had tobacco in his mouth.

"Woe be unto you, Simeon Lennox, if you can still think of the comfort of your poor body which will soon be ashes," cried his sister-in-law. She waved before him like a pale flame; her white face seemed fairly luminous.

Simeon shifted his tobacco into one cheek as he stared at her. "You'd better go to bed, Sophy Anne; you're gittin' highstericky," said he, and chewed again.

"Woe be unto you, fer the bed you shall lie on, unless you repent, Simeon Lennox!"

"Look at here, Sophy Anne," said Simeon, "'ain't you got no mince pies in the house?"

Mrs. Lennox looked at him, speechless, for a moment.

"If you have," Simeon went on, "I wish you'd give me a piece. I 'ain't had no mince pie fit to eat I dun'no' when. Abby Mosely wa'n't never much of a cook, and sence she's tuk to goin' to your meetin' here three times a day, it's much as ever's I get anything. It ain't no more'n fair, Sophy Anne, that you should give me a piece of mince pie, if you've got any."

Mrs. Lennox broke in upon him with a cry which was almost a shriek. "I shall make no more pies in this world, Simeon Lennox. Woe be unto you! Woe be unto you if you think of such things in the face of death and eternal condemnation!"

Solomon Lennox had followed the departing people into the yard. His exhorting voice could still be heard out there, for the doors were open.

Simeon looked around and shivered. "If you 'ain't got no mince pie, I wish you'd shet that door, Sophy Anne," he said.

Sophia Anne Lennox stood looking at him for a minute. He chuckled in her face. She snatched a candle from the shelf and went out of the room with an air of desperation.

Melissa rose up and crept after her, her face like a drooping white flower, gliding so closely in her mother's wake that she seemed to have no individual motion of her own. Simeon looked hard at her as she went.

"Sophy Anne is wiry," he said, when his brother came in. "She'll go it all right if the wires don't snap, an' I reckon they won't; but you'd better look out for Melissy. She can't stan' such tearin' work as this very long. She'll have a fever or somethin'."

"What matters that?" cried Solomon. "What matters any tribulation of the flesh when the end of all flesh is at hand?" His voice was hoarse with his long clamour. He leaned over and shook a nervous fist impressively before his brother's face.

Simeon chewed on, and looked at the fist without winking. "You don't mean to say, Solomon Lennox," said he at length, "that you believe all this darned tomfoolery?"

His brother looked at him with solemn wrath. "Do I believe revelation and the prophets?" he cried. "Woe be unto all scoffers, even though they be my own flesh and blood!"

"Now, Solomon, I'll jest stump ye to point out any passage in the Scriptures that says, up an' down, square an' fair, that the world's comin' to an end next Thursday. I'll jest stump ye to do it."

"There are passages that point to the truth, and I have repeated them tonight," replied Solomon, hotly.

"Passages that ye've had to twist hind-side foremost, an' bottom-side up, an' add, an' subtract, an' divide, an' multiply, an' hammer, an' saw, an' bile down, an' take to a grist-mill, afore you got at the meanin' you wanted," returned his brother, contemptuously. "That ain't the kind of passage I'm after. There's too much two-facedness an' double-dealin' about the Scriptures anyway, judgin' by some of you folks. What I want is a square up an' down passage that says, without no chance of its meanin' anything else, 'The world is comin' to an end next week Thursday.' I stump ye to show me sech a passage as that. *Ye can't do it!*"

The habits of a lifetime are strong even in strained and exalted states, acting like the lash of a familiar whip. Solomon Lennox was the younger brother; all his life he had borne a certain docility of attitude toward Simeon, which asserted itself now.

The fervid orator stood for a moment silent before this sceptical, sneering elder brother. "I'd like to know how you account for Lonny's drawin's," he said at length, in a tone which he might have used when bullied by Simeon in their boyhood.

"Drawin's," drawled Simeon, and sarcasm itself seemed to hiss in the final s—"dr-r-awin's! The little scamp is sharp as steel, an' he's watched an' he's eyed till he's put two an' two together. It's easy enough to account for the drawin's. The air here has been so thick lately with wings an' wheels an' horns an' trumpets an' everlastin' fire that anybody that wa'n't an idgit could breathe it in. An' I miss my guess if his mother 'ain't showed him the picturs in the big Bible mor'n once when you've been talkin', an' pointed out the hearth fire an' the candlesticks an' the powderhorn. Sophy Anne's sharp, an' she's done more to learn that boy than anybody knows of, though I've got my doubts now as to how straight he's really got it in his mind. Lord, them drawin's ain't nothin'. Solomon Lennox, you can't look me in the face an' say that you actilly believe all this darned tomfoolery!"

Solomon for these few minutes had been on the old level of a brotherly argument, but now he arose suddenly to his latter heights.

"I believe that the end of the world is near, that the great and dreadful day of the Lord is at hand, accordin' to prophecy and revelation," he proclaimed, and his eyes shone under his high forehead as under a majestic dome of thought and inspiration.

Simeon whistled. "Ye don't, though. Look at here, Solomon; tell ye what I'll do. I'll put ye to the test. Look at here, you say the world's comin' to an end next Thursday. Well, it stands to reason if it is, that you 'ain't got no more need of temporal goods. S'pose—you give me a deed of this 'ere farm?"

Solomon stared at his brother.

Simeon shook his fist at him slowly. "Ye won't do it," he said, with a triumphant chuckle.

"I will do it."

"Git Lawyer Bascombe to draw up the papers tomorrow?"

"I will."

"Me to take possession by daylight next Friday mornin', if the world don't come to an end Thursday night?"

"*Yes*," replied Solomon, hurling the word at his brother like a stone.

Simeon got up and buttoned his coat over his lean chest. "Well," said he, "I've had pretty hard luck. I've lost three wives, and I've been burnt out twice, an' the last house ain't none too tight. I'll move right in here next Friday mornin' at daylight. Mebbe I'll get married again."

"Much good will the heaping up of barns an' storehouses do when you hear the voice of the Lord saying, 'Thou fool, this night shall thy soul be required of thee,'" returned his brother; but he spoke the fervid words with a certain feebleness. All his life since he was a boy had Solomon Lennox toiled and saved to own this noble farm. The bare imagination of giving it up to another cost him much, although he firmly believed that in a week's space it would be only a modicum of the blackened ashes of a world. He stood the test of his faith, but he felt the scorch of sacrificial flame.

"It ain't me that's the fool," said Simeon, shrugging himself into his great-coat. "I ain't goin' to hang back with my soul when it's required of me, but I ain't goin' to keep chuckin' of it in the face of the Lord afore He's ready for it, like some folks I know. Them's the fools. When'll you be down to Lawyer Bascombe's tomorrow, Solomon, to deed away these barns an' storehouses that you 'ain't no more use for?"

"I'll be down there at nine o'clock tomorrow mornin'."

"All right; you can count on me," said Simeon. He went out, and Solomon bolted the door after him promptly. But he had no sooner returned to the kitchen than there came a sharp tap on the window, and there was Simeon's hard leering old face pressed against the pane. "You'll—have—to—fetch Sophy Anne down there tomorrow," he called. "She'll—have to sign that deed too, or it won't stan'."

"All right," shouted Solomon, and the face at the window, with a parting nod, disappeared.

Lawyer Bascombe's office was in the centre of the village, over the store. A steep flight of stairs at the right of the store led to it. Up these stairs, at nine o'clock the next morning, climbed Solomon Lennox and his wife Sophia Anne, with pale devoted faces, and signed away all their earthly goods as an evidence of their faith.

In some way the matter had become known in the village. When Solomon and Sophia Anne came down the stairs there was quite a crowd before the door, standing back with awed curiosity to let them pass. Simeon Lennox did not leave at once after the signing of the deed. When he appeared in the doorway with a roll of paper in his hand the crowd had dispersed.

Without any doubt this act of Solomon Lennox and his wife materially strengthened their cause. When it became known that they had actually signed away their property in their confidence that days of property-holding were over, even scoffers began to look serious. That evening the meeting at Solomon Lennox's house numbered a third more than usual. The next evening it was doubled, and the best room as well as the kitchen was filled. Solomon stood at the foot of the stairs in the entry between the rooms and exhorted, while the deaf-and-dumb boy's slate circulated among the awe-stricken people.

Isaac Penfield came to no more meetings, and he did not see Melissa again until Tuesday. Late Tuesday afternoon she went up to the village store with a basket of eggs. The days of barter were nearly over, as she had been taught to believe, but there was no molasses in the house, and the poor deaf-and-dumb boy was weeping for it with uncouth grief, and could not be comforted by the prospect of eternal joys. When Melissa came out of the store with the bottle of molasses in her basket, Isaac Penfield's bay mare and chaise were drawn up before the platform, and Isaac stood waiting. Melissa started and coloured when she saw him.

"Get in, please," he said, motioning her toward the chaise.

She looked at him falteringly.

"Get in, please, Melissa; I want to speak to you."

The bay mare was restive, tossing her head and pawing with one delicate fore foot. Isaac could scarcely keep her quiet until

163

Melissa got into the chaise. When he took the reins she gave a leap forward, and the chaise swung about with a lurch. Isaac threw himself back and held the reins taut; the mare flew down the road, pulling hard on her bits; the chaise rocked high on the frozen road. Melissa sat still, her delicate face retired within the dark depths of her silk hood.

Isaac did not speak to her until they reached the foot of a long hill. "I want to ask you something," he said then, with a wary eye still on the straining shoulders of the mare. "I want to ask you again to give this up."

Melissa did not speak.

"Won't you promise me?"

"I can't," she said, faintly.

"You can if you will." Suddenly Isaac leaned over her. "Won't you promise *me*, Melissa?"

She shrank away from him. "I—can't. I believe father."

"Melissa, you don't."

"I do," said she, with a despairing sob.

Isaac Penfield bent his face down close to hers. "Can't you believe me as well as your father? Melissa, look at me."

Melissa bent her head down over her hands.

"Look at me, Melissa."

She raised her head slowly as if there were a constraining hand under her chin, and her eyes met his.

"Can't you, Melissa?"

Fair locks of hair fell over Melissa's gentle cheeks; her soft mouth quivered. It seemed as if her piteous blue eyes were only upheld by the look in the young man's, and as if all the individual thought and purpose in her face and her whole soul were being overcast by his imperious will, but she shook her head.

"Can't you, Melissa?"

She shook her head again.

Isaac Penfield's face turned white. He touched the whip to the mare, and she gave a sharp bound forward. They had not much further to go. Neither of them spoke again until Isaac assisted Melissa out of the chaise at her own gate.

"Goodbye, Melissa," he said then, shortly.

Melissa looked up at him and caught her breath. She could not speak. Isaac sprang into his chaise, and was out of the yard with a sharp grate of wheels, and she went into the house.

Her mother was setting chairs in order for the evening meeting. She looked up sharply as Melissa entered.

"Who was that brought you home?" said she.

"Isaac Penfield," replied Melissa, turning her face from her mother's eyes.

"I hope you ain't letting your thoughts dwell on anything of that kind now," said her mother.

"I met him as I was coming out of the store, and he asked me to ride. I sha'n't ever see him again," Melissa returned, faintly.

The deaf-and-dumb boy had been dozing with gaping mouth in his chimney-corner. Now he waked, and caught sight of his sister and the basket, and hastened to her with a cry of uncouth hunger and greediness.

"In a minute, sonny," Melissa said, in a sobbing voice; "wait a minute." She held the basket aloof while she removed her hood and shawl.

"You may see him on his way to the outer darkness," said her mother, with solemn vindictiveness.

"Mother, he has repented; he is a member of the church," Melissa cried out, with sudden sharpness.

"Repentance avails nothing without faith," returned her mother, setting down a chair so heavily that the deaf-and-dumb boy started at the concussion and looked about him wonderingly.

"He has repented; he is a member of the church; he is safe," Melissa cried again.

"I tell you he is not," said her mother.

Melissa went into the pantry with her brother at her elbow, and prepared for him a plate of bread and molasses. The tears fell over her cheeks, but Alonzo noticed nothing. His greedy eyes were fixed on the food. When it was ready for him he sat down on his stool in the chimney-corner and devoured it with loud smacks of his lips. That was all the evening meal prepared in the Lennox house that night. After the chairs were set in order for the meeting, Melissa and her mother sat down close to the fire and sewed on some white stuff that flowed in voluminous folds over their knees to the floor. Solomon came in presently, and seated himself with the great Bible on his knees. He read silently, but now and then gesticulated fiercely, as if he read aloud.

The meeting began at half past six. About quarter of an hour before, the outer door was heard opening, and there was a shuffling step and a clearing cough in the entry.

"It's your uncle Simeon," whispered Mrs. Lennox to Melissa, and her mouth took on a severer tension.

Solomon frowned over the Holy Writ on his knees.

Simeon advanced into the room, his heavy boots clapping the floor with a dull clatter as of wood, dispelling the solemn stillness. His grinning old face, blue with the cold, was sunk in the collar of his great-coat. He rubbed his hands together as he approached the fire.

"Well, how are ye all?" he remarked, with a chuckle, as if there were a joke in the speech.

Nobody replied. Simeon pulled a chair up close to the fire and sat down.

"It's 'tarnal cold," said he, leaning over and spreading out his old hands to the blaze.

"The brands are all ready for the burning," said his sister-in-law, in a hollow, trembling voice. She drew a long thread through the white stuff on her knee.

Simeon turned suddenly and looked at her with a flash of small bright eyes. Then he laughed. "Lord bless ye, Sophy Anne, I forgot how 'tarnal hot you folks are calculatin' to have it day after tomorrow," said he. "Well, if you fail in your calculations, an' the cold continues, I shall be mighty glad to come in here. My house is darned cold this weather, and Abby Mosely ain't particular 'bout the doors; seems to me sometimes as if I was settin' in a hurricane the heft of the time, and as if my idees were gettin' on a slant. Abby thinks she's goin' up Thursday, and

I wish in thunder she would. I wouldn't have her another day, if she wa'n't a lone woman and nowheres to go. She ain't no kind of a cook. Look at here, Sophy Anne —"

Mrs. Lennox sewed on with compressed lips.

"Sophy Anne, look at here. You 'ain't got no mince pies on hand now, have you?"

"No, I 'ain't."

"Well, I didn't much s'pose you'd made any, you've been so busy gettin' ready to fly lately. Look at here, Sophy Anne, don't you feel as if you could roll me out a few meat pies tomorrow, hey?"

Mrs. Lennox looked at him.

"I dun'no' when I've eat a decent meat pie," pursued Simeon. "Abby Mosely keeps the commandments, but she can't make pies that's fit to eat. I 'ain't had a mince pie I could eat since my last wife died. I wish you'd contrive an' roll me out a few, Sophy Anne. Your mince pies used to go ahead of Maria's; she always said they did. If the world don't come to an end day after tomorrow, I'd take a sight of comfort with 'em, and I'll be darned, if it does come to an end, if I don't think I'd have a chance to eat one or two of 'em before the fire got round to me. Can't ye do it, Sophy Anne, nohow?"

"No, I can't."

"Can't ye roll me out jest half a dozen mince pies?"

"I will never roll out a meat pie for you, Simeon Lennox," said Sophia Anne, with icy fervour.

"Ye never will?"

"No, I never will." Sophia Anne's stern eyes in their hollow blue orbits met his.

Simeon chuckled; then he turned his brother. "Well, Sol'mon, s'pose you're flappin' all ready to fly?" he said.

Solomon made no reply. He frowned over the great volume on his knees. The deaf-and-dumb boy had set his empty plate on the hearth and fallen asleep again, with his head tilted against the jamb. Melissa sewed, her pale face bent closely over her work.

"Hear ye are goin' to fly from Penfield's hill?" said Simeon.

Still Solomon said nothing.

"Well, I s'pose that's as good a place as any," said Simeon, "though 'tain't a very high hill. I should 'most think you'd want a higher hill than Penfield's. I s'pose you'll be kind of unhandy with your wings at first, an' start off something like hens. But then I s'pose a few feet more or less won't make no odds when they get fairly to workin'. I heard the women was makin' flyin'-petticoats. Them what you're to work on, Sophy Anne, you and Melissy?"

Sophia Anne gave one look at him, then she took a stitch.

"Abby Mosely's to work on one, I guess," said Simeon. "She's ben a-settin' in a heap of white cloth a-sewin' for three days. I came in once, an' she was tryin' of it on, an' she slipped out of it mighty sudden. All I've got to say is she'll cut a queer figure flyin'. She's pretty hefty. I miss my guess if she don't find it a job to strike out at first. Now I should think you might take to flyin' pretty natural, Sophy Anne."

Mrs. Lennox's pale face was flushed with anger, but she sewed on steadily.

"As for Melissy," said Simeon, in his chuckling drawl, "I ruther guess she could fly without much practice too. She's built light; but it strikes me she'd better have a weddin'-gown than a flyin'-petticoat. Young Penfield goin' to fly with you, Melissy?"

Solomon Lennox closed the Bible with a great clap. "I'll have no more of this!" he said, with a shout of long-repressed fury.

"Now, Solomon, don't ye get riled so near the end of the world," drawled his brother, getting up slowly. "I'm a-goin'. I ain't goin' to be the means of makin' you backslide when ye're so nigh the top of Zion's Hill. I'm a-goin' home. I don't s'pose I shall get no supper on account of Abby's hurryin' up on her flyin'-petticoat. Sure you ain't goin' to make them meat pies for me, Sophy Anne?"

"Yes, I be sure."

The brother-in-law thrust his sharp old face down close to Sophia Anne's. "Sure?" he repeated.

Sophia Anne started back and stared at him. There was something strange in his manner.

The old man laughed, and straightened himself. "Well, I'm a-goin'," said he. "Goodbye. Mebbe I sha'n't see ye again before ye fly. Hope ye'll light easy. Goodbye."

After Simeon had closed the door, he opened it again, and thrust his sharp features through a narrow aperture. "Look at here, Solomon," said he. "Mind ye leave the key in the door when ye go out to fly Thursday night. I want to come right in." Then Simeon shut the door again, but his malicious laugh could be plainly heard in the entry.

He did not go straight home as he had said, but up the road to Lawyer Bascombe's office. When he returned, the meeting in his brother's house was in session, and the windows were dark with heads against the red firelight. Old Simeon stared up at them, and laughed aloud to himself as he went by. "Sophy Anne won't make me no meat pies. She's sure on't," he said, and laughed again.

The next day all the ordinary routine of life seemed at a standstill in the village. The storekeeper had become a convert, and the store was closed, and the green inside shutters up. Now and then a village loafer lounged disconsolately up, shook the door on its rattling lock, stared at the shuttered windows, then lounged away, muttering. The summer resting-place of his kind, the long, bewhittled wooden bench on the store platform, could not be occupied that wintry day. The air was clear, and the dry pastures were white and stiff with the hoar-frost; the slants of the roofs glistened with it in the sun. The breaths of the people going to and from Solomon Lennox's house were like white smoke. The meeting began at dawn.

Children were dragged hither at their parents' heels cold and breakfastless. Not a meal was cooked that day in the houses of Solomon Lennox's followers. All the precious hours were spent in fasting and prayer. Toward night the excitement deepened. There was present within the village a spiritual convulsion as real as any other convulsion of nature, and as truly although more subtly felt. Even they who had scoffed and laughed at this new movement from the first, and were now practically untouched by it, grew nervous and ill at ease toward night as from the gathering of a storm. The air seemed charged with electricity generated by the touch of human thought and faith with the Unknown. The unbelievers pressed their faces against the window-panes, shading their eyes from the light within as the dusk deepened, or stood out in their yards watching the sky, half fearful they should indeed see some sign or marvel therein.

But the night came on, and the stars shone out in their order as they had done from the first, and there was no sign but the old one of eternal love and beauty in the sky. The moon arose at nine o'clock, nearly at her full. That, from some interpretation of symbolical characters on the deaf-and-dumb boy's slate, had been fixed upon as the hour of meeting upon Penfield's hill. The solemn and dreadful moment which was to mark the climax of all creation was expected between that hour and dawn.

At half past eight white-robed figures begun to move along the road. People peeped around their curtains to see them pass; now and then belated children ran shrieking with terror into the houses at the sight of them.

Beside the road, close to the gate which led to the wide field at the foot of Penfield's hill, under the shadow of a clump of hemlocks, Isaac Penfield had been waiting since quarter past eight o'clock. When the white company came in sight he drew farther back within the shadow, scanning the people eagerly as they passed.

Solomon Lennox and Deacon Scranton let down the bars, and the people passed through silently, crowding each other whitely like a flock of sheep. Sophia Anne, the deaf-and-dumb boy holding fast to her hand, was among the first.

Isaac had expected to see Melissa close to her mother; but she had become separated from her and came among the last.

Her slender figure was hidden in her flowing white robes, but there was no mistaking her gently faltering gait and the delicate bend of her fair uncovered head.

Isaac stepped forward suddenly, threw his arm around Melissa, and drew her back with him within the shadow of the hemlocks. Nobody saw it but Abby Mosely, Simeon Lennox's housekeeper, and she was too panic-stricken to heed it intelligently; she went panting on after the others in her voluminous white robe, and left Melissa alone with Isaac Penfield.

Isaac pressed Melissa's head close to his breast, leaned his face down to hers, and whispered long in her ear. She listened trembling and unresisting; then she broke away from him weakly, "I can't, I can't," she moaned. But he caught her again, and whispered again with his lips close to her soft pale cheek, and frequent kisses between the words.

"Come, now, sweetheart," he said at length, and attempted to draw her with him into the road; but she pulled herself away from him again, and stood warding him off with her white-draped arms.

"I can't, I can't," she moaned again. "I must go with father and mother."

"I tell you they are wrong; can't you believe me?"

"I—must—go with them."

"No; come with me, Melissa."

Melissa, still with her arms raised against him, looked away over the meadow, full of moving white figures. The moon shone out over it, and it gleamed like a field of Paradise peopled with angels. Then she looked up in her lover's face, and suddenly it was to her as if she saw therein the new earth of all her dreams.

Solomon Lennox and his followers kept on to Penfield's hill, which arose before them crowned with silver, and Isaac Penfield hastened down the road to the village, half carrying Melissa's little white-clad figure, wrapped against the cold in his own gray cloak.

Early the next morning a small company of pallid shivering people crept through the village to their homes. Many had weakened and deserted long before dawn, chilled to their very thoughts and fancies by their long vigil on the hill-top. Young girls ran home, crying aloud like children, and men half dragged hysterical wives rigid with chills. Solomon Lennox and his wife

171

remained until the dawn light shone; then he beckoned to her and the whimpering deaf-and-dumb boy, and led the way down the hill without a word. He never looked at the rest of the company, but they followed silently.

The Penfield house was about a quarter of a mile from the pasture bars. When they reached it, Isaac stood waiting at the gate. He went up to Solomon, who was passing without a look, and touched his arm with an impatient yet respectful gesture. "You and Mrs. Lennox and Lonny had better come in here, I think," he said.

Solomon was moving on with dull obstinacy, but Isaac laid his hand on his arm. "I—think you have—forgotten," he said. "I am sorry, but—your brother Simeon has—taken possession of your house."

Solomon stared at him dully. He did not seem to comprehend. Sophia Anne looked as blue and bloodless in her white robe as if she were dead. She had scarce more control of her trembling tongue than if it were paralyzed, but her highly strung feminine nerves gave out vibrations still.

"Has Simeon took possession?" she demanded, fiercely.

Isaac Penfield nodded. "I think it would be pleasanter for you to come in here now," he said. Then he hesitated, and coloured suddenly. "Your daughter is in here," he added.

Sophia Anne gave a keen glance at him. Then she turned in at the gate with a sharp twitch at the arm of the deaf-and-dumb boy, who was making strange cries and moans, like a distressed animal. "Come, father," she called, impatiently; and Solomon also entered the Penfield gate with a piteous, dazed air.

In the great south room of the Penfield house were Melissa and Mrs. Martha Joyce, the housekeeper. Mrs. Joyce was mixing something in a steaming bowl; Melissa sat still, gazing at the fire. She was dressed in a blue satin gown and fine lace tucker, which had belonged to Isaac Penfield's mother. Madam Penfield had been nearly Melissa's size, and the gown fitted her slender figure daintily. She sat with her fair head bent, the colour coming and going in her soft cheeks, as if from her own thoughts.

Her little hands were folded in her blue satin lap, and on one finger gleamed a great pearl, which Madam Penfield had used to wear.

When the door opened and her parents entered, she half started up, with a great blush; then she sank back, trembling and pale.

Isaac Penfield crossed over to her, and laid his hand on her shoulder. "She is my wife," he said. "We were married last night."

Sophia Anne made a faint gesture, which might have expressed anything. Solomon staggered to a chair without a look. In truth, when they entered the warm room, and the long strain of resistance against cold and fatigue ceased, exhaustion overcame them. Mrs. Joyce administered hot porridge and cordials, and Melissa knelt down in her blue satin and rubbed her mother's benumbed hands.

Solomon took whatever was offered him, meekly, like a child. His face was changed; the look which it had worn during the greater part of his life, the expression of himself within his old worn channel, had returned.

He was sitting by the fire, sipping cordial, when his brother Simeon came in; he had not even noticed the brazen clang of the knocker.

Simeon came tiptoeing around in front of his brother, thrust down his face on a level with his, and peered at him with a sharp twinkle of black eyes. Then he looked at Sophia Anne, and chuckled. "'Pears to me wings didn't work very well," said he.

Simeon had a roll of paper in his hand. He went to the desk, and spread it out ostentatiously. Then he began to read in a high, solemn voice, with an undertone of merriment in it. "*Know all men by these presents*," began Simeon Lennox, and read straight through the deed, with all its strange legal formalities, by which his brother Solomon had conveyed his worldly goods to him.

Sophia Anne writhed in her chair as Simeon read. She was on a rack of torture, and every new word was a turn of the screw. Solomon set his tumbler of cordial on the hearth, and rested his head on his hands.

After Simeon had finished reading the deed, he paused for a moment. Sophia Anne gave a dry sob.

Then Simeon cleared his throat, and continued:

"The foregoing I do hereby declare null and void, and I do hereby remise, release, sell, and forever quitclaim, for myself and my heirs, by these presents, the aforementioned premises, with all the privileges and appurtenances thereunto belonging, to the said Solomon Lennox, his heirs and assigns forever, in consideration that Sophia Anne, the wife of said Solomon Lennox, shall, during the term of her natural life, unless she be prevented by sickness from so doing, make, mix, season, and bake for me with her own hands, with her best skill, according to her own conscience, seven mince pies during every week of the year, with one extra for every Independence and Thanksgiving day, and that the said Sophia Anne, the wife of the said Solomon Lennox, shall hereunto set her hand and seal."

Simeon looked at Sophia Anne. She stared back at him, speechless.

"Well, what ye goin' to do about it, Sophy Anne?" said Simeon.

Sophia Anne still looked at him as if he were a blank wall against which her very spirit had been brought to a standstill.

"Goin' to sign it, Sophy Anne?"

Sophia Anne got up. Her knees trembled, but she motioned back Isaac Penfield's proffered arm. She went to the desk, sat down, took the quill, dipped it carefully in the inkstand, and shook it lest it blot. Her lean arm crooked as stiffly as a stick, her lips were a blue line, but she wrote her name with sharply rippling strokes, and laid the pen down.

"Sure ye won't make them mince pies, Sophy Anne?" said Simeon.

Sophia Anne made no reply. She put her elbow on the desk, and leaned her head on her hand. Simeon looked at her a moment, then he gave her a rough pat on her shoulder and turned and went to the window, and stood there, staring out.

Melissa was weeping softly; Isaac stood beside her, smoothing her hair tenderly. The deaf-and-dumb boy's fair head hung helplessly over his shoulder. He had fallen asleep with the tears on his cheeks.

The morning sunlight shone broadly into the room over them all, but Solomon Lennox did not seem to heed that or anything that was around him, sitting sadly within himself: a prophet brooding over the ashes of his own prophetic fire.

A Pot of Gold

The moon came up over the mountain, and suddenly the shadows of the trees grew darker and more distinct. There were four great elm-trees in the Amesbury yard. Over across the road was a cemetery; back of that flowed the river; on the opposite bank of the river arose the mountain. The mountain was wooded to its summit. There were patches of silver on it, where some of the tree-tops waved in the moonlight.

Jonas Amesbury and his mother sat on the door-step; neither of them noticed the beautiful moonlight night much. Once the old woman remarked that the moon made it as bright as day, and Jonas did not even trouble himself to assent.

Jonas looked hardly more than a boy; his curly head had the blond lightness of a baby's; his round face was smooth and delicate. He sat on the lower door-stone, resting his elbows on his knees; his mother, a dark, sallow figure, sat on the upper one. She held herself rigidly, and did not lean against the door-casing. She was very tired, but her will would not let her old bones and muscles relax. Jane Amesbury never "lopped," as she termed it. She was, in her way, a student of human nature and a philosopher. She divided women into two classes: those who "lopped" and those who did not. "I wa'n't never one of the kind that lop," she used to say, with a backward lift of her head so forcible that it seemed as if her neck muscles were made of steel, and one listened for the click, "an' I ain't never thought much of them women that do lop."

One looking at her easily realized the truth of the statement.

Old as she was now, it was quite evident that Jane Amesbury had no more leaning necessity than a hardy tree over on the mountain. She required for her growth and support only a rude, stanch soil and a sky.

Her son Jonas seemed different; still, he had something of his mother's character. It was evident in a certain dignity and self-restraint with which he bore himself tonight. He was very unhappy. His mother was looking down upon him with tenderness and a kind of indignation. They had been silent for quite a while; when the moon arose it seemed a signal to them. It was with Jonas as if the shadows in his own soul deepened out, and it seemed as if his mother also saw them, for she began at once: "There ain't no use talkin' 'bout it," said she; "there ain't no sense in a fellar's settin' right down an' givin' up, 'cause he can't git one particular girl. Marryin' ain't everything there is in the world nohow, if folks do act as if 'twas. Folks act like poor fools sometimes. I guess I know."

The old woman gave her head a shake of rage and wisdom. Jonas said nothing. His face, in the moonlight, looked as fair and pretty as a girl's.

Presently his mother began again; she seemed to have a subtle ear for her son's thoughts, and to answer them like spoken arguments.

"I know she's a good-lookin' girl 'nough," said she, "an' she's smart 'nough. I dun know as there *is* anybody 'round here that quite comes up to her; but that don't make no difference. Looks ain't everything, an' smartness ain't everything. There's plenty of girls that's good 'nough, if they can't tear the airth up or set the river on fire. These dretful smart, handsome folks are just the ones that flax out sometimes. They ain't nothin' more'n Fourth of July fireworks; there's more sputter an' fizzle than anything else when you come to find out. I don't think I should give up eatin' an' sleepin', an' go round lookin' as if I'd lost my last friend, on account of one girl, when there's plenty more that would have me. There's Emma Jane Monk —"

Then the young man aroused himself. "I guess," said he,

"when you see me going with Emma Jane Monk you'll know it."

"Well, you can turn up your nose at Emma Jane Monk all you want to; she's as good as Rose Tenney any day."

"Mother!"

"What is it?"

"You can talk all you want to, but it ain't going to do any good. I suppose I ain't showing much spunk about it, and I know it ain't any worse for me than for other folks, and I ain't the first one that couldn't get the one he wanted. But I can't bear it, and I ain't going to; that's all there is about it."

"What you goin' to do?" asked his mother, in a stern voice that had in it a frightened inflection.

"I don't know any more than a tree in the wind. I ain't doing anything; I'm being done with."

"Jonas Amesbury, you make me mad talkin' such stuff. I don't see where you got such notions; for my part I know you didn't git 'em from me. Rose Tenney—h'm! S'pose she does curl her hair over her forehead, an' wear her dresses all girt in round her waist, an' act so dreadful soft an' sweet! Her folks ain't much, an' everybody knows it; everybody knows what old Joe Tenney is—stole all that land that belonged to his brother; everybody knowed he did it, if they couldn't prove it. I don't think Rose Tenney's got so very much to brag of nohow."

"I'd like to know what good you think it does talking that way, mother?"

"Oh, I don't s'pose it does any good. I s'pose if all Rose Tenney's relations were strung up on the gallows in a row, you'd want her just the same."

"Yes, I would," said Jonas, in a fervent tone, tossing back his head like his mother, with a defiant air. He could fancy himself wedding Rose under the shadow of her swinging relatives, and see nothing ridiculous; he was in such an intense mood that humour was entirely barred out.

"Yes, I s'pose you would; it would be just like you," returned his mother, sarcastically. Then she arose. "Well, I'm goin' in to set the bread a-risin'," said she. "I s'pose the bread might jest as well be riz, if you can't git Rose Tenney."

Jonas did not reply; he got up and went strolling off across the yard. His mother entered the house—the door opened directly into the kitchen. It was dark except for the moonlight. Jane spoke as she stepped over the threshold.

"You there?" said she.

"Yes."

"Where be yer?"

"Over here by the winder."

"Oh, yes, I see yer."

Jane stepped over to the window, where another woman was sitting, and peered out into the yard.

"He's gone out of the yard," said the sitting woman.

"You don't s'pose he's goin' down there, do ye?"

"No; he headed up the other way. I see him."

Jane then sat down in a chair near the other woman, who was her unmarried sister. Her name was Elvira Slawson. Elvira was ten years younger than her sister; her blond hair was scarcely gray; she wore it in twisted loops over her ears; she was tall and thin, and her clothes were so loose that all her outlines seemed wavering; one shoulder was a little higher than the other; she had a slow, high-pitched voice.

Jane looked at her; she was in the shadow herself. "I s'pose you heard me talkin' to him, didn't ye?" she remarked.

"I heard a little on't; I couldn't help it. I was settin' right here."

"Well, I dun know what he's goin' to do. I think it's a pretty piece of work, for my part."

"You don't s'pose he'll do anything desprit, do ye?"

"Desprit?—no. If he does, I'll shake him. Desprit! I ain't got no patience with sech kind of work. Ready to pull the house down, 'bout a girl. I s'pose it's what they call—*love!* H'm! it's 'nough to make anybody sick! Love!" Jane's voice as she said "love" had a contemptuous drawl.

Elvira, with her head gently inclined to one side, looked

doubtfully at her sister. Being supposed to have no acquaintance with love, she had more respect for him. "Well, I s'pose men do pretty desprit things sometimes on account of love," she said, in a shamefaced way. She was exceedingly timid about alluding to such matters before her sister.

"Desprit things! Well, I s'pose some that's poor fools do, an' I guess it's good riddance to 'em. Folks that can't see nothin' in this world but the one sugar-plum they ain't able to git had better git out of it. *Love!*"

Jane arose; she went to the shelf and struck a match. "Goin' to mix up bread?" asked her sister.

"Yes, I s'pose so. I thought I'd have some riz biscuit in the mornin', Jonas thinks so much of 'em; but I don't s'pose he'll tech 'em even if I make 'em. He ain't eat enough today to feed a fly."

The light flared out; Jane bent her brows over it to see if it were trimmed squarely. Then she went into the pantry for her mixing-bowl and flour. There was now and then a click as her heels struck the floor; the floor was worn into little hillocks, and the nails frequently protruded; one could see here and there one sparkle in the lamp-light. This was an old house; the underpinning sagged in places, and the rooms were full of crooked lines; not a door or window was straight.

Elvira watched her sister mix the bread. Jane did not lose a grain of flour in the process; her knotty fingers were deft and delicate from faithful practice. She left the mixing-bowl polished quite clean when she finally deposited the dough in the pans. There was little treasure in the Amesbury house, but none would be left clinging to the sides of it. Jane had made an appendix to the *Decalogue* to suit her own exigencies; one of the new sins was wastefulness. She did all the housework; she privately believed Elvira to be nothing of a housekeeper. Elvira knitted a great deal of lace edging, and she sold yards of it to people in the village. She also furnished a store with some. She had quite a local reputation for her knitted lace, and was looked upon somewhat in the line of an artist. It was even rumoured that she devised new patterns out of her own head. Her sister gave her her board, and all the money she spent was the proceeds of her lace-making. She knitted incessantly, and always had her lace with her in a little bag. Pretty soon she drew her chair up to the table where her sister was making the bread, and drew out her knitting.

"You ain't goin' to knittin' tonight?" remarked Jane, disapprovingly.

"I'm jest goin' to make one scallop."

This lace was considered Elvira's masterpiece, being very broad and intricate. She bent over it, and knitted with a frowning forehead. The light was not very good. She wore spectacles.

"You countin'?" said Jane presently.

"No."

"I'd like to know the hull truth of it 'bout Rose Tenney."

Elvira kept her eyes on her lace. "Do you s'pose she wouldn't have him?" she queried, timidly.

"I dun know; but I do know one thing: it wa'n't her fault if she wouldn't. I know a thing or two. I've had my eyes open. If that girl don't think 'nough of Jonas I'll miss my guess. I've seen her when he was round. A girl don't light up like a rainbow when she sees a fellar comin' if there ain't somethin' in the wind. She thinks 'nough of him. Old Joe Tenney's at the bottom of it. He don't think there's quite 'nough money here. I know him. Since he's got a little money himself, everybody else that ain't got it ain't any more than the dirt under his feet. Joe Tenney always thought more of money than anything else in the world. Cheated his own brother for the sake of it. I shouldn't think he'd want to say much."

Elvira still kept her eyes upon her lace; a red flush mounted on her soft, flabby cheeks. "There didn't nobody really know he cheated him," said she.

"Yes, they did know, too, well's they wanted to. Where did the deeds for that land go to, I'd like to know? They couldn't prove nothin', 'cause they wa'n't registered, but there wa'n't no doubt 'bout it."

"I s'pose he thought that land belonged to him anyhow. You know they said he'd lent Henry consider'ble money. I guess some thought Henry'd agreed to give him them deeds, an' then backed out."

"Elvira Slawson, if you want to stan' up for old Joe Tenney, you can. I should think you was 'bout old 'nough to be off the notion of that by this time."

"I—dun know what you mean, Jane."

"I know what I mean. Well, I s'pose it's—*love*."

Elvira said no more. She kept her meek suffused face close to her lace. It was quite true that years ago there had been a love affair between herself and Joseph Tenney, and it had come to naught. Her sister had never done twitting her with it: all the prickles in her nature seemed turned against sentiment, perhaps because of its fancied softness, which made her indignant. She had nursed Elvira faithfully through the severe illness which her disappointment had brought upon her, and then had tried a system of mental cauterization to cure the wound. Any symptoms that led her to believe the cure was not complete caused her to apply the iron anew. Now she kept glancing sharply at Elvira over her lace; her lips were compressed, her nose was elevated sarcastically. But soon her anxiety over her son drew her thoughts away from her sister.

"I don't see where he is," she said, standing in the door, after the bread was set away.

"Mebbe he's gone up to Jake Manson's."

"I don't think he has, this time of night. Oh, there he is!"

Neither of the women said anything to Jonas when he entered the kitchen, but they watched him furtively. He went across the room to the mantelshelf and lighted a candle. "Goin' to bed?" asked his mother then.

Jonas gave an affirmative grunt. He looked as if he had been walking fast, his face was flushed, and his fair hair lay damp and flat on the temples.

Pretty soon the women heard his steps on the stairs. "It's the greatest work I ever see," said Jane. She went about and slammed to the doors and locked them; Elvira put up her lace-work. Then they went to bed in the little bedroom that opened out of the kitchen—they slept together.

A little after midnight Elvira awoke her sister—"Jane, Jane, wake up!" she whispered, fearfully. The dark seemed to loom over her and make her voice echo like a mountain. Jane did not awaken very easily, she had to speak again and shake her a little. When Jane finally aroused it was with a jerk. She sat straight up in bed. "What's the matter?" asked she, in a loud, determined voice.

"Oh, Jane, lay down again; don't be scart. I've jest had the queerest dream."

"Elvira Slawson, you don't mean to say you made all this row an' waked me up out of a sound sleep for a dream!"

"You jest wait till you hear it. You lay down an' I'll tell you what 'twas."

"I don't want to hear it, an' I ain't goin' to. I ain't goin' to listen to any such tomfoolery—wakin' me up out of a sound sleep! I thought the house was afire, or somebody was gittin' in."

"I won't take but jest a minute, Jane."

"I ain't goin' to hear it, an' that's all there is about it." Jane lay down with a thud that made the feather-bed arise in billows.

Elvira begged hard, but she would not let her tell the dream. "If you don't stop carryin' on so I'll go in the spare bedroom an' leave you alone," said she; "I ain't goin' to be broke of my rest this way."

That threat silenced Elvira. All her life she had been afraid of the dark if she were alone in it.

With daylight she began again, but Jane was obdurate. She would not hear the dream at all. She did not believe in dreams. She had always had a contempt for them, and she held the opinion that repeating them caused one to dream more.

So Elvira carried about her dream all day, like a poet his unsung song. She would have told it to Jonas, but he was away all day haying in a distant field. The Amesburys owned this small farm, but their own haying was so meagre that it was done long ago. Now Jonas was hiring out to one of the neighbors. It was a relief to his mother to have him away all day; his miserable face stirred her to keenest agony and wrath. She was utterly distressed and despairing over his misery, and furious with him that he yielded to it.

"I don't see as he looked a mite different when he came home to supper," she told Elvira that night, "and he hadn't eat half what I give him for dinner."

"I wish you'd let me tell you that dream," returned Elvira, eagerly and mysteriously.

"Elvira Slawson, if you don't quit talkin' 'bout that dream I shall go ravin' crazy. I've got enough to stan' up under without that."

The two women were preparing for bed again, and Jane took the hair-pins out of her knot of hair with a conclusive air. Her hair hanging about her face gave her a fierce, haggard look.

"Well, of course I ain't a-goin' to tell it to you if you don't want to hear it," returned Elvira, with some trace of dignity.

"Well, I don't want to hear it, an' I hope you'll remember it."

But again Jane was awakened. This time Elvira clutched her desperately. "Jane," she called, "wake up, for massy sake! *I've dreamed it again.*"

Jane sat up, took hold of her sister, and laid her down peremptorily. Elvira in her excitement had raised herself, and was bending over her. "Now," said she, "you jest listen. I'm a-goin' to lay down again, an' if you speak another word I'm a-goin' into the spare bedroom. As for bein' broke of my rest again tonight, I won't."

Elvira gave a little gasp, but she said nothing more. Soon Jane began to breathe regularly. It was three o'clock in the morning when Elvira aroused her again. This time Elvira had a firm clutch on her arm; her voice was quite loud and decisive.

"Jane!"

"What do you mean actin' so?" Jane asked, feebly. She was now quite alarmed.

"I'm a-goin' to tell you my dream. *I've dreamed it again*."

"Well, do tell it, for massy sakes. I never see sech work."

"Jane, I've dreamed three times that I found a pot of gold in our field that joins Joe Tenney's oat field. It was under an apple-tree. I dug under it, and I found it."

"H'm!"

"It was an iron pot with a cover, like the one you boil beans in, an' it was chock-full of gold dollars."

"That all?"

"Jane, where you dream about the same thing three times, it comes true. I've always heard it did."

"I s'pose you believe it."

"I dun know as I really believe, but I've heard lots of folks say there was somethin' in it. Don't you remember how mother dreamed three times runnin' how father was goin' on a journey, before he died?"

"Well, if you want to believe sech stuff you can. I wish you'd stop talkin'. I've been broke of my rest 'bout all I want to be. I dun know but I'll go into the spare bedroom anyhow. I s'pose jest as I git fairly to sleep again you'll dream it over again an' grab me."

"Jane, don't you think it means somethin'?"

"It means I'm goin' into the spare bedroom, an' I ain't goin' to lay here talkin' 'bout it."

"Don't, Jane; I won't speak another word."

"You mind you don't, then."

Elvira kept her word. She said no more that night, nor did she the next morning. She never alluded to the dream. She assisted about the dish-washing after breakfast; then she sat down with her lace. After a while Jane went out to feed the hens. When she returned she caught a glimpse of Elvira stealing around the corner of the house. "Where you goin'?" she called.

"I ain't goin' far," answered Elvira, in a trembling voice. Jane strode after her, the hens' dough-dish in her hand. Elvira hustled along, but she soon caught up with her, and saw that she was carrying the shovel.

"Where are you going with that shovel?" asked Jane.

Suddenly Elvira faced her; she held the shovel like a staff. "*I'm—a-goin' to dig.*"

"Elvira Slawson, I never thought you was quite sech a perfect fool."

"I don't care what you say, Jane, I'm goin' to be sure that pot of gold ain't there."

"Well, you ain't goin' to dull up that new shovel diggin', nohow."

"I jest as soon take the old one."

Elvira went back and got the old shovel. Her sister sneered and argued all the way, but she paid no heed. There was on her mild face a kind of rapt expression, like a higher determination. She had gotten her revelation, however petty by comparison, Joan of Arc fashion, and was not to be turned back by banners and spears. Her mission was not to fight, but to dig, and she would dig.

She went forth with her shovel, and left Jane still talking. She did not return until noon; then her face was all flushed with the heat; she tried not to pant. There was a cup of tea and some bread and butter for dinner; they did not have a regular dinner when Jonas was not at home, and Jonas was still haying for the neighbour.

After dinner Elvira put on her sun-bonnet again.

"Then you ain't found the pot of gold yet?" remarked her sister, in a sweet, stinging voice. She had not spoken before except concerning food at the table.

"No," said Elvira, "I ain't found it yet."

"I should think you'd want to finish that lace you was workin' on some time. I should think you'd lose more money than you'll find in the wonderful pot."

"I can finish the lace tomorrow," replied Elvira, going out the door. She had left her shovel in the field. The afternoon passed, and she did not return. Jane got supper ready, and she had not come. Jane did not expect Jonas until late, and there was no one but herself at home for supper. She kept going to the road and looking. Finally she put on her sun-bonnet, and went down the road. It was not far to the field of Elvira's dream. On the farther side a stone wall divided it from Joseph Tenney's land; in the distance she could see the Tenney house—white-painted and *piazzaed*, a village mansion. The bars at the entrance of the field were let down; she passed through. There were five old apple-trees in the field. Around four of them were heaps of loose earth where Elvira had been digging. The fifth tree stood close to the wall that marked the Tenney land; its branches reached over it.

Under this tree crouched Elvira, examining something. Her shovel lay beside her on the ground. Jane approached stealthily. Just as she reached the tree she heard a quick rustle on the other side of the wall; she looked, and saw Joseph Tenney's face through branches of pink dog-bane and over masses of poison-ivy. It was a handsome old face, clean-shaven and blue-eyed, but it was deathly pale. Elvira saw him too. She and Jane looked at him, and he looked at them; then he turned about and went homeward across the wet field, with a step like a slow march. If it was a retreat, it was a dignified one.

The minute Joseph Tenney went away, Elvira sprang up and grasped the shovel. Jane peered around her. "What you got there?" she asked. Then she repeated the question in an excited tone: "Why, what is it? what have you found?" She had seen a small iron-bound chest, with loam clinging to it; it was open, and overflowing with unfolded papers. She stepped forward, but Elvira was before her in the path. She held the shovel uplifted. "*Don't you go near it!*"

"Course I'm goin' near it. I'd like to know what you mean; I guess I've got jest as good a right to know what 'tis as you have. I should laugh."

"*If you come one step nearer I'll kill you!*" Elvira's eyes were gleaming; there seemed to be sharp lights like steel in them; her face was white and resolute.

Jane started back: she was frightened. "Well, you can keep your old box if you want to," said she. Then she went off across the field. Her sun-bonnet was tilted until it looked of itself aggressive and rampant; she never turned around.

She had not been home long when Elvira returned, leaning upon the shovel. She could scarcely walk, she was so exhausted. When she sat down at the supper-table she turned faint; she laid her head down on the table with a low groan. Jane sprang and brought some water. "It's the greatest piece of work I ever did see," she said, bathing her sister's forehead.

Elvira began to weep. "Oh, Jane, I didn't mean to say such a dreadful thing to you!" she sobbed, weakly. "But I couldn't show it to you, nohow; I couldn't."

"We won't say nothin' more 'bout it," said Jane, shortly. "You'll be sick next. I don't care nothin' 'bout the old box."

After Elvira had had her tea, Jane made her go to bed. She said nothing about the matter to Jonas when he returned. She thought he seemed more depressed than ever.

The next day, in the afternoon, Jane went down to the store for a little shopping. She had a plan to buy some gray flannel and make a nice shirt for Jonas to do haying in. She thought that might perhaps please him and cheer him a little. She was gone an hour. When she returned she found Elvira sitting on the door-step knitting her lace. There was a grape-vine around the door, and some of the light green sprays hung down over Elvira's head. Her face, bent over her lace-work, looked fair and peaceful. Her old muslin dress fell around her in soft folds. She was sixty years old, but she looked maidenly.

When Jane stood before her she smiled up at her. Jane sank down on the door-step. "It's a dreadful hot day," she sighed. She eyed Elvira sharply. She felt irascible, and as if she must let go her tongue. Her face was glossy with perspiration, her hands were black from her cotton gloves. She suspected that the flannel was a poor bargain. She eyed Elvira a minute, then she spoke. "There wa'n't no need of your bein' so mighty private 'bout that box. I knowed well 'nough what 'twas all the time."

Elvira dropped the lace and looked at her.

"Mebbe you don't b'lieve it. Well, I'll tell you what 'twas: it was *them deeds.*"

Elvira was trembling violently. "Well, there ain't no harm in it if it was."

"Mebbe there ain't; but that's what was in that box—*them deeds.*"

"His brother's dead now, an' they're his anyway. You can't do nothin'."

"Oh, I ain't goin' to do nothin'. I wouldn't stir a step to tell it to a livin' soul. You needn't worry 'bout that. I ain't afeared but he'll git punishment 'nough some way. I sha'n't do nothin' to bring it on him."

Elvira looked fixedly at her sister; her soft, drawling voice became quite firm. "Jane, he didn't do nothin' wrong 'bout that. He's told me all 'bout it."

"Told you 'bout it? When?"

"Just now—this afternoon."

"Has Joe Tenney been here?"

"Yes."

"Come over 'cause he was scart, I s'pose."

"No, he didn't. He was goin' by, and I called him in. I wanted to tell him where I put it."

"Where did you put it?"

"Under the stone wall, on his side. He told me all 'bout it; jest how it was."

"I'd like to know how he 'counted for hidin' the deeds."

"I can't tell you; I said I wouldn't; but he wa'n't one mite to blame."

"Well, mebbe you believe it."

"Course I believe it."

Jane surveyed her blackened hands. Her right knee ached; she was rheumatic. "P'rhaps he'll have you yet, if you stick up for him so," said she.

Elvira quivered and shrank; her eyes suddenly looked red and weak. "Jane, you know I'm past all that. There ain't no call for you to say sech things as that. Sech a thing ain't never entered into his head. He's been married to a real nice woman, an' he ain't thought of me once a year. 'Twa'n't ever much to him anyway; he wa'n't nothin' but a boy. He don't want me, an' I wouldn't have him if he did. I ain't no fit person for him. He can git somebody that's younger an' smarter if he wants anybody. I ain't nothin' to be married, an' I know it well 'nough."

"You can talk that way all you want to; you'd have him fast enough if you had the chance."

Elvira looked quite solemnly at her sister. "Look a-here, Jane," said she, "mebbe you dun know jest what I mean; but it seems to me as if bein' sure that anybody was all right an' honest was the completest kind of bein' married that anybody could have."

Jane stared at her for a moment; then she looked away; she did not say any more.

Elvira knitted for a few minutes; then she looked up. "I ru-ther guess," said she, "that it will come out all right 'bout Jonas an' Rose."

"What do you mean?"

"We talked it over some. I guess he thought Jonas hadn't got much, an' there wa'n't much sense in it, in the first place, an' he told Rose she's got to give him up; but I shouldn't wonder if he was kinder thinkin' better of it."

"S'pose he's afraid we'll tell if he don't."

"No, that ain't it. If you knew what I know you wouldn't say so."

"Well, I dun know what you know, but you've got more faith in him than I have."

Elvira's face was lifted; she looked past her sister with an expression as if she were looking at a shrine. "I *know* Joe Tenney is a good man," said she.

The next day Jonas was at home working in the garden. In the afternoon a neighbour drove into the yard and called to him. He had brought a letter to him from the post-office.

Jane was peeping curiously from the window. "What is it?" she called out, after the neighbour had driven away.

Jonas stood out in the yard staring at the letter. "Oh, nothing much," he answered. But smiles were playing all over his face. He went back to the garden, and whistled as he worked.

After tea he went upstairs, and was gone quite a while. "I believe he's goin' somewhere," Jane said to Elvira. "He washed him real particular, an' he's shaved him. I don't believe but he's goin' down there."

When Jonas came downstairs he had on his best suit; his curly hair was damp and trained in careful locks over his smooth young forehead; his cheeks were fresh and rosy; he held his neck stiffly in his clean collar and white necktie.

He stood in the kitchen and brushed his hat carefully. His mother and aunt were in the sitting-room, and he stepped softly, hoping they would not come out; but his mother looked out into the kitchen. "Where you goin'?" she inquired.

Jonas blushed beautifully like a girl. Then he laughed. "Oh, I ain't goin' far," he replied, putting on his hat and passing out under the grapevine.

Jane and Elvira sat up until he returned, although it was quite late. They heard his step out in the yard, and were alert when he came in. He was radiant. He stood in the door looking at them and smiling. "Well," said his mother.

"I guess it's all right," said Jonas. "I shouldn't wonder if one of these days you had a daughter." His face was all pink and glowing, his yellow hair was dry, and the fluffy curls stood out around his forehead and caught the light. Elvira began to cry. His mother laughed and frowned together.

"Well, I hope you'll behave yourself an' eat somethin' now," said she.

After he had gone upstairs she went out into the kitchen to mix bread. "I guess I'll have some riz biscuit for breakfast," she said to Elvira. "He didn't eat none of them others, but I s'pose he'll eat these fast 'nough. It beats me, but I s'pose it's—*love.*" She tried to say "love" as if it were a clod of mud, but in spite of herself she said it as if it were a jewel.

The Twelfth Guest

"I *don't* see how it happened, for my part," Mrs. Childs said. "Paulina, you set the table."

"You counted up yesterday how many there'd be, and you said twelve; don't you know you did, mother? So I didn't count today. I just put on the plates," said Paulina, smilingly defensive.

Paulina had something of a helpless and gentle look when she smiled. Her mouth was rather large, and the upper jaw full, so the smile seemed hardly under her control. She was quite pretty; her complexion was so delicate and her eyes so pleasant. "Well, I don't see how I made such a blunder," her mother remarked further, as she went on pouring tea.

On the opposite side of the table were a plate, a knife and fork, and a little dish of cranberry sauce, with an empty chair before them. There was no guest to fill it.

"It's a sign somebody's comin' that's hungry," Mrs. Childs' brother's wife said, with soft effusiveness which was out of proportion to the words.

The brother was carving the turkey. Caleb Childs, the host, was an old man, and his hands trembled. Moreover, no one, he himself least of all, ever had any confidence in his ability in such directions. Whenever he helped himself to gravy, his wife watched anxiously lest be should spill it, and he always did. He spilled some today. There was a great spot on the beautiful clean table-cloth. Caleb set his cup and saucer over it quickly, with a little clatter because of his unsteady hand. Then he looked at his wife. He hoped she had not seen, but she had.

192

"You'd better have let John give you the gravy," she said, in a stern aside.

John, rigidly solicitous, bent over the turkey. He carved slowly and laboriously, but everybody had faith in him. The shoulders to which a burden is shifted have the credit of being strong. His wife, in her best black dress, sat smilingly, with her head canted a little to one side. It was a way she had when visiting. Ordinarily she did not assume it at her sister-in-law's house, but this was an extra occasion. Her fine manners spread their wings involuntarily. When she spoke about the sign, the young woman next her sniffed.

"I don't take any stock in signs," said she, with a bluntness which seemed to crash through the other's airiness with such force as to almost hurt itself. She was a distant cousin of Mr. Childs. Her husband and three children were with her. Mrs. Childs' unmarried sister, Maria Stone, made up the eleven at the table. Maria's gaunt face was unhealthily red about the pointed nose and the high cheek-bones; her eyes looked with a steady sharpness through her spectacles. "Well, it will be time enough to believe the sign when the twelfth one comes," said she, with a summary air. She had a judicial way of speaking. She had taught school ever since she was sixteen, and now she was sixty. She had just given up teaching. It was to celebrate that, and her final home-coming, that her sister was giving a Christmas dinner instead of a Thanksgiving one this year. The school had been in session during Thanksgiving week.

Maria Stone had scarcely spoken when there was a knock on the outer door, which led directly into the room. They all started. They were a plain, unimaginative company, but for some reason a thrill of superstitious and fantastic expectation ran through them. No one arose. They were all silent for a moment, listening and looking at the empty chair in their midst. Then the knock came again.

"Go to the door, Paulina," said her mother.

The young girl looked at her half fearfully, but she rose at once, and went and opened the door. Everybody stretched around to see. A girl stood on the stone step looking into the room. There she stood, and never said a word. Paulina looked around at her mother, with her innocent, half-involuntary smile.

"Ask her what she wants," said Mrs. Childs.

What do you want?" repeated Paulina, like a sweet echo.

Still the girl said nothing. A gust of north wind swept into the room. John's wife shivered, then looked around to see if any one had noticed it.

"You must speak up quick an' tell what you want, so we can shut the door; it's cold," said Mrs. Childs.

The girl's small sharp face was sheathed in an old worsted hood; her eyes glared out of it like a frightened cat's. Suddenly she turned to go. She was evidently abashed by the company.

"Don't you want somethin' to eat?" Mrs. Childs asked, speaking up louder.

"It ain't no matter." She just mumbled it.

"What?"

She would not repeat it. She was quite off the step by this time.

"You make her come in, Paulina," said Maria Stone, suddenly. "She wants something to eat, but she's half scared to death. You talk to her."

"Hadn't you better come in, and have something to eat?" said Paulina, shyly persuasive.

"Tell her she can sit right down here by the stove, where it's warm, and have a good plate of dinner," said Maria.

Paulina fluttered softly down to the stone step. The chilly snow-wind came right in her sweet, rosy face. "You can have a chair by the stove, where it's warm, and a good plate of dinner," said she.

The girl looked at her.

"Won't you come in?" said Paulina, of her own accord, and always smiling.

The stranger made a little hesitating movement forward.

"Bring her in, quick! and shut the door," Maria called out then. And Paulina entered with the girl stealing timidly in her wake.

"Take off your hood an' shawl," Mrs. Childs said, "an' sit down here by the stove, an' I'll give you some dinner." She spoke kindly. She was a warm-hearted woman, but she was rigidly built, and did not. relax too quickly into action.

But the cousin, who had been observing, with head alertly raised, interrupted. She cast a mischievous glance at John's wife—the empty chair was between them. "For pity's sake!" cried she; "you ain't goin' to shove her off in the corner? Why, here's this chair. She's the twelfth one. Here's where she ought to sit." There was a mixture of heartiness and sport in the young woman's manner. She pulled the chair back from the table. "Come right over here," said she.

There was a slight flutter of consternation among the guests. They were all narrow-lived country people. Their customs had made deeper grooves in their roads; they were more fastidious and jealous of their social rights than many in higher positions. They eyed this forlorn girl, in her in her faded and dingy woollens which fluttered airily and showed their pitiful thinness.

Mrs. Childs stood staring at the cousin. She did not think she could be in earnest.

But she was. "Come," said she; "put some turkey in this plate, John."

"Why, it's jest as the rest of you say," Mrs. Childs said, finally, with hesitation. She looked embarrassed and doubtful.

"Say! Why, they say just as I do," the cousin went on. "Why shouldn't they? Come right around here." She tapped the chair impatiently.

The girl looked at Mrs. Childs. "You can go an' sit down there where she says," she said, slowly, in a constrained tone.

"Come," called the cousin again. And the girl took the empty chair, with the guests all smiling stiffly.

Mrs. Childs began filling a plate for the newcomer.

Now that her hood was removed, one could see her face more plainly. It was thin, and of that pale brown tint which exposure gives to some blond skins. Still there was a tangible

195

beauty which showed through all that. Her fair hair stood up softly, with a kind of airy roughness which caught the light. She was apparently about sixteen.

"What's your name?" inquired the school-mistress sister, suddenly.

The girl started. "Christine," she said, after a second.

"What?"

"Christine."

A little thrill ran around the table. The company looked at each other. They were none of them conversant with the Christmas legends, but at that moment the universal sentiment of them seemed to seize upon their fancies. The day, the mysterious appearance of the girl, the name, which was strange to their ears—all startled them, and gave them a vague sense of the supernatural. They, however, struggled against it with their matter-of-fact pride, and threw it off directly.

"Christine what?" Maria asked further.

The girl kept her scared eyes on Maria's face, but she made no reply.

"What's your other name? Why don't you speak?"

Suddenly she rose.

"What are you goin' to do?"

"I'd—ruther—go, I guess."

"What are you goin' for? You ain't had your dinner."

"I—can't tell it," whispered the girl.

"Can't tell your name?"

She shook her head.

"Sit down, and eat your dinner," said Maria.

There was a strong sentiment of disapprobation among the company. But when Christine's food was actually before her, and she seemed to settle down upon it, like a bird, they viewed her with more toleration. She was evidently half starved. Their discovery of that fact gave them at once a fellow-feeling toward her on this feast-day, and a complacent sense of their own benevolence.

As the dinner progressed the spirits of the party appeared to rise, and a certain jollity which was almost hilarity prevailed. Beyond providing the strange guest plentifully with food, they seemed to ignore her entirely. Still nothing was more certain than the fact that they did not. Every outburst of merriment was yielded to with the most thorough sense of her presence, which appeared in some subtle way to excite it. It was as if this forlorn twelfth guest were the foreign element needed to produce a state of nervous effervescence in those staid, decorous people who surrounded her. This taste of mystery and unusualness, once fairly admitted, although reluctantly, to their unaccustomed palates, served them as wine with their Christmas dinner.

It was late in the afternoon when they arose from the table. Christine went directly for her hood and shawl, and put them on. The others, talking among themselves, were stealthily observant of her. Christine began opening the door.

"Are you goin' home now?" asked Mrs. Childs.

"No, marm."

"Why not?"

"I ain't got any."

"Where did you come from?"

The girl looked at her. Then she unlatched the door.

"Stop!" Mrs. Childs cried, sharply. "What are you goin' for? Why don't you answer?"

She stood still, but did not speak.

"Well, shut the door up, an' wait a minute," said Mrs. Childs.

She stood close to a window, and she stared out scrutinizingly. There was no house in sight. First came a great yard, then wide stretches of fields; a desolate gray road curved around them on the left. The sky was covered with still, low clouds; the sun had not shone out that day. The ground was all bare and rigid. Out in the yard some gray hens were huddled together in little groups for warmth; their red combs showed out. Two crows flew up, away over on the edge of the field.

"It's goin' to snow," said Mrs. Childs.

"I'm afeard it is," said Caleb, looking at the girl.

He gave a sort of silent sob, and brushed some tears out of his old eyes with the back of his hands.

"See here a minute, Maria," said Mrs. Childs.

The two women whispered together; then Maria stepped in front of the girl, and stood, tall and stiff and impressive.

"Now see here," said she; "we want you to speak up and tell us your other name, and where you came from, and not keep us waiting any longer."

"I—*can't.*" They guessed what she said from the motion of her head. She opened the door entirely then and stepped out.

Suddenly Maria made one stride forward and seized her by her shoulders, which felt like knife-blades through the thin clothes. "Well," said she, " we've been fussing long enough; we've got all these dishes to clear away. It's bitter cold, and it's going to snow, and you ain't going out of this house one step tonight, no matter what you are. You'd ought to tell us who you are, and it ain't many folks that would keep you if you wouldn't; but we ain't goin' to have you found dead in the road, for our own credit. It ain't on your account. Now you just take those things off again, and go and sit down in that chair."

Christine sat in the chair. Her pointed chin dipped down on her neck, whose poor little muscles showed above her dress, which sagged away from it. She never looked up. The women cleared off the table, and cast curious glances at her.

After the dishes were washed and put away, the company were all assembled in the sitting-room for an hour or so; then they went home. The cousin, passing through the kitchen to join her husband, who was waiting with his team at the door, ran hastily up to Christine.

"You stop at my house when you go tomorrow morning," said she. "Mrs. Childs will tell you where, 'tis half a mile below here."

When the company were all gone, Mrs. Childs called Christine into the sitting-room. "You'd better come in here and sit now," said she. "I'm goin' to let the kitchen fire go down; I ain't goin' to get another regular meal; I'm jest goin' to make a cup of tea on the sittin'-room stove by-an'-by."

The sitting-room was warm, and restrainedly comfortable with its ordinary village furnishings—its ingrain carpet, its little peaked clock on a corner of the high black shelf, its red-covered card-table, which had stood in the same spot for forty years. There was a little newspaper-covered stand, with some plants on it, before a window. There was one red geranium in blossom.

Paulina was going out that evening. Soon after the company went she commenced to get ready, and her mother and aunt seemed to be helping her. Christine was alone in the sitting-room for the greater part of an hour.

Finally the three women came in, and Paulina stood before the sitting-room glass for a last look at herself. She had on her best red cashmere, with some white lace around her throat. She had a red geranium flower with some leaves in her hair. Paulina's brown hair, which was rather thin, was very silky. It was apt to part into little soft strands on her forehead. She wore it brushed smoothly back. Her mother would not allow her to curl it.

The two older women stood looking at her. "Don't you think she looks nice, Christine?" Mrs. Childs asked, in a sudden overflow of love and pride, which led her to ask sympathy from even this forlorn source.

"Yes, marm." Christine regarded Paulina, in her red cashmere and geranium flower, with sharp, solemn eyes. When she really looked at any one, her gaze was as unflinching as that of a child.

There was a sudden roll of wheels in the yard.

"Willard's come!" said Mrs. Childs. "Run to the door an' tell him you'll be right out, Paulina, an' I'll get your things ready."

After Paulina had been helped into her coat and hood, and the wheels had bowled out of the yard with a quick dash, the mother turned to Christine.

"My daughter's gone to a Christmas tree over to the church," said she. "That was Willard Morris that came for her. He's a real nice young man that lives about a mile from here."

Mrs. Childs' tone was at once gently patronizing and elated. When Christine was shown to a little back bedroom that night, nobody dreamed how many times she was to occupy it. Maria and Mrs. Childs, who after the door was closed set a table against it softly and erected a tiltish pyramid of milkpans, to serve as an alarm in case the strange guest should try to leave her room with evil intentions, were fully convinced that she would depart early on the following morning.

"I dun know but I've run an awful risk keeping her," Mrs. Childs said. "I don't like her not tellin' where she come from. Nobody knows but she belongs to a gang of burglars, an' they've kind of sent her on ahead to spy out things an' unlock the doors for 'em."

"I know it," said Maria. "I wouldn't have had her stay for a thousand dollars if it hadn't looked so much like snow. Well, I'll get up an' start her off early in the morning."

But Maria Stone could not carry out this resolution. The next morning she was ill with a sudden and severe attack of erysipelas. Moreover, there was a hard snowstorm, the worst of the season; it would have been barbarous to have turned the girl out-of-doors on such a morning. Moreover, she developed an unexpected capacity for usefulness. She assisted Pauline about the housework with timid alacrity, and Mrs. Childs could devote all her time to her sister.

"She takes right hold as if she was used to it," she told Maria. "I'd rather keep her a while than not, if I only knew a little more about her."

"I don't believe but what I could get it out of her after a while if I tried," said Maria, with her magisterial air, which illness could not subdue.

However, even Maria, with all her well-fostered imperiousness, had no effect on the girl's resolution; she continued as much of a mystery as ever. Still the days went on, then the weeks and months, and she remained in the Childs family.

None of them could tell exactly how it had been brought about. The most definite course seemed to be that her arrival had apparently been the signal for a general decline of health in the family. Maria had hardly recovered when Caleb Childs was laid up with the rheumatism; then Mrs. Childs had a long spell of exhaustion from overwork in nursing. Christine proved exceedingly useful in these emergencies. Their need of her appeared to be the dominant, and only outwardly evident, reason for her stay; still there was a deeper one which they themselves only faintly realised—this poor young girl, who was rendered almost repulsive to these honest downright folk by her persistent cloak of mystery, had somehow, in a very short time, melted herself, as it were, into their own lives. Christine asleep of a night in her little back bedroom, Christine of a day stepping about the house in one of Paulina's old gowns, became a part of their existence, and a part which was not far from the nature of a sweetness to their senses.

She still retained her mild shyness of manner, and rarely spoke unless spoken to. Now that she was warmly sheltered and well fed, her beauty became evident. She grew prettier every day. Her cheeks became softly dimpled; her hair turned golden. Her language was rude and illiterate, but its very uncouthness had about it something of a soft grace.

She was really prettier than Paulina.

The two young girls were much together, but could hardly be said to be intimate. There were few confidences between them, and confidences are essential for the intimacy of young girls.

Willard Morris came regularly twice a week to see Paulina, and everybody spoke of them as engaged to each other.

Along in August Mrs. Childs drove over to town one afternoon and bought a piece of cotton cloth and a little embroidery and lace. Then some fine sewing went on, but with no comment in the household. Mrs. Childs had simply said, "I guess we may as well get a few things made up for you, Paulina, you're getting rather short." And Paulina had sewed all day long, with a gentle industry, when the work was ready.

There was a report that the marriage was to take place on Thanksgiving Day. But about the first of October Willard Morris stopped going to the Childs house. There was no explanation. He simply did not come as usual on Sunday night, nor the following Wednesday, nor the next Sunday. Paulina kindled her little parlour fire, whose sticks she had laid with maiden preciseness; she arrayed herself in her best gown and ribbons. When at nine o'clock Willard had not come, she blew out the parlour lamp, shut up the parlour stove, and went to bed. Nothing was said before her, but there was much talk and surmise between Mrs. Childs and Maria, and a good deal of it went on before Christine.

It was a little while after the affair of Cyrus Morris's note, and they wondered if it could have anything to do with that. Cyrus Morris was Willard's uncle, and the note affair had occasioned much distress in the Childs family for a month back. The note was for twenty-five hundred dollars, and Cyrus Morris had given it to Caleb Childs. The time, which was two years, had expired on the first of September, and then Caleb could not find the note.

He had kept it in his old-fashioned desk, which stood in one corner of the kitchen. He searched there a day and half a night, pulling all the soiled, creasy old papers out of the drawers and pigeonholes before he would answer his wife's inquiries as to what he had lost.

Finally he broke down and told. "I've lost that note of Morris's," said he. "I dun know what I'm goin' to do."

He stood looking gloomily at the desk with its piles of papers. His rough old chin dropped down on his breast.

The women were all in the kitchen, and they stopped and stared.

"Why, father," said his wife, "where have you put it?"

"I put it here in this top drawer, and it ain't there."

"Let me look," said Maria, in a confident tone. But even Maria's energetic and self-assured researches failed. "Well, it ain't here," said she. "I don't know what you've done with it."

"I don't believe you put it in that drawer, father," said his wife.

"It was in there two weeks ago. I see it."

"Then you took it out afterwards."

"I ain't laid hands on't."

"You must have; it couldn't have gone off without hands. You know you're kind of forgetful, father."

"I guess I know when I've took a paper out of a drawer. I know a leetle somethin' yit."

"Well, I don't suppose there'll be any trouble about it, will there?" said Mrs. Childs. "Of course he knows he give the note, an' had the money."

"I dun know as there'll be any trouble, but I'd ruther give a hundred dollar than had it happen."

After dinner Caleb shaved, put on his other coat and hat, and trudged soberly up the road to Cyrus Morris's. Cyrus Morris was an elderly man, who had quite a local reputation for wealth and business shrewdness. Caleb, who was lowly-natured and easily impressed by another's importance, always made a call upon him quite a formal affair, and shaved and dressed up. He was absent about an hour today. When he returned he went into the sitting-room, where the women sat with their sewing. He dropped into a chair, and looked straight ahead, with his forehead knitted.

The women dropped their work and looked at him, and then at each other.

"What did he say, father?" Mrs. Childs asked at length.

"Say! He's a rascal, that's what he is, an' I'll tell him so, too."

"Ain't he goin' to pay it?"

"No, he ain't."

"Why, father, I don't believe it! You didn't get hold of it straight," said his wife.

"You'll see."

"Why, what did he say?"

"He didn't say anything."

"Doesn't he remember he had the money and gave the note, and has been paying interest on it?" queried Maria.

"He jest laughed, an' said 'twa'n't accordin' to law to pay unless I showed the note an' give it up to him. He said he couldn't be sure but I'd want him to pay it over ag'in. *I know where that note is!*"

Caleb's voice had deep meaning in it. The women stared at him.

"Where?"

"*It's in Cyrus Morris's desk—that's where it is.*"

"Why, father, you're crazy!"

"No, I ain't crazy, nuther. I know what I'm talkin' about. I—"

"It's just where you put it," interrupted Maria, taking up her sewing with a switch; "and I wouldn't lay the blame onto anybody else."

"You'd ought to ha' looked out for a paper like that," said his wife. "I guess I should if it had been me. If you've gone an' lost all that money through your carelessness, you've done it, that's all I've got to say. I don't see what we're goin' to do."

Caleb bent forward and fixed his eyes upon the women. He held up his shaking hand impressively. "*If* you'll stop talkin' just a minute," said he, "I'll tell you what I was goin' to. Now I'd like to know just one thing: *Wa'n't Cyrus Morris alone in that kitchen as much as fifteen minutes a week ago today? Didn't you leave him there while you went to look arter me? Wa'n't the key in the desk? Answer me that!*"

His wife looked at him with cold surprise and severity.

"I wouldn't talk in any such way as that if I was you, father," said she. "It don't show a Christian spirit. It's jest layin' the blame of your own carelessness onto somebody else. You're all the one that's to blame. An' when it comes to it, you'd never ought to let Cyrus Morris have the money anyhow. I could have told you better. I knew what kind of a man he was."

"He's a rascal," said Caleb, catching eagerly at the first note of foreign condemnation in his wife's words. "He'd ought to be put in state's-prison. I don't think much of his relations nuther. I don't want nothin' to do with 'em, an' I don't want none of my folks to."

Paulina's soft cheeks flushed. Then she suddenly spoke out as she had never spoken in her life.

"It doesn't make it out because he's a bad man that his relations are," said she. "You haven't any right to speak so, father. And I guess you won't stop me having anything to do with them, if you want to."

She was all pink and trembling. Suddenly she burst out crying, and ran out of the room.

"You'd ought to be ashamed of yourself, father," exclaimed Mrs. Childs.

"I didn't think of her takin' on it so," muttered Caleb, humbly. "I didn't mean nothin'."

Caleb did not seem like himself through the following days. His simple old face took on an expression of strained thought, which made it look strange. He was tottering on a height of mental effort and worry which was almost above the breathing capacity of his innocent and placid nature. Many a night he rose, lighted a candle, and tremulously fumbled over his desk until morning, in the vain hope of finding missing note.

One night, while he was so searching, someone touched him softly on the arm.

He jumped and turned. It was Christine. She had stolen in silently.

"Oh, it's you!" said he.

"Ain't you found it?"

"Found it? No; an' I sha'n't, nuther." He turned away from her and pulled out another drawer. The girl stood watching him wistfully. "It was a big yellow paper," the old man went on—"a big yellow paper, an' I'd wrote on the back on't, 'Cyrus Morris's note.' An' the interest he'd, paid was set down on the back on't, too."

"It's too bad you can't find it," said she.

"It ain't no use lookin'; it ain't here, an' that's the hull on't. It's in *his* desk. I ain't got no more doubt on't than nothin' at all."

"Where—does he keep his desk?"

"In his kitchen; it's jest like this one."

"Would this key open it?"

"I dun know but 'twould. But it ain't no use. I s'pose I'll have to lose it." Caleb sobbed silently and wiped his eyes.

A few days later he came, all breathless, into the sitting room. He could hardly speak; but he held out a folded yellow paper, which fluttered and blew in his unsteady hand like a yellow maple-leaf in an autumn gale.

"Look-a-here!" he gasped—"look-a-here!"

"Why, for goodness' sake, what's the matter?" cried Maria. She and Mrs. Childs and Paulina were there, sewing peacefully.

"Jest look-a-*here*!"

"Why, for mercy's sake, what is it, father? Are you crazy?"

"It's—the *note*!"

"What note? Don't get so excited, father."

"Cyrus Morris's note. That's what note 'tis. Look-a-here!"

The women all arose and pressed around him, to look at it.

"Where *did* you find it, father?" asked his wife, who was quite pale.

"I suppose it was just where you put it," broke in Maria, with sarcastic emphasis.

"No, it wa'n't. No, it wa'n't, nuther. Don't you go to crowin' too quick, Maria. That paper was just where I told you 'twas. What do you think of that, hey?"

"Oh, father, you didn't!"

"It was layin' right there in his desk. That's where 'twas. Jest where I knew—"

"Father, you didn't go over there an' take it!"

The three women stared at him with dilated eyes.

"No, I didn't."

"Who did?"

The old man jerked his head towards the kitchen door. "She."

"Who?"

"Christiny."

"How did she get it?" asked Maria, in her magisterial manner, which no astonishment could agitate.

"She saw Cyrus and Mis' Morris ride past, an' then she run

over there, an' she got in through the window an' got it; that's how." Caleb braced himself like a stubborn child, in case any exception were taken to it all.

"It beats everything I ever heard," said Mrs. Childs, faintly.

"Next time you'll believe what I tell you!" said Caleb.

The whole family were in a state of delight over the recovery of the note; still Christine got rather hesitating gratitude. She was sharply questioned, and rather reproved than otherwise.

This theft, which could hardly be called a theft, aroused the old distrust of her.

"It served him just right, and it wasn't stealing, because it didn't belong to him; and I don't know what you would have done if she hadn't taken it," said Maria; "but, for all that, it went all over me."

"So it did over me," said her sister. " I felt just as you did, an' I felt as if it was real ungrateful too, when the poor child did it just for us."

But there were no such misgivings for poor Caleb, with his money, and his triumph over iniquitous Cyrus Morris. He was wholly and unquestioningly grateful.

"It was a blessed day when we took that little girl in," he told his wife.

"I hope it'll prove so," said she.

Paulina took her lover's desertion quietly. She had just as many soft smiles for everyone; there was no alteration in her gentle, obliging ways. Still her mother used to listen at her door, and she knew that she cried instead of sleeping many a night. She was not able to eat much, either, although she tried to with pleasant willingness when her mother urged her.

After a while she was plainly grown thin, and her pretty colour had faded. Her mother could not keep her eyes from her.

"Sometimes I think I'll go an' ask Willard myself what this kind of work means," she broke out with an abashed abruptness one afternoon. She and Paulina happened to be alone in the sitting-room.

"You'll kill me if you do, mother," said Paulina. Then she

began to cry.

"Well, I won't do anything you don't want me to, of course," said her mother. She pretended not to see that Paulina was crying.

Willard had stopped coming about the first of October; the time wore on until it was the first of December, and he had not once been to the house, and Paulina had not exchanged a word with him in the meantime.

One night she had a fainting-spell. She fell heavily while crossing the sitting-room floor. They got her on to the lounge, and she soon revived; but her mother had lost all control of herself. She came out into the kitchen and paced the floor.

"Oh, my darlin'!" she wailed. "She's goin' to die. What shall I do? All the child I've got in the world. An' he's killed her! That *scamp*! I wish I could get my hands on him. Oh, Paulina, Paulina, to think it should come to this!"

Christine was in the room, and she listened with eyes dilated and lips parted. She was afraid that shrill wail would reach Paulina in the next room.

"She'll hear you," she said, finally.

Mrs. Childs grew quieter at that, and presently Maria called her into the sitting-room.

Christine stood thinking for a moment. Then she got her hood and shawl, put on her rubbers, and went out. She shut the door softly, so nobody should hear. When she stepped forth she plunged knee-deep into snow. It was snowing hard, as it had been all day. It was a cold storm, too; the wind was bitter. Christine waded out of the yard and down the street. She was so small and light that she staggered when she tried to step firmly in some tracks ahead of her. There was a full moon behind the clouds, and there was a soft white light in spite of the storm. Christine kept on down the street, in the direction of Willard Morris's house. It was a mile distant. Once in a while she stopped and turned herself about, that the terrible wind might smite her back instead of her face. When she reached the house she waded painfully through the yard to the side-door and knocked. Pretty soon it opened, and Willard stood there in the entry, with a lamp in his hand.

"Good-evening," said he, doubtfully, peering out.

"Good-evenin'." The light shone on Christine's face.

The snow clung to her soft hair, so it was quite white. Her cheeks had a deep, soft colour, like roses; her blue eyes blinked a little in the lamp-light, but seemed rather to flicker like jewels or stars. She panted softly through her parted lips. She stood there, with the snow-flakes driving in light past her, and "She looks like an angel," came swiftly into Willard Morris's head before he spoke.

"Oh, it's you," said he.

Christine nodded.

Then they stood waiting. "Why, won't you come in?" said Willard, finally, with an awkward blush. "I declare I never thought. I ain't very polite."

She shook her head. "No, thank you," said she.

"Did—you want to see mother?"

"No."

The young man stared at her in increasing perplexity. His own fair, handsome young face got more and more flushed. His forehead wrinkled. "Was there anything you wanted?"

"No, I guess not," Christine replied, with a slow softness.

Willard shifted the lamp into his other hand and sighed. "It's a pretty hard storm," he remarked, with an air of forced patience.

"Yes."

"Didn't you find it terrible hard walking?"

"Some."

Willard was silent again. "See here, they're all well down at your house, ain't they?" said he, finally. A look of anxious interest had sprung into his eyes. He had begun to take alarm.

"I guess so."

Suddenly he spoke out impetuously. "Say, Christine, I don't know what you came here for; you can tell me afterwards. I don't know what you'll think of me, but—Well, I want to know something. Say—well, I haven't been 'round for quite a while.

You don't suppose they've cared much, any of them"

"I don't know."

"Well, I don't suppose you do, but—you might have noticed. Say, Christine, you don't think she—you know whom I mean— cared anything about my coming, do you?"

"I don't know," she said again, softly, with her eyes fixed warily on his face.

"Well, I guess she didn't; she wouldn't have said what she did if she had."

Christine's eyes gave a sudden gleam. "What did she say?"

"Said she wouldn't have anything more to do with me," said the young man, bitterly. "She was afraid I would be up to just such tricks as my uncle was, trying to cheat her father. That was too much for me. I wasn't going to stand that from any girl." He shook his head angrily.

"She didn't say it."

"Yes, she did; her own father told my uncle so. Mother was in the next room and heard it."

"No, she didn't say it," the girl repeated.

"How do you know?"

"I heard her say something different," Christine told him.

"I'm going right up there," cried he, when he heard that.

"Wait a minute, and I'll go along with you."

"I dun know as you'd better—tonight," Christine said, looking out towards the road evasively. "She—ain't been very well tonight."

"Who? Paulina? What's the matter?"

"She had a faintin'-spell jest before I came out," answered Christine, with stiff gravity.

"Oh! Is she real sick?"

"She was some better."

"Don't you suppose I could see her just a few minutes? I wouldn't stay to tire her," said the young man, eagerly.

"I dun know."

"I must, anyhow."

Christine fixed her eyes on his with a solemn sharpness.

"What makes you want to?"

"What makes me want to? Why, I'd give ten years to see her five minutes."

"Well, mebbe you could come over a few minutes."

"Wait a minute,!" cried Willard. "I'll get my hat."

"I'd better go first, I guess. The parlour fire'll be to light."

"Then had I better wait?"

"I guess so."

"Then I'll be along in about an hour. Say, you haven't said what you wanted."

Christine was off the step.

"It ain't any matter," murmured she.

"Say—she didn't send you?"

"No, she didn't."

"I didn't mean that. I didn't suppose she did," said Willard, with an abashed air. "What did you want, Christine?"

"There's somethin' I want you to promise," said she, suddenly.

"What's that?"

"Don't you say anything about Mr. Childs."

"Why, how can I help it?"

"He's an old man, an' he was so worked up he didn't know what he was sayin'. They'll all scold him. Don't say anything."

"Well, I won't say anything. I don't know what I'm going to tell her, though."

Christine turned to go.

"You didn't say what 'twas you wanted," called Willard again.

But she made no reply. She was pushing through the deep snow out of the yard.

It was quite early yet, only a few minutes after seven. It was eight when she reached home. She entered the house without anyone seeing her. She pulled off her snowy things, and went into the sitting-room.

Paulina was alone there. She was lying on the lounge. She was very pale, but she looked up and smiled when Christine entered.

Christine brought the fresh out-door air with her. Paulina noticed it. "Where have you been?" whispered she.

Then Christine bent over her, and talked fast in a low tone.

Presently Paulina raised herself and sat up. "Tonight?" cried she, in an eager whisper. Her cheeks grew red.

"Yes; I'll go make the parlour fire."

"It's all ready to light." Suddenly Paulina threw her arms around Christine and kissed her. Both girls blushed.

"I don't think I said one thing to him that you wouldn't have wanted me to," said Christine.

"You didn't—ask him to come?"

"No, I didn't, honest."

When Mrs. Childs entered, a few minutes later, she found her daughter standing before the glass.

"Why, Paulina!" cried she.

"I feel a good deal better, mother," said Paulina.

"Ain't you goin' to bed?"

"I guess I won't quite yet."

"I've got it all ready for you. I thought you wouldn't feel like sittin' up."

"I guess I will; a little while."

Soon the door-bell rang with a sharp peal. Everybody jumped—Paulina rose and went to the door.

Mrs. Childs and Maria, listening, heard Willard's familiar voice, then the opening of the parlour door.

"It's *him!*" gasped Mrs. Childs. She and Maria looked at each other.

It was about two hours before the soft murmur of voices in the parlour ceased, the outer door closed with a thud, and Paulina came into the room. She was blushing and smiling, but she could not look in any one's face at first.

"Well," said her mother, "who was it?"

"Willard. It's all right."

It was not long before the fine sewing was brought out again, and presently two silk dresses were bought for Paulina. It was known about that she was to be married on Christmas Day. Christine assisted in the preparation. All the family called to mind afterwards the obedience so ready as to be loving which she yielded to their biddings during those few hurried weeks. She sewed, she made cake, she ran of errands, she wearied herself joyfully for the happiness of this other young girl.

About a week before the wedding, Christine, saying goodnight when about to retire one evening, behaved strangely. They remembered it afterwards. She went up to Paulina and kissed her when saying goodnight. It was something which she had never before done. Then she stood in the door, looking at them all. There was a sad, almost a solemn, expression on her fair girlish face.

"Why, what's the matter?" said Maria.

"Nothin'," said Christine. "Goodnight."

That was the last time they ever saw her. The next morning Mrs. Childs, going to call her, found her room vacant. There was a great alarm. When they did not find her in the house nor the neighbourhood, people were aroused, and there was a search instigated. It was prosecuted eagerly, but to no purpose. Paulina's wedding evening came, and Christine was still missing.

Paulina had been married, and was standing beside her husband, in the midst of the chattering guests, when Caleb stole out of the room. He opened the north door, and stood looking out over the dusky fields. "Christiny!" he called; "Christiny!"

Presently he looked up at the deep sky, full of stars, and called again—"Christiny! Christiny!" But there was no answer save in light. When Christine stood in the sitting room door and said goodnight, her friends had their last sight and sound of her. Their Twelfth Guest had departed from their hospitality forever.

Silence

At dusk Silence went down the Deerfield street to Ensign John Sheldon's house. She wore her red blanket over her head, pinned closely under her chin, and her white profile showed whiter between the scarlet folds. She had been spinning all day, and shreds of wool still clung to her indigo petticoat; now and then one floated off on the north wind. It was bitterly cold, and the snow was four feet deep. Silence's breath went before her in a cloud; the snow creaked under her feet. All over the village the crust was so firm that men could walk upon it. The houses were half sunken in sharp, rigid drifts of snow; their roofs were laden with it; icicles hung from the eaves. All the elms were white on their windward sides, and the snow was so nearly ice and frozen to them so strongly that it was not shaken off when they were lashed by the fierce wind.

There was an odour of boiling meal in the air: the house-wives were preparing supper. Silence had eaten hers: she and her aunt, Widow Eunice Bishop, supped early. She had not far to go to Ensign Sheldon's. She was nearly there when she heard quick footsteps on the creaking snow behind her. Her heart beat quickly, but she did not look around. "Silence," said a voice. Then she paused, and waited, with her eyes cast down and her mouth grave, until David Walcott reached her. "What do you out this cold night, sweetheart?" he said.

"I am going down to Good wife Sheldon's," replied Silence. Then suddenly she cried out, wildly: "Oh, David, what is that on your cloak? What is it?"

David looked curiously at his cloak. "I see naught on my cloak save old weather stains," said he. "What mean you, Silence?"

Silence quieted down suddenly. "It is gone now," said she, in a subdued voice.

"What did you see, Silence?"

Silence turned toward him; her face quivered convulsively. "I saw a blotch of blood," she cried. "I have been seeing them everywhere all day. I have seen them on the snow as I came along."

David Walcott looked down at her in a bewildered way. He carried his musket over his shoulder, and was shrugged up in his cloak; his heavy flaxen moustache was stiff and white with frost. He had just been relieved from his post as sentry, and it was no child's play to patrol Deerfield village on a day like that, nor had it been for many previous days. The weather had been so severe that even the French and Indians, lurking like hungry wolves in the neighbourhood, had hesitated to descend upon the town, and had staid in camp.

"What mean you, Silence?" he said.

"What I say," returned Silence, in a strained voice. "I have seen blotches of blood everywhere all day. The enemy will be upon us."

David laughed loudly, and Silence caught his arm. "Don't laugh so loud," she whispered. Then David laughed again. "You be all overwrought, sweetheart," said he. "I have kept guard all the afternoon by the northern palisades, and I have seen not so much as a red fox on the meadow. I tell thee the French and Indians have gone back to Canada. There is no more need of fear."

"I have started all day and all last night at the sound of war-whoops," said Silence.

"Thy head is nigh turned with these troublous times, poor lass. We must cross the road now to Ensign Sheldon's house. Come quickly, or you will perish in this cold."

"Nay, my head is not turned," said Silence, as they hurried on

215

over the crust; "the enemy be hiding in the forests beyond the meadows. David, they be not gone."

"And I tell thee they be gone, sweetheart. Think you not we should have seen their camp smoke had they been there? And we have had trusty scouts out. Come in, and my aunt Hannah Sheldon shall talk thee out of this folly."

The front windows of John Sheldon's house were all flickering red from the hearth fire. David flung open the door, and they entered. There was such a goodly blaze from the great logs in the wide fireplace that even the shadows in the remote corners of the large keeping-room were dusky red, and the faces of all the people in the room had a clear red glow upon them.

Goodwife Hannah Sheldon stood before the fire, stirring some porridge in a great pot that hung on the crane; some fair-haired children sat around a basket shelling corn, a slight young girl in a snuff-yellow gown was spinning, and an old woman in a great quilted hood crouched in a corner of the fireplace, holding out her lean hands to the heat.

Goodwife Sheldon turned around when the door opened. "Good-day, Mistress Silence Hoit," she called out, and her voice was sweet, but deep like a man's. "Draw near to the fire, for in truth you must be near perishing with the cold."

"There'll be fire enough ere morning, I trow, to warm the whole township," said the old woman in the corner. Her small black eyes gleamed sharply out of the gloom of her great hood; her yellow face was all drawn and puckered toward the centre of her shrewdly leering mouth.

"Now you hush your croaking, Goody Crane," cried Hannah Sheldon. "Draw the stool near to the fire for Silence, David. I cannot stop stirring, or the porridge will burn. How fares your aunt this cold weather, Silence?"

"Well, except for her rheumatism," replied Silence. She sat down on the stool that David placed for her, and slipped her blanket back from her head. Her beautiful face, full of a grave and delicate stateliness, drooped toward the fire, her smooth fair hair was folded in clear curves like the leaves of a lily around her ears, and she wore a high, transparent, tortoise-shell comb like a coronet in the knot at the back of her head.

David Walcott had pulled off his cap and cloak, and stood looking down at her. "Silence is all overwrought by this talk of Indians," he remarked, presently, and a blush came over his weather-beaten blond face at the tenderness in his own tone.

"The Indians have gone back to Canada," said Goodwife Sheldon, in a magisterial voice. She stirred the porridge faster; it was smoking fiercely.

"So I tell her," said David.

Silence looked up in Hannah Sheldon's sober, masterly face. "Goodwife, may I have a word in private with you?" she asked, in a half-whisper.

"As soon as I take the porridge off," replied Goodwife Sheldon.

"God grant it be not the last time she takes the porridge off!" said the old woman.

Hannah Sheldon laughed. "Here be Goody Crane in a sorry mind tonight," said she. "Wait till she have a sup of this good porridge, and I trow she'll pack off the Indians to Canada in a half-hour!"

Hannah began dipping out the porridge. When she had placed smoking dishes of it on the table and bidden everybody draw up, she motioned to Silence. "Now, Mistress Silence," said she, "come into the bedroom if you would have a word with me."

Silence followed her into the little north room opening out of the keeping-room, where Ensign John Sheldon and his wife Hannah had slept for many years. It was icy cold, and the thick fur of frost on the little window-panes sent out sparkles in the candle-light. The two women stood beside the great chintz draped and canopied bed, Hannah holding the flaring candle. "Now, what is it?" said she.

"Oh, Goodwife Sheldon!" said Silence. Her face remained quite still, but it was as if one could see her soul fluttering beneath it.

"You be all overwrought, as David saith," cried Goodwife Sheldon, and her voice had a motherly harshness in it. Silence had no mother, and her lover, David Walcott, had none. Hannah was his aunt, and loved him like her son, so she felt toward Silence as toward her son's betrothed.

"In truth I know not what it is," said Silence, in a kind of reserved terror, "but there has been all day a great heaviness of spirit upon me, and last night I dreamed. All day I have fancied I saw blood here and there. Sometimes, when I have looked out of the window, the whole snow hath suddenly glared with red. Goodwife Sheldon, think you the Indians and the French have in truth gone back to Canada?"

Goodwife Sheldon hesitated a moment, then she spoke up cheerily. "In truth have they!" cried she. "John said but this noon that naught of them had been seen for some time."

"So David said," returned Silence; "but this heaviness will not be driven away. You know how Parson Williams hath spoken in warning in the pulpit and elsewhere, and besought us to be vigilant. He holdeth that the savages be not gone."

Hannah Sheldon smiled. "Parson Williams be a godly man, but prone ever to look upon the dark side," said she.

"If the Indians should come tonight—" said Silence.

"I tell ye they will not come, child. I shall lay me down in that bed a-trusting in the Lord, and having no fear against the time I shall arise from it."

"If the Indians should come—Goodwife Sheldon, be not angered, hear me. If they should come, I pray you keep David here to defend you in this house, and let him not out to seek me. You know well that our house be musket-proof as well as this, and it has long been agreed that they who live nearest, whose houses have not thick walls, shall come to ours and help us make defence. I pray you let not David out of the house to seek me, should there be a surprise tonight. I pray you give me your promise for this, Goodwife Sheldon."

Hannah Sheldon laughed. "In truth will I give thee the promise, if it make thee easier, child," said she. "At the very first war-screech will I tie David in the chimney-corner with my apron-string, unless you lend me yours. But there will be no war-screech tonight, nor tomorrow night, nor the night after that. The Lord will preserve His people that trust in Him. Today have I set a web of linen in the loom, and I have candles ready to dip tomorrow, and the day after that I have a quilting. I look not for Indians. If they come I will set them to work. Fear not for David, sweetheart. In truth you should have a bolder heart, an you look to be a soldier's wife some day."

"I would I had never been aught to him, that he might not be put in jeopardy to defend me!" said Silence, and her words seemed visible in a white cloud at her mouth.

"We must not stay here in the cold," said Goodwife Sheldon. "Out with ye, Silence, and have a sup of hot porridge, and then David shall see ye home."

Silence sipped a cup of the hot porridge obediently, then she pinned her red blanket over her head. Hannah Sheldon assisted her, bringing it warmly over her face. "'Tis bitter cold," she said. "Now have no more fear, Mistress Silence; the Indians will not come tonight; but do you come over tomorrow, and keep me company while I dip the candles."

"There'll be company enough—there'll be a whole house-ful," muttered the old woman in the corner, but nobody heeded her. She was a lonely and wretched old creature whom people sheltered from pity, although she was somewhat feared and held in ill repute. There were rumors that she was well versed in all the dark lore of witchcraft, and held commerce with unlawful beings. The children of Deerfield village looked askance at her, and clung to their mothers if they met her on the street, for they whispered among themselves that old Goody Crane rode through the air on a broom in the night-time.

Silence and David passed out into the keen night. "If you meet my Goodman, hasten him home, for the porridge is cool-ing," Hannah Sheldon called after them.

But they met not a soul on Deerfield street. They parted at Silence's door. David would have entered had she bidden him, but she said peremptorily that she had a hard task of spinning that evening, and then she wished him goodnight, and without a kiss, for Silence Hoit was chary of caresses. But tonight she called him back ere he was fairly in the street. "David," she called, and he ran back.

"What is it, Silence?" he asked.

She put back her blanket, threw her arms around his neck, and clung to him trembling.

"Why, sweetheart," he whispered, "what has come over thee?"

"You know—this house is made like—a fort," she said, bringing out her words in gasps, "and—there are muskets, and—powder stored in it, and—Captain Moulton, and his sons, and—John Carson will come, and make—a stand in it. I have—no fear should—the Indians come. Remember that I have no fear, and shall be safe here, David."

David laughed, and patted her clinging shoulders. "Yes, I will remember, Silence," he said; "but the Indians will not come."

"Remember that I am safe here, and have no fear," she repeated. Then she kissed him of her own accord, as if she had been his wife, and entered the house, and he went away, wondering.

Silence's aunt, Widow Eunice Bishop, did not look up when the door opened; she was knitting by the fire, sitting erect with her mouth pursed. She had a hostile expression, as if she were listening to some opposite argument. Silence hung her blanket on a peg; she stood irresolute a minute, then she breathed on the frosty window and cleared a little space through which she could look out. Her aunt gave a quick fierce glance at her, then she tossed back her head and knitted. Silence stood staring out of the little peep-hole in the frosty pane. Her aunt glanced at her again, then she spoke.

"I should think if you had been out gossiping and gadding for two hours, you had better get yourself at some work now," she said, "unless your heart be set on idling. A pretty housewife you'll make!"

"Come here quick, quick!" Silence cried out.

Her aunt started, but she would not get up; she knitted, scowling. "I cannot afford to idle if other folk can," said she. "I have no desire to keep running to windows and standing there gaping, as you have done all this day."

"Oh, aunt, I pray you to come," said Silence, and she turned her white face over her shoulder toward her aunt; "there is somewhat wrong surely."

Widow Bishop got up, still scowling, and went over to the window. Silence stood aside and pointed to the little clear circle in the midst of the frost. "Over there to the north," she said, in a quick, low voice.

Her aunt adjusted her horn spectacles and bent her head stiffly. "I see naught," said she.

"A red glare in the north!"

"A red glare in the north! Be ye out of your mind, wench! There be no red glare in the north. Everything be quiet in the town. Get ye away from the window and to your work. I have no more patience with such doings. Here have I left my knitting for nothing, and I just about setting the heel. You'd best keep to your spinning instead of spying out of the window at your own nightmares, and gadding about the town after David Walcott. Pretty doings for a modest maid, I call it, following after young men in this fashion!"

Silence turned on her aunt, and her blue eyes gleamed dark; she held up her head like a queen. "I follow not after young men," she said.

"Heard I not David Walcott's voice at the door? Went you not to Goody Sheldon's, where he lives? Was it not his voice—hey?"

"Yes, 'twas, an' I had a right to go there an I chose, an' 'twas naught unmaidenly," said Silence.

"'Twas unmaidenly in my day," retorted her aunt; "perhaps 'tis different now." She had returned to her seat, and was clashing her knitting-needles like two swords in a duel.

Silence pulled a spinning-wheel before the fire and fell to

work. The wheel turned so rapidly that the spokes were a revolving shadow; there was a sound as if a bee had entered the room.

"I staid at home, and your uncle did the courting," Widow Eunice Bishop continued, in a voice that demanded response.

But Silence made none. She went on spinning. Her aunt eyed her maliciously. "I never went after nightfall to his house that he might see me home," said she. "I trow my mother would have locked me up in the garret, and kept me on meal and water for a week, had I done aught so bold."

Silence spun on. Her aunt threw her head back, and knitted, jerking out her elbows. Neither of them spoke again until the clock struck nine. Then Widow Bishop wound her ball of yarn closer, and stuck in the knitting-needles, and rose. "'Tis time to put out the candle," she said, "and *I* have done a good day's work, and feel need of rest. They that have idled cannot make it up by wasting tallow." She threw open the door that led to her bedroom, and a blast of icy confined air rushed in. She untied the black cap that framed her nervous face austerely, and her gray head, with its tight rosette of hair on the crown, appeared. Silence set her spinning-wheel back, and raked the ashes over the hearth fire.

Then she took the candle and climbed the stairs to her own chamber. Her aunt was already in bed, her pale, white-frilled face sunk in the icy feather pillow. But she did not bid her goodnight: not on account of her anger; there was seldom any such formal courtesy exchanged between the women. Silence's chamber had one side sloping with the slope of the roof, and in it were two dormer-windows looking toward the north. She set her candle on the table, breathed on one of these windows, as she had on the one downstairs, and looked out. She stood there several minutes, then she turned away, shaking her head. The room was very cold. She let down her smooth fair hair, and her fingers began to redden; she took off her kerchief; then she stopped, and looked hesitatingly at her bed, with its blue curtains. She set her mouth hard, and put on her kerchief. Then she sat down on the edge of her bed and waited.

After a while she pulled a quilt from the bed and wrapped it around her. Still she did not shiver. She had blown out the candle, and the room was very dark. All her nerves seemed screwed tight like fiddle-strings, and her thoughts beat upon them and made terrific waves of sound in her ears. She saw sparks and flashes like diamond fire in the darkness. She had her hands clinched tight, but she did not feel her hands nor her feet—she did not feel her whole body. She sat so until two o'clock in the morning. When the clock down in the keeping-room struck the hours, the peals shocked her back for a minute to her old sense of herself; then she lost it again. Just after the clock struck two, while the silvery reverberation of the bell tone was still in her ears, and she was breathing a little freer, a great rosy glow suffused the frosty windows. A horrible discord of sound arose without. Above everything else came something like a peal of laughter from wild beasts or fiends.

Silence arose and went down stairs. Her aunt rushed out of her bedroom, shrieking, and caught hold of her. "Oh, Silence, what is it, what is it?" she cried.

"Get away till I light a candle," said Silence. She fairly pushed her aunt off, shovelled the ashes from the coals in the fireplace, and lighted a candle. Then she threw some wood on the smouldering fire. Her aunt was running around the room screaming. There came a great pound on the door.

"It's the Indians! it's the Indians! don't let 'em in!" shrieked her aunt. "Don't let them in! don't let them!" She placed her lean shoulder in her white bed-gown against the door. "Go away! go away!" she yelled. "You can't come in! O Lord Almighty, save us!"

"You stand off," said Silence. She took hold of her aunt's shoulders. "Be quiet," she commanded. Then she called out, in a firm voice, "Who is there?"

At the shout in response she drew the great iron bolts quickly and flung open the heavy nail-studded door. There was a press of frantic white-faced people into the room; then the door was slammed to and the bolts shot. It was very still in the room, except for the shuffling rush of the men's feet and now and then a stern gasping order. The children did not cry; all the noise was without. The house might have stood in the midst of some awful wilderness peopled with fiendish beasts, from the noise without. The cries seemed actually in the room. The children's eyes glared white over their mothers' shoulders.

The men hurriedly strengthened the window-shutters with props of logs, and fitted the muskets into the loop-holes. Suddenly there was a great crash at the door and a wilder yell outside. The muskets opened fire, and some of the women rushed to the door and pressed fiercely against it with their delicate shoulders, their white desperate faces turning back dumbly, like a spiritual phalanx of defence. Silence and her aunt were among them.

Suddenly Widow Eunice Bishop, at a fresh onslaught upon the door and a fiercer yell, lifted up her voice and shrieked back in a rage as mad as theirs. Her speech, too, was almost inarticulate, and the sense of it lost in a savage frenzy; her tongue stuttered over abusive epithets; but for a second she prevailed over the terrible chorus without. It was like the solo of a fury. Then louder yells drowned her out; the muskets cracked faster; the men rammed in the charges; the savages fell back somewhat; the blows on the door ceased.

Silence ran up the stairs to her chamber, and peeped cautiously out of a little dormer-window. Deerfield village was roaring with flames, the sky and snow were red, and leaping through the glare came the painted savages, a savage white face and the waving sword of a French officer in their midst. The awful war-whoops and the death-cries of her friends and neighbours sounded in her ears. She saw, close under her window, the dark sweep of the tomahawk, the quick glance of the scalping-knife, and the red starting of caps of blood. She saw infants dashed through the air, and the backward-straining forms of shrieking women dragged down the street; but she saw not David Walcott anywhere.

She eyed in an agony some dark bodies lying like logs in the snow. A wild impulse seized her to run out, turn their dead faces, and see that none of them was her lover's. Her room was full of red light; everything in it showed distinctly. The roof of the next house crashed in, and the sparks and cinders shot up like a volcano. There was a great outcry of terror from below, and Silence hurried down. The Indians were trying to fire the house from the west side. They had piled a bank of brush against it, and the men had hacked new loop-holes and were beating them back.

John Carson's wife clutched Silence as she entered the keeping-room. "They are trying to set the house on fire," she gasped, "and—the bullets are giving out!" The woman held a little child hugged close to her breast; she strained him closer. "They shall not have him, anyway," she said. Her mouth looked white and stiff.

"Put him down and help, then," said Silence. She began pulling the pewter plates off the dresser.

"What be you doing with my pewter plates?" screamed her aunt at her elbow.

Silence said nothing. She went on piling the plates under her arm.

"Think you I will have the pewter plates I have had ever since I was wed melted to make bullets for those limbs of Satan?"

Silence carried the plates to the fire; the women piled on wood and made it hotter. John Carson's wife laid her baby on the settle and helped, and Widow Bishop brought out her pewter spoons, and her silver cream-jug when the pewter ran low, and finally her dead husband's knee-buckles from the cedar chest. All the pewter and silver in Widow Eunice Bishop's house was melted down on that night. The women worked with desperate zeal to supply the men with bullets, and just before the ammunition failed, the Indians left Deerfield village, with their captives in their train.

The men had stopped firing at last. Everything was quiet outside, except for the flurry of musket-shots down on the meadow, where the skirmish was going on between the Hatfield men and the retreating French and Indians. The dawn was breaking, but not a shutter had been stirred in the Bishop house; the inmates were clustered together, their ears straining for another outburst of slaughter.

Suddenly there was a strange crackling sound overhead; a puff of hot smoke came into the room from the stairway. The roof had caught fire from the shower of sparks, and the stanch house that had withstood all the fury of the savages was going the way of its neighbours.

The men rushed up the stair, and fell back. "We can't save it!" Captain Isaac Moulton said, hoarsely. He was an old man, and his white hair tossed wildly around his powder-blackened face.

Widow Eunice Bishop scuttled into her bedroom, and got her best silk pelisse and her gilt-framed looking-glass. "Silence, get out the feather bed!" she shrieked.

The keeping-room was stifling with smoke. Captain Moulton loosened a window-shutter cautiously and peered out. "I see no sign of the savages," he said. They unbolted the door, and opened it inch by inch, but there was no exultant shout in response. The crack of muskets on the meadow sounded louder; that was all.

Widow Eunice Bishop pushed forward before the others; the danger by fire to her household goods had driven her own danger from her mind, which could compass but one terror at a time. "Let me forth!" she cried; and she laid the looking-glass and silk pelisse on the snow, and pelted back into the smoke for her feather bed and the best andirons.

Silence carried out the spinning-wheel, and the others caught up various articles which they had wit to see in the panic. They piled them up on the snow outside, and huddled together, staring fearfully down the village street. They saw, amid the smouldering ruins, Ensign John Sheldon's house standing.

"We must make for that," said Captain Isaac Moulton, and they started. The men went before and behind, with their muskets in readiness, and the women and children walked between. Widow Bishop carried the pelisse and looking-glass; somebody had helped her to bring out her feather bed, and she had dragged it to a clean place well away from the burning house.

226

The dawn-light lay pale and cold in the east; it was steadily overcoming the fire-glow from the ruins. Nobody would have known Deerfield village. The night before the sun had gone down upon the snowy slants of humble roofs and the peaceful rise of smoke from pleasant hearth fires. The curtained windows had gleamed out one by one with mild candle-light, and serene faces of white-capped matrons preparing supper had passed them. Now, on both sides of Deerfield street were beds of glowing red coals; grotesque ruins of door-posts and chimneys in the semblances of blackened martyrs stood crumbling in the midst of them, and twisted charred heaps, which the people eyed trembling, lay in the old doorways. The snow showed great red patches in the gathering light, and in them lay still bodies that seemed to move.

Silence Hoit sprang out from the hurrying throng, and turned the head of one dead man whose face she could not see. The horror of his red crown did not move her. She only saw that he was not David Walcott. She stooped and wiped off her hands in some snow.

"That is Israel Bennett," the others groaned.

John Carson's wife had been the dead man's sister. She hugged her baby tighter, and pressed more closely to her husband's back. There was no longer any sound of musketry on the meadows. There was not a sound to be heard except the wind in the dry trees and the panting breaths of the knot of people.

A dead baby lay directly in the path, and a woman caught it up, and tried to warm it at her breast. She wrapped her cloak around it, and wiped its little bloody face with her apron. "'Tis not dead," she declared, frantically; "the child is not dead!" She had not shed a tear nor uttered a wail before, but now she began sobbing aloud over the dead child. It was Goodwife Barnard's, and no kin to her. She was a single woman. The others were looking right and left for lurking savages. She looked only at the little cold face on her bosom. "The child breathes," she said, and hurried on faster that she might get succour for it.

The party halted before Ensign John Sheldon's house. The

stout door was fast, but there was a hole in it, as if hacked by a tomahawk. The men tried it and shook it. "Open, open, Goodwife Sheldon!" they hallooed. "Friends! friends! Open the door!" But there was no response.

Silence Hoit left the throng at the door, and began clambering up on a slant of icy snow to a window which was flung wide open. The window-sill was stained with blood, and so was the snow.

One of the men caught Silence and tried to hold her back. "There may be Indians in there," he whispered, hoarsely.

But Silence broke away from him, and was in through the window, and the men followed her, and unbolted the door for the women, who pressed in wildly, and flung it to again. And a child who was among them, little Comfort Arms, stationed herself directly with her tiny back against the door, with her mouth set like a soldier's, and her blue eyes gleaming fierce under her flaxen locks. "They shall not get in," said she. Somehow she had gotten hold of a great horse-pistol, which she carried like a doll.

Nobody heeded her, Silence least of all. She stared about the room, with her lips parted. Right before her on the hearth lay a little three-year-old girl, Mercy Sheldon, her pretty head in a pool of blood, but Silence cast only an indifferent glance when the others gathered about her, groaning and sighing.

Suddenly Silence sprang toward a dark heap near the pantry door, but it was only a woman's quilted petticoat.

The spinning-wheel lay broken on the floor, and all the simple furniture was strewn about wildly. Silence went into Goodwife Sheldon's bedroom, and the others followed her, trembling, all except little Comfort Arms, who stood unflinchingly with her back pressed against the door, and the single woman, Grace Mather; she staid behind, and put wood on the fire after she had picked up the quilted petticoat, and laid the dead baby tenderly wrapped in it on the settle. Then she pulled the settle forward before the fire, and knelt before it, and fell to chafing the little limbs of the dead baby, weeping as she did so.

Goodwife Sheldon's bedroom was in wild disorder. A candle still burned, although it was very low, on the table, whose linen cover had great red finger-prints on it. Goodwife Sheldon's decent clothes were tossed about on the floor; the curtains of the bed were half torn away. Silence pressed forward unshrinkingly toward the bed; the others, even the men, hung back. There lay Goodwife Sheldon dead in her bed. All the light in the room, the candle-light and the low daylight, seemed to focus upon her white frozen profile propped stiffly on the pillow, where she had fallen back when the bullet came through that hole in the door.

Silence looked at her. "Where is David, Goodwife Sheldon?" said she.

Eunice Bishop sprang forward. "Be you clean out of your mind, Silence Hoit?" she cried. "Know you not she's dead? She's dead! Oh, she's dead, she's dead! An' here's her best silk hood trampled underfoot on the floor!" Eunice snatched up the hood, and seized Silence by the arm, but she pushed her back.

"Where is David? Where is he gone?" she demanded again of the dead woman.

The other women came crowding around Silence then, and tried to soothe her and reason with her, while their own faces were white with horror and woe. Goodwife Sarah Spear, an old woman whose sons lay dead in the street outside, put an arm around the girl, and tried to draw her head to her broad bosom.

"Mayhap thou'lt will find him, sweetheart," she said. "He's not among the dead out there."

But Silence broke away from the motherly arm, and sped wildly through the other rooms, with the people at her heels, and her aunt crying vainly after her. They found no more dead in the house; naught but ruin and disorder, and bloody foot-prints and handprints of savages.

When they returned to the keeping-room, Silence seated herself on a stool by the fire, and held out her hands toward the blaze to warm them. The daylight was broad now, and the great clock that had come from overseas ticked; the Indians had not touched that.

Captain Isaac Moulton lifted little Mercy Sheldon from the hearth and carried her to her dead mother in the bedroom, and two of the older women went in there and shut the door. Little Comfort Arms still stood with her back against the outer door, and Grace Mather tended the dead baby on the settle.

"What do ye with that dead child?" a woman called out roughly to her.

"I tell ye 'tis not dead; it breathes," returned Grace Mather; and she never turned her harsh plain face from the dead child.

"An' I tell ye 'tis dead."

"An' I tell ye 'tis not dead. I need but some hot posset for it."

Goodwife Carson began to weep. She hugged her own living baby tighter. "Let her alone!" she sobbed. "I wonder our wits be not all gone." She went sobbing over to little Comfort Arms at the door. "Come away, sweetheart, and draw near the fire," she pleaded, brokenly.

The little girl looked obstinately up at her. "They shall not come in," she said. "The wicked savages shall not come in again."

"No more shall they, an the Lord be willing, sweet. But, I pray you, come away from the door now."

Comfort shook her head, and she looked like her father as he fought on the Deerfield meadows.

"The savages be gone, sweet."

But Comfort answered not a word, and Goodwife Carson sat down and began to nurse her baby. One of the women hung the porridge-kettle over the fire; another put some potatoes in the ashes to bake. Presently the two women came out of Goodwife Sheldon's bedroom with grave, strained faces, and held their stiff blue fingers out to the hearth fire.

Eunice Bishop, who was stirring the porridge, looked at them with sharp curiosity. "How look they?" she whispered.

"As peaceful as if they slept," replied Goodwife Spear, who

was one of the women.

"And the child's head?"

"We put on her little white cap with the lace frills."

Eunice stirred the bubbling porridge, scowling in the heat and steam; some of the women laid the table with Hannah Sheldon's linen cloth and pewter dishes, and presently the breakfast was dished up.

Little Comfort Arms had sunk at the foot of the nail-studded door in a deep slumber. She slept at her post like the faithless sentry whose slumbers the night before had brought about the destruction of Deerfield village. Goodwife Spear raised her up, but her curly head drooped helplessly.

"Wake up, Comfort, and have a sup of hot porridge," she called in her ear.

She led her over to the table, Comfort stumbling weakly at arm's-length, and set her on a stool with a dish of porridge before her, which she ate uncertainly in a dazed fashion, with her eyes filming and her head nodding.

They all gathered gravely around the table except Silence Hoit and Grace Mather. Silence sat still, staring at the fire, and Grace had dipped out a little cup of the hot porridge, and was trying to feed it to the dead baby, with crooning words.

"Silence, why come you not to the table?" her aunt called out.

"I want nothing," answered Silence.

"I see not why you should so set yourself up before the others, as having so much more to bear," said Eunice, sharply. "There be Goodwife Spear, with her sons unburied on the road yonder, and she doth eat her porridge with good relish."

John Carson's wife set her baby on her husband's knee, and carried a dish of porridge to Silence.

"Try and eat it, sweet," she whispered. She was near Silence's age.

Silence looked up at her. "I want it not," said she.

"But he may not be dead, sweet. He may presently be home. You would not he should find you spent and fainting. Perchance

231

he may have wounds for you to tend."

Silence seized the dish and began to eat the porridge in great spoonfuls, gulping it down fast.

The people at the table eyed her sadly and whispered, and they also cast frequent glances at Grace Mather bending over the dead baby. Once Captain Isaac Moulton called out to her in his gruff old voice, which he tried to soften, and she answered back, sharply: "Think ye I will leave this child while it breathes, Captain Isaac Moulton? In faith I be the only one of ye all that hath regard to it."

But suddenly, when the meal was half over, Grace Mather arose, and gathered up the little dead baby, carried it into Goodwife Sheldon's bedroom, and was gone some time.

"She has lost her wits," said Eunice Bishop. "Think you not we should follow her? She may do some harm."

"Nay, let her be," said Goodwife Spear.

When at last Grace Mather came out of the bedroom, and they all turned to look at her, her face was stern but quite composed. "I found a little clean linen shift in the chest," she said to Goodwife Spear, who nodded gravely. Then she sat down at the table and ate.

The people, as they ate, cast frequent glances at the barred door and the shuttered windows. The daylight was broad outside, but there was no glimmer of it in the room, and the candles were lighted. They dared not yet remove the barricades, and the muskets were in readiness: the Indians might return.

All at once there was a shrill clamour at the door, and men sprang to their muskets. The women clutched each other, panting.

"Unbar the door!" shrieked a quavering old voice. "I tell ye, unbar the door! I be nigh frozen a-standing here. Unbar the door! The Indians be gone hours ago."

"'Tis Goody Crane," cried Eunice Bishop.

Captain Isaac Moulton shot back the bolts and opened the door a little way, while the men stood close at his back, and Goody Crane slid in like a swift black shadow out of the daylight.

She crouched down close to the fire, trembling and groaning, and the women gave her some hot porridge.

"Where have ye been?" demanded Eunice Bishop.

"Where they found me not," replied the old woman, and there was a sudden leer like a light in the gloom of her great hood. She motioned toward the bedroom door.

"Goody Sheldon sleeps late this morning, and so doth Mercy," said she. "I trow she will not dip her candles today."

The people looked at each other; a subtler horror than that of the night before shook their spirits.

Captain Isaac Moulton towered over the old woman on the hearth. "How knew you Goodwife Sheldon and Mercy were dead?" he asked, sternly.

The old woman leered up at him undauntedly; her head bobbed. There was a curious grotesqueness about her blanketed and hooded figure when in motion. There was so little of the old woman herself visible that motion surprised, as it would have done in a puppet. "Told I not Goody Sheldon last night she would never stir porridge again?" said she. "Who stirred the porridge this morning? I trow Goody Sheldon's hands be too stiff and too cold, though they have stirred well in their day. Hath she dipped her candles yet? Hath she begun on her weaving? I trow 'twill be a long day ere Mary Sheldon's linen-chest be filled, if she herself go a-gadding to Canada and her mother sleep so late."

"Eat this hot porridge and stop your croaking," said Goodwife Spear, stooping over her.

The old woman extended her two shaking hands for the dish. "That was what she said last night," she returned. "The living echo the dead, and that be enough wisdom for a witch."

"You'll be burned for a witch yet, Goody Crane, an you be not careful," cried Eunice Bishop.

"There be fire enough outside to burn all the witches in the land," muttered the old woman, sipping her porridge. Suddenly she eyed Silence sitting motionless opposite. "Where be your sweetheart this fine morning, Silence Hoit?" she inquired.

Silence looked at her. There was a strange likeness between the glitter in her blue eyes and that in Goody Crane's black ones.

The old woman's great hood nodded over the porridge-dish. "I can tell ye, Mistress Silence," she said, thickly, as she ate. "He be gone to Canada on a moose-hunt, and unless I be far wrong, he hath taken thy wits with him."

"How know you David Walcott is gone to Canada?" cried Eunice Bishop; and Silence stared at her with her hard blue eyes.

Silence's soft fair hair hung all matted like uncombed flax over her pale cheeks. There was a rigid, dead look about her girlish forehead and her sweet mouth.

"I know," returned Goody Crane, nodding her head.

The women washed the pewter dishes, set them back on the dresser, and swept the floor. Little Comfort Arms had been carried up stairs and laid in the bed whence poor Mary Sheldon had been dragged and haled to Canada. The men stood talking near their stacked muskets. One of the shutters had been opened and the candles put out. The winter sun shone in the window as it had shone before, but the poor folk in Ensign Sheldon's keeping-room saw it with a certain shock, as if it were a stranger. That morning their own hearts had in them such strangeness that they transferred it like motion to all familiar objects. The very iron dogs in the Sheldon fireplace seemed on the leap with tragedy, and the porridge-kettle swung darkly out of some former age.

Now and then one of the men opened the door cautiously and peered out and listened. The reek of the smouldering village came in at the door, but there was not a sound except the whistling howl of the savage north wind, which still swept over the valley. There was not a shot to be heard from the meadows. The men discussed the wisdom of leaving the women for a short space and going forth to explore, but Widow Eunice Bishop interposed, thrusting in her sharp face among them.

"Here we be," scolded she, "a passel of women and children, and Hannah Sheldon and Mercy a-lying dead, and me with my house burnt down, and nothing saved except my silk pelisse and my looking-glass and my feather bed, and it's a mercy if that's not all smooched, and you talk of going off and leaving us!"

The men looked doubtfully at each other; then there was the hissing creak of footsteps on the snow outside, and Widow Bishop screamed. "Oh, the Indians have come back!" she proclaimed.

Silence looked up.

The door was tried from without.

"Who's there?" cried out Captain Moulton.

"John Sheldon," responded a hoarse voice. "Who's inside?"

Captain Moulton threw open the door, and John Sheldon stood there. His severe and sober face was painted like an Indian's with blood and powder grime; he stood staring in at the company.

"Come in, quick, and let us bar the door!" screamed Eunice Bishop.

John Sheldon came in hesitatingly, and stood looking around the room.

"Have you but just come from the meadows?" inquired Captain Moulton. But John Sheldon did not seem to hear him. He stared at the company, who all stood still staring back at him; then he looked hard and long at the doors, as if expecting some one to enter. The eyes of the others followed his, but no one spoke.

"Where's Hannah?" asked John Sheldon.

Then the women began to weep.

"She's in there," sobbed John Carson's wife, pointing to the bedroom door—"in there with little Mercy, Goodman Sheldon."

"Is—the child hurt, and—Hannah a-tending her?"

The women wept, and pushed each other forward to tell him, but Captain Isaac Moulton spoke out, and drove the knife home like an honest soldier, who will kill if he must, but not mangle.

"Goodwife Sheldon lies yonder, shot dead in her bed, and we found the child dead on the hearth-stone," said Isaac Moulton.

John Sheldon turned his gaze on him.

"The judgments of the Lord are just and righteous altogether," said Isaac Moulton, confronting him with stern defiance.

"Amen," returned John Sheldon. He took off his cloak, and hung it up on the peg where he was used.

"Where is David Walcott?" asked Silence, standing before him.

"David, he be gone with the Indians to Canada, and the boys, Ebenezer and Remembrance."

"Where is David?"

"I tell ye, lass, he be gone with the French and Indians to Canada; and you need be thankful he was but your sweetheart, and ye not wed, with a half-score of babes to be taken too. The curse that was upon the women of Jerusalem is upon the women of Deerfield." John Sheldon looked sternly into Silence's white wild face; then his voice softened. "Take heart, lass," said he. "Erelong I shall go to Governor Dudley and get help, and then after them to Canada, and fetch them back. Take heart; I will fetch thee thy sweetheart presently."

Silence returned to her seat in the fireplace. Goody Crane looked across at her. "He will come back over the north meadow," she whispered. "Keep watch over the north meadow; but 'twill be a long day ere ye see him."

Silence paid seemingly little heed. She paid little heed to Ensign John Sheldon relating how the French and Indians, with Hertel de Rouville at their head, were on the road to Canada with their captives; of the fight on the meadow between the retreating foe and the brave band of Deerfield and Hatfield men, who had made a stand there to intercept them; how they had been obliged to cease firing because the captives were threatened; and the pitiful tale of Parson John Williams, with two children dead, dragged through the wilderness with the others, and his sick wife.

"Had folk listened to him, we had all been safe in our good houses with our belongings," cried Eunice Bishop.

"They will not drag Goodwife Williams far," said Goody Crane, "nor the babe at her breast. I trow well it hath stopped wailing ere now."

"How know you that?" questioned Eunice Bishop, turning sharply on her.

But the old woman only nodded her head, and Silence paid no heed, for she was not there. Her slender girlish shape sat by the hearth fire in John Sheldon's house in Deerfield, her fair head showed like a delicate flower, but Silence Hoit was following her lover to Canada. Every step that he took painfully through pathless forests, on treacherous ice, and desolate snow fields, she took more painfully still; every knife gleaming over his head she saw. She bore his every qualm of hunger and pain and cold, and it was all the harder because they struck on her bare heart with no flesh between, for she sat in the flesh in Deerfield, and her heart went with her lover to Canada.

The sun stood higher, but it was still bitter cold; the blue frost on the windows did not melt, and the icicles on the eaves, which nearly touched the sharp snow-drifts underneath, did not drip. The desolate survivors of the terrible night began work among the black ruins of their homes. They cared as well as they might for the dead in Deerfield street, and the dead on the meadow where the fight had been. Their muscles were all tense with the cold, their faces seamed and blue with it, but their hearts were strained with a fiercer cold than that. Not one man of them but had one or more slain, with dead face upturned seeking his in the morning light or on that awful road to Canada. Ever as the men worked they turned their eyes northward, and met grimly the icy blast of the north wind, and sometimes to their excited fancies it seemed to bring to their ears the cries of their friends who were facing it also, and they stood still and listened.

Silence Hoit crept out of the house and down the road a little way, and then stood looking over the meadow toward the north. Her fair hair tossed in the wind, her pale cheeks turned pink, the wind struck full upon her delicate figure. She had come out without her blanket.

"David!" she called. "David! David! David!" The north wind bore down upon her, shrieking with a wild fury like a savage of the air; the dry branches of a small tree near her struck her in the face. "David!" she called again. "David! David!" She swelled out her white throat like a bird, and her voice was shrill and sweet and far-reaching. The men moving about on the meadow below, and stooping over the dead, looked up at her, but she did not heed them. She had come through a break in the palisades; on each side of her the frozen snow-drifts slanted sharply to their tops; over the drifts the enemy had passed the night before, and they glittered with blue lights like glaciers in the morning sun.

The men on the meadow saw Silence's hair blowing like a yellow banner between the drifts of snow.

"The poor lass has come out bareheaded," said Ensign Sheldon. "She is near out of her mind for David Walcott."

"A man should have no sweetheart in these times, unless he would her heart be broke," said a young man beside him. He was hardly more than a boy, and his face was as rosy as a girl's in the wind. He kept close to Ensign Sheldon, and his mind was full of young Mary Sheldon travelling to Canada on her weary little feet. He had often, on a Sabbath day, looked across the meeting-house at her, and thought that there was no maiden like her in Deerfield.

Ensign John Sheldon thought of his sweetheart lying with her heart still in her freezing bedroom, and stooped over a dead Hatfield man whose face was frozen into the snow.

The young man, whose name was Freedom Wells, bent over to help him. Then he started. "What's that?" he cried.

"'Tis only Silence Hoit calling David Walcott again," replied Ensign Sheldon.

The voice had sounded like Mary Sheldon's to Freedom. The tears rolled over his boyish cheeks as he put his hands into the snow and tried to dig it away from the dead man's face.

"David! David! David!" called Silence.

Suddenly her aunt threw a wiry arm around her. "Be you gone clean daft," she shrieked against the wind, "standing here calling David Walcott? Know you not he is a half-day's journey toward Canada, an the savages have not scalped him and left him by the way? Standing here with your hair blowing and no blanket! Into the house with ye!"

Silence followed her aunt unresistingly. The women in Ensign Sheldon's house were hard at work. They were baking in the great brick oven, spinning, and even dipping poor Goodwife Sheldon's candles.

"Bind up your hair, like an honest maid, and go to spinning," said Eunice, and she pointed to the spinning-wheel which had been saved from her own house. "We that be spared have to work, and not sit down and trot our own hearts on our knees. There be scarce a yard of linen left in Deerfield, to say naught of woollen cloth. Bind up your hair!"

And Silence bound up her hair, and sat down by her wheel meekly, and yet with a certain dignity. Indeed, through all the disorder of her mind, that delicate maiden dignity never forsook her, and there was never aught but respect shown her.

As time went on, it became quite evident that although the fair semblance of Silence Hoit still walked the Deerfield street, sat in the meeting-house, and toiled at the spinning-wheel and the loom, yet she was as surely not all there as though she had been haled to Canada with the other captives on that terrible February night. And it became the general opinion that Silence Hoit would never be quite her old self again and walk in the goodly company of all her fair wits unless David Walcott should be redeemed from captivity and restored to her. Then, it was accounted possible, the mending of the calamity which brought her disorder upon her might remove it.

"Ye wait," Widow Eunice Bishop would say, hetchelling flax the while as though it were the scalp-locks of the enemy—"ye wait. If once David Walcott show his face, ye'll see Silence Hoit be not so lacking. She hath a tenderer heart than some I could mention, who go about smiling when their nearest of kin lay in torment in Indian lodges. She cares naught for picking up a new sweetheart. She hath a steady heart that be not so easy turned as some. Silence was never a light hussy, a-dancing hither and thither off the bridle-path for a new flower on the bushes. An', for all ye call her lacking now, there be not a maid in Deerfield does such a day's task as she."

And that last statement was quite true. All the Deerfield women, the matrons and maidens, toiled unceasingly, with a kind of stern patience like that which served their husbands and lovers in the frontier cornfields, and which served all the dauntless border settlers, who were forced continually to rebuild after destruction, like wayside ants whose nests are always being trampled underfoot. There was need of unflinching toil at wheel and loom, for there was great scarcity of household linen in Deerfield, and Silence Hoit's shapely white maiden hands flinched less than any.

Nevertheless, many a day, in the morning when the snowy meadows were full of blue lights, at sunset when all the snow levels were rosy, but more particularly in wintry moonlight when the country was like a waste of silver, would Silence Hoit leave suddenly her household task, and hasten to the terrace overlooking the north meadow, and shriek out: "David! David! David Walcott!"

The village children never jeered at her, as they would sometimes jeer at Goody Crane if not restrained by their elders. They eyed with a mixture of wonder and admiration Silence's beautiful bewildered face, with the curves of gold hair around the pink cheeks, and the fret-work of tortoise-shell surmounting it. David Walcott had given Silence her shell comb, and she was never seen without it.

Many a time when Silence called to David from the terrace of the north meadow, some of the little village maids in their homespun pinafores would join her and call with her. They had no fear of her, as they had of Goody Crane.

Indeed, Goody Crane, after the massacre, was in worse repute than ever in Deerfield. There were dark rumours concerning her whereabouts upon that awful night. Some among the devout and godly were fain to believe that the old woman had been in league with the powers of darkness and their allies the savages, and had so escaped harm. Some even whispered that in the thickest of the slaughter, when Deerfield was in the midst of that storm of fire, old Goody Crane's laugh had been heard, and one, looking up, had spied her high overhead riding her broomstick, her face red with the glare of the fire. The old woman was sheltered under protest, and had Deerfield not been a frontier town, and graver matters continually in mind, she might have come to harm in consequence of the gloomy suspicions concerning her.

Many a night after the massacre would the windows fly up and anxious faces peer out. It was as if the ears of the people were tuned up to the pitch of the Indian war-whoops, and their very thoughts made the nights ring with them.

The palisades were well looked to; there was never a slope of frozen snow again to form foothold for the enemy, and the sentry never slept at his post. But the anxious women listened all winter for the war-whoops, and many a time it seemed they heard them. In the midst of their nervous terror it was often a sore temptation to consult old Goody Crane, since she was held to have occult knowledge.

"I'll warrant old Goody Crane could tell us in a twinkling whether or no the Indians would come before morning," Eunice Bishop said one fierce windy night that called to mind the one of the massacre.

"Knowledge got in unlawful ways would avail us naught," returned Goodwife Spear. "I trow the Lord be yet able to protect His people."

"I doubt not that," said Eunice Bishop, "but I would like well to know if I had best bury my pelisse and my spinning-wheel and looking-glass in a snow-drift to-night. I have no mind the Indians shall get them. I warrant she knoweth well."

But Eunice Bishop did not consult Goody Crane, although she watched her narrowly and had a sharp ear to her mutterings as she sat in the chimney-corner. Eunice and Silence were living in John Sheldon's house, as did many of the survivors for some time after the massacre. It was the largest house in the village, and most of its original inhabitants were dead or gone into captivity. The people all huddled together fearfully in the few houses that were left, and the women's spinning-wheels and looms jostled each other.

As soon as the weather moderated, the work of building new dwellings commenced, and went on bravely with the advance of the spring. The air was full of the calls of spring birds and the strokes of axes and hammers. A little house was built on the site of their old one for Widow Bishop and Silence Hoit. Widow Sarah Spear also lived with them, and Goody Crane took shelter at their fireside for the most part. So they were a household of women, with loaded muskets at hand, and spinning-wheels and looms at full hum. They had but a scanty household store, although Widow Bishop tried in every way to increase it. Several times during the summer she took perilous journeys to Hatfield and Squakheak, for the sake of bartering skeins of yarn or rolls of wool for household articles. In December, when Ensign Sheldon with young Freedom Wells went down to Boston to consult with Governor Dudley concerning an expedition to Canada to redeem the captives, Widow Eunice Bishop, having saved a few shillings, burdened him with a commission to purchase for her a new cap and a pair of bellows. She was much angered when he returned without them, having clean forgotten them in his press of business.

On the day when John Sheldon and Freedom Wells started upon their terrible journey of three hundred miles to redeem the captives, Eunice Bishop scolded well as she spun by her hearth fire.

"I trow they will bring back nobody," said she, her nose high in air, and her voice shrilling over the drone of the wheel; "an they could not do the bidding of a poor lone widow-woman, and fetch her not the cap and bellows from Boston, they'll fetch nobody home from Canada. I would I had ear of Governor Dudley. I trow men with minds upon their task would be sent."

Eunice kept jerking her head as she scolded, and spun like a bee angry with its own humming.

Silence sat knitting, and paid no heed. She had paid no heed to any of the talk about Ensign Sheldon's and Freedom Wells's journey to Canada. She had not seemed to listen when Widow Spear had tried to explain the matter to her. "It may be, sweetheart, if it be the will of the Lord, that they will bring David back to thee," she had said over and over, and Silence had knitted and made no response.

She was the only one in Deerfield who was not torn with excitement and suspense as the months went by, and the only one unmoved by joy or disappointment when in May John Sheldon and Freedom Wells returned with five of the captives. But David Walcott was not among them.

"Said I not 'twould be so?" scolded Eunice Bishop. "Knew I not 'twould be so when they forgot to get the cap and the bellows in Boston? The one of all the captives that could have saved a poor maid's wits they leave behind. There's Mary Sheldon come home, and she a-colouring red before Freedom Wells, and everybody in the room a-seeing it. I trow they might have done somewhat for poor Silence," and Eunice broke down and wailed and wept, but Silence shed not a tear. Before long she stole out to the terrace and called "David! David! David!" over the north meadow, and strained her blue eyes toward Canada, and held out her fair arms, but it was with no new disappointment and desolation.

There was never a day nor a night that Silence called not over the north meadow like a spring bird from the bush to her absent mate, and people heard her and sighed and shuddered. One afternoon in the last of the month of June, as Silence was thrusting her face between the leaves of a wild cherry-tree and calling "David! David! David!" David himself broke through the thicket and stood before her. He and three other young men had escaped from their captivity and come home, and the four, crawling half dead across the meadow, had heard Silence's voice from the terrace above, and David, leaving the others, had made his way to her.

"Silence!" he said, and held out his poor arms, panting.

But Silence looked past him. "David! David! David Walcott!" she called.

David could scarcely stand for trembling, and he grasped a branch of the cherry-tree to steady himself, and swayed with it.

"Know—you not—who I am, Silence?" he said.

But she made as though she did not hear, and called again, always looking past him. And David Walcott, being near spent with fatigue and starvation, wound himself feebly around the trunk of the tree, and the tears dropped over his cheeks as he looked at her; and she called past him, until some women came and led him away and tried to comfort him, telling him how it was with her, and that she would soon know him when he looked more like himself.

But the summer wore away and she did not know him, although he constantly followed her beseechingly. His elders even reproved him for paying so little heed to his work in the colony. "It is not meet for a young man to be so weaned from usefulness by grief for a maid," said they. But David Walcott would at any time leave his reaping-hook in the corn and his axe in the tree, leave aught but his post as sentry, when he heard Silence calling him over the north meadow. He would stand at her elbow and say, in his voice that broke like a woman's: "Here I be, sweetheart, at thy side. I pray thee turn thy head." But she would not let her eyes rest upon him for more than a second's space, but turned them ever past him toward Canada, and called in his very ears with a sad longing that tore his heart: "David! David! David!" It was as if her mind, reaching out ever and speeding fast in search of him, had gotten such impetus that she passed the very object of her search and knew it not.

Now and then would David Walcott grow desperate, fling his arms around her, and kiss her upon her cold delicate lips and cheeks as if he would make her recognize him by force; but she would free herself from him with a passionless resentment that left him helpless.

One day in autumn, when the borders of the Deerfield meadows were a smoky purple with wild asters, and golden-rods flashed out like golden flames in the midst of them, David Walcott had been pleading vainly with Silence as she stood calling on the north terrace. Suddenly he turned and rushed away, and his face was all convulsed like a weeping boy's. As he came out of the thicket he met the old woman Goody Crane, and would fain have hidden his face from her, but she stopped him.

"Prithee stop a moment's space, Master David Walcott," said she.

"What would you?" David cried out in a surly tone, and he dashed the back of his hand across his eyes.

"'Tis full moon tonight," said the old woman, in a whisper. "Come out here tonight when the moon shall be an hour high, and I promise ye she shall know ye."

The young man stared at her.

"I tell ye Mistress Silence Hoit shall know ye tonight," repeated the old woman. Her voice sounded hollow in the depths of her great hood, which she donned early in the fall. Her eyes in the gloom of it gleamed with a small dark brightness.

"I'll have no witch-work tried on her," said David, roughly.

"I'll try no witch-work but mine own wits," said Goody Crane. "If they would hang me for a witch for that, then they may. None but I can cure her. I tell ye, come out here tonight when the moon is an hour high; and mind ye wear a white sheep's fleece over your shoulders. I'll harm her not so much with my witch-work as ye'll do with your love, for all your prating."

The old woman pushed past him to where Silence stood calling, and waited there, standing in the shadow cast by the wild cherry-tree until she ceased and turned away. Then she caught hold of the skirt of her gown, and David stood, hidden by the thicket, listening.

"I prithee, Mistress Silence Hoit, listen but a moment," said Goody Crane.

Silence paused, and smiled at her gently and wearily.

"Give me your hand," demanded the old woman.

And Silence held out her hand, flashing white in the green gloom, as if she cared not.

The old woman turned the palm, bending her hooded head low over it. "He draweth near!" she cried out suddenly; "he draweth near, with a white sheep's fleece over his shoulders! He cometh through the woods from Canada. He will cross the meadow when the moon is an hour high tonight. He will wear a white sheep's fleece over his shoulders, and ye'll know him by that."

Silence's wandering eyes fastened upon her face.

The old woman caught hold of her shoulders and shook her to and fro. "David! David! David Walcott!" she screamed. "David Walcott with a white sheep's fleece on his back! On the meadow! Tonight when the moon's an hour high! Be ye out here tonight, Silence Hoit, if ye'd see him a-coming down from the north!"

Silence gasped faintly when the old woman released her and went muttering away. Presently she crept home, and sat down with her knitting-work in the chimney-place.

When Eunice Bishop hung on the porridge-kettle, Goody Crane lifted the latch-string and came in. It was growing dusky, but the moon would not rise for an hour yet. Goody Crane sat opposite Silence, with her eyes fixed upon her, and Silence, in spite of herself, kept looking at her. A gold brooch at the old woman's throat glittered in the firelight, and that seemed to catch Silence's eyes. She finally knitted with them fixed upon it.

She scarcely took her eyes away when she ate her supper; then she sat down to her knitting and knitted, and gazed, in spite of herself, at the gold spot on the old woman's throat.

The moon arose; the tree branches before the windows tossed half in silver light; the air was shrill with crickets. Silence stirred uneasily, and dropped stitches in her knitting-work. "He draweth near," muttered Goody Crane, and Silence quivered.

The moon was a half-hour high. Widow Bishop was spinning, Widow Spear was winding quills, and Silence knitted. "He draweth near," muttered Goody Crane.

"I'll have no witchcraft!" Silence cried out, suddenly and sharply. Her aunt stopped spinning, and Widow Spear started.

"What's that?" said her aunt. But Silence was knitting again.

"What meant you by that?" asked her aunt, sharply.

"I have dropped a stitch," said Silence.

Her aunt spun again, with occasional wary glances. The moon was three-quarters of an hour high. Silence gazed steadily at the gold brooch at Goody Crane's throat.

"The moon is near an hour high; you had best be going," said the old woman, in a low monotone.

Silence arose directly.

"Where go you at this time of night?" grumbled her aunt. But Silence glided past her.

"You'll lose your good name as well as your wits," cried Eunice. But she did not try to stop Silence, for she knew it was useless.

"A white sheep's fleece over his shoulders," muttered Goody Crane as Silence went out of the door; and the other women marvelled what she meant.

Silence Hoit went swiftly and softly down Deerfield street to her old haunt on the north meadow terrace. She pushed in among the wild cherry-trees, which waved, white with the moonlight, like ghostly arms in her face. Then she called, setting her face toward Canada and the north: "David! David! David!" But her voice had a different tone in it, and it broke with her heart-beats.

David Walcott came slowly across the meadow below; a white fleece of a sheep thrown over his back caught the moonlight. He came on, and on, and on; then he went up the terrace to Silence. Her face, white like a white flower in the moonlight, shone out suddenly close before him. He waited a second, then he spoke. "Silence!" he said.

Then Silence gave a great cry, and threw out her arms around his neck, and pressed softly and wildly against him with her wet cheek to his.

"Know you who 'tis, sweetheart?"

"Oh, David, David, 'tis thou, 'tis thou, 'tis thou!"

The trees arched like arbours with the weight of the wild grapes, which made the air sweet; the night insects called from the bushes; Deerfield village and the whole valley lay in the moonlight like a landscape of silver. The lovers stood in each other's arms, motionless, and seemingly fixed as the New England *flora* around them, as if they too might reappear hundreds of spring-times hence, with their loves as fairly in blossom.

The Wind in the Rose-Bush

Ford Village has no railroad station, being on the other side of the river from Porter's Falls, and accessible only by the ford which gives it its name, and a ferry line.

The ferry-boat was waiting when Rebecca Flint got off the train with her bag and lunch basket. When she and her small trunk were safely embarked she sat stiff and straight and calm in the ferry-boat as it shot swiftly and smoothly across stream. There was a horse attached to a light country wagon on board, and he pawed the deck uneasily. His owner stood near, with a wary eye upon him, although he was chewing, with as dully reflective an expression as a cow. Beside Rebecca sat a woman of about her own age, who kept looking at her with furtive curiosity; her husband, short and stout and saturnine, stood near her. Rebecca paid no attention to either of them. She was tall and spare and pale, the type of a spinster, yet with rudimentary lines and expressions of matronhood. She all unconsciously held her shawl, rolled up in a canvas bag, on her left hip, as if it had been a child. She wore a settled frown of dissent at life, but it was the frown of a mother who regarded life as a froward child, rather than as an overwhelming fate.

The other woman continued staring at her; she was mildly stupid, except for an over-developed curiosity which made her at times sharp beyond belief. Her eyes glittered, red spots came on her flaccid cheeks; she kept opening her mouth to speak, making little abortive motions. Finally she could endure it no longer; she nudged Rebecca boldly.

"A pleasant day," said she.

Rebecca looked at her and nodded coldly.

"Yes, very," she assented.

"Have you come far?"

"I have come from Michigan."

"Oh!" said the woman, with awe. "It's a long way," she remarked presently.

"Yes, it is," replied Rebecca, conclusively.

Still the other woman was not daunted; there was something which she determined to know, possibly roused thereto by a vague sense of incongruity in the other's appearance. "It's a long ways to come and leave a family," she remarked with painful slyness.

"I ain't got any family to leave," returned Rebecca shortly.

"Then you ain't—"

"No, I ain't."

"Oh!" said the woman.

Rebecca looked straight ahead at the race of the river.

It was a long ferry. Finally Rebecca herself waxed unexpectedly loquacious. She turned to the other woman and inquired if she knew John Dent's widow who lived in Ford Village. "Her husband died about three years ago," said she, by way of detail.

The woman started violently. She turned pale, then she flushed; she cast a strange glance at her husband, who was regarding both women with a sort of stolid keenness.

"Yes, I guess I do," faltered the woman finally.

"Well, his first wife was my sister," said Rebecca with the air of one imparting important intelligence.

"Was she?" responded the other woman feebly. She glanced at her husband with an expression of doubt and terror, and he shook his head forbiddingly.

"I'm going to see her, and take my niece Agnes home with me," said Rebecca.

Then the woman gave such a violent start that she noticed it.

"What is the matter?" she asked.

"Nothin', I guess," replied the woman, with eyes on her husband, who was slowly shaking his head, like a Chinese toy.

"Is my niece sick?" asked Rebecca with quick suspicion.

"No, she ain't sick," replied the woman with alacrity, then she caught her breath with a gasp.

"When did you see her?"

"Let me see; I ain't seen her for some little time," replied the woman. Then she caught her breath again.

"She ought to have grown up real pretty, if she takes after my sister. She was a real pretty woman," Rebecca said wistfully.

"Yes, I guess she did grow up pretty," replied the woman in a trembling voice.

"What kind of a woman is the second wife?"

The woman glanced at her husband's warning face. She continued to gaze at him while she replied in a choking voice to Rebecca:

"I—guess she's a nice woman," she replied. "I—don't know, I—guess so. I—don't see much of her."

"I felt kind of hurt that John married again so quick," said Rebecca; "but I suppose he wanted his house kept, and Agnes wanted care. I wasn't so situated that I could take her when her mother died. I had my own mother to care for, and I was school-teaching. Now mother has gone, and my uncle died six months ago and left me quite a little property, and I've given up my school, and I've come for Agnes. I guess she'll be glad to go with me, though I suppose her stepmother is a good woman, and has always done for her."

The man's warning shake at his wife was fairly portentous.

"I guess so," said she.

"John always wrote that she was a beautiful woman," said Rebecca.

Then the ferry-boat grated on the shore.

John Dent's widow had sent a horse and wagon to meet her sister-in-law. When the woman and her husband went down the road, on which Rebecca in the wagon with her trunk soon passed them, she said reproachfully:

"Seems as if I'd ought to have told her, Thomas."

"Let her find it out herself," replied the man. "Don't you go to burnin' your fingers in other folks' puddin', Maria."

"Do you s'pose she'll see anything?" asked the woman with a spasmodic shudder and a terrified roll of her eyes.

"See!" returned her husband with stolid scorn. "Better be sure there's anything to see."

"Oh, Thomas, they say—"

"Lord, ain't you found out that what they say is mostly lies?"

"But if it should be true, and she's a nervous woman, she might be scared enough to lose her wits," said his wife, staring uneasily after Rebecca's erect figure in the wagon disappearing over the crest of the hilly road.

"Wits that so easy upset ain't worth much," declared the man. "You keep out of it, Maria."

Rebecca in the meantime rode on in the wagon, beside a flaxen-headed boy, who looked, to her understanding, not very bright. She asked him a question, and he paid no attention. She repeated it, and he responded with a bewildered and incoherent grunt. Then she let him alone, after making sure that he knew how to drive straight.

They had travelled about half a mile, passed the village square, and gone a short distance beyond, when the boy drew up with a sudden Whoa! before a very prosperous-looking house. It had been one of the aboriginal cottages of the vicinity, small and white, with a roof extending on one side over a *piazza*, and a tiny "L" jutting out in the rear, on the right hand. Now the cottage was transformed by dormer windows, a bay window on the *piazzaless* side, a carved railing down the front steps, and a modern hard-wood door.

"Is this John Dent's house?" asked Rebecca.

The boy was as sparing of speech as a philosopher. His only response was in flinging the reins over the horse's back, stretching out one foot to the shaft, and leaping out of the wagon, then going around to the rear for the trunk. Rebecca got out and went toward the house. Its white paint had a new gloss; its blinds were an immaculate apple green; the lawn was trimmed as smooth as velvet, and it was dotted with scrupulous groups of hydrangeas and cannas.

"I always understood that John Dent was well-to-do," Rebecca reflected comfortably. "I guess Agnes will have considerable. I've got enough, but it will come in handy for her schooling. She can have advantages."

The boy dragged the trunk up the fine gravel-walk, but before he reached the steps leading up to the *piazza*, for the house stood on a terrace, the front door opened and a fair, frizzled head of a very large and handsome woman appeared. She held up her black silk skirt, disclosing voluminous ruffles of starched embroidery, and waited for Rebecca. She smiled placidly, her pink, double-chinned face widened and dimpled, but her blue eyes were wary and calculating. She extended her hand as Rebecca climbed the steps.

"This is Miss Flint, I suppose," said she.

"Yes, ma'am," replied Rebecca, noticing with bewilderment a curious expression compounded of fear and defiance on the other's face.

"Your letter only arrived this morning," said Mrs. Dent, in a steady voice. Her great face was a uniform pink, and her china-blue eyes were at once aggressive and veiled with secrecy.

"Yes, I hardly thought you'd get my letter," replied Rebecca. "I felt as if I could not wait to hear from you before I came. I supposed you would be so situated that you could have me a little while without putting you out too much, from what John used to write me about his circumstances, and when I had that money so unexpected I felt as if I must come for Agnes. I suppose you will be willing to give her up. You know she's my own blood, and of course she's no relation to you, though you must have got attached to her. I know from her picture what a sweet girl she must be, and John always said she looked like her own mother, and Grace was a beautiful woman, if she was my sister."

Rebecca stopped and stared at the other woman in amazement and alarm. The great handsome blonde creature stood speechless, livid, gasping, with her hand to her heart, her lips parted in a horrible caricature of a smile.

"Are you sick!" cried Rebecca, drawing near. "Don't you want me to get you some water!"

Then Mrs. Dent recovered herself with a great effort. "It is nothing," she said. "I am subject to—spells. I am over it now. Won't you come in, Miss Flint?"

As she spoke, the beautiful deep-rose colour suffused her face, her blue eyes met her visitor's with the opaqueness of turquoise—with a revelation of blue, but a concealment of all behind.

Rebecca followed her hostess in, and the boy, who had waited quiescently, climbed the steps with the trunk. But before they entered the door a strange thing happened. On the upper terrace close to the *piazza*-post, grew a great rose-bush, and on it, late in the season though it was, one small red, perfect rose.

Rebecca looked at it, and the other woman extended her hand with a quick gesture. "Don't you pick that rose!" she brusquely cried.

Rebecca drew herself up with stiff dignity.

"I ain't in the habit of picking other folks' roses without leave," said she.

As Rebecca spoke she started violently, and lost sight of her resentment, for something singular happened. Suddenly the rose-bush was agitated violently as if by a gust of wind, yet it was a remarkably still day. Not a leaf of the hydrangea standing on the terrace close to the rose trembled.

"What on earth—" began Rebecca, then she stopped with a gasp at the sight of the other woman's face. Although a face, it gave somehow the impression of a desperately clutched hand of secrecy.

"Come in!" said she in a harsh voice, which seemed to come forth from her chest with no intervention of the organs of speech. "Come into the house. I'm getting cold out here."

"What makes that rose-bush blow so when their isn't any wind?" asked Rebecca, trembling with vague horror, yet resolute.

"I don't see as it is blowing," returned the woman calmly. And as she spoke, indeed, the bush was quiet.

"It was blowing," declared Rebecca.

"It isn't now," said Mrs. Dent. "I can't try to account for everything that blows out-of-doors. I have too much to do."

She spoke scornfully and confidently, with defiant, unflinching eyes, first on the bush, then on Rebecca, and led the way into the house.

"It looked queer," persisted Rebecca, but she followed, and also the boy with the trunk.

Rebecca entered an interior, prosperous, even elegant, according to her simple ideas. There were Brussels carpets, lace curtains, and plenty of brilliant upholstery and polished wood.

"You're real nicely situated," remarked Rebecca, after she had become a little accustomed to her new surroundings and the two women were seated at the tea-table.

Mrs. Dent stared with a hard complacency from behind her silver-plated service. "Yes, I be," said she.

"You got all the things new?" said Rebecca hesitatingly, with a jealous memory of her dead sister's bridal furnishings.

"Yes," said Mrs. Dent; "I was never one to want dead folks' things, and I had money enough of my own, so I wasn't beholden to John. I had the old duds put up at auction. They didn't bring much."

"I suppose you saved some for Agnes. She'll want some of her poor mother's things when she is grown up," said Rebecca with some indignation.

The defiant stare of Mrs. Dent's blue eyes waxed more intense. "There's a few things up garret," said she.

"She'll be likely to value them," remarked Rebecca. As she spoke she glanced at the window. "Isn't it most time for her to be coming home?" she asked.

"Most time," answered Mrs. Dent carelessly; "but when she gets over to Addie Slocum's she never knows when to come home."

"Is Addie Slocum her intimate friend?"

"Intimate as any."

"Maybe we can have her come out to see Agnes when she's living with me," said Rebecca wistfully. "I suppose she'll be likely to be homesick at first."

"Most likely," answered Mrs. Dent.

"Does she call you mother?" Rebecca asked.

"No, she calls me Aunt Emeline," replied the other woman shortly. "When did you say you were going home?"

"In about a week, I thought, if she can be ready to go so soon," answered Rebecca with a surprised look.

She reflected that she would not remain a day longer than she could help after such an inhospitable look and question.

"Oh, as far as that goes," said Mrs. Dent, "it wouldn't make any difference about her being ready. You could go home whenever you felt that you must, and she could come afterward."

"Alone?"

"Why not? She's a big girl now, and you don't have to change cars."

"My niece will go home when I do, and not travel alone; and if I can't wait here for her, in the house that used to be her mother's and my sister's home, I'll go and board somewhere," returned Rebecca with warmth.

"Oh, you can stay here as long as you want to. You're welcome," said Mrs. Dent.

Then Rebecca started. "There she is!" she declared in a trembling, exultant voice. Nobody knew how she longed to see the girl.

"She isn't as late as I thought she'd be," said Mrs. Dent, and again that curious, subtle change passed over her face, and again it settled into that stony impassiveness.

Rebecca stared at the door, waiting for it to open. "Where is she?" she asked presently.

"I guess she's stopped to take off her hat in the entry," suggested Mrs. Dent.

Rebecca waited. "Why don't she come? It can't take her all

this time to take off her hat."

For answer Mrs. Dent rose with a stiff jerk and threw open the door.

"Agnes!" she called. "Agnes!" Then she turned and eyed Rebecca. "She ain't there."

"I saw her pass the window," said Rebecca in bewilderment.

"You must have been mistaken."

"I know I did," persisted Rebecca.

"You couldn't have."

"I did. I saw first a shadow go over the ceiling, then I saw her in the glass there"—she pointed to a mirror over the sideboard opposite—"and then the shadow passed the window."

"How did she look in the glass?"

"Little and light-haired, with the light hair kind of tossing over her forehead."

"You couldn't have seen her."

"Was that like Agnes?"

"Like enough; but of course you didn't see her. You've been thinking so much about her that you thought you did."

"You thought *you* did."

"I thought I saw a shadow pass the window, but I must have been mistaken. She didn't come in, or we would have seen her before now. I knew it was too early for her to get home from Addie Slocum's, anyhow."

When Rebecca went to bed Agnes had not returned. Rebecca had resolved that she would not retire until the girl came, but she was very tired, and she reasoned with herself that she was foolish. Besides, Mrs. Dent suggested that Agnes might go to the church social with Addie Slocum. When Rebecca suggested that she be sent for and told that her aunt had come, Mrs. Dent laughed meaningly.

"I guess you'll find out that a young girl ain't so ready to leave a sociable, where there's boys, to see her aunt," said she.

"She's too young," said Rebecca incredulously and indignantly.

"She's sixteen," replied Mrs. Dent; "and she's always been

great for the boys."

"She's going to school four years after I get her before she thinks of boys," declared Rebecca.

"We'll see," laughed the other woman.

After Rebecca went to bed, she lay awake a long time listening for the sound of girlish laughter and a boy's voice under her window; then she fell asleep.

The next morning she was down early. Mrs. Dent, who kept no servants, was busily preparing breakfast.

"Don't Agnes help you about breakfast?" asked Rebecca.

"No, I let her lay," replied Mrs. Dent shortly.

"What time did she get home last night?"

"She didn't get home."

"What?"

"She didn't get home. She stayed with Addie. She often does."

"Without sending you word?"

"Oh, she knew I wouldn't worry."

"When will she be home?"

"Oh, I guess she'll be along pretty soon."

Rebecca was uneasy, but she tried to conceal it, for she knew of no good reason for uneasiness. What was there to occasion alarm in the fact of one young girl staying overnight with another? She could not eat much breakfast. Afterward she went out on the little *piazza*, although her hostess strove furtively to stop her.

"Why don't you go out back of the house? It's real pretty—a view over the river," she said.

"I guess I'll go out here," replied Rebecca. She had a purpose: to watch for the absent girl.

Presently Rebecca came hustling into the house through the sitting-room, into the kitchen where Mrs. Dent was cooking.

"That rose-bush!" she gasped.

Mrs. Dent turned and faced her.

"What of it?"

"It's a-blowing."

"What of it?"

"There isn't a mite of wind this morning."

Mrs. Dent turned with an inimitable toss of her fair head. "If you think I can spend my time puzzling over such nonsense as—" she began, but Rebecca interrupted her with a cry and a rush to the door.

"There she is now!" she cried. She flung the door wide open, and curiously enough a breeze came in and her own gray hair tossed, and a paper blew off the table to the floor with a loud rustle, but there was nobody in sight.

"There's nobody here," Rebecca said.

She looked blankly at the other woman, who brought her rolling-pin down on a slab of pie-crust with a thud.

"I didn't hear anybody," she said calmly.

"I saw somebody pass that window!"

"You were mistaken again."

"I *know* I saw somebody."

"You couldn't have. Please shut that door."

Rebecca shut the door. She sat down beside the window and looked out on the autumnal yard, with its little curve of footpath to the kitchen door.

"What smells so strong of roses in this room?" she said presently. She sniffed hard.

"I don't smell anything but these nutmegs."

"It is not nutmeg."

"I don't smell anything else."

"Where do you suppose Agnes is?"

"Oh, perhaps she has gone over the ferry to Porter's Falls with Addie. She often does. Addie's got an aunt over there, and Addie's got a cousin, a real pretty boy."

"You suppose she's gone over there?"

"Mebbe. I shouldn't wonder."

"When should she be home?"

"Oh, not before afternoon."

Rebecca waited with all the patience she could muster. She kept reassuring herself, telling herself that it was all natural, that the other woman could not help it, but she made up her mind that if Agnes did not return that afternoon she should be sent for.

When it was four o'clock she started up with resolution. She had been furtively watching the onyx clock on the sitting-room mantel; she had timed herself. She had said that if Agnes was not home by that time she should demand that she be sent for. She rose and stood before Mrs. Dent, who looked up coolly from her embroidery.

"I've waited just as long as I'm going to," she said. "I've come 'way from Michigan to see my own sister's daughter and take her home with me. I've been here ever since yesterday—twenty-four hours—and I haven't seen her. Now I'm going to. I want her sent for."

Mrs. Dent folded her embroidery and rose.

"Well, I don't blame you," she said. "It is high time she came home. I'll go right over and get her myself."

Rebecca heaved a sigh of relief. She hardly knew what she had suspected or feared, but she knew that her position had been one of antagonism if not accusation, and she was sensible of relief.

"I wish you would," she said gratefully, and went back to her chair, while Mrs. Dent got her shawl and her little white headtie. "I wouldn't trouble you, but I do feel as if I couldn't wait any longer to see her," she remarked apologetically.

"Oh, it ain't any trouble at all," said Mrs. Dent as she went out. "I don't blame you; you have waited long enough."

Rebecca sat at the window watching breathlessly until Mrs. Dent came stepping through the yard alone. She ran to the door and saw, hardly noticing it this time, that the rose-bush was again violently agitated, yet with no wind evident elsewhere.

"Where is she?" she cried.

Mrs. Dent laughed with stiff lips as she came up the steps over the terrace. "Girls will be girls," said she. "She's gone with Addie to Lincoln. Addie's got an uncle who's conductor on the train, and lives there, and he got 'em passes, and they're goin' to stay to Addie's Aunt Margaret's a few days. Mrs. Slocum said Agnes didn't have time to come over and ask me before the train went, but she took it on herself to say it would be all right, and—"

"Why hadn't she been over to tell you?" Rebecca was angry, though not suspicious. She even saw no reason for her anger.

"Oh, she was putting up grapes. She was coming over just as soon as she got the black off her hands. She heard I had company, and her hands were a sight. She was holding them over sulphur matches."

"You say she's going to stay a few days?" repeated Rebecca dazedly.

"Yes; till Thursday, Mrs. Slocum said."

"How far is Lincoln from here?"

"About fifty miles. It'll be a real treat to her. Mrs. Slocum's sister is a real nice woman."

"It is goin' to make it pretty late about my goin' home."

"If you don't feel as if you could wait, I'll get her ready and send her on just as soon as I can," Mrs. Dent said sweetly.

"I'm going to wait," said Rebecca grimly.

The two women sat down again, and Mrs. Dent took up her embroidery.

"Is there any sewing I can do for her?" Rebecca asked finally in a desperate way. "If I can get her sewing along some—"

Mrs. Dent arose with alacrity and fetched a mass of white from the closet. "Here," she said, "if you want to sew the lace on this nightgown. I was going to put her to it, but she'll be glad enough to get rid of it. She ought to have this and one more before she goes. I don't like to send her away without some good underclothing."

Rebecca snatched at the little white garment and sewed feverishly.

That night she wakened from a deep sleep a little after midnight and lay a minute trying to collect her faculties and explain to herself what she was listening to. At last she discovered that it was the then popular strains of "The Maiden's Prayer" floating up through the floor from the piano in the sitting-room below.

She jumped up, threw a shawl over her nightgown, and hurried downstairs trembling. There was nobody in the sitting-room; the piano was silent. She ran to Mrs. Dent's bedroom and called hysterically:

"Emeline! Emeline!"

"What is it?" asked Mrs. Dent's voice from the bed. The voice was stern, but had a note of consciousness in it.

"Who—who was that playing 'The Maiden's Prayer' in the sitting-room, on the piano?"

"I didn't hear anybody."

"There was someone."

"I didn't hear anything."

"I tell you there was someone. But—*there ain't anybody there.*"

"I didn't hear anything."

"I did—somebody playing 'The Maiden's Prayer' on the piano. Has Agnes got home? I *want to know.*"

"Of course Agnes hasn't got home," answered Mrs. Dent with rising inflection. "Be you gone crazy over that girl? The last boat from Porter's Falls was in before we went to bed. Of course she ain't come."

"I heard—"

"You were dreaming."

"I wasn't; I was broad awake."

Rebecca went back to her chamber and kept her lamp burning all night.

The next morning her eyes upon Mrs. Dent were wary and blazing with suppressed excitement. She kept opening her mouth as if to speak, then frowning, and setting her lips hard. After breakfast she went upstairs, and came down presently with her coat and bonnet.

"Now, Emeline," she said, "I want to know where the Slocums live."

Mrs. Dent gave a strange, long, half-lidded glance at her. She was finishing her coffee.

"Why?" she asked.

"I'm going over there and find out if they have heard anything from her daughter and Agnes since they went away. I don't like what I heard last night."

"You must have been dreaming."

"It don't make any odds whether I was or not. Does she play 'The Maiden's Prayer' on the piano? I want to know."

"What if she does? She plays it a little, I believe. I don't know. She don't half play it, anyhow; she ain't got an ear."

"That wasn't half played last night. I don't like such things happening. I ain't superstitious, but I don't like it. I'm going. Where do the Slocums live?"

"You go down the road over the bridge past the old grist mill, then you turn to the left; it's the only house for half a mile. You can't miss it. It has a barn with a ship in full sail on the cupola."

"Well, I'm going. I don't feel easy."

About two hours later Rebecca returned. There were red spots on her cheeks. She looked wild. "I've been there," she said, "and there isn't a soul at home. Something *has* happened."

"What has happened?"

"I don't know. Something. I had a warning last night. There wasn't a soul there. They've been sent for to Lincoln."

"Did you see anybody to ask?" asked Mrs. Dent with thinly concealed anxiety.

"I asked the woman that lives on the turn of the road. She's stone deaf. I suppose you know. She listened while I screamed at her to know where the Slocums were, and then she said, 'Mrs. Smith don't live here.' I didn't see anybody on the road, and that's the only house. What do you suppose it means?"

"I don't suppose it means much of anything," replied Mrs. Dent coolly. "Mr. Slocum is conductor on the railroad, and he'd be away anyway, and Mrs. Slocum often goes early when he does, to spend the day with her sister in Porter's Falls. She'd be more likely to go away than Addie."

"And you don't think anything has happened?" Rebecca asked with diminishing distrust before the reasonableness of it.

"Lord, no!"

Rebecca went upstairs to lay aside her coat and bonnet. But she came hurrying back with them still on.

"Who's been in my room?" she gasped. Her face was pale as ashes.

Mrs. Dent also paled as she regarded her.

"What do you mean?" she asked slowly.

"I found when I went upstairs that—little nightgown of—Agnes's on—the bed, laid out. It was—*laid out.* The sleeves were folded across the bosom, and there was that little red rose between them. Emeline, what is it? Emeline, what's the matter? Oh!"

Mrs. Dent was struggling for breath in great, choking gasps. She clung to the back of a chair. Rebecca, trembling herself so she could scarcely keep on her feet, got her some water.

As soon as she recovered herself Mrs. Dent regarded her with eyes full of the strangest mixture of fear and horror and hostility.

"What do you mean talking so?" she said in a hard voice.

"It *is there.*"

"Nonsense. You threw it down and it fell that way."

"It was folded in my bureau drawer."

"It couldn't have been."

"Who picked that red rose?"

"Look on the bush," Mrs. Dent replied shortly.

Rebecca looked at her; her mouth gaped. She hurried out of the room. When she came back her eyes seemed to protrude. (She had in the meantime hastened upstairs, and come down with tottering steps, clinging to the banisters.)

"Now I want to know what all this means?" she demanded.

"What what means?"

"The rose is on the bush, and it's gone from the bed in my room! Is this house haunted, or what?"

"I don't know anything about a house being haunted. I don't believe in such things. Be you crazy?" Mrs. Dent spoke with gathering force. The colour flashed back to her cheeks.

"No," said Rebecca shortly. "I ain't crazy yet, but I shall be if this keeps on much longer. I'm going to find out where that girl is before night."

Mrs. Dent eyed her.

"What be you going to do?"

"I'm going to Lincoln."

A faint triumphant smile overspread Mrs. Dent's large face.

"You can't," said she; "there ain't any train."

"No train?"

"No; there ain't any afternoon train from the Falls to Lincoln."

"Then I'm going over to the Slocums' again tonight."

However, Rebecca did not go; such a rain came up as deterred even her resolution, and she had only her best dresses with her. Then in the evening came the letter from the Michigan village which she had left nearly a week ago. It was from her cousin, a single woman, who had come to keep her house while she was away. It was a pleasant unexciting letter enough, all the first of it, and related mostly how she missed Rebecca; how she hoped she was having pleasant weather and kept her health; and how her friend, Mrs. Greenaway, had come to stay with her since she had felt lonesome the first night in the house; how she hoped Rebecca would have no objections to this, although nothing had been said about it, since she had not realized that she might be nervous alone. The cousin was painfully conscientious, hence the letter. Rebecca smiled in spite of her disturbed mind as she read it, then her eye caught the postscript. That was in a different hand, purporting to be written by the friend, Mrs. Hannah Greenaway, informing her that the cousin had fallen down the cellar stairs and broken her hip, and was in a dangerous condition, and begging Rebecca to return at once, as she herself was rheumatic and unable to nurse her properly, and no one else could be obtained.

Rebecca looked at Mrs. Dent, who had come to her room with the letter quite late; it was half-past nine, and she had gone upstairs for the night.

"Where did this come from?" she asked.

"Mr. Amblecrom brought it," she replied.

"Who's he?"

"The postmaster. He often brings the letters that come on the late mail. He knows I ain't anybody to send. He brought yours about your coming. He said he and his wife came over on the ferry-boat with you."

"I remember him," Rebecca replied shortly. "There's bad news in this letter."

Mrs. Dent's face took on an expression of serious inquiry.

"Yes, my Cousin Harriet has fallen down the cellar stairs—they were always dangerous—and she's broken her hip, and I've got to take the first train home tomorrow."

"You don't say so. I'm dreadfully sorry."

"No, you ain't sorry!" said Rebecca, with a look as if she leaped. "You're glad. I don't know why, but you're glad. You've wanted to get rid of me for some reason ever since I came. I don't know why. You're a strange woman. Now you've got your way, and I hope you're satisfied."

"How you talk."

Mrs. Dent spoke in a faintly injured voice, but there was a light in her eyes.

"I talk the way it is. Well, I'm going tomorrow morning, and I want you, just as soon as Agnes Dent comes home, to send her out to me. Don't you wait for anything. You pack what clothes she's got, and don't wait even to mend them, and you buy her ticket. I'll leave the money, and you send her along. She don't have to change cars. You start her off, when she gets home, on the next train!"

"Very well," replied the other woman. She had an expression of covert amusement.

"Mind you do it."

"Very well, Rebecca."

Rebecca started on her journey the next morning. When she arrived, two days later, she found her cousin in perfect health. She found, moreover, that the friend had not written the postscript in the cousin's letter. Rebecca would have returned to Ford Village the next morning, but the fatigue and nervous strain had been too much for her. She was not able to move from her bed. She had a species of low fever induced by anxiety and fatigue. But she could write, and she did, to the Slocums, and she received no answer. She also wrote to Mrs. Dent; she even sent numerous telegrams, with no response. Finally she wrote to the postmaster, and an answer arrived by the first possible mail. The letter was short, curt, and to the purpose. Mr. Amblecrom, the postmaster, was a man of few words, and especially wary as to his expressions in a letter.

He wrote :

Dear madam, your favour rec'ed. No Slocums in Ford's Village. All dead. Addie ten years ago, her mother two years later, her father five. House vacant. Mrs. John Dent said to have neglected stepdaughter. Girl was sick. Medicine not given. Talk of taking action. Not enough evidence. House said to be haunted. Strange sights and sounds. Your niece, Agnes Dent, died a year ago, about this time.

           Yours truly,

                      Thomas Amblecrom.

The Love of Parson Lord

On Monday morning Love Lord sat on the side-door step, stitching some fine linen shirt bands for her father. It was a day in early May, moving from dawn to dark with a rush of strong fresh winds, made almost as palpable as wings by the apple and cherry blossoms which they loosened and bore away from the trees. There was a fine apple-orchard in full bloom in the rear of Parson Reuben Lord's gray shingled house, three large white-plumed cherry-trees stood in the side yard, but Love would never taste the apples and cherries therefrom, unless perchance some scanty measure of poor fruit could not be readily sold. All of Parson Lord's alabaster boxes of life were sold, and the proceeds devoted to foreign missions. Love had never questioned the wisdom of it; she had never questioned the wisdom of any of the orderings of her life. She regarded them as indirectly ordained by Providence through her father, and not to be cavilled at, except possibly in one instance. Love at twelve years of age had had many lacks of life, but only one active sorrow, and that sense of loss and deprivation after the delight of possession which induces rebellion.

Love had lost her mother when she was scarce more than a baby; she had been brought up by a rigorous widow, a distant relative of her father's, who had trained her according to all letters of law and faith. So inexorable had been her method, so thoroughly had Love been taught to perform her duties, that there had seemed to be danger of their losing the distinction of hand and individual work. Little Love had lived as under the self-regulating motive power of an automaton, her native inclinations, whether toward grace or perversity, being wholly amenable to her instructress, as to a spiritual sun and wind. Cousin Daphne Weatherhead, as the widow was called, was the only person with whom she was brought in close contact through her childhood. Of her father she saw very little except at meals, at family prayers, and on Sabbath days, when she sat for hours, with her solemn innocent eyes intent upon him, as he proclaimed the truths of the Word and the terrors of the law from his beetling pulpit.

Parson Reuben Lord was so closely welded to his faith and his devotion that he seemed to gain therefrom a strange stiffness, almost ossification, of spirit. People, while holding him in utmost respect for his stern consistency of life, yet regarded him with awe which had in it something of terror. His fervent zeal for the cause of missions seemed the ruling passion of his life. His two brothers were still labouring in foreign fields. It had been the sorest trial of his life that delicate health in his youth had kept him at home in narrower and more peaceful tillage. It had also been a sore trial to him that his first-born child had not been a son, whom he could devote, with more certainty of the acceptability of the sacrifice, to the cause of Christ in heathen lands.

There was, however, a belief in the village that he had so devoted his first-born daughter, Elizabeth. When the child died, at the early age of seven, after a most wonderful life and precocious maturity of religious experience, afterward celebrated in a memoir which became a village classic, people were strengthened in this belief. It was also reported, on the authority of Aunt Betsey Ware, who had officiated at both births, that the parson made a similar dedication to the Lord of his second daughter, Love, in spite of the expostulations of his poor wife Mehitable, whose maternal affection overcame her religious ardour.

It was even said that Mehitable Lord had faded away and died because of her preying grief over the loss of her first-born, and the fear lest the second, who was delicate, and had that sensitiveness of disposition which is sometimes thought prophetic of early death, should follow her. However that may have been, Mehitable Lord died when Love was too young to have anything but that vague sense of loss of love in the abstract which, while it changes the whole savour of life, does not rend it with bitterness. Love had no little mates during her childhood.

Cousin Daphne Weatherhead, seemingly with the best of motives, kept her aloof from them. "You are the minister's daughter, and should endeavour to follow in the footsteps of your sainted sister," Cousin Daphne would remark if the little maid seemed to cast a wistful eye toward the frolics of the young of her kind. Poor little Love used, for she learned to read at an early age, to strive to console and amuse herself with the perusal of the memoir of her sainted sister. Sitting in her little chair, with the book on her small aproned knees, she bent her childish brows over its pious pages, and pondered gravely its every word.

Love's childhood, which might well have been considered somewhat dull and joyless, though so straightly ordered in the paths of righteousness and peace, held, however, but one grief. When she was six years old she had had a doll presented to her by a loving old dame who had brought up a family of fourteen children. The doll had belonged to her youngest daughter, and was a homely, rustic specimen of her race; but Love took it to her heart with a great content and the most credulous admiration. She was guilty of the one act of deception and the one lie of her childhood for the protection of this poor doll which had come to her for motherhood. She hid the fact of its possession from Cousin Daphne, and then she told a falsehood when questioned.

The pleased old grandmother who had given it to her told of it here and there with innocent garrulity, not dreaming it would do harm. But when Cousin Daphne heard the news, home she came, and poor little Love underwent a miniature inquisition, and remained firm under her rack and thumb-screw. "No, Grandma Streeter didn't ever give me any doll," declared she, with blue eyes looking straight into Cousin Daphne's, yet with a recoil glance of horror at her own wickedness. The word of the small sister of a departed saint was pitted against that of an ancient mother in Israel, but Cousin Daphne made diligent search, and discovered the doll hidden away under Love's feather bed. When she held it before Love, and the child saw the beloved symbolic baby, never of any beauty whatever, and now battered and marred by the caresses and corrections of many mothers, until only a little girl in whom the first strength of maternal imagination can encompass miracles could hold her of any account whatever, she expressed no shame or contrition; she only stretched out her arms with a cry of love and agony: "Give her to me! oh, give her to me! Don't take her away, Cousin Daphne!"

That confirmed matters. Love did not see the doll again for years; and she knelt, in company with her father and Cousin Daphne, until, out of docility and terror, her soul was melted within her with contrition for her heinous sin. Poor little Love seemed to almost see the lapping of the infernal fires around her, and she could not even hold the doll in her arms for comfort. She used often to wonder where it was, what Cousin Daphne had done with it; but she would no more have asked her than she would have taken the name of the Lord in vain. And as for asking her father, she would never forget till her dying day his countenance of stern wretchedness and condemnation when Cousin Daphne had told him of her wickedness, and the almost despairing fervour of his prayer. She would as soon have asked for a little graven image.

Love was twelve years old when Cousin Daphne was found one afternoon sitting stiffly in her chair, with her knitting-work in her motionless hands. She did not come to prayers, and when Love went to call her, Cousin Daphne's face looked at her unseeingly out of the gathering dusk. After Cousin Daphne's death she lived alone with her father, it being held that with her fine training she was able to keep his house at the age of twelve. Love knelt with her father an hour every morning and evening, and listened to his reading of the Scriptures and prayers. She prepared his frugal meals, and sat timidly and respectfully opposite him at table. The rest of the time he remained alone in his study, walled in, as it were, with the thoughts of dead divines and fathers of the Church in mummy-cases of old calf-skin, and was in sore labour over his many-headed sermons.

Love kept his house, as she had been taught, as if it were her own soul; she cleaned it as she would have cleaned her heart of sin; she made all the poor furnishings shine as if they had been the trappings of the Temple, and acquitted herself like a housewife of twice her age, to the approbation of all the village matrons. This morning, although it was still early, the house was neatly set in order from garret to cellar, and there were two hours for the fine stitching before dinner. She sat there, hearing the soft rush of the spring wind and breathing in the flurrying sweetness of the cherry blossoms, but with no consciousness thereof. She set the beautiful stitches, like a little row of pearls, with the precision of a machine, her fingers working with no aid from her mind, which was intent upon a dream she had the night before about her lost doll.

As Love sat there the dream was to her what the perfume was to the cherry blossom, and would have been as evident to a sense made for its perception. Love had dreamed, the night before, that she was up in the garret of her father's house, when she heard a little wail, like that of a young baby. She started and looked around, and it came again, seemingly from the vicinity of an old hair trunk which her father had carried to college in his youth. An experience which she had had at church that day had possibly, by some obscure system of suggestion, induced the dream. That Sunday Love had seen for the first time the squire's new wife. The squire had lately married for the second time, a woman from the city, elderly, but very beautiful and stately. She had brought her orphan grandson to live with her. This grandson, Richard Pierce, was a boy of fourteen, large for his age and forward of understanding. He was nearly fitted to enter Harvard College. That Sunday, young Richard, sitting in the squire's pew, looked across at Love, sitting all alone in the parson's pew. Love was slim and tall, but with a pretty roundness under her little drab spencer cape, with apple curves of pink cheeks under her scooping bonnet, tied under her sweet chin with a sober-coloured ribbon like her cape. Not a bright tint was there about Love, except in her face and hair.

Young Master Richard looked at her with the half-indifferent, half-earnest gaze of an intellectual boy whose mind is devoted to matters in his estimation more important than the faces of girls, and yet has at times, in his own despite, his heart stirred faintly with the instincts and imaginations of his kind. At last Love, compelled perhaps by his gaze, looked at him, though it was in the midst of a fiery appeal from the pulpit. She gazed at the boy with an utter calmness and unconsciousness of scrutiny, as if he were something inanimate. Indeed, to this young Love, with her perfect innocence of ignorance and the long training of her mind on spiritual lines, a boy did not mean as much as a girl, nor much more than a rose-bush or an apple-tree. Richard, as if something in himself, of which he had not known, was discovered by her gaze, looked away with a great blush, and then Love turned her eyes from him towards his grandmother. They were suddenly alert, full of the most timid yet ardent admiration.

The one love with which the child had any acquaintance, and for which she had as yet any yearning, was in the face of that elderly dame. It shone plain to her sight when she glanced at the grandson by her side, and it beamed forth, like a light in the windows of a home, when she saw little Love gazing at her in such timidly beseeching and admiring wise. Love cast down her eyes before the sweet mother-look of the squire's lady, her heart leaped, her mouth quivered as if she would weep. She thought that never, never since her own mother, whose caresses she remembered better than her face, had there been any one as beautiful as this woman. That morning Love heard no more of her father's discourse. She was conscious of nothing except that mother-presence, which seemed to pervade the whole church. The inexorable fatherhood of God, as set forth in the parson's sermon, was not as evident to the hungry little heart in His sanctuary as the motherhood of the squire's lady.

She continued to gaze at her at intervals, with softly furtive eyes of adoration, as if the lady were the Blessed Mary, and she a little papist; and when she sometimes received a tenderly benignant glance in return, she scarcely knew where her body was, such was the elation of her spirit. When, after meeting, she was going down the aisle, and came abreast of the wonderful lady, and the soft sweep of her velvet cloak brushed her face like a wing, she could not help an involuntary nestle against her side, as if she were a baby. Then the squire's lady bent down, her beautiful old face framed in gray curls, and smiled, and lifted her hand, and patted Love gently on the smooth curve of her cheek. Love could have gone down at her feet. Nobody since her mother's death had ever caressed her to that extent. She gave a quick look up at the lady with something between a sob and a smile, then shrank back, followed her out of church, and watched her drive away with the squire and Master Richard, though she did not see them at all.

Somehow this encounter with the squire's lady set Love to thinking, more strenuously than usual, of the lost doll of her childhood, and that night she dreamed that she went over to the old trunk, and suddenly her doll peeped at her from behind it. It wore the same muslin frock sprigged with green which she remembered well, and the same bonnet made of pasteboard covered with green satin; but the little face, which looked up at her with the lips parted in a wail, was, curiously enough, that of the squire's lady, gray curls and all, with the tiny cheeks crumpled delicately in pink and white, like an old rose-bud. When Love awoke, she could scarcely believe that the dream was not true, being one of those for whom dreams are separated from the real by insensible shadings rather than sharp divisions.

Love pondered over it all the morning, and that afternoon, her father being away, she stole guiltily up to the garret, and stood listening, breathless, in the midst of the great stretch of space, with the triangle of rafters converging over her head. There was only one small window, and the afternoon was growing old. On either side of the garret, under the eaves, lay long shadows of dark mystery, which to the child's excited fancy seemed often stirring to arise. The garret, like the rest of the house, was very clean and sparse. All the small store of discarded household furnishings was stowed away neatly against the eaves, and the middle space was bare. Love could see the great arc of an old tow-wheel which had not been used for many a year, and near it a cedar chest which contained her mother's meagre wardrobe, two barrels full of old sermons, and the little hair trunk. There was not much besides, except a *surtout* which had belonged to her grandfather, which hung on a nail over the trunk.

Love stood listening, she scarcely knew for what, but the influence of her dream was strong upon her. She was like a little statue of fearful attention, in her straight blue gown, her hands clutching nervously at her sides, her eyes dilating to the dusk and her own fears. Finally Love went over to the trunk and peered behind it. There was no doll there, at once to her disappointment and her relief. She opened the trunk, and it was full of old letters. Love straightened herself, and in so doing jostled her grandfather's *surtout*. One sleeve swung out and hit her cheek with a curious impetus for anything so presumably soft and light. Love started back; a sense of the uncanny thrilled her; then she caught hold of the sleeve eagerly, and there was her doll. Cousin Daphne had been a subtle concealer; people had seldom found out anything which she wished to keep secret. She had doubtless many curious hiding-places in empty habits and meaningless forms for the privacies of her own character, and she was at no loss, working from within out to practical illustrations, to find a concealment for poor Love's doll.

Love slipped up the sleeve, and looked irresolutely at the clumsy rag feet; she looked at the pantalets edged with knitted lace, and the hem of the green-sprigged muslin skirt. Love removed the doll and looked at it tremblingly. It was the same old doll. Love went over to the front window and sat down on the floor, clasping it closely. She felt unutterably guilty, still there was a sweet comfort from the feeling of the doll in her arms which she could not help realizing, in spite of her conviction of sin. There was in her consciousness a savour, faint and diluted, of the joy of a mother united to a long-lost child. She gazed at its poor old rag face, its wide mouth painted grotesquely with poke-berry juice, its staring eyes outlined in circles of India ink. She stroked lovingly the scanty locks made from a ravelled brown silk stocking. She knew that the doll was miserably ugly, but, by a sort of under-knowledge of love, she also knew she was fair. She pressed her closely to her childish bosom, throbbing with a sense of shame and guilt, and yet with defiant joy. She kissed her as she had never kissed any living thing.

That night Parson Lord's supper was an hour late. He, working by candle-light in his study, felt that vague uneasiness which results from the interruption of a habit upon which no especial stress of mind has been laid, although it may have continued through a lifetime. Through his surfeit of spiritual food, he had scarcely ever been conscious of any desire for that of the flesh. He had never looked forward impatiently to his supper hour, and it was doubtful if he had ever partaken of the meal with a full perception of its quality or quantity, being always more or less abstracted from all material things. Tonight he fidgeted over his sixthly without knowing why. He did not even know, when his daughter came trembling to his study door, that the meal was late, but followed her without a word, and took his place at the table, and bowed his head for the solemnly muttered blessing. The meal was frugal, as all meals were at Parson Lord's—just a brown loaf, a pitcher of milk, and tea made of steeped sage leaves. Genuine tea was not to be thought of, with foreign missions in such sore need.

That night Parson Lord ate his supper with a curious mechanical gusto, as if his body, through its long fast, might be asserting itself without the knowledge or connivance of his mind. He did not notice that his daughter ate nothing, nor her disturbed face. After he had done he bowed his head reverently again, gave thanks to the Lord for His mercies in a lengthy list, and returned to his study.

An hour afterward, when Love had washed and put away the supper dishes and set the bread to rising, she knocked at the study door, twice and thrice before her father heard her. At last he bade her enter, and looked up absently when the door opened, expecting to see some brother or sister in quest of spiritual aid, as was often the case. Instead, there stood his own daughter, pale and trembling piteously, holding the old doll in her arms. Parson Lord stared at her, took off his spectacles, wiped them, and stared again. "What do you want, my child?" he inquired.

Before he had finished speaking, Love came to his side and stood there in an agony of contrition, displaying the doll. "I found her where Cousin Daphne hid her," she said, in a strained, quick way; then she sobbed; all her staidness and propriety of demeanour had failed her.

The parson stared at her, his thin lips parted, his high fore-head knitted. He had entirely forgotten the episode of the doll. Poor Love had to repeat the whole story. A light of understand-ing came into the parson's eyes as he listened. "And you found it, you say, this afternoon?" he said, in a curious voice.

"Yes, father," replied Love. Then she cried, with a great sob of appeal, "Oh, father, may I keep her now?"

Parson Lord's face quivered a little as he looked at her, then settled again into its usual lines of ascetic sternness and gravity. None but his Maker knew if it cost him a struggle, but he re-fused the child; he bade her carry the doll back where she had found it. Love obeyed without a demur. She took a candle, went slowly up the steep garret stairs, stole tremblingly through the dark flickering stretch of shadows to the old *surtout* hanging with an awful semblance of life from the nail in the rafters, gave the poor doll one last fervent caress, and thrust it back in the sleeve, pinning it therein as before. That night Reuben Lord knelt long with his daughter in earnest prayer; her old sins of disobedience and deception were rekindled to their full enormity, until they shone before her as in characters of fire. That night Love slept little, being kept awake by the war between her innocent members and her fierce New England conscience. Many a time, as she lay there, it seemed to her that she must arise, steal upstairs, rescue the doll from the darkness and loneliness, and hold it through the rest of the night close in her arms.

The next day was the Sabbath, and Love, sitting alone in the parson's pew, was much paler and soberer of countenance than usual. Once in a while, though she strove to keep her mind upon the sermon, her mouth quivered when she thought of the doll. Perhaps it was that which led the squire's lady to favour her with such special and gracious notice at the close of the services. That beautiful and stately lady, when she reached Love lingering at the door of the pew, actually put caressingly about her an arm draped with silk shimmering with purples like the breast of a dove, and bade her a "Good-morning, my dear child." Love never knew whether she answered her or not. She went home in a sort of ecstasy, as of first love.

The squire's lady was in reality her first love. However fond she might be again of others, the affection would go forth in a worn channel. The girl heard that tender voice multiplying into infinite cadences of love and comfort in all the voices of the spring day. Love's cheeks were so flushed and her eyes so strange with happiness that even her father noticed it when she sat opposite him at the dinner table.

His mind had been intent upon his afternoon discourse, when suddenly he looked up as if at a touch upon the shoulder. His daughter sat before him just as usual, dressed in her little homely gown of a dull drab-colour, with never a ribbon bow to brighten it. Her pretty fair hair, braided so smoothly and tightly that the very colour seemed compressed, was crossed in the usual flat mat at the back of her head, and brought over her ears in two satinlike folds, with high lights of polish at the sides. Her father saw nothing unusual in her except that blue shining of eyes which seemed almost wild, and that flush of cheeks which seemed almost fever, and an involuntary curving of lips into smiles which seemed almost levity.

First the parson inquired of his daughter if she were ailing, and then if she were in a state of mind befitting the day. To both inquiries Love replied dutifully, her colour deepening, to the former with a respectful negative, to the latter with a modest hesitancy of hope that she might be, which was reassuring. However, her father continued to gaze at her now and then in the same curious and anxious way. He looked not only at her face, but at her dress and her hair, as if he saw them for the first time. He continued to gaze at her in the same fashion later on when they walked to the meeting-house for the afternoon service. He seemed to see the patient, sober young figure at his side with ever-recurring surprise. He scanned again and again the homely dun-coloured gown, falling in scanty folds to the clumsy little shoes, the Boer bonnet tied with dull ribbon. Then he looked from her to some gayer figures moving along the road with flutters of bright streamers and flounces.

Love would have been disturbed by this unwonted notice of her father had not her whole mind been intent upon the squire's lady, who was not there, indeed, but whose presence seemed more vital to her than that of any who sat under the parson's preaching. Until the sermon began she watched anxiously for the object of her adoration to enter, and when she became certain that she was not coming, she felt a pang at heart the like of which she had never known before. She could have wept when she saw Master Richard Pierce coming up the aisle alone. She could not bear to look at the squire's pew; once when young Richard's persistent gaze of admiration forced her unwilling attention, she almost scowled at him, so sad and impatient was she, and jealous of her own self for the sake of the squire's lady. However, after a while she became in a manner reconciled to her disappointment, and fell to musing tenderly over past joy, and building air-castles for the future.

Love's face then took on such an expression that the boy in the squire's pew gazed at her as if fascinated, seeing for the first time the dream of love in a young girl's face. Richard that day managed to be at the door of the parson's pew when Love emerged; he cast a keen though somewhat shamefaced glance at her, but she did not see him at all. "I don't think that girl is very pretty, come to see her close to," he reflected, on his way home. He resolved not to take the trouble to look at her again, with the unconfessed masculine assurance of her annoyance in that case.

Love would not at that time have known whether he looked or not, having eyes for his grandmother only; and the next day but one something happened to distract her still farther. Upon that day Love had the first great and beautiful surprise of her life. She had been alone since morning, as she had been the day before. On Monday and Tuesday of every week the parson travelled to neighbouring towns, where they had not the benefit of regular Sabbath services in a church of his own denomination, and gave them a week-day rendering of his Lord's-day sermon. On Tuesday afternoon Love grew weary of her needle-work, and thought that she would have a change of task by way of harmless recreation. So thinking, she went up to her chamber to get a sampler which she was working. When Love had crossed the threshold of her chamber she stopped short with a gasp.

There in her little chair sat a doll, not the old rag doll, but a new, resplendent creature—a very ideal of dollhood. No unskilled hands had ever fashioned this radiant thing of blooming wax and real flaxen ringlets, of sweetest smiles of baby candour and innocence, of blue eyes intently beaming at the whole world of child-women without a special glance of favor for one, of pink satins and ribbons, of fine linens and laces. Love stood looking, her eyes dilated, her breath coming short and quick. At length she gained courage, and went nearer and knelt down before the wonderful thing. Her face was rapt. It was long before she dared to touch the doll, to do anything but drink in its beauty with her eyes and embrace it with her soul. Finally she rose, with a great sigh of delicious terror, took up the doll, and seated herself.

As she sat there, with the little flaxen head on her shoulder, fingering with gentle, reverent fingers the delicate mysteries of the fine apparel, she was, for the first time in her life, in a state of actual bliss. She had experienced ecstasy at the caressing touch of the squire's lady and her loving words, but this was fruition and realization of the vague sweet promise of that touch and word. Love did not doubt for one minute that the doll came from the bountiful hand of the squire's lady. She reasoned away easily enough all difficulties in the way of its having been brought secretly to the house and deposited in her chamber. Love had that order of mind which springs to conviction, and afterward proves the route to it by a facile imagination. Old Aunt Betsey Ware was then living at the squire's.

"Aunt Betsey," reasoned Love, conclusively, "is well acquainted with this house; she knows well where my chamber is, and I have been at work in the kitchen, where I could not have heard anyone enter, had they stepped softly." Moreover, that very forenoon Love had seen Aunt Betsey hurrying down the road, with head averted, as if she did not wish to be noticed. Love *knew* that the squire's lady had given her the doll. When she heard her father open the door she rose without a second's hesitation, and still clasping the doll, followed him into the study before he had seated himself at his desk.

When the parson turned at the sound of the opening door and saw his daughter standing there, with the great doll in her arms, a strange expression came over his face, the like of which she had never seen there before. But Love did not heed that, neither did she fairly know the matter of her father's answer to her quivering statement concerning the doll, and her pitiful petition that she be allowed to keep it. In truth, it was a long and somewhat stilted speech which Parson Lord made to his trembling daughter, and it was not singular that Love, in her agitation, should grasp only the gist of it—that she might keep the doll. Love, with her New England shamefacedness as to all demonstration, only dropped a prim little courtesy, said "Thank you, sir," and went out, with the doll's pink face looking over her shoulder; but there might well have been a perceptible darkening of the room, so much joy went with her.

Love that night was fairly possessed with affection and gratitude; she loved her father as she had never loved him before, and he seemed nearer to her. She had not mentioned her belief that the squire's lady was the donor of the precious gift. She thought, jumping at that conclusion as she had done at the other, that her father must know it as well as she. Who but the squire's lady could have given her the doll?

Love then entered at once upon a new epoch in her life. It seemed a strange thing that the possession of a plaything of childhood should all at once transform her character from that of a child to that of a woman, but such was apparently the case. Love never played, in the strictest sense of the word, with her doll; she never tended it with that sweet make-believe of motherhood in dressing and nursing; but the doll surely sent her heart into blossom, being perhaps the little stimulus of love needed for that end. At this time there came into the girl's face that expression of sweet intelligence and gentle comprehension, instead of the mere innocent outlook of childhood. People meeting Love in those days used to look at her carelessly, as one looks at any wonted object, then look again and again with growing wonder, as at a change which they could not define. Some, after meeting her so, said she had grown tall, some that she had grown pretty, some that she grew to look more like her mother, or father, or Cousin Daphne. Whatever they said, people noticed her more. A few weeks after she had come into the possession of her doll, the squire's lady, one morning, sent over Aunt Betsey Ware with a formally worded message.

"Mrs. Squire Hawkes desires her compliments to Miss Love Lord, and would be pleased to have her company at tea this afternoon," said Aunt Betsey, with a fine and consequential pucker, and Love could only courtesy in unquestioning gratitude and acquiescence, like one who is bidden to an audience with a queen.

That very morning Master Richard Pierce had departed for college, and his grandmother, feeling sad and lonely, had bethought herself of the parson's sweet little daughter whom she had noticed so often in meeting, that it would be a comfort to have another young face at her tea table that night.

Love had never been in the squire's house since the advent of this second wife. This was to institute a new order of things. She sat at the dainty tea table opposite the squire's lady—the squire himself was confined to his room with rheumatism—ate gingerly and delicately of the cream biscuits, the quince sauce, and the pound-cake. She sipped her tea from the blue china cup, with timid lifts, over the rim, of blue eyes at the kind and gracious face opposite; she spoke modestly when she was spoken to, and if she volunteered a remark, did so with a sweet deference which was pretty to behold. The squire's lady was even more pleased with the child than she had thought to be.

"She is a dear child," she told the squire when Love had gone, and she was in his chamber mixing the sleeping-cup for which she had a dainty hand. "She is a dear child. I mean to have her often to tea. 'Tis a treat to her, too. I hear the good parson keeps her close and is over-strict with her."

"Did she tell you so?" asked the squire, beginning to sip his spiced and comforting drink from his silver cup.

"No; she said nothing; she never would, unless I mistake her greatly," replied his wife. "I had it from Aunt Betsey, who formerly lived there." The squire's lady, beautiful and gracious though she was, still got some savour to life from a little harmless gossip.

"Well, 'tis true enough," said the squire, "true enough. The parson has driven her with a mighty tight rein, and taught her to shy at the first scent of the devil." The squire had been in his day, and was still, a great lover of horseflesh. "Why, bless you, my dear," said the squire, "I don't suppose that child ever had anything but the drippings of the contribution-box to eat or wear or make merry with. Every cent that the parson can save goes to foreign missions. Why, he sells every apple in his orchard—all except the windfalls—and sends the proceeds to India's burning strand; never one left for that poor child to have a bite of, fine apples too, a rare kind, brought from overseas by his grandfather. I've tried to graft from 'em, and couldn't. I don't suppose that child ever has a lollypop or a sweet-cake unless it's given her, and I don't know but her father would make her sell it then and drop in the penny next Sabbath day. Never a ribbon flying, or a frill setting her off. I've noticed her myself. I used to know her mother; used to think sometimes—I was perfectly satisfied with my own wife, you know, my dear—but I used to think that if I had been a young man, and my wife had married somebody else, I would have known how to look out for her better than the man who had her—one of the prettiest girls anywhere about.

"I wonder if the parson intends to send his daughter to Burmah or the Fiji Islands? Well, he is a good man, and he has stepped along in his path of duty without a kick or a shy, and I suppose he is sure of finding his heavenly pasture at last. I wish some other people were as sure." The squire finished his cup as he spoke, and handed it to his wife for replenishment.

"It would be a cruel thing for him to send that little wild rose of a girl to any of those deadly climates; she looks as if she might have inherited delicacy from her mother too. I can't believe he will," said she, tilting the china pitcher carefully. "I shall invite her to tea again next week. I think the poor child will be benefited by it."

So it came to pass that every Wednesday afternoon Love went to take tea at the squire's house. Her father gave his consent, Love could not help thinking, with a certain constraint of pleasure at the invitation. "The squire's wife is a godly woman, and, I hear, a notable housekeeper; her example may profit you in some things, as your mother's would have done," the parson said.

Love thought that her father seemed pleased when some fresh gifts, which she attributed, like the others, to the bounty of the squire's lady, arrived. A few days after her first tea-drinking at the squire's, on a warm night in early May, there was a loud knock at the front door, and when Love answered it, no one was there, but a dainty package was swinging by a cord to the latch.

Love, after opening it in the sitting-room, carried it to her father, who sat over his sermon in the study, and displayed, with rapture and terror at what he might say, the fine India muslin for a gown, the beautiful blue ribbon to tie around her waist, and the little morocco shoes. Her father, much to her astonishment, did not withhold his permission for her to keep the gifts, yet he spoke almost sternly regarding them, and impressed upon her her duty in not placing undue importance upon such frivolities, in view of the serious life work before her.

Love went clad in her new finery to take tea with the squire's lady, and her heart was in such a flutter of gratitude she made no expression of it, except by an eloquent look at her friend when she praised the beauty of her gown.

"Why, my dear, what have we here, a little white rose instead of a little Quaker lady?" the squire's wife asked, smiling at Love, fluttering before her in her muslin frills; and Love only smiled back at her, and blushed with modest pride and affection.

Love had a delicacy, perhaps exaggerated and misplaced, about returning open thanks for surreptitious benefits. She said never a word to the squire's wife about the gifts. Indeed, a number of times Mrs. Squire Abner Hawkes gave the child presents with no pretence of secrecy; there were three old gowns of her own among them—one, the pride of Love's heart, of a blue figured satin. Love altered these gowns to fit her slender shape, and wore them to the admiration and somewhat to the wonder of all beholders. They thought it strange that Parson Lord should allow his daughter to go dressed so gayly, especially to the house of God. Love, who was henceforth always a bird of fine plumage, never talked much about these showers of surreptitious benefits to her father. She never mentioned the squire's lady in that connection, except now and then to remark upon her kindness, once especially when she wore for the first time the remodelled gown of blue figured satin. It was on a Wednesday, when she was going to take tea at the squire's, and it was four years after her first visit there. The squire's wife was a faithful friend, and Love a faithful admirer.

Parson Lord might have pleaded, with truth, the strength of the temptation, had he felt some purely temporal pride in the appearance of his daughter as she stood before him in that gown, shimmering with blue lights from shoulder to heel, and her lovely head shining with a golden crown of braids. In fact, a smile of that utter weakness and fondness which would have better suited her mother's face came over her father's, to Love's wonder. But he enjoined her as sternly as ever not to allow her heart to dwell upon such vanities, but to remember that it was only her poor dying body which was so adorned, then turned again with his usual grave dignity to his sermon.

Mr. Richard Pierce was to be at the tea-drinking that afternoon, and Love did not anticipate the occasion with quite as much pleasure as usual. Now, she thought, it would be goodby to her pleasant sittings and her confidential talks with the squire's lady. She had confessed as much to her friend, who had only patted her cheek fondly and smiled. Love was afterward afraid that she had been rude and forgetful of the claims upon her gratitude and deference. There, she had actually as good as told her that she was sorry her grandson was coming home, when she had not seen him for so long.

Mr. Richard Pierce, having developed within himself an amazing spirit of independence, had been away the greater part of his vacations, earning money as tutor, and possibly in other capacities. There were those who claimed to have seen Mr. Richard Pierce, the squire's step-grandson, following the plough on a farm twenty miles away like any farmer's son. During his last vacation he had been in the old country with two boys whom he was fitting for college; the one before that, when he had been home for a few weeks, Love had been housed with a quinsy sore throat, and had not seen him. Indeed, with the exception of a few chance encounters with him at his grandmother's, when he had just arrived or was just leaving, the girl had not seen him at all.

When she reached the squire's house, and entered the stately old sitting-room, hung, as to its walls, with dim old oil-paintings and blurred engravings in heavy frames, furnished with old mahogany pieces reflecting the light, as in little pools, from their polished surfaces, it was at first so dark to her, coming out of the afternoon sunlight, that she could see nobody. The shutters were nearly closed, because the squire's wife had a headache. Love saw her friend's face smiling dimly out of the gloom, heard her voice greeting her fondly, and felt her soft lips on her cheek; then she was presented formally to Mr. Richard Pierce, and curtsied vaguely before a bowing shadow. After Love had removed her worked muslin cape and her bonnet, she seated herself and took out her needle-work—a fine handkerchief which she was hem-stitching for her father, having coveted a little daintiness for him as well as herself. She worked industriously, answering modestly and prettily the squire's wife when she spoke to her, and frequently giving her fond glances; but she looked very seldom at Mr. Richard, and replied in gentle but cool monosyllables when he ventured to address her.

The young man could scarcely take his eyes from her, though he strove hard not to stare rudely. It seemed to him that he had never in his whole life seen anything quite so fair and wonderful as this girl, who seemed to sit in a sort of blue radiance, with a shaft of sunlight from the open upper half of the shutter gilding her head. All the courtly ease of manner for which he had been quite famed among his associates deserted him. He heard his voice tremble when he addressed this unresponsive girl; he knew that his remarks were boyish commonplaces. It seemed to him that his grandmother's fair guest was in a mood not of maiden shyness only, but of decided aversion toward himself. He wondered in what way he could have offended her so soon.

He wondered if she simply objected to him on the score of his personal appearance. It had always been considered fair beyond the average, but it might easily not be so regarded by her. Richard was not a large man; he considered that fact uneasily. He straightened himself to his fullest height when he crossed the room to open a shutter. However, his pains were thrown away; Love did not look at him at all. Still, although she was apparently oblivious of his presence, she was, in reality, fully aware of it.

The moment Love had entered the room, she had been conscious of a strange and pungent odour. She did not know what it was, but Mr. Richard smoked tobacco, and the scent of it was in his clothes. Love did not find it disagreeable, but she perceived it with every breath she drew, and it gave her a strange impulse of maiden rebellion, quite out of proportion to the cause, as if this man were fairly forcing his presence upon her, making it a part of her, whether she would or not.

Love, with a little impatient air foreign to her, removed the lid from a potpourri-jar on a stand near her, and bent her face over it. The scent of rose leaves, lavender, and spices seemed like a reassertion of the flavour of her own maiden individuality, which this man in his tobacco-scented garments, with his glances of hitherto unknown masculine pleading, was striving to overcome.

"It is too pleasant an afternoon for you to sit here in this dark room with your needle-work," said the squire's lady, presently. "Put it away, my dear, and Richard will take you out for a stroll in the garden."

Love started. "Thank you," she faltered, "I would rather remain here with you, if you please."

"Do as I bid you, my dear," repeated the squire's wife, with her air of gentle authority which no one ever gainsaid.

Love, with no further demur, folded her needle-work and put it in her bead bag, and went with Mr. Richard into the garden at the back of the house.

Up and down the long box-bordered paths they paced. Love kept her eyes downcast, and face turned, so that only the pink curve of it was visible to her companion. She answered in soft monosyllables, a yes, sir, or a no, sir, when he addressed her with anxious deference. It spoke well for her charms that this young man, who had been heretofore treated very kindly by her sex, should have had a relish for this strolling in his grandmother's garden with one so sparing of responsive words and smiles. But Mr. Richard Pierce, far from appearing bored or dull, wore a look of rapture, as he paced the tortuous garden paths, Love's blue flounces rustling against him, no matter how far she shrank away, the pungent odor of the rank box, which was waist-high in places, in his nostrils, and now and then, like the melody triumphing over the swell of the bass, a breath of lavender from Love's garments.

They threaded the green maze of the garden, Richard more adoring at every step; he held Love's parasol jealously between her face and the sun. It would have pleased him, doubtless, had the snapdragons in the garden beds been real ones, that he might have slain them in her defence. He ventured to pick a nosegay and offer it to her. She accepted it with courtesy, and when they returned to the house, gave it to his grandmother.

The tea-drinking that afternoon was a sore embarrassment and trial to Love. The squire was away, and his lady's headache had waxed so severe that she had been obliged to retire to her room and leave her guest to sup alone with her grandson.

So she and Mr. Richard sat alone at the table, Love behind the tea-tray with its silver cream-jug and sugar-bowl and blue cups and saucers. She poured out the tea, tilting the silver pot with a dainty turn of her round elbow, and inquired politely as to the number of lumps of sugar, but volunteered scarcely a word beside.

She sipped her tea delicately, and made a pretence at her biscuit and a glass of syllabub and a square of sponge-cake, but was all the time anxiously furtive as to Richard's progress, that she might rise from the table.

Even after tea Love was not as soon quit of her admirer as she had expected, for he must needs walk home with her to guard her from the deadly perils of the village street at dusk. She began to fear that she would not be rid of him at her house door, knowing that it would be incumbent upon her, unless she violated her sense of courtesy and hospitality, to invite him to enter. However, the young man, desirous as he might have been to accept the invitation, had the wisdom to refuse.

When Mr. Richard Pierce returned to Boston, some six weeks later, to take up the study of the law, Love had smiled in his face a few times, she had addressed him of her own accord upon as many occasions as he could count on his fingers, and twice when returning in his company from tea-drinkings at his grand-mother's, she had strolled with him a half-mile past her house. Once, coming on some errand for his grandmother, and having met with no response to his knocks, he had peered around the house and caught a glimpse of something blue through the trees in the apple orchard. He had followed up that glimpse of blue, and found Love seated with her needle-work in a natural arbour made by the growth of a wild grape-vine over an old apple-tree, and had ventured to throw himself on the grass at her feet. Love cast a startled glance at him, half rose as if to run away, then set-tled herself and resumed her needle-work. Love's eyes were so intent upon this work that presently the young man dared still further. He gently laid hold of the hem of her blue muslin gown and kissed it fervently.

Love was on her feet in a flash, and her work—a lace tuck-er which she was embroidering—her scissors, her emery, her thread, were on the ground. "I will never come here again, never, never," said she, in a voice between anger and tears, and then was gone, flying like a blue-clad nymph through the green distance to the house.

There was a certain shrewdness about Richard Pierce, al-though he seemed such a humble lover. He doubtless was abashed and conscience-stricken before Love's indignation, but he argued hopefully from her declaration that she would never visit the arbour again. "She must have thought of the possibility of my meeting her here," reasoned Richard Pierce.

Richard was to leave for Boston the next day but one. The following afternoon he repaired full of hope to the grape-ar-bour, reaching it by a circuitous way across the fields, lest Love spy him from her window, and so not be able to excuse her coming to herself.

Richard waited long, but Love did not come; finally he re-paired boldly to the house and knocked; but no one opened the door. The parson was away; and as for Love, she had been weeping so bitterly that not for the whole world would she have faced Richard Pierce with her red eyes.

Richard came again that evening, and then the parson admitted him, and ushered him into the study, concluding, as a matter of course, that the young man was there upon some errand connected with his soul's salvation.

Richard, after a period of solemn waiting, on the parson's part, for the unburdening of his spirit, inquired somewhat awkwardly if Miss Love were at home. The parson directly inferred that he had come on some errand for his grandmother, and replied that his daughter had retired to her room, suffering with a severe headache, but that he would deliver the message in the morning.

Richard, for very shame before this man so unconscious of his selfish designs, must needs plunge himself still further into deceit and invent a message, and thereby also accomplish a purpose of his own. He took out of his pocket a neat little parcel in silver-paper, and stated wickedly that his grandmother desired her compliments to Miss Love, and here was a little gift which she begged her to accept, the said gift being a most exquisite and dainty tucker of wrought lace, and a pair of embroidery-scissors, and an emery of painted velvet in an ivory case, for all of which treasures he had ridden hard that morning to the next market-town.

Love, up in her chamber, knew perfectly well who was downstairs; she heard him come and heard him go; and although she would not go down to see him and bid him goodbye, she wept because she would not.

The next morning, when her father gave her the parcel, she knew at once from whom it had come, in spite of that deceptive message. She colored so hotly that her father looked at her in a puzzled way, and she never thanked Madam Diantha (she had come to call the squire's lady by that name), though here was a fine chance with such an openly presented gift.

That night in his prayer the parson betrayed the fact that, however oblivious he had seemed, he had possibly conceived suspicions. He prayed fervently to the effect that his beloved child might ever be mindful of the daily fulfilment of her duty to the Lord. He quoted Saint Paul in terms rendered somewhat covert by sacred imagery; he declared the blessedness of going into the world and preaching the gospel to every living creature in preference to the joys of this life. He petitioned that she might not forget the example of her sainted sister, that pattern of early piety, and might have strength to follow in that path which she would perchance have trod had her life been spared.

When Love rose from her knees she was very pale. Up in her own chamber, she took the lace tucker and the ivory case, folded them carefully in the silver-paper, and put them in a box of painted satinwood which had belonged to her mother. Then she folded the blue muslin gown whose hem Richard had kissed, daintily in a linen towel, and packed it away with the satinwood box in the very bottom of her chest.

Love did not sleep that night, and looked wan and pale the next morning. Even her father's prayer, which was a sort of triumphant homily upon the joys which await them who overcome, did not seem to raise her flagging spirits. Sometimes that prospect of pearly gate and golden street, of eternal chorals of triumphant praise, seem all too splendid to a little humble soul who would fain have offered to itself a smaller reward for sacrifice.

If, instead of the sea of jasper and those pavements of gold, Love had had pictured some little door of home, and her mother standing in it with outstretched arms of welcome, it might have filled her with a deeper sense of comfort.

When Richard had been gone a week, he wrote a letter to Love in which he humbly begged her pardon for his boldness the afternoon before he left, and craved the honour of a correspondence.

Love had debated long as to whether her duty demanded that she show this letter to her father and ask his advice in the matter. Finally, being led to a decision largely by the reasoning that her duty it must be since it was such a sore trial, she took the letter to his study, and stood waiting at his elbow, a patient, downcast young figure, while he read it.

The candle-light flickered over the parson's long, pale, heavily corrugated face as he read. It was a face expressive of all the stern resignation and persistency in sacrifice, and of none of its triumphant self-consciousness. Most truly did Parson Lord serve his Maker through pure obedience to His will, and never for the sake of his own. Finally the parson folded the letter, and stated his mind to his daughter, with his usual circumlocution of scriptural imagery. When he had finished, Love curtsied, took her letter, and went back to her chamber.

Poor Richard Pierce received no answer from his divinity, but, instead, a lengthy epistle from her father, assuring him of the receipt of his distinguished favour, which had been submitted to his inspection by his daughter, for whom he had, he begged leave to say, views connected with her spiritual welfare and her true duty in life which rendered it inadvisable, according to his poor judgment, for her to engage in a correspondence of the nature proposed, which might perchance cause her to waste precious time and strength which should be devoted to higher aims, and possibly in the end divert her mind from the favourable contemplation of the one true and acceptable sacrifice of her life. The parson concluded with a few words of pious exhortation to his young friend.

It was quite possible that Richard felt some irritation at that very sweet docility, which he would have so admired if directed toward himself, which led Love to show his letter to her father and allow him to answer it. He did not again subject himself to a similar rebuff, nor endeavour to see Love until the following summer.

Then, at the first sight of the girl, grown far prettier, and with a helpless blush and tremor before his eyes, he felt his resentment vanish, and his admiration and love revive. However, he progressed not at all in his wooing. If he went to call upon Love, he was entertained by her father with a relentless persistency of pious conversation, and he went many a time to the grape-arbour in the hope that Love might be there with her needlework, but she never was. During the three weeks he was at home she came only once to take tea with his grandmother, and then her father came for her, and himself escorted her home.

Richard could not but feel that he was avoided, and finally went back to Boston, resolved that he would waste no more thought upon a girl who so persistently flouted him.

After Richard had gone, Love grew thin and pale. The subtle inconsistency of reasoning power of her sex was strongly marked in her. Underneath all her keeping to the letter of the law she had a feeling of wonder and grief and injury that her lover should so take her at her word. She would have had him come when he was told not. She would have had him force her to a *tête-à-tête* in that grape-arbour, and make it out of her power to say him nay. She would have had him correspond with her when such correspondence had been forbidden, and somehow ease her conscience of any blame. She would have had him take her love all the more, since she withheld it. She told herself that he did not care now; he had seen a fairer face in Boston; she would sternly put him from her mind, and strive to gain sufficient earthly bliss in the hope of that of heaven.

Now and then she talked to her father of her uncles in Burmah and India, how old were their wives when they accompanied them, how old was it necessary for a female missionary to be before the American Board would think it judicious to send her to those far-off lands? Reuben Lord had not always that expression of quick sympathy and joy with which he might have been expected to hear remarks so evidently tending toward the accomplishment of his cherished wish. Instead, he looked at his daughter with a sternly anxious knitting of brows, and replied that it was not so much a matter of years which was in question, as preparation and fitness of spirit and body to perform such work with acceptance to the Lord.

Love reflected humbly that her father considered that she was not spiritually fit for so great a trust; of her bodily state she thought not at all. She wondered why the squire's lady looked at her with such wistful intentness; she wondered why she always insisted upon her drinking a glass of port-wine when she first arrived at her house.

In those days more mysterious gifts than ever were showered upon the girl—a warm fur tippet for her delicate throat, a great muff wherein to nestle her little hands, a warmly wadded cloak, a hood of blue silk edged with swan's-down, and many luxuries to tempt her appetite—oranges and pineapples, and often a plump partridge or quail.

Love's gratitude to the squire's lady seemed to warm her whole heart. She often speculated as to the advisability of thanking her friend for her anonymous gifts, and once she consulted her father. "Do you think it advisable to thank a person for a gift who has given it secretly, sir?" she asked. And her father stared a little, and replied,

"No, daughter; no, certainly it is not advisable," and was again intent upon Doddridge.

All winter, when the stage-coach came in with the mail, Love had a forlorn hope that it might bring a letter from Richard, but it never did. Sometimes the squire's lady used to read extracts from her grandson's letters to Love, both to her delight and her fear. Always her heart was beating loud in her ears with the fear lest Richard had written of some beautiful Boston lady who had won his heart. It was in such wise that she betrayed herself one afternoon in late June.

It being a fine day, she and Madam Diantha were walking in the garden when the squire came with the mail, and there was a letter from Richard.

The squire was a fine, handsome old gentleman, red-cheeked and clear-eyed, with a silver fleece of hair. Though he limped somewhat on account of his rheumatic joints, yet he advanced with an almost boyish impetuosity. He was of rather smaller stature than his wife, who moved with slow state between the roses, in a wide inflorescence of lavender flounces and softly floating laps and frills of lace.

"Open the letter at once, my dear," cried the squire, "and let us hear if the boy is coming, or if some fair Boston lady has him at her silk apron strings."

Love had moved aside in the garden path to make room for the squire, and Madam Diantha saw the girl's face go white and red.

"Read it aloud, my dear, if you please," repeated the squire, eagerly.

His wife began to read in her soft voice.

The box in that place was as high as Love's waist, and some branches of roses were hooping over it. She turned her face away and smelled of a rose as she listened.

The letter was short. Richard could not come just yet, not until next month, possibly not until August. He was very much occupied; the weather was very warm. He had been to dine at Mr. Solomon Purdy's house the week before, and was to go there to a party tomorrow. Mr. Purdy had two daughters, most amiable young ladies, and a son whom he found a most desirable companion—

"'Tis one of the most amiable young ladies!" interrupted the squire, with a loud laugh. "An amiable young lady and a pretty little apron, and Mr. Richard Pierce stumbling at the length of the strings. I knew it. She has him fast. Well, 'tis hard lines for us when we thought to see the lad's face at the table a month ago, and now—Why, Diantha, my dear, what is the matter with the child?" For Love was half hanging over the green wall of box, like a broken rose branch.

"Why, my dear, what is the matter? Are you ill?" cried Madam Diantha, and put her arm around the girl, supporting her tenderly on her broad motherly bosom. Love was gasping faintly, and her lips were white.

"What do you think is the matter?" asked the squire, anxiously: he was very fond of Love.

"It is nothing, I think," said his wife: "she is not very strong, and the sun is hot. Will you please go to the house and get the camphor-bottle on my dressing-table?"

The squire's lady put her mouth close to the girl's ear when her husband had gone. "My precious child," she whispered, but said no more of comfort; she dared not, since she knew not but the squire's surmise was correct. So she only kissed and patted and soothed as best she could, and repeated that the sun was hot, and she not strong, and no wonder that she was faint.

Poor Love would have given the world to run home and hide herself, but she responded, with a proud impulse toward concealment, to her friend's subterfuge. She owned that she had felt the heat of the sun; she submitted to all that was done for her, and remained to tea as usual, eating obediently as much as she was able of a little bird which the squire had ordered to be specially prepared.

"What ailed the child?" the squire asked his wife, after Love had gone home. "No, don't say the sun, my dear, unless you spell it with an o," and the squire laughed with boyish glee at his own joke.

"Hush, my dear, we have no reason —" his wife began; but he nodded obstinately.

"The poor little soul was distressed at the mention of the amiable Purdy," said he; "but I hope you told her that it was nothing particular."

"Oh, but, my dear, it may be!" said his wife.

"I don't believe a word of it," declared the squire, stoutly. "Well, if the boy should want her, and she him, I would venture ten to one that the parson would try to separate them with the contribution-box."

The next week Love forced herself to go to the squire's, lest they suspect the reason if she stayed away, but after that she did not go any more. Then July came and passed, and August was there, and Richard returned.

Love saw him first as she was walking down the street. He was out driving with his grandmother and the squire. He had come unexpectedly the night before. When Love first lifted her eyes at the roll of wheels and saw Richard, she went so white that Madam Diantha gave an involuntary start as if she would go to her. She thought for a second that the girl would fall. But Love recovered herself quickly, and curtsied prettily, and they had passed.

Richard's grandmother glanced covertly at him, but he looked quite unconcerned, and her heart sank. However, Richard had seen, and the image of Miss Catharine Purdy, which he had rather urged upon his heart of late, faded.

Love wore that day a white muslin gown—one of her mysterious gifts—a little white cape, and a hat with a white ribbon; she looked for all the world like a flying white flower as she came down the street, her white draperies blown in the wind.

The squire had been shrewdly observant. "The parson's daughter looks more like an angel than a thing of flesh and blood," he remarked presently, "and I fear she'll be one in earnest if they don't look out for her."

Richard stared at the landscape. "Is she out of health?" he inquired, in a somewhat constrained tone.

"She was always delicate, dear," his grandmother replied, evasively.

"Not like this," maintained the squire.

That evening, when he and Richard were sitting together after supper, he turned suddenly upon the young man with a motion of defiance, as if he were throwing secrecy and prudence to the winds. "Well, my boy, your grandmother would have me say nothing, but I am going to get to the bottom of this. Our little Love Lord fainted away when your grandmother read a letter of yours in which you spoke of the Misses Purdy something particularly, and we knew—Now, sir, if you have trifled —"

"Trifled, sir!" cried Richard, staring. "Why, sir, she will have none of me. She has shown me so plainly that there is no mistaking it."

"Then it's the parson," said the squire, reflectively.

"No; it is she herself."

"Go there and see her, and you will find out that I am right, my boy," said the squire.

"I go not the second time where I have as good as had the door in my face, though it was heaven, and an angel shutting it," replied Richard, and was true to his resolution for some little time.

Poor Love staid close at home, and always, when the weather was fine, repaired of an afternoon to the grape-arbor, and sat there until tea-time, with an eye of wistful hope for a young man coming across the field; but he never came.

But one afternoon, during the last of August, Love went into her father's study, bringing a letter in which Mr. Richard Pierce begged her to be in the grape-arbour at eight o'clock, for the purpose of conversation upon a matter pertaining to them both. He concluded by stating that he would consider her failure to be there as final, and would hence forth obtrude himself no further upon her, whose obedient servant he would ever be.

Parson Reuben Lord read the letter, while his daughter looked at him with that same expression with which she had pleaded for the doll.

"Daughter, you know what my will has been for you from your youth up," said the parson, solemnly.

Love went out without a word; her father heard her sob on the stairs. She ate no supper, though a little crock of honey had mysteriously come for her late that afternoon. She went up to her room at half past seven o'clock.

Parson Lord stood listening at the foot of the stairs leading to his daughter's chamber; now and then he heard a stifled sob. He put foot on the stair, as if to ascend, then drew back; at every sob his own face was convulsed. At last he took his hat and went out, shutting the front door softly.

That night the sky was overcast and the dusk was early. When Richard, at eight o'clock, crossed the fields, all the trees were forgathering in shadows, and all white flower bushes and white house walls in the distance seemed luminous. Long before he reached the arbour he saw something white shining therein, and his heart leaped for joy, he thinking it was surely Love's white gown and she had come. But when he went in, it was only a soft lavender-scented mass of silken shawl.

"She has been here and gone," thought Richard, in a great turmoil of grief and wrath. "She has been here and not waited. I will have no more of her. If she loves me not, I will not follow her any longer; and if she loves me, she has no spirit which is worthy of the love. The clock has not yet struck eight, and she did not wait—"

Then, just as Richard spoke, the town clock struck the half-hour after eight. And here it may be said that the next day, when the Boston stage-coach came in, there was great amazement all over the village to find that the town clock was a half-hour fast.

But Richard Pierce, that night when he heard the half-hour strike, went straight to the parson's house and let fall the knocker with a bold clang, and when the parson came, demanded to see his daughter.

"She has retired, I fear," replied the parson, who was strangely pale, and whose voice quivered convulsively. "Will you walk into my study, sir?"

But Richard would not come in, and would see his daughter at the door.

Love did not know the voice in which her father called; she asked, tremblingly, who had spoken.

"Come down, daughter," said her father, still in that strange voice. "There is some one at the door who is desirous of speaking with you." Then he went into his study and shut the door.

Love went down, and Richard's face shone white framed in the doorway against a background of night gloom. He flung an arm around her and drew her outside.

"We have had enough of this, dear," he said, shortly. "If you love me, tell me so now, for God's sake!"

"Oh, it is not right! I fear it is not right!" Love gasped, and trembled in his arms.

"Let the right alone. Tell me!"

"I must not!"

"Let the must not alone. Tell me!"

"Yes," said Love, with a sigh, and then tried with a faint assertion of maiden dignity to ward off Richard's kisses. "It can be no more than—this," she whispered, brokenly. "We cannot be—married, Richard."

"Why not?" demanded Richard. "Why not, sweetheart?"

"Father—father has vowed—He does not wish me to marry, Richard."

"Well, marry you will, nevertheless, sweetheart."

"Never without his consent. I cannot, Richard."

"With or without, you shall marry me, Love; but he will consent."

"Oh, he will not, unless —" Love looked with sudden courage in his face. "Oh," she whispered—"oh, Richard, if you would only be a missionary!"

Richard Pierce laughed so loud that the gay ring of it penetrated to the parson in the study. "I will not be a missionary, and yet marry me you shall, now I know that you love me, sweetheart," said he; then, before Love knew it, they were standing before her father.

"Sir," said Richard, speaking with a fine manly air, "I should have come to you before and asked for your daughter's hand had she not been so desirous of following your wishes instead of her own, and concealing her feelings from me so well that I judged it to be useless. Now we know that we love each other, and I beg that you will give me your daughter for my wife."

"My daughter has long known that my plans for her were otherwise than the married estate," said Parson Lord, looking past them and speaking with stiff lips.

"Is the soul of your daughter yours to command in a matter like this, sir?" inquired the young man, hotly, and yet with some show of deference.

"I cannot give my consent," Parson Lord said, and turned to his sermon.

"Cannot you reconsider this, sir?"

"I cannot give my consent," repeated the parson. "It is final."

"Then," said Richard, drawing Love's arm firmly through his own, "marry without your consent we must, sir, for marry her I will, now I know that she loves me."

The next Sunday the banns between Richard Pierce, Esquire, and Love Lord, spinster, were published—not proclaimed from the pulpit, but copied neatly on a fair sheet, and hung in the frame used for that purpose beside the meeting-house door, where all who entered might read. The parson might have discerned a greater spirit of astonishment and gossip in the faces of his audience than of pious attention to the precepts of the gospel, had he been interested to decipher it.

His plans for his daughter were well known, and here were her banns published. Had the parson yielded unto the pleading of earthly affection, or was this without his knowledge or approval? Public opinion rather inclined to the latter view, although far from sure that the banns could be set up, even with the squire to manage matters, without the parson's knowledge. Love was not at meeting, but Richard Pierce was sitting between his grandmother and the squire, and holding up his head with a gallant air, looking straight at the parson, as if he were weighing every word of the discourse.

The banns were published three Sundays, and on Monday following the third, the squire, the squire's lady, and Mr. Richard Pierce drove in the coach to Parson Reuben Lord's house. When they entered the study, having been ushered therein by the parson with a grave dignity, Richard looked around anxiously, but Love was not there. He glanced imploringly at his grandmother. "Where is Love, sir?" she asked the parson, in her sweetly imperative voice.

"In her chamber," he replied. When he was dead, Parson Lord would be no whiter.

"I will call her," said Madam Diantha, and called "Love! Love, dear child!" And when the girl did not come for the calling, she went upstairs, and found her weeping and moaning that she could not wed without her father's consent, and he would never give it, and if he would, he would fly in the face of his own conscience, and bring a curse upon himself for breaking his solemn promise to the Lord.

Thus the poor child, in her bewilderment of love and conscience, until the squire's lady would hear no more, but bathed her eyes and led her downstairs to Richard, who took her hand

302

with an air as if he challenged the whole world.

Then Squire Hawkes spoke to the parson. "Sir," he said, "my grandson loves your daughter, and she returns his love. The banns have been published for the requisite length of time, as you are aware, and they stand before you humbly beseeching that you give them your blessing and unite them in matrimony."

"I cannot do so, sir," replied Parson Lord, in a set sad voice. "I cannot, sir."

"May I inquire why not, sir?"

"When my child was born, I solemnly dedicated her to God. I vowed that she should be set apart for the service of the Lord, should she be spared to me," replied the Parson. "I can break my vow no more than Jephthah of old."

"Damn Jephthah!" shouted the squire, who had an uncompromising tongue when aroused. "You are mad, sir."

The parson remained silent.

"Will you, or will you not, marry them?" demanded the squire.

"I cannot."

"Will you give your consent, then?"

"I cannot."

Love was clinging weakly to her lover's arm. The squire faced them suddenly. "'Tis the rankest folly," he cried, "and the cruellest! What are you, Reuben Lord, to dispose of your daughter, heart and soul, as you propose? How dare you come thrusting your damned covenant like a wedge between two young things who love each other in the fear of the Lord, and refusing to make them happy, because you are afraid you will go to hell for it? How dare you tamper with the holiest feeling of the human heart? Here is your daughter, an angel if ever there was one, loving this young man, and ready and willing to honour and obey him all the days of her life, comfort him in sorrow, and nurse him in sickness, are you not, sweetheart?"

Love nodded, sobbing.

"And here is my grandson, with all his heart set upon loving, cherishing, and protecting her in sickness or health, and cleaving to her for better or worse, are you not, Richard?"

"Yes, sir, I am," replied Richard, with a start of amazement.

"Then," said the squire, his voice changing suddenly from a tone of easy interrogation to one of solemn proclamation, "in virtue of the authority vested in me as justice of the peace of this township, I pronounce you man and wife."

The squire gave a loud laugh of triumph, which he checked suddenly as he saw Parson Reuben Lord's face. It was shocked beyond words, and with a strange expression of guilt.

"Before the Lord, sir," cried Squire Hawkes, "neither your daughter nor my grandson nor my wife was a party to this, nor I myself, until the fancy struck me. I saw in a flash 'twas the only way; unless she had been trapped thus, she would never have brought herself to wed without your consent."

Parson Lord went over to his daughter, kissed her solemnly on her forehead, said "God bless you, my daughter! May you and the husband you have chosen dwell together in the love of the Lord, and may the day be sanctified to you!" and went out.

A crowd which had gathered outside, gaping silently out of the shadows, stood back in a very hush of wonder when the bridal party emerged from the parson's house, got into the coach, and were driven away. "She's coming! She's married to him!" said one exclaiming voice, and then no more.

For days the village was thrilled to its fullest capacity for excitement by the wedding of the squire's grandson and the parson's daughter; but no one ever knew the full particulars, for principals and witnesses kept them to themselves.

Everybody agreed that the parson aged fast after his daughter's marriage, and that his whole character seemed strangely changed. Whereas he had moved among his people, discharging his religious duties toward them with a stern rigidity of faithfulness, he now bore himself with a meek lovingness which caused folk to turn and stare at him as at a stranger. Moreover, his sermons lost their directness of application concerning the justice and righteous judgments of the Lord, and some feared lest he might be falling off in the doctrines.

Aunt Betsey Ware, who kept house for him, said never was such a change in mortal man before, and when a sour-apple tree begun to bear sweetings, 'twas a sure sign that it would blossom next spring in another world. She was right in that case, for Parson Reuben Lord died very suddenly the spring after his daughter's marriage.

Love was sent for, and came with her husband, and mourned for her father, though in somewhat unwonted fashion. It was as if she grieved more sorely for that father whom she had never had than for him whom she had lost.

Then, a few days after the funeral, she found among his papers his journal, which she read, and had therefrom a revelation. When her husband came in she ran and clung to him, weeping and trembling in a passion of remorseful love and pity.

"Oh," she cried—"oh, Richard! it was father—it was father!"

"What do you mean, sweetheart?"

"It was father who gave me the doll, and not Madam Diantha. It was father who gave me the pretty gowns and the bonnets and the ribbons. It was father who gave me everything! Oh, Richard, it was poor father! Look at this—look!"

Richard took the parson's journal and read, here and there, where she indicated:

******

March 6.—I have purchased the doll. Alas! I am weak and selfish, and under the sway of my natural affection. The price of the toy should have gone elsewhere; but the heart of the child is sore, and I cannot have it. Oh, her face as she stood there holding the old treasure of her childhood, which she had found, and which I could not let her keep for very consistency in discipline! Daphne was too hard upon such a tender heart of such a little girl.

God forgive me if I have erred through too great love for my child! Methinks I could have been burned at the stake in Thy cause, I could have been broken upon the wheel, but this martyrdom of pain in the heart of the child of my love I cannot bear.

March 7.—She looks as I have never seen her; the joy in her face causes my heart to leap. I have given her the toy in a manner secretly, hoping that she will not confound me with her innocent delight and thanks, which would convey to me such reproaches; and she was delicately mindful of my wish. She is wise beyond her years. How can I crave forgiveness when I do not truly repent, remembering the child's face and the joy in it? Right or wrong, I would do it over again. Oh, my poor heart!

July 8.—Have purchased a gown of white muslin for my daughter. The ornament of a meek and quiet spirit should have been sufficient for her, but she was not attired as others of her age, and it perchance has tried her: the heart of a maid is a tender and unknown thing. Oh, my weak and degenerate nature! May it not foster in her too great love of dress and the pleasures of the world; for myself it matters not, so she be innocently glad.

September 6.—She is grieving because of that youth to whom her heart has turned, as I have known for some time, to my great sadness. What will become of that tender heart, yielding so helplessly and so guilelessly unto the great call of life? I cannot give my consent; I dare not break my vow unto the Lord. Herein, at least, I must stand firm. She has no appetite. I have purchased delicacies for her. It may be that I do wrong, when the heathen starve for the milk of the word; but she is my only child.

January 9.—She is very poor in health. She shivers in the cold meeting-house. I have purchased a fur tippet for her, and a large muff, and a wadded cloak, at a price which would have done incalculable good in purchasing spiritual raiment for the needy in foreign fields. The child does not put me to shame with her openly expressed gratitude, but takes her gift, as usual, with her sweet docility and meek grace.

March 18.—I have today purchased a new gown of fine texture and a pretty colour. She still pines and grieves, and I strive to render her content with these little gewgaws, which, I have understood, sweeten the greater lacks of life to the feminine heart. May God forgive me for yielding to this so great weakness, and striving to temper the sorrow which may be ordained for her good to my daughter, and even perchance awakening thereby a love for vanity in her heart!

July 26.—The youth upon whom she has fixed her affections is in the village; she is watching for him and he does not come. Can I keep to my resolution and see her unhappy?

August 27.—All is over. I have yielded to the strength of my paternal love. They have met and plighted their vows, and by my means. I myself, in spite of everything, have brought about a meeting between them, and that by methods which bring me to shame. I resorted to subterfuge, even to deception. I cannot recall even to myself the means which I used, involving, as they did, deception and trickery, without the deepest mortification and the most painful prickings of conscience, and yet I acknowledge, to my still deeper humiliation, that I do not regret the result which was brought about by such means, and I confess that I am sure, in the depths of my guilty and self-betraying heart, that, for the sake of her happiness, I would repeat, as long as I drew the breath of life, my folly and my fault.

September 30.—My daughter is wedded to the man of her choice. The letter of my vow I kept, yet broke it undeniably in the spirit. I humbly confess to my Maker my joy and exceeding happiness that the vow be not fulfilled, sinful though it may be. In spite of my backsliding, my lack of steadfastness, and my weakness of the flesh, I have upon me a deep peace and certainty of good to come which will not be gainsaid by any self-blame. I marvel greatly if I perchance have rightfully estimated the love of God toward us, which may—an I be not led astray by my evil imagination—acknowledge as its own offspring all the natural affections of the human heart, and the human weakness therefrom be thus forgiven by the divine love.

The Southwest Chamber

"That schoolteacher from Acton is coming today," said the elder Miss Gill, Sophia.

"So she is," assented the younger Miss Gill, Amanda.

"I have decided to put her in the southwest chamber," said Sophia.

Amanda looked at her sister with an expression of mingled doubt and terror. "You don't suppose she would—" she began hesitatingly.

"Would what?" demanded Sophia, sharply. She was more incisive than her sister. Both were below the medium height, and stout, but Sophia was firm where Amanda was flabby. Amanda wore a baggy old muslin (it was a hot day), and Sophia was uncompromisingly hooked up in a starched and boned cambric over her high shelving figure.

"I didn't know but she would object to sleeping in that room, as long as Aunt Harriet died there such a little time ago," faltered Amanda.

"Well!" said Sophia, "of all the silly notions! If you are going to pick out rooms in this house where nobody has died, for the boarders, you'll have your hands full. Grandfather Ackley had seven children; four of them died here to my certain knowledge, besides grandfather and grandmother. I think Great-grandmother Ackley, grandfather's mother, died here, too; she must have; and Great-grandfather Ackley, and grandfather's unmarried sister, Great-aunt Fanny Ackley. I don't believe there's a room nor a bed in this house that somebody hasn't passed away in."

"Well, I suppose I am silly to think of it, and she had better go in there," said Amanda.

"I know she had. The northeast room is small and hot, and she's stout and likely to feel the heat, and she's saved money and is able to board out summers, and maybe she'll come here another year if she's well accommodated," said Sophia. "Now I guess you'd better go in there and see if any dust has settled on anything since it was cleaned, and open the west windows and let the sun in, while I see to that cake."

Amanda went to her task in the southwest chamber while her sister stepped heavily down the back stairs on her way to the kitchen.

"It seems to me you had better open the bed while you air and dust, then make it up again," she called back.

"Yes, sister," Amanda answered, shudderingly.

Nobody knew how this elderly woman with the untrammelled imagination of a child dreaded to enter the southwest chamber, and yet she could not have told why she had the dread. She had entered and occupied rooms which had been once tenanted by persons now dead. The room which had been hers in the little house in which she and her sister had lived before coming here had been her dead mother's. She had never reflected upon the fact with anything but loving awe and reverence. There had never been any fear. But this was different. She entered and her heart beat thickly in her ears. Her hands were cold. The room was a very large one. The four windows, two facing south, two west, were closed, the blinds also. The room was in a film of green gloom. The furniture loomed out vaguely. The gilt frame of a blurred old engraving on the wall caught a little light. The white counterpane on the bed showed like a blank page.

Amanda crossed the room, opened with a straining motion of her thin back and shoulders one of the west windows, and threw back the blind. Then the room revealed itself an apartment full of an aged and worn but no less valid state. Pieces of old mahogany swelled forth; a peacock-patterned chintz draped the bedstead. This chintz also covered a great easy chair which had been the favourite seat of the former occupant of the room. The closet door stood ajar. Amanda noticed that with wonder. There was a glimpse of purple drapery floating from a peg inside the closet. Amanda went across and took down the garment hanging there. She wondered how her sister had happened to leave it when she cleaned the room. It was an old loose gown which had belonged to her aunt. She took it down, shuddering, and closed the closet door after a fearful glance into its dark depths. It was a long closet with a strong odour of lovage. The Aunt Harriet had had a habit of eating lovage and had carried it constantly in her pocket. There was very likely some of the pleasant root in the pocket of the musty purple gown which Amanda threw over the easy chair.

Amanda perceived the odour with a start as if before an actual presence. Odour seems in a sense a vital part of a personality. It can survive the flesh to which it has clung like a persistent shadow, seeming to have in itself something of the substance of that to which it pertained. Amanda was always conscious of this fragrance of lovage as she tidied the room. She dusted the heavy mahogany pieces punctiliously after she had opened the bed as her sister had directed. She spread fresh towels over the wash-stand and the bureau; she made the bed. Then she thought to take the purple gown from the easy chair and carry it to the garret and put it in the trunk with the other articles of the dead woman's wardrobe which had been packed away there; *but the purple gown was not on the chair!*

Amanda Gill was not a woman of strong convictions even as to her own actions. She directly thought that possibly she had been mistaken and had not removed it from the closet. She glanced at the closet door and saw with surprise that it was open, and she had thought she had closed it, but she instantly was not sure of that. So she entered the closet and looked for the purple gown. *It was not there!*

Amanda Gill went feebly out of the closet and looked at the easy chair again. The purple gown was not there! She looked wildly around the room. She went down on her trembling knees and peered under the bed, she opened the bureau drawers, she looked again in the closet. Then she stood in the middle of the floor and fairly wrung her hands.

"What does it mean?" she said in a shocked whisper.

She had certainly seen that loose purple gown of her dead Aunt Harriet's.

There is a limit at which self-refutation must stop in any sane person. Amanda Gill had reached it. She knew that she had seen that purple gown in that closet; she knew that she had removed it and put it on the easy chair. She also knew that she had not taken it out of the room. She felt a curious sense of being inverted mentally. It was as if all her traditions and laws of life were on their heads. Never in her simple record had any garment not remained where she had placed it unless removed by some palpable human agency.

Then the thought occurred to her that possibly her sister Sophia might have entered the room unobserved while her back was turned and removed the dress. A sensation of relief came over her. Her blood seemed to flow back into its usual channels; the tension of her nerves relaxed.

"How silly I am," she said aloud.

She hurried out and downstairs into the kitchen where Sophia was making cake, stirring with splendid circular sweeps of a wooden spoon a creamy yellow mass. She looked up as her sister entered.

"Have you got it done?" said she.

"Yes," replied Amanda. Then she hesitated. A sudden terror overcame her. It did not seem as if it were at all probable that Sophia had left that foamy cake mixture a second to go to Aunt Harriet's chamber and remove that purple gown.

"Well," said Sophia, "if you have got that done I wish you would take hold and string those beans. The first thing we know there won't be time to boil them for dinner."

Amanda moved toward the pan of beans on the table, then she looked at her sister.

"Did you come up in Aunt Harriet's room while I was there?"

she asked weakly.

She knew while she asked what the answer would be.

"Up in Aunt Harriet's room? Of course I didn't. I couldn't leave this cake without having it fall. You know that well enough. Why?"

"Nothing," replied Amanda.

Suddenly she realized that she could not tell her sister what had happened, for before the utter absurdity of the whole thing her belief in her own reason quailed. She knew what Sophia would say if she told her. She could hear her.

"Amanda Gill, have you gone stark staring mad?"

She resolved that she would never tell Sophia. She dropped into a chair and begun shelling the beans with nerveless fingers. Sophia looked at her curiously.

"Amanda Gill, what on earth ails you?" she asked.

"Nothing," replied Amanda. She bent her head very low over the green pods.

"Yes, there is, too! You are as white as a sheet, and your hands are shaking so you can hardly string those beans. I did think you had more sense, Amanda Gill."

"I don't know what you mean, Sophia."

"Yes, you do know what I mean, too; you needn't pretend you don't. Why did you ask me if I had been in that room, and why do you act so queer?"

Amanda hesitated. She had been trained to truth. Then she lied.

"I wondered if you'd noticed how it had leaked in on the paper over by the bureau, that last rain," said she.

"What makes you look so pale then?"

"I don't know. I guess the heat sort of overcame me."

"I shouldn't think it could have been very hot in that room when it had been shut up so long," said Sophia.

She was evidently not satisfied, but then the grocer came to the door and the matter dropped.

For the next hour the two women were very busy. They kept no servant. When they had come into possession of this fine old place by the death of their aunt it had seemed a doubtful blessing. There was not a cent with which to pay for repairs and taxes and insurance, except the twelve hundred dollars which they had obtained from the sale of the little house in which they had been born and lived all their lives. There had been a division in the old Ackley family years before. One of the daughters had married against her mother's wish and had been disinherited. She had married a poor man by the name of Gill, and shared his humble lot in sight of her former home and her sister and mother living in prosperity, until she had borne three daughters; then she died, worn out with overwork and worry.

The mother and the elder sister had been pitiless to the last. Neither had ever spoken to her since she left her home the night of her marriage. They were hard women.

The three daughters of the disinherited sister had lived quiet and poor, but not actually needy lives. Jane, the middle daughter, had married, and died in less than a year. Amanda and Sophia had taken the girl baby she left when the father married again. Sophia had taught a primary school for many years; she had saved enough to buy the little house in which they lived. Amanda had crocheted lace, and embroidered flannel, and made tidies and pincushions, and had earned enough for her clothes and the child's, little Flora Scott.

Their father, William Gill, had died before they were thirty, and now in their late middle life had come the death of the aunt to whom they had never spoken, although they had often seen her, who had lived in solitary state in the old Ackley mansion until she was more than eighty. There had been no will, and they were the only heirs with the exception of young Flora Scott, the daughter of the dead sister.

Sophia and Amanda thought directly of Flora when they knew of the inheritance.

"It will be a splendid thing for her; she will have enough to live on when we are gone," Sophia said.

She had promptly decided what was to be done. The small house was to be sold, and they were to move into the old Ackley house and take boarders to pay for its keeping. She scouted the idea of selling it. She had an enormous family pride. She had always held her head high when she had walked past that fine old mansion, the cradle of her race, which she was forbidden to enter. She was unmoved when the lawyer who was advising her disclosed to her the fact that Harriet Ackley had used every cent of the Ackley money.

"I realize that we have to work," said she, "but my sister and I have determined to keep the place."

That was the end of the discussion. Sophia and Amanda Gill had been living in the old Ackley house a fortnight, and they had three boarders: an elderly widow with a comfortable income, a young Congregationalist clergyman, and the middle-aged single woman who had charge of the village library. Now the school-teacher from Acton, Miss Louisa Stark, was expected for the summer, and would make four.

Sophia considered that they were comfortably provided for. Her wants and her sister's were very few, and even the niece, although a young girl, had small expenses, since her wardrobe was supplied for years to come from that of the deceased aunt. There were stored away in the garret of the Ackley house enough voluminous black silks and satins and bombazines to keep her clad in somber richness for years to come.

Flora was a very gentle girl, with large, serious blue eyes, a seldom-smiling, pretty mouth, and smooth flaxen hair. She was delicate and very young—sixteen on her next birthday.

She came home soon now with her parcels of sugar and tea from the grocer's. She entered the kitchen gravely and deposited them on the table by which her Aunt Amanda was seated stringing beans. Flora wore an obsolete turban-shaped hat of black straw which had belonged to the dead aunt; it set high like a crown, revealing her forehead. Her dress was an ancient purple-and-white print, too long and too large except over the chest, where it held her like a straight waistcoat.

"You had better take off your hat, Flora," said Sophia. She turned suddenly to Amanda. "Did you fill the water-pitcher in that chamber for the schoolteacher?" she asked severely. She was quite sure that Amanda had not filled the water-pitcher.

Amanda blushed and started guiltily. "I declare, I don't believe I did," said she.

"I didn't think you had," said her sister with sarcastic emphasis.

"Flora, you go up to the room that was your Great-aunt Harriet's, and take the water-pitcher off the wash-stand and fill it with water. Be real careful, and don't break the pitcher, and don't spill the water."

"In *that* chamber?" asked Flora. She spoke very quietly, but her face changed a little.

"Yes, in that chamber," returned her Aunt Sophia sharply. "Go right along."

Flora went, and her light footstep was heard on the stairs. Very soon she returned with the blue-and-white water-pitcher and filled it carefully at the kitchen sink.

"Now be careful and not spill it," said Sophia as she went out of the room carrying it gingerly.

Amanda gave a timidly curious glance at her; she wondered if she had seen the purple gown.

Then she started, for the village stagecoach was seen driving around to the front of the house. The house stood on a corner.

"Here, Amanda, you look better than I do; you go and meet her," said Sophia. "I'll just put the cake in the pan and get it in the oven and I'll come. Show her right up to her room."

Amanda removed her apron hastily and obeyed. Sophia hurried with her cake, pouring it into the baking-tins. She had just put it in the oven, when the door opened and Flora entered carrying the blue water-pitcher.

"What are you bringing down that pitcher again for?" asked Sophia.

"She wants some water, and Aunt Amanda sent me," replied Flora.

Her pretty pale face had a bewildered expression.

"For the land sake, she hasn't used all that great pitcherful of water so quick?"

"There wasn't any water in it," replied Flora.

Her high, childish forehead was contracted slightly with a puzzled frown as she looked at her aunt.

"Wasn't any water in it?"

"No, ma'am."

"Didn't I see you filling the pitcher with water not ten minutes ago, I want to know?"

"Yes, ma'am."

"What did you do with that water?"

"Nothing."

"Did you carry that pitcherful of water up to that room and set it on the washstand?"

"Yes, ma'am."

"Didn't you spill it?"

"No, ma'am."

"Now, Flora Scott, I want the truth! Did you fill that pitcher with water and carry it up there, and wasn't there any there when she came to use it?"

"Yes, ma'am."

"Let me see that pitcher." Sophia examined the pitcher. It was not only perfectly dry from top to bottom, but even a little dusty. She turned severely on the young girl. "That shows," said she, "you did not fill the pitcher at all. You let the water run at the side because you didn't want to carry it upstairs. I am ashamed of you. It's bad enough to be so lazy, but when it comes to not telling the truth—"

The young girl's face broke up suddenly into piteous confusion, and her blue eyes became filmy with tears.

"I did fill the pitcher, honest," she faltered, "I did, Aunt Sophia. You ask Aunt Amanda."

"I'll ask nobody. This pitcher is proof enough. Water don't go off and leave the pitcher dusty on the inside if it was put in ten minutes ago. Now you fill that pitcher full quick, and you carry it upstairs, and if you spill a drop there'll be something besides talk."

Flora filled the pitcher, with the tears falling over her cheeks. She snivelled softly as she went out, balancing it carefully against her slender hip. Sophia followed her.

"Stop crying," said she sharply; "you ought to be ashamed of yourself. What do you suppose Miss Louisa Stark will think. No water in her pitcher in the first place, and then you come back crying as if you didn't want to get it."

In spite of herself, Sophia's voice was soothing. She was very fond of the girl. She followed her up the stairs to the chamber where Miss Louisa Stark was waiting for the water to remove the soil of travel. She had removed her bonnet, and its tuft of red geraniums lightened the obscurity of the mahogany dresser. She had placed her little beaded cape carefully on the bed. She was replying to a tremulous remark of Amanda's, who was nearly fainting from the new mystery of the water-pitcher, that it was warm and she suffered a good deal in warm weather.

Louisa Stark was stout and solidly built. She was much larger than either of the Gill sisters. She was a masterly woman inured to command from years of school-teaching. She carried her swelling bulk with majesty; even her face, moist and red with the heat, lost nothing of its dignity of expression.

She was standing in the middle of the floor with an air which gave the effect of her standing upon an elevation. She turned when Sophia and Flora, carrying the water-pitcher, entered.

"This is my sister Sophia," said Amanda tremulously.

Sophia advanced, shook hands with Miss Louisa Stark and bade her welcome and hoped she would like her room. Then she moved toward the closet. "There is a nice large closet in this room—the best closet in the house. You might have your trunk—" she said, then she stopped short.

The closet door was ajar, and a purple garment seemed suddenly to swing into view as if impelled by some wind.

"Why, here is something left in this closet," Sophia said in a mortified tone. "I thought all those things had been taken away."

She pulled down the garment with a jerk, and as she did so

Amanda passed her in a weak rush for the door.

"I am afraid your sister is not well," said the school-teacher from Acton. "She looked very pale when you took that dress down. I noticed it at once. Hadn't you better go and see what the matter is? She may be going to faint."

"She is not subject to fainting spells," replied Sophia, but she followed Amanda.

She found her in the room which they occupied together, lying on the bed, very pale and gasping. She leaned over her.

"Amanda, what is the matter; don't you feel well?" she asked.

"I feel a little faint."

Sophia got a camphor bottle and began rubbing her sister's forehead.

"Do you feel better?" she said.

Amanda nodded.

"I guess it was that green apple pie you ate this noon," said Sophia. "I declare, what did I do with that dress of Aunt Harriet's? I guess if you feel better I'll just run and get it and take it up garret. I'll stop in here again when I come down. You'd better lay still. Flora can bring you up a cup of tea. I wouldn't try to eat any supper."

Sophia's tone as she left the room was full of loving concern. Presently she returned; she looked disturbed, but angrily so. There was not the slightest hint of any fear in her expression.

"I want to know," said she, looking sharply and quickly around, "if I brought that purple dress in here, after all?"

"I didn't see you," replied Amanda.

"I must have. It isn't in that chamber, nor the closet. You aren't lying on it, are you?"

"I lay down before you came in," replied Amanda.

"So you did. Well, I'll go and look again."

Presently Amanda heard her sister's heavy step on the garret stairs. Then she returned with a queer defiant expression on her face.

"I carried it up garret, after all, and put it in the trunk," said, she. "I declare, I forgot it. I suppose your being faint sort of put it out of my head. There it was, folded up just as nice, right where I put it."

Sophia's mouth was set; her eyes upon her sister's scared, agitated face were full of hard challenge.

"Yes," murmured Amanda.

"I must go right down and see to that cake," said Sophia, going out of the room. "If you don't feel well, you pound on the floor with the umbrella."

Amanda looked after her. She knew that Sophia had not put that purple dress of her dead Aunt Harriet in the trunk in the garret.

Meantime Miss Louisa Stark was settling herself in the southwest chamber. She unpacked her trunk and hung her dresses carefully in the closet. She filled the bureau drawers with nicely folded linen and small articles of dress. She was a very punctilious woman. She put on a black India silk dress with purple flowers. She combed her grayish-blond hair in smooth ridges back from her broad forehead. She pinned her lace at her throat with a brooch, very handsome, although somewhat obsolete—a bunch of pearl grapes on black onyx, set in gold filigree. She had purchased it several years ago with a considerable portion of the stipend from her spring term of school-teaching.

As she surveyed herself in the little swing mirror surmounting the old-fashioned mahogany bureau she suddenly bent forward and looked closely at the brooch. It seemed to her that something was wrong with it. As she looked she became sure. Instead of the familiar bunch of pearl grapes on the black onyx, she saw a knot of blonde and black hair under glass surrounded by a border of twisted gold. She felt a thrill of horror, though she could not tell why. She unpinned the brooch, and it was her own familiar one, the pearl grapes and the onyx. "How very foolish I am," she thought. She thrust the pin in the laces at her throat and again looked at herself in the glass, and there it was again—the knot of blond and black hair and the twisted gold.

Louisa Stark looked at her own large, firm face above the

brooch and it was full of terror and dismay which were new to it. She straightway began to wonder if there could be anything wrong with her mind. She remembered that an aunt of her mother's had been insane. A sort of fury with herself possessed her. She stared at the brooch in the glass with eyes at once angry and terrified. Then she removed it again and there was her own old brooch. Finally she thrust the gold pin through the lace again, fastened it and turning a defiant back on the glass, went down to supper.

At the supper table she met the other boarders—the elderly widow, the young clergyman and the middle-aged librarian. She viewed the elderly widow with reserve, the clergyman with respect, the middle-aged librarian with suspicion. The latter wore a very youthful shirt-waist, and her hair in a girlish fashion which the school-teacher, who twisted hers severely from the straining roots at the nape of her neck to the small, smooth coil at the top, condemned as straining after effects no longer hers by right.

The librarian, who had a quick acridness of manner, addressed her, asking what room she had, and asked the second time in spite of the school-teacher's evident reluctance to hear her. She even, since she sat next to her, nudged her familiarly in her rigid black silk side.

"What room are you in, Miss Stark?" said she.

"I am at a loss how to designate the room," replied Miss Stark stiffly.

"Is it the big southwest room?"

"It evidently faces in that direction," said Miss Stark.

The librarian, whose name was Eliza Lippincott, turned abruptly to Miss Amanda Gill, over whose delicate face a curious colour compounded of flush and pallor was stealing.

"What room did your aunt die in, Miss Amanda?" asked she abruptly.

Amanda cast a terrified glance at her sister, who was serving a second plate of pudding for the minister.

"That room," she replied feebly.

"That's what I thought," said the librarian with a certain triumph. "I calculated that must be the room she died in, for it's the best room in the house, and you haven't put anybody in it before. Somehow the room that anybody has died in lately is generally the last room that anybody is put in. I suppose *you* are so strong-minded you don't object to sleeping in a room where anybody died a few weeks ago?" she inquired of Louisa Stark with sharp eyes on her face.

"No, I do not," replied Miss stark with emphasis.

"Nor in the same bed?" persisted Eliza Lippincott with a kittenish reflection.

The young minister looked up from his pudding. He was very spiritual, but he had had poor pickings in his previous boarding place, and he could not help a certain abstract enjoyment over Miss Gill's cooking.

"You would certainly not be afraid, Miss Lippincott?" he remarked, with his gentle, almost caressing inflection of tone. "You do not for a minute believe that a higher power would allow any manifestation on the part of a disembodied spirit—who we trust is in her heavenly home—to harm one of His servants?"

"Oh, Mr. Dunn, of course not," replied Eliza Lippincott with a blush. "Of course not. I never meant to imply—"

"I could not believe you did," said the minister gently. He was very young, but he already had a wrinkle of permanent anxiety between his eyes and a smile of permanent ingratiation on his lips. The lines of the smile were as deeply marked as the wrinkle.

"Of course dear Miss Harriet Gill was a professing Christian," remarked the widow, "and I don't suppose a professing Christian would come back and scare folks if she could. I wouldn't be a mite afraid to sleep in that room; I'd rather have it than the one I've got. If I was afraid to sleep in a room where a good woman died, I wouldn't tell of it. If I saw things or heard things I'd think the fault must be with my own guilty conscience." Then she turned to Miss Stark. "Any time you feel timid in that room I'm ready and willing to change with you," said she.

"Thank you; I have no desire to change. I am perfectly satisfied with my room," replied Miss Stark with freezing dignity, which was thrown away upon the widow.

"Well," said she, "any time, if you should feel timid, you know what to do. I've got a real nice room; it faces east and gets the morning sun, but it isn't so nice as yours, according to my way of thinking. I'd rather take my chances any day in a room anybody had died in than in one that was hot in summer. I'm more afraid of a sunstroke than of spooks, for my part."

Miss Sophia Gill, who had not spoken one word, but whose mouth had become more and more rigidly compressed, suddenly rose from the table, forcing the minister to leave a little pudding, at which he glanced regretfully.

Miss Louisa Stark did not sit down in the parlour with the other boarders. She went straight to her room. She felt tired after her journey, and meditated a loose wrapper and writing a few letters quietly before she went to bed. Then, too, she was conscious of a feeling that if she delayed, the going there at all might assume more terrifying proportions. She was full of defiance against herself and her own lurking weakness.

So she went resolutely and entered the southwest chamber. There was through the room a soft twilight. She could dimly discern everything, the white satin scroll-work on the wall paper and the white counterpane on the bed being most evident. Consequently both arrested her attention first. She saw against the wall-paper directly facing the door the waist of her best black satin dress hung over a picture.

"That is very strange," she said to herself, and again a thrill of vague horror came over her.

She knew, or thought she knew, that she had put that black satin dress waist away nicely folded between towels in her trunk. She was very choice of her black satin dress.

She took down the black waist and laid it on the bed preparatory to folding it, but when she attempted to do so she discovered that the two sleeves were firmly sewed together. Louisa Stark stared at the sewed sleeves. "What does this mean?" she asked herself. She examined the sewing carefully; the stitches were small, and even, and firm, of black silk.

She looked around the room. On the stand beside the bed was something which she had not noticed before: a little old-fashioned work-box with a picture of a little boy in a pinafore on the top. Beside this work-box lay, as if just laid down by the user, a spool of black silk, a pair of scissors, and a large steel thimble with a hole in the top, after an old style. Louisa stared at these, then at the sleeves of her dress. She moved toward the door. For a moment she thought that this was something legitimate about which she might demand information; then she became doubtful. Suppose that work-box had been there all the time; suppose she had forgotten; suppose she herself had done this absurd thing, or suppose that she had not, what was to hinder the others from thinking so; what was to hinder a doubt being cast upon her own memory and reasoning powers?

Louisa Stark had been on the verge of a nervous breakdown in spite of her iron constitution and her great will power. No woman can teach school for forty years with absolute impunity. She was more credulous as to her own possible failings than she had ever been in her whole life. She was cold with horror and terror, and yet not so much horror and terror of the supernatural as of her own self. The weakness of belief in the supernatural was nearly impossible for this strong nature. She could more easily believe in her own failing powers.

"I don't know but I'm going to be like Aunt Marcia," she said to herself, and her fat face took on a long rigidity of fear.

She started toward the mirror to unfasten her dress, then she remembered the strange circumstance of the brooch and stopped short. Then she straightened herself defiantly and marched up to the bureau and looked in the glass. She saw reflected therein, fastening the lace at her throat, the old-fashioned thing of a large oval, a knot of fair and black hair under glass, set in a rim of twisted gold. She unfastened it with trembling fingers and looked at it. It was her own brooch, the cluster of pearl grapes on black onyx. Louisa Stark placed the trinket in its little box on the nest of pink cotton and put it away in the bureau drawer.

Only death could disturb her habit of order.

Her fingers were so cold they felt fairly numb as she unfastened her dress; she staggered when she slipped it over her head. She went to the closet to hang it up and recoiled. A strong smell of lovage came in her nostrils; a purple gown near the door swung softly against her face as if impelled by some wind from within. All the pegs were filled with garments not her own, mostly of sombre black, but there were some strange-patterned silk things and satins.

Suddenly Louisa Stark recovered her nerve. This, she told herself, was something distinctly tangible. Somebody had been taking liberties with her wardrobe. Somebody had been hanging some one else's clothes in her closet. She hastily slipped on her dress again and marched straight down to the parlour. The people were seated there; the widow and the minister were playing backgammon. The librarian was watching them. Miss Amanda Gill was mending beside the large lamp on the centre table. They all looked up with amazement as Louisa Stark entered. There was something strange in her expression. She noticed none of them except Amanda.

"Where is your sister?" she asked peremptorily of her.

"She's in the kitchen mixing up bread," Amanda quavered; "is there anything—" But the school-teacher was gone.

She found Sophia Gill standing by the kitchen table kneading dough with dignity. The young girl Flora was bringing some flour from the pantry. She stopped and stared at Miss Stark, and her pretty, delicate young face took on an expression of alarm.

Miss Stark opened at once upon the subject in her mind.

"Miss Gill," said she, with her utmost school-teacher manner, "I wish to inquire why you have had my own clothes removed from the closet in my room and others substituted?"

Sophia Gill stood with her hands fast in the dough, regarding her. Her own face paled slowly and reluctantly, her mouth stiffened.

"What? I don't quite understand what you mean, Miss Stark," said she.

"My clothes are not in the closet in my room and it is full of things which do not belong to me," said Louisa Stark.

"Bring me that flour," said Sophia sharply to the young girl, who obeyed, casting timid, startled glances at Miss Stark as she passed her. Sophia Gill began rubbing her hands clear of the dough. "I am sure I know nothing about it," she said with a certain tempered asperity. "Do you know anything about it, Flora?"

"Oh, no, I don't know anything about it, Aunt Sophia," answered the young girl, fluttering.

Then Sophia turned to Miss Stark. "I'll go upstairs with you, Miss Stark," said she, "and see what the trouble is. There must be some mistake." She spoke stiffly with constrained civility.

"Very well," said Miss Stark with dignity. Then she and Miss Sophia went upstairs. Flora stood staring after them.

Sophia and Louisa Stark went up to the southwest chamber. The closet door was shut. Sophia threw it open, then she looked at Miss Stark. On the pegs hung the schoolteacher's own garments in ordinary array.

"I can't see that there is anything wrong," remarked Sophia grimly.

Miss Stark strove to speak but she could not. She sank down on the nearest chair. She did not even attempt to defend herself. She saw her own clothes in the closet. She knew there had been no time for any human being to remove those which she thought she had seen and put hers in their places. She knew it was impossible. Again the awful horror of herself overwhelmed her.

"You must have been mistaken," she heard Sophia say.

She muttered something, she scarcely knew what. Sophia then went out of the room. Presently she undressed and went to bed. In the morning she did not go down to breakfast, and when Sophia came to inquire, requested that the stage be ordered for the noon train. She said that she was sorry, but was ill, and feared lest she might be worse, and she felt that she must return home at once. She looked ill, and could not take even the toast and tea which Sophia had prepared for her. Sophia felt a certain pity for her, but it was largely mixed with indignation. She felt that she knew the true reason for the school-teacher's illness and sudden departure, and it incensed her.

"If folks are going to act like fools we shall never be able to keep this house," she said to Amanda after Miss Stark had gone; and Amanda knew what she meant.

Directly the widow, Mrs. Elvira Simmons, knew that the school-teacher had gone and the southwest room was vacant, she begged to have it in exchange for her own. Sophia hesitated a moment; she eyed the widow sharply. There was something about the large, roseate face worn in firm lines of humour and decision which reassured her.

"I have no objection, Mrs. Simmons," said she, "if—"

"If what?" asked the widow.

"If you have common sense enough not to keep fussing because the room happens to be the one my aunt died in," said Sophia bluntly.

"Fiddlesticks!" said the widow, Mrs. Elvira Simmons.

That very afternoon she moved into the southwest chamber. The young girl Flora assisted her, though much against her will.

"Now I want you to carry Mrs. Simmons' dresses into the closet in that room and hang them up nicely, and see that she has everything she wants," said Sophia Gill. "And you can change the bed and put on fresh sheets. What are you looking at me that way for?"

"Oh, Aunt Sophia, can't I do something else?"

"What do you want to do something else for?"

"I am afraid."

"Afraid of what? I should think you'd hang your head. No; you go right in there and do what I tell you."

Pretty soon Flora came running into the sitting-room where Sophia was, as pale as death, and in her hand she held a queer, old-fashioned frilled nightcap.

"What's that?" demanded Sophia.

"I found it under the pillow."

"What pillow?"

"In the southwest room."

Sophia took it and looked at it sternly.

"It's Great-aunt Harriet's," said Flora faintly.

"You run down street and do that errand at the grocer's for me and I'll see that room," said Sophia with dignity. She carried the nightcap away and put it in the trunk in the garret where she had supposed it stored with the rest of the dead woman's belongings. Then she went into the southwest chamber and made the bed and assisted Mrs. Simmons to move, and there was no further incident.

The widow was openly triumphant over her new room. She talked a deal about it at the dinner-table.

"It is the best room in the house, and I expect you all to be envious of me," said she.

"And you are sure you don't feel afraid of ghosts?" said the librarian.

"Ghosts!" repeated the widow with scorn. "If a ghost comes I'll send her over to you. You are just across the hall from the southwest room."

"You needn't," returned Eliza Lippincott with a shudder. "I wouldn't sleep in that room, after—" she checked herself with an eye on the minister.

"After what?" asked the widow.

"Nothing," replied Eliza Lippincott in an embarrassed fashion.

"I trust Miss Lippincott has too good sense and too great faith to believe in anything of that sort," said the minister.

"I trust so, too," replied Eliza hurriedly.

"You did see or hear something—now what was it, I want to know?" said the widow that evening when they were alone in the parlour. The minister had gone to make a call.

Eliza hesitated.

"What was it?" insisted the widow.

"Well," said Eliza hesitatingly, "if you'll promise not to tell."

"Yes, I promise; what was it?"

"Well, one day last week, just before the school-teacher came, I went in that room to see if there were any clouds. I wanted to wear my gray dress, and I was afraid it was going to rain, so I wanted to look at the sky at all points, so I went in there, and—"

"And what?"

"Well, you know that chintz over the bed, and the valance, and the easy chair; what pattern should you say it was?"

"Why, peacocks on a blue ground. Good lord, I shouldn't think anyone who had ever seen that would forget it."

"Peacocks on a blue ground, you are sure?"

"Of course I am. Why?"

"Only when I went in there that afternoon it was not peacocks on a blue ground; it was great red roses on a yellow ground."

"Why, what do you mean?"

"What I say."

"Did Miss Sophia have it changed?"

"No. I went in there again an hour later and the peacocks were there."

"You didn't see straight the first time."

"I expected you would say that."

"The peacocks are there now; I saw them just now."

"Yes, I suppose so; I suppose they flew back."

"But they couldn't."

"Looks as if they did."

"Why, how could such a thing be? It couldn't be."

"Well, all I know is those peacocks were gone for an hour that afternoon and the red roses on the yellow ground were there instead."

The widow stared at her a moment, then she began to laugh rather hysterically.

"Well," said she, "I guess I sha'n't give up my nice room for any such tomfoolery as that. I guess I would just as soon have red roses on a yellow ground as peacocks on a blue; but there's no use talking, you couldn't have seen straight. How could such a thing have happened?"

"I don't know," said Eliza Lippincott; "but I know I wouldn't sleep in that room if you'd give me a thousand dollars."

"Well, I would," said the widow, "and I'm going to."

When Mrs. Simmons went to the southwest chamber that night she cast a glance at the bed-hanging and the easy chair. There were the peacocks on the blue ground. She gave a contemptuous thought to Eliza Lippincott.

"I don't believe but she's getting nervous," she thought. "I wonder if any of her family have been out at all."

But just before Mrs. Simmons was ready to get into bed she looked again at the hangings and the easy chair, and there were the red roses on the yellow ground instead of the peacocks on the blue. She looked long and sharply. Then she shut her eyes, and then opened them and looked. She still saw the red roses. Then she crossed the room, turned her back to the bed, and looked out at the night from the south window. It was clear and the full moon was shining. She watched it a moment sailing over the dark blue in its nimbus of gold. Then she looked around at the bed hangings. She still saw the red roses on the yellow ground.

Mrs. Simmons was struck in her most vulnerable point. This apparent contradiction of the reasonable as manifested in such a commonplace thing as chintz of a bed-hanging affected this ordinarily unimaginative woman as no ghostly appearance could have done. Those red roses on the yellow ground were to her much more ghostly than any strange figure clad in the white robes of the grave entering the room.

She took a step toward the door, then she turned with a resolute air. "As for going downstairs and owning up I'm scared and having that Lippincott girl crowing over me, I won't for any red roses instead of peacocks. I guess they can't hurt me, and as long as we've both of us seen 'em I guess we can't both be getting loony," she said.

Mrs. Elvira Simmons blew out her light and got into bed

and lay staring out between the chintz hangings at the moonlit room. She said her prayers in bed always as being more comfortable, and presumably just as acceptable in the case of a faithful servant with a stout habit of body. Then after a little she fell asleep; she was of too practical a nature to be kept long awake by anything which had no power of actual bodily effect upon her. No stress of the spirit had ever disturbed her slumbers. So she slumbered between the red roses, or the peacocks, she did not know which.

But she was awakened about midnight by a strange sensation in her throat. She had dreamed that some one with long white fingers was strangling her, and she saw bending over her the face of an old woman in a white cap. When she waked there was no old woman, the room was almost as light as day in the full moonlight, and looked very peaceful; but the strangling sensation at her throat continued, and besides that, her face and ears felt muffled. She put up her hand and felt that her head was covered with a ruffled nightcap tied under her chin so tightly that it was exceedingly uncomfortable. A great qualm of horror shot over her. She tore the thing off frantically and flung it from her with a convulsive effort as if it had been a spider. She gave, as she did so, a quick, short scream of terror. She sprang out of bed and was going toward the door, when she stopped.

It had suddenly occurred to her that Eliza Lippincott might have entered the room and tied on the cap while she was asleep. She had not locked her door. She looked in the closet, under the bed; there was no one there. Then she tried to open the door, but to her astonishment found that it was locked—bolted on the inside. "I must have locked it, after all," she reflected with wonder, for she never locked her door. Then she could scarcely conceal from herself that there was something out of the usual about it all. Certainly no one could have entered the room and departed locking the door on the inside. She could not control the long shiver of horror that crept over her, but she was still resolute. She resolved that she would throw the cap out of the window. "I'll see if I have tricks like that played on me, I don't care who does it," said she quite aloud. She was still unable to believe wholly in the supernatural. The idea of some human agency was still in her mind, filling her with anger.

She went toward the spot where she had thrown the cap— she had stepped over it on her way to the door—but it was not there. She searched the whole room, lighting her lamp, but she could not find the cap. Finally she gave it up. She extinguished her lamp and went back to bed. She fell asleep again, to be again awakened in the same fashion. That time she tore off the cap as before, but she did not fling it on the floor as before. Instead she held to it with a fierce grip. Her blood was up.

Holding fast to the white flimsy thing, she sprang out of bed, ran to the window which was open, slipped the screen, and flung it out; but a sudden gust of wind, though the night was calm, arose and it floated back in her face. She brushed it aside like a cobweb and she clutched at it. She was actually furious. It eluded her clutching fingers. Then she did not see it at all. She examined the floor, she lighted her lamp again and searched, but there was no sign of it.

Mrs. Simmons was then in such a rage that all terror had disappeared for the time. She did not know with what she was angry, but she had a sense of some mocking presence which was silently proving too strong against her weakness, and she was aroused to the utmost power of resistance. To be baffled like this and resisted by something which was as nothing to her straining senses filled her with intensest resentment.

Finally she got back into bed again; she did not go to sleep. She felt strangely drowsy, but she fought against it. She was wide awake, staring at the moonlight, when she suddenly felt the soft white strings of the thing tighten around her throat and real-ized that her enemy was again upon her. She seized the strings, untied them, twitched off the cap, ran with it to the table where her scissors lay and furiously cut it into small bits. She cut and tore, feeling an insane fury of gratification.

"There!" said she quite aloud. "I guess I sha'n't have any more trouble with this old cap."

She tossed the bits of muslin into a basket and went back to bed. Almost immediately she felt the soft strings tighten around her throat. Then at last she yielded, vanquished. This new refutal of all laws of reason by which she had learned, as it were, to spell her theory of life, was too much for her equilibrium. She pulled off the clinging strings feebly, drew the thing from her head, slid weakly out of bed, caught up her wrapper and hastened out of the room. She went noiselessly along the hall to her own old room: she entered, got into her familiar bed, and lay there the rest of the night shuddering and listening, and if she dozed, waking with a start at the feeling of the pressure upon her throat to find that it was not there, yet still to be unable to shake off entirely the horror.

When daylight came she crept back to the southwest chamber and hurriedly got some clothes in which to dress herself. It took all her resolution to enter the room, but nothing unusual happened while she was there. She hastened back to her old chamber, dressed herself and went down to breakfast with an imperturbable face. Her colour had not faded. When asked by Eliza Lippincott how she had slept, she replied with an appearance of calmness which was bewildering that she had not slept very well. She never did sleep very well in a new bed, and she thought she would go back to her old room.

Eliza Lippincott was not deceived, however, neither were the Gill sisters, nor the young girl, Flora. Eliza Lippincott spoke out bluntly.

"You needn't talk to me about sleeping well," said she. "I know something queer happened in that room last night by the way you act."

They all looked at Mrs. Simmons, inquiringly—the librarian with malicious curiosity and triumph, the minister with sad incredulity, Sophia Gill with fear and indignation, Amanda and the young girl with unmixed terror. The widow bore herself with dignity.

"I saw nothing nor heard nothing which I trust could not have been accounted for in some rational manner," said she.

"What was it?" persisted Eliza Lippincott.

"I do not wish to discuss the matter any further," replied Mrs. Simmons shortly. Then she passed her plate for more creamed potato. She felt that she would die before she confessed to the ghastly absurdity of that nightcap, or to having been disturbed by the flight of peacocks off a blue field of chintz after she had scoffed at the possibility of such a thing. She left the whole matter so vague that in a fashion she came off the mistress of the situation. She at all events impressed everybody by her coolness in the face of no one knew what nightly terror.

After breakfast, with the assistance of Amanda and Flora, she moved back into her old room. Scarcely a word was spoken during the process of moving, but they all worked with trembling haste and looked guilty when they met one another's eyes, as if conscious of betraying a common fear.

That afternoon the young minister, John Dunn, went to Sophia Gill and requested permission to occupy the southwest chamber that night.

"I don't ask to have my effects moved there," said he, "for I could scarcely afford a room so much superior to the one I now occupy, but I would like, if you please, to sleep there tonight for the purpose of refuting in my own person any unfortunate superstition which may have obtained root here."

Sophia Gill thanked the minister gratefully and eagerly accepted his offer.

"How anybody with common sense can believe for a minute in any such nonsense passes my comprehension," said she.

"It certainly passes mine how anybody with Christian faith can believe in ghosts," said the minister gently, and Sophia Gill felt a certain feminine contentment in hearing him. The minister was a child to her; she regarded him with no tincture of sentiment, and yet she loved to hear two other women covertly condemned by him and she herself thereby exalted.

That night about twelve o'clock the Reverend John Dunn essayed to go to his nightly slumber in the southwest chamber. He had been sitting up until that hour preparing his sermon.

He traversed the hall with a little night-lamp in his hand, opened the door of the southwest chamber, and essayed to enter. He might as well have essayed to enter the solid side of a house. He could not believe his senses. The door was certainly open; he could look into the room full of soft lights and shadows under the moonlight which streamed into the windows. He could see the bed in which he had expected to pass the night, but he could not enter. Whenever he strove to do so he had a curious sensation as if he were trying to press against an invisible person who met him with a force of opposition impossible to overcome. The minister was not an athletic man, yet he had considerable strength. He squared his elbows, set his mouth hard, and strove to push his way through into the room. The opposition which he met was as sternly and mutely terrible as the rocky fastness of a mountain in his way.

For a half hour John Dunn, doubting, raging, overwhelmed with spiritual agony as to the state of his own soul rather than fear, strove to enter that southwest chamber. He was simply powerless against this uncanny obstacle. Finally a great horror as of evil itself came over him. He was a nervous man and very young. He fairly fled to his own chamber and locked himself in like a terror-stricken girl.

The next morning he went to Miss Gill and told her frankly what had happened, and begged her to say nothing about it lest he should have injured the cause by the betrayal of such weakness, for he actually had come to believe that there was something wrong with the room.

"What it is I know not, Miss Sophia," said he, "but I firmly believe, against my will, that there is in that room some accursed evil power at work, of which modern faith and modern science know nothing."

Miss Sophia Gill listened with grimly lowering face. She had an inborn respect for the clergy, but she was bound to hold that southwest chamber in the dearly beloved old house of her fathers free of blame.

"I think I will sleep in that room myself tonight," she said, when the minister had finished.

He looked at her in doubt and dismay.

"I have great admiration for your faith and courage, Miss Sophia," he said, "but are you wise?"

"I am fully resolved to sleep in that room tonight," said she conclusively. There were occasions when Miss Sophia Gill could put on a manner of majesty, and she did now.

It was ten o'clock that night when Sophia Gill entered the southwest chamber. She had told her sister what she intended doing and had been proof against her tearful entreaties. Amanda was charged not to tell the young girl, Flora.

"There is no use in frightening that child over nothing," said Sophia.

Sophia, when she entered the southwest chamber, set the lamp which she carried on the bureau, and began moving about the rooms pulling down the curtains, taking off the nice white counterpane of the bed, and preparing generally for the night.

As she did so, moving with great coolness and deliberation, she became conscious that she was thinking some thoughts that were foreign to her. She began remembering what she could not have remembered, since she was not then born: the trouble over her mother's marriage, the bitter opposition, the shutting the door upon her, the ostracizing her from heart and home. She became aware of a most singular sensation as of bitter resentment herself, and not against the mother and sister who had so treated her own mother, but against her own mother, and then she became aware of a like bitterness extended to her own self. She felt malignant toward her mother as a young girl whom she remembered, though she could not have remembered, and she felt malignant toward her own self, and her sister Amanda, and Flora. Evil suggestions surged in her brain—suggestions which turned her heart to stone and which still fascinated her. And all the time by a sort of double consciousness she knew that what she thought was strange and not due to her own volition. She knew that she was thinking the thoughts of some other person, and she knew who. She felt herself possessed.

But there was tremendous strength in the woman's nature. She had inherited strength for good and righteous self-assertion, from the evil strength of her ancestors. They had turned their own weapons against themselves. She made an effort which seemed almost mortal, but was conscious that the hideous thing was gone from her. She thought her own thoughts. Then she scouted to herself the idea of anything supernatural about the terrific experience. "I am imagining everything," she told herself. She went on with her preparations; she went to the bureau to take down her hair. She looked in the glass and saw, instead of her softly parted waves of hair, harsh lines of iron-gray under the black borders of an old-fashioned head-dress.

She saw instead of her smooth, broad forehead, a high one wrinkled with the intensest concentration of selfish reflections of a long life; she saw instead of her steady blue eyes, black ones with depths of malignant reserve, behind a broad meaning of ill will; she saw instead of her firm, benevolent mouth one with a hard, thin line, a network of melancholic wrinkles. She saw instead of her own face, middle-aged and good to see, the expression of a life of honesty and good will to others and patience under trials, the face of a very old woman scowling forever with unceasing hatred and misery at herself and all others, at life, and death, at that which had been and that which was to come. She saw instead of her own face in the glass, the face of her dead Aunt Harriet, topping her own shoulders in her own well-known dress!

Sophia Gill left the room. She went into the one which she shared with her sister Amanda. Amanda looked up and saw her standing there. She had set the lamp on a table, and she stood holding a handkerchief over her face. Amanda looked at her with terror.

"What is it? What is it, Sophia?" she gasped.

Sophia still stood with the handkerchief pressed to her face.

"Oh, Sophia, let me call somebody. Is your face hurt? Sophia, what is the matter with your face?" fairly shrieked Amanda.

Suddenly Sophia took the handkerchief from her face.

"Look at me, Amanda Gill," she said in an awful voice.

Amanda looked, shrinking.

"What is it? Oh, what is it? You don't look hurt. What is it, Sophia?"

"What do you see?"

"Why, I see you."

"Me?"

"Yes, you. What did you think I would see?"

Sophia Gill looked at her sister. "Never as long as I live will I tell you what I thought you would see, and you must never ask me," said she.

"Well, I never will, Sophia," replied Amanda, half weeping with terror.

"You won't try to sleep in that room again, Sophia?"

"No," said Sophia; "and I am going to sell this house."

The Prism

There had been much rain that season, and the vegetation was almost tropical. The wayside growths were jungles to birds and insects, and very near them to humans. All through the long afternoon of the hot August day, Diantha Fielding lay flat on her back under the lee of the stone wall which bordered her stepfather's, Zenas May's, south mowing-lot. It was pretty warm there, although she lay in a little strip of shade of the tangle of blackberry-vines, poison-ivy, and the gray pile of stones; but the girl loved the heat. She experienced the gentle languor which is its best effect, instead of the fierce unrest and irritation which is its worst. She left that to rattlesnakes and nervous women. As for her, in times of extreme heat, she hung over life with tremulous flutters, like a butterfly over a rose, moving only enough to pre-serve her poise in the scheme of things, and realizing to the full the sweetness of all about her.

She heard, as she lay there, the voice of a pine-tree not far away—a solitary pine which was full of gusty sweetness; she smelled the wild grapes, which were reluctantly ripening across the field over the wall that edged the lane; she smelled the black-berry-vines; she looked with indolent fascination at the virile sprays of poison-ivy. It was like innocence surveying sin, and wondering what it was like. Once her stepmother, Mrs. Zenas May, had been poisoned with ivy, and both eyes had been closed thereby. Diantha did not believe that the ivy would so serve her. She dared herself to touch it, then she looked away again.

She heard a far-carrying voice from the farmhouse at the

left calling her name. "Diantha! Diantha!" She lay so still that she scarcely breathed. The voice came again. She smiled triumphantly. She knew perfectly well what was wanted: that she should assist in preparing supper. Her stepmother's married daughter and her two children were visiting at the house. She preferred remaining where she was. Her sole fear of disturbance was from the children. They were like little ferrets. Diantha did not like them. She did not like children very well under any circumstances. To her they seemed always out of tune; the jar of heredity was in them, and she felt it, although she did not know enough to realize what she felt. She was only twelve years old, a child still, though tall for her age.

The voice came again. Diantha shifted her position a little; she stretched her slender length luxuriously; she felt for something which hung suspended around her neck under her gingham waist, but she did not then remove it. "Diantha! Diantha!" came the insistent voice.

Diantha lay as irresponsive as the blackberry-vine which trailed beside her like a snake. Then she heard the house door close with a bang; her ears were acute. She felt again of that which was suspended from her neck. A curious expression of daring, of exultation, of fear, was in her face. Presently she heard the shrill voices of children; then she lay so still that she seemed fairly to obliterate herself by silence and motionlessness.

Two little girls in pink frocks came racing past; their flying heels almost touched her, but they never saw her.

When they were well past, she drew a cautious breath, and felt again of the treasure around her neck.

After a while she heard the soft padding of many hoofs in the heavy dust of the road, a dog's shrill bark, the tinkle of a bell, the absent-minded shout of a weary man. The hired man was driving the cows home. The fragrance of milk-dripping udders, of breaths sweetened with clover and meadow-grass, came to her. Suddenly a cold nose rubbed against her face; the dog had found her out. But she was a friend of his. She patted him, then pushed him away gently, and he understood that she wished to remain concealed. He went barking back to the man. The cows broke into a clumsy gallop; the man shouted. Diantha smelled the dust of the road which flew over the field like smoke. She heard the children returning down the road behind the cows. When the cows galloped, they screamed with half-fearful delight. Then it all passed by, and she heard the loud clang of a bell from the farmhouse.

Then Diantha pulled out the treasure which was suspended from her neck by an old blue ribbon, and she held it up to the low western sun, and wonderful lights of red and blue and violet and green and orange danced over the shaven stubble of the field before her delighted eyes. It was a prism which she had stolen from the best-parlour lamp—from the lamp which had been her own mother's, bought by her with her school-teaching money before her marriage, and brought by her to grace her new home.

Diantha Fielding, as far as relatives went, was in a curious position. First her mother died when she was very young, only a few months old; then her father had married again, giving her a stepmother; then her father had died two years later, and her stepmother had married again, giving her a stepfather. Since then the stepmother had died, and the stepfather had married a widow with a married daughter, whose two children had raced down the road behind the cows. Diantha often felt in a sore bewilderment of relationships. She had not even a cousin of her own; the dearest relative she had was the daughter of a widow whom a cousin of her mother's had married for a second wife. The cousin was long since dead. The wife was living, and Diantha's little step second cousin, as she reckoned it, lived in the old homestead which had belonged to Diantha's grandfather, across the way from the May farm-house. It was a gambrel-roof, half-ruinous structure, well banked in front with a monstrous growth of lilacs, and overhung by a great butternut-tree.

Diantha knew well that she was heaping up vials of cold wrath upon her head by not obeying the supper-bell, but she lay still. Then Libby came—Libby, the little cousin, stepping very cautiously and daintily; for she wore slippers of her mother's, which hung from her small heels, and she had lost them twice already.

She stopped before Diantha. Her slender arms, terminating in hands too large for them, hung straight at her sides in the folds of her faded blue-flowered muslin. Her pretty little heat-flushed face had in it no more speculation than a flower, and no more changing. She was like a flower, which would blossom the same next year, and the next year after that, and the same until it died. There was no speculation in her face as she looked at Diantha dangling the prism in the sunlight, merely unimaginative wonder and admiration.

"It's a drop off your best-parlour lamp," said she, in her thin, sweet voice.

"Look over the field, Libby!" cried Diantha, excitedly.

Libby looked.

"Tell me what you see, quick!"

"What I see? Why, grass and things."

"No, I don't mean them; what you see from this."

Diantha shook the prism violently.

"I see a lot of different colours dancing," replied Libby, "same as you always see. Addie Green had an ear-drop that was broken off their best-parlour lamp. Her mother gave it to her."

"Don't you see anything but different lights?"

"Of course I don't. That's all there is to see."

Diantha sighed.

"That drop ain't broken," said the other little girl. "How did she happen to let you have it?" By "she" Libby meant Diantha's stepmother.

"I took it," replied Diantha. She was fastening the prism around her neck again.

Libby gasped and stared at her. "Didn't you ask her?"

"If I'd asked her, she'd said no, and it was my own mother's lamp. I had a right to it."

"What'll she do to you?"

"I don't know, if she finds out. I sha'n't tell her, if I can help it without lying."

Diantha fastened her gingham frock securely over the prism. Then she rose, and the two little girls went home across the dry stubble of the field.

"I didn't go when she called me, and I didn't go when the supper-bell rang," said Diantha.

Libby stared at her wonderingly. She had never felt an impulse to disobedience in her life; she could not understand this other child, who was a law unto herself. She walked very carefully in her large slippers.

"What'll she do to you?" she inquired.

Diantha tossed her head like a colt.

"She won't do anything, I guess, except make me go without my supper. If she does, I ain't afraid; but I guess she won't, and I'd a heap rather go without my supper than go to it when I don't want to."

Libby looked at her with admiring wonder. Diantha was neatly and rigorously, rather than tastefully, dressed. Her dark blue-and-white gingham frock was starched stiffly; it hung exactly at the proper height from her slender ankles; she wore a clean white collar; and her yellow hair was braided very tightly and smoothly, and tied with a punctilious blue bow. In strange contrast with the almost martial preciseness of her attire was the expression of her little face, flushed, eager to enthusiasm, almost wild, with a light in her blue eyes which did not belong there, according to the traditions concerning little New England maidens, with a feverish rose on her cheeks, which should have been cool and pale. However, that had all come since she had dangled the prism in the rays of the setting sun.

"What did you think you saw when you shook that ear-drop off the lamp?" asked Libby; but she asked without much curiosity.

"Red and green and yellow colours, of course," replied Diantha, shortly.

When they reached Diantha's door, Libby bade her good night, and sped across the road to her own house. She stood a little in fear of Diantha's stepmother, if Diantha did not. She knew just the sort of look which would be directed toward the other little girl, and she knew from experience that it might include her. From her Puritan ancestry she had a certain stubbornness when brought to bay, but no courage of aggression; so she ran.

Diantha marched in. She was utterly devoid of fear.

Her stepmother, Mrs. Zenas May, was washing the supper dishes at the kitchen sink. All through the house sounded a high sweet voice which was constantly off the key, singing a lullaby to the two little girls, who had to go to bed directly after they had finished their evening meal.

Mrs. Zenas May turned around and surveyed Diantha as she entered. There was nothing in the least unkind in her look; it was simply the gaze of one on a firm standpoint of existence upon another swaying on a precarious balance—the sort of look a woman seated in a car gives to one standing. It was irresponsible, while cognizant of the discomfort of the other person.

"Where were you when the supper-bell rang?" asked Mrs. Zenas May. She was rather a pretty woman, with an exquisitely cut profile. Her voice was very even, almost as devoid of inflections as a deaf-and-dumb person's. Her gingham gown was also rigorously starched. Her fair hair showed high lights of gloss from careful brushing; it was strained back from her blue-veined temples.

"Out in the field," replied Diantha.

"Then you heard it?"

"Yes, ma'am."

"The supper-table is cleared away," said Mrs. May. That was all she said. She went on polishing the tumblers, which she was rinsing in ammonia water.

Diantha glanced through the open door and saw the dining-room table with its chenille after-supper cloth on. She made no reply, but went upstairs to her own chamber. That was very comfortable—the large south one back of her step-parents'. Not a speck of dust was to be seen in it; the feather-bed was an even mound of snow. Diantha sat down by the window, and gazed out at the deepening dusk. She felt at the prism around her neck, but she did not draw it out, for it was of no use in that low light. She could not invoke the colours which it held. Her chamber door was open. Presently she heard the best-parlour door open, and heard quite distinctly her stepmother's voice. She was speaking to her stepfather.

"There's a drop broken off the parlour lamp," said she.

There was an unintelligible masculine grunt of response.

"I wish you'd look while I hold the lamp, and see if you can find it on the floor anywhere," said her stepmother. Her voice was still even. The loss of a prism from the best-parlour lamp was not enough to ruffle her outward composure.

"Don't you see it?" she asked, after a little.

Again came the unintelligible masculine grunt.

"It is very strange," said Mrs. May. "Don't look any more."

She never inquired of Diantha concerning the prism. In truth, she believed one of her grandchildren, whom she adored, to be responsible for the loss of the glittering ornament, and was mindful of the fact that Diantha's mother had originally owned that lamp. So she said nothing, but as soon as might be purchased another, and Diantha kept her treasure quite unsuspected.

She did not, however, tremble in the least while the search was going on downstairs. She had her defence quite ready. To her sense of justice it was unquestionable. She would simply say that the lamp had belonged to her own mother, consequently to her; that she had a right to do as she chose with it. She had not the slightest fear of any reproaches which Mrs. May would bring to bear upon her. She knew she would not use bodily punishment, as she never had; but she would have stood in no fear of that.

Diantha did not go to bed for a long time. There was a full moon, and she sat by the window, leaning her two elbows on the sill, making a cup of her hands, in which she rested her peaked chin, and peered out.

It was nearly nine o'clock when someone entered the room with heavy, soft movements, like a great tame dog. It was her stepfather, and he had in his hand a large wedge of apple-pie.

"Diantha," he said, in a loud whisper, "you gone to bed?"

"No, sir," replied Diantha. She liked her stepfather. She was always aware of a clumsy, covert partisanship from him.

"Well," said he, "here's a piece of pie. You hadn't ought to go to bed without any supper. You'd ought to come in when the bell rings another time, Diantha."

"Thank you, father," said Diantha, reaching out her hand for the pie.

Zenas May, who was large and shaggily blond, with a face like a great blank of good nature, placed a heavy hand on her little, tightly braided head, and patted it.

"Better eat your pie and go to bed," he said. Then he shambled downstairs very softly, lest his wife hear him.

Diantha ate her pie obediently, and went to bed, and with the first morning sunlight she removed her prism from her neck, and flashed it across the room, and saw what she saw, or what she thought she saw.

Diantha kept the prism, and nobody except Libby knew it, and she was quite safe with a secret. While she did not in the least comprehend, she was stanch. Even when she grew older and had a lover, she did not tell him; she did not even tell him when she was married to him that Diantha Fielding always carried a drop off the best-parlour lamp, which belonged to her own mother, and when she flashed it in the sunlight she thought she saw things. She kept it all to herself. Libby married before Diantha, before Diantha had a lover even. Young men, for some reason, were rather shy of Diantha, although she had a little property in her own right, inherited from her own father and mother, and was, moreover, extremely pretty. However, her prettiness was not of a type to attract the village men as quickly as Libby's more material charms. Diantha was very thin and small, and her colour was as clear as porcelain, and she gave a curious impression of mystery, although there was apparently nothing whatever mysterious about her.

But her turn came. A graduate of a country college, a farmer's son, who had worked his own way through college, had now obtained the high school. He saw Diantha, and fell in love with her, although he struggled against it. He said to himself that she was too delicate, that he was a poor man, that he ought to have a more robust wife, who would stand a better chance of discharging her domestic and maternal duties without a break-down. Reason and judgment were strongly developed in him. His passion for Diantha was entirely opposed to both, but it got the better of him. One afternoon in August when Diantha was almost twenty, he, passing by her house, saw her sitting on her front doorstep, stopped, and proposed a little stroll in the woods, and asked her to marry him.

"I never thought much about getting married," said Diantha. Then she leaned toward him as if impelled by some newly developed instinct. She spoke so low that he could not hear her, and he asked her over.

"I never thought much about getting married," repeated Diantha, and she leaned nearer him.

He laughed a great triumphant laugh, and caught her in his arms.

"Then it is high time you did, you darling," he said.

Diantha was very happy.

They lingered in the woods a long time, and when they went home, the young man, whose name was Robert Black, went in with her, and told her stepmother what had happened.

"I have asked your daughter to marry me, Mrs. May," he said, "and she has consented, and I hope you are willing."

Mrs. May replied that she had no objections, stiffly, without a smile. She never smiled. Instead of smiling, she always looked questioningly even at their beloved grandchildren. They had lived with her since their mother's death, two pretty, boisterous girls, pupils of Robert Black, who had had their own inevitable little dreams regarding him, as they had had regarding every man who came in their way.

When their grandmother told them that Diantha was to marry the hero who had dwelt in their own innocently bold air-castles of girlish dreams, they started at first as from a shock of falling imaginations; then they began to think of their attire as bridesmaids.

Mrs. Zenas May was firmly resolved that Diantha should have as grand a wedding as if she had been her own daughter.

"Folks sha'n't say that she didn't have as good an outfit and wedding as if her own mother had been alive to see to it," she said.

As for Diantha, she thought very little about her outfit or the wedding, but about Robert. All at once she was possessed by a strong angel of primal conditions of whose existence she had never dreamed. She poured out her very soul; she made revelations of the inmost innocences of her nature to this ambitious, faithful, unimaginative young man. She had been some two weeks betrothed, and they were walking together one afternoon, when she showed him her prism.

She no longer wore it about her neck as formerly. A dawning unbelief in it had seized her, and yet there were times when to doubt seemed to doubt the evidence of her own senses.

That afternoon, as they were walking together in the lonely country road, she stopped him in a sunny interval between the bordering woods, where the road stretched for some distance between fields foaming with wild carrot and mustard, and swarmed over with butterflies, and she took her prism out of her pocket and flashed it full before her wondering lover's eyes.

He looked astonished, even annoyed; then he laughed aloud with a sort of tender scorn.

"What a child you are, dear!" he said. "What are you doing with that thing?"

"What do you see, Robert?" the girl cried eagerly, and there was in her eyes a light not of her day and generation, maybe inherited from some far-off Celtic ancestor—a strain of imagination which had survived the glaring light of latter days of commonness.

He eyed her with amazement; then he looked at the gorgeous blots and banners of colour over the fields.

347

"See? Why, I see the prismatic colours, of course. What else should I see?" he asked.

"Nothing else?"

"No. Why, what else should I see? I see the prismatic colours from the refraction of the sunlight."

Diantha looked at the dancing tints, then at her lover, and spoke with a solemn candour, as if she were making confession of an alien faith. "Ever since I was a child, I have seen, or thought so—" she began.

"What, for heaven's sake?" he cried impatiently.

"You have read about—fairies and—such things?"

"Of course. What do you mean, Diantha?"

"I have seen, or thought so, beautiful little people moving and dancing in the broken lights across the fields."

"For heaven's sake, put up that thing, and don't talk such nonsense, Diantha!" cried Robert, almost brutally. He had paled a little.

"I have, Robert."

"Don't talk such nonsense. I thought you were a sensible girl," said the young man.

Diantha put the prism back in her pocket.

All the rest of the way Robert was silent and gloomy. His old doubts had revived. His judgment for the time being got the upper hand of his passion. He began to wonder if he ought to marry a girl with such preposterous fancies as those. He began to wonder if she were just right in her mind.

He parted from her coolly, and came the next evening, but remained only a short time. Then he stayed away several days. He called on Sunday, then did not come again for four days. On Friday Diantha grew desperate. She went by herself out in the sunny field, walking ankle-deep in flowers and weeds, until she reached the margin of a little pond on which the children skated in winter. Then she took her prism from her pocket and flashed it in the sunlight, and for the first time she failed to see what she had either seen, or imagined, for so many years.

She saw only the beautiful prismatic colours flashing across the field in bars and blots and streamers of rose and violet, of orange and green. That was all. She stooped, and dug in the oozy soil beside the pond with her bare white hands, and made, as it were, a little grave, and buried the prism out of sight. Then she washed her hands in the pond, and waved them about until they were dry. Afterward she went swiftly across the field to the road which her lover must pass on his way from school, and, when she saw him coming, met him, blushing and trembling.

"I have put it away, Robert," she said. "I saw nothing; it was only my imagination."

It was a lonely road. He looked at her doubtfully, then he laughed, and put an arm around her.

"It's all right, little girl," he replied; "but don't let such fancies dwell in your brain. This is a plain, common world, and it won't do."

"I saw nothing; it must have been my imagination," she repeated. Then she leaned her head against her lover's shoulder. Whether or not she had sold her birthright, she had got her full measure of the pottage of love which filled to an ecstasy of satisfaction her woman's heart.

She and Robert were married, and lived in a pretty new house, from the western windows of which she could see the pond on whose borders she had buried the prism. She was very happy. For the time being, at least, all the mysticism in her face had given place to an utter revelation of earthly bliss. People said how much Diantha had improved since her marriage, what a fine housekeeper she was, how much common sense she had, how she was such a fitting mate for her husband, whom she adored.

Sometimes Diantha, looking from a western window, used to see the pond across the field, reflecting the light of the setting sun, and looking like an eye of revelation of the earth; and she would remember that key of a lost radiance and a lost belief of her own life, which was buried beside it. Then she would go happily and prepare her husband's supper.

The Vacant lot

When it became generally known in Townsend Centre that the Townsends were going to move to the city, there was great excitement and dismay. For the Townsends to move was about equivalent to the town's moving. The Townsend ancestors had founded the village a hundred years ago. The first Townsend had kept a wayside hostelry for man and beast, known as the "Sign of the Leopard." The sign-board, on which the leopard was painted a bright blue, was still extant, and prominently so, being nailed over the present Townsend's front door. This Townsend, by name David, kept the village store. There had been no tavern since the railroad was built through Townsend Centre in his father's day. Therefore the family, being ousted by the march of progress from their chosen employment, took up with a general country store as being the next thing to a country tavern, the principal difference consisting in the fact that all the guests were transients, never requiring bedchambers, securing their rest on the tops of sugar and flour barrels and codfish boxes, and their refreshment from stray nibblings at the stock in trade, to the profitless de-plenishment of raisins and loaf sugar and crackers and cheese.

The flitting of the Townsends from the home of their an-cestors was due to a sudden access of wealth from the death of a relative and the desire of Mrs. Townsend to secure better advantages for her son George, sixteen years old, in the way of education, and for her daughter Adrianna, ten years older, better matrimonial opportunities. However, this last inducement for leaving Townsend Centre was not openly stated, only ingeniously surmised by the neighbours.

"Sarah Townsend don't think there's anybody in Townsend Centre fit for her Adrianna to marry, and so she's goin' to take her to Boston to see if she can't pick up somebody there," they said. Then they wondered what Abel Lyons would do. He had been a humble suitor for Adrianna for years, but her mother had not approved, and Adrianna, who was dutiful, had repulsed him delicately and rather sadly. He was the only lover whom she had ever had, and she felt sorry and grateful; she was a plain, awkward girl, and had a patient recognition of the fact.

But her mother was ambitious, more so than her father, who was rather pugnaciously satisfied with what he had, and not easily disposed to change. However, he yielded to his wife and consented to sell out his business and purchase a house in Boston and move there.

David Townsend was curiously unlike the line of ancestors from whom he had come. He had either retrograded or advanced, as one might look at it. His moral character was certainly better, but he had not the fiery spirit and eager grasp at advantage which had distinguished them. Indeed, the old Townsends, though prominent and respected as men of property and influence, had reputations not above suspicions. There was more than one dark whisper regarding them handed down from mother to son in the village, and especially was this true of the first Townsend, he who built the tavern bearing the Sign of the Blue Leopard. His portrait, a hideous effort of contemporary art, hung in the garret of David Townsend's home. There was many a tale of wild roistering, if no worse, in that old roadhouse, and high stakes, and quarrelling in cups, and blows, and money gotten in evil fashion, and the matter hushed up with a high hand for inquirers by the imperious Townsends who terrorized everybody.

David Townsend terrorized nobody. He had gotten his little competence from his store by honest methods—the exchanging of sterling goods and true weights for country produce and country shillings. He was sober and reliable, with intense self-respect and a decided talent for the management of money. It was principally for this reason that he took great delight in his sudden wealth by legacy. He had thereby greater opportunities for the exercise of his native shrewdness in a bargain. This he evinced in his purchase of a house in Boston.

One day in spring the old Townsend house was shut up, the Blue Leopard was taken carefully down from his lair over the front door, the family chattels were loaded on the train, and the Townsends departed. It was a sad and eventful day for Townsend Centre. A man from Barre had rented the store—David had decided at the last not to sell—and the old familiars congregated in melancholy fashion and talked over the situation. An enormous pride over their departed townsman became evident. They paraded him, flaunting him like a banner in the eyes of the new man. "David is awful smart," they said; "there won't nobody get the better of him in the city if he has lived in Townsend Centre all his life. He's got his eyes open. Know what he paid for his house in Boston? Well, sir, that house cost twenty-five thousand dollars, and David he bought it for five. Yes, sir, he did."

"Must have been some out about it," remarked the new man, scowling over his counter. He was beginning to feel his disparaging situation.

"Not an out, sir. David he made sure on't. Catch him gettin' bit. Everythin' was in apple-pie order, hot an' cold water and all, and in one of the best locations of the city—real high-up street. David he said the rent in that street was never under a thousand. Yes, sir, David he got a bargain—five thousand dollars for a twenty-five-thousand-dollar house."

"Some out about it!" growled the new man over the counter.

However, as his fellow townsmen and allies stated, there seemed to be no doubt about the desirableness of the city house which David Townsend had purchased and the fact that he had secured it for an absurdly low price. The whole family were at first suspicious. It was ascertained that the house had cost a round sum only a few years ago; it was in perfect repair; nothing whatever was amiss with plumbing, furnace, anything. There was not even a soap factory within smelling distance, as Mrs. Townsend had vaguely surmised. She was sure that she had heard of houses being undesirable for such reasons, but there was no soap factory. They all sniffed and peeked; when the first rainfall came they looked at the ceiling, confidently expecting to see dark spots where the leaks had commenced, but there were none. They were forced to confess that their suspicions were allayed, that the house was perfect, even overshadowed with the mystery of a lower price than it was worth.

That, however, was an additional perfection in the opinion of the Townsends, who had their share of New England thrift. They had lived just one month in their new house, and were happy, although at times somewhat lonely from missing the society of Townsend Centre, when the trouble began. The Townsends, although they lived in a fine house in a genteel, almost fashionable, part of the city, were true to their antecedents and kept, as they had been accustomed, only one maid. She was the daughter of a farmer on the outskirts of their native village, was middle-aged, and had lived with them for the last ten years. One pleasant Monday morning she rose early and did the family washing before breakfast, which had been prepared by Mrs. Townsend and Adrianna, as was their habit on washing-days. The family were seated at the breakfast table in their basement dining-room, and this maid, whose name was Cordelia, was hanging out the clothes in the vacant lot.

This vacant lot seemed a valuable one, being on a corner. It was rather singular that it had not been built upon. The Townsends had wondered at it and agreed that they would have preferred their own house to be there. They had, however, utilized it as far as possible with their innocent, rural disregard of property rights in unoccupied land.

"We might just as well hang out our washing in that vacant lot," Mrs. Townsend had told Cordelia the first Monday of their stay in the house. "Our little yard ain't half big enough for all our clothes, and it is sunnier there, too."

So Cordelia had hung out the wash there for four Mondays, and this was the fifth. The breakfast was about half finished—they had reached the buckwheat cakes—when this maid came rushing into the dining-room and stood regarding them, speechless, with a countenance indicative of the utmost horror. She was deadly pale. Her hands, sodden with soapsuds, hung twitching at her sides in the folds of her calico gown; her very hair, which was light and sparse, seemed to bristle with fear. All the Townsends turned and looked at her. David and George rose with a half-defined idea of burglars.

"Cordelia Battles, what is the matter?" cried Mrs. Townsend. Adrianna gasped for breath and turned as white as the maid. "What is the matter?" repeated Mrs. Townsend, but the maid was unable to speak. Mrs. Townsend, who could be peremptory, sprang up, ran to the frightened woman and shook her violently. "Cordelia Battles, you speak," said she, "and not stand there staring that way, as if you were struck dumb! What is the matter with you?"

Then Cordelia spoke in a fainting voice.

"There's—somebody else—hanging out clothes—in the vacant lot," she gasped, and clutched at a chair for support.

"Who?" cried Mrs. Townsend, rousing to indignation, for already she had assumed a proprietorship in the vacant lot. "Is it the folks in the next house? I'd like to know what right they have! We are next to that vacant lot."

"I—dunno—who it is," gasped Cordelia. "Why, we've seen that girl next door go to mass every morning," said Mrs. Townsend. "She's got a fiery red head. Seems as if you might know her by this time, Cordelia."

"It ain't that girl," gasped Cordelia. Then she added in a horror-stricken voice, "I couldn't see who 'twas."

They all stared.

"Why couldn't you see?" demanded her mistress. "Are you struck blind?"

"No, ma'am."

"Then why couldn't you see?"

"All I could see was—" Cordelia hesitated, with an expression of the utmost horror.

"Go on," said Mrs. Townsend, impatiently.

"All I could see was the shadow of somebody, very slim, hanging out the clothes, and—"

"What?"

"I could see the shadows of the things flappin' on their line."

"You couldn't see the clothes?"

"Only the shadow on the ground."

"What kind of clothes were they?"

"Queer," replied Cordelia, with a shudder.

"If I didn't know you so well, I should think you had been drinking," said Mrs. Townsend. "Now, Cordelia Battles, I'm going out in that vacant lot and see myself what you're talking about."

"I can't go," gasped the woman.

With that Mrs. Townsend and all the others, except Adrianna, who remained to tremble with the maid, sallied forth into the vacant lot. They had to go out the area gate into the street to reach it. It was nothing unusual in the way of vacant lots. One large poplar tree, the relic of the old forest which had once flourished there, twinkled in one corner; for the rest, it was overgrown with coarse weeds and a few dusty flowers. The Townsends stood just inside the rude board fence which divided the lot from the street and stared with wonder and horror, for Cordelia had told the truth. They all saw what she had described—the shadow of an exceedingly slim woman moving along the ground with up-stretched arms, the shadows of strange, nondescript garments flapping from a shadowy line, but when they looked up for the substance of the shadows nothing was to be seen except the clear, blue October air.

"My goodness!" gasped Mrs. Townsend. Her face assumed a strange gathering of wrath in the midst of her terror. Suddenly she made a determined move forward, although her husband strove to hold her back.

"You let me be," said she. She moved forward. Then she recoiled and gave a loud shriek. "The wet sheet flapped in my face," she cried. "Take me away, take me away!" Then she fainted. Between them they got her back to the house. "It was awful," she moaned when she came to herself, with the family all around her where she lay on the dining-room floor. "Oh, David, what do you suppose it is?"

"Nothing at all," replied David Townsend stoutly. He was remarkable for courage and staunch belief in actualities. He was now denying to himself that he had seen anything unusual.

"Oh, there was," moaned his wife.

"I saw something," said George, in a sullen, boyish bass.

The maid sobbed convulsively and so did Adrianna for sympathy.

"We won't talk any about it," said David. "Here, Jane, you drink this hot tea—it will do you good; and Cordelia, you hang out the clothes in our own yard. George, you go and put up the line for her."

"The line is out there," said George, with a jerk of his shoulder.

"Are you afraid?"

"No, I ain't," replied the boy resentfully, and went out with a pale face.

After that Cordelia hung the Townsend wash in the yard of their own house, standing always with her back to the vacant lot. As for David Townsend, he spent a good deal of his time in the lot watching the shadows, but he came to no explanation, although he strove to satisfy himself with many.

"I guess the shadows come from the smoke from our chimneys, or else the poplar tree," he said.

"Why do the shadows come on Monday mornings, and no other?" demanded his wife.

David was silent.

Very soon new mysteries arose. One day Cordelia rang the dinner-bell at their usual dinner hour, the same as in Townsend Centre, high noon, and the family assembled. With amazement

Adrianna looked at the dishes on the table.

"Why, that's queer!" she said.

"What's queer?" asked her mother.

Cordelia stopped short as she was about setting a tumbler of water beside a plate, and the water slopped over.

"Why," said Adrianna, her face paling, "I—thought there was boiled dinner. I—smelt cabbage cooking."

"I knew there would something else come up," gasped Cordelia, leaning hard on the back of Adrianna's chair.

"What do you mean?" asked Mrs. Townsend sharply, but her own face began to assume the shocked pallor which it was so easy nowadays for all their faces to assume at the merest suggestion of anything out of the common.

"I smelt cabbage cooking all the morning up in my room," Adrianna said faintly, "and here's codfish and potatoes for dinner."

The Townsends all looked at one another. David rose with an exclamation and rushed out of the room. The others waited tremblingly. When he came back his face was lowering.

"What did you—" Mrs. Townsend asked hesitatingly.

"There's some smell of cabbage out there," he admitted reluctantly. Then he looked at her with a challenge. "It comes from the next house," he said. "Blows over our house."

"Our house is higher."

"I don't care; you can never account for such things."

"Cordelia," said Mrs. Townsend, "you go over to the next house and you ask if they've got cabbage for dinner."

Cordelia switched out of the room, her mouth set hard. She came back promptly.

"Says they never have cabbage," she announced with gloomy triumph and a conclusive glance at Mr. Townsend. "Their girl was real sassy."

"Oh, father, let's move away; let's sell the house," cried Adrianna in a panic-stricken tone.

"If you think I'm going to sell a house that I got as cheap as this one because we smell cabbage in a vacant lot, you're mistaken," replied David firmly.

"It isn't the cabbage alone," said Mrs. Townsend.

"And a few shadows," added David. "I am tired of such nonsense. I thought you had more sense, Jane."

"One of the boys at school asked me if we lived in the house next to the vacant lot on Wells Street and whistled when I said 'Yes,'" remarked George.

"Let him whistle," said Mr. Townsend.

After a few hours the family, stimulated by Mr. Townsend's calm, common sense, agreed that it was exceedingly foolish to be disturbed by a mysterious odour of cabbage. They even laughed at themselves.

"I suppose we have got so nervous over those shadows hanging out clothes that we notice every little thing," conceded Mrs. Townsend.

"You will find out some day that that is no more to be regarded than the cabbage," said her husband.

"You can't account for that wet sheet hitting my face," said Mrs. Townsend, doubtfully.

"You imagined it."

"I *felt* it."

That afternoon things went on as usual in the household until nearly four o'clock. Adrianna went downtown to do some shopping. Mrs. Townsend sat sewing beside the bay window in her room, which was a front one in the third story. George had not got home. Mr. Townsend was writing a letter in the library. Cordelia was busy in the basement; the twilight, which was coming earlier and earlier every night, was beginning to gather, when suddenly there was a loud crash which shook the house from its foundations. Even the dishes on the sideboard rattled, and the glasses rang like bells. The pictures on the walls of Mrs. Townsend's room swung out from the walls. But that was not all: every looking-glass in the house cracked simultaneously—as nearly as they could judge—from top to bottom, then shivered into fragments over the floors.

Mrs. Townsend was too frightened to scream. She sat huddled

in her chair, gasping for breath, her eyes, rolling from side to side in incredulous terror, turned toward the street. She saw a great black group of people crossing it just in front of the vacant lot. There was something inexpressibly strange and gloomy about this moving group; there was an effect of sweeping, wavings and foldings of sable draperies and gleams of deadly white faces; then they passed. She twisted her head to see, and they disappeared in the vacant lot. Mr. Townsend came hurrying into the room; he was pale, and looked at once angry and alarmed.

"Did you fall?" he asked inconsequently, as if his wife, who was small, could have produced such a manifestation by a fall.

"Oh, David, what is it?" whispered Mrs. Townsend.

"Darned if I know!" said David.

"Don't swear. It's too awful. Oh, see the looking-glass, David!"

"I see it. The one over the library mantel is broken, too."

"Oh, it is a sign of death!"

Cordelia's feet were heard as she staggered on the stairs. She almost fell into the room. She reeled over to Mr. Townsend and clutched his arm. He cast a sidewise glance, half furious, half commiserating at her.

"Well, what is it all about?" he asked.

"I don't know. What is it? Oh, what is it? The looking-glass in the kitchen is broken. All over the floor. Oh, oh! What is it?"

"I don't know any more than you do. I didn't do it."

"Lookin'-glasses broken is a sign of death in the house," said Cordelia. "If it's me, I hope I'm ready; but I'd rather die than be so scared as I've been lately."

Mr. Townsend shook himself loose and eyed the two trembling women with gathering resolution.

"Now, look here, both of you," he said. "This is nonsense. You'll die sure enough of fright if you keep on this way. I was a fool myself to be startled. Everything it is is an earthquake."

"Oh, David!" gasped his wife, not much reassured.

"It is nothing but an earthquake," persisted Mr. Townsend. "It acted just like that. Things always are broken on the walls, and the middle of the room isn't affected. I've read about it."

Suddenly Mrs. Townsend gave a loud shriek and pointed.

"How do you account for that," she cried, "if it's an earth-quake? Oh, oh, oh!"

She was on the verge of hysterics. Her husband held her firmly by the arm as his eyes followed the direction of her rigid pointing finger. Cordelia looked also, her eyes seeming converged to a bright point of fear. On the floor in front of the broken looking-glass lay a mass of black stuff in a grewsome long ridge.

"It's something you dropped there," almost shouted Mr. Townsend.

"It ain't. Oh!"

Mr. Townsend dropped his wife's arm and took one stride toward the object. It was a very long crape veil. He lifted it, and it floated out from his arm as if imbued with electricity.

"It's yours," he said to his wife.

"Oh, David, I never had one. You know, oh, you know I— shouldn't—unless you died. How came it there?"

"I'm darned if I know," said David, regarding it. He was dead-ly pale, but still resentful rather than afraid.

"Don't hold it; don't!"

"I'd like to know what in thunder all this means?" said David. He gave the thing an angry toss and it fell on the floor in exactly the same long heap as before.

Cordelia began to weep with racking sobs. Mrs. Townsend reached out and caught her husband's hand, clutching it hard with ice-cold fingers.

"What's got into this house, anyhow?" he growled.

"You'll have to sell it. Oh, David, we can't live here."

"As for my selling a house I paid only five thousand for when it's worth twenty-five, for any such nonsense as this, I won't!"

David gave one stride toward the black veil, but it rose from the floor and moved away before him across the room at exactly the same height as if suspended from a woman's head. He pursued it, clutching vainly, all around the room, then he swung himself on his heel with an exclamation and the thing fell to the floor again in the long heap. Then were heard hurrying feet on the stairs and Adrianna burst into the room. She ran straight to her father and clutched his arm; she tried to speak, but she chattered unintelligibly; her face was blue. Her father shook her violently.

"Adrianna, do have more sense!" he cried.

"Oh, David, how can you talk so?" sobbed her mother.

"I can't help it. I'm mad!" said he with emphasis. "What has got into this house and you all, anyhow?"

"What is it, Adrianna, poor child," asked her mother. "Only look what has happened here."

"It's an earthquake," said her father staunchly; "nothing to be afraid of."

"How do you account for *that?*" said Mrs. Townsend in an awful voice, pointing to the veil.

Adrianna did not look—she was too engrossed with her own terrors. She began to speak in a breathless voice.

"I—was—coming—by the vacant lot," she panted, "and—I—I—had my new hat in a paper bag and—a parcel of blue ribbon, and—I saw a crowd, an awful—oh! a whole crowd of people with white faces, as if—they were dressed all in black."

"Where are they now?"

"I don't know. Oh!" Adrianna sank gasping feebly into a chair.

"Get her some water, David," sobbed her mother.

David rushed with an impatient exclamation out of the room and returned with a glass of water which he held to his daughter's lips.

"Here, drink this!" he said roughly.

"Oh, David, how can you speak so?" sobbed his wife.

"I can't help it. I'm mad clean through," said David.

Then there was a hard bound upstairs, and George entered. He was very white, but he grinned at them with an appearance of unconcern.

"Hullo!" he said in a shaking voice, which he tried to control.

"What on earth's to pay in that vacant lot now?"

"Well, what is it?" demanded his father.

"Oh, nothing, only—well, there are lights over it exactly as if there was a house there, just about where the windows would be. It looked as if you could walk right in, but when you look close there are those old dried-up weeds rattling away on the ground the same as ever. I looked at it and couldn't believe my eyes. A woman saw it, too. She came along just as I did. She gave one look, then she screeched and ran. I waited for someone else, but nobody came."

Mr. Townsend rushed out of the room.

"I daresay it'll be gone when he gets there," began George, then he stared round the room. "What's to pay here?" he cried.

"Oh, George, the whole house shook all at once, and all the looking-glasses broke," wailed his mother, and Adrianna and Cordelia joined.

George whistled with pale lips. Then Mr. Townsend entered.

"Well," asked George, "see anything?"

"I don't want to talk," said his father. "I've stood just about enough."

"We've got to sell out and go back to Townsend Centre," cried his wife in a wild voice. "Oh, David, say you'll go back."

"I won't go back for any such nonsense as this, and sell a twenty-five thousand dollar house for five thousand," said he firmly.

But that very night his resolution was shaken. The whole family watched together in the dining-room. They were all afraid to go to bed—that is, all except possibly Mr. Townsend. Mrs. Townsend declared firmly that she for one would leave that awful house and go back to Townsend Centre whether he came or not, unless they all stayed together and watched, and Mr. Townsend yielded. They chose the dining-room for the reason that it was nearer the street should they wish to make their egress hurriedly, and they took up their station around the dining-table on which Cordelia had placed a luncheon.

"It looks exactly as if we were watching with a corpse," she said in a horror-stricken whisper.

"Hold your tongue if you can't talk sense," said Mr. Townsend.

The dining-room was very large, finished in oak, with a dark blue paper above the wainscotting. The old sign of the tavern, the Blue Leopard, hung over the mantelshelf. Mr. Townsend had insisted on hanging it there. He had a curious pride in it. The family sat together until after midnight and nothing unusual happened. Mrs. Townsend began to nod; Mr. Townsend read the paper ostentatiously. Adrianna and Cordelia stared with roving eyes about the room, then at each other as if comparing notes on terror. George had a book which he studied furtively. All at once Adrianna gave a startled exclamation and Cordelia echoed her. George whistled faintly. Mrs. Townsend awoke with a start and Mr. Townsend's paper rattled to the floor.

"Look!" gasped Adrianna.

The sign of the Blue Leopard over the shelf glowed as if a lantern hung over it. The radiance was thrown from above. It grew brighter and brighter as they watched. The Blue Leopard seemed to crouch and spring with life. Then the door into the front hall opened—the outer door, which had been carefully locked. It squeaked and they all recognized it. They sat staring. Mr. Townsend was as transfixed as the rest. They heard the outer door shut, then the door into the room swung open and slowly that awful black group of people which they had seen in the afternoon entered. The Townsends with one accord rose and huddled together in a far corner; they all held to each other and stared.

The people, their faces gleaming with a whiteness of death, their black robes waving and folding, crossed the room. They were a trifle above mortal height, or seemed so to the terrified eyes which saw them. They reached the mantel-shelf where the sign-board hung, then a black-draped long arm was seen to rise and make a motion, as if plying a knocker. Then the whole company passed out of sight, as if through the wall, and the room was as before. Mrs. Townsend was shaking in a nervous chill,

Adrianna was almost fainting, Cordelia was in hysterics. David Townsend stood glaring in a curious way at the sign of the Blue Leopard. George stared at him with a look of horror. There was something in his father's face which made him forget everything else. At last he touched his arm timidly.

"Father," he whispered.

David turned and regarded him with a look of rage and fury, then his face cleared; he passed his hand over his forehead.

"Good Lord! What DID come to me?" he muttered.

"You looked like that awful picture of old Tom Townsend in the garret in Townsend Centre, father," whimpered the boy, shuddering.

"Should think I might look like 'most any old cuss after such darned work as this," growled David, but his face was white. "Go and pour out some hot tea for your mother," he ordered the boy sharply. He himself shook Cordelia violently. "Stop such actions!" he shouted in her ears, and shook her again. "Ain't you a church member?" he demanded; "what be you afraid of? You ain't done nothin' wrong, have ye?"

Then Cordelia quoted Scripture in a burst of sobs and laughter.

"Behold, I was shapen in iniquity; and in sin did my mother conceive me," she cried out. "If I ain't done wrong, mebbe them that's come before me did, and when the Evil One and the Powers of Darkness is abroad I'm liable, I'm liable!" Then she laughed loud and long and shrill.

"If you don't hush up," said David, but still with that white terror and horror on his own face, "I'll bundle you out in that vacant lot whether or no. I mean it."

Then Cordelia was quiet, after one wild roll of her eyes at him. The colour was returning to Adrianna's cheeks; her mother was drinking hot tea in spasmodic gulps.

"It's after midnight," she gasped, "and I don't believe they'll come again tonight. Do you, David?"

"No, I don't," said David conclusively.

"Oh, David, we mustn't stay another night in this awful

364

house."

"We won't. Tomorrow we'll pack off bag and baggage to Townsend Centre, if it takes all the fire department to move us," said David.

Adrianna smiled in the midst of her terror. She thought of Abel Lyons.

The next day Mr. Townsend went to the real estate agent who had sold him the house.

"It's no use," he said, "I can't stand it. Sell the house for what you can get. I'll give it away rather than keep it."

Then he added a few strong words as to his opinion of parties who sold him such an establishment. But the agent pleaded innocent for the most part.

"I'll own I suspected something wrong when the owner, who pledged me to secrecy as to his name, told me to sell that place for what I could get, and did not limit me. I had never heard anything, but I began to suspect something was wrong. Then I made a few inquiries and found out that there was a rumour in the neighbourhood that there was something out of the usual about that vacant lot. I had wondered myself why it wasn't built upon. There was a story about it's being undertaken once, and the contract made, and the contractor dying; then another man took it and one of the workmen was killed on his way to dig the cellar, and the others struck. I didn't pay much attention to it. I never believed much in that sort of thing anyhow, and then, too, I couldn't find out that there had ever been anything wrong about the house itself, except as the people who had lived there were said to have seen and heard queer things in the vacant lot, so I thought you might be able to get along, especially as you didn't look like a man who was timid, and the house was such a bargain as I never handled before. But this you tell me is beyond belief."

"Do you know the names of the people who formerly owned the vacant lot?" asked Mr. Townsend.

"I don't know for certain," replied the agent, "for the original owners flourished long before your or my day, but I do know that the lot goes by the name of the old Gaston lot. What's the matter? Are you ill?"

"No; it is nothing," replied Mr. Townsend. "Get what you can for the house; perhaps another family might not be as troubled as we have been."

"I hope you are not going to leave the city?" said the agent, urbanely.

"I am going back to Townsend Centre as fast as steam can carry me after we get packed up and out of that cursed house," replied Mr. David Townsend.

He did not tell the agent nor any of his family what had caused him to start when told the name of the former owners of the lot. He remembered all at once the story of a ghastly murder which had taken place in the Blue Leopard. The victim's name was Gaston and the murderer had never been discovered.

The Lost Ghost

Mrs. John Emerson, sitting with her needlework beside the window, looked out and saw Mrs. Rhoda Meserve coming down the street, and knew at once by the trend of her steps and the cant of her head that she meditated turning in at her gate. She also knew by a certain something about her general carriage—a thrusting forward of the neck, a bustling hitch of the shoulders—that she had important news. Rhoda Meserve always had the news as soon as the news was in being, and generally Mrs. John Emerson was the first to whom she imparted it. The two women had been friends ever since Mrs. Meserve had married Simon Meserve and come to the village to live.

Mrs. Meserve was a pretty woman, moving with graceful flirts of ruffling skirts; her clear-cut, nervous face, as delicately tinted as a shell, looked brightly from the plumy brim of a black hat at Mrs. Emerson in the window. Mrs. Emerson was glad to see her coming. She returned the greeting with enthusiasm, then rose hurriedly, ran into the cold parlour and brought out one of the best rocking-chairs. She was just in time, after drawing it up beside the opposite window, to greet her friend at the door.

"Good-afternoon," said she. "I declare, I'm real glad to see you. I've been alone all day. John went to the city this morning. I thought of coming over to your house this afternoon, but I couldn't bring my sewing very well. I am putting the ruffles on my new black dress skirt."

"Well, I didn't have a thing on hand except my crochet work," responded Mrs. Meserve, "and I thought I'd just run over a few minutes."

"I'm real glad you did," repeated Mrs. Emerson. "Take your things right off. Here, I'll put them on my bed in the bedroom. Take the rocking-chair."

Mrs. Meserve settled herself in the parlour rocking-chair, while Mrs. Emerson carried her shawl and hat into the little adjoining bedroom. When she returned Mrs. Meserve was rocking peacefully and was already at work hooking blue wool in and out.

"That's real pretty," said Mrs. Emerson.

"Yes, I think it's pretty," replied Mrs. Meserve.

"I suppose it's for the church fair?"

"Yes. I don't suppose it'll bring enough to pay for the worsted, let alone the work, but I suppose I've got to make something."

"How much did that one you made for the fair last year bring?"

"Twenty-five cents."

"It's wicked, ain't it?"

"I rather guess it is. It takes me a week every minute I can get to make one. I wish those that bought such things for twenty-five cents had to make them. Guess they'd sing another song. Well, I suppose I oughtn't to complain as long as it is for the Lord, but sometimes it does seem as if the Lord didn't get much out of it."

"Well, it's pretty work," said Mrs. Emerson, sitting down at the opposite window and taking up her dress skirt.

"Yes, it is real pretty work. I just *love* to crochet."

The two women rocked and sewed and crocheted in silence for two or three minutes. They were both waiting. Mrs. Meserve waited for the other's curiosity to develop in order that her news might have, as it were, a befitting stage entrance. Mrs. Emerson waited for the news. Finally she could wait no longer.

"Well, what's the news?" said she.

"Well, I don't know as there's anything very particular," hedged the other woman, prolonging the situation.

"Yes, there is; you can't cheat me," replied Mrs. Emerson.

"Now, how do you know?"

"By the way you look."

Mrs. Meserve laughed consciously and rather vainly.

"Well, Simon says my face is so expressive I can't hide anything more than five minutes no matter how hard I try," said she. "Well, there is some news. Simon came home with it this noon. He heard it in South Dayton. He had some business over there this morning. The old Sargent place is let."

Mrs. Emerson dropped her sewing and stared.

"You don't say so!"

"Yes, it is."

"Who to?"

"Why, some folks from Boston that moved to South Dayton last year. They haven't been satisfied with the house they had there—it wasn't large enough. The man has got considerable property and can afford to live pretty well. He's got a wife and his unmarried sister in the family. The sister's got money, too. He does business in Boston and it's just as easy to get to Boston from here as from South Dayton, and so they're coming here. You know the old Sargent house is a splendid place."

"Yes, it's the handsomest house in town, but—"

"Oh, Simon said they told him about that and he just laughed. Said he wasn't afraid and neither was his wife and sister. Said he'd risk ghosts rather than little tucked-up sleeping-rooms without any sun, like they've had in the Dayton house. Said he'd rather risk *seeing* ghosts, than risk being ghosts themselves. Simon said they said he was a great hand to joke."

"Oh, well," said Mrs. Emerson, "it is a beautiful house, and maybe there isn't anything in those stories. It never seemed to me they came very straight anyway. I never took much stock in them. All I thought was—if his wife was nervous."

"Nothing in creation would hire me to go into a house that I'd ever heard a word against of that kind," declared Mrs. Meserve with emphasis. "I wouldn't go into that house if they would give me the rent. I've seen enough of haunted houses to last me as long as I live."

Mrs. Emerson's face acquired the expression of a hunting hound.

"Have you?" she asked in an intense whisper.

"Yes, I have. I don't want any more of it."

"Before you came here?"

"Yes; before I was married—when I was quite a girl."

Mrs. Meserve had not married young. Mrs. Emerson had mental calculations when she heard that.

"Did you really live in a house that was—" she whispered fearfully.

Mrs. Meserve nodded solemnly.

"Did you really ever—see—anything—"

Mrs. Meserve nodded.

"You didn't see anything that did you any harm?"

"No, I didn't see anything that did me harm looking at it in one way, but it don't do anybody in this world any good to see things that haven't any business to be seen in it. You never get over it."

There was a moment's silence. Mrs. Emerson's features seemed to sharpen.

"Well, of course I don't want to urge you," said she, "if you don't feel like talking about it; but maybe it might do you good to tell it out, if it's on your mind, worrying you."

"I try to put it out of my mind," said Mrs. Meserve.

"Well, it's just as you feel."

"I never told anybody but Simon," said Mrs. Meserve. "I never felt as if it was wise perhaps. I didn't know what folks might think. So many don't believe in anything they can't understand, that they might think my mind wasn't right. Simon advised me not to talk about it. He said he didn't believe it was anything supernatural, but he had to own up that he couldn't give any explanation for it to save his life. He had to own up that he didn't believe anybody could. Then he said he wouldn't talk about it. He said lots of folks would sooner tell folks my head wasn't right than to own up they couldn't see through it."

"I'm sure I wouldn't say so," returned Mrs. Emerson reproachfully. "You know better than that, I hope."

"Yes, I do," replied Mrs. Meserve. "I know you wouldn't say so."

"And I wouldn't tell it to a soul if you didn't want me to."

"Well, I'd rather you wouldn't."

"I won't speak of it even to Mr. Emerson."

"I'd rather you wouldn't even to him."

"I won't."

Mrs. Emerson took up her dress skirt again; Mrs. Meserve hooked up another loop of blue wool. Then she begun:

"Of course," said she, "I ain't going to say positively that I believe or disbelieve in ghosts, but all I tell you is what I saw. I can't explain it. I don't pretend I can, for I can't. If you can, well and good; I shall be glad, for it will stop tormenting me as it has done and always will otherwise. There hasn't been a day nor a night since it happened that I haven't thought of it, and always I have felt the shivers go down my back when I did."

"That's an awful feeling," Mrs. Emerson said.

"Ain't it? Well, it happened before I was married, when I was a girl and lived in East Wilmington. It was the first year I lived there. You know my family all died five years before that. I told you."

Mrs. Emerson nodded.

"Well, I went there to teach school, and I went to board with a Mrs. Amelia Dennison and her sister, Mrs. Bird. Abby, her name was—Abby Bird. She was a widow; she had never had any children. She had a little money—Mrs. Dennison didn't have any—and she had come to East Wilmington and bought the house they lived in. It was a real pretty house, though it was very old and run down. It had cost Mrs. Bird a good deal to put it in order. I guess that was the reason they took me to board. I guess they thought it would help along a little. I guess what I paid for my board about kept us all in victuals. Mrs. Bird had enough to live on if they were careful, but she had spent so much fixing up the old house that they must have been a little pinched for awhile.

371

"Anyhow, they took me to board, and I thought I was pretty lucky to get in there. I had a nice room, big and sunny and furnished pretty, the paper and paint all new, and everything as neat as wax. Mrs. Dennison was one of the best cooks I ever saw, and I had a little stove in my room, and there was always a nice fire there when I got home from school. I thought I hadn't been in such a nice place since I lost my own home, until I had been there about three weeks.

"I had been there about three weeks before I found it out, though I guess it had been going on ever since they had been in the house, and that was most four months. They hadn't said anything about it, and I didn't wonder, for there they had just bought the house and been to so much expense and trouble fixing it up.

"Well, I went there in September. I begun my school the first Monday. I remember it was a real cold fall, there was a frost the middle of September, and I had to put on my winter coat. I remember when I came home that night (let me see, I began school on a Monday, and that was two weeks from the next Thursday), I took off my coat downstairs and laid it on the table in the front entry. It was a real nice coat—heavy black broadcloth trimmed with fur; I had had it the winter before. Mrs. Bird called after me as I went upstairs that I ought not to leave it in the front entry for fear somebody might come in and take it, but I only laughed and called back to her that I wasn't afraid. I never was much afraid of burglars.

"Well, though it was hardly the middle of September, it was a real cold night. I remember my room faced west, and the sun was getting low, and the sky was a pale yellow and purple, just as you see it sometimes in the winter when there is going to be a cold snap. I rather think that was the night the frost came the first time. I know Mrs. Dennison covered up some flowers she had in the front yard, anyhow. I remember looking out and seeing an old green plaid shawl of hers over the verbena bed. There was a fire in my little wood-stove. Mrs. Bird made it, I know. She was a real motherly sort of woman; she always seemed to be the happiest when she was doing something to make other folks happy and comfortable. Mrs. Dennison told me she had always been so. She said she had coddled her husband within an inch of his life. 'It's lucky Abby never had any children,' she said, 'for she would have spoilt them.'

"Well, that night I sat down beside my nice little fire and ate an apple. There was a plate of nice apples on my table. Mrs. Bird put them there. I was always very fond of apples. Well, I sat down and ate an apple, and was having a beautiful time, and thinking how lucky I was to have got board in such a place with such nice folks, when I heard a queer little sound at my door. It was such a little hesitating sort of sound that it sounded more like a fumble than a knock, as if someone very timid, with very little hands, was feeling along the door, not quite daring to knock. For a minute I thought it was a mouse. But I waited and it came again, and then I made up my mind it was a knock, but a very little scared one, so I said, 'Come in.'

"But nobody came in, and then presently I heard the knock again. Then I got up and opened the door, thinking it was very queer, and I had a frightened feeling without knowing why.

"Well, I opened the door, and the first thing I noticed was a draught of cold air, as if the front door downstairs was open, but there was a strange close smell about the cold draught. It smelled more like a cellar that had been shut up for years, than out-of-doors. Then I saw something. I saw my coat first. The thing that held it was so small that I couldn't see much of anything else. Then I saw a little white face with eyes so scared and wishful that they seemed as if they might eat a hole in anybody's heart. It was a dreadful little face, with something about it which made it different from any other face on earth, but it was so pitiful that somehow it did away a good deal with the dreadfulness. And there were two little hands spotted purple with the cold, holding up my winter coat, and a strange little far-away voice said: 'I can't find my mother.'

"'For Heaven's sake,' I said, 'who are you?'

"Then the little voice said again: 'I can't find my mother.'

"All the time I could smell the cold and I saw that it was about the child; that cold was clinging to her as if she had come out of some deadly cold place. Well, I took my coat, I did not know what else to do, and the cold was clinging to that. It was as cold as if it had come off ice. When I had the coat I could see the child more plainly. She was dressed in one little white garment made very simply. It was a nightgown, only very long, quite covering her feet, and I could see dimly through it her little thin body mottled purple with the cold. Her face did not look so cold; that was a clear waxen white. Her hair was dark, but it looked as if it might be dark only because it was so damp, almost wet, and might really be light hair. It clung very close to her forehead, which was round and white. She would have been very beautiful if she had not been so dreadful.

"'Who are you?' says I again, looking at her.

"She looked at me with her terrible pleading eyes and did not say anything.

"'What are you?' says I. Then she went away. She did not seem to run or walk like other children. She flitted, like one of those little filmy white butterflies, that don't seem like real ones they are so light, and move as if they had no weight. But she looked back from the head of the stairs. 'I can't find my mother,' said she, and I never heard such a voice.

"'Who is your mother?' says I, but she was gone.

"Well, I thought for a moment I should faint away. The room got dark and I heard a singing in my ears. Then I flung my coat onto the bed. My hands were as cold as ice from holding it, and I stood in my door, and called first Mrs. Bird and then Mrs. Dennison. I didn't dare go down over the stairs where that had gone. It seemed to me I should go mad if I didn't see somebody or something like other folks on the face of the earth. I thought I should never make anybody hear, but I could hear them stepping about downstairs, and I could smell biscuits baking for supper. Somehow the smell of those biscuits seemed the only natural thing left to keep me in my right mind. I didn't dare go over those stairs. I just stood there and called, and finally I heard the entry door open and Mrs. Bird called back:

"'What is it? Did you call, Miss Arms?'

"'Come up here; come up here as quick as you can, both of you,' I screamed out; 'quick, quick, quick!'

"I heard Mrs. Bird tell Mrs. Dennison: 'Come quick, Amelia, something is the matter in Miss Arms' room.' It struck me even then that she expressed herself rather queerly, and it struck me as very queer, indeed, when they both got upstairs and I saw that they knew what had happened, or that they knew of what nature the happening was.

"'What is it, dear?' asked Mrs. Bird, and her pretty, loving voice had a strained sound. I saw her look at Mrs. Dennison and I saw Mrs. Dennison look back at her.

"'For God's sake,' says I, and I never spoke so before—'for God's sake, what was it brought my coat upstairs?'

"'What was it like?' asked Mrs. Dennison in a sort of failing voice, and she looked at her sister again and her sister looked back at her.

"'It was a child I have never seen here before. It looked like a child,' says I, 'but I never saw a child so dreadful, and it had on a nightgown, and said she couldn't find her mother. Who was it? What was it?'

"I thought for a minute Mrs. Dennison was going to faint, but Mrs. Bird hung onto her and rubbed her hands, and whispered in her ear (she had the cooingest kind of voice), and I ran and got her a glass of cold water. I tell you it took considerable courage to go downstairs alone, but they had set a lamp on the entry table so I could see. I don't believe I could have spunked up enough to have gone downstairs in the dark, thinking every second that child might be close to me. The lamp and the smell of the biscuits baking seemed to sort of keep my courage up, but I tell you I didn't waste much time going down those stairs and out into the kitchen for a glass of water. I pumped as if the house was afire, and I grabbed the first thing I came across in the shape of a tumbler: it was a painted one that Mrs. Dennison's Sunday school class gave her, and it was meant for a flower vase.

"Well, I filled it and then ran upstairs. I felt every minute as if something would catch my feet, and I held the glass to Mrs. Dennison's lips, while Mrs. Bird held her head up, and she took a good long swallow, then she looked hard at the tumbler.

"'Yes,' says I, 'I know I got this one, but I took the first I came across, and it isn't hurt a mite.'

"'Don't get the painted flowers wet,' says Mrs. Dennison very feebly, 'they'll wash off if you do.'

"'I'll be real careful,' says I. I knew she set a sight by that painted tumbler.

"The water seemed to do Mrs. Dennison good, for presently she pushed Mrs. Bird away and sat up. She had been laying down on my bed.

"'I'm all over it now,' says she, but she was terribly white, and her eyes looked as if they saw something outside things. Mrs. Bird wasn't much better, but she always had a sort of settled sweet, good look that nothing could disturb to any great extent. I knew I looked dreadful, for I caught a glimpse of myself in the glass, and I would hardly have known who it was.

"Mrs. Dennison, she slid off the bed and walked sort of tottery to a chair. 'I was silly to give way so,' says she.

"'No, you wasn't silly, sister,' says Mrs. Bird. 'I don't know what this means any more than you do, but whatever it is, no one ought to be called silly for being overcome by anything so different from other things which we have known all our lives.'

"Mrs. Dennison looked at her sister, then she looked at me, then back at her sister again, and Mrs. Bird spoke as if she had been asked a question.

"'Yes,' says she, 'I do think Miss Arms ought to be told—that is, I think she ought to be told all we know ourselves.'

"'That isn't much,' said Mrs. Dennison with a dying-away sort of sigh. She looked as if she might faint away again any minute. She was a real delicate-looking woman, but it turned out she was a good deal stronger than poor Mrs. Bird.

"'No, there isn't much we do know,' says Mrs. Bird, 'but what little there is she ought to know. I felt as if she ought to when

376

she first came here.'

"'Well, I didn't feel quite right about it,' said Mrs. Dennison, 'but I kept hoping it might stop, and any way, that it might never trouble her, and you had put so much in the house, and we needed the money, and I didn't know but she might be nervous and think she couldn't come, and I didn't want to take a man boarder.'

"'And aside from the money, we were very anxious to have you come, my dear,' says Mrs. Bird.

"'Yes,' says Mrs. Dennison, 'we wanted the young company in the house; we were lonesome, and we both of us took a great liking to you the minute we set eyes on you.'

"And I guess they meant what they said, both of them. They were beautiful women, and nobody could be any kinder to me than they were, and I never blamed them for not telling me before, and, as they said, there wasn't really much to tell.

"They hadn't any sooner fairly bought the house, and moved into it, than they began to see and hear things. Mrs. Bird said they were sitting together in the sitting-room one evening when they heard it the first time. She said her sister was knitting lace (Mrs. Dennison made beautiful knitted lace) and she was reading the Missionary Herald (Mrs. Bird was very much interested in mission work), when all of a sudden they heard something. She heard it first and she laid down her Missionary Herald and listened, and then Mrs. Dennison she saw her listening and she drops her lace. 'What is it you are listening to, Abby?' says she. Then it came again and they both heard, and the cold shivers went down their backs to hear it, though they didn't know why. 'It's the cat, isn't it?' says Mrs. Bird.

"'It isn't any cat,' says Mrs. Dennison.

"'Oh, I guess it *must* be the cat; maybe she's got a mouse,' says Mrs. Bird, real cheerful, to calm down Mrs. Dennison, for she saw she was 'most scared to death, and she was always afraid of her fainting away. Then she opens the door and calls, 'Kitty, kitty, kitty!' They had brought their cat with them in a basket when they came to East Wilmington to live. It was a real handsome tiger cat, a tommy, and he knew a lot.

"Well, she called 'Kitty, kitty, kitty!' and sure enough the kitty came, and when he came in the door he gave a big yawl that didn't sound unlike what they had heard.

"'There, sister, here he is; you see it was the cat,' says Mrs. Bird. 'Poor kitty!'

"But Mrs. Dennison she eyed the cat, and she give a great screech.

"'What's that? What's that?' says she.

"'What's what?' says Mrs. Bird, pretending to herself that she didn't see what her sister meant.

"'Somethin's got hold of that cat's tail,' says Mrs. Dennison. 'Somethin's got hold of his tail. It's pulled straight out, an' he can't get away. Just hear him yawl!'

"'It isn't anything,' says Mrs. Bird, but even as she said that she could see a little hand holding fast to that cat's tail, and then the child seemed to sort of clear out of the dimness behind the hand, and the child was sort of laughing then, instead of looking sad, and she said that was a great deal worse. She said that laugh was the most awful and the saddest thing she ever heard.

"Well, she was so dumfounded that she didn't know what to do, and she couldn't sense at first that it was anything supernatural. She thought it must be one of the neighbour's children who had run away and was making free of their house, and was teasing their cat, and that they must be just nervous to feel so upset by it. So she speaks up sort of sharp.

"'Don't you know that you mustn't pull the kitty's tail?' says she. 'Don't you know you hurt the poor kitty, and she'll scratch you if you don't take care. Poor kitty, you mustn't hurt her.'

"And with that she said the child stopped pulling that cat's tail and went to stroking her just as soft and pitiful, and the cat put his back up and rubbed and purred as if he liked it. The cat never seemed a mite afraid, and that seemed queer, for I had always heard that animals were dreadfully afraid of ghosts; but then, that was a pretty harmless little sort of ghost.

"Well, Mrs. Bird said the child stroked that cat, while she and

Mrs. Dennison stood watching it, and holding onto each other, for, no matter how hard they tried to think it was all right, it didn't look right. Finally Mrs. Dennison she spoke.

"'What's your name, little girl?' says she.

"Then the child looks up and stops stroking the cat, and says she can't find her mother, just the way she said it to me. Then Mrs. Dennison she gave such a gasp that Mrs. Bird thought she was going to faint away, but she didn't. 'Well, who is your mother?' says she. But the child just says again 'I can't find my mother—I can't find my mother.'

"'Where do you live, dear?' says Mrs. Bird.

"'I can't find my mother,' says the child.

"Well, that was the way it was. Nothing happened. Those two women stood there hanging onto each other, and the child stood in front of them, and they asked her questions, and everything she would say was: 'I can't find my mother.'

"Then Mrs. Bird tried to catch hold of the child, for she thought in spite of what she saw that perhaps she was nervous and it was a real child, only perhaps not quite right in its head, that had run away in her little nightgown after she had been put to bed.

"She tried to catch the child. She had an idea of putting a shawl around it and going out—she was such a little thing she could have carried her easy enough—and trying to find out to which of the neighbours she belonged. But the minute she moved toward the child there wasn't any child there; there was only that little voice seeming to come from nothing, saying 'I can't find my mother,' and presently that died away.

"Well, that same thing kept happening, or something very much the same. Once in awhile Mrs. Bird would be washing dishes, and all at once the child would be standing beside her with the dish-towel, wiping them. Of course, that was terrible. Mrs. Bird would wash the dishes all over. Sometimes she didn't tell Mrs. Dennison, it made her so nervous. Sometimes when they were making cake they would find the raisins all picked over, and sometimes little sticks of kindling-wood would be found laying beside the kitchen stove. They never knew when they would come across that child, and always she kept saying over and over that she couldn't find her mother. They never tried talking to her, except once in awhile Mrs. Bird would get desperate and ask her something, but the child never seemed to hear it; she always kept right on saying that she couldn't find her mother.

"After they had told me all they had to tell about their experience with the child, they told me about the house and the people that had lived there before they did. It seemed something dreadful had happened in that house. And the land agent had never let on to them. I don't think they would have bought it if he had, no matter how cheap it was, for even if folks aren't really afraid of anything, they don't want to live in houses where such dreadful things have happened that you keep thinking about them. I know after they told me I should never have stayed there another night, if I hadn't thought so much of them, no matter how comfortable I was made; and I never was nervous, either. But I stayed. Of course, it didn't happen in my room. If it had I could not have stayed."

"What was it?" asked Mrs. Emerson in an awed voice.

"It was an awful thing. That child had lived in the house with her father and mother two years before. They had come—or the father had—from a real good family. He had a good situation: he was a drummer for a big leather house in the city, and they lived real pretty, with plenty to do with. But the mother was a real wicked woman. She was as handsome as a picture, and they said she came from good sort of people enough in Boston, but she was bad clean through, though she was real pretty spoken and most everybody liked her. She used to dress out and make a great show, and she never seemed to take much interest in the child, and folks began to say she wasn't treated right.

"The woman had a hard time keeping a girl. For some reason one wouldn't stay. They would leave and then talk about her awfully, telling all kinds of things. People didn't believe it at first; then they began to. They said that the woman made that little thing, though she wasn't much over five years old, and small and babyish for her age, do most of the work, what there was done; they said the house used to look like a pig-sty when she didn't have help. They said the little thing used to stand on a chair and wash dishes, and they'd seen her carrying in sticks of wood most as big as she was many a time, and they'd heard her mother scolding her. The woman was a fine singer, and had a voice like a screech-owl when she scolded.

"The father was away most of the time, and when that happened he had been away out West for some weeks. There had been a married man hanging about the mother for some time, and folks had talked some; but they weren't sure there was anything wrong, and he was a man very high up, with money, so they kept pretty still for fear he would hear of it and make trouble for them, and of course nobody was sure, though folks did say afterward that the father of the child had ought to have been told.

"But that was very easy to say; it wouldn't have been so easy to find anybody who would have been willing to tell him such a thing as that, especially when they weren't any too sure. He set his eyes by his wife, too. They said all he seemed to think of was to earn money to buy things to deck her out in. And he about worshiped the child, too. They said he was a real nice man. The men that are treated so bad mostly are real nice men. I've always noticed that.

"Well, one morning that man that there had been whispers about was missing. He had been gone quite a while, though, before they really knew that he was missing, because he had gone away and told his wife that he had to go to New York on business and might be gone a week, and not to worry if he didn't get home, and not to worry if he didn't write, because he should be thinking from day to day that he might take the next train home and there would be no use in writing. So the wife waited, and she tried not to worry until it was two days over the week, then she run into a neighbour's and fainted dead away on the floor; and then they made inquiries and found out that he had skipped—with some money that didn't belong to him, too.

"Then folks began to ask where was that woman, and they found out by comparing notes that nobody had seen her since the man went away; but three or four women remembered that she had told them that she thought of taking the child and going to Boston to visit her folks, so when they hadn't seen her around, and the house shut, they jumped to the conclusion that was where she was. They were the neighbours that lived right around her, but they didn't have much to do with her, and she'd gone out of her way to tell them about her Boston plan, and they didn't make much reply when she did.

"Well, there was this house shut up, and the man and woman missing and the child. Then all of a sudden one of the women that lived the nearest remembered something. She remembered that she had waked up three nights running, thinking she heard a child crying somewhere, and once she waked up her husband, but he said it must be the Bisbees' little girl, and she thought it must be. The child wasn't well and was always crying. It used to have colic spells, especially at night. So she didn't think any more about it until this came up, then all of a sudden she did think of it. She told what she had heard, and finally folks began to think they had better enter that house and see if there was anything wrong.

"Well, they did enter it, and they found that child dead, locked in one of the rooms. (Mrs. Dennison and Mrs. Bird never used that room; it was a back bedroom on the second floor.)

"Yes, they found that poor child there, starved to death, and frozen, though they weren't sure she had frozen to death, for she was in bed with clothes enough to keep her pretty warm when she was alive. But she had been there a week, and she was nothing but skin and bone. It looked as if the mother had locked her into the house when she went away, and told her not to make any noise for fear the neighbours would hear her and find out that she herself had gone.

"Mrs. Dennison said she couldn't really believe that the woman had meant to have her own child starved to death. Probably she thought the little thing would raise somebody, or folks would try to get in the house and find her. Well, whatever she thought, there the child was, dead.

"But that wasn't all. The father came home, right in the midst of it; the child was just buried, and he was beside himself. And— he went on the track of his wife, and he found her, and he shot her dead; it was in all the papers at the time; then he disappeared. Nothing had been seen of him since. Mrs. Dennison said that she thought he had either made way with himself or got out of the country, nobody knew, but they did know there was something wrong with the house.

"'I knew folks acted queer when they asked me how I liked it when we first came here,' says Mrs. Dennison, 'but I never dreamed why till we saw the child that night.'

"I never heard anything like it in my life," said Mrs. Emerson, staring at the other woman with awestruck eyes.

"I thought you'd say so," said Mrs. Meserve. "You don't wonder that I ain't disposed to speak light when I hear there is anything queer about a house, do you?"

"No, I don't, after that," Mrs. Emerson said.

"But that ain't all," said Mrs. Meserve.

"Did you see it again?" Mrs. Emerson asked.

"Yes, I saw it a number of times before the last time. It was lucky I wasn't nervous, or I never could have stayed there, much as I liked the place and much as I thought of those two women; they were beautiful women, and no mistake. I loved those women. I hope Mrs. Dennison will come and see me sometime.

"Well, I stayed, and I never knew when I'd see that child. I got so I was very careful to bring everything of mine upstairs, and not leave any little thing in my room that needed doing, for fear she would come lugging up my coat or hat or gloves or I'd find things done when there'd been no live being in the room to do them. I can't tell you how I dreaded seeing her; and worse than the seeing her was the hearing her say, 'I can't find my mother.' It was enough to make your blood run cold. I never heard a living child cry for its mother that was anything so pitiful as that dead one. It was enough to break your heart.

"She used to come and say that to Mrs. Bird oftener than to anyone else. Once I heard Mrs. Bird say she wondered if it was possible that the poor little thing couldn't really find her mother in the other world, she had been such a wicked woman.

"But Mrs. Dennison told her she didn't think she ought to speak so nor even think so, and Mrs. Bird said she shouldn't wonder if she was right. Mrs. Bird was always very easy to put in the wrong. She was a good woman, and one that couldn't do things enough for other folks. It seemed as if that was what she lived on. I don't think she was ever so scared by that poor little ghost, as much as she pitied it, and she was 'most heartbroken because she couldn't do anything for it, as she could have done for a live child.

"'It seems to me sometimes as if I should die if I can't get that awful little white robe off that child and get her in some clothes and feed her and stop her looking for her mother,' I heard her say once, and she was in earnest. She cried when she said it. That wasn't long before she died.

"Now I am coming to the strangest part of it all. Mrs. Bird died very sudden. One morning—it was Saturday, and there wasn't any school—I went downstairs to breakfast, and Mrs. Bird wasn't there; there was nobody but Mrs. Dennison. She was pouring out the coffee when I came in. 'Why, where's Mrs. Bird?' says I.

"'Abby ain't feeling very well this morning,' says she; 'there isn't much the matter, I guess, but she didn't sleep very well, and her head aches, and she's sort of chilly, and I told her I thought she'd better stay in bed till the house gets warm.' It was a very cold morning.

"'Maybe she's got cold,' says I.

"'Yes, I guess she has,' says Mrs. Dennison. 'I guess she's got cold. She'll be up before long. Abby ain't one to stay in bed a minute longer than she can help.'

"Well, we went on eating our breakfast, and all at once a shadow flickered across one wall of the room and over the ceiling the way a shadow will sometimes when somebody passes the window outside. Mrs. Dennison and I both looked up, then out of the window; then Mrs. Dennison she gives a scream.

"'Why, Abby's crazy!' says she. 'There she is out this bitter cold morning, and—and—' She didn't finish, but she meant the child. For we were both looking out, and we saw, as plain as we ever saw anything in our lives, Mrs. Abby Bird walking off over the white snow-path with that child holding fast to her hand, nestling close to her as if she had found her own mother.

"'She's dead,' says Mrs. Dennison, clutching hold of me hard. 'She's dead; my sister is dead!'

"She was. We hurried upstairs as fast as we could go, and she was dead in her bed, and smiling as if she was dreaming, and one arm and hand was stretched out as if something had hold of it; and it couldn't be straightened even at the last—it lay out over her casket at the funeral."

"Was the child ever seen again?" asked Mrs. Emerson in a shaking voice.

"No," replied Mrs. Meserve; "that child was never seen again after she went out of the yard with Mrs. Bird."

The Little Maid at the Door

Joseph Bayley and his wife Ann came riding down from Salem village. They had started from their home in Newbury the day before, and had stayed overnight with their relative, Sergeant Thomas Putnam, in Salem village; they were on their way to the election in Boston. The road wound along through the woods from Salem to Lynn; it was some time since they had passed a house.

May was nearly gone; the pinks and the blackberry vines were in flower. All the woods were full of an indefinite and composite fragrance, made up of the breaths of myriads of green plants and seen and unseen blossoms, like a very bouquet of spring. The newly leaved trees cast shadows that were as much a part of the tender surprise of the spring as the new flowers. They flickered delicately before Joseph Bayley and his wife Ann on the grassy ridges of the road, but they did not remark them. Their own fancies cast gigantic projections which eclipsed the sweet show of the spring and almost their own personalities. That year the leaves came out and the flowers bloomed in vain for the people in and about Salem village. There was epidemic a disease of the mind which deafened and blinded to all save its own pains.

Ann Bayley on the pillion snuggled closely against her husband's back; her fearful eyes peered at the road around his shoulder. She was a young and handsome woman; she had on her best *mantle* of sad-coloured silk, and a fine black hood with a topknot, but she did not think of that.

"Joseph, what is that in the road before us?" she whispered, timorously.

He pulled up the horse with a great jerk.

"Where?" he whispered back.

"There! there! at the right; just beyond that laurel thicket. 'Tis some what black, an' it moves. There! there! Oh, Joseph!"

Joseph Bayley sat stiff and straight in his saddle, like a soldier; his face was pale and stern, his eyes full of horror and defiance.

"See you it?" Ann whispered again. "There! now it moves. What is it?"

"I see it," said Joseph, in a loud, bold voice. "An' whatever it be, I will yield not to it; an' neither will you, Goodwife."

Ann reached around and caught at the reins. "Let us go back," she moaned, faintly. "Oh, Joseph, let us not pass it. My spirit faints within me. I see its back among the laurel blooms. 'Tis the black beast they tell of. Let us turn back, Joseph, let us turn back!"

"Be still, woman!" returned her husband, jerking the reins from her hand. "What think ye 'twould profit us to turn back to Salem village? I trow if there be one black beast here, there is a full herd of them there. There is naught left but to ride past it as best we may. Sit fast, an' listen you not to it, whatever it promise you." Joseph looked down the road towards the laurel bushes, his muscles now as tense as a bow. Ann hid her face on his shoulder. Suddenly he shouted, with a great voice like a herald: "Away with ye, ye cursed beast! away with ye! We are not of your kind; we are gospel folk. We have naught to do with you or your master. Away with ye!"

The horse leaped forward. There was a great cracking among the laurel bushes at the right, a glossy black back and some white horns heaved over thorn, then some black flanks plunged heavily out of sight.

"Oh!" shrieked Ann, "has it gone? Goodman, has it gone?"

"The Lord hath delivered us from the snare of the enemy," answered Joseph, solemnly.

"What looked it like, Joseph, what looked it like?"

"Like no beast that was saved in the ark."

"Had it fiery eyes?" asked Ann, trembling.

"'Tis well you did not see them."

"Ride fast! oh, ride fast!" Ann pleaded, clutching hard at her husband's cloak. "It may follow on our track." The horse went down the road at a quick trot. Ann kept peering back and starting at every sound in the woods. "Do you mind the tale Samuel Endicott told last night?" she said, shuddering. "How on his voyage to Barbadoes he, sitting on the windlass on a bright moonshining night, was shook violently, and saw the appearance of that witch Goody Bradbury, with a white cap and a white neckcloth on her? It was a dreadful tale."

"It was naught to the sight of Mercy Lewis and Sergeant Thomas Putnam's daughter Ann, when they were set upon and nigh choked to death by Goody Proctor. Know you that within a half-mile we must pass the Proctor house?"

Ann gave a shuddering sigh. "I would I were home again," she moaned. "They said 'twas full of evil things, and that the black man himself kept tavern there since Goodman Proctor and his wife were in jail. Did you mind what Goodwife Putnam said of the black head, like a hog's, that Goodman Perley saw at the keeping-room window as he passed, and the rumbling noises, and the yellow birds that flow around the chimney and twittered in a psalm tune? Oh, Joseph, there is a yellow bird now in the birch-tree-see! see!"

They had come into a little space where the woods were thinner. Joseph urged his horse forward.

"We will not slack our pace for any black beasts nor any yellow birds," he cried, in a valiant voice.

There was a passing gleam of little yellow wings above the birch-tree.

"He has flown away," said Ann. "'Tis best to front them as you do, Goodman, but I have not the courage. That looked like a common yellowbird; his wings shone like gold. Think you it has gone forward to the Proctor house?"

"It matters not, so it but fly up before us," said Joseph Bayley.

He was somewhat older than Ann; fair-haired and fair-beard-ed, with blue eyes set so deeply under heavy brows that they looked black. His face was at once stern and nervous, showing not only the spirit of warfare against his foes, but the elements of strife within himself.

They rode on, and the woods grew thicker; the horse's hoofs made only a faint liquid pad on the mossy road. Suddenly he stopped and whinnied. Ann clutched her husband's arm; they sat motionless, listening; the horse whinnied again.

Suddenly Joseph started violently, and stared into the woods on the left, and Ann also. A long defile of dark evergreens stretched up the hill, with mysterious depths of blue-black shad-ows between them; the air had an earthy dampness.

Joseph shook the reins fiercely over the horse's back, and shouted to him in a loud voice.

"Did you see it?" gasped Ann, when they had come into a lighter place. "Was it not a black man?"

"Fear not; we have outridden him," said her husband, setting his thin intense face proudly ahead.

"I would we were safe home in Newbury," Ann moaned. "I would we had never set out. Think you not Dr. Mather will ride back from Boston with us to keep the witches off? I will bide there forever, if he will not. I will never come this dreadful road again, else. What is that? Oh, what is that? 'Tis a voice coming out of the woods like a great roar. *Joseph!* What is *that?* That was a black cat run across the road into the bushes. 'Twas a black cat. Joseph, let us turn back! No; the black man is behind us, and the beast. What shall we do? What shall we do? Oh, oh, I begin to twitch like Ann and Mercy last night! My feet move, and I cannot stop them! Now there is a pin thrust in my arm! I am pinched! There are fingers at my throat! Joseph! Joseph!"

"Go to prayer, sweetheart," shouted Joseph. "Go to prayer. Be not afraid. 'Twill drive them away. Away with ye, Goody Brad-bury! Away, Goody Proctor! Go to prayer, go to prayer!"

Joseph bent low in the saddle and lashed the horse, which sprang forward with a mighty bound; the green branches rushed in their faces. Joseph prayed in a loud voice. Ann clung to him convulsively, panting for breath. Suddenly they came out of the woods into a cleared space.

"The Proctor house! the Proctor house!" Ann shrieked. "Mercy Lewis said 'twas full of devils. What shall we do?" She hid her face on her husband's shoulder, sobbing and praying.

The Proctor house stood at the left of the road; there were some peach-trees in front of it, and their blossoms showed in a pink spray against the gray unpainted walls. On one side of the house was the great barn, with its doors wide open; on the other, a deep ploughed field, with the plough sticking in a furrow. John Proctor had been arrested and thrown into jail for witchcraft in April, before his spring planting was done.

Joseph Bayley reined in his horse opposite the Proctor house. "Ann," he whispered, and his whisper was full of horror.

"What is it?" she returned, wildly.

"Ann, Goodman Proctor looks forth from the chamber window, and Goody Proctor stands outside by the well, and they are both in jail in Boston." Joseph's whole frame shook in a strange rigid fashion, as if his joints were locked. "Look, Ann!" he whispered.

"I cannot."

"Look!"

Ann turned her head. "Why," she said, and her voice was quite natural and sweet, it had even a tone of glad relief in it, "I see naught but a little maid in the door."

"See you not Goodman Proctor in the window?"

"Nay," said Ann, smiling; "I see naught but the little maid in the door. She is in a blue petticoat, and she has a yellow head, but her little cheeks are pale, I trow."

"See you not Goodwife Proctor in the yard by the well?" asked Joseph.

"Nay, Goodman; I see naught but the little maid in the door. She has a fair face, but now she falls a-weeping. Oh, I fear lest she be all alone in the house."

"I tell you, Goodman Proctor and Goodwife Proctor are both

there," returned Joseph. "Think you I see not with my own eyes? Goodman Proctor has on a red cap, and Goodwife Proctor holds a spindle." He urged on the horse with a sudden cry. "Now the prayers do stick in my throat," he groaned. "I would we were out of this devil's nest!"

"Joseph," implored Ann, "prithee wait a minute! The little maid is calling 'mother' after me. Saw you not how she favoured our little Susanna who died? Hear her! There was naught there but the little maid. Joseph, I pray you, stop."

"Nay; I'll ride till the nag drops," said Joseph Bayley, with a lash. "This last be too much. I tell ye they are there, and they are also in jail. 'Tis hellish work."

Ann said no more for a little space; a curve in the road hid the Proctor house from sight. Suddenly she raised a great cry. "Oh! oh!" she screamed, "'tis gone; 'tis gone from my foot." Joseph stopped. "What is gone?"

"My shoe; but now I missed it from my foot. I must alight, and go back for it."

Joseph started the horse again.

Ann caught at the reins. "Stop, Goodman," she cried, imperatively. "I tell you I must have my shoe."

"And I tell you I'll stop for no shoe in this place, were it made of gold."

"Goodman, you know not what shoe 'tis. 'Tis one of my fine shoes, in which I have never taken steps. They have the crimson silk lacings. I have even carried them in my hand to the meeting-house on a Sabbath, wearing my old ones, and only put them on at the door. Think you I will lose that shoe? Stop the nag."

But Joseph kept on grimly.

"Think you I will go barefoot or with one shoe into Boston?" said Ann. "Know you that these shoes, which were a present from my mother, cost bravely? I trow you will needs loosen your purse strings well before we pass the first shop in Boston. Well, go on, an' you will, when 'tis but a matter of my slipping down from the pillion and running back a few yards."

Joseph Bayley turned his horse about; but Ann remonstrated.

"Nay," said she; " I want not to go thus. I am tired of the saddle. I would like to feel my feet for a space."

Her husband looked around at her with wonder and suspicion. Dark thoughts came into his mind.

She laughed. "Nay," said she, "make no such face at me. I go not back to meet any black man nor sign any book. I go for my fine shoe with the crimson lacing."

"'Tis but a moment since you were afraid," said Joseph. "Have you no fear now?" His blue eyes looked sharply into hers.

She looked back at him soberly and innocently. "In truth, I feel no such fear as I did," she answered. "If I mistake not, your bold front and your prayers drove away the evil ones. I will say a psalm as I go, and I trow naught will harm me."

Ann slipped lightly down from the pillion, and pulled off her one remaining shoe and her stockings; they were her fine worked silk ones, and she could not walk in them over the rough road. Then she set forth very slowly, peering here and there in the undergrowth beside the road, until she passed the curve and the reach of her husband's eyes. Then she gathered up her crimson taffeta petticoat and ran like a deer, with long, graceful leaps, looking neither to right nor left, straight back to the Proctor house.

In the door of the house stood a tiny girl with a soft shock of yellow hair. She wore a little straight blue gown, and her baby feet were bare, curling over the sunny door-step. When she saw Ann coming she started as if to run; then she stood still, her soft eyes wary, her mouth quivering .

Ann Bayley ran up quickly, and threw her arms around her, kneeling down on the step.

What is your name, little maid?" said she, in a loving, agitated voice.

"Abigail Proctor," replied the little maid, shyly, in her sweet childish treble. Then she tried to free herself, but Ann held her fast.

"Nay, be not afraid, sweet," said she. "I love you. I once had a little maid like you for my own. Tell me, dear heart, are you all alone in the house?"

Then the child fell to crying again, and clung around Ann's neck.

"Is there anybody in the house, sweet?" Ann whispered, fondling her, and pressing the wet baby cheek to her own. "The constables came and took them," sobbed the little maid. "They put my poppet down the well, and they pulled mother and Sarah down the road. They took father before that, and Mary Warren did gibe and point. The constables pulled Benjamin away too. I want my mother."

"Your mother shall come again," said Ann. "Take comfort, dear little heart, they cannot have the will to keep her long away. There, there, I tell you she shall come. You watch in the door, and you will see her come down the road."

She smoothed back the little maid's yellow hair, and wiped the tears from her little face with a corner of her beautiful embroidered neckerchief. Then she saw that the face was all grimy with tears and dust, and she went over to the well, which was near the door, and drew a bucket of water swiftly with her strong young arms; then she wet the corner of the neckerchief and scrubbed the little maid's face, bidding her shut her eyes. Then she kissed her over and over.

"Now you are sweet and clean," said she. "Dear little heart, I have some sugar cakes in my bag for you, and then I must be gone."

The little maid looked at her eagerly, her cheeks were waxen, and the blue veins showed in her full childish forehead. Ann pulled some little cakes out of a red velvet satchel she wore at her waist, and Abigail reached out for one with a hungry cry. The tears sprang to Ann's eyes; she put the rest of the cakes in a little pile on the door-stone, and watched the child eat. Then she gathered her up in her arms.

"Goodbye, sweetheart," she said, kissing the soft trembling mouth, the sweet hollow under the chin, and the clinging hands.

"Before long I shall come this way again, and do you stand in the door when I go past."

She put her down and hastened away, but little Abigail ran after her. Ann stopped and knelt and fondled her again.

"Go back, deary," she pleaded; "go back, and eat the sugar cakes."

But this beautiful kind vision in the crimson taffeta, with the rosy cheeks and sweet black eyes looking out from the French hood, with the gleam of gold and delicate embroidery between the silken folds of her *mantilla*, with the ways like her mother's, was more to little deserted Abigail Proctor than the sugar cakes, although she was sorely hungry for them. She stood aloof with pitiful determined eyes until Ann's back was turned, then, as she followed, Ann looked around and saw her and caught her up again.

"My dear heart, my dear heart," she said, and she was half sobbing, "now must you go back, else I fear harm will come to you. My Goodman is waiting for me yonder, and I know not what he will do or say. Nay; you must go buck. I would I could keep you, my little Abigail, but you must go back." Ann Bayley put the little maid down and gave her a gentle push. "Go back," she said, smiling, with her eyes full of tears; "go back, and eat the sugar cakes."

Then she sped on swiftly; as she neared the curve in the road she thrust a band in her pocket, and drew forth a dainty shoe with dangling lacings of crimson silk. She glanced around with a smile and a backward wave of her hand the glowing crimson of her petticoat showed for a minute through the green mist of the undergrowth; then she disappeared.

The little maid Abigail stood still in the road, gazing after her, her soft pink mouth open, her hands clutching at her blue petticoat, as if she would thus hold herself back from following. She heard the tramp of a horse's feet beyond the curve; then it died away. She turned about and went back to the house, with the tears rolling over her cheeks; but she did not sob aloud, as she would have done had her mother been near to hear. A pitiful conviction of the hopelessness of all the appeals of grief was stealing over her childish mind. She had been alone in the house three nights and two days, ever since her sister Sarah and her brother Benjamin had been arrested for witchcraft and carried to jail. Long before that her parents, John and Elizabeth Proctor, had disappeared down the Boston road in charge of the constables. None of the family was spared save this little Abigail, who was deemed too young and insignificant to have dealings with Satan, and was therefore not thrown into prison, but was left alone in the desolate Proctor house in the midst of woods said to be full of evil spirits and witches, to die of fright or starvation as she might. There was but little mercy shown the families of those accused of witchcraft.

"Let some of Goody Proctor's familiars minister unto the brat," one of the constables had said, with a stern laugh, when Abigail had followed wailing after her brother and sister on the day of their arrest.

"Yea," said another; " she can send her yellow-bird or her black hog to keep her company. I wot her tears will be soon dried."

Then the stoutly tramping horses had borne out of sight and bearing the mocking faces of the constables; Sarah's fair agonized one turned backward towards her little deserted sister, and Benjamin raised a brave youthful clamour of indignation.

"Let us loose!"' Abigail heard him shout; "let us loose, I tell ye! Ye are fools, rather than we are witches; ye are fools and murderers! Let us loose, I tell ye!"

Abigail waited long, thinking her brother's words would prevail; but neither he nor Sarah returned, and the sounds all died away, and she went back to the house sobbing. The damp spring night was settling down in a palpable mist, and the woods seemed full of voices. The little maid had heard enough of the terrible talk of the day to fill her innocent head with vague superstitious horror. She threw her apron over her head and fled blindly through the woods, and now and then she fell down and bruised herself, and rose up lamenting sorely, with nobody to hear her.

As soon as she was in the house she shut the doors, and barred them with the great bars that had been made as protection against Indians, and now might wax useless against worse than savages, according to the belief of the colony.

All night long the little maid shrieked and sobbed, and called on her father and her mother and her sister and her brother. Men faring in the road betwixt Boston and Salem village heard her with horror, and fled past with psalm and prayer, their blood cold in their veins. They related the next day to the raging, terror-stricken people how at midnight the accursed Proctor house was full of flitting infernal lights, and howling with devilish spirits, and added a death-dealing tale of some godly woman of the village who outrode their horses on a broomstick and disappeared in the Proctor house.

The next day the little maid unbarred the door, and stood there watching up and down the road for her mother or some other to come. But they came not, although she watched all day. That night she did not sob and call out; she had become afraid of her own voice, and discovered that it had no effect to bring her help. Then, too, early in the night, she heard noises about the house which frightened her, and made her think that perchance the dreadful black beast of which she had heard them discourse was abroad.

The next morning she found that the two horses and the cow and calf were gone from the barn; also that there was left scarce anything for her to eat in the house. There had been some loaves of bread, some boiled meat, and some cakes; now they were all gone, and also all the meal from the chest, and the potatoes and pork from the cellar. But for that last she did not care, since she was not old enough to make a fire and cook. She had left for food only a little cold porridge in a blue bowl, and that she ate up at once and had no more, and a little buttermilk in a crock, which, she being not over-fond of it, served her longer. But that was all she had had for a day and a night, until Goodwife Ann Bayley gave her the sugar cakes. These she ate up at once on her return to the house. Then again she stood watching in the door, but nothing passed along the road save a partridge or a squirrel. It was accounted a bold thing for any solitary traveller to come this way, save a witch, and she, it was supposed, might find many comrades in the woods beside the road and in the Proctor house, which was held to be a sort of devils' tavern. But now no witch came, nor any of her uncanny friends, unless indeed the squirrel and the partridge were familiar demons in disguise. Nothing was too harmless and simple to escape that imputation of the devil's mask.

Abigail took her little pewter porringer from the cupboard, and got herself a drink of water from the bucketful that Goodwife Bayley had drawn; then she stood on a stone, and peered into the well, leaning over the curb. Her poppet was in there, her dear rag doll that Sarah had made for her, and dressed in a beautiful silver brocade made from a piece of a wedding-gown that was brought from England. One of the constables had caught sight of little Abigail Proctor's poppet, and being straightway filled with suspicion that it was an image whereby Goody Proctor afflicted her victims by proxy, had seized it and thrown it into the well. The other constables had chidden him for such rashness, saying it should have been carried to Boston and produced as evidence at the trial; and little Abigail had shrieked out in a panic for her poppet.

She could see nothing of it now, and she went back to her watching-place in the door.

In the afternoon she felt sorely hungry again, and searched through the house for food; then she went out in the sunny fields behind the house, and found some honeysuckles on the rocks, and sucked the honey greedily from their horns. On her return to the house she found a corn-cob, which she snatched up and folded in her apron, and began tending. She sat down in the doorway in her little chair, which she dragged out of the keeping-room, and hugged the poor poppet close, and crooned over it.

"Be not afraid," said she. "I'll not let the black beast harm you; I promise you I will not."

That night she formed a new plan for her solace and protection in the lonely darkness. All the garments of her lost parents and sister and brother that she could find she gathered together, and formed in a circle on the keeping-room floor; then she crept inside with her corn-cob poppet, and lay there hugging it all night. The next day she watched again in the door; but now she was weak and faint, and her little legs trembled so under her that she could not stand to watch, but sat in her small straight-backed chair, holding her poppet and peering forth wistfully.

In the course of the day she made shift to creep out into the fields again, and lying flat on the sun-heated rocks, she sucked some more honey drops from the honeysuckles. She found, too, on the edge of the woods, some young wintergreen leaves, and she even pulled some blue violets and ate them. But the delicate, sweet, and aromatic fare in the spring larder of nature was poor nourishment for a human baby.

Poor little Abigail Proctor could scarcely creep home, still clinging fast to her poppet; scarcely lift herself into her chair in the door; scarcely crawl inside her fairy-ring of her loved ones' belongings at night. She rolled herself tightly in an old cloak of her father's, and it was a sweet and harmless outcome of the dreadful superstition of the day, grafted on an innocent childish brain, that it seemed to partake of the bodily presence of her father, and protect her.

All night long, as she lay there, her mother cooked good meat and broth and sweet cakes, and she ate her fill of them; but in the morning she was too weak to turn her little body over. She could not get to her watching-place in the door, but that made no difference to her, for she did not fairly know that she was not there. It seemed to her that she sat in her little chair looking up the road and down the road; she saw the green branches weaving together, and hiding the sky to the northward and the southward; she saw the flushes of white and rose in the flowering undergrowth; she saw the people coming and going.

There were her father and mother now coming with store

of food and presents for her, now following the constables out of sight. There was that fine pageant passing, as she had seen it pass once before, of the two magistrates, their worshipful masters John Hathorne and Jonathan Corwin, with the marshal, constables, and aids, splendid and awe-inspiring in all their trappings of office, to examine the accused in the Salem meeting-house. There were the ministers Parris and Noyes coming, with severe malignant faces, to question her mother as to whether she had afflicted Mary Warren, their former maidservant, who was now bewitched. There went Benjamin, clamoring out boldly at his captors. There came Sarah with the poppet, which she had drawn out of the well, shaking the water from its silver brocade.

All this the little maid Abigail Proctor saw through her half-delirious fancy as she lay weakly on the keeping-room floor, but she saw not the reality of her sister Sarah coming about four o'clock in the afternoon.

Sarah Proctor, tall and slender, in her limp bedraggled dress, with her fair severe face set in a circle of red shawl, which she had pinned under her chin, came resolutely down the road from Boston, driving a black cow before her with a great green branch. She was nearly fainting with weariness, but she set her dusty shoes down swiftly among the road weeds, and her face was as unyielding as an Indian's.

When she came in sight of the Proctor house she stopped a second. "Abigail!" she called; "Abigail!"

There was no answer, and she went on more swiftly than before. When she reached the house she called again, "Abigail!" but did not wait except while she tied the black cow, by a rope which was around her neck, to a peach-tree. Then she ran in, and found the little maid, her sister Abigail, on the floor in the keeping-room.

She got down on her knees beside her, and Abigail smiled up in her face waveringly. She still thought herself in the door, and that she had just seen her sister come down the road.

"Abigail, what have they done to you?" asked Sarah, in a sharp voice; and the little maid only smiled.

"Abigail, Abigail, what is it?" Sarah took hold of the child's shoulders and shook her; but she got no word back, only the smile ceased, and the eyelids drooped faintly.

"Are you hungry, Abigail?"

The little maid shook her head softly.

"It cannot be that," said Sarah, as if half to herself; "there was enough in the house; but what is it? Abigail, look at me; how long is it since you have eaten? Abigail!"

"Yesterday," whispered the little maid, dreamily.

"What did you eat then?"

"Some posies and leaves out in the field."

"What became of all the bread that was baked, and the cakes, and the meat?"

"I—have forgot."

"No, you have not. Tell me, Abigail."

"The black beast came in the night and did eat it all up, and the cow, and calf, and the horses, too."

"The black beast!"

"I heard him in the night, and in the morning 'twas gone."

Sarah sprang up. "Robbers and murderers!" she cried, in a fierce voice; but the little maid on the floor did not start; she shut her eyes again, and looked up and down the road.

Sarah got a bucket quickly, and went out in the yard to the cow. Down on her knees in the grass she went and milked; then she carried in the bucket, strained the milk with trembling haste, and poured some into Abigail's little pewter porringer. "She was wont to love it warm," she whispered, with white lips.

She bent close over the little maid, and raised her on one arm, while she put the porringer to her mouth. "Drink, Abigail," she said, with tender command. "'Tis warm—the way you love it."

The little maid tried to sip, but shut her mouth, and turned her head with weak loathing, and Sarah could not compel her. She laid her back, and got a spoon and fed her a little, by dint of much pleading to make her open her mouth and swallow.

Afterwards she undressed her, and put her to bed in the south-front room, but the child was so uneasy without the ring of garments which she had arranged, that Sarah was forced to put them around her on the bed; then she fell asleep directly, and stood in her dream watching in the door.

Sarah herself stood in the door, looking up and down the road. There was the sound of a galloping horse in the distance; it came nearer and nearer. She went down to the road and stood waiting. The horse was reined in close to her, and the young man who rode him sprang off the saddle.

"It is you, Sarah; you are safe home," he cried, eagerly, and would have put his arm about her; but she stood aloof sternly.

"For what else did you take me—my apparition?" she said, in a hard voice.

"Sweetheart!"

Know you that I have but just come from the jail in Boston, where I have lain fast chained for witchcraft? See you my fine apparel with the prison air in it? Know you that they called me a witch, and said that I did afflict Mary Warren and the rest? I marvel not that you kept your distance, David Carr; I might perchance have hurt you, and they might have accused you, since you were in fellowship with a witch. I marvel not at that. I would have no harm come to you, though far greater than this came to me, but wherefore did you let my little sister Abigail starve? That can I not suffer, coming from you, David."

The young man took her in his arms with a decided motion; and indeed she did not repulse him, but began to weep.

"Sarah," said he, earnestly, "I was in Ipswich. I knew naught of you and Benjamin being cried out upon until within this hour, when I returned home, and my mother told me. I knew not you were acquitted, and was on my way to Boston to you when I saw you at the gate. And as for Abigail, I knew naught at all; and so 'twas with my mother, for she but now wept when she said the poor little maid had been taken with the rest. But you mean not that, sweetheart; she has not been let to starve?"

"They stole away the food in the night," said Sarah, "and the horses and the cow and calf. I found the cow straying in the woods but now, on my way home, and drove her in and milked her; but Abigail would take scarce a spoonful of the warm milk. She has had but little to eat for three days, and has been distracted with fear, being left alone. She has ever been but a delicate child, and now I fear she has a fever on her, and will die, with her mother away."

"I will go for my mother, sweetheart," said David Carr, eagerly.

"Bring her under cover of night, then," said Sarah; "else she may be suspected if she come to this witch tavern, as they call it. Oh, David, think you she will come? I am in a sore strait."

"I will bring her without fail, sweet, and a flask of wine also, and needments for the little maid," cried David. "Only do you keep up good heart. Perchance, sweet, the child will amend soon, and the others be soon acquit. Nay, weep not, poor lass! poor lass! Thou hast me, whatever else fail thee, poor solace though that be, and I will fetch thee my mother right speedily. She has ever set great store by the little maid, and knows much about ailments; and I doubt not they will be soon acquit."

"They

say my mother will," answered Sarah, tearfully; "and Benjamin is acquit now, but had best keep for a season out of Salem village. But my father will not be acquit; he has spoken his mind too boldly before them all."

"Nay, sweetheart," said David Carr, mounting, "'twill all have passed soon; 'Tis but a madness. Go in to the little maid, and be of good comfort."

Sarah went sobbing into the house, but her face was quite calm when she stood over little Abigail. The child was still asleep, and she could arouse her only for a moment to take a few spoonfuls of milk; then she turned her head on her pillow with weary obstinacy, and shut her eyes again. She still held the poor corncob poppet fast.

Sarah washed herself, braided her hair, and changed her prison dress for a clean blue linen one; then she sat beside Abigail, and waited for David Carr and his mother, who came within an hour.

Goodwife Carr was renowned through Salem village for her knowledge of medicinal herbs and her nursing. She had a gentle sobriety and decision of manner which placed her firmly in her neighbours' confidences, they seeing how she abode firmly in her own, and arguing from that. Then she had too the good fortune to have made no enemies, consequently her ability had not incurred for her the suspicion of being a witch.

Goodwife Carr brought a goodly store of healing herbs, of bread and cakes and meat, and she brewed drinks, and bent her face, pale and soberly faithful, in her close white cap, untiringly over Abigail Proctor. But the little maid never arose again. A fever, engendered by starvation and fright and grief, had seized upon her, and she lay in the bed with her little corn-cob baby a few days longer, and then died.

They made a straight white gown for her, and dressed her in it, after washing her and smoothing her yellow hair; and she lay, looking longer and older than in life, all set about with flowers—pinks and lilacs and roses—from Goodwife Carr's garden, until she was buried. And they had the Ipswich minister come for the funeral, for David Carr cried out in a fury that Minister Parris, who had prosecuted this witchcraft business, was her murderer, and blood would flow from her little body if he stood beside it, and that it was the same with Minister Noyes; and Sarah Proctor's pale face had flushed up fiercely in assent.

The morning after the little maid Abigail Proctor was buried, Joseph Bayley and his wife Ann came riding down the road from Boston, and they were in brave company, and needed to have but little fear of witches; for the great minister Cotton Mather rode with them, his Excellency the Governor of the colony, two worshipful magistrates, and two other ministers—all on their way to a witch trial in Salem.

And is they neared the Proctor house there was much discourse concerning it and the inmates thereof, many strange and dreadful accounts, and much godly denunciation. And as they reached the curve in the road they came suddenly insight of a young man and a tall fair maid standing together at the side by some white-flowering bushes. And Sarah Proctor, even with her little sister Abigail dead and her parents in danger of death, was smiling for a second's space in David Carr's face, for the love and hope in tragedy that make God possible, and the selfishness of love that makes life possible, were upon her in spite of herself.

But when she saw the cavalcade approaching, saw the gleam of rich raiment, and heard the tramp and jingling, the smile faded straightway from her face, and she stood behind David in the white alder bushes. And David stood before her, and gazed with a stern and defiant scowl at the gentry as they passed by. And the great Cotton Mather gazed back at that beautiful white face rising like another flower out of the bushes, and he speculated with himself if it were the face of a witch.

But Goodwife Ann Bayley thought only on the little maid at the door. And when they came to the Proctor house she leaned eagerly from the pillion, and she smiled and kissed her hand.

"Why do you thus, Ann?" her husband asked, looking about at her.

"See you not the little maid in the door?" she whispered low, for fear of the goodly company. "I trow she looks better than she did. The roses are in her cheeks, and they have combed her yellow hair, and put a clean white gown on her. She holds a little doll, too."

"I see nobody," said Joseph Bayley, wonderingly.

"Nay, but she stands there. I never saw naught shine like her hair and her white gown; the sunlight lies full in the door. See! see! she is smiling! I trow all her griefs be well over."

The cavalcade passed the Proctor house, but Goodwife Ann Bayley's sweet face was turned backward until it was out of sight, towards the little maid in the door.

The Buckley Lady

The dark slate stones that now slant to their falls in the old burying-ground, or are fallen already, then stood straight. The old inscriptions, now blurred over by moss and lichen, or worn back into the face of the stone by the wash of the heavy coast rains, were then quite plain. The winged cherubim and death-heads—the terrible religious symbols of the Old Testament, made realistic by New England minds under stress of grief— were quite fresh from the artist's hands.

The funeral urns and weeping-willows, a very art of sorrow in themselves, with their every curve the droop of a mourner's head, and all their flowing lines of tears, were yet distinct. Indeed, the man who had graven many of them was still alive, and not yet past his gloomy toil. He lived in his little house not far beyond the burying-ground, and his name was Ichabod Buckley. He had a wife Sarah, a son Ichabod, and three daughters, Submit, Rebecca, and Persis. When Persis was twelve years old a great change and a romance came into her life. She was the youngest of the family; her brother was ten years older than she; her sisters were older still. She had always been to a certain extent petted and favoured from her babyhood; still, until she was twelve, she had not been exempt from her own little duties and privations.

She had gathered drift-wood on the shore, her delicate little figure buffeted and shaken by rough winds. She had dug quahaugs, wading out in the black mud, with her petticoats kilted high over her slender childish legs. She had spun her daily stint, and knitted faithfully on harsh blue yarn socks for her father and brother. In the early autumn, when she was twelve years old, all that was changed.

One morning in September it was hot inland, but cool on the point of land reaching out into the sea where the Buckley house stood. The son, Ichabod, had gone to sea in a whaling-vessel; the father was at home, working in the little slanting shed behind the house. One could hear the grating slide of his chisel down the boughs of a weeping-willow on a new gravestone. A very old woman of the village had died that week.

At the left of the house there was a bright unexpected glint from a great brass kettle which the eastern sun struck. Ichabod Buckley's wife had her dye-kettle out there on forked sticks over a fire. She was dyeing some cloth an indigo-blue, and her two elder daughters were helping her. The two daughters Submit and Rebecca looked like their mother. The three, from their figures, seemed about of an age—all tall and meagre and long-limbed, moving in their scanty petticoats around the kettle with a certain dry pliability, like three tall brown weeds on the windy marsh.

Persis came up from the shore at the front of the house with her arms full of drift-wood. She was just crossing the front yard when she heard a sound that startled her, and she stood still and listened, inclining her head toward the woods on the right. In the midst of these woods was the cleared space of the graveyard; past it ran the rough path to the main road.

Seldom any but horseback riders came that way; but now Persis was sure that she heard the rumble of carriage-wheels, as well as the tramp of horses' feet. She turned excitedly to run to her mother and sisters; but all at once the splendid coach and four emerged with a great flourish on the open space before the house, and she stood still.

The short coarse grass in the yard had gotten a perpetual slant from the wind. Just now it was still, but that low bending sweep of the grass toward the west made it seem as if the wind were transfixed there. Persis stood there in the midst of this still show of wind, her slender childish figure slanting a little also.

All her fair hair was tucked away tidily under a little blue hood tied under her chin. The oval of her face showed like the oval of a pearl in this circle of blue, and it had a beauty that could draw the thoughts of people away from their own hearts. Even the folk of this old New England village, who had in their stern doctrines no value for a fair face, turned for a second, as if by some compelling gleam of light under their eyelids, when this little Buckley maid entered the meeting-house; and her mother and sisters, although they saw her every day, would stop some-times their work or speech when her face came suddenly before their eyes.

Persis had her little looking-glass. She looked in it when she had washed her face to see if it were clean, and when she braided her hair to see if it were smooth. Sometimes she paused herself and eyed her face with innocent wonder, but she did not know its value. She was like a child with a precious coin which had its equivalent in goods beyond her ken.

Today Persis had no idea why these fine strangers in the grand coach sat still with their eyes riveted upon her face.

She stood there in the windy grass, in her little straight blue gown, clasping her bundle of drift-wood to her breast, and stared, turning her back altogether upon her own self, at the coach and the trappings, and the black coachman in his livery, with his head like a mop of black sheep's wool, and his white rolling eyes, which half frightened her. She looked a little more curiously at this black coachman than at the gentleman and lady in the coach, although they were grand enough; and, moreover, the gentleman was very handsome, and not old. He thrust his fair head, which had on it a slight silvery sheen of powder, out of the coach window, and the pale old face and velvet hood of the lady showed over his shoulder, and they both stared at Per-sis's face.

Then the gentleman spoke, and Persis started, and blushed, and dropped a courtesy. She had forgotten that until now, and felt overcome with shame. "Good-day, my pretty maid," said the gentleman; and as he spoke he stepped out of the coach and approached Persis. She saw, with half-dazzled eyes, his grand fair head, his queue tied with a blue silk ribbon, his jewelled knee-buckles and silk hose, his flowered waistcoat, and the deep falls of lace over his long white hands. No such fine gentleman as this had ever come within her vision. She curtsied again, and looked up in his face when he reached her. Then she looked down again quickly, and the strange salt savour of the drift-wood, overpowering a sweet perfume about the stranger's rich attire, came up in her blushing face. The gentleman looked very kind, and his eyes were very gay and blue, yet somehow she was frightened and abashed. It was as if he saw something within herself of which she had not dreamed, and suddenly forced her to see it also, to her own confusion.

The gentleman laughed softly when she looked down. "Is it the first time you have had another pair of eyes for your looking-glass, little maid?" he asked, with a kind of mocking caress in his tone.

Persis did not lift her eyes from the drift-wood. She blushed more deeply, and her sweet mouth trembled.

"Nay, tease not the child. Ask if her father be in the house," called the lady's soft voice, with a little impatient ring in it, from the coach.

"'Tis but the fault of my eyes, your ladyship," retorted the gentleman, gayly. "They are ever as lakes reflecting flowers in the presence of beauty, and I doubt much if this little maid hath ever seen herself so clearly before, if eyes like mine have come in her way."

Persis's mouth quivered more. She wanted to run away, and did not dare; but suddenly the gentleman spoke again, quite gravely and coldly, and all the gay banter in his voice was gone.

"Is your father, Ichabod Buckley, within, my good maid?" he said.

Persis felt as if a spell which had been cast over her were broken. She dropped a courtesy.

"Please, sir, my father is yonder, cutting a weeping-willow on old Widow Nye's gravestone," she replied, pointing toward the rear of the house; and she spoke with that punctilious courtesy with which she had been taught to address strangers.

"Will you bid him come this way? I would speak with him," said the gentleman.

"And bid him hasten, for this air from the sea is full cold for me!" called the lady from the coach.

Persis dipped another affirmative courtesy toward her, then fled swiftly around the corner of the house. She met her mother and her sister Submit face to face, with a shock. They had been peeping around the corner at the grand folk. Rebecca had run into the house to put on her shoes and a clean kerchief, in case one of the elder women had to go forward to speak to them.

"Father! the gentleman wants father," said Persis, with soft pants. "Oh, mother!"

Her mother caught her arm with a jerk. "Who be they?" she hissed in her ear.

"I—don't know—such—grand folks, and—the coach and the four, and the black man—oh, mother!"

"Go bid your father come quick."

Sarah Buckley gave her daughter a push, and Persis flew on toward the shed where her father kept his stock of gravestones and worked. But Rebecca had already given him the alarm, and he was at the well washing the slate dust from his hands.

"Go quick, father; they want you," panted Persis.

"Who be they?" queried Ichabod Buckley. His voice was as nervous as a woman's, and he was small and delicately made like one. He shook the water from his small hands, his fingers twitching. The muscles on the backs glanced under the thin brown skin; the muscles on his temples and neck glanced also. Ichabod Buckley had, when nervously excited, a look as if his whole body were based on a system of brown wires.

Persis danced up and down before him, as if his nervous excitement communicated itself to her. "I know not who they be," she panted; "but, oh, father, they be such grand folk!"

When Ichabod Buckley, striving to pace with solemn dignity, as befitted his profession, but breaking, in spite of himself, into nervous runs, went around to the front of the house, Persis slunk at his heels, but her mother arrested her at the corner. "Stay where you be, and not go out there staring at the gentle-folk like a bold hussy!" she ordered. So Persis staid, peeping around the corner with her mother and Submit; and presently Rebecca in her shoes, with her kerchief pinned over her lean bosom, joined them.

Once Persis, advancing her beautiful face a little farther around the corner, caught the gentleman's gay blue eyes full upon her, and she drew back with a great start and a blush.

Listen as they might, the women could not catch one word of Ichabod Buckley's and the gentleman's discourse—they stood too far away. But presently they saw the black coachman turn the coach and four around with a wide careful sweep, and then the gentleman got in beside the lady, and Ichabod beside the coachman, and then the horses leaped forward, and the whole was out of sight behind the spray of pine woods.

Ichabod Buckley was gone about three-quarters of an hour. When he returned he at once told his curious women-folks somewhat that had passed, but his face was locked over more. "You have not told us all," said his wife, sharply. "It may well be, as you say, that the gentle-folk wished to find the grave of the man who was their kin, and died here in the first of the town, but that is not all."

"I pointed out the grave to them beyond a question," said Ichabod, "though there was no stone to it. I knew it well from hearsay. And I am to make at once a fine stone, with a round top and a winged head, and here is the pay already."

Ichabod jingled for the dozenth time a gold coin and some small silver ones in his nervous hand, and his wife frowned.

"You have told us all this before," said she. "There is something else that you keep back."

Ichabod was smiling importantly. He could not control his mouth, but he went back without another word to old Widow Nye's gravestone, and the weeping-willow thereon grew apace under his hands.

However, he could not keep anything to himself long, least of all from his wife, with her imperative curiosity. After dinner that noon he beckoned her into the front room.

"What do you want of me?" she said. "I have the work to do." She felt that his previous silence demanded some show of dignity upon her part.

Ichabod glanced at his staring daughters, and beckoned beseechingly.

"Well, I can't waste much time," said Sarah; but she followed him eagerly into the front room. They were shut in there some time. The daughters, tidying up the kitchen, could hear the low murmur of their parents' voices, but that was all. Persis was polishing the brasses on the hearth—the andirons and the knobs on the shovel and tongs. That was always her task. It roughened her small hands, but nobody ever minded that. Today, as she was scouring away sturdily, her mother came suddenly out of the front room and caught her plying arm.

"There!" said she; "you need do no more of this. 'Twill get your hands all out of shape, and make them rough. They be too small for such work. Submit, come here and finish scouring the brasses."

Persis looked up at her mother and then at her little red grimy hands in a bewildered way.

"Go and wash your hands, and then rub some Injun meal on them, and see if it will not make them a little softer," ordered her mother. "Submit, make haste."

Submit, although she was herself puzzled, and might well have been resentful, knelt obediently down on the hearth, and fell to work on the brasses, rubbing vigorously with salt and vinegar.

Persis washed her hands as her mother bade her, and afterward rubbed on some Indian meal. Then she was ordered to put on her pink-flowered chintz gown, and sit down in the front room with her sampler. Her mother braided her fair hair for her in two tight smooth braids, and crossed them neatly at the back. She even put her own beautiful high tortoise-shell comb in her daughter's head.

"You may wear it a spell if you want to," said she.

Persis smiled delightedly. Her chief worldly ambition had been to wear a shell comb like her mother's.

The window was open. She could hear faintly the rasp of her father's chisel upon the boughs of old Widow Nye's weeping-willow. She could hear the voices of her mother and sisters, who had gone back to their work over the dye-kettle. After a while she saw Submit going down to the shore for more drift-wood. "That is my work," she thought to herself with wonder. She could not understand her mother's treatment of her. It was very pleasant and grand to be sitting in state in the best room, with the tortoise-shell comb in her hair, working her sampler, and be rid of all ruder toil, yet she finally grew uneasy.

She laid down her sampler, and pulled open the front door, which was seldom used, and hard to move, being swollen with the sea dampness. Then she stole around the house toward the group at the dye-kettle. She felt scared and uncertain without knowing why. Her mother called out sharply when she caught sight of her, and waved her back. "Can't I go down for more drift-wood?" pleaded Persis, timidly.

"Back into the house!" ordered her mother, speaking against the wind, which was now blowing hard. "Back with ye! Out here in this wind! Would you be as black as an Injun? Go back to your sampler!"

Persis crept back, bewildered. The other two daughters looked at each other. Then Rebecca spoke out boldly.

"Mother, what is all this?" said she.

"Perhaps you will know sometime," replied Sarah Buckley, smiling mysteriously, and she would say no more.

Persis continued to sit at the front-room window, with her sampler in her hands. She cross-stitched a letter forlornly and laboriously, with frequent glances out at the rosy wind-swept marshes and the blue dazzle of sea beyond. She never dreamed of disputing her mother's wishes farther. Persis Buckley, although full of nervous force, had also a strange docility of character. She stitched on her sampler all the afternoon. When it came time to prepare supper, her mother would not even then let her out in the kitchen to help, as was her wont. "Stay where you be," said she, when Persis appeared on the threshold. And the little maid remained in her solitary state until the meal was ready, and she was bidden forth to it. There was a little sweet cake beside her plate on the table, one of those which her mother kept in a stone jar for company. Nobody else had one. Persis looked at it doubtfully when she had finished her bread. "Eat it," said her mother, and Persis ate it, but it tasted strange to her. She wondered if her mother had put anything different in the sweet cake.

Persis had lately sat up until the nine-o'clock bell rang, knitting or paring sweet apples to dry, but now her mother sent her off to bed at half past seven.

"Can't I sit up and help Submit and Rebecca pare apples?" she begged, but her mother was inexorable.

"I am not going to have your hands spoilt with apple juice," said she. "Besides, if you go to bed early 'twill make you grow faster and keep your cheeks red." There was an unusual softness in Sarah Buckley's voice, and she coloured and smiled foolishly, as if she were ashamed of it.

Ichabod Buckley sat on the hearth whittling chips with lightning jerks of his clasp-knife. He did everything swiftly. "Do as your mother bids you," he said to Persis. He chuckled nervously, and looked meaningly at his wife.

Persis went laggingly out of the room.

"Stand up straight," ordered her mother. "The first thing you know you'll be all bent over like an old woman."

Persis threw back her weak girlish shoulders until her slender back hollowed. She had been trained to obedience. She clattered slowly up the stairs in her little heavy shoes, still trying to keep her shoulders back, when her mother called again.

"Come back here, Persis," called her mother, and Persis returned to the kitchen. "Sit down here," said her mother, pointing to a chair, and Persis sat down. She did not ask any questions; she felt a curious terror and intimidation. She waited, sitting meekly with her eyes cast down. She heard the snip of shears and the rattle of stiff paper at her back, then she felt a sharp tug at her hair. She winced a little.

"You keep still," said her mother at her back, rolling a lock of hair vigorously. "I ain't going to have your hair as straight as a broom if I can help it."

When Persis went to bed her head was covered with hard papered knots of hair, all straining painfully at the roots. When she laid her head uncomfortably on her pillow, she remembered in a bewildered way how her mother had smoothed and smoothed and smoothed her hair in former days, and how she had said many a time that rough and frowsly locks were not modest or becoming. Her first conviction of the inconsistency of the human heart was upon little Persis Buckley, and she was dazed. The whole of this strange experience did not seem real enough to last until the next day.

But the days went on and on, and she continued to live a life as widely different from her old one as if she had been translated into another world. She sat at the front-room window, with her beautiful face looking out meekly from under her crown of curl-papers. Her mother had a theory that a long persistency in the use of the papers might produce a lasting curl, and Persis was seldom freed from them. She walked abroad on a pleasant day at a genteel pace, with a thick black embroidered veil over her face to protect her complexion. She never ran barefoot, and even her thick cowhide shoes were discarded. She wore now dainty high-heeled red morocco shoes, which made her set her feet down as delicately as some little pink-footed pigeon. All her coarse home-spun gowns were laid away in a chest. She wore now fine chintz or soft boughten wool of a week-day, and she even had a gown of silken stuff and a fine silk pelisse for Sabbath days.

Going into the meeting-house beside her soberly clad parents and sisters, she looked like some gay-feathered bird which had somehow gotten into the wrong nest. All the Buckley family seemed to have united in a curious reversed tyranny toward this beautiful child. She was set up as a queen among them, whether she would or no, and she was made to take the best in their lot, whether she wanted it or not.

When Persis was fourteen, her sister Rebecca went some fifty miles away to keep house for a widowed uncle and take care of his family of children. She was not needed at home, and in this way the cost of her support was saved for Persis. Submit was a dull woman, and hard work was making her duller. She broadened her patient back for her own and her sister's burdens without a murmur, and became a contented drudge that Persis might sit in state in the front room, keeping her hands soft and white.

As for Persis's brother Ichabod, nearly all his savings were given to her, but, after all, not with any especial self-denial. This beautiful young sister represented all the faint ambition in his life; he had none left for himself, and nobody had tried to arouse any. He made perilous voyages on a whaling-ship for his living. When he came home, with his face browned and stiffened by his hard fight with the icy winds of the North Atlantic, he sat down by the fire in his father's kitchen. Then he chewed tobacco, and never stirred if he could help it until his next voyage.

At thirty, Ichabod had become as old as his father. All the dreams of youth had gone out of him, and he slumbered in the present like a very old man. Always as he sat chewing by the fire his face wore that look of set resistance, as if the lash of the North Atlantic wind still threatened it. Ever since she could remember, Persis Buckley had seen her brother sit there between his voyages, a dull reflective bulk before the hearth, like some figure-head of a stranded whaler.

The morning after his return from his voyage, Persis, passing her brother, would be arrested by an inarticulate command, and would pause while he dragged out his old leather bag, heavy with his hard-earned coins. Then Persis would hold up her apron by the two lower corners, and he would pour in a goodly portion of his wealth, while his face looked more smiling and animated than she ever saw it at any other time. "'Twill buy you something as good as anybody when you go among the grand folk," he would say, with a half-chuckle, when Persis thanked him.

Sarah Buckley hid away all this money for Persis in the till of the chest. "It will come handy some day," she would say, with a meaning smile. This fund was not drawn upon for the purchase of Persis's daily needs and luxuries. Her father's earnings and her mother's thrift provided them, and with seemingly little stint. People said that the materials for Persis Buckley's crewel-work alone cost a pretty sum. After she had finished her sampler she worked a mourning-piece, and after that a great picture, all in cross-stitch, which was held to be a marvel.

Persis's very soul flagged over the house and the green trees, the river, and the red rose-bushes, and the blue sky, all wrought with her needle, stitch by stitch. Once in the depths of her docile heart a sudden wish, which seemed as foreign to her as an impious spirit, leapt up that all this had never been created, since she was forced to reproduce it in cross-stitch.

"I wish," said Persis, quite out loud to herself when she was all alone in the front room—"I wish the trees had never been made, nor the roses, nor the river, nor the sky, then I shouldn't have had to work them." Then she fairly trembled at her wickedness, and counted the stitches in a corner of the sky with renewed zeal and faithfulness.

When Persis was sixteen, her mother, in her zeal to provide her with accomplishments, went a step beyond all previous efforts, and a piano was bought for her. It was the very first piano which had ever come to this little seaport town. Ichabod had commissioned a sea-captain to purchase it in England.

When it was set up on its slender fluted legs in the Buckley front room, all the people came and craved permission to see it, and viewed its satiny surface and inlaid-work in mother-of-pearl with admiration and awe. Then they went away, and discoursed among themselves as to the folly and sinful extravagance of Ichabod Buckley and his wife.

There was in the village an ancient maiden lady who had lived in Boston in her youth, and had learned to play several tunes on the harpsichord. These, for a small stipend, she imparted to Persis. They were simple and artless melodies, and Persis had a ready ear. In a short time she had learned all the maiden lady knew. She could sing three old songs, innocently imitating her teacher's quaver with her sweet young voice, and she could finger out quite correctly one battle piece and two jigs. The two jigs she played very slowly, according to her teacher's instructions. Persis herself did not know why, but this elderly maiden was astute. She did not wish Ichabod Buckley and his family to be tormented with scruples themselves, neither did she wish to be called to account for teaching light and worldly tunes.

"Play these very slowly, my dear," she said. She shook the two bunches of gray curls which bobbed outside her cap over her thin red cheeks; her old blue eyes winked with a light which Persis did not understand.

"Be they psalm tunes?" she inquired, innocently.

"'Tis according to the way you play them," replied her teacher, evasively.

And Persis never knew, nor any of her family, that she played jigs. However, one worldly amusement which was accounted distinctly sinful was Persis taught with the direct connivance of her parents.

This old maiden lady, although she was constant in the meeting-house on the Sabbath day, and was not seen to move a muscle of dissent when the parson proclaimed the endless doom of the wicked, had Unitarian traditions, and her life in her youth had been more gayly and broadly ordered than that of those about her. It had always been whispered that she had played cards, and had even danced, in days gone by. To the most rigidly sanctified nostrils there was always perceptible a faint spiritual odour of past frivolity when she came into the meeting-house, although she seemed to subscribe faithfully to all the orthodox tenets. The parson often felt it his duty to call upon her, and enter into wordy expounding of the truth, and tempt her with argument. She never questioned his precepts, and never argued, yet a suspicion as to her inmost heresy was always abroad. Had it not been so, Sarah Buckley would never have dared make one proposition to her with regard to her daughter's accomplishments.

One day the shutters in the Buckley front room were carefully closed, as if someone lay dead therein; the candles were lighted, and this ancient maiden lady, holding with both hands her petticoats above her thin ankles in their black silk hose, taught Persis Buckley some dancing steps. That, nobody in the village ever knew. All the parties concerned would have been brought before the church had that secret been disclosed. The Buckleys scarcely dared mention it to each other.

This old teacher of Persis Buckley had still some relatives left in Boston, and now and then she went to them on a visit. On one of these occasions Sarah Buckley commissioned her to purchase some books for Persis. All the literature in the Buckley house consisted of the Bible, Watts's Hymns, and Doddridge's *Rise and Progress*, and Sarah fancied that another book or two of possibly an ornamental and decorative tendency might be of use in her daughter's education.

When Mistress Tabitha Hopkins returned from Boston she brought with her a volume of Young's *Night Thoughts* and one of Richardson's *Clarissa Harlowe*. The first she presented with confidence, the second with some excuses.

"I know well that the poetry is of a nature that will elevate her soul and tend to form her mind," said she, "and I have myself no doubt as to the other. If it be a tale, 'tis one she can read to her profit, and the pleasure she may take in it may lead her to peruse it more closely. 'Tis well sometimes to season hard doctrines with sugar if you would have them gulped down at all." Mistress Hopkins made a wry face, as if the said doctrines were even then like bitter pills in her mouth, and Sarah Buckley glanced at her suspiciously. However, she took the books, and paid for them a goodly sum, and Persis was henceforth made acquainted with the lofty admonitions to Lorenzo and the woes of the unfortunate and virtuous Clarissa.

It might well have been that Tabitha Hopkins's recommendation of the story of poor Clarissa Harlowe and her desperate experience at the hands of a faithless lover had its object. Mistress Tabitha Hopkins's single life had not predisposed her to implicit reliance upon the good faith or the motives of gay gallants who, in the course of some little trip out of their world, chanced to notice a beautiful rustic maiden. Everybody in the village knew now the reason for Ichabod Buckley's and his wife's strange treatment of their daughter Persis. They knew that the grand gentleman who had come to town with the coach and four had seen Persis, and cried out at her beauty, and made her father give his promise that she should be kept for him until she was grown up, when he would come over seas from England and marry her.

Ichabod had vainly tried to keep this secret, but he had told it before a week had passed to old Thomas Knapp, who was helping him to set Widow Nye's gravestone.

Then the sun had not set before the news was widely spread. Marvellous tales were told of this gentleman and his lady mother, who had come in the coach with him. Persis, when she was wedded, would dwell in marble halls, wear satin and velvet of a week-day, and eat off gold and silver dishes. No wonder that Ichabod Buckley and his wife Sarah were doing their poor best to fit their daughter for such a high estate! No wonder that they kept her all day in the best room embroidering and reading poetry and playing music! No wonder that they never let her walk abroad without morocco shoes and a veil over her face!

"It ain't likely," said old man Knapp, "that she'll ever have any call to so much as dye a hank of yarn or dip a candle arter she's married."

Still, although people acquiesced in the wisdom of fitting Persis for this grand station, if there was any prospect of her reaching it, they were mostly incredulous or envious.

The incredulous said quite openly that Ichabod Buckley always did hear things five times as big as they were, and they doubted much if the grand gentleman ever really meant or said he would come back for Persis. The envious said that if he did come they mistrusted that it would not be for any good and honest purpose, for he would never think Persis Buckley his equal, in spite of all her fine accomplishments and her gaudy attire. And her face might by that time be no more beautiful than some others, after all.

The incredulous moved the parson to preach many a discourse upon the folly of worldly ambition and trust in the vain promises of princes. The envious instigated sermons upon the sin of any other ornament or accomplishment than a meek and quiet spirit for the daughters of Zion.

Poor little Persis, in her silken attire, lifting her wonderful face to the parson, never dreamed that the discourse was directed at her and her parents, but Ichabod and Sarah knew, and sat up with bristling stiffness. After that they withdrew themselves largely from intercourse with their neighbours. They felt as if the spiritual watch-dog had been set upon them, and they were justly indignant. Sarah Buckley had always been given to staying at home and minding the affairs of her own household; now she kept herself more closely than ever. Ichabod was by nature sociable, and liked to fraternize with his kind; but now almost his only dealing with people outside his own family lay in his work upon their gravestones.

The Buckleys lived by themselves in their little house on the windy land past the graveyard, following out their own end in life, and all the time were under, as it were, a subtle spiritual bombardment of doubt and envy and disapproval from their neighbors in the village.

People talked much about Submit's patient drudgery, and felt for her the resentment which she did not feel for herself. "It is a shame the way they make that poor girl do all the work to keep her sister in idleness!" said they. They began to call Persis in derision "The Buckley Lady."

Poor Persis Buckley, shut out of the free air and away from all the mates of her youth, was leading the life of a forlorn princess in a fairy tale. She would have given all the money which her brother Ichabod brought her for his privilege of a cruise over the wild seas. Year after year she waited in her prison, cast about and bound, body and spirit, by the will and ambition of her parents, like steel cobwebs, for the prince who never came.

At first the romance of it all had appealed to her childish imagination. When the high destiny which awaited her had been disclosed, her heart leapt. She had been amused and pleased. She liked to watch out for that grand coach and four. When she remembered the gay blue flash of that grand gentleman's eyes she blushed, and laughed to herself.

But after a while all that failed. She did not grow incredulous, for she had a simple and long-suffering faith in her parents, but quietly and secretly frightened at the prospect before her. Poor Persis Buckley sometimes felt herself turn fairly cold with dread at the thought of entering that splendid coach and driving away forever out of her old life at that strange gentleman's side. He became to her as cold and formless as a moving column of mist on the marsh, and even the dreams which sprang of themselves in her girlish heart could not invest him with love and life again.

She did not dare confide her fears to her mother. Sometimes her mother filled her with a vague alarm. Sarah Buckley in ten years grew old, and the eagerness in her face waxed so bright and sharp that one shrank before it involuntarily, as before some blinding on-coming headlight of spirit.

All those years she waited and watched and listened for that grand coach and four which would bring her fortune in her daughter's. All the ambition of her earthly life, largely balked for herself, had centred in this. Her lot in the world had been to tread out a ceaseless round of sordid toil in her poor little home on the stormy coast, but her beautiful daughter could take a flight above it, and her eyes and something of herself could follow her.

She never gave up, although year after year she watched and listened in vain; but finally her body failed under this long strain of the spirit. When Persis was twenty-three her mother died, after a short illness. Then Persis found her father as keen a guardian as her mother had been. Sarah had given him her farewell charges, and during her lifetime had imbued his nervous receptive nature with a goodly portion of her own spirit.

He wrought for his dead wife a fine tall stone, and set thereon a verse of his own composition. Ichabod Buckley was somewhat of a poet, publishing himself his effusions upon his gloomy stone pages. Then he fulfilled his own and her part toward their daughter Persis.

Sarah Buckley had been dead two years, and the Buckley Lady was twenty-five years old, sitting at her window in the front room, watching for the prince who never came.

"The fine gentleman will find an old maid waiting for him if he does not come before long," people said, with sniffs.

But Persis had really grown more and more beautiful. Her complexion, although she had lived so much within-doors, was not sickly, but pale and fine as a white lily. Her eyes were like dark stars, and her hair was a braided cap of gold, with light curls falling from it around her face and her sweet neck. Of late Persis had rebelled upon one minor point: she never, even of a morning, would sit at the window with her hair rolled up in curl-papers. She argued with her father, with a duplicity which was unlike her, that should the gentleman arrive suddenly, she would have no time to take them down before he saw her. But that was not the reason. Ichabod never suspected, neither did the stupid Submit, padding faithfully in her household tracks; the son, Ichabod, was away at sea. Nobody knew how the Buckley Lady, sitting in her window watching, had seen Darius Hopkins pass by, with never a coach and four, but striding bravely along on his own stalwart young legs, and how her heart had gone out to him and followed him, whether she would or not.

Darius Hopkins was Mistress Tabitha Hopkins's nephew, and he had come from Boston to pay his aunt a visit. People whispered that he had expectations, and had come with a purpose. Mistress Tabitha had had within two years a legacy, nobody knew how large, by the death of a relative. However that may have been, the young man treated his aunt with exceeding deference and tenderness. Her pride and delight were great. She held her head high, and swung out her slim foot with almost the motion of her old dancing steps when she went up the meeting-house aisle on a Sabbath day, leaning on her nephew's arm. Darius was finely dressed, and he was also a personable young man of whom she might well be proud. She kept glancing at him almost with the shy delight of a sweetheart. Darius had a glossy dark head and a dark complexion, but his eyes were blue and light, and somewhat, as she fondly thought, like her own.

Darius had arrived on a Thursday, and it was on that day Persis Buckley had seen him, and he had seen her at her window. Tabitha Hopkins's house was past the Buckleys', fairly out at sea, on the point, across the marshy meadows.

The young man glanced up carelessly at the Buckley house as he passed; then he started, and fairly stopped, and his heart leapt almost with fear, for it actually seemed to him that he saw the face of an angel in the window.

"Who was the maid in the window of the house back yonder?" he said to his aunt as soon as he had greeted her. He waved his hand carelessly backward, and tried to speak as carelessly, but his aunt gave him a sharp look.

"It must have been Persis Buckley," said she.

"There is not another face like that in the whole country," said the young man, and in spite of himself his tongue betrayed him.

"Yes, it is generally considered that she has a fair face," said Tabitha, dryly. "She has accomplishments also. She can play music, and she has a pretty voice for a song. She can dance, though that's not to be spoke of in this godly town, and she is well versed in polite literature. Persis Buckley is fitted to adorn any high estate to which she may be called."

There was a mysterious tone in Tabitha's voice, and her nephew looked at her with eager inquiry.

"What mean you, aunt?" he said.

"What I have said," replied she, aggravatingly, and would tell him no more. She was secretly a little jealous that her nephew had shortened his greeting to her to inquire about Persis. Old single woman though she was, her feminine birth-right of jealousy of the love of men, be they lovers or sons or nephews, still survived in her heart.

The young man dared not ask her any more questions, but the next day he passed the Buckley house many a time with sidelong glances at the window where Persis sat. He would not stare too boldly at that fair vision. And in the evening he stole out and strolled slowly over the meadows, and came to the Buckley house again. She was not at the window then, but the sweet tinkle of her piano came out to him from the candle-lit room, and he listened in rapture to her tender little voice trilling and quavering. Then peeping cautiously, he saw her graceful head thrown back, and her white throat swelling with her song like a bird's.

When he returned, his aunt looked at him sharply, but she did not ask where he had been. When he took his candle to retire for the night, her old blue eyes twinkled at him suddenly.

"How did the little bird sing tonight?" she said.

The young man stared at her a second, then he blushed and laughed. "Bravely, aunt, bravely," he replied.

"'Tis a bird in the bush, nephew," said she, and her voice was mocking, yet shrewdly tender.

Darius's face fell. "What mean you, aunt?" he said.

"'Tis a bird that will always sing in the bush, and never in hand."

Darius made as if he would question his aunt further, but he did not. He bade her goodnight in a downcast and confused manner, and was out of the room like a shy girl.

Mistress Tabitha chuckled to herself, then she looked grave, and sat in her rocking-chair for a long time thinking.

Darius Hopkins marvelled much what his aunt could mean by her warning, and was uneasy over it. But the next day also he had many an errand across the meadows, down the forest road, to the village, and always he saw, without seeming to see, Persis at the window, and always she saw, without seeming to see, him.

On the Sabbath day, when he and his aunt went by the Buckley house on their way to meeting, Persis was not at the window. His aunt surprised his sly glances. "They go to meeting early," said she, demurely. Darius laughed in a shamefaced fashion.

After he and his aunt were seated in the meeting-house, he scarcely dared look up for a while, for he feared, should he see Persis suddenly and near at hand, his face might alter in spite of himself. And, in truth, when he did look up, and saw Persis close before him in a pew at the side of the pulpit, a tremor ran over him, his lips twitched, and all the colour left his face. His aunt pressed her bottle of salts into his hand, and he pressed it back almost sharply, and turned red as a girl to the roots of his black hair. Then he sat up straight and looked over almost defiantly at Persis. Her face in her blue satin bonnet, with its drooping blue plume and lace veil thrown to one side, was fair enough to stir the heart of any mortal man who looked at her.

There were, indeed, in that meeting-house, certain godly men who kept their eyes sternly turned away, and would not look upon her, thinking it a sin, although it was a sin to their own hearts alone.

But many a young man besides Darius Hopkins, although he had seen her in that selfsame place Sabbath after Sabbath, still regarded her furtively with looks of almost startled adoration. Not one of them had ever spoken to her or heard her speak, or seen her except in the meeting-house, or at her window, or thickly veiled on the village street.

Persis to-day kept her eyes fixed upon the parson, exhorting under his echoing sounding-board. She never looked around, although she knew that Darius was sitting beside his aunt in her pew. She also was afraid, and she never recovered courage, like Darius. Her father, Ichabod, fiercely intent upon the discourse, his nervous face screwed to a very point of attention, sat on one side; her sister Submit, her back bowed like an old woman's, on the other.

When meeting was over, Ichabod shot down the aisle, with his daughters following, as was his wont, and reached the door before many that sat farther back.

When Darius and his aunt came out of the meeting-house, the Buckleys were quite out of sight. When they emerged from the road past the graveyard through the woods, Persis was already at the window, with her bonnet off, but she kept her head turned far to one side, as if intent upon something in the room, and only the pink curve of one cheek was visible.

Darius had grown bold in the meeting-house; this time he looked, and forgot himself in looking.

"She is a pretty maid, but she is not for you, nor for any other young man unless he come for her with a coach and four, with a black gentleman a-driving," said his aunt's voice half mockingly at his side.

Then the young man turned and questioned her quite boldly. "I beg of you to tell me what you mean, aunt," he said.

Then Mistress Tabitha Hopkins, holding her Sabbath gown high above her hooped satin petticoat as she stepped along, unfolded to her nephew Darius Hopkins the strange romance of Persis Buckley's life.

"'Tis a shame!" cried the young man, indignantly, when she had finished—"a shame, to keep her a prisoner in this fashion!"

"'Tis only a prince with a coach and four can set her free. A prince from over seas, with a black gentleman a-driving," said his aunt.

Darius turned, and stared back across the flat meadow-land at Ichabod Buckley's house. It was late August now, and the meadow had great rosy patches of marsh-rosemary flung upon it like silken cloaks of cavaliers, and far-seen purple plumes of blazing-star. Darius studied slowly the low gray walls and long slant of gray roofs in the distance.

"A strong right arm and a willing heart might free her, were he prince or not!" said he. And he flung out his own right arm as if it were the one to do it.

"Were the maid willing to be freed," said Mistress Tabitha, softly.

Darius coloured. "That is true, aunt," he said, with a downcast and humbled air, and he turned and went on soberly.

Mistress Tabitha looked at her nephew's handsome face, and thought to herself, with loving but jealous pride, that no maid could refuse him as a deliverer. But she would not tell him so, for her heart was still sore at his preference of Persis to herself.

Darius Hopkins had an uneasy visit at his aunt Tabitha's. He did not speak again of Persis Buckley, but he thought the more. Useless, as he told himself, as either hopes or fears were, they sprang up in his heart like persistent flames, and could not be trodden out.

He told himself that it was not sensible to think that the grand Englishman would ever come for Persis after all these years, and that it was nothing to him if he did. Yet he often trembled when he came in sight of her house lest he see a coach and four standing before it, and see her carried away before his very eyes.

And sometimes he would look at his own comely face in the glass, and look into his own heart, and feel as if the love therein must compel her even against her will; for beautiful as she was, not an angel or a goddess, after all, but only a mortal woman. "She cannot love this man whom she has not seen since she was a child, and he must be an old man now," reasoned Darius, viewing his own gallant young face in the glass. And he smiled with hope, although he knew that he could not reasonably expect to have more of Persis than the sight of her face in the meeting-house or at the window were he to stay in the village a year.

For a long time Darius was not sure that Persis even noticed him when he passed by, but there came a day when he had that at least for his comfort. That day he had not passed her house until late; on the day before her face had been so far turned from the window that his heart had sunk. He had said to himself that he would be such a love-cracked fool no longer; he would not pass her house again unless of a necessity. So all that day he had sat moodily with his aunt, but just before dusk his resolution had failed him. He had strolled slowly across the meadow, while his aunt watched him, smiling shrewdly in her window.

He had not meant to glance even when he passed the Buckley house, but in spite of himself his eyes turned. And there was

Persis at the window, leaning toward him, with her face all radiant with joy. It was only a second, and she was gone. Darius had no time for anything but that one look, but that was enough. He felt as if he had already routed the gallant with the coach and four. He meditated all sorts of audacious schemes as he went home. What could he not do, if Persis would only smile upon him? He felt like marching straight upon her house, like a soldier upon a castle, and demanding her of her father, who was her jailer.

But the next day his heart failed him again, for she was not at her window—nor the next, nor the next. He could not know that she was peeping through the crack in the shutter, and that her embroidery and her reading and her old thoughts were all thrown aside for his sake. Persis Buckley could do nothing, day nor night, but think of Darius Hopkins, and watch for him to pass her window.

She did not know why, but she did not like to look fairly out of the window at him any longer. She could only peep through the crack in the shutter, with her colour coming and going, and her heart beating loud in her ears.

But when Darius saw no more of Persis at the window, he told himself that his conceit had misled him; that no such marvellous creature as that could have looked upon him as he had thought, and that his bold stare had affronted her.

So he did not pass the Buckley house for several days, and Persis watched in vain. One afternoon she rose up suddenly, with her soft cheek all creased where she had leaned it against the shutter. "He will not come; I will watch no longer," she said to herself, half angrily. And she got out her green silk pelisse and her bonnet, and prepared to walk abroad. She went through the kitchen, and her sister Submit stared up at her from the hearth, which she was washing.

"You have not got on your veil, Persis," said she.

"I want no veil," Persis returned, impatiently.

"But you will get burned in the wind; father will not like it," said Submit, with wondering and dull remonstrance.

"Well," sighed Persis, resignedly. And Submit got the black-wrought veil, and tied it over her sister's beautiful face.

Poor Persis, when she was out of the house, glanced hastily through the black maze of leaves and flowers across the meadow, but she saw no one coming. Then she strolled on away down the road through the woods. Just that side of the burying-ground there was an oak grove, and she went in there and sat down a little way from the road, with her back against a tree. It was very cool for the time of year, but the sun shone bright. All the oak-trees trilled sharply with the insects hidden in them, and the leaves rustled together.

Persis sat very stiffly under the oak-tree. Her petticoat was of green flowered chintz, and her *pelisse* and her bonnet of green silk. She was as undistinguishable as a green plant against the trunk of the tree, and neither Darius Hopkins nor his aunt Tabitha saw her when they passed. Persis heard their voices before they came in sight. She scarcely breathed. She seemed to be fairly hiding within herself, and forcing her very thoughts away from the eyes of Darius and his aunt.

Mistress Tabitha came down the wood, stepping with her fine mincing gait, and leaning upon her nephew's arm. They never dreamed that Persis was near. The green waving lines of the forest met their eyes on either hand, but all unnoted, being as it were the revolutions of that green wheel of nature of which long acquaintance had dimmed their perception. Only an unusual motion therein could arouse their attention when their thoughts were elsewhere, and they were talking busily.

As they came opposite Persis, Mistress Tabitha cried out suddenly, and her voice was full of dismay. "Not tomorrow!" she cried out. "You go not tomorrow, Darius!"

And Darius replied, sadly: "I must, Aunt Tabitha. I must go back to Boston by the Thursday stage-coach, and today is Wednesday."

Persis heard no more. She felt faint, and there was a strange singing in her ears. As soon as the aunt and nephew were well past, she got up and hastened back to the house. She took off her bonnet and *pelisse*, and sat down in her old place at the window, where she had watched so many years through her strange warped youth. When she saw Darius and his aunt returning, all her soul seemed to leap forward and look out of her great dark eyes. But Darius never glanced her way. He knew she was there, for his aunt said, "There is Persis Buckley," and nodded; but he dared not look, for fear lest he look too boldly, and she be offended.

Persis did not nod in response to Mistress Tabitha. She only looked, and looked at the slight, straight figure of the young man moving past her and out of her life. She thought that it was the last time that she should ever see him—the Boston stage left at daybreak. It seemed to her that he would never come again; and if he did, that she could not live until the time, but should ride away first from her old home forever, in gloomier state than had been planned for so many years.

When Darius and his aunt were out of sight she heard her father's voice in the kitchen, and she arose and went out there with a sudden resolve. "Father," she said, standing before Ichabod.

He looked at her in a curious startled way. There was a strange gleam in her soft eyes, and a strange expression about her docile mouth.

"What is it?" he said.

"He will never come, father. I want to be different."

"Who will never come? What do you mean, Persis?"

"The—gentleman—the grand gentleman with—the coach and four. He will never come for me now. I want to be different, father. I want to work with Submit, and not stay in there by myself. If I have to any longer I shall die, I think. I want to be different. He will never come now, father."

Ichabod Buckley trembled with long convulsive tremors, which seemed to leave him rigid and stiff as they passed. "He will come!" he returned, and he shouted out the words like an oath.

Submit, who was preparing supper, stopped, and stood pale

and staring.

Persis quailed a little, but she spoke again.

"It is too long now, father," she said. "He has forgotten me. He has married another in England. He will never come, and I want to be different. And should he come, after all, I should be sorely afraid to go with him now. I could never go with him now, father."

Ichabod turned upon her, and spoke with such force that she shrank, as if before a stormy blast. "I tell ye he will come!" he shouted, hoarsely. "He will come, and you shall go with him, whether you will or no! He will come, and you shall sit there in that room and wait for him until he comes! You should wait there until you were dead, if he came not before. But he will, I tell ye—*he will come!*"

Persis fled before her father back to the best room, and sat there in the gathering dusk. Across the meadows the light of Tabitha Hopkins's evening candle shone out suddenly like a low-hung star, and Persis sat watching it. When Submit called, in a scared voice, that supper was ready, she went out at once, and took her place at the table. There were pink spots in her usually pale cheeks; she spoke not a word, and scarcely tasted the little tid-bits grouped as usual around her plate. Her father swallowed his food with nervous gulps, then he left the table and went out. Soon Persis heard the grate of his tools on the gravestone slate, and knew that he had gone to work by candle-light, something he seldom did.

"Father is put out," Submit said, with a half-scared, half-reproachful look at Persis.

"Oh, Submit!" Persis cried out, with the first appeal she had ever made in her life to her slow-witted elder sister, "I must be different, or I think I shall die!"

"Maybe he will come soon," said Submit, who did not understand her sister's appeal. "Maybe he will come soon, Persis. Father thinks so," she repeated, as she rose from the table and padded heavily about, removing the supper dishes.

Then she added something which filled her sister's soul with fright and dismay.

"Father he dreamt a dream last night," said Submit, in her thick drone. "He dreamt that the grand gentleman came with the coach and four, and the black gentleman a-driving, and the grand lady in a velvet hood, just as he came before, and you got in and rode away. And he dreamt he came on a Thursday."

"Tomorrow is Thursday," gasped Persis.

Submit nodded. "Father thinks he will come tomorrow," said she. "He bade me not tell you, but I will for your comfort."

Submit stared wonderingly at her sister's distressed face as she ran out of the room; then she went on with her work. She presently, in sweeping the hearth, made a long black mark thereon, and straightway told herself that there was another sign that the gentleman was coming. Submit was well versed in New England domestic superstition, that being her only exercise of imagination.

Persis did not light the candles in the best room. She sat at the window in the dark, and watched again Mistress Tabitha's candle-light across the meadow. She also stared from time to time in a startled way in the other direction toward the woodland road. Persis also was superstitious. She feared lest her father's dream come true. She seemed almost to see now and then that stately equipage emerge as of old from the woods. She almost thought that she heard the far-away rumble of the wheels. She kept reminding herself that it was Wednesday, and her father's dream said Thursday; but what if she did have to go away forever with that strange gentleman only the next day!

She thought suddenly, not knowing why, of Clarissa Harlowe and Lovelace in her book. Mistress Tabitha's purpose had not wholly failed in its effect. A great vague horror of something which she was too ignorant to see fairly came over her. The face of that fine strange gentleman, dimly remembered before through all the years, shaped itself suddenly and plainly out of the darkness like the face of a demon. Persis looked away, shuddering, to the candle-gleam over the meadow, and Darius Hopkins's eyes seemed to look wistfully and lovingly into hers.

Persis Buckley arose softly, groped her way across the room in the dark, sliding noiselessly like a shadow, felt for the latch of the door that led into the front entry, lifted it cautiously, stole out into the entry, then opened the outer door with careful pains by degrees, and was out of the house.

Persis fled then past the plumy gloom of the pine-trees that skirted the wood, over the meadow, straight toward that candle-gleam in the Hopkins window.

There was a dry northeaster blowing, and it struck her as she fled, and lashed her clothing about her. She had on no outer wraps, and her head and her delicate face, which had always been veiled before a zephyr, were now all roughened and buffeted by this strong wind, which carried the sting of salt in it.

She never thought of it nor minded it. She fled on and on like a love-compelled bird, with only one single impulse in her whole being. The measure of freedom is always in proportion to the measure of previous restraint. Persis Buckley had been under a restraint which no maiden in this New England village had ever suffered, and she had gotten from it an impetus for a deed which they would have blushed to think of.

She fled on, forcing her way against the wind, which sometimes seemed to meet her like a moving wall, and sometimes like the rushing legions of that Prince of the Powers of the Air of whom she had read in the Bible, making as if they would lift her up bodily and carry her away among them into unknown tumult and darkness.

When Persis reached Tabitha Hopkins's door, she was nearly spent. Her life had not trained her well for a flight in the teeth of the wind. She leaned against the door for a minute faint and gasping.

Then she raised the knocker, and it fell with only a slight clang; but directly she heard an inner door open, and a step.

Then the door swung back before her, and Darius Hopkins stood there in the dim candle-light shining from the room within.

He could not see Persis's face plainly at first, only her little white hands reaching out to him like a child's from the gloom.

"Who is it?" he asked, doubtfully, and his voice trembled.

Persis made a little panting sound that was half a sob. Darius bent forward, peering out. Then he cried out, and caught at those little beseeching hands.

"It is not you!" he cried. "It is not you! You have not come to me! It is not you!"

Darius Hopkins, scarcely knowing what he did, he was so stirred with joy and triumph and doubt and fear, led Persis into the house and the candle-lit room. Then, when he saw in truth before him that beautiful face which he had worshipped from afar, the young man trembled and fell down upon his knees before Persis as if she were indeed a queen, or an angel who had come to bless him, and kissed her hand.

But Persis stood there, trembling and pale, before him, with the tears falling from her wonderful eyes, and her sweet mouth quivering. "Do not let him carry me away," she pleaded, faintly.

Then Darius sprang to his feet and put his arms around her. "Who is it would carry you away?" he said, angrily and tenderly. "No one shall have you. Who is it?"

"The—gentleman—from over-seas," whispered Persis. Her soft wet cheek was pressed against Darius's.

"He has not come?" he asked, starting fiercely.

"No; but—father has dreamed that he will—tomorrow."

Then Darius laughed gayly. "Dreams go by contraries," he said.

"Do not let him carry me away," Persis pleaded again, and she sobbed on his shoulder, and clung to him.

Darius held her more closely. "He shall never carry you away, even if he comes, against your will," he said. "Do not fear."

"I will go with nobody but you," whispered Persis in his ear.

And he trembled, scarcely believing that he heard aright. And, indeed, he scarcely believed even yet that he was not dreaming, and that he held this beautiful creature in his arms, and, more than all, that she had come to him of her own accord.

"You—do—not—mean—You cannot—oh, you cannot

mean—You are an angel. There is no one like you. You cannot—you cannot feel so about me?" he whispered, brokenly, at length.

Persis nodded against his breast.

"And—that was why—you came?"

Persis nodded again.

Darius bent her head back until he could see her beautiful, tearful face. He gazed at it with reverent wonder, then he kissed her forehead, and gently loosed her arm from his neck, and led her over to a chair.

He knelt down before her then as if she were a queen upon a throne, and held her hands softly. Then he questioned her as to how she had come, and whether any one knew, and more about the expected coming of her strange gentleman suitor, and she answered him like a docile child.

Mistress Tabitha Hopkins stood for quite a time in the doorway, and neither of them saw her. Then she spoke up.

"I want to know what this means," said she. "How came she here?" She pointed a sharp forefinger at Persis, who shrank before it.

But Darius arose quickly and went forward, blushing, but full of manly confidence. "Come out with me a moment, Aunt Tabitha," he said; "I have something to say to you privately." He took his aunt's arm and led her out of the room, and, as he went, smiled back at Persis. "Do not be afraid, sweetheart," he said.

"Sweetheart!" sniffed Mistress Tabitha, before the door closed.

Persis Buckley had been gone no longer than an hour from her own home when Darius and his aunt Tabitha escorted her back. She was wrapped then in a warm cloak of Mistress Tabitha's, and clung to her lover's arm, and he leaned between her and the rough wind, and sheltered her all he could. Poor Mistress Tabitha, with her skirts whipping about her and her ears full of wind, forced often by the onset of the gale at her back into staggering runs, pressed along after them. She had declined with some asperity her nephew's proffered assistance. "You look out for her," she said, shortly. And then she added, to temper her refusal, that she could better keep her cloak around her if both her arms were free. All her life had Mistress Tabitha Hopkins seen love only from the outside shining in her neighbour's window. It was to her credit tonight if she was not all bitter when its light fell on her solitary old maiden face, but got a certain reflected warmth and joy from it.

Nobody had missed Persis. Submit was fairly knitting in her sleep by the kitchen fire. Ichabod was still out in his shed at work.

Mistress Tabitha stood back a little while her nephew bade Persis good-by at her door. "Remember, do not be frightened, whatever happens to+morrow," he whispered in her ear. "If the gentleman comes with the coach and four, go with him, and trust in me."

"I will do whatever you bid me," whispered Persis. Then Darius kissed her hand, and she stole softly through the dark doorway into the gloom of the house, while her faith in her lover was as a lamp to all her thoughts.

On the next afternoon there was a sensation in this little seaport town. A grand coach and four, with a black man driving, a fine gentleman's head at one window, and a fine lady's at another, came dashing through the place at two o'clock. The women all ran to the doors and windows. Lounging old men straightened themselves languidly to stare, and turned their vacant faces over their shoulders. A multitude of small lads, with here and there a little petticoat among them, collected rapidly, and pelted along in the wake of this grand equipage. They followed it quite through the town to the road that led through the woods, past the graveyard, to the Buckley house, then up the road, panting but eager, the smaller children dragging at the hands of their elder brothers.

When they reached the Buckley house, this small rabble separated itself into decorously silent, primly curtseying rows on either side of the way. Then the grand coach and four at length turned about, and moved between the curtseying rows of children, while Ichabod Buckley stood proudly erect in his best green *surtout* watching it, and poor Submit, with a scrubbing-cloth in her hand, peeped around the house corner, and the Buckley Lady rode away.

And all the people saw the coach and four dash at a rattling pace back through the town, with the Buckley Lady's face set like a white lily in a window, and her grand suitor's fair head opposite. They also saw another lady beside Persis; her face was well hidden in her great velvet hood and wrought veil, but she sat up with a stately air.

The children followed the coach on the Boston road as far as they were able, then they straggled homeward, and the coach went out of sight in a great billow of dust.

It was several days before the people knew what had really happened—that Persis Buckley had gone away with Darius Hopkins, with a fair wig over his black hair, and the fine lady in the velvet hood had been nobody but Mistress Tabitha.

Darius Hopkins had sent a letter to the parson, and begged him to acquaint Ichabod Buckley with the truth, and humbly to crave his pardon for himself and Persis, who was now his wife, for the deceit they had practised. "But, in truth," wrote Darius Hopkins, "my beloved wife was not acquaint with the plan at all, it being contrived by my aunt, who hath a shrewd head, and carried out by myself; and I doubt much if she fairly knew with whom she went at the very first, being quite overcome by her fright and bewilderment." And Darius Hopkins begged the parson also to acquaint Ichabod Buckley, for his comfort, with this fact: Although his daughter Persis had not wedded with a gentleman of high estate from over-seas, yet he, Darius Hopkins, was of no mean birth, and had a not inconsiderable share of this world's goods, with more in expectation, as his esteemed aunt bade him mention.

And furthermore, Darius Hopkins stated that had he believed any other way than the one he had taken to be available for the purpose of winning his beloved wife and freeing her from a hard and unhappy lot, he would much have preferred it. But he had taken this believing there was no other, in all honesty and purity of purpose, and he again humbly begged Ichabod Buckley's pardon.

One afternoon the parson paced solemnly up to the Buckley house with the great red-sealed letter in his hand. Ichabod was not at work. His nervous old face was visible at the window where his daughter's beautiful one had been so long, and the parson went in the front door.

It was two hours before he came out, and went with his head bent gravely down the road. He never told exactly what had passed between himself and Ichabod Buckley, but it was whispered that the parson had striven in prayer for him for the space of an hour and a half, but had not reconciled him to his disappointment.

After his daughter had departed in state, Ichabod Buckley, while not returning to his old garrulous ways, but comporting himself with a dignity that would have befitted a squire, was seen frequently in the store and on the street, and he wore always his best green *surtout*, which he had heretofore kept for Sabbath days.

But after the truth was revealed to him Ichabod Buckley was seen no more abroad. He shut himself up in his poor workshed, and all day long his chisel rasped on the dark slate. Persis wrote to him, and Darius, and he read the letters, scowling fiercely and painfully through his iron-bowed spectacles, then put them away in his beetling old desk in the kitchen, and fell to work again.

It was not three weeks after Persis went away when Submit, with her apron over her head, went one morning through the woods with lumbering swiftness and called the doctor, for her father lay on his bed as motionless as if he were dead, and could not speak.

They sent for Persis, but her father was dead before she reached her old home and went weeping over the threshold, leaning on her young husband's arm. Not a word did she have of blame or forgiveness from her father's lips; but she knew his last mind toward her when she saw what his work had been since the day she left him.

Out in Ichabod Buckley's workshop stood a tall slate stone, shaped like the one he had erected for his dearly beloved wife. On it were cut his name, and the years of his birth and death, and under that a verse. In his own poor brain, strained almost asunder with its awful stress of one idea in life, he had devised this verse; with his poor old failing hands he had cut it on the stone:

Stranger, view well this speaking stone,
And drop a pitying tear;
Ingratitude had overthrown,
And Death then laid me here.

Ichabod Buckley had left a space below, as if he had designed to make still larger his appeal to the pity of those who should pause in the future by his grave; and thereon did Darius Hopkins, to comfort his wife Persis, who grieved as if she could never be comforted when she read the first, cut another verse.

When the stone was set up over Ichabod's grave, people kneeling before it read, after the piteous complaint and prayer for sympathy of the dead man, Darius's verse:

Who doth his clearer sight possess
In brighter realms above,
May come his earthly woe to bless,
And know that all was Love.

And it has so happened, because Darius cut with his strong young hands more firmly and deeply his verse in the stone, that his has endured and can be read, while Ichabod's is all worn away by the rain-storms of the years, as it might have been by the tears of mortal life.

The Jade Bracelet

Lawrence Evarts was on his way home from his law-office in Somerset when he caught sight of the inexplicable circle in the snow. The snow was hard and smooth, and the circle immediately arrested his attention. It was just outside the compact snow of the sidewalk, in what would have been the gutter had there been any gutters in Somerset.

Lawrence carried a neatly-folded umbrella. He was exceedingly punctilious in all his personal habits. It had threatened snow earlier in the day, although now the sky was brilliantly clear, and the stars were shining out, one by one, in the ineffable rose, violet and yellow tints of the horizon.

Lawrence poked with the steel point of his umbrella at the circle, and struck something hard. He endeavoured to lift whatever it was with the umbrella-point, but was unable to do so. Then, frowning a little, he removed his English glove, plunged his hand into the snow and drew it up again with the jade bracelet. It was beautiful, cabbage-green jade, cut out of the solid stone and very large—a man's bracelet, and rather large for his own hand. Evarts had a small hand.

He stood staring at it. He immediately remembered having seen somewhere, in a Chinese laundry, a Chinaman wearing a bracelet of a similar design. But there was no Chinese laundry in Somerset; he could not remember that there was one in Lloyds, which was the only other village for miles large enough to support a laundry.

Once a Chinaman had penetrated to Somerset, but the hood-

440

lum element, which was large and flourishing, had routed him out. He had disappeared, presumably for more peaceable fields of cleanliness, although there had been dark rumours which had died away, both for lack of substantiation, and of interest in the uncanny heathen—as most of the citizens adjudged him.

Lawrence stood gazing at the thing with wonder; then obeying some unaccountable impulse, he slipped it over his right hand, the one from which he had removed the glove. Immediately the horror was upon him. He realized, although fighting hard against the realization, that there was another hand beside his own in the jade bracelet. He gave his hand a sharp jerk to rid himself of the sensation, but it remained. He could feel the other hand and wrist, although he could see absolutely nothing. Only his sense of touch was reached, and one other, his sense of smell. Overpowering the clear, frosty atmosphere came the strange pungency of opium and sandalwood. But worse than the uncanny assailing of the senses—far worse—was something else. Into his clear Western mind, trained from infancy to logical inferences, Christian belief, and right estimates of things, stole something foreign and antagonistic. Strange memories, strange outlooks, seemed misting over his own familiar ones, as smoke mists a window.

Evarts snatched the bracelet from his wrist and gave it a fling back into the snow. Then something worse happened. He still had the feel of the thing on his wrist, but the pull of the other hand and wrist became stronger, he fairly choked with the opium smoke, and the strange cloud dimmed his own personality with greater force. He drew on his glove, but unmistakably it would not go on over the invisible bracelet.

"What the devil!" Evarts said quite aloud. He could see in the snow the clearly-cut circle where the bracelet had fallen. He withdrew his glove, picked up the thing again, put it on and walked along, shaking the snow from his hand. It was unmistakably better on than off. The strange sensations were not so pronounced. Still, it was bad enough, in all conscience.

Presently, as he walked along, Evarts met a friend, who stared at him after he had said good-evening.

"What is the matter? Are you ill?" he asked, turning back.

"No," replied Evarts shortly.

"You look like the deuce," his friend remarked wonderingly. Evarts was conscious that the man stood still a moment staring at him, but he did not turn. He walked on, feeling as if he were in handcuffs with the devil. It became more and more horrible.

When he reached his boarding-house he went straight to his room, and did not go down to dinner. No one came to ask why he did not. He had not any intimates in the house, and, indeed, was one who was apt to keep himself to himself, regulate his own actions and resent questions concerning them.

He turned on his electric light and tried to write a letter. He was able to do that, as far as the mere mechanical action was concerned. The other hand moved in accordance with his. But what he wrote —! Evarts stared incredulously at the end of the first page. What he had written was in a language unfamiliar to him, both in words and characters, and yet the meaning was horribly clear. He could not conceive of the possibility of his writing things of such hideous significance, and, moreover, of a significance hitherto unknown to him.

He tore up the sheet and threw it into the waste-paper basket; then he lit his pipe and tried to smoke, but the scent of opium came in his nostrils instead of tobacco. He flung his pipe aside and took up the evening paper, but to his horror he read in a twofold fashion, as one may see double. There were horrors enough, as usual, but there were horrors besides, which dimmed them.

He tossed the paper to the floor, and sat for a few moments looking about him. He had rather luxurious apartments: a large sitting-room, bedroom and bath; and he had gathered together some choice things in the way of furniture and bric-a-brac. He had rather a leaning to Oriental treasures, and there were some good things in the way of Persian rugs and hangings. Just before his chair was a fine prayer-rug, with its graceful triangle which should point toward the Holy City.

Suddenly he seemed to see, kneeling there, not a Moslem but a small figure in a richly-wrought robe, with a long slimy braid, and before it sat a squat, grinning bronze god. That was too much.

"Good God!" Evarts muttered to himself, and sprang up. He got his coat and hat, put them on hurriedly and rushed out of the room and the house, all the time with that never-ceasing sensation of the other hand and wrist in the jade bracelet. He hurried down the street until he reached the office of a physician, a friend of his, perhaps the closest he had in Somerset. There was a light in the office, and Evarts entered without ceremony.

Dr. Van Brunt was alone. He had just finished his dinner and was having his usual smoke, leaning back luxuriously in a very old Morris chair, well-worn to all the needs of his figure. He was a short man, heavily blond-bearded.

"Thank God, I smell tobacco instead of that cursed other thing!" was Evarts' first salutation. Van Brunt looked at him, then he jumped up with heavy alacrity. "For Heaven's sake, what's to pay, old man?" he said.

"The devil, I rather guess," answered Evarts, settling himself in a forlorn hunch on the nearest chair.

Dr. Van Brunt remained standing, looking at him with consternation.

"You look like the devil," he remarked finally.

"I feel like him, I reckon," responded Evarts gloomily. Now that he was there, he shrank from confidence. He felt a decided tug on his wrist, and hardly seemed to realize himself at all, because of the cloud of another personality before his mental vision.

Dr. Van Brunt stood before him, scowling with perplexity, his fuming pipe in hand. Then he said suddenly: "What in thunder is that thing you've got on your wrist?"

"Some token from hell, I begin to think," answered Evarts.

"Where did you get it?"

"I found it in the snow near the corner of State Street, and I was fool enough to put the infernal thing on."

"Why on earth don't you take it off, if it bothers you?"

"I have tried it, and the second state is worse than the first. Look here" —

"What is it?"

"You know I never drink, except an occasional glass of wine at a dinner, and an occasional pint of beer, mostly to keep you company."

"Of course I do. What —?"

"You know I am not in any sense a drinking man."

"Of course I know it. Why?"

"Why?" Evarts faced him fiercely. "Why, then, do I see things that nobody, except men who have sold their souls and wits for drink, see?"

"You don't."

"Yes, I do. I must be mad. For God's sake, Van Brunt, tell me if I am mad, and do something for me if you can!"

Van Brunt sat down again in his chair and took a whiff of his pipe, but he did not remove his great blue eyes from Evarts.

"Mad, nothing!" he said. "Don't you suppose I know a maniac when I see him? What on earth are you ranting about, anyway? And what is it about that green thing on your arm, and why don't you take it off?"

"I tell you I am in the innermost circles of hell when it is off!" cried Evarts.

"What made you put the thing on, anyway?"

"I don't know. My evil angel, I reckon."

Dr. Van Brunt leaned forward and looked closely at the jade bracelet. "It is a fine specimen," he said. "I have never seen anything like it, except"—he hesitated a moment, and was evidently endeavouring to recall something. "I know where I saw one like it," he said suddenly. "That poor devil of a Chinaman who started a laundry here five years ago, and was routed out of town, had its facsimile. I remember noticing it one day, just before he was run out. Don't you remember?"

"I don't know what I remember," replied Evarts. He jerked

the bracelet angrily as he spoke, then gave a great start of horror, for the invisible thing which he felt had seemed to come closer at the jerk.

"Why on earth don't you take that thing off?" asked Van Brunt again. He continued to smoke and to watch his friend closely.

"Didn't I tell you it was worse off than on? Then he gets so close, ugh!"

"He? Who?"

"Don't ask me. How do I know? The devil, I think, or one of his friends."

"Rot!"

"It's so."

"Sit down, Evarts, and have a pipe, and put that nonsense out of your head."

"Put it out of my head?" repeated Evarts bitterly. Suddenly a thought struck him. "See here; you don't believe that I am talking rationally," he said.

"I think something has happened to upset you," replied Van Brunt guardedly.

"I see. Well, try the thing yourself."

Evarts as he spoke withdrew the bracelet with a jerk. He paled perceptibly as he did so, and set his mouth hard, as if with pain or disgust. He extended the shining green circle toward Van Brunt, who took it, laughing, although there was an anxious gleam in his eyes.

Van Brunt, oddly enough, since he was a large man, had small hands. The bracelet slipped on his wrist as easily as it had done on Evarts'. He sat quite still for a second. He gave one more puff at his pipe, then he laid it on the table. His great blond face changed. He looked at Evarts.

"What is this infernal thing, anyhow?" he said.

"Don't ask me. I am as wise as yourself. But now you know what torment I am in." Evarts spoke with a feeble triumph.

"You don't mean you feel it without the bracelet?"

"Try it."

Van Brunt took off the bracelet and laid it on the table beside his pipe. His face contracted. "My God!" he ejaculated.

"Now you know."

"Good Lord! I am remembering devilish things which never happened. I am going backward like a crab."

Evarts nodded.

"You mean you feel the same thing?"

"Don't I?"

"As if some infernal thing was handcuffed to you?"

Evarts nodded.

"Well," said Van Brunt slowly. "I did not think I believed in much of anything, but now I believe in the devil." He took up the bracelet. Evarts made a sudden gesture of remonstrance. "For the love of God! let me have it on again," he said hoarsely. "I don't think I can stand this much longer."

Van Brunt gave the bracelet to Evarts, who slipped it over his hand, immediately an expression of something like relief came over his face.

"You don't feel quite so—with it on?" asked Van Brunt.

"No, but it is bad enough anyway. And you?"

Van Brunt grimaced. "As for me, I am handcuffed to a fiend," he said.

Evarts sat down, with the bracelet still on his wrist. "Van Brunt, what does it mean?" he asked helplessly.

"Ask me what is on the other side of the moon."

"You honestly don't know?"

"I can't diagnose the case, or cases, unless you are crazy and the microbe has hit me, too, for I am as crazy as you are."

Evarts looked down at the shining green circle on his wrist.

"I wish I'd let the thing alone," said he.

"So do I."

Suddenly Van Brunt arose. He was a man of a less sensitive nervous organization than the other, and his mouth was set hard, and even his hands clenched, as for a fight. "See here, old fellow," he said, "we've had enough of this. It is time to put a stop to it. Have you had any dinner?"

"Do you think—?" began Evarts.

"Well, you've got to eat dinner, whether you want to or not. This is nonsense!"

Van Brunt struck the call-bell on his table violently and his man entered. A look of surprise overspread his face as he looked at his master and Evarts, but he said nothing.

"Tell Hannah, if there was any soup left over from dinner to warm it immediately, and send up whatever else was left. Mr. Evarts has not dined. Tell her to be as quick as possible."

"Yes, sir," replied the man.

"And, Thomas."

"Yes, sir."

"Get a bottle of that old port, and open it."

"Yes, sir."

After the man had gone Evarts and Van Brunt sat in a moody silence. Both were pale, and both had expressions of suffering and disgust, as if from the contact of some loathsome thing, but Van Brunt still kept his mouth set hard. He even resumed his pipe.

It was not long before dinner was announced and he sprang to his feet, and laid his hand on Evarts' shoulder. "Now, come, old man," he said. "When you've got some good roast beef and old port in your stomach the mists will leave your brain."

"The mists are on your brain, and you have the good roast beef in your stomach," returned Evarts bitterly, but he arose.

"But I haven't the old port," said Van Brunt with an attempt at jocularity, as the two men entered the dining-room. Van Brunt kept bachelor's hall, and a neat maid was in attendance. Her master saw her quick glance of amazement at their altered faces.

"You may go, Katie," said Van Brunt. "Mr. Evarts and I will wait upon ourselves."

After the maid had left Evarts leaned his elbows on the table and bent his head forward with a despairing gesture. "I can't eat," he almost moaned.

"You can and will!" replied Van Brunt, and ladled out the smoking soup. Evarts did eat mechanically, and both men drank of the old port. They sat side by side at the table, for the greater convenience of serving.

After Evarts had finished his dinner, and the two men had despatched the wine, they looked at each other. Evarts gave a glance of horror at the green thing on his wrist. "Well?" he said, with a kind of interrogative bitterness.

Van Brunt tried to laugh. "Take that confounded thing off and put it out of your mind," he said.

"You want to wear it yourself," Evarts returned almost savagely.

Van Brunt laughed. "No, I don't. I can stand it," he said, "but I'll be hanged if I believe I could suffer much more in hell. The devilish thing is converting me, paradoxically."

"What does it mean?" asked Evarts again.

"Don't know. If it keeps up much longer I'll try a narcotic for both of us."

"Not"—Evarts shuddered.

"No, not opium, if I know myself."

As he spoke, Van Brunt had his eyes fixed upon a spot directly in front of the fireplace, and Evarts knew that he saw what he himself saw—the horrible, prostrate figure covered with embroideries, and the grinning idol.

"You see?" he gasped.

"Yes, I do see, confound it! I'll do something before long."

"You feel as if—"

"Yes."

"there is something between us?"

"Yes. Don't talk about it. I'll do something soon, if it keeps up."

Evarts made a quick gesture. He grasped the table-knife beside him.

"I'll do something now!" he cried, and made a thrust.

Van Brunt's face whitened. Almost simultaneously he grasped another knife and did the same thing. Then the two men drew long breaths and looked at each other.

"It's gone," said Evarts, and he almost sobbed.

Van Brunt was still pale, but he recovered his equilibrium more quickly.

"What was it?" gasped Evarts. "Oh! what was it? Am I going mad?"

"Going mad? No."

"There's a reason why I ask. It concerns someone very dear to me. I have not said much about Agnes Leeds to you; in fact, I have not said much to her; but sometimes I think that she—I have thought that I—when my practice was a little better. Good God! Van Brunt, I am not mad, am I? That would make marriage impossible for us.

"You are no more mad than I am," said Van Brunt. He gazed at his friend scrutinizingly. "What case have you on hand now?" he asked.

"The Day girl's; the murder case, you know."

Van Brunt nodded. "Just so. You have had that horrible murder thing on your mind, and—say, old fellow, your collar looks somewhat the worse for wear" —

"Yes, my laundress failed me this week, and I have been so horribly busy today that I have not had time to buy some fresh ones before the stores closed."

"Just so. And you wished that there was a Chinese laundry here, I'll be bound!"

"I don't know but I did," admitted Evarts, with a dawning expression of relief. Then his face fell again. "But what of the jade bracelet?" he said. He glanced at his wrist and gave a great start, "Good God! it's gone," he cried.

"Of course it is gone," said Van Brunt coolly. "It never was there."

"But you—saw it?"

"Thought I saw it. My dear fellow, the whole thing is a clear case of hypnotism; something for the Psychical Research. You were all overwrought with your work, nerves in a devil of a state, and you hypnotized yourself, and then—you hypnotized me."

Evarts sat staring at Van Brunt, with the look of one who is trying to turn a corner of mentality. Then the door was flung open violently, and Van Brunt's man rushed in, pale and breathless.

"Doctor!" he gasped.

"What is it?"

"Oh, Dr. Van Brunt, there's a Chinaman dead right out in front of the office door, and he's got two stabs in his side, and he's got a green bracelet on his wrist!"

Dr. Van Brunt turned ashy white. "Nonsense!" he said.

"It's so, doctor."

"Well, I'll come," said Van Brunt in a voice which he kept steady. "You run and get the police, Thomas. Maybe he isn't dead. I'll come."

"He's stone dead!" said the man in a shocked voice as he hurried out.

"Oh, my God!" said Evarts. "If we—if I—killed him, what about Agnes?"

"I can tell quickly enough which of us killed him," said Van Brunt rising. Both men hurried out of the room.

There was already a crowd around the ghastly thing, and police uniforms glittered among them. The fact that the dead Chinaman happened to be in front of his office had no significance for anybody present. There was no question of suspicion for either himself or Evarts. Some men held lanterns while Van Brunt examined the dead Chinaman. It was soon done, and the body was carried away in an undertaker's wagon, with the crowd in tow.

Then Van Brunt and Evarts entered the office. Evarts looked at his friend, and he was as white as the dead man himself.

"Well?" he stammered.

Van Brunt laughed, and clasped him on the shoulder. "It's all right, old man," he said. "My knife did the deed."

"But"—stammered Evarts, "I was on the heart side."

"What if you were? Your knife went nowhere near the heart. Mine cut the heart clean. I lunged around to the front of the thing. Don't you remember?"

"Are you sure?"

"I know it. You can rest easy now."

"But—you?" said Evarts in a voice from which, for very shame, he tried to suppress the joy.

Van Brunt laughed again. "It was a poisonous thing," he said. "Did you see his face?" he shuddered in spite of himself. "Men kill snakes of a right," he added.

"But how do you explain —?"

"I don't explain. All you have to consider is that you did not do it; and all I have to consider is that I have set my heel on something which would have bruised it."

As he spoke he was preparing a powder, which he presently handed to Evarts. "Now, go home, old man," he said. "Take a warm bath, and this, and go to bed and dream of Agnes Leeds."

After Evarts was gone Van Brunt stood still for a moment. His face had suddenly turned ghastly, and all the assumed lightness had vanished. He struck the bell and told his man to bring up another bottle of the old port. When it came he poured out a glass for himself and gave one to the man. "You've got a turn, too, Thomas," he said.

The man, who was shivering from head to foot, looked at his master.

"Did you see its face, sir?" he whispered.

"Better put it out of your mind."

"He looked like a fiend. I doubt if I can ever stop seeing him," said the man. Then he swallowed the wine and went out.

Van Brunt settled himself again in his old Morris chair, and lit his pipe. He gave a few whiffs, then stopped and gazed straight ahead of him with horror. The face of the dead Chinaman was vividly before his eyes again.

"Thank God, he does not know he did it!" he whispered, and a good smile came over his great blond face.

The Hall Bedroom

My name is Mrs. Elizabeth Jennings. I am a highly respectable woman. I may style myself a gentlewoman, for in my youth I enjoyed advantages. I was well brought up, and I graduated at a young ladies' seminary. I also married well. My husband was that most genteel of all merchants, an apothecary. His shop was on the corner of the main street in Rockton, the town where I was born, and where I lived until the death of my husband. My parents had died when I had been married a short time, so I was left quite alone in the world. I was not competent to carry on the apothecary business by myself, for I had no knowledge of drugs, and had a mortal terror of giving poisons instead of medicines. Therefore I was obliged to sell at a considerable sacrifice, and the proceeds, some five thousand dollars, were all I had in the world.

The income was not enough to support me in any kind of comfort, and I saw that I must in some way earn money. I thought at first of teaching, but I was no longer young, and methods had changed since my school days. What I was able to teach, nobody wished to know. I could think of only one thing to do: take boarders. But the same objection to that business as to teaching held good in Rockton. Nobody wished to board. My husband had rented a house with a number of bedrooms, and I advertised, but nobody applied. Finally my cash was running very low, and I became desperate. I packed up my furniture, rented a large house in this town and moved here. It was a venture attended with many risks. In the first place the rent was exorbitant, in the next I was entirely unknown. However, I am a person of considerable ingenuity, and have inventive power, and much enterprise when the occasion presses.

I advertised in a very original manner, although that actually took my last penny, that is, the last penny of my ready money, and I was forced to draw on my principal to purchase my first supplies, a thing which I had resolved never on any account to do. But the great risk met with a reward, for I had several applicants within two days after my advertisement appeared in the paper. Within two weeks my boarding-house was well established, I became very successful, and my success would have been uninterrupted had it not been for the mysterious and bewildering occurrences which I am about to relate. I am now forced to leave the house and rent another.

Some of my old boarders accompany me, some, with the most unreasonable nervousness, refuse to be longer associated in any way, however indirectly, with the terrible and uncanny happenings which I have to relate. It remains to be seen whether my ill luck in this house will follow me into another, and whether my whole prosperity in life will be forever shadowed by the Mystery of the Hall Bedroom. Instead of telling the strange story myself in my own words, I shall present the journal of Mr. George H. Wheatcroft. I shall show you the portions beginning on January 18 of the present year, the date when he took up his residence with me. Here it is:

******

January 18, 1883. Here I am established in my new boarding-house. I have, as befits my humble means, the hall bedroom, even the hall bedroom on the third floor. I have heard all my life of hall bedrooms, I have seen hall bedrooms, I have been in them, but never until now, when I am actually established in one, did I comprehend what, at once, an ignominious and sternly uncompromising thing a hall bedroom is. It proves the ignominy of the dweller therein. No man at thirty-six (my age) would be domiciled in a hall bedroom, unless he were himself ignominious, at least comparatively speaking. I am proved by this means incontrovertibly to have been left far behind in the race. I see no reason why I should not live in this hall bedroom for the rest of my life, that is, if I have money enough to pay the landlady, and that seems probable, since my small funds are invested as safely as if I were an orphan-ward in charge of a pillar of a sanctuary.

After the valuables have been stolen, I have most carefully locked the stable door. I have experienced the revulsion which comes sooner or later to the adventurous soul who experiences nothing but defeat and so-called ill luck. I have swung to the opposite extreme. I have lost in everything—I have lost in love, I have lost in money, I have lost in the struggle for preferment, I have lost in health and strength. I am now settled down in a hall bedroom to live upon my small income, and regain my health by mild potations of the mineral waters here, if possible; if not, to live here without my health—for mine is not a necessarily fatal malady—until Providence shall take me out of my hall bedroom. There is no one place more than another where I care to live. There is not sufficient motive to take me away, even if the mineral waters do not benefit me.

So I am here and to stay in the hall bedroom. The landlady is civil, and even kind, as kind as a woman who has to keep her poor womanly eye upon the main chance can be. The struggle for money always injures the fine grain of a woman; she is too fine a thing to do it; she does not by nature belong with the gold grubbers, and it therefore lowers her; she steps from heights to claw and scrape and dig. But she can not help it oftentimes, poor thing, and her deterioration thereby is to be condoned. The landlady is all she can be, taking her strain of adverse circumstances into consideration, and the table is good, even conscientiously so. It looks to me as if she were foolish enough to strive to give the boarders their money's worth, with the due regard for the main chance which is inevitable. However, that is of minor importance to me, since my diet is restricted.

It is curious what an annoyance a restriction in diet can be even to a man who has considered himself somewhat indifferent to gastronomic delights. There was today a pudding for dinner, which I could not taste without penalty, but which I longed for. It was only because it looked unlike any other pudding that I had ever seen, and assumed a mental and spiritual significance. It seemed to me, whimsically no doubt, as if tasting it might give me a new sensation, and consequently a new outlook. Trivial things may lead to large results: why should I not get a new outlook by means of a pudding? Life here stretches before me most monotonously, and I feel like clutching at alleviations, though paradoxically, since I have settled down with the utmost acquiescence. Still one can not immediately overcome and change radically all one's nature.

Now I look at myself critically and search for the keynote to my whole self, and my actions, I have always been conscious of a reaching out, an overweening desire for the new, the untried, for the broadness of further horizons, the seas beyond seas, the thought beyond thought. This characteristic has been the primary cause of all my misfortunes. I have the soul of an explorer, and in nine out of ten cases this leads to destruction. If I had possessed capital and sufficient push, I should have been one of the searchers after the North Pole. I have been an eager student of astronomy. I have studied botany with avidity, and have dreamed of new *flora* in unexplored parts of the world, and the same with animal life and geology. I longed for riches in order to discover the power and sense of possession of the rich.

I longed for love in order to discover the possibilities of the emotions. I longed for all that the mind of man could conceive as desirable for man, not so much for purely selfish ends, as from an insatiable thirst for knowledge of a universal trend. But I have limitations, I do not quite understand of what nature—for what mortal ever did quite understand his own limitations, since a knowledge of them would preclude their existence?—but they have prevented my progress to any extent. Therefore behold me in my hall bedroom, settled at last into a groove of fate so deep that I have lost the sight of even my horizons. Just at present, as I write here, my horizon on the left, that is my physical horizon, is a wall covered with cheap paper. The paper is an indeterminate pattern in white and gilt.

"There are a few photographs of my own hung about, and on the large wall space beside the bed there is a large oil painting which belongs to my landlady. It has a massive tarnished gold frame, and, curiously enough, the painting itself is rather good. I have no idea who the artist could have been. It is of the conventional landscape type in vogue some fifty years since, the type so fondly reproduced in chromos—the winding river with the little boat occupied by a pair of lovers, the cottage nestled among trees on the right shore, the gentle slope of the hills and the church spire in the background—but still it is well done. It gives me the impression of an artist without the slightest originality of design, but much of technique. But for some inexplicable reason the picture frets me. I find myself gazing at it when I do not wish to do so. It seems to compel my attention like some intent face in the room. I shall ask Mrs. Jennings to have it removed. I will hang in its place some photographs which I have in a trunk.

January 26. I do not write regularly in my journal. I never did. I see no reason why I should. I see no reason why anyone should have the slightest sense of duty in such a matter. Some days I have nothing which interests me sufficiently to write out, some days I feel either too ill or too indolent. For four days I have not written, from a mixture of all three reasons. Now, today I both feel like it and I have something to write. Also I am distinctly better than I have been. Perhaps the waters are benefiting me, or the change of air. Or possibly it is something else more subtle. Possibly my mind has seized upon something new, a discovery which causes it to react upon my failing body and serves as a stimulant.

All I know is, I feel distinctly better, and am conscious of an acute interest in doing so, which is of late strange to me. I have been rather indifferent, and sometimes have wondered if that were not the cause rather than the result of my state of health. I have been so continually balked that I have settled into a state of inertia. I lean rather comfortably against my obstacles. After all, the worst of the pain always lies in the struggle. Give up and it is rather pleasant than otherwise. If one did not kick, the pricks would not in the least matter. However, for some reason, for the last few days, I seem to have awakened from my state of quiescence. It means future trouble for me, no doubt, but in the meantime I am not sorry.

It began with the picture—the large oil painting. I went to Mrs. Jennings about it yesterday, and she, to my surprise—for I thought it a matter that could be easily arranged—objected to having it removed. Her reasons were two; both simple, both sufficient, especially since I, after all, had no very strong desire either way. It seems that the picture does not belong to her. It hung here when she rented the house. She says if it is removed, a very large and unsightly discoloration of the wall-paper will be exposed, and she does not like to ask for new paper. The owner, an old man, is travelling abroad, the agent is curt, and she has only been in the house a very short time. Then it would mean a sad upheaval of my room, which would disturb me. She also says that there is no place in the house where she can store the picture, and there is not a vacant space in another room for one so large.

So I let the picture remain. It really, when I came to think of it, was very immaterial after all. But I got my photographs out of my trunk, and I hung them around the large picture. The wall is almost completely covered. I hung them yesterday afternoon, and last night I repeated a strange experience which I have had in some degree every night since I have been here, but was not sure whether it deserved the name of experience, but was not rather one of those dreams in which one dreams one is awake. But last night it came again, and now I know. There is something very singular about this room. I am very much interested. I will write down for future reference the events of last night. Concerning those of the preceding nights since I have slept in this room, I will simply say that they have been of a similar nature, but, as it were, only the preliminary stages, the prologue to what happened last night.

I am not depending upon the mineral waters here as the one remedy for my malady, which is sometimes of an acute nature, and indeed constantly threatens me with considerable suffering unless by medicine I can keep it in check. I will say that the medicine which I employ is not of the class commonly known as drugs. It is impossible that it can be held responsible for what I am about to transcribe. My mind last night and every night since I have slept in this room was in an absolutely normal state. I take this medicine, prescribed by the specialist in whose charge I was before coming here, regularly every four hours while awake. As I am never a good sleeper, it follows that I am enabled with no inconvenience to take any medicine during the night with the same regularity as during the day.

It is my habit, therefore, to place my bottle and spoon where I can put my hand upon them easily without lighting the gas. Since I have been in this room, I have placed the bottle of medicine upon my dresser at the side of the room opposite the bed. I have done this rather than place it nearer, as once I jostled the bottle and spilled most of the contents, and it is not easy for me to replace it, as it is expensive. Therefore I placed it in security on the dresser, and, indeed, that is but three or four steps from my bed, the room being so small. Last night I wakened as usual, and I knew, since I had fallen asleep about eleven, that it must be in the neighbourhood of three. I wake with almost clock-like regularity and it is never necessary for me to consult my watch.

I had slept unusually well and without dreams, and I awoke fully at once, with a feeling of refreshment to which I am not accustomed. I immediately got out of bed and began stepping across the room in the direction of my dresser, on which I had set my medicine-bottle and spoon.

To my utter amazement, the steps which had hitherto sufficed to take me across my room did not suffice to do so. I advanced several paces, and my outstretched hands touched nothing. I stopped and went on again. I was sure that I was moving in a straight direction, and even if I had not been I knew it was impossible to advance in any direction in my tiny apartment without coming into collision either with a wall or a piece of furniture. I continued to walk falteringly, as I have seen people on the stage: a step, then a long falter, then a sliding step. I kept my hands extended; they touched nothing. I stopped again. I had not the least sentiment of fear or consternation. It was rather the very stupefaction of surprise. 'How is this?' seemed thundering in my ears. 'What is this?'

The room was perfectly dark. There was nowhere any glimmer, as is usually the case, even in a so-called dark room, from the walls, picture-frames, looking-glass or white objects. It was absolute gloom. The house stood in a quiet part of the town. There were many trees about; the electric street lights were extinguished at midnight; there was no moon and the sky was cloudy. I could not distinguish my one window, which I thought strange, even on such a dark night. Finally I changed my plan of motion and turned, as nearly as I could estimate, at right angles. Now, I thought, I must reach soon, if, I kept on, my writing-table underneath the window; or, if I am going in the opposite direction, the hall door. I reached neither. I am telling the unvarnished truth when I say that I began to count my steps and carefully measure my paces after that, and I traversed a space clear of furniture at least twenty feet by thirty—a very large apartment.

And as I walked I was conscious that my naked feet were pressing something which gave rise to sensations the like of which I had never experienced before. As nearly as I can express it, it was as if my feet pressed something as elastic as air or water, which was in this case unyielding to my weight. It gave me a curious sensation of buoyancy and stimulation. At the same time this surface, if surface be the right name, which I trod, felt cool to my feet with the coolness of vapour or fluidity, seeming to overlap the soles. Finally I stood still; my surprise was at last merging into a measure of consternation. 'Where am I?' I thought. 'What am I going to do?' Stories that I had heard of travellers being taken from their beds and conveyed into strange and dangerous places, Middle Age stories of the Inquisition flashed through my brain.

I knew all the time that for a man who had gone to bed in a commonplace hall bedroom in a very commonplace little town such surmises were highly ridiculous, but it is hard for the human mind to grasp anything but a human explanation of phenomena. Almost anything seemed then, and seems now, more rational than an explanation bordering upon the supernatural, as we understand the supernatural. At last I called, though rather softly, 'What does this mean?' I said quite aloud, 'Where am I? Who is here? Who is doing this? I tell you I will have no such nonsense. Speak, if there is anybody here.' But all was dead silence. Then suddenly a light flashed through the open transom of my door. Somebody had heard me—a man who rooms next door, a decent kind of man, also here for his health. He turned on the gas in the hall and called to me. 'What's the matter?' he asked, in an agitated, trembling voice. He is a nervous fellow.

"Directly, when the light flashed through my transom, I saw that I was in my familiar hall bedroom. I could see everything quite distinctly—my tumbled bed, my writing-table, my dresser, my chair, my little wash-stand, my clothes hanging on a row of pegs, the old picture on the wall. The picture gleamed out with singular distinctness in the light from the transom. The river seemed actually to run and ripple, and the boat to be gliding with the current. I gazed fascinated at it, as I replied to the anxious voice:

'Nothing is the matter with me,' said I. 'Why?'

'I thought I heard you speak,' said the man outside. 'I thought maybe you were sick.'

'No,' I called back. 'I am all right. I am trying to find my medicine in the dark, that's all. I can see now you have lighted the gas.'

'Nothing is the matter?'

'No; sorry I disturbed you. Goodnight.'

'Goodnight.' Then I heard the man's door shut after a minute's pause. He was evidently not quite satisfied. I took a pull at my medicine-bottle, and got into bed. He had left the hall-gas burning. I did not go to sleep again for some time. Just before I did so, some one, probably Mrs. Jennings, came out in the hall and extinguished the gas. This morning when I awoke everything was as usual in my room. I wonder if I shall have any such experience tonight.

January 27. I shall write in my journal every day until this draws to some definite issue. Last night my strange experience deepened, as something tells me it will continue to do. I retired quite early, at half-past ten. I took the precaution, on retiring, to place beside my bed, on a chair, a box of safety matches, that I might not be in the dilemma of the night before. I took my medicine on retiring; that made me due to wake at half-past two. I had not fallen asleep directly, but had had certainly three hours of sound, dreamless slumber when I awoke. I lay a few minutes hesitating whether or not to strike a safety match and light my way to the dresser, whereon stood my medicine-bottle. I hesitated, not because I had the least sensation of fear, but because of the same shrinking from a nerve shock that leads one at times to dread the plunge into an icy bath. It seemed much easier to me to strike that match and cross my hall bedroom to my dresser, take my dose, then return quietly to my bed, than to risk the chance of floundering about in some unknown limbo either of fancy or reality.

At last, however, the spirit of adventure, which has always been such a ruling one for me, conquered. I rose. I took the box of safety matches in my hand, and started on, as I conceived, the straight course for my dresser, about five feet across from my bed. As before, I travelled and travelled and did not reach it. I advanced with groping hands extended, setting one foot cautiously before the other, but I touched nothing except the indefinite, unnameable surface which my feet pressed. All of a sudden, though, I became aware of something. One of my senses was saluted, nay, more than that, hailed, with imperiousness, and that was, strangely enough, my sense of smell, but in a hitherto unknown fashion. It seemed as if the odour reached my mentality first. I reversed the usual process, which is, as I understand it, like this: the odour when encountered strikes first the olfactory nerve, which transmits the intelligence to the brain.

It is as if, to put it rudely, my nose met a rose, and then the nerve belonging to the sense said to my brain, 'Here is a rose.' This time my brain said, 'Here is a rose,' and my sense then recognized it. I say rose, but it was not a rose, that is, not the fragrance of any rose which I had ever known. It was undoubtedly a flower-odour, and rose came perhaps the nearest to it. My mind realized it first with what seemed a leap of rapture. 'What is this delight?' I asked myself. And then the ravishing fragrance smote my sense. I breathed it in and it seemed to feed my thoughts, satisfying some hitherto unknown hunger. Then I took a step further and another fragrance appeared, which I liken to lilies for lack of something better, and then came violets, then mignonette. I can not describe the experience, but it was a sheer delight, a rapture of sublimated sense. I groped further and further, and always into new waves of fragrance.

I seemed to be wading breast-high through flower-beds of Paradise, but all the time I touched nothing with my groping hands. At last a sudden giddiness as of surfeit overcame me. I realized that I might be in some unknown peril. I was distinctly afraid. I struck one of my safety matches, and I was in my hall bedroom, midway between my bed and my dresser. I took my dose of medicine and went to bed, and after a while fell asleep and did not wake till morning.

January 28. Last night I did not take my usual dose of medicine. In these days of new remedies and mysterious results upon certain organizations, it occurred to me to wonder if possibly the drug might have, after all, something to do with my strange experience.

"I did not take my medicine. I put the bottle as usual on my dresser, since I feared if I interrupted further the customary sequence of affairs I might fail to wake. I placed my box of matches on the chair beside the bed. I fell asleep about quarter past eleven o'clock, and I waked when the clock was striking two—a little earlier than my wont. I did not hesitate this time. I rose at once, took my box of matches and proceeded as formerly. I walked what seemed a great space without coming into collision with anything. I kept sniffing for the wonderful fragrances of the night before, but they did not recur. Instead, I was suddenly aware that I was tasting something, some morsel of sweetness hitherto unknown, and, as in the case of the odour, the usual order seemed reversed, and it was as if I tasted it first in my mental consciousness. Then the sweetness rolled under my tongue. I thought involuntarily of '*Sweeter than honey or the honeycomb*' of the Scripture.

I thought of the Old Testament manna. An ineffable content as of satisfied hunger seized me. I stepped further, and a new savour was upon my palate. And so on. It was never cloying, though of such sharp sweetness that it fairly stung. It was the merging of a material sense into a spiritual one. I said to myself, 'I have lived my life and always have I gone hungry until now.' I could feel my brain act swiftly under the influence of this heavenly food as under a stimulant. Then suddenly I repeated the experience of the night before. I grew dizzy, and an indefinite fear and shrinking were upon me. I struck my safety match and was back in my hall bedroom. I returned to bed, and soon fell asleep. I did not take my medicine. I am resolved not to do so longer. I am feeling much better.

January 29. Last night to bed as usual, matches in place; fell asleep about eleven and waked at half-past one. I heard the half-hour strike; I am waking earlier and earlier every night. I had not taken my medicine, though it was on the dresser as usual. I again took my match-box in hand and started to cross the room, and, as always, traversed strange spaces, but this night, as seems fated to be the case every night, my experience was different. Last night I neither smelled nor tasted, but I heard—my Lord, I heard! The first sound of which I was conscious was one like the constantly gathering and receding murmur of a river, and it seemed to come from the wall behind my bed where the old picture hangs. Nothing in nature except a river gives that impression of at once advance and retreat. I could not mistake it.

On, ever on, came the swelling murmur of the waves, past

and ever past they died in the distance. Then I heard above the murmur of the river a song in an unknown tongue which I recognized as being unknown, yet which I understood; but the understanding was in my brain, with no words of interpretation. The song had to do with me, but with me in unknown futures for which I had no images of comparison in the past; yet a sort of ecstasy as of a prophecy of bliss filled my whole consciousness. The song never ceased, but as I moved on I came into new sound-waves. There was the pealing of bells which might have been made of crystal, and might have summoned to the gates of heaven. There was music of strange instruments, great harmonies pierced now and then by small whispers as of love, and it all filled me with a certainty of a future of bliss.

At last I seemed the centre of a mighty orchestra which constantly deepened and increased until I seemed to feel myself being lifted gently but mightily upon the waves of sound as upon the waves of a sea. Then again the terror and the impulse to flee to my own familiar scenes was upon me. I struck my match and was back in my hall bedroom. I do not see how I sleep at all after such wonders, but sleep I do. I slept dreamlessly until daylight this morning.

January 30. I heard yesterday something with regard to my hall bedroom which affected me strangely. I can not for the life of me say whether it intimidated me, filled me with the horror of the abnormal, or rather roused to a greater degree my spirit of adventure and discovery. I was down at the Cure, and was sitting on the veranda sipping idly my mineral water, when somebody spoke my name. 'Mr. Wheatcroft?' said the voice politely, interrogatively, somewhat apologetically, as if to provide for a possible mistake in my identity. I turned and saw a gentleman whom I recognized at once. I seldom forget names or faces. He was a Mr. Addison whom I had seen considerable of three years ago at a little summer hotel in the mountains. It was one of those passing acquaintances which signify little one way or the other.

If never renewed, you have no regret; if renewed, you accept the renewal with no hesitation. It is in every way negative. But just now, in my feeble, friendless state, the sight of a face which beams with pleased remembrance is rather grateful. I felt distinctly glad to see the man. He sat down beside me. He also had a glass of the water. His health, while not as bad as mine, leaves much to be desired.

Addison had often been in this town before. He had in fact lived here at one time. He had remained at the Cure three years, taking the waters daily. He therefore knows about all there is to be known about the town, which is not very large. He asked me where I was staying, and when I told him the street, rather excitedly inquired the number. When I told him the number, which is 240, he gave a manifest start, and after one sharp glance at me sipped his water in silence for a moment. He had so evidently betrayed some ulterior knowledge with regard to my residence that I questioned him.

'What do you know about 240 Pleasant Street?' said I.

'Oh, nothing,' he replied, evasively, sipping his water.

After a little while, however, he inquired, in what he evidently tried to render a casual tone, what room I occupied. 'I once lived a few weeks at 240 Pleasant Street myself,' he said. 'That house always was a boarding-house, I guess.'

'It had stood vacant for a term of years before the present occupant rented it, I believe,' I remarked. Then I answered his question. 'I have the hall bedroom on the third floor,' said I. 'The quarters are pretty straitened, but comfortable enough as hall bedrooms go.'

But Mr. Addison had showed such unmistakable consternation at my reply that then I persisted in my questioning as to the cause, and at last he yielded and told me what he knew. He had hesitated both because he shrank from displaying what I might consider an unmanly superstition, and because he did not wish to influence me beyond what the facts of the case warranted. 'Well, I will tell you, Wheatcroft,' he said. 'Briefly all I know is this: When last I heard of 240 Pleasant Street it was not rented because of foul play which was supposed to have taken place there, though nothing was ever proved. There were two disappearances, and—in each case—of an occupant of the hall bed-room which you now have.

The first disappearance was of a very beautiful girl who had come here for her health and was said to be the victim of a profound melancholy, induced by a love disappointment. She obtained board at 240 and occupied the hall bedroom about two weeks; then one morning she was gone, having seemingly vanished into thin air. Her relatives were communicated with; she had not many, nor friends either, poor girl, and a thorough search was made, but the last I knew she had never come to light. There were two or three arrests, but nothing ever came of them. Well, that was before my day here, but the second disap-pearance took place when I was in the house—a fine young fellow who had overworked in college. He had to pay his own way. He had taken cold, had the grip, and that and the overwork about finished him, and he came on here for a month's rest and recuperation.

He had been in that room about two weeks, a little less, when one morning he wasn't there. Then there was a great hullabaloo. It seems that he had let fall some hints to the effect that there was something queer about the room, but, of course, the police did not think much of that. They made arrests right and left, but they never found him, and the arrested were discharged, though some of them are probably under a cloud of suspicion to this day. Then the boarding-house was shut up. Six years ago nobody would have boarded there, much less occupied that hall bedroom, but now I suppose new people have come in and the story has died out. I dare say your landlady will not thank me for reviving it.'

I assured him that it would make no possible difference to me. He looked at me sharply, and asked bluntly if I had seen anything wrong or unusual about the room. I replied, guarding myself from falsehood with a quibble, that I had seen nothing in the least unusual about the room, as indeed I had not, and have not now, but that may come. I feel that that will come in due time. Last night I neither saw, nor heard, nor smelled, nor tasted, but I felt. Last night, having started again on my exploration of, God knows what, I had not advanced a step before I touched something. My first sensation was one of disappointment. 'It is the dresser, and I am at the end of it now,' I thought. But I soon discovered that it was not the old painted dresser which I touched, but something carved, as nearly as I could discover with my unskilled finger-tips, with winged things.

There were certainly long keen curves of wings which seemed to overlay an arabesque of fine leaf and flower work. I do not know what the object was that I touched. It may have been a chest. I may seem to be exaggerating when I say that it somehow failed or exceeded in some mysterious respect of being the shape of anything I had ever touched. I do not know what the material was. It was as smooth as ivory, but it did not feel like ivory; there was a singular warmth about it, as if it had stood long in hot sunlight. I continued, and I encountered other objects I am inclined to think were pieces of furniture of fashions and possibly of uses unknown to me, and about them all was the strange mystery as to shape. At last I came to what was evidently an open window of large area. I distinctly felt a soft, warm wind, yet with a crystal freshness, blow on my face. It was not the window of my hall bedroom, that I know. Looking out, I could see nothing. I only felt the wind blowing on my face.

Then suddenly, without any warning, my groping hands to the right and left touched living beings, beings in the likeness of men and women, palpable creatures in palpable attire. I could feel the soft silken texture of their garments which swept around me, seeming to half enfold me in clinging meshes like cobwebs. I was in a crowd of these people, whatever they were, and whoever they were, but, curiously enough, without seeing one of them I had a strong sense of recognition as I passed among them. Now and then a hand that I knew closed softly over mine; once an arm passed around me. Then I began to feel myself gently swept on and impelled by this softly moving throng; their floating garments seemed to fairly wind me about, and again a swift terror overcame me. I struck my match, and was back in my hall bedroom. I wonder if I had not better keep my gas burning tonight? I wonder if it be possible that this is going too far? I wonder what became of those other people, the man and the woman who occupied this room? I wonder if I had better not stop where I am?

January 31. Last night I saw—I saw more than I can describe, more than is lawful to describe. Something which nature has rightly hidden has been revealed to me, but it is not for me to disclose too much of her secret. This much I will say, that doors and windows open into an out-of-doors to which the outdoors which we know is but a vestibule. And there is a river; there is something strange with respect to that picture. There is a river upon which one could sail away. It was flowing silently, for tonight I could only see. I saw that I was right in thinking I recognized some of the people whom I encountered the night before, though some were strange to me. It is true that the girl who disappeared from the hall bedroom was very beautiful. Everything which I saw last night was very beautiful to my one sense that could grasp it. I wonder what it would all be if all my senses together were to grasp it? I wonder if I had better not keep my gas burning tonight? I wonder—

★★★★★★

This finishes the journal which Mr. Wheatcroft left in his hall bedroom. The morning after the last entry he was gone. His friend, Mr. Addison, came here, and a search was made. They even tore down the wall behind the picture, and they did find something rather queer for a house that had been used for boarders, where you would think no room would have been let run to waste. They found another room, a long narrow one, the length of the hall bedroom, but narrower, hardly more than a closet. There was no window, nor door, and all there was in it was a sheet of paper covered with figures, as if somebody had been doing sums.

They made a lot of talk about those figures, and they tried to make out that the fifth dimension, whatever that is, was proved, but they said afterward they didn't prove anything. They tried to make out then that somebody had murdered poor Mr. Wheatcroft and hid the body, and they arrested poor Mr. Addison, but they couldn't make out anything against him. They proved he was in the Cure all that night and couldn't have done it. They don't know what became of Mr. Wheatcroft, and now they say two more disappeared from that same room before I rented the house.

The agent came and promised to put the new room they discovered into the hall bedroom and have everything new-papered and painted. He took away the picture; folks hinted there was something queer about that, I don't know what. It looked innocent enough, and I guess he burned it up. He said if I would stay he would arrange it with the owner, who everybody says is a very queer man, so I should not have to pay much if any rent. But I told him I couldn't stay if he was to give me the rent. That I wasn't afraid of anything myself, though I must say I wouldn't want to put anybody in that hall bedroom without telling him all about it; but my boarders would leave, and I knew I couldn't get any more. I told him I would rather have had a regular ghost than what seemed to be a way of going out of the house to nowhere and never coming back again. I moved, and, as I said before, it remains to be seen whether my ill luck follows me to this house or not. Anyway, it has no hall bedroom.

Seventoes' Ghost

"You needn't waste any more time talkin' about it, Benjamin; you can jest take that puppy-dog and carry him off. I don't care what you do with him; you can carry him back where you got him, or give him away, or swap him off; but jest as sure as you leave him here half an hour longer, I'll call Jimmy up from the hay field and have him shoot him. I won't have a dog round the place, nohow. Couldn't keep Seventoes a minute; he's dreadful scart of dogs."

"Grandsir—"

"Take that puppy-dog and go along, I tell ye. I won't have any more talk about it."

Benjamin Wellman, small and slight, sandy-haired and blue-eyed, stood before his grandfather, who sat in his big armchair in the east door. Benjamin held in his right hand an old rope, which was attached to a leather strap around a puppy's neck. The puppy pulled at the rope, keeping it taut all the time. He also yelped shrilly. He did not like to be tied. The puppy was not a pretty one, being yellow and very clumsy; but Benjamin thought him a beauty. He had urged to his grandfather that there would not be a dog to equal him in the neighbourhood when he was grown up, but the old man had not been moved.

There were tears in Benjamin's pretty blue eyes, but his square chin looked squarer. He tried to speak again. "Grandsir —" he began.

"Not another word," said his grandfather.

Benjamin looked past his grandfather into the kitchen. His

mother sat in there stemming currants. He went around to the other door and entered, dragging the puppy after him.

"Mother," he said, in a low voice, "can't I keep him?"

His grandfather in the east door looked around suspiciously, but he could hear nothing; he was somewhat deaf.

"No; not if your grandfather don't want you to," said his mother; "you know I can't let you, Benjamin."

The puppy was whining piteously, and Benjamin seemed to echo it when he spoke. "I don't see why he don't want me to. It ain't as if Cæsar was a common puppy. You ask him, mother."

"No," returned his mother; "it won't do any good. You know how much he thinks of Seventoes, and the dog might kill him when he was grown."

"Wouldn't care if he did," muttered Benjamin; "nothing but a cross old stealing cat; don't begin to be worth what this puppy is."

"Now, Benjamin, you mustn't talk any more about it," said his mother, severely. "Grandsir does too much for you and me for you to make any fuss about a thing like this. Take that puppy and run right along with it, as he tells you to."

Grandsir's suspicions suddenly took shape then. "Benjamin, you run right along," he called out; "don't stand there teasing your mother about it."

So Benjamin gathered the puppy up into his arms with a jerk—it was impossible to lead him any distance—and plunged out of the house. He gave two or three little choking sobs as he hurried along. It was a hot day, and he was tired and disappointed and discouraged. He had walked three miles over to the village and back to get that puppy, and now he had to walk a mile more to give it away. He had no doubt whatever as to the disposal of it; he knew Sammy Tucker would give it a hearty welcome, for there was an understanding to that effect. Benjamin had been a little doubtful as to the reception the puppy might have from his grandfather; but when Mr. Dyer, who kept the village grocery store, had offered it to him three weeks before, he had not had the courage to refuse. Sammy Tucker, too, had been in the store,

buying three bars of soap for his mother, and he had looked on
admiringly and enviously. When Benjamin had mentioned hesitatingly his doubts about his grandfather, Sammy had pricked
up his ears.

"Say, Ben, you give him to me if your grandfather won't let
you keep him," he had whispered, with a nudge. "Father said I
might have a dog soon as there was a good chance, and Mr. Dyer
won't want it back. He's giv away all but this, and he wants to
get rid of 'em. They're common kind of dogs, anyhow. I heard
him say so."

Benjamin had looked at him stiffly. "Oh, I guess grandsir'll
let me keep this puppy, he's such a smart one," he had answered,
with dignity.

"Well, you ask him, and if he won't, I'll take him," said Sammy.

But Benjamin had not asked his grandfather. He had not
had courage to run the risk. He had waited the three weeks
which the store-keeper had said must elapse before the little
dog could leave its mother, and then had gone over to the village and brought it home, without a word to any one, trusting
to the puppy's own attractions to plead for it. It had seemed to
Benjamin that nobody could resist that puppy. But Grandfather
Wellman had all his life preferred cats to dogs, and now he was
childishly fond of Seventoes. Benjamin's mother often said that
she didn't know what grandsir would do if anything happened
to Seventoes.

Benjamin, going out of the yard with the puppy under his
arm, could see Seventoes sitting on the shed roof. That and the
ledge of the old well behind the barn were his favourite perches.
Grandfather Wellman thought he chose them because he was so
afraid of dogs. Benjamin looked at him, and wished Cæsar was
big enough to shake him. He had named the puppy Cæsar on
his way home from the village. There was a great mastiff over
there by the same name. Benjamin had always admired this big
Cæsar, and now thought he would name his dog after him. It
was the same principle reduced on which Benjamin himself had

been named after Benjamin Franklin.

Benjamin trudged down the road, kicking up the dust with his toes. That was something he had been told not to do, so now in this state of mind he liked to do it. The sun beat down fiercely upon his small red cropped head in the burned straw hat, and his slender shoulders in the calico blouse. The puppy was large and fat for his age, and made his arms ache. The stone walls on both sides of the road were hidden with wild-rose and mead-owsweet bushes; the fields were dotted with hay-makers; now and then a loaded hay-cart loomed up in the road. Many boys no older than Benjamin had to work hard in the hay fields, but Grandfather Wellman was too careful of him; he would not let him work much in vacation; he had never been considered very strong. But Benjamin did not think of that. One grievance will outweigh a hundred benefits. He hugged the struggling puppy tight in his arms and trudged on painfully, brooding over his wrongs.

He muttered to himself as he went, "Wanted a dog ever since I was born. All the other boys have got 'em. 'Ain't never had nothing but an old cat. Sha'n't never have a chance to get such a dog as this again. Wish something would happen to that old cat; shouldn't care a mite." He stubbed more fiercely into the dust, and it flew higher; a squirrel ran across the road, and he looked at it with an indifferent scowl.

When he reached Sammy Tucker's house he saw Sammy out in the great north yard raking hay with his father. Sammy looked up and saw Benjamin coming.

"Hullo!" he sang out, eagerly. Then he dropped his rake and raced into the road. His black eyes winked fast with excitement. "Say, won't he let you keep him, Ben?" he cried.

"No; he won't let me keep nothing."

"Going to let me have him, then?"

"S'pose so."

Sammy reached forth his eager hands, and took the kicking puppy from Benjamin's reluctant arms. "Nice fellar—nice little fellar," said he, tenderly.

"I've named him Cæsar," said Benjamin.

"That's a good name," assented Sammy. "Hi, Cæsar! Hi, sir!"

Sammy's father came smilingly forward to the fence; he was fond of dogs. He also took the puppy, and talked to it. Benjamin thought to himself that he wished his grandfather was more like Sammy's father. He looked on gloomily.

"Hate to give it up, don't you, Ben?" said Mr. Tucker, kindly.

"Sha'n't never have such a chance again."

"Oh yes, you will; your grandfather'll let you have a dog sometime."

"No; he won't never let me have nothing."

"Oh, don't you give up yet, Ben."

Benjamin shook his head like a discouraged old man, and turned to go home.

"Sammy'll feed him, and take real good care of him, and you can come over here and see him," Mr. Tucker called after him, as he went down the road.

Benjamin thought to himself that he should not want to, as he marched wearily homeward. His arms were lightened of the puppy, but his heart seemed heavy within him. Two boys whom he knew sang out to him from a load of hay, but he gave only a grim nod in response. "*They've* got a dog," he muttered; and indeed the pretty shepherd dog was following after the load.

Benjamin, when he came in sight of home, thought he would take a short-cut through the orchard. He meditated stealing up the back stairs to his chamber, staying up there, and saying that he did not want any supper; he was not hungry. They had not cut the grass in the orchard, and he plunged through clover, feathery grass, and daisies to his waist. He felt pleased to think how he was making a furrow through his grandfather's hay. He emerged from the orchard, and went on toward the barn; directly back of it was the old well. When he reached that he stopped short. There was Seventoes—beautiful great yellow cat—stretched in the sun, all his wonderful seven-toed paws spread out. The ledge of the old well was a strange place for a cat, but Seventoes was fond of it, and staid there much of the time when he was not on the shed roof.

Benjamin walked close to the well and looked at Seventoes. His small face was burning red with the heat; his blue eyes gleamed angrily. "You lazy old cat," said he. He stood a second longer; then he thrust out his right hand and gave Seventoes a push. There was a piteous yawl and a great clawing, and Seventoes was out of sight. Benjamin ran. He gasped; a white streak was settling around his mouth. He was well versed in Bible stories, and he thought of Cain. What had he done? What would happen to him? Could he ever get away from his guilt, run fast as he would? Benjamin ran as he had never run before, his heart pounding, although he did not know clearly what he was running for. He tore around the barn, through the pasture bars, towards the house. When he came in sight of the shed a great qualm of guilt and remorse forced him to glance up at the place where poor Seventoes had so loved to sit, and where he would sit no more. Benjamin glanced, then he stood stock-still, fairly aghast with awe and terror—*there sat Seventoes!*

All the red faded out of Benjamin's cheeks. He had never been encouraged in superstitious beliefs, but he was an imaginative child, and just now bewildered and unstrung. He stared at the shed roof. Yes! he saw Seventoes there, and Seventoes was at the bottom of the old well. Had he not seen him fall, clawing, down?

Benjamin rushed staggering into the kitchen. "Oh, grandsir! oh, mother!" he wailed—"oh, I've pushed Seventoes into the old well and drowned him, and his ghost's sitting on the shed roof! Oh, mother!"

Grandfather Wellman was confined to his chair with rheumatism, but he arose. "Pushed Seventoes into the well," he repeated, while Benjamin's mother turned as pale as her son.

"I have—I have," sobbed Benjamin. "I didn't know I was going to, but I have. And he's in the well, and he's sitting on the shed roof too. Oh!"

"What do you mean?" his mother gasped. "Stop acting so, and tell me what you've done."

475

"I pushed Seventoes into the old well. I didn't know I was going to, but I did; and he's dead in there and he's on the shed roof. Oh, mother!"

"You 'ain't pushed that cat into the well?" groaned Grandfather Wellman. "If you have —" He was trying to limp across the kitchen with his cane. He too was pale, and trembling from head to foot. "Hannah," he said to Benjamin's mother, "you come right along quick, and see if we can't get him out. I wouldn't take a hundred dollars for that cat."

Benjamin's mother started. Benjamin, sobbing and trembling, was clinging to her. Just then *Seventoes walked in through the east door*, his splendid ringed tail waving a little uneasily, but not a hair of him was hurt. A frightened cat can run faster than a guilty little boy, and Seventoes had found his unusual number of claws of good service in climbing a well and retarding his progress toward the bottom.

They all looked.

"Is it—Seventoes?" gasped Benjamin, with wild eyes.

"Of course it's Seventoes," growled his grandfather. "I'd like to know what you've been cutting up so for. Pussy, pussy, pussy."

Benjamin's mother took him over to the sink, and put some water on his head and made him drink some. "There's no such thing as a ghost, and you're acting very silly," said she; "but I don't wonder you are scared, when you've done such a dreadful thing. It scares me to think of it. It was 'most as bad as killing somebody. I never thought a boy of mine would do such a thing. Grandsir good as he is to you, too."

"I—won't ever do so—again," sobbed Benjamin, all trembling. "I'm sorry; I *am* sorry."

Benjamin was not whipped, the scourging of his own conscience had been severe enough, but he sat pale and sober in the kitchen, while grandsir, with Seventoes on his knees, and his mother talked to him.

"If you ever do anything like this again, Benjamin," said his grandfather, "I shall be ha'sh with you, ha'sher than I've ever been, and you must remember it."

"I guess he must," said his mother. "It was a dreadful wicked thing, and he should be punished now if I didn't think he'd suffered enough from his own guilty conscience for this time, and would never as long as he lived do such a terrible thing again."

"I won't—I—won't!" choked Benjamin.

At supper-time, when the new milk was brought in from the barn, Benjamin filled a saucer with it and carried it to the door for Seventoes. He filled it so full that he spilled it all the way over the clean kitchen floor, but his mother said nothing. Seventoes lapped his milk happily; Benjamin, with his little contrite, tearstained face, stood watching him, and grandsir sat in his armchair. Over in the fields the hay-makers were pitching the last loads into the carts; the east sky was red with the reflected colour of the west. Everything was sweet and cool and peaceful, and the sun was not going down on Benjamin's childish wrath. His grandfather put out his hand and patted his little red cropped head, "You're always going to be a good boy after this, ain't you, sonny?"

"Yes, sir," said Benjamin, and he got down on his knees and hugged Seventoes.

Giles Corey, Yeoman
A Play

CAST OF CHARACTERS.

Giles Corey.

Paul Bayley, *Olive Corey's lover.*

Samuel Parris, *minister in Salem Village.*

John Hathorne, *magistrate.*

Jonathan Corwin, *magistrate.*

Olive Corey, *Giles Corey's daughter.*

Martha Corey, *Giles Corey's wife.*

Ann Hutchins, *Olive's friend and one of the Afflicted Girls.*

Widow Eunice Hutchins, *Ann's mother.*

Phœbe Morse, *little orphan girl, niece to Martha Corey.*

Mercy Lewis, *one of the Afflicted Girls.*

Nancy Fox, *an old serving-woman in Giles Corey's house.*

Afflicted Girls, Constables, Marshal, People of Salem Village, Messengers, etc.

ACT 1.

Scene 1.—*Salem Village. Living-room in* Giles Corey's *house.* Olive Corey *is spinning.* Nancy Fox, *the old servant, sits in the fireplace paring apples. Little* Phœbe Morse, *on a stool beside her, is knitting a stocking.*

Phœbe (starting). What is that? Oh, Olive, what is that?

Nancy. Yes, what is that? Massy, what a clatter!

Olive (spinning). I heard naught. Be not so foolish, child. And you, Nancy, be of a surety old enough to know better.

Nancy. I trow there was a clatter in the chimbly. There 'tis again! Massy, what a screech!

Phœbe (*running to* Olive *and clinging to her*). Oh, Olive, what is it? what is it? Don't let it catch me. Oh, Olive!

Olive. I tell you 'twas naught.

Nancy. Them that won't hear be deafer than them that's born so. Massy, what a screech!

Phœbe. Oh, Olive, Olive! Don't let 'em catch me!

Olive. Nobody wants to catch you. Be quiet now, and I'll sing to you. Then you won't think you hear screeches.

Nancy. We won't, hey?

Olive. Be quiet! This folly hath gone too far. (*Sings spinning song.*)

SPINNING SONG.

I'll tell you a story; a story of one,
'Twas of a great prince whose name was King John.
A great prince was he, and a man of great might
In putting down wrong and in setting up right.
To my down, down, down, derry down.

Nancy. Massy, what screeches! (*Screams violently.*)

Phœbe. Oh, Nancy, 'twas you screeched then.

Nancy. It wasn't me; 'twas a witch in the chimbly. (*Screams again.*) There, hear that, will ye? I tell ye 'twa'n't me. I 'ain't opened my mouth.

Olive. Nancy, I will bear no more of this. If you be not quiet, I will tell my mother when she comes home. Now, Phœbe, sing the rest of the song with me, and think no more of such folly. (*Sings with* Phœbe.)

This king, being a mind to make himself merry,
He sent for the Bishop of Canterbury.
'Good-morning, Mr. Bishop,' the king did say.
'Have you come here for to live or to die?'
To my down, down, down, derry down.

'For if you can't answer to my questions three,
Your head shall be taken from your body;

479

And if you can't answer unto them all right,
Your head shall be taken from your body quite.'
To my down, down, down, derry down.

Nancy (*wagging her head in time to the music*). I know some words that go better with that tune.

Phœbe. What are they?

Nancy. Oh, I'm forbid to tell.

Phœbe. Who forbade you to tell, Nancy?

Nancy. The one who forbade me to tell, forbade me to tell who told me.

Olive. Don't gossip, or you won't get your stints done before mother comes home.

Phœbe (*sulkily*). I won't finish my stint. Aunt Corey set me too long a stint. I won't. Oh, there she is now! (*Knits busily*).

Enter Ann Hutchins.

Olive (*rising*). Well done, Ann. I was but now wishing to see you. Sit you down and lay off your cloak. Why, how pale you look, Ann! Are you sick?

Ann. You know best.

Olive. I? Why, what mean you, Ann?

Ann. You know what I mean, in spite of your innocent looks. Oh, open your eyes wide at me, if you want to! Perhaps you don't know what makes them bigger and bluer than they used to be.

Olive. Ann!

Ann. Oh, I mean nothing. I am not sick. Something frightened me as I came through the wood.

Olive. Frightened you! Why, what was it?

Phœbe. Oh, what was it, Ann?

Ann. I know not; something black that hustled quickly by me and raised a cold wind.

Phœbe. Oh, oh!

Olive. 'Twas a cat or a dog, and your own fear raised the cold wind. Think no more of it, Ann. Wait a moment while I go to the north room. I have something to show you. (*Exit* Olive *with a candle.*)

Phœbe. What said the black thing to you, Ann?

Ann. I know not.

Nancy. Said it not: "Serve me; serve me?"

Ann. I know not. I was deaf with fear.

Phœbe. Oh, Ann, did it have horns?

Ann. I tell you I know not. You pester me, child.

Phœbe. Did it have hoofs and a tail?

Ann. Be quiet, I tell you, or I'll cuff your ears.

Nancy. She needn't be so topping. It will be laying in wait for her when she goes home. I'll warrant it won't let her off so easy.

> Enter Olive, *bringing an embroidered muslin cape.*
> *She puts it gently over* Ann's *shoulders.*

Ann (*throwing it off violently*). Oh! oh! Take it away! take it away!

Olive. Why, Ann, what ails you?

Ann. Take it away, I say! What mean you by your cursed arts?

Olive. Why, Ann! I have been saving a long time to buy it for you. 'Tis like my last summer's cape that you fancied so much. I sent by father to Boston for it.

Ann. I need it not.

Olive. I thought 'twould suit well with your green gown.

Ann. 'Twill suit well enough with a green gown, but not with a sore heart.

Nancy. I miss my guess but it 'll suit well enough with her heart too. I trow that's as green as her gown; green's the jealous colour.

Olive. You be all unstrung by your walk hither through the wood, Ann. I'll fold the cape up nicely for you, and you can take it when you go home. And mind you wear it next Sabbath day, sweet. Now I must to my wheel again, or I shall not finish my stint by nine o'clock.

Ann. Your looks show that you were up later than nine o'clock last night.

Phœbe. Oh, Ann, did you see the light in the fore room?

Ann. That did I. I stood at my chamber and saw it shine through the wood.

Nancy. You couldn't see so far without spectacles.

Ann. It blinded me. I could get no sleep.

Nancy. You think your eyes are mighty sharp. Maybe your ears are too? Maybe you heard 'em kissing at the door when he went home?

Olive. Nancy, be quiet!

Nancy. You needn't colour up and shake your head at me, Olive. They stood kissing there nigh an hour, and he with his arm round her waist, and she with hers round his neck. They'd kiss, then they'd eye each other and kiss again. I know I woke up and thought 'twas Injuns, and I peeked out of my chamber window. Such doings! You'd ought to have seen 'em, Ann.

Phœbe. Oh, Nancy, why didn't you wake me up?

Olive. Nancy, I'll have no more of this.

Nancy. That's what she ought to have said last night—hadn't she, Ann? But she didn't. Oh, I'll warrant she didn't! I know you would, Ann.

Olive. Nancy! (*A noise is heard outside*).

Phœbe. Oh, what's that noise? What is coming?

Enter Giles Corey, *panting.*
He flings the door to violently and slips the bolt.

Nancy. Massy! what's after ye?

Phœbe. Oh, Uncle Corey, what's the matter?

Giles. The matter is there be too many evil things abroad nowadays for a man to be out after nightfall. When things that can be hit by musket balls lay in wait, old Giles Corey is as brave as any man; but when it comes to devilish black beasts and black men that musket balls bound back from—What! you here, Ann Hutchins? What be you out after dark for?

Ann. I came over to see Olive, Goodman Corey.

Giles. You'd best stayed by your own hearth if you've got one. Young women have no call to be out gadding after dark in these times.

Phœbe. Oh, Uncle Corey, something did frighten Ann as she came through the wood. A black beast, with horns and a tail and eyes like balls of fire, jumped out of the bushes at her, and bade her sign the book in a dreadful voice.

Giles. What! Was't so, Ann?

Ann. I know not. There was something.

Olive (laughing). 'Twas naught but Ann's own shadow that her fear gave a voice and a touch to. Say naught to frighten Ann, father; she is the most timorous maid in Salem Village now.

Giles. There is some wisdom in fear nowadays. You make too light of it, lass.

Olive (laughing). Nay, father, I'll turn to and hang up my own shadow in the chimbly-place for a witch, an you say so.

Giles. This be no subject for jest. Said you the black beast spoke to you, Ann?

Ann. I know not. Once I thought I heard Olive calling. I know not what I heard.

Giles. You'd best have stayed at home. Where is your mother, Olive?

Olive. She has gone to Goodwife Bishop's with a basket of eggs.

Giles. Gone three miles to Goodwife Bishop's this time of night? Is the woman gone out of her senses?

Olive. She is not afraid.

Giles. I'll warrant she is not afraid. So much the worse for her. Mayhap she's gone riding on a broomstick herself. How is the cat?

Olive. She is better.

Giles. She was taken strangely, if your mother did make light of it. And the ox, hath he fell down again?

Olive. Not that I have heard.

Giles. The ox was taken strangely, if your mother did pooh at it. The ox was better when she went out of the yard.

Phœbe. There's Aunt Corey now. Who is she talking to?

Enter Martha Corey.

Phœbe. Who were you talking to, Aunt Corey?

Martha. Nobody, child. Good-evening, Ann.

Phœbe. I heard you talking to somebody, Aunt Corey.

Martha. Be quiet, child. I was talking to nobody. You hear too much nowadays. (*Takes off her cloak.*)

Nancy. Mayhap she hears more than folk want her to. I heard a voice too, a gruff voice like a pig's.

Giles. I thought I heard talking too. Who was it, Martha?

Martha. I tell you 'twas no one. Are you all out of your wits? (*Gets some knitting-work out of a cupboard and seats herself.*)

Phœbe. Weren't you afraid coming through the wood, Aunt Corey?

Martha (*laughing*). Afraid? Why, no, child. Of what should I be afraid?

Giles. I trow there's plenty to be afraid of. How did you get home so quick? 'Tis a good three miles to Goody Bishop's.

Martha. I walked at a good speed.

Giles. I thought perhaps you galloped a broomstick.

Martha. Nay, Goodman, I know not how to manage such a strange steed.

Giles. I thought perhaps one had taught you, inasmuch as you have naught to say against the gentry that ride the broomstick of a night.

Martha. Fill not the child's head with such folly. How fares your mother, Ann?

Ann. Well, Goodwife Corey.

Giles. She lacks sense, or she would have kept her daughter at home. Out after nightfall, and the woods full of the devil knoweth what.

Martha. Nay, goodman, there be no danger. The scouts are in the fields.

Giles. I meant not Injuns. There be worse than Injuns. There be evil things and witches!

Martha (*laughing*). Witches! Goodman, you are a worse child than Phœbe here.

Giles. I tell ye, wife, you talk like a fool, ranting thus against witches. I would you had been where I have been tonight, and heard the afflicted maids cry out in torment, being set upon by Sarah Good and Sarah Osborn. I would you had seen Mercy Lewis strangled almost to death, and the others testifying 'twas Sarah Good thus afflicting her. But I'll warrant you'd not have believed them.

Martha (laughing). That I would not, Goodman. I would have said that the maids should be sent home and soundly trounced, then put to bed, with a quart bowl of sage tea apiece.

Giles. Talk so if you will. One of these days folk will say you be a witch yourself. You were ever hard-skulled, and could knock your head long against a truth without being pricked by it. Hold out if you can, when only this morning the ox and the cat were took so strangely here in our own household.

Martha. Shame on you, Goodman! The ox and the cat themselves would laugh at you. The cat ate a rat, and it did not set well on her stomach, and the ox slipped in the mire in the yard.

Nancy. 'Twas more than that. I know, I know.

Giles. Laugh if you will, wife. Mayhap you know more about it than other folk. You never could abide the cat. I am going to bed, if I can first go to prayer. Last night the words went from me strangely! But you will laugh at that. (*Lights a candle. Exit.*)

Phœbe. Aunt Corey, may I eat an apple?

Martha. Not tonight. 'Twill give you the nightmare.

Phœbe. No, 'twill not.

Martha. Be still!

There is a knock. Olive *opens the door. Enter* Paul Bayley. Ann *starts up.*

Paul. Good-evening, goodwife. Good-evening, Olive. Good-evening, Ann. 'Tis a fine night out.

Ann. I must be going; 'tis late.

Olive. Nay, Ann, 'tis not late. Wait, and Paul will go home with you through the wood.

Ann. I must be going.

Paul (hesitatingly). Then let me go with you, Mistress Ann! I can well do my errand here later.

Ann. Nay, I can wait whilst you do the errand, if you are

speedy. I fear lest the delay would make you ill at ease.

Martha (*quickly*). There is no need, Paul. I will go with Ann. I want to borrow a hood pattern of Goodwife Nourse on the way.

Paul. But will you not be afraid, goodwife?

Martha. Afraid, and the moon at a good half, and only a short way to go?

Paul. But you have to go through the wood.

Martha. The wood! A stretch as long as this room—six ash-trees, one butternut, and a birch sapling thrown in for a witch spectre. Say no more, Paul. Sit you down and keep Olive company. I will go, if only for the sake of showing these silly little hussies that there is no call for a gospel woman with prayer in her heart to be afraid of anything but the wrath of God. (*Puts a blanket over her head.*)

Ann. I want no company at all, Goodwife Corey.

Phœbe. Aunt Corey, let me go, too; my stint is done.

Martha. Nay, you must to bed, and Nancy too. Off with ye, and no words.

Nancy. I'm none so old that I must needs be sent to bed like a babe, I'd have you know that, Goody Corey. (*Sets away apple pan; exit, with* Phœbe *following sulkily.*)

Martha. Come, Ann.

Ann. I want no company. I have more fear with company than I have alone.

Martha. Along with you, child.

Olive. Oh, Ann, you are forgetting your cape. Here, mother, you carry it for her. Goodnight, sweetheart.

Ann. I want no company, Goodwife Corey. (Martha *takes her laughingly by the arm and leads her out.*)

Paul. It is a fine night out.

Olive. So I have heard.

Paul. You make a jest of me, Mistress Olive. Know you not when a man is of a sudden left alone with a fair maid, he needs to try his speech like a player his fiddle, to see if it be in good tune for her ears; and what better way than to sound over and over again the praise of the fine weather? What ailed Ann that she seemed so strangely, Olive?

Olive. I know not. I think she had been overwrought by coming alone through the woods.

Paul. She seemed ill at ease. Why spin you so steadily, Olive?

Olive. I must finish my stint.

Paul. Who set you a stint as if you were a child?

Olive. Mine own conscience, to which I will ever be a child.

Paul. Cease spinning, sweetheart.

Olive. Nay.

Paul. Come over here on the settle, there is something I would tell thee.

Olive. Tell it, then. I can hear a distance of three feet or so.

Paul. I know thou canst, but come.

Olive. Nay, I will not. This is no courting night. I cannot idle every night in the week.

Paul. Thou wouldst make a new commandment. A maid shall spin flax every night in the week save the Sabbath, when she shall lay aside her work and be courted. There be young men here in Salem Village, though you may credit it not, Olive, who visit their maids twice every week, and have the fire in the fore room kindled.

Olive. My mother thinks it not well that I should sit up oftener than once a week, nor do I; but be not vexed by it, Paul.

Paul. I love thee better for it, sweetheart.

Olive. My stint is done.

Paul. Then come. (*She obeys.*) Now for the news. This morning I bought of Goodman Nourse his nine-acre lot for a homestead. What thinkest thou of that?

Olive. It is a pleasant spot.

Paul. 'Tis not far from here, and thou wilt be near thy mother.

Olive. Was it not too costly?

Paul. I had saved enough to pay for it, and in another year's time, and I have the help of God in it, I shall have saved enough for our house. What thinkest thou of a gambrel-roof and a lean-to, two square front rooms, both fire-rooms, and a living-room? And peonies and hollyhocks in the front yard, and two popple-trees, one on each side of the gate?

Olive. We shall need not a lean-to, Paul, and one fire-room will serve us well; but I will have laylocks and red and white roses as well as peonies and hollyhocks in the front yard, and some mint under the windows to make the house smell sweet; and I like well the popple-trees at the gate.

Paul. The house shall be built of fairly seasoned yellow pine wood, with a summer tree in every room, and fine panel-work in the doors and around the chimbleys.

Olive. Nay, Paul, not too fine panel-work; 'twill cost too high.

Paul. Cupboards in every room, and fine-laid white floors.

Olive. We need a cupboard in the living-room only, but I have learned to sand a floor in a rare pattern. (Paul *attempts to embrace* Olive. *She repulses him.*)

Paul. I trow you are full provident of favours and pence, Olive.

Olive. I would save them for thee, Paul.

Paul. And thou shalt not be hindered by me to any harm, sweetheart. Was't thy mother taught thee such wisdom, or thine own self, Olive?

Olive. 'Twas my mother.

Paul. Nay, 'twas thine own heart; that shall teach me, too. (*Nine-o'clock bell rings.*)

Olive. Oh, 'tis nine o'clock, and 'tis not a courting night. Paul, be off; thou must! (*They jump up and go to the door*).

Paul (*putting his arm around* Olive). Give me but one kiss, Olive, albeit not a courting night, for good speed on my homeward walk and my tomorrow's journey.

Olive. Where go you tomorrow, Paul?

Paul. To Boston, for a week's time or more.

Olive. Oh, Paul, there may be Injuns on the Boston path! Thou wilt be wary?

Paul (*laughing*). Have no fear for me, sweetheart. I shall have my musket.

Olive. A week?

Paul. 'Tis a short time, but long enough to need sweetening with a kiss when folk are absent from one another.

Olive (kisses him). Oh, be careful, Paul!

Paul. Fear not for me, sweetheart, but do thou too be careful, for sometimes danger sneaks at home, when we flee it abroad. Keep away from this witchcraft folly. Goodbye, sweetheart. (*They part.* Olive *sets a candle in the window after* Paul's *exit. Nine-o'clock bell still rings as curtain falls.*)

Scene 2.—*Twelve o'clock at night. Living-room at* Giles Corey's *house, lighted only by the moon and low fire-light. Enter* Nancy Fox *with a candle,* Phœbe *following with a large rag doll.* Nancy *sets the candle on the dresser.*

Nancy. Be ye sure that Goody Corey is asleep, and Goodman Corey?

Phœbe (dances across to the door, which she opens slightly, and listens). They be both a-snoring. Hasten and begin, I pray you, Nancy.

Nancy. And Olive?

Phœbe. She is asleep, and she is in the south chamber, and could not hear were she awake. Here is my doll. Now show me how to be a witch. Quick, Nancy!

Nancy. Whom do you desire to afflict?

Phœbe (considers). Let me see. I will afflict Uncle Corey, because he brought me naught from Boston today; Olive, because she gave that cape to Ann instead of me; and Aunt Corey, because she set me such a long stint, because she would not let me eat an apple tonight, and because she sent me to bed. I want to stick one pin into Uncle Corey, one into Olive, and three into Aunt Corey.

Nancy. Take the doll, prick it as you will, and say who the pricks be for. (Phœbe *sticks a pin into the doll.*)

Phœbe. This pin be for Uncle Corey, and this pin be for Olive, and this pin for Aunt Corey, and this pin for Aunt Corey, and this pin for Aunt Corey. Pins! pins!! pins!!! (*Dances.*) In truth, Nancy,

489

'tis rare sport being a witch; but I stuck not in the pins very far, lest they be too sorely hurt.

Nancy. Is there any other whom you desire to afflict?

Phœbe. I fear I know not any other who has angered me, and I could weep for 't. Stay! I'll afflict Ann, because she hath the cape; and I'll afflict Paul Bayley, because I'm drove forth from the fore room Sabbath nights when he comes a-courting; and I'll afflict Minister Parris, because he put me too hard a question from the catechism; that makes three more. Oh, 'tis rare sport! (*Seizes the doll and sticks in three pins.*) This pin be for Ann, this pin be for Paul, and this pin be for Minister Parris. Deary me, I can think of no more! What next, Nancy?

Nancy. I'll do some witchcraft now. I desire to afflict your aunt Corey, because she doth drive me hither and thither like a child, and sets no value on my understanding; Olive, because she made a jest of me; and Goody Bishop, because she hath a fine silk hood.

Phœbe. Here is the doll, Nancy.

Nancy. Nay, I have another way, which you be too young to understand. (Nancy *takes the candle, goes to the fireplace, and courtesies three times, looking up the chimney.*)

Nancy. Hey, black cat! hey, my pretty black cat! Go ye and sit on Goody Corey's breast, and claw her if she stirs. Do as I bid ye, my pretty black cat, and I'll sign the book.

Phœbe. Oh, Nancy, I hear the black cat yawl!

Nancy (*after curtseying three times*). Hey, black dog! hey, my pretty black dog! Go ye and howl in Mistress Olive's ear, so she be frighted in her dreams, and so get a little bitter with the sweet. Do as I bid ye, my pretty black dog, and I'll sign the book.

Phœbe. Oh, Nancy, I hear the black dog howl!

Nancy (*after curtseying three times*). Hey, yellow bird! hey, my pretty yellow bird! Go ye and peck at Goody Bishop's fine silk hood and tear it to bits. Do as I bid ye, my pretty yellow bird, and I'll sign the book.

Phœbe. Oh, Nancy, I hear the yellow bird twitter up chimbly!

Nancy. 'Tis rare witchcraft.

Phœbe. Is that all, Nancy?

Nancy. All of this sort. I've given them all they can do to-night.

Phœbe. Then sing the witch song, Nancy.

Nancy. I'll sing the witch song, and you can dance on the table.

Phœbe. But 'tis sinful to dance, Nancy!

Nancy. 'Tis not sinful for a witch.

Phœbe. True; I forgot I was a witch. (*Gets upon the table and dances, dangling her doll, while* Nancy *sings.*)

WITCH SONG.

(Same air as Spinning Song.)

I'll tell you a story, a story of one;
'Twas of a dark witch, and the wizard her son.
A dark witch was she, and a dark wizard he,
With yellow birds singing so gay and so free.
To my down, down, down, derry down.

The clock was a-striking, a-striking of one.
The witches came out, and the dancing begun.
They courtesied so fine, and they drank the red wine—
The wizards were three and the witches were nine.
To my down, down, down, derry down.

Halloo, the gay dancers! Halloo, I was one;
The goody that prayed and the maiden that spun!
The yellow birds chirped in the boughs overhead,
And fast through the bushes the black dog sped.
To my down, down, down, derry down.

(*A noise is heard.* Phœbe *jumps down from the table.*)

Phœbe. Oh, Nancy, something's coming! Run, run quick, or it'll catch us! (*Both run out. Curtain falls.*)

ACT 2

Best room in the house of Widow Eunice Hutchins, Ann's *mother.* John Hathorne *and* Minister Parris *enter, shown in by* Widow

Hutchins.

Hutchins. I pray you, sirs, to take some cheers the while I go for a moment's space to my poor afflicted child. I heard her cry out but now. (*Exit.*)

(Hathorne *and* Parris *seat themselves,*
but Hathorne *quickly springs up, and begins walking.*)

Hathorne. I cannot be seated in this crisis. I would as lief be seated in an onset of the savages. I must up and lay about me. We have heretofore been too lax in this dreadful business; the powers of darkness be almost over our palisades. I tell thee there must be more action!

Parris (*pounding with his cane*). Yea, Master Hathorne, I am with thee. Verily, this last be enough to make the elect themselves quake with fear. This Martha Corey is a woman of the covenant.

Hathorne. There must be no holding back. The powers of darkness be let loose amongst us, and they that be against them must be up. We must hang, hang, hang, till we overcome!

Parris. Yea, we must not falter, though all the woods of Massachusetts Bay be cut for gallows-trees, and the country be like Sodom. Verily, Satan hath manifested himself at the head of our enemies; the colonies were never in such peril as now. We must strive as never before, or all will be lost. The wilderness full of malignant savages, who be the veritable servants of Satan, closes us in, and the cloven footmark is in our midst. There must be no dallying as we would save the colonies. Widow Hutchins saith her daughter is grievously pressed. (*A scream.*) There, heard you that?

Hathorne. It is dreadful, dreadful, that an innocent maid should be so tormented by acts which her guileless fancy could never compass!

Parris. Verily, malignity hath ever cowardice in conjunction with it. Satan loveth best to afflict those who can make no defence, and fastens his talons first in the lambs.

Enter Widow Hutchins *with the embroidered cape.*

Hutchins. Here, your worships, is the cape.

Hathorne (*examines it*). I have seen women folk wear its like on the Sabbath day. I can see naught unwonted about it.

Parris. It looketh like any cape.

Hutchins. I fear it be not like any cape. Had your worships seen my poor child writhe under it, and I myself, when I would try it on, bent down to my knees as under a ton weight, your worships would not think it like any cape.

Parris. I suspect there be verily evil work in the cape, and a witch's bodkin hath pierced these cunning eyelets. It goeth so fast now that erelong every guileless, senseless thing in our houses, down to the tinder-box and the candle-stick, will find hinges and turn into a gate, whereby witchcraft can enter. You say, Widow Hutchins, that Olive Corey gave this cape to your daughter?

Hutchins. That did she. Yesterday evening Ann went down to Goody Corey's house for a little chat; she and Olive have been gossips ever since they were children, though lately there hath been somewhat of bitterness betwixt them.

Parris. How mean you?

Hutchins. I have laid it upon my mind ere now to tell you, being much wrought up concerning it, and thinking that you might give me somewhat of spiritual consolation and advice. It was in this wise. Paul Bayley, who, they say, goeth every Sabbath night to Goody Corey's house and sitteth up until unseemly hours with Olive, looked once with a favourable eye upon my daughter Ann. Had your worships seen him, as I saw him one day in the meeting-house, look at Ann when she wore her green *paduasoy*, you had not doubted. Youths look not thus upon maidens unless they be inclined toward them. But this hussy Olive Corey did come between Paul and my Ann, and that not of her own merits. There is nobody in Salem Village who would say that Olive Corey's looks be aught in comparison with my Ann's, but I trow Goody Corey hath arts which make amends for lack of beauty. I trow all ill-favoured folk might be fair would they have such arts used upon them.

493

Hathorne. What mean you by that saying?

Hutchins. I mean Goody Corey hath devilish arts whereby she giveth her daughter a beauty beyond her own looks, wherewith she may entice young men.

Hathorne. You say that this cape caused your daughter torment?

Hutchins. Your worships, it lay on her neck like a fire-brand, and she thought she should die ere she cast it off.

Hathorne. Widow Hutchins, will you now put on the cape?

Hutchins. Oh, your worship, I dare not put it on! I fear it will be the death of me if I do.

Hathorne. Minister Parris, wilt thou put on the cape?

Parris. Good Master Hathorne, it would ill behoove a minister of the gospel to put himself in jeopardy when so many be depending upon him to lead them in this dreadful conflict with the powers of darkness. But do thou put on the mantle the while I go to prayer to avert any ill that may come of it.

Hathorne. Nay, I will make no such jest of my office of magistrate as to put this woman's gear on my shoulders. I doubt if there be aught in it. Prithee, Widow Hutchins, when did this torment first come upon the young woman?

Hutchins. Your worship, she went, as I have said, to Goody Corey's yester-evening to have a little chat with her gossip, Olive, and Paul Bayley came in also, and some of them did talk strangely about this witchcraft, Olive and Goody Corey nodding and winking, and making light of it. And then when Ann said she must be home, Paul rose quickly and made as though he would go with her, but Goody Corey would not let him, and herself went with Ann. And she did practise her devilish arts upon my poor child all the way home, and when my poor child got on the door-stone she burst open the door, and came in as though all the witches were after her, and she hath not been herself since. She hath ever since been grievously tormented, being set upon now by Goody Corey, and now by Olive, being choked and twisted about until I thought she would die, and so I fear she will, unless they be speedily put in chains. It seemeth flesh and blood cannot endure it. Mercy Lewis is just come in, and she saw Goody Corey and Olive upon her when she opened the door.

Hathorne. This evil work must be stopped at all hazards, and this monstrous brood of witches gotten out of the land.

Parris. Yea, verily, although we have to reach under the covenant for them. (*Screams.*)

Hutchins. Oh, your worships, my poor child will have no peace until they be chained in prison.

Hathorne. They shall be chained in prison before the sun sets. I will at once go forth and issue warrants for the arrest of Martha Corey and her daughter. (*More violent screams and loud voices overhead.*

Parris. Would it not be well, good Master Hathorne, for us to see the afflicted maid before we depart?

Hutchins. Oh, I pray you, sirs, come up stairs to my poor child's chamber and see yourselves in what grievous torment she lies. She hath often called for Minister Parris, saying they dared not so afflict her were he there.

Hathorne. It would perchance be as well. Lead the way, if you will, Widow Hutchins. (*Exeunt. Screams continue*)

Enter Nancy Fox *and* Phœbe Morse *stealthily from other door.* Phœbe *carries her rag doll.*)

Nancy. Massy sakes, hear them screeches!

Phœbe (clinging to Nancy). Oh, Nancy, won't they catch us too! I'm afraid!

Nancy. They can't touch us; we're witches too.

Phœbe. Massy sakes! I forgot we were witches.

Nancy. Hear that, will ye? Ain't she a-ketchin' it?

Phœbe. Nancy, do you suppose it's the pin I stuck in my doll makes Ann screech that way?

Nancy. Most likely 'tis. Stick in another, and see if she screeches louder.

Phœbe. No, I won't. I'll pull the pin out; 'twas this one in my doll's arm. (*Pulls out pin and flings it on the floor.*) I won't have Ann hurt so bad as that if Olive did give her the cape. Why don't she stop screeching now, Nancy? Oh, Nancy, somebody's coming! I hear somebody at the door. Crawl under the bed—quick! quick!

(Phœbe *gets down and begins to crawl under the bed.*
Nancy *tries to imitate her, but cannot bend herself.*

Nancy. Oh, massy! I've got a crick in my back, and I can't double up. What shall I do? (*Tries to bend.*) I can't; no, I can't! 'Tis like a hot poker. Massy! What'll I do?

Phœbe. You've got to, Nancy. Quick! the latch is lifting. Quick! quick! I'll push you. No; I'll pull you. Here!

(*Pulls* Nancy *down upon the floor, and rolls her under the bed; gets under herself just as the door is pushed open.*)
Enter Giles Corey *in great excitement.*

Giles (*running across the room, and listening at the door leading to the chamber stairs*). Devil take them! why don't they put an end to it? Why do they let the poor lass be set upon this way? Screeching so you can hear her all over Salem Village! There! hear that, will ye? Out upon them! Widow Hutchins! Widow Hutchins! Can't you give her some physic? Sha'n't I come up there with my musket? Why don't they find out who is so tormenting her and chain her up in prison? 'Tis some witch or other. Oh, I'd hang her; I'd tie the rope myself. Poor lass! poor lass! (*The door is pushed open, and* Giles *starts back.*

Enter John Hathorne, Minister Parris, *and* Widow Hutchins.

Giles. Good-day, Widow Hutchins. Shall I go up there with my musket?

Parris. I trow there be too many of thy household up there now.

Giles. I'd lay about me till I hit some of 'em. I'll warrant I would. Oh, the poor lass! hear that!

Parris. She is a grievous case.

Giles. I heard the screeches out in the wood, and I ran in thinking I might do somewhat. I would Martha were here. I'll be bound she'd laugh and scoff at it no longer!

Hathorne. Laugh and scoff, say you?

Giles. That she doth. Martha acts as if the devil were in her about it. She doth nothing but laugh at and make light of the afflicted children, and saith there be no witches. She would not even believe 'twas aught out of the common when our ox and cat were took strangely. If she were herself a witch she could be no more stiff-necked.

Parris. Doth she go out after nightfall?

Giles. That she doth, in spite of all I can say. She hath no fear that an honest gospel woman should have in these times. She went out last night, and I was so angered that I charged her with galloping a broomstick home.

Hathorne. Did she deny it?

Giles. She laughed as she is wont to do. She even made a jest on't, when I could not when I would go to prayer, and the words stayed beyond my wits. I would she could be here now, and hear this!

Parris. Perchance she doth.

Giles. I'll warrant she'd lose somewhat of her stiff-neckedness. Hear that! Can't ye chain up the witch that's tormenting the poor lass! Is't Goody Osborn?

Hathorne. The witch will be chained and in prison before nightfall. Come, Minister Parris, we can do no good by abiding longer here. Methinks we have sufficient testimony.

Parris. Verily the devil hath played into our hands. (*They turn to leave.*)

Hutchins. Oh, your worships, ye will use good speed for the sake of my poor child.

Giles. Ay, be speedy about it. Put the baggage in prison as soon as may be, and load her down well with irons.

Hathorne. I will strive to obey your commands well, Goodman Corey. Good-day, Widow Hutchins; your daughter shall soon find relief.

Parris. Good-day, Widow Hutchins, and be of good cheer.

(*Exeunt* Hathorne *and* Parris,
while Widow Hutchins *courtesies.*)

Giles. Well, I must even be going too. I have my cattle to water. I but bolted in when I heard the poor lass screech, thinking I might do somewhat. But good Master Hathorne will see to it. Hear that! Do ye go up to her, widow, and mix her up a bowl of yarb tea, till they put the trollop in prison. I'm off to water my cattle, then devil take me if I don't give the sheriffs a hand if they need it. Goody Osborn's house is nigh mine. Good-day, widow. (*Exit* Giles.)

Hutchins (*laughing*). Give the sheriffs a hand, will he? Perchance he will, but I doubt me if 'tis not a fisted one. He sets his life by Goody Corey, however he rate her. (*A scream from above of* "Mother! Mother!") Yes, Ann, I'm coming, I'm coming! (*Exit.*)

Phœbe (*crawls out from under the bed*). Now, Nancy, we've got a chance to run. Come out, quick! Oh, if Uncle Corey had caught us here!

Nancy. I can't get out. Oh! oh! The rheumatiz stiffened me so I couldn't double up, and now it has stiffened me so I can't undouble. No, 'tis not rheumatiz, 'tis Goody Bishop has bewitched me. I can't get out.

Phœbe. You must, Nancy, or somebody'll come and catch us. Here, I'll pull you out.

(*Tugs at* Nancy's *arms, and drags her out, groaning.*)

Nancy. Here I am out, but I can't undouble. I'll have to go home on all-fours like a cat. Oh! oh!

Phœbe. Give me your hands and I'll pull you up. Think you 'tis witchcraft, Nancy?

Nancy. I know 'tis. 'Tis Goody Bishop in her fine silk hood afflicts me. Oh, massy!

Phœbe. There, you are up, Nancy.

Nancy. I ain't half undoubled.

Phœbe. You can walk so, can't you, Nancy? Oh, come, quick! I think I hear somebody on the stairs. (*Catches up her doll and seizes* Nancy's *hand.*) Quick! quick!

Nancy. I tell ye I can't go quick; I ain't undoubled enough. Devil take Goody Bishop!

(*Exit, hobbling and bent almost double,*
Phœbe *urging her along. Curtain falls.*)

Act 3.

The Meeting-house in Salem Village. Enter People of Salem Village *and take seats. The* Afflicted Girls, *among whom are* Ann Hutchins *and* Mercy Lewis, *occupy the front seats.* Nancy Fox *and* Phœbe. *Enter the magistrates* John Hathorne *and* Jonathan Corwin *with* Minister Parris, *escorted by the* Marshal, Aids, *and four* Constables. *They place themselves at a long table in front of the pulpit.*

Hathorne (*rising*). We are now prepared to enter upon the examination. We invoke the blessing of God upon our proceedings, and call upon the Marshal to produce the bodies of the accused.

(*Exeunt* Marshal *and* Constables.
Afflicted Girls *twist about and groan.*
Great excitement among the people.

Enter Marshal *and* Constables *leading* Martha *and* Olive Corey *in chains.* Giles *follows. The prisoners are placed facing the assembly, with the* Constables *holding their hands.* Giles *stands near. The* Afflicted Girls *make a great clamour.*

Ann. Oh, they are tormenting! They will be the death of me! I will not! I will not!

Giles. Hush your noise, will ye, Ann Hutchins!

Parris. Peace, Goodman Corey!

Hathorne. Martha Corey, you are now in the hands of authority. Tell me now why you hurt these persons.

Martha. I do not. I pray your worships give me leave to go to prayer.

Hathorne. We have not sent for you to go to prayer, but to confess that you are a witch.

Martha. I am no witch. I am a gospel woman. There is no such thing as a witch. Shall I confess that I am what doth not exist? It were not only a lie, but a fool's lie.

Mercy. There is a black man whispering in her ears.

Hathorne. What saith the black man to you, Goodwife?

Martha. I pray your worships to ask the maid. Perchance, since she sees him, she can also hear what he saith better than I.

Hathorne. Why do you not tell how the devil comes in your shape and hurts these maids?

Martha. How can I tell how? I was never acquaint with the ways of the devil. I leave it to those wise maids who are so well acquaint to tell how. Perchance he hath whispered it in their ears.

Afflicted Girls. Oh, there is a yellow bird! There is a yellow bird perched on her head!

Hathorne. What say you to that, Goodwife Corey?

Martha. What can I say to such folly?

Hathorne. Constables, let go the hands of Martha Corey.

(*The* Constables *let go her hands, and immediately there is a great outcry from the* Afflicted Girls.)

Afflicted Girls. She pinches us! Hold her hands! Hold her hands again! Oh! oh!

Ann. She is upon me again! She digs her fingers into my throat! Hold her hands! Hold her hands! She will be the death of me!

Giles. Devil take ye, ye lying trollop! 'Tis a pity somebody had not been the death of ye before this happened!

Hathorne. Constables, hold the hands of the accused.

(Constables *obey, and at once the afflicted are quiet.*

Hathorne. Goodwife Corey, what do you say to this?

Martha. I see with whom we have to do. May the Lord have mercy upon us!

Hathorne. What say you to the charges that your husband, Giles Corey, hath many a time brought against you in the presence of witnesses—that you hindered him when he would go to prayer, causing the words to go from him strangely; that you were out after nightfall, and did ride home on a broomstick; and that you scoffed at these maids and their affliction, as if you were a witch yourself?

Giles. I said not so! Martha, I said it not so!

Hathorne. What say you to your husband's charge that you did afflict his ox and cat, causing his ox to fall in the yard, and the cat to be strangely sick?

Giles. Devil take the ox and the cat! I said not that she did afflict them.

Hathorne. Peace, Goodman Corey; you are now in court.

Martha. I say, if a gospel woman is to be hung as a witch for every stumbling ox and sick cat, 'tis setting a high value upon oxen and cats.

Giles. I would mine had all been knocked in the head, lass, and me too!

Hathorne. Peace! Ann Hutchins, what saw you when Goodwife Corey went home with you through the wood?

Ann. Hold fast her hands, I pray, or she will kill me. The trees were so full of yellow birds that it sounded as if a mighty wind passed over them, and the birds lit on Goody Corey's head. And black beasts ran alongside through the bushes, which did break and crackle, and they were at Goody Corey and me to go to the witch dance on the hill. And they said to bring Olive Corey and Paul Bayley. And Goody Corey told them how she and Olive would presently come, but not Paul, for he never would sign the book, not even though Olive trapped him by the arts they had taught her. And Goody Corey showed me the book then, and besought me to sign, and go with her to the dance. And when I would not, she and Olive also afflicted me so grievously that I thought I could not live, and have done so ever since.

Hathorne. What say you to this, Goodwife Corey?

Martha. I pray your worship believe not what she doth charge against my daughter.

Corwin. Mercy Lewis, do you say that you have seen both of the accused afflicting Ann Hutchins?

Mercy. Yes, your worship, many a time have I seen them pressing her to sign the book, and afflicting when she would not.

Corwin. How looked the book?

Mercy. 'Twas black, your worship, with blood-red clasps.

Corwin. Read you the names in it?

Mercy. I strove to, your worship, but I got not through the C's; there were too many of them.

Hathorne. Let the serving-woman, Nancy Fox, come hither.

(Nancy Fox *makes her way to the front.*

Hathorne. Nancy, I have heard that your mistress afflicts you.

Nancy. That she doth.

Hathorne. In what manner?

Nancy. She sendeth me to bed at first candlelight as though I were a babe; she maketh me to wear a woollen petticoat in winter-time, though I was not brought up to't; and she will never let me drink more than one mug of cider at a sitting, and I nigh eighty, and needing on't to warm my bones.

Corwin. Hath she ever afflicted you? Your replies be not to the point, woman.

Nancy. Your worship, she hath never had any respect for my understanding, and that hath greatly afflicted me.

Hathorne. Hath she ever shown you a book to sign?

Nancy. Verily she hath; and when I would not, hath afflicted me with sore pains in all my bones, so I cried out, on getting up, when I had set awhile.

Hathorne. Hath your mistress a familiar?

Nancy. Hey?

Hathorne. Have you ever seen any strange thing with her?

Nancy. She hath a yellow bird which sits on her cap when she churns.

Hathorne. What else have you seen with her?

Nancy. A thing like a cat, only it went on two legs. It clawed up the chimbly, and the soot fell down, and Goody Corey set me to sweeping on't up on the Lord's day.

Giles. Out upon ye, ye lying old jade!

Hathorne. Silence! Nancy, you may go to your place. Phœbe Morse, come hither.

(Phœbe Morse *approaches with her apron over her
face, sobbing. She has her doll under her arm.*

Hathorne. Cease weeping, child. Tell me how your aunt Corey treats you. Hath she ever taught you otherwise than you have learned in your catechism?

Phœbe (weeping). I don't know. Oh, Aunt Corey, I didn't mean to! I took the pins out of my doll, I did. Don't whip me for it.

Hathorne. What doll? What mean you, child?

Phœbe. I don't know. I didn't stick them in so very deep, Aunt Corey! Don't let them hang me for it!

Hathorne. Did your aunt Corey teach you to stick pins into your doll to torment folk?

Phœbe (sobbing convulsively). I don't know! I don't know! Oh, Aunt Corey, don't let them hang me! Olive, you won't let them! Oh! oh!

Corwin. Methinks 'twere as well to make an end of this.

Hathorne. There seemeth to me important substance under this froth of tears. (*To* Phœbe.) Give me thy doll, child.

Phœbe (clutching the doll). Oh, my doll! my doll! Oh, Aunt Corey, don't let them have my doll!

Martha. Peace, dear child! Thou must not begrudge it. Their worships be in sore distress just now to play with dolls.

Parris. Give his worship the doll, child. Hast thou not been taught to respect them in authority?

(Phœbe *gives the doll to* Hathorne, *whimpering.* Hathorne, Corwin, *and* Parris *put their heads together over it.*

Hathorne (holding up the doll). There be verily many pins in this image. Goodwife Corey, what know you of this?

Martha. Your worship, such a weighty matter is beyond my poor knowledge.

Hathorne. Know you whence the child got this image?

Martha. Yes, your worship. I myself made it out of a piece of an old homespun blanket for the child to play with. I stuffed it with lamb's wool, and sewed some green ravellings on its head for hair. I made it a coat out of my copperas-coloured petticoat, and coloured its lips and cheeks with pokeberries.

Hathorne. Did you teach the child to stick in these pins wherewith to torment folk?

Martha. It availeth me naught to say no, your worship.

Mercy (screams). Oh, a sharp pain shoot through me when I look at the image! 'Tis through my arms! Oh!

Hathorne (*examining the doll*). There is a pin in the arms.

Ann. I feel sharp pains, like pins, in my face; oh, 'tis dreadful!

Hathorne (*examining the doll*). There are pins in the face.

Phœbe (*sobbing*). No, no! Those are the pins I stuck in for Aunt Corey. Don't let them hang me, Aunt Corey.

Parris. That is sufficient. She has confessed.

Hathorne. Yes, methinks the child hath confessed whether she would or no. Goodwife Corey, Phœbe hath now plainly said that she did stick these pins in this image for you. What have you to say?

Martha (*courtesying*). Your worship, the matter is beyond my poor speech.

(Hathorne *tosses the doll on the table,*
Phœbe *watching anxiously.*)

Hathorne. Go to your place, child.

Phœbe. I want my doll.

Parris. Go to thy place as his worship bids thee, and think on the precepts in thy catechism. (Phœbe *returns sobbing.*)

Afflicted Girls. Oh, Goody Corey turns her eyes upon us! Bid her turn her eyes away!

Ann. Oh, I see a black cat sitting on Goody Corey's shoulder, and his eyes are like coals. Now, now, he looks at me when Goody Corey does! Look away! look away! Oh, I am blind! I am blind! Sparks are coming into my eyes from Goody Corey's. Make her turn her eyes away, your worships; make her turn her eyes away!

Hathorne. Goody Corey, fix your eyes upon the floor, and look not at these poor children whom you so afflict.

Martha. May the Lord open the eyes of the magistrates and ministers, and give them sight to discover the guilty!

Parris. Why do you not confess that you are a witch?

Martha (*with sudden fervour*). I am no witch. There is no such thing as a witch. Oh, ye worshipful magistrates, ye ministers and good people of Salem Village, I pray ye hear me speak for a moment's space. Listen not to this testimony of distracted children, this raving of a poor lovesick, jealous maid, who should be treated softly, but not let to do this mischief. Ye, being in your fair wits and well acquaint with your own knowledge, must know, as I know, that there be no witches. Wherefore would God let Satan after such wise into a company of His elect? Hath He not guard over His own precinct? Can He not keep it from the power of the Adversary as well as we from the savages? Why keep ye the scouts out in the fields if the Lord God hath so forsaken us? Call in the scouts! If we believe in witches, we believe not only great wickedness, but great folly of the Lord God. Think ye in good faith that I verily stand here with a black cat on my shoulder and a yellow bird on my head?

Why do ye not see them as well as these maids? I would that ye might if they be there. Black cat, yellow bird, if ye be upon my shoulder and my head, as these maids say, I command ye to appear to these magistrates! Otherwise, if I have signed the book, as these maids say, I swear unto ye that I will cross out my name, and will serve none but the God Almighty. Most worshipful magistrates, see ye the black cat? See ye any yellow bird? Why are ye not afflicted as well as these maids, when I turn my eyes upon ye? I pray you to consider that. I am no saint; I wot well that I have but poorly done the will of the Lord who made me, but I am a gospel woman and keep to the faith according to my poor measure.

Can I be a gospel woman and a witch too? I have never that I know of done aught of harm whether to man or beast. I have spared not myself nor minded mine own infirmities in tasks for them that belonged to me, nor for any neighbour that had need. I say not this to set myself up, but to prove to you that I can be no witch, and my daughter can be no witch. Have I not watched nights without number with the sick? Have I not washed and dressed new-born babes? Have I not helped to make the dead ready for burial, and sat by them until the cock crew? Have I ever held back when there was need of me? But I say not this to set myself up. Have I not been in the meeting-house every Lord's day? Have I ever stayed away from the sacrament? Have I not gone in sober apparel, nor wasted my husband's substance? Have

I not been diligent in my household, and spun and wove great store of linen? Are not my floors scoured, my brasses bright, and my cheese-room well filled? Look at me! Can I be a witch?

Ann. A black man hath been whispering in her ear, telling her what to say.

Hathorne. What say you to that, Goody?

Martha. I say if that be so, he told me not to his own advantage. I see with whom I have to do. I pray you give me leave to go to prayer.

Hathorne. You are not here to go to prayer. I much fear that your many prayers have been to your master, the devil. Constables, bring forward the body of the accused.

(Afflicted Girls *shriek.* Constables *lead* Olive *forward.* Martha *is led to one side.*)

Martha. Be of good cheer, dear child.

Giles. Yes, be not afraid of them, lass; thy father is here.

Hathorne. Silence! Olive Corey, why do you so afflict these other maids?

Olive. I do not, your worship.

Ann. She is looking at me. Oh, bid her look away, or she will kill me!

Olive. Oh, Ann, I do not! What mean you, dear Ann?

Hathorne. I charge you, Olive Corey, keep your eyes upon the floor.

Giles. Look where you please, lass, and thy old father will uphold thee in it; and I only wish your blue eyes could shoot pins into the lying hussies.

Hathorne. Goodman, an ye disturb the peace again, ye shall be removed from court. Ann Hutchins, you have seen this maid hurt you?

Ann. Many a time she hath hurt me nigh to death.

Olive. Oh, Ann, I hurt thee?

Ann. There is a flock of yellow birds around her head.

(Olive *moves her head involuntarily, and looks up.*

Afflicted Girls. See her look at them!

Hathorne. What say you to that, Olive?

Olive. I did not see them.

Hathorne. Ann Hutchins, did you see this maid walking in the wood with a black man last week?

Ann. Yes, your worship.

Hathorne. How did he go?

Ann. In black clothes, and he had white hair.

Hathorne. How went the accused?

Ann. She went in her flowered petticoat, and the flowers stood out, and smelt like real ones; her kerchief shone like a cobweb in the grass in the morning, and gold sparks flew out of her hair. Goody Corey fixed her up so with her devilish arts to trap Paul Bayley.

Hathorne. What mean you?

Ann. To trap the black man, your worship. I knew not what I said, I was in such torment.

Hathorne. Olive Corey, did your mother ever so change your appearance by her arts?

Olive. My mother hath no arts, your worship.

Ann. Her cheeks were redder than was common, and her eyes shone like stars.

Hathorne. Olive, did your mother so change your looks?

Olive. No, your worship; I do not know what Ann may mean. I fear she be ill.

Hathorne. Mercy Lewis, did you see Olive Corey with the black man?

Mercy. Yes, your worship; and she called out to me to go with them to the dance, and I should have the black man for a partner; and when I would not she afflicted me, pulling my hair and pinching me.

Hathorne. How appeared she to you?

Mercy. She was dressed like a puppet, finer than I had ever seen her.

Hathorne. Olive, what did you wear when you walked with the black man?

Olive. Your worship, I walked with no black man.

Ann. There he is now, standing behind her, looking over her shoulder.

Hathorne. What say you to that, Olive?

Olive (looking in terror over her shoulder). I see no one. I pray you, let my father stand near me.

Parris. Nay; the black man is enough for you.

Giles (forcing his way to his daughter). Here I be, lass; and it will go hard if the hussies can see the black man and old Giles in one place. Where be the black man now, jades?

Hathorne (angrily). Marshal!

Corwin (interposing). Nay, good Master Hathorne, let Goodman Corey keep his standing. The maid looks near swooning, and albeit his manner be rude, yet his argument hath somewhat of force. In truth, he and the black man cannot occupy one place. Mercy Lewis, see you now this black man anywhere?

Mercy. Yes, your worship.

Corwin. Where?

Mercy. Whispering in your worship's ear.

Parris. May the Lord protect his magistrates from the wiles of Satan, and maintain them in safety for the weal of his afflicted people!

Hathorne. This be going too far. This be presumption! Who of you now see the black man whispering to the worshipful esquire Jonathan Corwin?

Mercy. He is gone now out of the meeting-house. 'Twas but for a moment I saw him.

Corwin. Speak up, children. Did any other of ye see the black man whispering to me?

Afflicted Girls. No! no! no!

Corwin. Mercy Lewis, you say of a truth you saw him?

Mercy. Your worship, it may have been Minister Parris's shadow falling across the platform.

Corwin. This is but levity, and hath naught to do with the trial.

Hathorne. We will proceed with the examination. Widow Eunice Hutchins, produce the cape.

(Widow Hutchins *comes forward, holding the cape by a corner.*)

Hathorne. Put it over your daughter's shoulders.

Hutchins. Oh, your worships, I pray you not! It will kill her!

Ann. Oh, do not! do not! It will kill me! Oh, mother, do not! Oh, your worships! Oh, Minister Parris!

Parris. Why put the maid to this needless agony?

Corwin. Put the cape over her shoulders.

> (Widow Hutchins *approaches* Ann *hesitatingly,*
> *and throws the cape over her shoulders.*
> Ann *sinks upon the floor, shrieking.*)

Ann. Take it off! Take it off! It burns! It burns! Take it off! Have mercy! I shall die! I shall die!

Hathorne. Take off the cape; that is enough. Olive Corey, what say you to this? This is the cape you gave Ann Hutchins.

Olive. Oh, mother! mother!

Martha (pushing forward). Nay, I will speak again. Ye shall not keep me from it; ye shall not send me out of the meeting-house! (*The afflicted cry out.*) Peace, or I will afflict ye in earnest! I *will* speak! If I be a witch, as ye say, then ye have some reason to fear me, even ye most worshipful magistrates and ministers. It might happen to ye even to fall upon the floor in torment, and it would ill accord with your offices. Ye shall hear me. I speak no more for myself—ye may go hang me—I speak for my child. Ye shall not hang her, or judgment will come upon ye. Ye know there is no guile in her; it were monstrous to call her a witch. It were less blasphemy to call her an angel than a witch, and ye know it. Ye know it, all ye maids she hath played with and done her little kindnesses to, ye who would now go hang her.

That cape—that cape, most worshipful magistrates, did the dear child earn with her own little hands, that she might give it to Ann, whom she loved so much. Knowing, as she did, that Ann was poor, and able to have but little bravery of apparel, it was often on her mind to give her somewhat of her own, albeit that was but scanty; and she hath toiled overtimes at her wheel all winter, and sold the yarn in Salem, and so gained a penny at a time wherewithal to buy that cape for Ann. And now will it hang her, the dear child?

Dear Ann, dost thou not remember how thou and my Olive have spent days together, and slept together many a night, and lain awake till dawn talking? Dost thou not remember how thou couldst go nowhere without Olive, nor she without thee, and how no little junketing were complete to the one were the other not there? Dost thou not remember how Olive wept when thy father died? Mercy Lewis, dost thou not remember how my Olive came over and helped thee in thy work that time thou wert ailing, and how she lent thee her shoes to walk to Salem?

Oh, dear children, oh, maids, who have been playmates and friends with my dear child, ye will not do her this harm! Do ye not know that she hath never harmed ye, and would die first? Think of the time when this sickness, that is nigh to madness, shall have passed over, and all is quiet again. Then will ye sit in the meeting-house of a Lord's day, and look over at the place where my poor child was wont to sit listening in her little Sabbath best, and ye will see her no more, but will say to yourselves that ye have murdered her. And then of a weekday ye will see her no more spinning at her wheel in the doorway, nor tending the flowers in her garden.

She will come smiling in at your doors no more, nor walk the village street, and ye will always see where she is not, and know that ye have murdered her. Oh, poor children, ye are in truth young, and your minds, I doubt not, sore bewildered! If I have spoken harshly to ye, I pray ye heed it not, except as concerns me. I wot well that I am now done with this world, and I feel already the wind that bloweth over Gallows Hill in my face. But consider well ere ye do any harm to my dear child, else verily the day will come when ye will be more to be pitied than she. Oh, ye will not harm her! Ye will take back your accusation! Oh, worshipful magistrates, oh, Minister Parris, I pray you have mercy upon this child! I pray you mercy as you will need mercy! (*Falls upon her knees.*)

Hathorne. Rise, woman; it is not now mercy, but justice that has to be considered.

Parris. In straits like this there is no mercy in the divine will.

510

Shall mercy be shown Satan?

Corwin. Mercy Lewis, is it in truth Olive Corey who afflicts you?

Mercy (*hesitating*). I am not so sure as I was.

Other Afflicted Girls. Nor I! nor I! nor I!

Mercy. Last time I was somewhat blinded and could not see her face. Methinks she was something taller than Olive.

Ann (*shrieks*). Oh, Olive is upon me! The sun shines on her face! I see her, she is choking me! Oh! oh!

Mercy (*to* Ann). Hush! If she be put away you'll not get Paul Bayley; I'll tell you that for a certainty, Ann Hutchins.

Ann. Oh! oh! she is killing me!

Mercy. I see her naught; 'tis a taller person who is afflicting Ann. (*To* Ann.) Leave your outcries or I will confess to the magistrates. (Ann *becomes quiet.*)

Corwin. Ann Hutchins, saw you in truth Olive Corey afflicting you?

Ann (*sullenly*). It might have been Goody Corey.

Corwin. Mercy Lewis, saw you of a certainty Olive Corey walking in the wood with a black man?

Mercy. It was the wane of the moon; I might have been mistaken. It might have been Goody Corey; their carriage is somewhat the same.

Corwin. Give me the cape, Widow Hutchins. (Widow Hutchins *hands him the cape; he puts it over his shoulders.*) Verily I perceive no great inconvenience from the cape, except it is an ill fit.

(*Takes it off and lays it on the table.*
The two magistrates and Minister Parris *whisper together.*)

Hathorne. Having now received the testimony of the afflicted and the witnesses, and duly weighted the same according to our judgment, being aided to a decision, as we believe, by the divine wisdom which we have invoked, we declare the damsel Olive Corey free and quit of the charges against her. And Martha Corey, the wife of Giles Corey, of Salem Village, we commit unto the jail in Salem until—

Giles. Send Martha to Salem jail! Out upon ye! Why, ye be

gone clean mad, magistrates and ministers and all! Send Martha to jail! Why, she must home with me this night and get supper! How think ye I am going to live and keep my house? Load Martha down with chains in jail! Martha a witch! Then, by the Lord, she keeps His company overmuch for one of her trade, for she goes to prayer forty times a day. Martha a witch! Think ye Goodwife Martha Corey gallops a broomstick to the hill of a night, with her decent petticoats flapping? Who says so? I would I had my musket, and he'd not say so twice to Giles Corey.

And let him say so twice as 'tis, and meet my fist, an he dares. I be an old man, but I could hold my own in my day, and there be some of me left yet. Who says so twice to old Giles Corey? Martha a witch! Verily she could not stop praying long enough to dance a jig through with the devil. Martha! Out upon ye, ye lying devil's tool of a parson, that seasons murder with prayer! Out upon ye, ye magistrates! your hands be redder than your fine trappings! Martha a witch! Ye yourselves be witches, and serving Satan, and he a-tickling in his sleeve at ye. Send Martha in chains to Salem jail, ye will, will ye? (*Forces his way to* Martha, *and throws his arm around her.*) Be not afraid, good lass, thy man will save thee.

Thou shalt not go to jail! I say thou shalt not! I'll cut my way through a whole king's army ere thou shalt. I'll raise the devil myself ere thou shalt, and set him tooth and claw on the whole brood of them. I'll—(*One of the afflicted shrieks.* Giles *turns upon them.*) Why, devil take ye, ye lying hussies, ye have done this! Ye should be whipped through the town at the tail of a cart, every one of ye. Ye ill-favoured little jades, puling because no man will have ye, and putting each other up to this d— mischief for lack of something better. Out upon ye, ye little—

Mercy (*jumping up and screaming in agony*). Oh, Giles Corey is upon me! He is afflicting me grievously! Oh, I will not! Chain him! chain him! chain him!

Ann. Oh, this is worse than the others! This is dreadful! He's strangling me! I—Oh—your—worships! Oh—help!—help! (*Falls upon the floor*).

Afflicted Girls. Chain him! chain him!

Hathorne. Marshal, take Giles Corey into custody and chain him.

(Marshal *and* Constables *advance. Tableau—Curtain falls.*)

ACT 4

The living-room in Giles Corey's *house.* Nancy Fox *and the child* Phœbe Morse *sit beside the hearth; each has her apron over her face, weeping.*

Phœbe (sobbing). I—want my Aunt—Corey and—my Uncle Corey. Why don't they come? Oh, deary me!

(Phœbe *jumps up and runs to the window.*)

Nancy. See you anybody coming?

Phœbe. There is a dame in a black hood coming past the popple-trees. Oh, Nancy, come quick; see if it be Aunt Corey!

Nancy. Where be my spectacles—where be they? (*Runs about the room searching.*) Oh Lord, what's the use of living to be so old that you're scattered all over the house like a seed thistle! Having to hunt everywhere for your eyes and your wits whenever you want to use 'em, and having other folks a-meddling with 'em! Where be the spectacles? They be not in the cupboard; they be not on the dresser. Where be they? I trow this be witch-work. I know well enough what has become of my good horn spectacles. Goody Bishop hath witched them away, thinking they would suit well with her fine hood. I know well that I—

Phœbe (sobbing aloud). Oh, Nancy, it is not Aunt Corey. It is only Goodwife Nourse.

Nancy. May the black beast catch her! Be you sure?

Phœbe. Yes; she is passing our gate. Oh, Nancy, what shall we do? what shall we do?

Nancy. I would that I had my fingers in old man Hathorne's fine wig. I would yank it off for him, and fling it to the pigs. A-sending master and mistress to jail, and they no more witches than I be!

Phœbe. Oh, Nancy, be we witches? They have not sent us to jail.

Nancy. I know not what we be. My old head will not hold it all. It is time they came home. There is not a crumb of sweet-cake in the house, and the stopple is so tight in the cider-barrel that I cannot stir it a peg. (*Weeps.*)

Phœbe. Nancy, did they send Aunt Corey and Uncle Corey to jail because I stuck the pins in my doll?

Nancy. I know not. I tell ye my old head spins round like a flax-wheel; when I put my finger on one spoke 'tis another one. These things be too much for a poor old woman like me. It takes folks like their worships the magistrates and Minister Parris to deal with black men and witches, and keep their wits in no need of physic.

Phœbe. Oh, Nancy, I know what I will do! Oh, 'tis well I snatched my doll off the meeting-house table that day after the trial, and ran home with it under my apron! (*Runs to the settle, takes up the doll, which is lying there, and kisses it.*) Here is one kiss for Aunt Corey, here is another kiss for Aunt Corey, here is another, and another, and another. Here is one kiss for Uncle Corey, and here is another kiss for Uncle Corey, and here is another, and another, and another. There, Nancy! will not this do away with the pin pricks, and they be let out of jail?

Nancy. I know not. My old head bobs like a pumpkin in a pond. I would master and mistress were home. These be troublous times for an old woman. I would I could stir the stopple in the cider-barrel. Look again, and see if mistress be not coming up the road.

Phœbe. It is of no use. I have looked for a whole week, and she has not come in sight. I want my Aunt Corey! Nancy, have I not done away with the pin pricks? Tell me, will she be not let out of jail? Oh, there's Paul coming past the window! He's got home! Olive! Olive!

Enter Paul Bayley. Phœbe *runs to him.*

Phœbe. Oh, Paul, they've put Aunt Corey and Uncle Corey in Salem jail while you were gone! Can't you get them out, Paul, can't you?

Paul. Where is Olive?

Phœbe. She is in her chamber. She stays there all the time at prayer. Olive! Olive! Paul is come.

(*Calls at the foot of chamber stairs.*)

Paul. Olive!

Olive *comes slowly down the stairs and enters.*

Paul (seizing her in his arms). Oh, my poor lass, what is this that hath come to thee?

Olive. This is what thou feared when we parted, Paul, and more.

Paul. I but heard of it as I came through Salem on my way hither. Oh, 'tis devilish work!

Olive. They let me loose, but father and mother are in Salem jail.

Paul. Poor lass!

Olive. Can you do naught to help them, Paul?

Paul. Olive, I will help them, if there be any justice or un-clouded minds left in the colony.

Olive. Thou art in truth here, Paul; it is thy voice.

Paul. Whose voice should it be, dear heart?

Olive. I know not. For a week I have thought I heard so many voices. The air seemed full of voices a-calling me, but I heeded them not, Paul. I kept all the time at prayer and heeded them not.

Paul. Of course thou didst not. There were no voices to heed.

Olive. Sometimes I thought I heard birds twittering, and sometimes I thought there was something black at my elbow, and in the night-time faces at my window. Paul, was there aught there?

Paul. No, no; there was naught there. Birds and black beasts and faces! This be all folly, Olive!

Olive. They saw a black man by my side in the meeting-house—Ann saw him. She cried out that the cape I gave her put her to dreadful torment. Can I have been a witch unknowingly, and so done this great evil to my father and mother? Tell me, Paul.

Paul. Call up thy wits, Olive! I tell thee thou art no witch. There was no black man at thy side in the meeting-house. Black man! I would one would verily lay hands on that lying hussy. Thou art no witch.

(Phœbe *rushes to* Olive, *and clings to her, sobbing.*)

Phœbe. You are not a witch, Olive. You are not. If Ann says so I will pinch her and scratch her. I will! yes, I will—I will scratch her till the blood runs. You are not a witch. I was the one that got them into jail. I stuck pins into my doll, but I have made up for it now. They'll be let out. Don't cry, Olive.

Nancy. Don't you fret yourself, Olive. I trow there's no witch-mark on you. It's Goody Bishop in her fine silk hood that's at the bottom on't. I know, I know. Perchance Paul could loose the stopple in the cider-barrel. I am needful of somewhat to warm my old bones. This witch-work makes them to creep with chills like long snakes.

Olive. They say my mother will soon be hanged, and I per-chance a witch, and the cause of it. I cannot get over it. (*Moves away from them.*) If I be a witch, I shall hurt thee, as I perchance have hurt them. (*Weeps*)

Paul. Olive Corey, what is that?

Olive (looking up). What? What mean you, Paul? (Nancy *and* Phœbe *stare.*)

Paul. There, over the cupboard. Is it— Yes, 'tis—cobwebs. I trow I never saw such a sight in Goodwife Corey's house be-fore.

Olive. I will brush them down, Paul.

Paul (looking at the floor). And I doubt me much if the floor has been swept up this week past, and the hearth is all strewn with ashes. I trow Goodwife Corey would weep could she see her house thus.

Olive. I will get the broom, Paul.

Paul. I know well thou hast not spun this last week, that the cream is too far gone to be churned, and the cheeses have not been turned.

Nancy. 'Tis so, Paul; and there's no sweet-cake in the house, either.

Paul. Thou art no such housewife as thy mother, Olive Corey! One would say she had not taught thee. I trow she was a good housewife, and notable among the neighbours; but this will take from her reputation that she hath so brought thee up. I trow could she see this house 'twould give her a new ache in her heart among all the others.

Olive. I will mind the house, Paul.

Paul. Ay, mind the house, poor lass! Know you, Olive, that there is a rumour abroad in Salem that your father will refuse to plead, and will stand mute at his trial?

Olive. Wherefore will he do that?

Paul. I scarcely know why. Has he made a will, 'twill not be valid were he to plead at a criminal trial; there will be an attainder on it. They say that is one reason, and that he thinks thus to show his scorn of the whole devilish work, and of a trial that is no trial.

Olive. What is the penalty if he stand mute?

Paul. 'Tis a severe one; but he shall not stand mute.

Phœbe. Oh, Paul, get Aunt Corey out of jail! Can't you get Aunt Corey out of jail?

Nancy. Perchance you could pry up the hook of the jail door with the old knife. It will be dark to-night. There is no moon until three o'clock in the morning.

Olive. Paul, think you not that my father's sons-in-law might do somewhat? They are men of influence. Their wives are but my half-sisters, but they are his own daughters. I marvel they have not come to me since this trouble.

Paul. Olive, his sons-in-law have sent in their written testimony against him and your mother.

Olive. Paul, it cannot be so!

Paul. They have surely so testified. There is no help to be had from them. I have a plan.

Olive. All is useless, Paul. His sons-in-law, his own daughters' husbands, have turned against him! There is no help anywhere. My mother will soon be hanged. Minister Parris said so last night when he came. And he knelt yonder and prayed that I might no longer practise witchcraft. My father and mother are lost, and I have brought it upon them. Talk no more to me, Paul.

Paul. Then, perchance your mother be a witch, Olive Corey.

Olive. My mother is not a witch.

Paul. Doth not Minister Parris say so? And if he speak truth when he calls you a witch, why speaks he not truth of your mother also? I trow, if you be a witch, she is.

Olive. My mother is no witch, and I am no witch, Paul Bayley!

Paul. Mind you stick to that, poor lass! Now, I go to Boston to the governor. There lies the only hope for thy parents.

Olive. Think you the governor will listen? Oh, he must listen! Thou hast a masterful way with thee, Paul. When wilt thou start? Oh, if I had not thee!

Paul. I would I could make myself twenty-fold 'twixt thee and evil, sweet. I will get Goodman Nourse's horse and start tonight.

Olive. Then go, go! Do not wait!

Paul. I will not wait. Goodbye, dear heart. Keep good courage, and put foolish fancies away from thee. (*Embraces her.*

Olive (freeing herself). This is no time for love-making, Paul. I will mind the house well and keep at prayer. Thou need'st not fear. Now, haste, haste! Do not wait!

Paul. I will be on the Boston path in a half-hour. Goodbye Olive. Please God, I'll bring thee back good news. (*Exit* Paul.

(Olive *stands in the door watching him depart.* Phœbe *steals up to her and throws her arms around her.* Olive *turns suddenly and embraces the child.*)

Olive. Come, sweet; while Paul sets forth to the governor, we will go to prayer. Nancy, come, we will go to prayer that the governor may lend a gracious ear, and our feet be kept clear of the snares of Satan. Come, we will go to prayer; there is naught left for us but to go to prayer!

Tableau—Curtain falls.

Act 5.

Six weeks later. Giles Corey's *cell in Salem jail. It is early morning.* Giles, *heavily chained, is sleeping upon his bed. A noise is heard at the door.* Giles *stirs and raises himself.*

Giles. Yes, Martha, I'm coming. (*Noise continues.*) I'm coming, Martha. (*Stares around the cell.*) God help me, but I thought 'twas Martha calling me to supper, and 'tis a month since she died on Gallows Hill. I verily thought that I smelt the pork frying and the pan-cakes.

The door is opened and the Guard, *bringing a dish of porridge, enters; he sets it on the floor beside the bed, then examines* Giles's *chains.*

Giles. Make sure they be strong, else it will verily go hard with the hussies. They will screech louder yet, and be more like pin-cushions than ever. Art sure they be strong? 'Twere a pity such guileless and tender maids should suffer, and old Giles Corey's hands be rough. He hath hewn wood and handled the plough for nigh eighty years with them, and now these pretty maids say he hurts their soft flesh. In truth, they must be sore afflicted. Prithee are the chains well riveted? I thought last night one link seemed somewhat loose as though it might be forced, and old Giles Corey hath still some strength; and hath he witchcraft, as they say, it might well make him stronger. Be wary about the chains for the sake of those godly and tender maids.

(*Exit* Guard. Giles *takes the dish of porridge and eats.*

Giles (*making a wry face*). This be rare porridge; it be rare enough to charge the cook on't with witchcraft. It might well have been scorched in some hell-fire. I trow Martha would have flung it to the pigs. I verily thought 'twas Martha calling me to supper, and I smelt the good food cooking, and Martha hung a month since on Gallows Hill. Who's that at the door now?

(Guard *opens the door and* Paul Bayley *enters.* Giles *takes another spoonful of porridge.*)

Paul. Good-day, Goodman Corey.

Giles. Taste this porridge, will ye.

Paul (*tastes the porridge*). 'Tis burned.

Giles. It be rare food to keep up the soul of an old man who hath set himself to undergo what I have set myself to undergo. But it matters not. I trow old Giles Corey may well have eat all his life unknowingly to this end, and hath now somewhat of strength to fall back upon. He needs no dainty fare to make him strong to undergo what he hath set himself. How fares my daughter?

Paul. As well as she can fare, poor lass! I saw her last evening. She is now calmer in her mind, and she goeth about the house like her mother.

Giles. Her mother set great store by her. She would often strive in prayer that she should not make an idol of her before the Lord.

Paul. Goodman, it goes hard to tell you, but I had an audience yesterday again with Governor Phipps, an' 'twas in vain.

Giles (*laughing*). In vain, say ye 'twas in vain? Why, I looked to see the pardon sticking out of your waistcoat pocket! Why went ye again to Boston? Know ye not that this whole land is now a bedlam, and the governors and the magistrates swell the ravings? Seek ye in bedlam for justice of madmen? It is not now pardon or justice that we have to think on, but death, and the best that can be made out on't. Know ye that my trial will be held this afternoon?

Paul. Yes, Goodman Corey.

Giles. Sit ye down on this stool. I have much I would say to ye.

(Paul *seats himself on a stool.* Giles *sits on his bed.*)

Giles. Master Bayley, ye have been long a-courting my daughter. Do ye propose in good faith to take her to wife?

Paul. With the best faith that be in me.

Giles. Then I tell ye, man, take her speedily—take her within three weeks.

Paul. I would take her with all my heart, goodman, would she be willing.

Giles. She must needs be willing. Why, devil take it! be ye not smart enough to make her willing? It will all go for naught if she be not willing. Tell her her father bids her. She hath ever minded her father.

Paul. I will tell her so, goodman.

Giles. Tell her 'tis the last command her father gives her. If she say no, hear it yes. Do not ye give it up if ye have to drag her to 't. Why, she must not be left alone in the world. It be a hard world. Old Giles hath gone far in it, and found it ever a hard world. Verily it be not cleared any more than the woods of Massachusetts. It be hard enough for a man; a young maid must needs have somebody to hold aside the boughs for her. Wed her, if she will or no. I have somewhat to show ye, Master Bayley. (*Draws a document from his waistcoat.*) See ye this?

(Paul *takes the document and examines it.*)

Giles. See ye what 'tis?

Paul. It is a deed whereby you convey all your property to me, so I be Olive's husband. Wherefore?

Giles. It be drawn up in good form. It be duly witnessed. You see that it be all in good form, Paul.

Paul. I see. But wherefore?

Giles. It will stand in law; there will be no getting loose from it. It be a good and trusty document. But—so be it that this afternoon I stand trial for witchcraft, and plead guilty or not guilty, this same good and trusty document will be worth less than the parchment 'tis writ on. 'Tis so with the law. There will be an attainder on 't. My sons-in-law that testified to the undoing of Martha and me will have their share, and thou and Olive perchance have naught in this bedlam. I bear no ill will toward my sons-in-law and my daughters, who have been put up by them to deal falsely with Martha and me, but I would not that they have my goods. I bear no ill will; it becometh not a man so near death to bear ill will. But they shall not have my goods; I say they shall not. There shall be no attainder on this document. I will stand mute at my trial.

Paul. Goodman Corey, know you the penalty?

Giles. I trow I know it better than the catechism. 'Tis to be pressed beneath stone weights until I be dead.

Paul. I say you shall not do this thing. What think you I care for your goods? I'll have naught to do with them, nor will Olive. This is madness!

Giles. 'Tis not all for the goods. I would Olive had them, and not those foul traitors; but 'tis not all. Were there no goods and no attainder, I would still do this thing. Paul, they say that Martha spake fair words when they had her there on Gallows Hill.

Paul. She spake like a martyr at the door of heaven.

Giles. Did they let her speak long?

Paul. They cut her short, Minister Parris saying, "Let not this firebrand of hell burn longer."

Giles. Then they put the rope to her neck. Martha had a fair neck when she was a maid. Did she struggle much?

Paul. Not much.

Giles. Then they left her hanging there a space. It was a wet day, and the rain pelted on her. I remember it was a wet day. The rain pelted on her, and the wind blew, and she swung in it. I swear to thee, lass, I will make amends! I will suffer twenty pangs for thy one.

Paul. 'Tis not you who should make amends.

Giles. I tell ye I did Martha harm. When she chid my folly and the folly of others, I did bawl out at her, and say among folk things to her undoing, though I meant it not as they took it. Now I will make amends, and the king himself shall not stop me. Martha was a good wife. I know not how I shall make myself seemly for the court this afternoon. My coat has many stitches loose in it. She was a good wife. I will make amends to thee, lass; I swear I shall make amends to thee! I will come where thou art by a harder road than the one I made thee go.

Paul. It was not you, Goodman. You overblame yourself. Those foul-mouthed jades did it, and those bloodthirsty magistrates.

Giles. I tell ye I did part on't. I was wroth with her that she made light of this witch-work over which I was so mightily wrought up, and I said words that they twisted to her undoing.

Verily, words can be made to fit all fancies. 'Twere safer to be mute—as I'll be this afternoon.

Paul. Goodman Corey, you must not think of this thing. There is still some hope from the trial. They will not dare murder you too.

Giles. There be some things in this world folks may not bear, but there be no wickedness they'll stick at when they get started on the way to 't. 'Tis death in any case, and what would ye have me do? Stand before their mad worships and those screeching jades, and plead as though I were before folk of sound mind and understanding? Think ye I would so humble myself for naught?

Paul. But Olive! I tell you 'twill kill her! There may be a chance yet, and you should throw not away however small a one for Olive's sake. She can bear no more.

Giles. There is no chance, and if there were—I tell ye if I had a hundred daughters, and every one such a maid as she, and every one were to break her heart, I would do this thing I have set myself to do. There be that which is beyond human ties to force a man, there be that which is at the root of things.

Paul. We will have none of your goods, I tell you that, Giles Corey!

Giles. Goods. The goods be the least of it! Old Giles Corey be not a deep man. I trow he hath had a somewhat hard skull, but when a man draws in sight of death he hath a better grasp at his wits than he hath dreamed of. This be verily a mightier work than ye think. It shall be not only old Giles Corey that lies pressed to death under the stones, but the backbone of this great evil in the land shall be broke by the same weight. I tell ye it will be so. I have clearer understanding, now I be so near the end on't. They will dare no more after me. Today shall I stand mute at my trial, but my dumbness shall drown out the clamour of my accusers. Old Giles Corey will have the best on't. 'Tis for this, and not for the goods, I will stand mute; for this, and to make amends to Martha.

Paul. Giles Corey, you shall not die this dreadful death. If death it must be, and it may yet not be, choose the easier one.

Giles. Think ye I cannot do it? (*Rises.*) Master Paul Bayley, you see before you Giles Corey. He be verily an old man, he be over eighty years old, but there be somewhat of the first of him left. He hath never had much power of speech; his words have been rough, and not given to pleasing. He hath been a rude man, an unlettered man, and a sinner. He hath brawled and blasphemed with the worst of them in his day. He hath given blow for blow, and I trow the other man's cheek smarted sorer than old Giles's. Now he be a man of the covenant, but he be still stiff with his old ways, and hath no nimbleness to shunt a blow. Old Giles Corey hath no fine wisdom to save his life, and no grace of tongue, but he hath power to die as he will, and no man hath greater.

Paul. Goodman Corey, I— (Guard *opens the door*).

Guard. Here is your daughter to see you, Goodman Corey.

Giles. Tell her I will see her not. What brought her here? I know. Minister Parris hath sent her, thinking to tempt me from my plan. I will see her not.

Olive (from without). Father, you cannot send me away.

Giles. Why come you here? Go home and mind the house.

Olive. Father, I pray you not to send me away.

Paul. If you be hard with her, you will kill her.

Giles. Come in.

Enter Olive.

Olive. What is this you will do, father?

Giles. My duty, lass.

Olive. Father, you will not die this dreadful death?

Giles. That will I, lass.

Olive. Then I say to you, father, so will I also. The stones will press you down a few hours' space, and they will press me down so long as I may live. You will be soon dead and out of the pains, but you will leave your death with the living.

Giles. Then must the living bear it.

Olive. Father, you may yet be acquitted. Plead at your trial.

Giles. Work the bellows in the face of the north wind. Oh, lass, why came you here? 'Tis worse than the stones. Talk no more to me, good lass; womenkind should meddle not with men's plans. But promise me you will wed with Paul here within three weeks.

Olive. I will never wed.

Giles. Ye will not, hey? Ye will wed with Master Paul Bayley within three weeks. 'Tis the last command your father gives thee.

Olive. Think you I can wed when you—

Giles. Ay, I do think so, lass, and so ye will.

Olive. Father, I will not. But if you plead I will, I promise you I will.

Giles. I will not, and you will. Lass, since you be here, I pray you set a stitch in this seam in my coat. I would look tidy at the trial, for thy mother's sake. Hast thou thy huswife with thee?

Olive. Yes, father.

(Olive *threads a needle, and standing beside her father,*
sets the stitch; weeps as she does so.)

Giles. Know you every tear adds weight to the stones, lass?

Olive. Then will I weep not. (*Mends.*)

Giles. Be the child and the old woman well?

Olive. Yes, father.

Giles. Look out for them as you best can. And see to 't the little maid's linen chest is well filled, as your mother would have.

(Olive *breaks off the thread.*)

Giles. Be the stitch set strong?

Olive. Yes, father.

Giles (*turning and folding her to his arms*). Oh, my good lass, the stones be naught, but this cometh hard, this cometh hard! Could they not have spared me this?

Olive. Father, listen to me, listen to me—

Giles. Lass, I must listen to naught but the voice of God. 'Tis that speaks, and bids me do this thing. Thou must come not betwixt thy father and his God.

Olive. Father! father!

Giles. Go, Olive, I can bear no more. Tell me thou wilt wed as I command you.

Olive. As thou wilt, father! father! but I will love no man as I love thee.

Giles. Go, lass. Give me a kiss. There, now go! I command thee to go! Paul, take her hence. I charge ye do by her when her father be dead and gone, as ye would were he at thy elbow. Take her hence. I would go to prayer.

(*Exeunt* Paul *and* Olive.)

Olive (*as the door closes*). Father! father!

(Giles Corey *stands alone in cell. Curtain falls.*)

ACT 6

Three weeks later. Lane near Salem overhung by blossoming apple-trees. Enter Hathorne, Corwin, *and* Parris.

Corwin. 'Tis better here, a little removed from the field where they are putting Giles Corey to death. I could bear the sight of it no longer.

Hathorne. You are fainthearted, good Master Corwin.

Corwin. Fainthearted or not, 'tis too much for me. I was brought not up in the shambles, nor bred butcher by trade.

Parris. Your worship, you should strive in prayer, lest you falter not in the strife against Satan.

Corwin. I know not that I have faltered in any strife against Satan.

Parris. Perchance 'tis but your worship's delicate frame of body causeth you to shrink from this stern duty.

Hathorne. This torment of Giles Corey's can last but a little space now. He hath still his chance to speak and avert his death, and he will do it erelong. They have increased the weights mightily. Fear not, good Master Corwin, Giles Corey will not die; erelong his old tongue will wag like a millwheel.

Corwin. I doubt much, good Master Hathorne, if Giles Corey speak. And if he does not speak, and so be put to death, as is decreed, I doubt much if the temper of the people will stand more. There are those who have sympathy with Giles Corey. I heard many murmurs in the streets of Salem this morning.

Hathorne. Let them murmur.

Parris. Ay, let them murmur, so long as we wield the sword of the Lord and of Gideon.

Enter first Messenger.

Hathorne. Here comes a man from the field. How goes it now with Giles Corey?

Messenger. Your worship, Giles Corey has not spoken.

Parris. And he hath been under the weights since early light. Truly such obstinacy is marvellous. (*Exit* Messenger.)

Hathorne. Satan gives a strength beyond human measure to his disciples.

Enter Olive *and* Paul Bayley, *appearing in the distance.*
Olive *wears a white gown and white bonnet.*

Hathorne. Who is that maid coming in a bride bonnet?

Corwin. 'Tis Corey's daughter. I marvel that Paul lets her come hither. 'Tis no place for her, so near. Master Hathorne, let us withdraw a little way. I would not see her distress. I am somewhat shaken in nerve this morning.

(Corwin, Hathorne, *and* Parris *exeunt at other end of lane.*)

Olive (*as she and* Paul *advance*). Who were those men, Paul?

Paul. The magistrates and Minister Parris, sweet.

Olive. Are they gone?

Paul. Yes, they are quite out of sight. Oh, why wouldst thou come here, dear heart?

Olive. Thou thinkest to cheat me, Paul; but thou canst not cheat me. Three fields away to the right have they dragged my father this morning. I knew it, I knew it, although you strove so hard to keep it from me. I'll be as near my father's death-bed on my wedding-day as I can.

Paul. I pray thee, sweetheart, come away with me. This will do no good.

Olive. Loyalty doth good to the heart that holds it, if to no other. Think you I'll forsake my father because 'tis my wedding-day, Paul? Oh, I trow not, I trow not, or I'd make thee no true wife.

527

Paul. It but puts thee to needless torment.

Olive. Torment! torment! Think of what he this moment bears! Oh, my father, my father! Paul Bayley, why have I wedded you this dreadful day!

Paul. Hush! Thy father wished it, sweetheart.

Olive. I swear to you I'll never love any other than my father. I love you not.

Paul. Thou needst not, poor lass!

Olive (clinging to him). Nay, I love thee, but I hate myself for it on this day.

Paul (caressing her). Poor lass! Poor lass!

Olive. Why wear I this bridal gear, and my father over yonder on his dreadful death-bed? Why could you not have gone your own way and let me gone mine all the rest of my life in black apparel, a-mourning for my father? That would have beseemed me. This needed not have been so; it needed never have been so.

Paul. Never? I tell thee, sweet, as well say to these apple blossoms that they need never be apples, and to that rose-bush against the wall that its buds need not be roses. In faith, we be far set in that course of nature, dear, with the apple blossoms and the rose-buds, where the beginning cannot be without the end. Our own motion be lost, and we be swept along with a current that is mightier than death, whether we would have it so or not.

Olive. I know not. I only know I would be faithful to my poor father. But 'twas his last wish that I should wed thee thus.

Paul. Yes, dear.

Olive. He said so that morning before his trial. Oh, Paul, I can see it now, the trial! I have been to the trial every day since. Shall I go every day of my life? Perchance thou may often come home and find thy wife gone to the trial, and no supper. I will go on my wedding-day; my father shall have no slights put upon him. I can see him stand there, mute. They cry out upon him and mock him and lay false charges upon him, and he stands mute. The judge declares the dreadful penalty, and he stands mute. Oh, my father, my poor father! I tell ye my father will not mind anything. The governor and the justices may command him as they will, the afflicted may clamour and gibe as they will, and I may pray to him, but he will not mind, he will stand mute. I tell ye there be not power enough in the colony to make him speak. Ye know not my father. He will have the best of it.

Paul. Thou speakest like his daughter now. Keep thyself up to this, sweet. The daughter of a hero should have some brave stuff in her. Thy father does a greater deed than thou knowest. His dumbness will save the colonies from more than thou dreamest of. 'Twill put an end to this dreadful madness; he himself hath foretold it. (*A clamour is heard.*)

Olive. Paul, Paul, what is that?

Paul. Naught but some boys shouting, sweet.

Olive. 'Twas not. Oh, my father, my father!

Paul. Olive, thou must not stay here.

Olive. I must stay. Who is coming? (Paul *and* Olive *step aside*).

> *Enter second* Messenger. Hathorne, Corwin,
> *and* Parris *advance to meet him.*

Hathorne. How goes it now with Giles Corey?

Messenger. Your worship, Giles Corey hath not spoken.

Hathorne. What! Have they not increased the weights?

Messenger. They have doubled the weights, your worship.

Parris. I trow Satan himself hath put his shoulder under the stones to take off the strain. (*Exit* Messenger.)

Hathorne. 'Tis a marvel the old tavern-brawler endures so long, but he'll soon speak now.

Corwin. Hush, good master, his daughter can hear.

Hathorne. Let her then withdraw if it please her not. I'll warrant he cannot bear much more; he will soon speak.

Parris. Yea, he cannot withstand the double weight unless his master help him.

> (Corwin *speaks aside to* Paul *and motions him
> to take* Olive *away.* Paul *takes her by the arm. S
> he shakes her head and will not go.*)

Hathorne. I trow 'twill take other than an unlettered clown like Giles Corey to stand firm under this stress. He'll speak soon.

Parris. Yea, that he will. He can never hold out. He hath not the mind for it.

Hathorne. It takes a man of finer wit than he to undergo it. He will speak. Oh yes, fear ye not, he will speak.

Olive (breaking away from Paul). My father will *not* speak!

Hathorne. Girl!

Olive. My father will *not* speak. I tell ye there be not stones enough in the provinces to make him speak. Ye know not my father. My father will have the best of ye all.

(*Enter third* Messenger, *running.*)

Hathorne. How goes it now with Giles Corey?

Messenger. Giles Corey is dead, and he has not spoken.

Olive *clings to* Paul *as curtain falls.*